A Kiss For Luck!
A Novel
by
Ken Blaisdell

Copyright © 2014 by Ken Blaisdell
ken@kenblaisdell.com

ISBN: 978-0-9849257-5-9
All rights reserved.
Neither the whole nor any part
of this work may be reproduced
in any form without the
written permission of the author.

Published by

LIGHTKEEPER
PRESS™

Gilbert, AZ
USA

Original Cover Art by JLB Designs

Printed in USA

A Kiss For Luck!

Dedication

This book is dedicated to the memory of the late *Don Blaisdell*, my father. His time in the US Merchant Marine during the final year of WWII is the inspiration for the character Frank Hendricks in *Part II: The Crossing*. I only wish that he could have read this work; I think he would have been proud.

Ken Blaisdell

To BRIAN,

BEST OF LUCK!

A Kiss For Luck!

The sound of a kiss is not so loud as that of a cannon, but its echo lasts a great deal longer.

Oliver Wendell Holmes, Sr.
1809 – 1894

A Kiss For Luck!

Part I:
The Assembly Line

Chicago, Illinois
Christmas Eve, Friday, December 24, 1943
Five months before D-Day

Betty was upstairs in her bedroom when she heard the jangle of the crank-style bell in the middle of the front door. One long and two short bursts.

"Josh is here!" her mother called out from the kitchen, recognizing his signature ring.

"Tell him I'll be right there!" Betty shouted down.

"I'll get it," Betty's father called out as he pushed himself up out of the easy chair in the living room. As he walked to the door, he sang along with the tune that was playing on the radio next to his chair. "... *just like the ones I used to know* ..." He had all the words right, but he wasn't hitting quite the same notes as Bing.

"Hi, Mr. Hancock," Josh said when the door opened. "Merry Christmas! Is Betty ready?"

"Has she ever been on time?" her father asked motioning the tall young man to come inside.

Josh laughed. "She's worth the wait," he said, used to Mr. Hancock's teasing of his only daughter. "I'll just wait out here on the porch, if that's alright. I don't want to warm up and then have to come back out into the cold, again."

"Suit yourself," Mr. Hancock said with a shrug as he closed the door. "... *to heeear sleigh bells in the snooow* ..."

"Where's Josh?" Betty asked as she bounded down the stairs, having heard the front door open and close.

"Said he wanted to wait outside in the cold," her father said with a shake of his head. "I swear, sometimes that boy don't seem to have the sense that God gave a goose." As he retreated back to his chair, he continued to abuse the song. " ... *I'm dreaming of a white Christmas* ..."

Josh stood on the porch looking out at the few strings of blue, red, green, and yellow Christmas lights on the houses across the street. He had been praying all month that there would be snow tonight, but there wasn't even any on the ground. He remembered, years ago, Father Jacob telling his Sunday school class, that God answered *all* prayers ... but sometimes the answer was *no*. He wasn't disappointed, really; it's just that a gently falling snow would have made the night that much better, even more magical.

As Betty pulled on her coat, she got up on her tiptoes and peeked out at Josh through one of the high windows in the front door. He was just standing there, his back to the house, with his hands stuffed into his coat pockets. Was he mad because she was making him wait out in the cold? He *could* have come inside.

She pulled on her knit hat, flipped her scarf around her neck, and pulled on her mittens. She checked herself in the small mirror on the wall, adjusted her hat a bit, and then pulled open the door.

Josh turned as she stepped outside, and she gave him her best smile as she said, "Sorry to keep you waiting. You should have come inside where it's warm. It's *freezing* out here!"

He just looked at her and slowly shook his head.

Her smile faded, and she began to formulate another iteration of her apology, but he spoke first.

"Could you *possibly* look any more adorable?" he said as he looked at the face he had known since the third grade; the lips he had first kissed in the fifth grade; the nose he had accidentally broken their sophomore year in high school; and the green eyes that twinkled like the tinsel on a Christmas tree.

Her pretty face peeked out from within the soft frame of a knitted hat of white wool pulled low over her ears and all the way down to her eyebrows, and a matching scarf slung around her neck that snuggled up under her chin.

Her smile spread across her face, once again, and she reached out her mittened hands to him. "I was afraid you were mad because you had to wait out in the cold."

Smiling, he shook his head, and turned her toward the display of multi-colored lights. "Look at that," he said. "I just love Christmas. I didn't want to miss a second of it. I'm so glad people have put their lights up again this year. Remember in '41, right after Pearl? Everyone thought we needed to be blacked out. It was so bleak. It didn't seem like Christmas at all that year."

"I love it, too," she said. "But don't you wish it was snowing? Like Bing Crosby is dreaming about?"

He laughed. "You have no idea how much I wish that. But you know, even if he got the snow he's dreaming about he'd still be missing the best part." He bent down and kissed her lips. "Someone to share it with," he said.

He took her mitten in his glove, and led her down the steps into the crisp, clear night.

"Are the hat and scarf new?" he asked as they walked. "I don't remember seeing them before."

"My Mom made them for me for Christmas, but she gave them to me early so I could wear them to choir practice tonight. The mittens, too. Do you like them?"

"They're adorable, and you're adorable all wrapped up in them," he repeated. "I'll have to remember to thank your mother."

As they walked along the sidewalk, their breath visible in the glow of the street lamps and Christmas lights, Betty began to sing, "*I'm dreaming of a white Christmas ...*"

Josh smiled as he listened to her. He suspected that she had inherited her *love* for music from her father, but he was grateful that her dad's inability to carry a tune had politely skipped a generation. When she finished the first verse, he joined her in harmony on the second. They loved to sing together.

After they had finished the song, they walked for a while in silence. The night was so quite and peaceful—a near perfect Christmas Eve—that it almost seemed inappropriate to disturb it with talking.

At the end of the block, the church steeple came into sight, and Josh knew that there was never going to be a better time to say what he had been rehearsing in his head and in front of his mirror for two weeks.

"I've decided that I'm going to join the Army, rather than the Navy," he began as they walked on.

"Really?" Betty said. "Why?"

That he was going to enlist was not the least bit surprising; just about every guy she knew was joining up as soon as they turned 18, and Josh's birthday was February 14th. But Josh had always talked about going into the Navy, like his father had in World War I, and like his two older brothers had right after Pearl Harbor.

"Well," Josh said, "I figure that if I join the Navy, all I'm going to get to see is a lot of water. In the Army, I'll get to see Europe—or at least what's left of it. My Dad says they're going to need lots of soldiers to round up the Nazis after we make the big invasion."

"When will that be?" Betty asked. She secretly hoped it would be before the middle of February, so Josh didn't have to be part of it.

"Don't know," he shrugged. "Whenever the Brits and our fly boys get done bombing, I guess."

"How long will you be over there, do you think?" she asked. She knew that he couldn't know the answer to that question; nobody could. She was just hoping for some assurance that he *would* be coming home.

"I read in the paper where some general said that he figured our boys would all be home for next Christmas."

"That's still a long time with people shooting at you," she said.

"I'll keep my head down," he joked, trying to soften her fears, but having the very same fears himself.

"Maybe you'll meet some cute girl in England or Italy, and you won't want to come home at all," she kidded him ... but only half in jest. That too was a very real worry for her. And one of the reasons she was more comfortable with him joining the Navy; there would be far fewer girls to meet.

Although he could tell from her voice that she was teasing him—at least partially—her comment surprised him. The whole conversation that had played over and over in his head for the past week revolved around his fear that *she* would meet someone new while he was gone. Finding that she was apparently as worried about losing him as he was about losing her gave him just the boost of confidence that he needed to go ahead with what he had been rehearsing.

"Don't worry about me meeting somebody else over there," he said as they passed under the next streetlight. "You're the only girl in the whole world for me."

With that, he stopped and faced her, and then took his gloves off and got down in front of her on one knee.

When he stopped her and knelt down, she thought he needed to tie his shoe. But then she realized he was wearing his winter boots, and the proverbial light came on.

Josh reached into his jacket pocket and took out a small square box. He tilted the top of the box back, and said, "Betty Hancock, will you wait for me until I get back, and then do me the honor of being my bride?"

She looked down at the delicate gold band in the box, topped with a small green stone that seemed to sparkle in the dull glow of the streetlight as if a tiny magical fire was captured inside it.

Josh looked up at her face, framed by her white hat and scarf, and silhouetted by the glow from the streetlight above. He was quite sure that no angel in heaven ever looked more beautiful.

She looked from the ring to Josh's face, and as her smile spread from ear to ear, and her eyes began to fill with tears, she found that her voice was completely failing her, and all she could do was nod.

As he watched the smile spread across her face, and her eyes fill with tears, he caught the same twinkle in her green eyes that he had seen in the emerald in the jewelry store.

It was only when he noticed her silent nod that he realized that he'd been holding his breath since he had asked her to marry him. He finally exhaled, and along with his breath, he felt the nearly suffocating anxiety of her saying *no* leave his body at the same time.

With a smile mirroring hers, he took the mitten off her left hand, and still on one knee, he slid the ring onto her finger.

As he slipped the mitten off of her hand, her eyes were so full of joyful tears that she could hardly see what he was doing. But when she felt the ring slide over her finger, she suddenly understood why the ancient Greeks thought that there was a vein that ran directly from the third finger of the left hand right to the heart.

He stood up, took her in his arms, and said, "I am the happiest and luckiest man in the world." Then he kissed her lips long and passionately.

When their lips finally parted, with happy tears streaming down her cheeks, she said, "I'm going to write you every day while you're gone, and I'm going to seal every letter with a kiss just like that one."

"That'll be my daily kiss for luck!" he said. "It'll be way better than any rabbit's foot or four leaf clover!"

They started off toward the church, once again, but she refused to put her mitten back on. She wanted to feel his hand in hers, and know that both of their fingers were entwined around the ring that would bind their hearts together forever.

"I'm sorry I couldn't afford a diamond," he said as they neared the church. "The emerald reminded me so much of your eyes, though, that I thought it would be a nice substitute, for now. I'm going to save my Army pay, and when I get back I'll buy you a *real* engagement ring, I promise."

"Fat chance of that!" she said. "Not you or anyone else is getting this ring off my finger! Ever!"

Rock-Ola Manufacturing Corporation
Chicago, Illinois
Monday, May 8, 1944: 11:58 p.m.
One month before D-Day

"Okay, girls!" Maggie called out. "I think that's it. Let's let the line clear out. Fantastic job tonight! 388! That even breaks *day* shift's record! Fantastic!"

"One more, Maggie!" Betty pleaded as she looked up at the factory clock. "It's two minutes to twelve; we can get one more rifle down the line." Without waiting for a reply from Maggie, Betty called out to the other girls, "Come on! One more, one more! We can do it! Lydia, get a recoil plate into the stock, Come on, let's go! One more!"

When the clock clicked over to midnight and the shift bell rang, 389 M1 Carbine rifles had cleared the assembly line, and would soon be on their way to GIs headed for Europe and the build up for the long-awaited and much-anticipated invasion of Europe.

Maggie Kelly was the 24-year-old swing-shift supervisor of Rock-Ola's M1 Carbine final assembly line, but 19-year-old Betty Hancock was the line's cheerleader.

Betty, Maggie, and the rest of the girls felt pretty darned good as they punched out on the time clock and stepped out of the factory into the cold Chicago air that night. Their shift—the 4:00 p.m. to midnight "swing shift"—had just assembled 389 rifles in eight hours. Not only had they broken their *own* shift record, they had taken the day shift's record away, too! And not by just a little. They had cranked out 20 more rifles than the previous factory high, and 31 more than their own shift ever had.

Of course, even 389 was a long way from the 500 rifles per shift that the Army had set as Rock-Ola's production goal, but nobody really saw that mark as being attainable anymore. Even eternally-optimistic Maggie had lowered her sights to 400.

At the front gate, Betty wished the other girls a good night, and went to retrieve her bicycle for the four and a half mile ride home. The bright red Schwinn had been her older brother's paper route transportation until he started high school, but now, even though it was a boy's bike, it served her perfectly. And although Betty was old enough to get her driver's license now, war rationing of gasoline and the scarcity of cars made having it rather pointless.

The temperature had been cool and clear when Betty arrived at the factory in the afternoon—not unusual for early May in Chicago—but now at midnight, as she walked to the bike lot, she felt a few drops of rain. And it was so cold that she was only a little surprised that it wasn't *snow*! In *May*! Stupid lake-effect weather! She hoped that she could make it home before it really started coming down. In a light coat, with a knit hat and mittens, she wasn't dressed for a downpour.

Betty's buoyant mood about her shift's success was dulled by the surprising change in weather, but it positively plunged when she reached the lot, and she saw that the rear tire on her bike was flat. She would have to walk it all the way home and, unless her father had a tire patch that he wasn't saving for one of the nearly bald tires on his Hudson, she would have to walk *back* to work tomorrow.

A mile into her walk home the rain changed from sprinkles to a constant cold drizzle. A half mile after that it was coming down like it really meant it. The wind was picking up, blowing the rain directly at her, stinging her exposed face. And her feet were soaked and freezing! With no mention of a storm in the paper this morning, Betty had not bothered to wear her overshoes or a raincoat, or to pack an umbrella.

She stopped for a minute and hid under a big elm tree, the wide trunk of which also shielded her from the wind and driving rain. She was so cold that she wasn't sure that she was going to be able to make it home pushing the bicycle. With the wind and the uneven sidewalk, it took both hands to guide the bike, so she couldn't put even one hand in front of her face to shield it. But she couldn't just leave the bike there. It would surely be stolen, and then she'd have to walk to and from work *every* day.

She looked around for some place to hide it, but in the dark of the night and with the veil of rain, she couldn't see more than ten or fifteen feet away.

She finally resigned herself to pushing onward with the bicycle.

Just before she turned from her shelter behind the tree, she noticed a pair of headlights coming toward her through the rain. She considered stepping to the curb and sticking her thumb out to hitch a ride. But she hesitated, thinking how horrified her mother would be at such unladylike behavior. Hitchhiking was something that hobos did, not respectable young women. And there was still the problem of the bike.

Still, the car would likely be so warm ... and dry ...

Finally, she decided and she turned away from the approaching lights, and kept her thumbs to herself.

To her surprise, the car pulled to the side of the road and stopped abreast of her. The passenger window rolled down, and then a familiar voice called out from the interior.

"Betty! What are you doing standing out here in the cold? You got a flat tire there?"

It was Bob Devers, the swing-shift assembly manager from the factory. He had also been her older brother's best friend throughout high school.

"Yeah. And right in the middle of a surprise storm," she answered as she hurried over to the open window. The warm air that billowed from the car felt wonderful on her aching face.

"You must be freezing! Come on, get in the car out of that cold," he said, pushing the door open. "Let me give you a ride home."

She didn't need to be asked twice. She climbed into the car, closed the door, and quickly rolled up the window. "Thank you, Bob! My feet feel like ice cubes."

"Lucky I came along when I did, I'd say," he said.

She hesitated a moment, not wanting to seem ungrateful for just being in the warm car, but then said, "What about my bike? I don't want to just leave it there."

"Heck no," he said. "Somebody would steal it for sure. I'll put it in the rumble seat."

"You're sure? I wouldn't want it to ruin the cushions or anything."

"It'll be fine," he said as he pulled up the hood of the slicker he was wearing and got out. She watched through the back window as he opened the trunk to expose the fold-up seat, then pulled a heavy canvas tarp up over the upholstery. He then retrieved the bike, picked it up, and carefully slid the back wheel down into the foot well, allowing the handlebars to hook over the back of the seat after he doubled the canvas to protect the paint.

"There!" he said, when he climbed back into the car. "Perfect fit."

"Thank you so much," Betty said. She had never really cared for Bob—she had always felt a little uncomfortable around him when he was hanging out with her brother—but she was sure glad to be sitting next to him right now.

When war was declared after Pearl Harbor, Betty's brother, Donny, and Bob had made a pact that after graduation they would join the Navy together and go fight the Japs. In their senior year, Bob was injured playing football, and spent the last month of his school year in the hospital. He received his diploma in a wheelchair, but was permanently deferred from active military service. Donny and Bob ended up joining the Army with several other buddies, and while they shipped out to Europe, Bob, as a corporal in the quartermaster corps, worked stateside to make the weapons that would help his former classmates beat the Krauts.

"You and the girls did a bang up job, today," Bob said as he pulled the car out onto the street. "389 rifles, and only three of them didn't pass inspection. And that was just because of a loose pin in the front sight. Those'll be fixed tonight, so we'll ship the full 389 to the Army. How the devil did you do it, anyway? Did you work through your lunch break or something?"

"Nope," she replied, more than just a little proud to be able to explain her idea. As she positioned her freezing feet directly in front of the heater under the dashboard, she explained, "You know how we all sit at the long table and each of us puts our part into the rifle and then slides it along to the next girl?"

"Sure," he said. "Classic assembly line."

"Okay, so Sally Higgins—I don't know if you know her, she's the first girl at the final assembly table—she screws the buttplate onto the end of the stock, and sets the recoil plate into the top of it. Then she slides the rifle to Lydia Howe, who holds the nut for the recoil plate screw under the stock, and then puts in the screw and tightens it. Then she slides the rifle to Lucy Katz, who puts the barrel assembly into the stock, making sure it's latched under the recoil plate.

"Then it's my turn," she went on. "Only thing is that the rifle is pointing *away* from the first girls, and Lucy has to turn the whole thing around as she slides it to me so the barrel end is pointing *toward* me. She has to do that because that's the easiest way for me to put on the hand guard and the bayonet band.

"Well, today, I asked Maggie if we could try something, and she said okay. So we pulled the table away from the wall, and Sally, Lydia, and Lucy sat on the other side. Only Lydia was first, and she screwed the recoil plate into the stock then passed it to Lucy, who put in the barrel assembly. Sally was sitting right across from me, and when she got the rifle from Lucy, the barrel was already pointing at me, so we didn't have to turn it around. Then, she put on the butt plate at the same time that I put on the hand guard and bayonet band. Without the turning and with two of us putting our parts on at the same time, it took us a few less seconds to finish the whole rifle."

"That is brilliant!" Bob said. "And so utterly simple! You're a genius!"

Betty blushed and gave a little shrug. "My dad says I have a gift for organizing. Of course, he won't let me organize his garage—he say's he'd never be able to find anything."

"So, did you show the graveyard girls what you came up with?" Bob asked.

"Oh, sure," Betty said. "We showed them, and they'll show day shift when they come in. Plus Maggie is putting it in her report."

"I'll put it in mine, too," Bob said, "*and* recommend you for a citation. The Army appreciates it when somebody performs above and beyond the call of duty."

"Gee, that would be swell! Thanks, Bob. Will I get a raise?"

"Probably not," Bob chuckled. "Just a fancy piece of paper and a handshake from Colonel Nathan."

Betty shrugged. "Better than a stick in the eye, I guess. Besides, it's really all about making more rifles for our boys to use."

"It'll sure look good in your employment folder," Bob said as he turned the car into Betty's driveway. Stopping in front of the garage, he turned off the engine and headlights so as not to wake up Betty's folks or the neighbors at one in the morning.

Betty jumped out and ran for the cover of the breezeway that connected the house to the garage.

Bob extracted the bike from the rumble seat, then walked it under the breezeway, leaning it against the kitchen steps.

"Thanks for stopping to give me a lift, Bob," Betty said as she started up the steps. "It was getting pretty cold. And the citation thing is great, too. I guess I'll see you tomorrow at work, huh?"

"Hey, doesn't your knight in shining armor get a kiss for coming to your rescue?" Bob asked with an overacted look of hurt.

Betty groaned inwardly, but forced a smile and a slight chuckle to make sure that Bob knew that she didn't take him too seriously. "Of course," she said.

"Isn't that the code of damsels in distress?" She leaned down and gave him a quick kiss on the cheek.

"I take it that's for rescuing your bicycle," he said. "Now one for saving *you* from the cold," he added and puckered his lips.

"Bob, you know I'm engaged," she said, trying to keep a lightness in her voice to mask her rising revulsion. "I don't think Josh would want me going around kissing other men." To try to break the tension, she added with a chuckle, "I sure don't want him kissing other girls!"

"Oh, I'm sure Josh would be okay with a friendly little kiss since I probably saved you from getting frostbite. It's a little hard to go for hand-in-hand walks along the lakefront after they've amputated your feet. I'm sure he'd want you to treat me right for watching out for you."

Realizing that he was not going to be talked out of this, Betty saw that she had two choices. She could turn and go into the house—in which case she would probably anger him so much that he might try to get her fired or something—or she could give in and kiss him, and then explain it to Josh in the letter she would write to him in the morning, and hope that he would understand and forgive her.

"You're probably right," she said with a smile that was even harder to force than the first one.

She leaned down to give him a quick peck on the lips, but as soon as their lips touched, she felt his hand on the back of her head holding her from pulling away as he pressed his lips forcefully into hers.

Leaning down from the step, she was off balance, and unable to pull away for several long seconds. When he finally released her, she jerked away, and raised her hand to slap him across his grinning face.

She stopped herself, however, as she realized that a slap with her mittened hand—soaking wet though it was—would inflict no pain whatsoever, and might antagonize him to a point where he would strike back. She had seen eruptions of his temper, before.

Instead, she snarled at him, "That was rude, Bob Devers! Josh is not going to be happy when I tell him!" She pulled the kitchen door open and stormed inside, but before the door closed, she heard Bob laughing as he walked back to his car.

Inside, she leaned with her back against the door as tears of anger, frustration, and humiliation filled her eyes. "*You son of a bitch!*" she hissed under her breath.

When she had gotten out of the car, her only thought was to get inside and stand next to the warm kitchen stove to drive the cold from her bones before she went upstairs to crawl into bed. Now, with her adrenaline pumping, she felt neither cold *nor* tired.

She took off her coat, hat, and mittens, and hung them up to dry. She slid off her shoes, pushed them under the stove, and then went upstairs to her room. She changed out of her wet clothes, and into her pajamas, toweled her hair, and then wrapped herself in her bathrobe and pushed her feet into her slippers.

She took several sheets of stationery and two envelopes from her dresser drawer, and headed back down to the warm kitchen. She found a couple of pencils in the drawer, ground them to fine points in the wall mounted sharpener, and sat down at the table to begin to write.

When she had first started writing to Donny while he was in basic training and then in Africa, she had used her father's fountain pen. The letters looked so elegant.

Now that he was in Italy, where it seemed to rain constantly, if a letter got wet, the ink would run, and he would end up with little more than a sheet of blue-smudged paper. A letter written in pencil could be read even soaking wet.

She decided to write her daily letter to her brother first, hoping that she would be a little more calm when she wrote the one to Josh.

> Dearest Brother,
>
> I hope this letter finds you safe and well, warm and dry. We are all well here, and I am warming up, which I'll tell you about in a minute. But first the good news. I can't talk about the details in this letter, of course, but I'm sure you'll be happy to hear that my shift at the factory set a production record tonight! And not just for swing shift, but for all three shifts! And it was all because of my idea!"

She thought about mentioning the citation that Bob had promised, but figured if he had been serious in the car, he probably wouldn't go through with it, now.

> As you can imagine, I was pretty happy when I left the plant at midnight, but that changed quickly when I found that the back tire on your old bicycle was flat. Then, while I was pushing the bike home, it started raining freezing-cold cats and dogs! And the wind was blowing it straight sideways! By the time I made it to Grenshaw Street, I thought my feet were going to freeze solid, and I could hardly feel my nose at all! Just when I didn't think I could go on, Bob Devers happened to drive by.

Writing those last few words made her think of something that she hadn't before. Bob lived in the other direction from the plant. Why would he *just happen by* in the middle of a storm miles out of his own way home? Had he seen her walking her bike when she left the factory, and then waited for her to get good and cold before *happening by* to come to her rescue? Then something he said when he stopped came back to her. He seemed to have known that she had a flat tire. Why wouldn't he suspect a broken chain or some other malfunction? She remembered the bike standing in a puddle; he couldn't have seen the bottom of the tire to see that it was flat.

Suddenly, a memory from years ago popped into her head. She pulled on her father's dry coat, took the flashlight from the shelf next to the door, and went outside. Protected by the breezeway, she wheeled her bike into the cold garage through the side door.

Under the glow of a single bare bulb, and working in the narrow space beside her father's car, Betty rotated the back wheel around until the valve stem was at the bottom where she could look at it with the flashlight. Even before she flicked the light on, she noticed that the valve cap was missing.

She knelt down and looked closely at the valve, and she could see a small sharp stone wedged into stem, holding the valve open.

It would probably never have occurred to her to even look for something like that, except that she remembered her brother, when he was about 12, having done that same thing to one of their father's car tires as a practical joke. It was the only time she recalled her father ever being so mad that he used his belt on Donny.

The sound of Donny's crying had upset her so much that she had run to the garage and locked herself in the car where she cried and cried out of fear that her father was going to kill Donny, and then *he* would go to prison, leaving her mother and her all alone!

She suddenly wondered if maybe Bob had put Donny up to that little stunt all those years ago, and then let Donny take the punishment all by himself.

She found an awl in her father's tool rack, and pried the stone out of the valve. She then got the tire pump out of the Hudson's trunk, and two minutes later had the tire fully inflated. She waited another couple of minutes, but the tire showed no signs of deflating, again.

"*You son of a bitch!*" she repeated.

She returned to the kitchen, more furious than ever, and went back to the letter she was writing to her brother, ready to tell him what Bob had done.

As she touched the pen to the paper, she realized that what she was about to write was going to make her brother very angry when there wasn't a darned thing he could do about it.

If he was here she was sure he would at least punch Bob in the nose, but with him being half a world away in Italy, knowing that his supposed best friend was picking on his little sister would only frustrate him. It might even distract him from being a smart soldier, and she didn't want to even think about the consequences of losing your concentration when people were shooting at you!

As she stared at the unfinished letter, she recalled the poster that hung next to the time clock at the factory. It was a serious looking young woman with her hair in a bandana, holding a wrench and working on a big machine of some sort. Below her were the words, "*She's A WOW! And She Can Do It!*" WOW stood for Woman Ordinance Worker, and Betty was proud to be one of the millions of women who were accomplishing goals every day that they would never have been allowed to even attempt before the war, and which they themselves would hardly have thought possible a few years ago.

She crumbled the letter to her brother and threw it into the waste basket. She had planned to write a similar letter to Josh, but decided against that on the same what-can-he-do-about-it grounds. She would write both of the men in her life letters tomorrow—as she did every day—but neither of them would show the anger she had felt tonight.

She put the pencils away and went up to bed.

As she climbed the stairs, she reflected on how she had learned self-reliance and analytical thinking from her father, had inherited moral strength and conviction from her mother, and had been taught to be tough by her brother. Although she didn't know how, just yet, she felt confident that she was going to be able to handle this all on her own. The feeling made her smile.

Tuesday, May 9, 1944

When Betty got up at a quarter to eight the next morning, her father was long gone to his job as an inspector at the Champlain Valve Company, and her mother was already hard at work at Grey Brothers Textiles sewing military uniforms.

Betty took a pan from the cupboard, put in a cup of water, and lit the burner under it on the stove. She measured out a serving of oatmeal, and while she waited for the water to boil, she got out her paper and pencils to write her letters to Josh and Donny.

When her oatmeal was ready to eat, she poured herself half a glass of milk, and then filled it the rest of the way with water from the fridge. She took a sip, and made a face. She had gotten used to a lot of things during wartime rationing, but watered-down milk was not one of them.

She decided to write her letter to Josh, first.

> My Dearest Josh,
>
> I hope this letter finds you safe and well, warm and dry wherever you are.
>
> You would be so proud of me! I made a suggestion yesterday at the factory that allowed my shift to set a new record for production! And not just for swing shift, but for **all** shifts! As you can imagine, I was pretty happy when I left the plant, but that soon changed when I saw my bicycle. The back tire was flat!
>
> While I was pushing the bike home, it started raining cats and dogs! <u>Freezing-cold</u> cats and dogs! And the wind was blowing it straight sideways! The morning paper hadn't said anything about a storm, so I didn't wear my boots or scarf, or carry my umbrella. (You'd think that growing up in Chicago, I'd know better!) By the time I reached Grenshaw Street, my feet were like blocks of ice, and I couldn't feel my nose at all! Just

when I didn't think I could go on, Bob Devers happened to drive by.

In case you don't remember, Bob is with the quartermaster corps and works for the colonel who is in charge of all the plants that make those same things we make. He said he was going to recommend to the colonel that I get a citation for my idea at the factory! Pretty swell, don't you think? I'll let you know if it happens.

Oh, and I fixed the tire myself, by the way!

Cindy Marshall <u>finally</u> had her baby! It's a boy and they named him Roger Jr. I'd sure like to be there when Roger Sr. gets home and sees his son for the first time!

Not much more to talk about today. I'm going to write a letter to Donny, now, and I have to get the laundry done before I go back to work, so I'm going to say goodbye for now.

Please take care, and be safe. You are in my thoughts and prayers always!

All my love.
Betty

She then wrote a very similar letter to her brother. She set the two letters side by side on the kitchen counter, went into the bathroom, and applied a coat of glossy red lipstick. Returning to the letters, she leaned over and pressed her lips to each of them, leaving a bright red lip print near the bottom.

Across the lip prints she wrote, *A Kiss For Luck!* in big bold cursive letters. She had been ending her letters to Donny this way since he sailed for Africa, and *all* of Josh's letters had gotten her special kiss.

She folded the letters and slid them into their envelopes, addressed them, and affixed a two-cent stamp to each one. She then went to the front door to stick them in the mailbox that hung on the front of the house next to the door.

As she lifted the cover to the mailbox she noticed that Mr. Hale, the postman, was walking up the sidewalk two houses down. She decided to wait for him.

As he came up her walk, he held up an Army-issue envelope. "Letter here from Donny!" he said. "I hope it's good news."

"I hope so," Betty replied. "How is Larry? Have you heard from him lately?" Larry was Mr. Hale's only son and was stationed in England as a B-17 bomber pilot.

"Forty-eight missions!" Mr. Hale answered with obvious pride. "Two more and he'll rotate home to become an instructor."

"I'll remember him in my prayers, tonight," Betty said.

"Thank you, sweetheart," he said. "All our boys could use that."

In the kitchen, Betty put the other mail in her father's stack, but opened the letter from Donny.

> Dear Mom, Dad, and Sis,
>
> Having a great time! Wish you were here! Ha, ha! I don't wish anyone was here - especially me! Of course, I can't tell you were "here" is, except to tell you that we're still in Italy; no big secret there!
>
> I don't have much time to write, we're moving out in the morning, and I need to get some shut-eye. I just wanted to tell Betty that her "kiss for luck" that she puts on all my letters sure works!
>
> Yesterday, our company got the assignment to take out a Nazi artillery piece that was up in the hills, and giving our supply ships a hard time. Before we moved out, one of my buddies saw me kissing Betty's good luck lips on my letter, and he made me pass it around to every guy in my unit. (If your lips were sore one night a couple of weeks ago, now you know why! Ha, ha!)
>
> It was a hard fight and we lost too many of our boys, but not one guy from my unit was even wounded! Not a scratch! Needless to say, each and every guys now sees Betty's letters and her lips as being almost as valuable as fresh ammunition!
>
> I have to go now, the sarge is collecting our letters. Keep your letters coming, Betty, and whatever you do, don't run out of that lipstick!
>
> Love and hugs to all,
> Donny

Betty read the letter over twice more, smiling just as much each time. It had never occurred to her when she kissed her letters to send good luck to Donny that he would kiss them, as well, to receive it. That Donny's whole unit had done it—and it had apparently worked—thrilled her beyond anything she could have imagined when she first slicked her lips and started the silly ritual.

She put the letter back in its envelope and set it on the table for her mom and dad to read when they got home. She then went to start the laundry.

As she scrubbed at a stain in her father's work pants with a bar of Fels Naptha soap, she imagined Josh kissing her lip prints when he read her letters, too. He wasn't in combat yet, but she pictured him with her latest letter in his shirt pocket, right over his heart, ready to take out and kiss when the big European invasion finally did start. She wished that every GI could have a kiss for luck from a sweetheart, a wife, or even a sister to take with them when they jumped off the boat or out of the plane, or however they were going to get to Europe to fight.

She stopped in mid-scrub as she was suddenly struck with a wonderful idea!

For the rest of the morning Betty sped through her chores so she would have time to execute her plan before she had to get ready for work.

Betty got to the plant early that afternoon, and the first thing she wanted to know was whether day sift had managed to take their record away. The big tote board just inside the main entrance read: Day: 387, Swing: 389, Night: 372. They still held the record!

Betty looked around for someone to share her excitement with, and saw Maggie walking toward her through the horde of swing shift workers, most of whom Betty knew only in passing.

"Maggie! Did you see that," she said pointing to the board. "Day shift wasn't able to beat us! Isn't that swell? And I'll bet we can do even better tonight."

"That *is* swell," Maggie said as she gave Betty a hug. "You should be really proud. Between the three shifts, the factory put out 88 more rifles yesterday than the previous best day. And it was all your idea. That was great thinking, Betty."

There wasn't quite as much excitement behind Maggie's words as Betty had expected, but she was too eager to tell Maggie about her *new* idea to dwell on it.

"Thanks!" Betty said. "I'm glad it worked out so well, because I have another idea. Only this one isn't about *making* rifles; it's something for the boys who are going to be *using* our rifles.

"So, whenever I write to Donny or Josh," Betty began to explain, "down at the bottom corner of the letter ..."

"Did I hear right that you had a flat tire on your bicycle when you left the plant last night?" Maggie interrupted her in mid-sentence.

Betty was surprised at being cut off by her friend—a usually ultra-polite woman—with such a banal question.

"Yeah, but I got it fixed okay," Betty answered. "Why?"

20

"Did Bob Devers happen by on your way home, and offer you a ride?" Maggie asked.

Betty looked at her very curiously, and replied, "Yes. How did you know that?"

Maggie ignored her question and asked her own. "And did he demand a kiss as a reward for having *rescued* you when he dropped you off?"

Betty's mouth hung open. "How did you know that?" she asked at the same instant that the obvious answer was forming in her own head.

"Because he did the same thing to me about two weeks ago," Maggie said. "When Lucy told me a few minutes ago about your flat tire, I just had to ask you."

"That son of a ..." Betty stopped short of cussing in front of Maggie. "Was there an actual hole in your tire?" Betty asked. "Or was there just something stuck in the valve that let all the air out?"

"I don't know," Maggie said. "I took it to Henderson's Garage to have it fixed. But he didn't charge me for a patch or anything, so maybe there *wasn't* a hole in it!"

"Did he take your bike home for you? In the rumble seat?" Betty asked.

"Yes."

"And did he just *happen* to have a big sheet of canvas that he pulled over the seat to protect it?"

"That's exactly what he did!" Maggie said. "Did he do ..."

"Hello ladies!" Bob's voice came from behind them, startling both women. "I'm glad I found you two together. Did you see the board? Swing still holds the shift record, and the whole factory hit a new high yesterday, thanks to you two! I couldn't be more proud of my girls! So, come along with me before your shift starts. I've got a little surprise for the both of you."

He inserted himself between the two women, and put an arm over each of their shoulders as they walked.

"What's the surprise?" Betty asked as he led them away from the factory floor toward the office and warehouse area of the plant. After the previous night's events, Betty would have been a little suspicious of Bob's motives. But with Maggie's story thrown on top of it, she was decidedly wary, now. She was only going along with Bob because Maggie was with her.

"Colonel Nathan heard about the production numbers," Bob said, "and was in the area, so he dropped by to see what caused the spike and to see if he could use whatever our secret weapon was in his other rifle plants. I told him that I'd introduce him to my secret weapons personally. He's upstairs in Mr. Wilson's office waiting for us."

Todd Wilson was the factory's general manager—and Bob's uncle. It was widely suspected among the girls that that was how Bob had gotten his job in the first place, and how he kept it despite his marginal qualifications.

"Is this that citation you told me about?" Betty asked, surprised that he would still be going through with it.

"Nope. The Colonel found out before I had a chance to write up my report and recommend you," Bob said. "This could be even better, though. The Colonel is known for making snap field promotions, so in about ten minutes time, Betty, you could be supervisor of your whole line, and Mags, you could be a shift super on *days*. How would that be, huh?"

"He can just do that?" Maggie said. Betty picked up on the concern in Maggie's tone, but Bob was apparently oblivious to it.

"Well, since you girls are actually civilians," Bob replied, "all the Colonel can do is *recommend* that you get promoted. But don't worry, what he wants, he usually gets."

"But what if I don't ..." Maggie began.

"Don't think you deserve a promotion?" Betty interrupted her. "Don't be modest!" She then surprised her by pulling her out from under Bob's arm and pushing her toward the lady's room door they were passing.

To an equally surprised Bob, Betty said, "We need to freshen up before we see the Colonel and Mr. Wilson. Just be a minute."

As the restroom door swung closed behind them, Maggie said, "I was going to say that I don't *want* a promotion. I like where I am. Besides, if he wanted a kiss just for giving us a ride home, what would he ..."

Betty stopped Maggie from talking so loudly by putting a finger to her own lips, and pointing to the three occupied stalls. Fortunately, two of the girls in adjacent stalls were carrying on a conversation, so no one overheard Maggie's comment.

Maggie leaned closer, and continued in a whisper, "If he wanted a kiss just for giving us a ride home, what is he going to think a *promotion* deserves?"

"I don't want a promotion, either. I love the girls I work with, Maggie, and we all love working for you," Betty whispered in reply. "But I've got an idea. When we get up there in front of the Colonel, we should ..." But she had to stop mid-sentence as the door to the end stall creaked open.

Betty had seen the woman who came out of the stall in the factory, but didn't actually know her. Maggie, being a line supervisor, did know her, however, and the woman greeted her by name, then asked, "Who's next?" indicating the vacated stall.

"You take it," Betty said to Maggie. As the woman washed her hands, she and Betty exchanged pleasantries, and then the woman left.

Hearing Betty say goodbye to the woman, Maggie came back out of the stall. Before Betty could resume telling her her plan, however, two more ladies came into the restroom. Both women knew Maggie, and one of them said, "You know Bob Devers is outside waiting for you?"

Betty quickly realized that she was not going to be able explain her idea to Maggie in private, and indicated that they should leave. Leaning close to Maggie's ear as she opened the door for her, Betty whispered, "Just follow my lead when we get up there."

When they emerged, Bob was standing there looking at his watch.

"Sorry," Betty said. "There was a line."

He just shook his head as he hurried them along to the stairway.

Upstairs, Bob knocked on the open door of his uncle's office.

"Come in! Come in!" Mr. Wilson boomed, interrupting his conversation with Colonel Nathan.

"So, these are the little ladies you told me about," the Colonel said.

"Yes, sir," Bob answered. "Colonel Nathan, may I introduce Betty Hancock and Maggie Kelly. Rock-Ola's secret weapons to higher production."

The Colonel reached out and shook the women's hands. "You girls should be very proud," he said. "What you did allowed this company to show the biggest single-day jump in production that there's ever been in any of my rifle plants. That's the kind of initiative and good old fashioned Yankee ingenuity that gets rewarded in my factories."

Betty looked between the Colonel and Mr. Wilson with her best what-the-heck-are-you-talking-about look.

Then, as if it suddenly became clear to her, she turned to Bob, and said, "Oh, no, Bob. Not again. Not about something as important as this."

She quickly turned back to the other men to keep from laughing at Bob's baffled expression.

"Bob is always doing this," she lied to his superiors. "He's always giving us girls more credit than we ought to have when he's the one who really makes the swing shift click. If anyone deserves to be rewarded here, it's Bob. Moving us around to get more work done with the same number of girls was *his* idea."

The Colonel and Mr. Wilson looked at Bob.

Betty could see that he was trying to figure out why she was telling such blatant lies, and before he could make any kind of reply, she added some reinforcement to her fabrication.

Pointing back and forth between herself and Maggie, she said, "Do you really think a couple of girls could come up with something as clever as that?"

Betty knew that that would be an easily accepted pretense, because although women had been allowed into the wartime factories to take on what had previously been men-only jobs, most men still didn't think that women were very bright about anything mechanical or industrial.

The two men looked at Maggie, who just shrugged, and said, "She's right. It was Bob's idea."

Betty got the impression that Maggie still wasn't sure what she was doing, but at least she was playing along.

The men looked back at Bob, but again, before he could muster a reply, Betty took the initiative.

"I don't know anything about how factories are supposed to work, or anything," she lied, "but it seems to me that you need someone like Bob at *all* your plants. Why, with someone like that at your *best* factory, I'll bet you'd get even *more* production out of them."

Betty nearly laughed at the change in Bob's expression as his confusion was replaced by the comprehension of what she was trying to do. The last thing he would want is for the Colonel to promote him out from under his uncle's protective wing.

Risking one more layer of pure bull, Betty went on, "And Bob doesn't just look out for us girls at work, either. Why just last night he gave me a ride home in the rain, miles out of his way, because my bicycle had a flat tire."

Finally understanding what Betty was doing, Maggie jumped in with both feet.

"She's right about him looking out for us like a big brother," she said. "He even took the time to teach me how to supervise the girls on the line to get more out of them than they ever thought they could give. Just look at the tote board; numbers don't lie."

Bob just stood there dumbstruck. Betty could see in his eyes that he was searching for some way to respond, but she knew that he couldn't very well tell the Colonel and his uncle, "*Don't believe a word of what they're saying! I'm really just an incompetent lecher who lets the air out of girls' tires to trick them into kissing me!*"

The Colonel looked at Bob, and said, "I commend what you tried to do for your girls here, Bob, but I guess I should have known from the start that an idea like that wouldn't come from the little ladies on the line, but from a man who understands manufacturing and organization."

He turned to Betty and Maggie, and said, "You young women did the right thing by bringing Bob's little fib to our attention. I know that you just want him to get the credit that he really deserves, but I'm afraid your loyalty might have backfired on you. Innovative thinkers like Bob don't grow on trees. I think I'm going to need to put his obvious talents to work at one of my *less* productive plants, now that I know what he can do."

To Betty, he patiently explained, "You may not understand it, but born leaders like Bob aren't needed in the *best* plants; they can have a much bigger impact getting the *worst* plant to run better."

"I *guess* I see that," Betty said, putting on her best worried look. "And I'm sure that Bob can do that, but who's going to take his place *here*? What are *we* supposed to do? I don't want our numbers to start going *down*."

"Don't you worry your pretty little heads about that," Mr. Wilson said. "We'll see to it that you ladies don't have to fend for yourselves. That would just never do, now would it?" He looked at his watch, and added, "Looks like you have just enough time to make it downstairs before your shift starts, so you'd better run along and put rifles together, and let us men do what *we* do best."

"Thank you ladies," the Colonel added. "I'm sorry that you'll be losing your friend here, but I'm sure you realize that it's the best thing for the war effort."

"Yes, sir," Betty said. "Whatever will get our boys home even one day sooner is worth any sacrifice we need to make."

As the two women left, they overheard Mr. Wilson saying as he closed the office door, "I'm proud of you, son. I always knew you were holding something back. I finally understand what you've been doing."

24

Hurrying down the stairs, Maggie laughed, "That was a stroke of genius! How did you know that's what the Colonel would do if you gave Bob credit for your idea?"

"Probably eighteen years of watching my Mom get my Dad to do whatever she wants and having him think it was *his* idea," Betty said. The two women laughed as they ran toward the assembly line.

"What was the other idea you wanted to tell me about?" Maggie asked as they ran. "If it's anything like your last two, I'm already all for it!"

"Let's get some rifles going down the line," she said to Maggie as she slid into her seat at the assembly table just as the factory's master clock clicked over to four o'clock and the shift bell rang. "Then I'll explain my idea to you and all the girls at the same time."

The girls fell into their usual rhythm almost right away. The tempo of the clicks, clacks, snaps, and swishes of metal and wood parts being fit together told all of the girls that they were in sync without them even looking.

As Betty passed the sixth rifle down the line to where it would have its front sight keyed and pinned in place, she began to explain her newest idea to the rest of the girls.

"I write a letter to Josh and Donny every day, and at the bottom, I always write 'A Kiss For Luck!' on top of a lip print I kiss onto the page with my best red lipstick." She then told them about her brother's letter from Italy, and how her kiss apparently *had* brought him and his unit good luck.

"So, I got to thinking," she went on, "wouldn't it be swell if every GI who got one of our rifles got a kiss for luck to go with it?" She then took a small stack of paper slips from her shirt pocket, and put them on the table between the girls.

Hardly missing a beat in their mechanical symphony, each girl slid one of the slips over to look at it. Each slip was about an inch wide, and a little over two inches long. In the middle was a pair of bright red lips, that had been smooched onto the paper after Betty had written, "A kiss for luck!" in her best flowing cursive.

"I want to stick one of these under the barrel of every rifle we put together," Betty told them, "right in front of the slide pocket in the stock."

Maggie laughed. "I love it!" she said. "Just like a box of Cracker Jack; a prize in every rifle."

"But it will fall out the first time the soldier takes his rifle apart to clean it," Lucy pointed out.

"Probably," Betty agreed. "But when the lucky GI does find it, I'm hoping he'll maybe stick it in his pocket, and give it a kiss every time he's headed into battle. It sure seemed to work for my brother and *his* unit."

"It sure can't hurt!" Maggie said.

With only six sheets of 5 ½ inch by 8 ½ inch stationery that she felt she could spare, Betty had only been able to make 96 slips, so only about one fourth of their night's production would get lucky prizes.

Blaming it on the time it took them to work out the best way to add the slip-insertion into their routine, the women were only able to tie their previous night's record, but vowed to do better the next night. They also agreed that each girl would bring in a stack of slips cut from their own paper, and with their own handwriting and lip prints on each one.

The next night, even though they had added the slip's insertion step to the assembly process, the swing-shift girls, by virtue of their renewed motivation, managed to break their own record with 392 rifles, and to keep day shift from retaking the lead.

While every one of the 392 rifles went down the line with a lucky talisman inside it, the girls were left with only eight slips for the next day, and none of them had any more spare stationery.

Betty, Maggie, and the other three girls were standing near the time clock, having just punched out, trying to figure out where they could get more writing paper for the next day's production.

They were discussing whether Mr. Levy, who owned the drugstore a block from Betty's house, might donate a pad or two of writing paper if Betty explained what the girls wanted it for. Betty thought the idea had a pretty good chance of working, because Mr. Levy had two sons in the Army, himself.

With a plan of action, the girls were saying their goodbyes when Kyle Olson walked up and took Maggie aside.

Kyle was a sergeant with the Army's quartermaster corps, and worked as a final inspector for rifles being crated for shipment from Rock-Ola. He and Maggie had dated a couple of times. Once, they had gone to see *Double Indemnity* with Fred MacMurray and Barbara Stanwyck, and another time he'd taken her to the Saturday night dance at the USO.

Maggie liked Kyle well enough, but she wasn't sure that she wanted to get involved with someone whose career could see him transferred out of her life at a moment's notice.

Kyle, on the other hand, was hopelessly in love with Maggie. When he kissed her lips at the end of their second date, he knew that he had met the girl he was going to marry.

Kyle looked around to see that no one was within casual listening distance, then he said to Maggie, "I was just doing a random-sample teardown to inspect one of the rifles that came off your line tonight, and I found this." He took a slip of paper from his pocket, and handed it to her.

She recognized it immediately as one of the slips that she had written and kissed herself.

"I guess you'd like an explanation," she said.

"Not really," he replied. "I understand what you're trying to do. And off the record, I think it's a great idea to send our boys an encouraging note from the girls they left behind. Officially, though, it's against Army regs for there to be *anything* in a weapon that is not listed in its bill of materials.

"Now, *I* know that that little piece of paper," he went on, "isn't going to have the slightest effect on the performance of the rifle it's in, and I also know that it could have a *profound* and positive effect on the morale of any soldier who might find it. But the Army doesn't care what *I* think, they just want their rules followed.

"And the rule against foreign objects—which even a little slip of paper constitutes—is that the affected weapon or weapons must be returned to the manufacturer for disassembly, 100% inspection of the entire lot, repair if necessary, and resubmittal along with a corrective action report to the quartermaster for re-inspection."

"Every ..." Maggie managed, barely above a whisper. "every *one* of them?" Her normally rosy complexion turned ashen, and her mouth hung slightly agape.

Kyle had suspected that the slip he found was not an isolated incident. Maggie's reaction told him he was right, which put him in a very conflicted spot.

On the one hand was the Army regulation against foreign objects. It was clear and to the point. Countering that, Kyle knew that the slips would do no harm, and he felt that they could actually be *good* foreign objects, although the Army had no such definition.

Then there were the production numbers. Rejecting an entire shift of rifles—for such a minor infraction—was not good for the war effort. Nor would it be for the morale of the girls who had broken another plant record putting the rifles together. And it would certainly not ingratiate them with upper management or Army brass.

And that segued into Kyle's adoration of Maggie. Rejection of nearly 400 rifles from the line that she was supervising would probably get her fired. It would certainly get her demoted.

He needed to be very careful how he phrased his next question to be sure that Maggie could give him the answer he needed to hear.

Standing next to the plant door, Betty had been watching Maggie and Kyle talk. Betty knew that the two had gone out a couple of times, and so she imagined that he was asking her out on another date. Maybe to celebrate two record breaking shifts and a tie. Betty thought they would make a swell couple, so she was happy watching them chat.

Then she saw Kyle hand Maggie a slip of paper with a bright red lip print. A few moments later, she saw the blood drain from Maggie's face, and watched her whole body slump as if a huge weight had been dropped on her shoulders.

Betty hurried in her direction. She didn't know what was wrong, but if it had anything to do with the *Kiss For Luck!* slip, she knew it was her fault.

"Hey you two," Betty said with a smile and make-believe naiveté as she approached, "what's all the kibitzing? If Kyle's asking you on a date, I strongly recommend you accept."

Maggie looked at Betty with an almost dazed look, and began to say something so softly that Betty almost didn't catch it. As she spoke, her voice cracked, and she ended up sobbing the last part. It took a moment for Betty to decipher that Maggie had said, "Kyle is going to send all of our rifles over to rework! The whole shift!" Maggie put her hands to her face and sobbed, "I'm sorry. I'm so sorry. I should have known better."

Kyle reached out and put his hand gently on Maggie's shoulder. He would have preferred to wrap his arms around her and hold her close to comfort her, but that would have been inappropriate workplace *and* Army behavior.

"Maggie," he said consolingly, "I didn't say that. I was only talking about a situation with one rifle, which is already addressed."

"What was wrong with the rifle?" Betty asked him innocently.

"A slip of paper *somehow* got inside it," he said. "I removed it and cleared the weapon to ship, but ..."

"A little piece of paper," Betty interrupted him, "isn't going to effect how ..."

He held up his hand to stop her. "I know all that," he said. "And off the record, I actually think it's a clever idea. But that's not the point. It's an Army regulation, and I can't knowingly ignore it."

"But that means a whole shift of ..."

Again, he cut her off. "My inspection," he began in an official tone, "has found one single weapon in violation, and as I mentioned, that discrepancy has been corrected. Now, because the potential for this particular deviation to pose any significant quality issue is extremely low, I can make the determination that it is not necessary to tear down the other 391 rifles to look for identical deviations if I have verbal assurance from the line supervisor *that the slip that I found would not be found in any other rifles.*"

Betty heard the inflection that he put on the last part of his statement, but she wasn't sure what he was getting at. He obviously knew that there were quite likely more slips in the other rifles. Was he suggesting that Maggie lie about it? She looked at Maggie and got the impression that her shock had probably not worn off sufficiently for her to pick up on Kyle's meaning, either.

Kyle read the confusion in Betty's face, and pointed to the note that Maggie still held in her fingers. He asked Betty, "If I were to open another rifle from your line, would I find *that* slip of paper?"

"*That* slip of paper?" Betty repeated. "Of course not. It's in Maggie's hand. How could it be in two ..." She stopped as the reason behind his seemingly odd phrasing became clear. She gave him a smile, and nodded her head in understanding.

Betty turned to Maggie, and said, "Do you understand what Kyle's asking you about that piece of paper?"

Maggie sniffed, and let out a long, resigned sigh. "Yes," she said. "He wants to know how many rifles have one of ..."

"No," Betty cut her off, pointing to the slip in her hand. "He wants to know how many rifles have *that* piece of paper in them. Just *that* piece."

Maggie's fog of shock was apparently lifting enough that she realized that what Betty was asking was a rather silly question. "What do you mean? None of the other rifles could have *this* piece of ..."

Betty smiled at the change in Maggie's expression as an understanding of the odd question finally fell into place for her.

Maggie turned to Kyle, and he carefully asked her again, "So, Miss Kelly, how many rifles that went down your line today had that slip of paper in them?"

"Only one," she said.

"You're sure of that?" he asked.

"*Positive*," she replied seriously.

"Well, that's good enough for me," he said with a smile and a wink. "That's going to save me a lot of paperwork, it's going to keep the production numbers up, *and* it should make 400 or so GIs feel pretty darned lucky."

"Maybe as many as 487," Betty said, mentally doing the math from her first 96 slips plus today's total, minus the slip that Maggie held.

Betty reached out and took the paper from Maggie, and pushed it into Kyle's pocket. "488," she said, then leaned over and kissed him on the cheek. "Thanks Kyle. And I'm sorry I kicked this hornets' nest to start with. This was all my idea, so please don't blame Maggie."

"Blame?" he said. "Like I told you, I personally think it's a great idea. But until it comes down from Washington in a fifty page order, it's not an *Army* idea. So, until that happens, no more slips, okay?"

"Promise!" Betty said holding up her hand like she was taking an oath.

Kyle turned to Maggie. She was smiling at him, and said, "I promise, too, Kyle. And thank you." She then leaned over and kissed his other cheek.

He hesitated there for a moment, and Betty was half expecting him—actually *hoping* for him—to take Maggie's face in his hands and kiss her full on the lips.

But he didn't. Stupid Army regulations!

"Well, I guess all's well that ends well," he said. "You ladies take care going home, now." Then he turned to walk back to his office.

Betty leaned over and whispered into Maggie's ear, "Don't let him just walk away! Ask him to take you to the USO dance Friday."

"You really think I should?" Maggie whispered in reply.

"If I wasn't already engaged, *I'd* ask him!" Betty said. "Look at how he fits that uniform! *Hubba, hubba!*"

"I don't know. What if he says ..."

"Hey, Kyle!" Betty called out, "wait a second."

He stopped and turned.

"You just stuck your neck out to do us a huge favor," Betty said as she walked toward him, dragging Maggie by the hand, "so we'd like to do something to repay you. We want to take you to the USO dance Friday. What do you say?"

"Both of you want to take me?" he said.

"Well, technically, you'd be taking us, since you're the one with the uniform," Betty said, "but yes, both of us. Of course," she added with a wink, "I am engaged, so Maggie would be the one doing most of the dancing ... if that would be okay."

He smiled at Betty, and then looked over at Maggie. "I think that would be just swell," he said.

They said their good-byes to Kyle, and as Betty and Maggie walked toward the exit door, Maggie said, "You're quite the fixer, aren't you? You fixed the line so we can make more rifles, you fixed it so Bob won't be around to bother us any more, and you fixed me up with a date with Kyle. What's next?"

"I don't know. But whatever it is, like the poster says," Betty replied with a laugh as they passed the time clock, "I'm a WOW! I can do it!"

Of the 228,500 M1 Carbine rifles that were shipped by the Rock-Ola Manufacturing Corporation during World War II, 487 contained *A Kiss For Luck!* slip. The majority of them were lost the first time the rifle was disassembled in the field. Many, as Betty had hoped, were regarded as lucky charms by the soldiers who discovered them, and were carried into combat. Some of those eventually turned into pocket lint, but some made it all the way back to the states protected in the wallets of returning GIs.

One rifle, serial number 6,152,649, retained one of Betty's *A Kiss For Luck!* slips through the entire war, and would eventually find its way back to the city of its birth.

End of Part I

A Kiss For Luck!

Part II:
The Crossing

Boston Massachusetts
Monday, May 15, 1944

"So, you think you want to be a sailor, huh?" the old man asked Frank as they ate the last breakfast they would have ashore for several weeks. They sat in the crowded dining room of a crowded boarding house near crowded Boston Harbor.

"I want to do my part for the war, you know?" the 18 year old answered. "Plus, I grew up on a farm; I'm ready for something different."

The old sailor laughed, and a bit of chewed pancake landed on the table.

"Oh! It'll be different, all right! You can *bet* the farm on that!" He took a swig from his coffee cup, and asked, "So, why the merchant fleet, kid? Why not join the Navy? Their ships sail in the same water and they're a damned sight bigger, better, and faster than the tubs we put to sea in."

"I want to go to England," Frank said. "In the Navy, with my luck, I'd probably get sent to the Pacific. Besides, in the merchant marines, if I find out I don't like the sea I don't have to sign on for another trip, and I can enlist in the Army. In the Navy I'd be stuck with water for the whole war, like it or not."

"Got it all worked out, huh kid?" the old man said as he stuffed another half of a pancake into his mouth. He chewed a few times, and then asked around the mush, "So, what ship did you sign on?"

"The *Donald E. Shea*," Frank said. "She's a Liberty ship."

"Well, ain't it a small-ass world!" the old man laughed.

Frank pulled his coffee cup away just in time to avoid catching some flying pancake in it.

"That's my ship, too!" the old man said.

"No kidding?"

"Honest to God," the old seaman replied. Then he asked the kid what seemed like an innocent question: "So, when is it we sail, anyway?"

Frank looked at his watch, and said, "Today at ..."

The old timer reached across the table with surprising speed and slapped the youngster across the face. It wasn't a hard slap, and it surprised Frank much more than it hurt him.

"What the hell was that for?!" Frank demanded as he rubbed his cheek.

"If you ain't already aboard your ship, don't *ever* talk about when you're sailing! *Ever*! I could be a goddamned Nazi spy for all you know. So could anybody in here, just waiting to send a message out to a U-boat about when to expect his next target. Ain't you ever heard that loose lips sink ships, back on the farm?"

"I heard it!" Frank said defensively. "I just figured that since you were ..."

"Don't try figuring, kid," the old man interrupted him. "You ain't even cut yourself shaving, yet. You'll be better off if you just listen."

Frank began to get up from the table, but the old man caught his arm. "Sit down, kid," he said. "You ain't finished your breakfast. Trust me, after a week of eating aboard ship in the Atlantic, you'll miss a table that sits still through your whole meal."

Frank pulled his arm away from the man's hand, but he slowly sat down.

"What's your job on the *Shea*?" the old man asked as if the past 30 seconds had never transpired.

"You gonna hit me again if I tell you?"

The old man roared with laughter, and Frank threw his hand over the top of his cup. "No spy's gonna have the slightest interest in what a landlubber farm boy is trying to do to get his sea legs."

"I'm an oiler. I'm going to take care of the engine," Frank answered.

"You ever even seen a triple-expansion steam engine, kid? It ain't no puny tractor motor made for plowing your garden. It's got power enough to push a fifteen thousand ton steel bathtub through the water at fifteen knots when she has to!" Rudy said, rounding the tonnage and speed up a bit in boastful exaggeration.

"Yeah, I've seen one. They taught us all about them down in Sheeps ..." He stopped abruptly and leaned back out of the old man's reach, wary of another smack in the face.

The old man laughed, again. "Sheepshead Bay?" he said. "Don't worry; that ain't no secret military base or something, but I'm glad you get the idea about keeping your mouth shut. And I hope you were paying real close attention down there, 'cause the engine you're gonna be wiping belongs to me." He reached out his big rough right hand, and said, "Name's Rudy Norcross; Chief Engineer on the *Shea*. Pleased to meet you, kid."

"Frank Hendricks," the boy replied, shaking Rudy's hand.

"You any relation to Jack Hendricks from Baltimore?"

"I don't think so," Frank answered.

"Good! He's a liar and a cheat, and he owes me twenty bucks."

"Then I'm *sure* I'm not related," Frank said.

Rudy laughed. "I like you, kid. You may not know a slide valve from a sow's ass, but I think you can learn, and I'm just the old salt to teach you."

"How come you're here?" Frank said. "I'd have thought you'd be on board by now."

"Just got the call from the union hall this morning," Rudy answered after a swig of coffee. "They took the chief I'm replacing off to the hospital last night with appendicitis. How about you? Why ain't you on board?"

"The train up from New York got delayed," Frank said around a forkful of eggs. "A couple of Navy sailors I was with in the taxi said it was too late to get aboard and I should stay here the night, and that somebody would be by to pick me up in the morning."

Rudy laughed, again. "Bell-bottomed little pricks. They were bullshitting you, kid. You should have reported to the ship no matter what time it was. The ship and the whole port's open for business 24 hours. There's no such thing as *too late* unless the ship's already sailed."

As he spoke, Rudy reached out for the salt shaker in the middle of the table, and Frank unwittingly did a double-take when he noticed that the old man was missing the index and middle fingers of his left hand. Frank quickly looked away, his eyes uncomfortably flitting from his coffee to his eggs to his sausage, trying to find something else to focus on.

"Finally noticed my *claw*, huh?" Rudy said with a chuckle. "Don't be embarrassed about looking at it; look at it and learn something. I learned it the hard way, but you can learn it without all the pain and the blood if you're smart."

Rudy held his hand out over Frank's plate so he really had little choice *but* to look at it.

The places where the fingers should have been were not even stumps, but were just a single flat plateau covered by a reddish scar with patches that were almost purple, some streaks of white, and a few spots that were nearly black.

"Ask me how my fingers got cut off," Rudy said, still holding his hand above Frank's breakfast.

"Okay. How'd your fingers get cut off?" Frank asked dutifully.

"They didn't!" Rudy answered with a laugh. "They got *pulled* off! Pulled right out of the knuckles! All that was left was blood pissing out, and a couple of dangly little white worm things."

"Probably your tendons," Frank said as he cut a piece of sausage on his plate that would have been hidden if Rudy hadn't been missing fingers.

"Yeah. That's what they called 'em," Rudy said, as he retracted his hand. He was obviously disappointed in the kid's stoic reaction. That description, especially when eating, always got a gag from new sign-ons. "How'd you come to know that?" Rudy asked. "You a medic or something?"

"Same kind of thing happened to my uncle on a hay bailer," Frank said as he popped the sausage into his mouth.

Rudy looked at him for a moment, and then went back to his pancake without saying anything more.

Frank realized he had screwed up. He was trying to show he wasn't some green kid who'd faint at the first sight of blood, but he had unwittingly taken the wind out of Rudy's sail by not being surprised and disgusted by his story. His uncle was exactly the same way when he retold *his* story. If he didn't get at least a cringe out of the listener—no matter how many times they had heard the tale—he would actually sulk. But given the cost of the story—two missing fingers—Frank figured that Rudy and his uncle had a right to want to impress people with it.

"What's with the scar, though?" Frank asked. "My uncle's hand doesn't look like that after the accident." In fact, it looked almost just like Rudy's, and Frank knew why. But he was hoping that if he reacted appropriately to the gruesome second half of the story, he could get back in Rudy's good graces as a humble pupil and willing listener. It was obvious that Ruby was someone that he wanted on his side.

Rudy brightened immediately, and he stuck his hand back out for Frank to see. "Something you might want to remember about freighters, kid" he said, "is that there ain't no fancy hospital on board, and no real doctor, either. This is the kind of doctoring you can expect if you're careless enough to get yourself hurt."

Frank gave Rudy a suitably worried look, and asked, "Who did that then?"

"The cook!" Rudy said. "Turns out the guy's old man was an animal doctor, and one time he helped him fix up a dog that got his leg cut off by a train."

"That's not much medical training," Frank said. "Weren't you worried?"

"Hell, yeah! Until they poured half a bottle of whiskey into me," Rudy said with a chuckle. "Then I didn't give a shit about *anything*!"

"What did he do?" Frank asked making a face, and sounding as if he didn't really want to hear.

Picking up his butter knife from the table, Rudy held it up and began, "The cook takes one of his big steel knives—three or four times the size of this—and he puts it on top of one of the burners on his stove. Then the first mate takes hold of me from behind, around the middle, and the chief holds my arm down on the table. He tells me to make a fist with what fingers I got left, and says for me to look down at my shoes. Drunk as a skunk, I'm staring at the blood on my shoes, and the cook comes over and slaps that red hot knife right down on my hand! He just squashed it right down on all that blood and guts hanging out and melted my skin right back together!"

Frank grimaced and sucked in his breath just as he knew he should; just as people did when they heard his uncle's similar story for the first time.

"Didn't that *hurt*?" Frank asked with well-acted horror.

"Sweet Jesus, hell-yes it hurt!" Rudy roared with a laugh. "I ain't never sobered up so quick in all my life! And the smell! I will never ever forget that God-awful smell of my own skin burning!"

Frank knew the smell that Rudy was talking about. It had taken him a long while to get over it himself after he had witnessed basically the same cauterizing *operation* performed on his uncle.

"That must have been *horrible*!" Frank said, not pretending about that part. "How long ago did it happen?" The scar looked pretty old.

"Happened back in the summer of '19; twenty-five years ago, now. I'd been sailing just long enough to think I knew what I was doing. I thought I could wipe between the eccentrics as the first one came around and get in and get out before the second one came by. Got pretty good at it, too. Got the timing down like a good watch. In—wipe—out, in—wipe—out. Then one time my shirt cuff got hooked on one of the bolts on the strap, and it broke my rhythm. In the extra second it took for me to tug twice on my shirt, the other strap came around far enough so it caught my hand coming out, and sucked me right back in. Then *Pop!* and my fingers were gone."

Rudy held is hand up, again, and said, "A big ship is like the sea herself, kid; neither one forgives stupid mistakes."

The taxi dropped Rudy, Frank, and two sailors off in front of the East Boston Port Authority Building. The driver said the fare was on him, because they were all probably shipping out soon, and he knew some of them might not be coming back.

"I got two nephews in the merchant marines," the old driver said. "They told me what it's like out there in them floating targets, never knowing if a U-boat is right on your tail and having nothing but a few Navy boys onboard with pea-shooters for defense. You fellows got a lot more crust than most, I'll tell you that."

The old driver wasn't exaggerating; by the time the war would end, the US Merchant Marine Service would lose a higher percentage of men than any other branch of the military in any of the countries in the conflict.

All of the men thanked the driver, but Rudy pulled a five dollar bill from his pants pocket and pressed it into the man's hand. "I appreciate it, pops—we all do—but you gotta eat, too." Rudy said.

Frank watched in surprise as the driver took the bill and tore it in two.

He then handed Rudy back half of it, and said, "You look me up when you get back, mister, and we'll put it back together and we'll have us a drink. What do you say?"

Rudy shook the old man's hand and slapped him on the back. "You got yourself a deal!" he said with a laugh. "What's your name?"

"Harold Dow. You ask anybody driving a cab in Boston when you get back and they'll tell you where to find me."

Rudy and Frank then made their way to the guard shack in front of the Port Authority Building, and showed their passports and sailing papers to one of the Marines who were guarding the entrance. The sergeant looking over their papers wore a .45 automatic on his hip, but his partner, a few feet away, held a Thompson submachine gun in his hands.

Frank had read everything he could find about "Tommy guns," but this was the first time he had ever actually seen one. Having hunted with everything from a slingshot, to a shotgun, to a .30-06 rifle, he had always wondered what it would be like to hunt with a Tommy gun. How could you possibly miss firing six-hundred rounds a minute?

Once on the other side of the building, Frank was surprised at how crowded and busy the dock area was. It appeared to be general chaos with men and trucks going in all different directions; orders being shouted, whistles blowing, and big ships' horns sounding. After finishing their training at Sheepshead Bay, Frank and a couple of buddies had taken a one-day detour to see New York City before heading for their respective assignments, and Frank had been in awe of the city and the frantic pace of everyone there. But that seemed almost calm compared to this.

"This way, kid," Rudy said as he headed toward one of the piers. "That's the *Shea* on the starboard side there. Some people call Liberties *Ugly Ducklings* 'cause FDR said that once, but not me. She may not be a racing yacht, but by God she gets her job done. I've sailed on the *Shea* before, and she's brought me back every time. That's beauty in my book."

As they walked toward the gangway they watched one of the *Shea's* several cargo booms lift a pallet of four crated Jeeps off of a flatbed rail car and swing it over the deck's edge where it quickly disappeared from view down into the aftermost hold.

As the Jeeps went out of sight Frank's eyes were drawn to the deck gun mounted atop the after deckhouse; exposed to the elements except for a thin splinter shield that surrounded it to provide some protection to the gun crew.

Four men in Navy uniforms busied themselves about the gun, wiping, checking, and lubricating its many parts, Frank presumed. He wondered if any of them were the sailors from yesterday's taxi ride.

Frank elbowed Rudy, and said as he pointed, "That's a lot bigger than the three-inch-fifty that we trained with down at Sheepshead Bay. I sure wouldn't want to be on the receiving end of *that*!"

"And if you were ten miles away, you'd *still* be on the receiving end of it," Rudy said. "That's a five-inch-thirty-eight. I've seen them showing up on *Liberty* ship decks for about a year, now. Takes 15 men to really make her sing, but what a song!

"Back in '42, she was brand new then, and I was First Engineer on her on that trip. I was just coming off my watch down in the engine room one night when the lookout calls out that he's seen the conning tower of a U-boat off the starboard stern quarter.

Between the Navy boys and a few of us mariners, we had that gun throwing shells out at whatever he saw for a quarter of an hour. I was the hot case man, and I was catching spent casings coming out of that gun every four or five seconds sometimes, just barely keeping up with the Navy boys who were loading and firing her."

"Did you get her?" Frank asked. "Did you sink the sub?" He wanted to know, not just because it was an interesting sea story, but because if they *had* sunk the sub it meant there was one less out there to hunt them on *this* trip.

"Don't know," Rudy said. "It was dark and we never saw an explosion out there bigger than our own shells. But we never got torpedoed, either. Could have been that the lookout was seeing things; we could have sunk her; or we could have scared her off. Doesn't matter too much which; we made it to Murmansk in one piece. *That's* what matters."

At the bottom of the *Shea's* gangway they showed their papers to another armed Marine guard, and then made their way to the bridge where they reported for duty.

Rudy had never met the captain, before, but he had sailed with the first mate, Adam Jones. After introductions, Jones had a seaman show the two new crew members to their respective quarters, so they could stow their gear.

Rudy's state room was one level below the bridge, on the boat deck, but Frank would be sharing quarters with two other oilers, on the ship's upper deck, one more level down.

As Rudy and Frank separated on Rudy's deck, Rudy said to Frank, "You haven't been assigned to a watch section yet, kid, but make your way below to the engine room as soon as you get your gear stowed. I'll see you down there."

As Chief Engineer, Rudy himself, had no specific watch assignment; he was *always* on duty.

As he changed out of his civvies and into his khaki work uniform, Rudy looked out his porthole over the forward deck of the ship. The number-two hatch had been closed, and between the small forest of masts, crane booms, and cables, he watched a P-38 Lightning, with its wing tips removed, being lowered on top of the hatch.

As he intently watched the fighter being maneuvered some 70 feet forward, he was startled by a big dark mass that swung past his porthole, not ten feet from his nose.

He quickly refocused and watched the five-ton cargo boom, located right in front of the number three hold, lower its load of rectangular wooden boxes stacked at least thirty high on an eight-foot square pallet.

From the size and shape of the boxes Rudy's guess was that they contained rifles. But they *could* have been just about anything from artillery shells to mortars to spare parts for airplanes to burners for field kitchens. Almost everything that was needed to wage war—including soldiers—got there on a merchant ship ... which is why stopping them was such a high priority for the Germans.

If Rudy had been really curious, he could have gone and looked at the ship's cargo manifest to see what was in those crates. If he had, he would have seen that they had come from a factory in Chicago named the Rock-Ola Manufacturing Corporation, and that they contained "Rifles; M1 Carbine; Caliber .30".

Five years ago, rifles from a company that made juke boxes might have seemed quite odd, but there were very few manufacturers anywhere in the country now who were still making whatever it was they had made before the war.

The manifest would *not* have told him that the crate nestled into the top forward corner on the starboard side of the pallet contained a rifle with the serial number 6,152,649. And it would certainly not have explained how the weapon had been especially blessed by a number of special young ladies, to carry good luck. Like most seamen, Rudy was very superstitious, and had he known that his ship was carrying a lucky talisman, he would have gone down and touched it.

As the pallet sank down into the hold, Rudy turned from the porthole, donned his chief engineer's cap, and went into his office through the connecting door. He was much more interested in going down to inspect his machinery and meet his crew than watching cargo being loaded. From his desk, he picked up a clipboard with the ship's crew manifest attached and the First Engineer's previous day's report. He then headed for the engine room, forty feet below.

The engine room was warm and uncharacteristically crowded as Rudy made his way down the first ladder to the generator landing. From there he could see that most of the men from all three watches of the engineering department were there at the same time—11 men including Rudy—all wanting to get a close look before shoving off, at the equipment they would be living with for the next month or two. Only the Second Assistant Engineer and the Deck Engineer were topside, keeping an eye on the winches, cargo booms, and other deck machinery that Rudy's crew was also responsible for.

From where he stood, he could see that the two boilers had a full head of superheated steam—220 pounds of pressure at 440-degrees—which was being fed sparingly through the main engine cylinders to warm them up. Two of the three electric generators beside Rudy were running, powering the winches, lights, and radio equipment. The third would be started when the ship left dock to power the massive array of degaussing wires built into the hull.

Those demagnetizing coils would make the German's magnetic mines much less dangerous. And such mines were not only encountered in the war zones of the North Sea, the English Channel, and the Mediterranean. Daring German submarines had also been known to lay the electronic mines in the approaches and even *inside* several of the east coast harbors, including Boston.

Rudy stood watching from the landing for almost a full minute before his first assistant—addressed by the crew in typical merchant marine vernacular as "First"—noticed him and called out, "Hey, Chief! Glad you could join us. I was thinking I was going to get a promotion and move into your stateroom on this trip."

The man's name was Howard Walsh, and Rudy had sailed with him three other times. "If you could keep your skinny ass out of jail every time you're in port," Rudy replied as he started down the ladder to the engine room floor, "you'd probably be a ship's master by now, let alone a chief."

Rudy liked Walsh, and he was glad to have him on his ship, again. He was an excellent engineer who could fix anything aboard a ship, and he was as professional a sailor as he had ever met. But once he got on dry land and he started drinking, his Mr. Hyde side came out, and a barroom fistfight was inevitable. It was only the war's desperate need for experienced sailors that got him sprung from the hoosegow every time.

At First's acknowledgement of the Chief, the rest of the crew turned, and greeted him, as well. Besides First and Frank, Rudy saw four other familiar faces. He had sailed with two of the three firemen and the third assistant engineer.

Rudy made his way among the men and machinery, looking at boiler pressure and temperature dials, water-level gauges, and fuel pressure needles. He flipped open the inspection cover on each of the oil burners, and looked at the bright yellow flame that each was blasting under the boilers.

He turned to Walsh, and said, "Number three starboard is a little uneven. Probably a dirty sprayer plate."

"Really?" Walsh said walking toward the boiler. "We just swapped out all the burners at the start of the watch."

"Well, let's get it changed out, again. And check the strainers, too. If we get a U-boat coming up our butt between here and Novi, and the bridge calls for all-ahead-full, I don't want to be giving them *almost* all-ahead-full because that burner's spittin' and sputterin' like your grandmother trying to whistle *Dixie* when she ain't got her teeth in."

"Hey, hey! Watch what you're saying about my grandmother, there, Chief," Walsh shot back, "Nana Walsh can whistle *The Star Spangled Banner* with a mouthful of chaw, and never spit a drop. With or without her choppers in!"

The banter between the two men was typical for them and good natured, but the youngsters weren't quite sure. To them, the two men seemed angry at each other.

Walsh turned to the three firemen, and bellowed, "You heard the Chief! Hooker, kill that burner and close the air register. Reilly, you watch the water and pressure in the boiler. Patterson, get your wrenches and get your asbestos gloves on. Hop to it!"

As the three men jumped into action, Rudy turned toward Frank, who was standing nearby with two other boys about his own age, and said, "Who's oiler on watch?"

"I ... I am, Chief," the tall skinny redhead next to Frank said. His nervousness was obvious. He undoubtedly thought he had screwed something up and was about to get his rear end chewed.

"Looks good in here," Rudy said. "Oil cups all topped off, the generators all look fine, and the main looks like its ready to start turning as soon as the pilot calls down for power. Good job. What're you gonna do next?"

"Um ... as long as the other guys are here to keep an eye on things, I was going to make my way down the shaft alley and check the spring bearings before I go off watch," he said. Then he added, timidly, "Un ... unless you want me to do something else, Chief." He was clearly intimidated by Rudy's quick and accurate grasp of conditions in the engine room after only a seemingly cursory look.

"No," Rudy said. "I like it." He turned to Frank and the other oiler, a stocky kid with slicked-back wavy brown hair who was trying desperately to grow a mustache, and said, "That's how I want all of your watch changes to go. Be down here early to make sure you know what's been goin' on during the last watch, and then your mate who's goin' off can walk the shaft alley. Clear enough?"

"Clear, Chief." "Yes, sir." and "Sure thing, Chief." came the three replies.

As Rudy went to talk with First, again, Frank turned to the redhead, extended his hand, and said "Frank Hendricks. I'm from Wisconsin. What's your name?"

"Richie St. Jacques," he said. "But everybody calls me Narrow. I'm from Arizona."

"Narrow? What kind of name is that?"

"Everybody in the group I hung around with at school had a nickname, but we already had a Skinny and a Slim, so they took to calling me Narrow. They thought it was real funny, but it stuck. Even my old man calls me that, now." He looked at his wrist watch and said, "I'm going to go check the bearings, and then go topside and watch what's going on there. I can't wait to get underway."

"First voyage?" Frank asked. "It's mine."

"Second," Narrow said. "I love the pitch and roll of the ship when we're out at sea. You'll see what I mean." With a laugh, he added, "Either that, or you'll be seasick all the time, and you'll hate it." Then with a wave, he said, "I'll talk to you later."

Narrow then made his way to the aft of the engine, and turned the wheel on the watertight hatch that led to the shaft alley. He pulled the hatch open, stepped inside, and swung it closed behind himself. Frank watched the wheel spin as Narrow sealed the hatch from the other side. While the hatch was momentary open, Frank could look down what in his mind was an almost endless, dimly lit, cramped, steel-encased tunnel that was located underwater. A little shiver ran down Frank's spine.

The last item that was scheduled to be loaded aboard the *Shea*—a ten-ton bulldozer—was in midair when a blue Navy jeep pulled along side the ship's gangway. A man in his mid-thirties hopped out, grabbed his sea bag from the back, and thanked the young sailor for the lift.

While the Marine guard at the bottom of the gangway checked the new arrival's sailing orders and passport the man watched the big olive-drab machine swing smoothly through the air and over the deck.

"Cutting it a little close," the guard said as he handed back the seaman's papers.

"First time in Boston," the man said. "I got lost."

Before the guard could reply—if he even intended to—a voice came from behind him half way up the gangway.

"Who the hell are you?" Chief Mate Jones asked. He had come down the gangway to attach lifting cables to the on-shore end of it in preparation for shoving off.

"Craig O'Hara," the man said, holding out his papers. "Able-bodied seaman, reporting for duty."

"I think you got the wrong ship, fella." Jones said as he reached up to grab one of the two steel hooks that were dangling over his head from one of the *Shea's* booms. "There's no O'Hara on the *Shea's* manifest. We got our crew." He latched a hook onto each side of the gangway and gave the signal to the seaman on deck to take the slack out of the cable.

"I think if you look at my papers, Mr. Jones, you'll see I'm on the right ship," the man said as he held out the folded documents.

As they spoke, the cable went taut and the gangway began to rise off the pier. The man hopped onto it as it moved.

Listening to the exchange, the guard put his hand on his sidearm when the man jumped onto the gangway next to Jones.

Riding the gangway as it was raised was against all safety regulations, and with it about three feet in the air, Jones gave a wave to the boom operator to stop.

"How do you know my name?" Jones asked, looking at the man skeptically.

"If you'll look at my papers, I think you'll understand," the man answered.

Jones unfolded the stranger's sailing orders, and inside—along with the passport that the guard *had* seen—was a black leather wallet that the man had *not* shown him.

Jones flipped the wallet open and stared at a gold star and a photo ID, both emblazoned with the letters, "FBI."

Jones looked up at the man who put his finger to his lips, obviously indicating that he didn't want him to say anything about the badge.

Jones refolded the papers and said, "What's this all about?"

"If you'll take me to Captain Hill I'll explain everything," O'Hara said. "Permission to come aboard?"

Jones looked at him with equal parts skepticism and curiosity. "Alright," he said finally, "I'll take you to see the captain." He then gave a nod to the guard, and led the way up the gangway. At the top he signaled the seaman to start the winch again.

As they stepped onto the deck O'Hara opened his pea coat to slide his wallet into an inside pocket, and when he did Jones caught a glimpse of a revolver in a shoulder holster. Jones was pretty sure that O'Hara intended for him to see it.

With preparations nearly complete for getting underway, Captain Hill was just getting ready to leave his office and take command on the bridge.

Jones knocked on the open door, and said, "Excuse me, Captain. We have a new crew member who'd like a word with you."

"Not now, Mr. Jones. We're about to get underway," the captain said as he came around his desk. Then what Jones had said registered completely. "What do you mean a new crew member?" Hill said looking at the man standing behind Jones in the doorway. Looking back at Jones, he said, "I believe you told me that all of our crew was aboard already."

O'Hara reached past Jones with his open ID wallet, and said quietly, "I'm from Washington, Captain Hill. There's a problem on your ship."

"Washington?" the captain repeated. "What do you mean *problem*? What kind of problem?"

"We need to talk in private," O'Hara replied. "I'm authorized to talk about this only with you and Mr. Jones. Nobody else can know why I'm here." As he spoke, he stepped into the cabin, forcing Jones into the room in front of him. Inside, he reached back, and closed and locked the door.

"You have a saboteur aboard, Captain," O'Hara said flatly.

"A saboteur? In the crew? Who is it?" the captain demanded. He stole a glance at Jones as if he should have known about this.

"We don't know," O'Hara said as he lowered himself into one of the captain's guest chairs without being invited to do so. "That's why I'm here."

"What do you mean you don't know? Then how do you know there even *is* one?" the captain said.

O'Hara stretched out his legs and leaned his head back against the bulkhead. He looked relaxed to the point of being almost bored. The captain was taking a very quick dislike to the man.

"We broke up a Nazi spy ring down in Baltimore about a week ago," O'Hara began. "After some *persuasive interrogation*, one of the things that we discovered this group was doing was putting agents on merchant ships to cripple them at sea."

"You mean sink them?" Jones said. "How did they do it?"

"Sinking a ship this size without several pounds of TNT would be pretty hard," O'Hara replied. "And not very subtle. But you don't need to sink a ship to take it out of action. If you can cripple it in some way it's almost as good; the supplies on board don't get to the troops, and the war is a little more lost."

"How do you mean *cripple* it?" the captain asked.

"Damage the engine?" O'Hara offered. "Contaminate the fuel with seawater? Do something to the boilers? I don't really know." He looked at the two men and said, "You're the sailors; how would *you* stop this ship?"

"I'd refuse to give the order to cast off!" the captain said. "And that's exactly what I'm going to do!"

"That's the one thing you *can't* do, Captain," O'Hara said without lifting his head from the wall. "If we don't sail we'll never find out who the agent is."

"I don't give a damn about one Nazi spy if catching him is going to put my ship and fifty-seven men's lives at risk."

"We're not talking about just one spy here, Captain," O'Hara replied. "If we can catch him we can make him give up the names of others who, in turn, will give up the names of others, and so on and so on. We're looking at a spy ring here that's operating on all three coasts, East, West, and Gulf."

"I'm sorry," Hill said. "I can't allow it. You can question the crew if you'd like, but I won't give the order to cast off until I know your spy has been taken off my ship."

"This isn't a request, Captain," O'Hara replied calmly. "It's an order direct from Washington DC. This ship and its entire crew are now part of a federal investigation into a Nazi plot to cripple the war effort. I'm with the FBI, remember? If you won't follow my orders, then I have the authority to make a call and have you replaced as captain."

That was a complete lie on O'Hara's part. The authority to replace a duly-licensed captain on a ship carrying war material rested solely with the Coast Guard and the War Shipping Administration.

But the aura that had come to surround the FBI through J. Edgar Hoover's masterful manipulation of the agency's public-image led most people to believe that the organization had supreme authority and was completely omnipotent when it came to anything involving a crime, especially a federal one. It made it very easy for agents like O'Hara to get their way, and they rarely had their bluff called or even questioned.

Which is not to say that O'Hara *couldn't* have gotten Hill replaced, but it would have taken a lot more than a phone call.

"So, how is our being at sea going to make it any easier for you to catch this spy ?" the captain asked. "You think he's going to get seasick and you're just going to arrest the first man you see puking over the side?"

"Nope," O'Hara replied, ignoring the captain's obvious attempt to bait him. "We're going to let him sabotage the ship, and then figure out who aboard had the means and opportunity to do whatever he did, and that will give us our man. Or at least a few candidates. Once we have it narrowed down, I know how to get the answers I need."

"You want me to put to sea and then knowingly let someone sabotage my ship? Are you insane? What if he cripples us mid-crossing? We'd be a sitting duck to any U-boats out there."

"That's how important catching this guy is, Captain," O'Hara replied. "It's a risk the FBI is willing to take."

"The *FBI* is willing to take the risk?" Jones repeated. "What about the crew? Shouldn't they have a vote on that? The last time I looked this was still a democracy."

"The last time *I* looked we were still at war," O'Hara answered, "and war involves extreme measures and extreme sacrifices. I'm on the ship, too, you know; you think I want to drop my ass in the North Atlantic any more than you do? Shit, I can't even swim!

"But speaking of the crew ..." O'Hara said as he reached into the inside pocket of his jacket and pulled out a folded sheet of paper.

When he opened his jacket Captain Hill saw the pistol in its leather holster as Jones had earlier. He made a mental note, but didn't say anything.

"This is a copy of your crew manifest," O'Hara said as he handed the sheet to Jones. "The names that have a checkmark beside them have been investigated and cleared by our office in Washington. We can be pretty sure that they're not Nazi sympathizers."

Jones scanned down the alphabetically arranged list as Hill looked over his shoulder. Of the 43 crewmember's names on the sheet only eight had checkmarks, including Hill's and Jones'. Another four had an "X" next to them, and the rest were blank. Below the crew's names were listed the names and ranks of the seventeen members of the Navy Armed Guard who were aboard. All of them had checkmarks.

"What do the X's mean?" Captain Hill asked.

"Those are men that we know have some tie back to Germany," O'Hara said.

"What kind of ties?" Jones asked.

"They might have a family member there or maybe they traveled there before the war."

"They're seamen for Pete's sake!" Jones said. "They travel all over the world! It's their job!"

"We're not fools, Mr. Jones," O'Hara said. "I'm not talking about a couple of weeks in a port city getting drunk and picking up whores. Crowley there spent three months in Berlin and then six in Nuremberg in 1933. He may have been at *Der Fuehrer's* big rally there in September."

"That doesn't make him a goddamned Nazi!" Jones shot back. "I listen to President Roosevelt's Fireside Chats; that doesn't make me a *Democrat*!"

O'Hara replied, "You really think that none of those men could be a Nazi sympathizer just because they're fellow sailors and don't have a swastika tattooed on their arm? Are you really that naïve?"

"I've sailed with Crowley before," Jones replied, his voice getting more forceful. "And more than once. He's no more a Nazi spy than I am or you are! Hell, I'd trust *him* over *you* if it came to that!"

"I don't give a damn how much you trust him!" O'Hara said as he came up out of the chair. "If you breathe one word of this to him I'll shoot you myself for obstructing an FBI investigation! Is that clear?"

"Calm down! Both of you!" Captain Hill told them with an authority in his voice that didn't require loudness. He stepped around his desk and said to O'Hara, "Nobody is going to shoot anybody on my ship." He reached out his hand and said, "I'll take the gun. It goes in the safe with the others."

O'Hara couldn't believe that he'd heard him correctly. "What?" he said.

"No one is allowed to carry small arms on my ship," Hill said. "Not even the Navy boys. All pistols and the trigger assemblies from their rifles are kept in my safe, right here, for the duration of the voyage. They get them back if we're docked in a port that doesn't already have an Army, Navy, or Marine guard. Which pretty much means Russia."

"Are you out of your goddamned mind, Captain?" O'Hara said incredulously. "There's a war on! How the hell do you expect the Navy to defend this tub if you take their guns away?"

"With the deck guns," the Captain said calmly. " That's what they're for. No one ever sank a submarine or a surface raider with a rifle, much less a pistol. The very fact that you've already threatened one of my officers gives me every reason to disarm you, Mr. O'Hara."

The captain continued to hold his hand out, but O'Hara made no move to put anything in it.

"Several years ago, before the war," Hill began without moving his hand, "I was Chief Mate on a tramp steamer called the D'Elia Marie. One night an argument broke out in the crew's mess and it turned into a fist fight pretty quickly. Before I or any of the other officers could break it up, both of the men pulled pistols out of their pockets and started firing at one another.

"Five men in that room were shot that night," Hill went on, "including me, but *not* including the men doing the shooting. Three of those men died before we could get to port.

"As we buried those men at sea I swore that when I finally got my own ship no crewman of mine would be allowed to carry a gun." He moved his fingers in a give-it-here gesture, and said, "You'll get it back when we reach port or if there's any trouble that warrants it."

The two men stared at each other for a long while, before O'Hara finally reached into his coat, and said, "Alright, but at the first sniff of trouble I want it back."

"Agreed," Hill said as he took the pistol and turned to set it on his desk.

The captain then picked up the papers that O'Hara had brought with him. He studied them silently for a half a minute. Without looking up from them, he said, "What's a snatch block, Mr. O'Hara?"

"What?"

"A snatch block," Hill repeated as he turned back to face O'Hara again. "What is it used for?"

"Snatching things!" O'Hara said sarcastically. "How the hell should I know?"

"It says here you're an able seaman; that's how you'd know," the captain replied. "Are you really the best the FBI could come up with to put on a merchant ship? Have you ever actually *been* to sea before?"

"Yeah, I've sailed before," O'Hara answered defensively, but offered nothing more.

"What ship?" the captain asked.

O'Hara hesitated, and then said, "The *Franconia*."

"The *passenger* ship?" Jones asked. "What the hell, did you get a cruise to Europe for graduation?"

"No, smartass! I worked my way across!"

"Doing what? Waiting tables?"

O'Hara just stared at him without replying.

"You've got to be buggy-juggin' me!" Jones said, "You were a waiter on a passenger ship and you think you can pass yourself off as an able seaman on a freighter? You got balls bigger than your brain, you know that?"

"I'll get by!" O'Hara snapped. "You just ..."

"You won't last ten minutes," the captain cut him off, "and then I'll have to explain why I've allowed a man on board pretending to be something he's obviously not. This crew's not stupid; they're likely to think that *you're* a spy." He picked up a pen and wrote something on O'Hara's paperwork. "I'm assigning you to the steward's department; you should be able to fit in as a messman, I should think."

"Is that supposed to be funny, Captain?" O'Hara said.

"There is nothing the least bit humorous about any part of this," Hill replied. Picking up O'Hara's list of names, the captain went on, "One of the names you checked off here is Roberto Delano, my Chief Steward. That means that we can let him in on the secret, and he can make sure you fit in with the rest of his crew.

"And you'll be surprised at what you'll hear in the crew's mess," the captain went on, "if you can bring yourself to listen more than you talk. Maybe we'll even get lucky and you'll overhear something that will let you figure out who this spy is *before* he damages my ship."

The captain lifted his well-worn uniform cap from a hook on the bulkhead, and set it on his head at an angle that had the rim nearly touching his right ear. "Mr. Jones, please take our new crewman down to meet Roberto. Find a private corner and explain what's going on, and then meet me on the bridge." Movement outside of his porthole caught the captain's attention, and he looked to see a loaded Victory ship heading for the harbor entrance. He added to Jones, "I want to catch up with the rest of the ships well before dusk."

Although the threat of U-boat attack between the US ports and Nova Scotia wasn't nearly what it had been in the spring of '43, they were still out there, and dusk and dawn were their favorite hunting times when ships were easily silhouetted against the horizon. And stragglers were their favorite prey.

Although not on duty, Frank wanted to be in the engine room when the *Shea* got underway. To keep busy while waiting, he climbed the ladder to the platform where the two generators were running, took an oil can from a rack on the bulkhead, and gave each of their main-bearing oil cups an unnecessary squirt. They might actually *need* a squirt half way through his watch—which didn't actually start until 2200 hours—10:00 p.m. on his twelve-hour watch—but for now, it was just something to do on the only piece of running machinery in the engine room.

He secured the oil can and walked over to look at the big main engine, quiet and still, but like a sleeping mythical beast, ready to be awakened and set loose with unimaginable power.

As much as Frank wanted to see the beast stretch from its slumber and come alive, while it sat peaceful and benign, he wanted to see if he could figure out where Rudy had lost his fingers. Although he had said that it happened 25 years ago, Frank knew that these giant workhorses dated back to the 1890's and had not fundamentally changed since.

Frank went back down the ladder, walked to the forward end of the engine, and leaned over the guardrail. He put his hand in between the two eccentrics, which, because the engine wasn't turning, were stationary and perfectly safe. His hand fit between them, but just barely. He could easily see how Rudy's bigger hand could have gotten caught in there.

But then something didn't add up. Frank couldn't figure out what had pulled off only two of Rudy's fingers. If he'd lost his whole hand he could understand it, but even Rudy's fingers weren't big enough to get caught by the eccentrics.

Lost in thought, Frank didn't notice First come up behind him.

"Whatcha doin' there kid?" First said, then laughed like hell when Frank jumped and almost fell over into the crankpit.

Stepping back from the rail, Frank wiped his hands on the rag in his back pocket, and said, "I was just trying to see where the Chief lost his fingers. I don't want that to happen to me."

"He told you he lost his fingers in *there*?" First replied. He laughed, and said, "That happened in a bar in Havana!" He laughed again, and said, "I wish I had a dime for every different place he said he lost them two fingers!"

Just then, the engine telegraph rang two times, and every man in the engine room turned to look at it. The needle in the center had moved from "Finished with Engines" to "Stand By."

"Stand by!" First shouted. "Make ready to get underway." As he stepped to the telegraph to reply to the bridge, he told Frank, "Make sure the crankpit is clear, kid. Then make sure the jacking gear worm is out."

The three firemen on watch had just finished changing the oil burner, and had lit it off. As one of them adjusted the air register, another checked the water and steam gauges on the boiler, and the third moved about checking various valves and gauges on the engine.

After acknowledging the bridge's order to stand by, First moved over to the high-pressure end of the huge reciprocating engine. With his left hand he operated the reversing engine and with his right, he controlled the cylinder bypass valves above his head.

As if he was playing the iron behemoth like a musical instrument the size of a locomotive, he carefully jockeyed the engine forward and backward—ahead and astern—in partial revolutions until he was sure that any water that had collected in the three cylinders had been pumped out. He would leave all of the bypass valves open so the steam could bleed through the cylinders until the order came down from the bridge to start the engine turning so they could pull away from the dock.

"Reilly!" he called out to one of the firemen, "Stand-by the telegraph." He turned to Frank, and asked, "What's your name, kid?"

"Hendricks, sir. Frank Hendricks."

"Okay, Hendricks, get ready to check the bearing temps on the degaussing generator when the Second Engineer puts 'er on line."

Frank climbed the ladder once again, and stood by the still idle number three generator, with an oil can in his hand.

Every man in the engine room waited at his station, watching the telegraph, waiting for its pointer to swing around, and listening for its bell to set them and the ship in motion.

After a full, interminable, two minutes the bell rang and the pointer swung around to "Slow Astern."

"Slow astern!" Reilly called out as he pulled the telegraph handle forward and back so its pointer matched a duplicate on the bridge.

First pulled the lever on the reversing engine to shift the slide valves so that the main engine would start in reverse. Next, he turned the throttle wheel, letting a little more steam blow through the high-pressure—the HP—cylinder. He then turned the bypass valve closed on the HP, and almost immediately, the massive engine began to turn slowly, almost silently, in reverse. He left the mid and low-pressure cylinder bypass valves open, creating what was called a *maneuvering engine*. By running on only one cylinder out of the three, the engine would stop and reverse much faster when the bridge called for a change, which could happen often and quickly while in the harbor.

At the stern of the ship, deep below the waterline, the enormous four-bladed propeller began to turn, cutting into the water of Boston Harbor. Frank felt a shudder run through the ship as the *Shea* began to move away from the dock.

"Uh oh," Frank heard Patterson say as he climbed the ladder to the generator platform. "That ain't a good sign."

"What ain't?" Frank asked, looking down at him.

"You feel that just now?" Patterson said.

"Yeah," Frank answered. "She's just settling from being under her own power finally."

"That's what they might tell you down at the Sheepshead Bay," he replied, "but that's the same as the shiver that runs down your spine when you hear a scary show on the radio or you walk past a graveyard on a dark night. She's scared. She knows we're in for a rough crossing."

Frank wasn't sure whether the older fireman was being serious, or if he was just teasing him because this was his first sailing; one of the many "rights-of-passage" new guys had to endure. Patterson never cracked a smile, however ... and that concerned Frank.

The lightly-escorted 15-ship convoy stretched out for four miles as it sailed north-northeast 100 miles off the coast of Maine. Due to its slightly delayed departure, the *Shea* was the last ship in the line except for a "PY" bringing up the rear.

PY stood for "patrol yacht." It was an oceangoing size private yacht that had been outfitted with some simple sonar equipment, a couple of depth charges, and a small deck gun. PYs were supposed to run interference for the cargo ships, but the U-boat captains were apparently not terribly intimidated by them.

Being at the end of the convoy, even with a PY behind them, was a position that Captain Hill would not envy under *normal* conditions. With the threat of a saboteur aboard planning who-knows-what, it was nerve wracking.

The water was calm and the sky was solid grey except for a narrow break on the western horizon. When the sun began to set in about half an hour, it would silhouette the ships for any U-boats on their starboard side, and light them up like props on a stage for subs on their port. It was a potentially disastrous set of circumstances, so Hill ordered every available man out on deck to stand watch.

The sailors of the Navy Armed Guard were at their battle stations, manning the five-inch gun at the stern, the three-inch at the bow, and the 20mm "ack-ack" anti-aircraft guns along the higher decks and in smaller gun tubs flanking the 5 and 3-inchers. Every member of the ship's civilian company not on watch was on deck scanning a sector of the ocean for any sign of a periscope or conning tower ... or an incoming torpedo.

Frank had never been more excited or more nervous in his life. Most of him didn't want a U-boat to appear out there, but if there was one, another piece of him wanted to be the one to see it first and sound the alarm. It would make him the hero of the ship! ... assuming that the Navy boys were able to fend off the attack, of course.

Not being part of the normal engine room watch at that time, Frank was free to serve as an extra lookout. But he did not have a pair of binoculars.

Stationed amidships on the port side of the ship's boat deck, he found himself looking directly into the setting sun. He didn't think to grab his cap when he was told to go and watch for submarines, so he improvised a visor by holding his hand up to his forehead. He angled it so that it just blocked the sun but left his view of the water unobstructed. That helped, but the sunlight glinting and dancing across the low waves, made it painful to watch the water for any length of time. But that was exactly what the commander of any lurking U-boat would be hoping for, so Frank had no choice but to keep staring.

By the time the ocean had swallowed half of the sun, Frank's eyes were burning and watering constantly. He had to keep blinking in order to keep his assigned section of the ocean in focus.

Suddenly, through tearing eyes, he saw something! A small vertical line, dark against the brilliance of the sun's glare on the water. He blinked twice and stared hard to be sure his eyes weren't playing tricks ... but then the line was gone.

His heart pounded in his chest. Had he seen a periscope just before it had been pulled back below the surface having marked its target? Had no one else seen it? There were no alarms being yelled across the ship.

His mind was racing as he stared hard at the spot where he had seen ... *thought* he had seen the periscope. Should he sound the alarm, *just in case*? If he was wrong he would send the ship into a panic for no reason ... and become the boy who cried wolf.

If he was right—and they had been targeted—the warning might give the captain just enough time to change course now that the sub could no longer see them, and avoid a fatal torpedo strike.

Then the solution occurred to him. He would shout, "*Possible* periscope sighted ..." As he filled his lungs for what he hoped would be the loudest shout of his life he suddenly saw it again.

The sunlight backlit a spray of water and a second later the slim grey periscope broke the surface. It appeared to be heading directly at him. Then the dark curve of the top of the conning tower broke the surface! And it was much closer than he had been told a sub needed to be to fire a torpedo! It must be out of torpedoes and it was going to be a surface attack! That meant the Navy boys could fire back! If they could bring their guns around quickly enough, they might even score a hit before the sub's gun crew could get on deck!

Frank refilled his lungs and let loose, "SUBMARINE PORT AMIDSHIPS! ESTIMATED TWO HUNDRED YARDS!"

Two seconds later the ship's klaxon started barking the warning to the whole crew that the ship was under attack.

Frank looked forward and saw the three-inch cannon swinging around to port. He looked aft and saw the five-inch doing the same.

He turned back to the ocean, hoping to see the first shell hit the sub, but it was gone again!

Could the enemy have heard the ship's alarm and been warned off? Maybe the captain of the U-boat saw the guns swinging around through the periscope and knew he'd lost the element of surprise.

A Kiss For Luck!

Frank would rather have seen the sub sunk, but if his keen-sighted alarm had only prevented an attack, he still felt pretty heroic.

His heart still racing, he continued to stare at the water where the sub had disappeared, hoping *not* to see the bubble trail of a torpedo appear.

Suddenly, the periscope appeared again and at nearly the same time the water directly in front of it erupted in a huge glittering spray lit up by the sun. The Navy boys had put a shell almost right on top of it! Only ... Frank hadn't heard the gun go off. He had been there during practice firing at Sheepshead Bay and he knew they made a *lot* of noise. How could he miss *that*?

His mind had only a second or so to ponder that conundrum when he saw the top of the conning tower appear again.

This time the marauder wasn't headed directly at him, however, but had turned slightly to his right, and it suddenly registered what he was really looking at. It was the dorsal fin and the back of a huge fish! A killer whale to be precise—an Orca. Although Frank had never even seen a picture of such an animal, it was clear to him now that it was no submarine.

From the aft gun tub, 200 feet away, Frank faintly heard the order to "Hold fire!" as the aiming officer obviously made the same identification. At almost the same instant, the forward three-inch gun went off and Frank jumped at the unexpected noise. He turned to see a splash 20 or 30 yards beyond the whale, followed by a geyser of water caused by the exploding shell. At the same moment that the shell went off, two of the anti-aircraft guns above Frank's head started firing, sending rips of water into the air where the whale had been seconds before.

Immediately, Frank heard shouts of, "Cease firing! Cease firing!" and in a moment all he could hear was the indistinguishable shouts of men trying to figure out what the hell had just gone on.

After the darkness of the night had completely enveloped the blacked-out freighter, and everyone felt just a bit safer, word of what had happened spread pretty quickly through the ship. When Frank returned to his quarters he found a sheet of paper taped up on the bulkhead above his bunk. On it, below the hand-drawn silhouette of a U-boat was the word "FOE". Below that was the profile of a whale and the word "FRIEND."

Rudy teasingly took to calling him "Ahab" after that.

Earlier, as soon as the *Shea* and her PY escort had cleared Boston's harbor defenses—the shore-controlled mines and the submarine nets—and was in open ocean, Captain Hill and First Mate Jones sought out each of the officers who were on O'Hara's check-marked list, and privately explained the Nazi saboteur dilemma.

Hill had decided against a single meeting as it would have been unusual and it might have aroused the suspicion of the spy. Now, after dinner had been served, a gathering of the officers would not be out of the ordinary, and so eight men sat and stood in Hill's state room to discuss the situation. The group included Hill, Jones, Rudy, First Assistant Engineer Walsh, Second A.E., Moschella, Deck Engineer Chase, Chief Steward Delano, Navy Armed Guard Lt. Kendricks, and O'Hara.

"I'd like to have a special little chat with that kid who had us hunting whales this afternoon," O'Hara said from his seat beside Hill's bunk. "That was no accident. Nobody mistakes a goddamned fish for a U-boat! I think he wanted us to break radio silence telling the other ships we were under attack so his Nazi friends out there could get a fix on us."

"I doubt that," Rudy said. "He's hardly the first nervous kid to see something that wasn't there on his first watch. Besides, I'd rather see Kendricks' boys blow a whale out of the water because a kid's too eager, than take a torpedo 'cause he's scared of making a mistake."

"Give me five minutes with him," O'Hara said, "and I'll show him what scared is. I'll get the truth out of him."

"No," Hill said. "You'll leave him alone. I think the Chief is right; it was an honest mistake by a nervous kid who's never seen anything bigger than a catfish. We can all keep a close eye on him, but I doubt he's your man."

"What do you suggest we do then?" O'Hara asked.

"Not that I actually *like* the idea, but just what you suggested in the first place," Captain Hill answered. "We watch and wait. Between us we should be able to notice anything strange or unusual short of a sudden explosion. All we can do is hope that your spy really does want to be subtle so he can move on and fry other fish after us."

"Speaking of frying," Jones said, happy for a segue to poke a barb into O'Hara's ego, "Have you overheard anything while you've been feeding the crew, *messman* O'Hara?"

"Only that they're pretty sure that the first mate's a queer and they don't like that very much," O'Hara replied with a smirk.

Jones, who had been leaning against the aft bulkhead of the state room, pushed himself off the wall and started toward O'Hara. "I'll show you who's a queer you FBI pussy!"

O'Hara started up out of his chair to meet Jones' advance.

Hill, who was seated on the edge of his bunk, grabbed O'Hara by the shoulder and pushed him down in his chair. At about the same instant, Rudy grabbed Jones by the back of his shirt and pulled him back.

"Knock it off, you two!" the captain said. "You want to put the gloves on and settle your differences when we get to Halifax, that's fine. But for now, try acting professional instead of like a couple of school boys."

There was a few seconds of tense silence as the two men stared at each other, and then Hill said to O'Hara, "*Have* you heard anything from the crew?"

O'Hara took a moment to relax in his chair before answering. The question made him the center of attention again, and he wanted to milk it. He stretched out his legs as if the whole thing was suddenly boring and then said, "The kid named Billy was asking some of the old-timers how far they thought we were from land. I asked him why he wanted to know and he said he was just curious.

Seems like an odd thing to be curious about to me. I think he wanted to know when we were far enough from any port so it would take a good long while to get help to us if we *mysteriously* broke down."

"Any of you know him?" Hill asked as he looked around at his officers.

"He's an oiler on first watch," Rudy answered. "This is his first trip, I think. But he seems pretty much on the ball."

"It may be nothing," Hill said, "probably is, but you never can tell. Keep an eye on him, all of you. And keep your eyes and ears open in general. You see or hear anything that doesn't seem to fit, I want to know about it, pronto."

Frank and Narrow leaned against the starboard railing at the stern, just below the aft gun tub, looking out into the darkness of the starless, moonless night. It was just coming up on 2100. Frank's watch in the engine room began at 2200, but he would be there a half hour early to perform a detailed shift turnover with Billy.

"Boy, I really screwed the pooch this afternoon," Frank said to Narrow. "I've never even seen a *picture* of a whale that looked like *that* before."

Narrow shrugged. "Could have happened to anyone," he said. "If you ain't nervous as a cat when you think there might be a sub around, you got a few screws loose."

"That's kind of what the chief said," Frank replied. "But he said he's gonna keep calling me Ahab just so I don't forget the lesson."

Narrow laughed. "Like I said, could have happened to anyone ... but I'm glad it was you and not me!"

Frank gave him a jab in the arm. "Thanks! With friends like you, who needs enemies?"

The two stared out into the darkness in silence for a while. Finally, Frank asked, "Are you claustrophobic?"

"You mean scared of small places? Nah. We got old abandoned mines all over the desert back in Arizona; I used to love exploring them. Some of them go for a mile or more under ground. Why? Are you?"

"I never thought so, but we don't have any mines or caves around the farm. I'll tell you, though, that that shaft alley gives me the heebie-jeebies! When I climb in there and pull the hatch closed behind me I feel like I'm running out of air the whole time I'm in there. I can't wait to get the bearings checked, and get the hell out!"

Narrow chuckled. "That's funny, 'cause that's one of my favorite places on the whole ship. I wouldn't mind stringing up a hammock and sleeping down there."

Frank gave a mock shudder and said, "You're *weird*! What if we got hit by a torpedo while you were in there?"

"That's what the escape trunk is for. If you can't get out through the engine room, you climb straight up and come out right here." He turned and jerked his thumb toward the watertight hatch below the gun tub that looked like the door to a small broom closet.

"I know that's what's *supposed* to happen," Frank replied. "But what happens after you've climbed thirty feet straight up that three-foot square chimney with water coming up right behind you and you can't get the hatch open 'cause it's jammed or something?" At that thought, Frank shuddered again, but it wasn't put on; the thought scared the hell out of him.

Narrow laughed again, unable to comprehend that level of fear about something as benign as a small space. "Hey, I'll tell you what. If it bothers you all that much to be in the alley, I'll go in and check the bearings for you at the end of your watch, which is really the beginning of mine, anyway."

"Really?" Frank said, amazed that anyone would *volunteer* to go into that cold steel tunnel below the waterline when they didn't have to. "You think it'll be okay with the chief?"

"As long as the bearings get checked and oiled every watch, why should he care who does it?"

"I guess," Frank said with an uncertain shrug. "Are you sure you don't mind?"

"Nah. What are friends for, huh? I'll check the bearings at the end of your watch, and then again at the end of my own. Billy will be checking them just before he goes off duty, so they'll all get checked every eight hours, same as always. No problem."

"Speaking of Billy ..." Frank said as he looked at his watch. The luminous dial was still visible, but just barely. "I better be getting below deck. See you at 0530"

"0530," Narrow repeated. Looking at his own watch, he said, "That's going to come early; I should probably hit the sack myself."

As Frank headed down to the engine room, Narrow headed forward and climbed up the one deck to the quarters that he shared with Frank and Billy. Rather than getting ready to turn in, however, he took his empty duffle bag from his locker and unfolded it. He reached down to its very bottom, and fingered a seemingly stray length of thread. He pulled on the thread and it unraveled the locking chain stitch that went all the way around a false bottom of the bag. He lifted out the circle of canvas, and then reached in and removed two rolls of wiping rags. Each was about as big as his forearm.

He put the duffle bag away, and then he stuffed one roll into each of his front pants pockets. He immediately took them out. If he walked out on deck that way, even in the dark almost anyone would have noticed them bulging and sticking out the top of the pockets.

He opened his jacket and unbuttoned his shirt. He took the two rolls and wedged them into the waistband of his pants, inside his shirt. He rebuttoned his shirt and then zipped up his jacket. The bulges still showed, but not nearly as obviously as they had in his pockets. He put his hands in his jacket pockets on top of the rags, and found that he could pretty much make the bulges disappear as long as someone wasn't looking too closely.

He looked at his watch. It was nearly 2200 hours. Billy would be in the shaft alley right now, and Frank would be in the engine room. Narrow left their quarters and went down onto the upper deck. He made his way aft, winding his way through and around the heaps of cargo that were lashed to the deck alongside and even atop each cargo hatch.

As he passed hold number four Narrow encountered another sailor heading toward him. Narrow stopped, turned, and made the pretense of checking the knot in one of the lines that secured a big "deuce and a half" truck to the top of the hatch cover.

The other man squeezed passed Narrow and went on his way without speaking. Narrow guessed that he was probably on his way to the crew's mess after his watch. Or maybe to the head. It didn't matter as long as he was gone.

Narrow walked toward the stern to where he and Frank had been talking at the rail earlier. Three Navy boys were in the gun tub above him, but if they noticed he was there they didn't say anything to him. He walked into the passageway under the tub and stood next to the watertight door that sealed off the upper end of the shaft alley escape trunk. It was nearly pitch black under the gun platform, but Narrow easily found the locking handles on the hatch by feel.

Earlier in the day, after his watch in the engine room was over, he had "busied himself" by going around the ship oiling the hinges, dogs, and wheels on every watertight hatch. The deck engineer had commended him for his initiative, but the real reason he had done it was so that when he opened this one hatch in the dead of the night it would be silent.

His efforts paid off. Only the fourth and final dog made any noise at all when it released the full weight of the sealed door. And that noise was easily swallowed up by the creaks and groans of the rolling ship and the sounds of the sea.

He swung the hatch open, stepped onto the ladder inside the three foot square vertical shaft, and pulled the hatch closed. It was as black inside as the deepest mine shaft he had ever been in back in Arizona, but he didn't bother to turn on the flashlight that he carried in his back pocket. He would need to save its batteries for later. Instead, he felt for the dogs, and turned each one, sealing himself inside.

At an unhurried and even pace he began to descend the ladder in total darkness. After twenty or so rungs he stopped, took out the flashlight and took a quick look down to see how far he was from the bottom. He had ten or twelve feet to go. He had to be careful not to walk off the end of the suspended ladder in the darkness. If he fell the five or six feet to the steel deck and twisted an ankle it would be a disaster. He wished that he had thought to count the rungs on the ladder sometime earlier, but it was too late now.

He counted ten more rungs and then took out the flashlight, turned it on, and held it in his hand pointing downward as he climbed down the last few rungs. Finally standing on the steel grating that ran the length of the alley, he set the light down on top of the huge iron pedestal that held the last shaft bearing before the shaft disappeared through a bulkhead and passed through the tail bearing assembly. Beyond that, the eighteen foot diameter, four-blade bronze propeller screwed its way through the cold Atlantic, pushing the fifteen-thousand ton *Shea* ahead of it.

Narrow didn't want to turn on the overhead lights in the alley, so he needed to use his flashlight sparingly. Although the watertight hatches would certainly have contained the light, if someone did happen to come in while he was working, he would have perhaps thirty seconds of darkness to react from the time he heard the hatch opening until the person switched the lights on. It could be enough to save his life.

Next to where Narrow stood, the steel propeller shaft—more than a foot in diameter—turned at a steady 65 RPM. It was not particularly dangerous to be standing there because the shaft's surface was smooth and if one were to lean against it, all they would get is a little dirty. Between the last bearing pedestal and the bulkhead, however, was an even larger diameter pair of steel flanges, bolted together. It was one of seven pairs that connected the twenty-foot sections of the shaft together, and it was the only one that was not guarded by a sheet-metal housing.

Those flanges were attached to one another with six massive bolts, the heads of which protruded from one side, with the nuts on the other. It was those bolt heads and nuts that were dangerous. If one were to get their clothing caught up in them somehow, the shaft would pull the unlucky victim around and around, beating their body, like a rag doll, against the port bulkhead and the steel deck faster than time every second. And it would not slow the propeller one iota.

It was directly above that spinning flange that Narrow needed to work.

He took off his coat and draped it over an electrical conduit. He opened his shirt and took out the rolls of rags, and then took his shirt off, draping it over his jacket. Next, he took off his shoes and socks, and then his pants. In less than a minute he was completely naked, with all of his clothes hanging well off the deck over various pipes and tubes.

It was cold and clammy down there below the waterline, and although eliminating the possibility of getting his clothes snagged by one of the flange bolts would make his planned task a little safer, the main reason for his nakedness was so that his clothes would not get saturated with oil, and leave a dripping trail when he left. What he was about to do was going to be messy and there was no way to avoid it. And he could wipe the oil off his skin with his rags much easier than he could wring it from his clothes.

He unrolled the two bundles of rags on the deck grating. Inside one was a pair of short open-end wrenches. Inside the other was a length of pipe about a foot long and 5/8 of an inch in diameter.

Also in the rags was a pipe union. This was a heavy iron three-piece fitting consisting of two threaded flanges, and a nut that held them together. In normal plumbing, the flanges were screwed onto the ends of two pipes that needed to be joined, and the nut held them tightly together, forming a seal. Just about every run of pipe on the ship would have one somewhere. This union was different from all of those, however, in that both ends were plugged; nothing could pass through it.

The last item in the rags was a length of wooden dowel about a half inch in diameter that was just a little longer than the piece of pipe.

All of the items together constituted the sabotage kit that his spy handlers had given him, and that he had trained with to a point of proficiency. In a mock-up of this part of the ship in a backstreet warehouse in Baltimore, Narrow and half a dozen other young men had practiced over and over the whole process that Narrow was about to perform, even before they had reported to Sheepshead Bay.

He had no idea who had come up with this particular way of sabotaging a cargo ship, but he considered the plan to be genius (which was only natural from the master-race from which he was descended on his mother's side).

Narrow picked up the flashlight and shined it on the steel plate above his head. On land it would have been called the ceiling of the shaft alley, but on a ship it was called the *overhead*. This particular section of the overhead was also the bottom of a huge oil tank built into the structure of the ship.

Protruding straight down out of the tank was a pipe that was about as big in diameter as Narrow's thumb. Through a series of fittings, a valve, and other lengths of pipe, it fed a constant supply of oil to the propeller shaft tail-bearing. It also had a small petcock teed into it, for dispensing oil into the can that hung below it, for topping off the spring bearings.

The propeller shaft tail-bearing was a massive bronze cylinder almost four feet long and more that a foot in diameter. Directly ahead of the bearing, inside its cast iron housing, was a hollow chamber that was filled with oil delivered by the pipes. As the polished steel shaft turned within the bronze bearing a thin film of oil migrated from the chamber into the bearing. It was this film of oil—thinner than a piece of paper—that kept the thousands of pounds of force generated by the propeller shaft from fusing the steel and bronze together as if they were welded.

If that happened, either the shaft would stop turning—held solid by the frozen bearing, or the shaft would tear the bearing loose from the tight fit in its housing and keep right on spinning.

If the former happened, the ship would stop because the propeller would stop. If the latter occurred, all the shaft seals would be torn apart and seawater would begin to pour in through the ever-widening gap between the bearing and the damaged housing, flooding the shaft alley. When the crew discovered that happening, they would have to seal off the shaft alley and shut the engine down to prevent even more damage.

Either way the ship would be stopped. And either scenario would be impossible to repair at sea. It would require that the ship be towed to port somewhere, have all of its cargo unloaded onto another ship, and put into dry-dock for repairs.

There was a saying in wartime that you're better off wounding an enemy soldier than killing him, because it takes more resources to care for the wounded than the dead. That was not quite the same for crippling a ship versus sinking it, but it had its advantages. With sinking, the ship and cargo were gone forever, possibly with some of the crew. But crippling still put a huge drain on war-making assets by tying up valuable manpower, other ships, and shipbuilding facilities. It would delay vital war materials from reaching England, and it was a lot safer for the saboteur ... assuming he didn't get caught.

Narrow examined the series of pipes and fittings that made up the oil line. One of the fittings was a gate valve that could be turned to regulate or shut off the oil to the tail bearing.

Compared to what Narrow was about to do, closing the valve and jamming it somehow would have been an easy way to starve the shaft's tail-bearing of oil. But it would also have been easy to repair if it was discovered before fatal damage was done to the bearing. That was the brilliance of *this* plan.

Beyond the valve, the pipe continued for a couple of feet and then disappeared through the shaft alley's aft bulkhead.

The bulkhead formed the forward wall of what was called the "after peak tank." This was an empty area at the very aft end of the ship, specially reinforced inside with steel plates and bracing to be able to support the enormous stresses put into the ship by the propeller and the rudder.

Because the area was full of bracing it was not much use for storing cargo, but it could be filled with water if the ship needed extra ballast. Fully loaded, the last thing the *Shea* needed was any more weight, and so the tank was empty for this crossing.

Inside the tank, which was sealed off by an access plate that was bolted in place, the horizontal oil line made a 90-degree turn downward, and connected to the tail-bearing oil chamber.

While all Liberty ships were built from the same basic set of plans, they each had subtle differences in their small details. Every Liberty ship would have this oil line, but the exact arrangement of fittings and lengths of pipe would be up to the pipe fitter who worked on the ship. This section of oil line would be as unique to the *Shea* as a fingerprint. It was why Narrow couldn't just smuggle aboard a section of pre-sabotaged piping and swap it out. The process could only be carried out *in situ*.

Narrow took the pipe union from his rags and disassembled it. He would only need one half of the fitting for his plan, but he couldn't know which half until he was here, looking at the pipes. He put the top half and the nut back in the rags, and then balanced the bottom half on a steel brace, within easy reach.

Next, he took his two wrenches and fit them onto the identical union in the ship's oil line. Using his length of pipe as a lever, he forced the wrenches in opposite directions, loosening the nut.

As soon as the nut broke loose, oil started to seep out of the unsealed fitting under the pressure from the 200 gallon tank above. Most of the oil was running down the pipe and into the can that hung there, but some traveled across the horizontal pipe until it hit the valve and dripped onto the deck. The faster he could perform this next part of the operation, the smaller the mess would be that he would have to wipe up later.

He dropped the wrenches and the pipe onto his rags, and then, by hand, he spun the nut all the way off the bottom half of the union.

The oil poured out from between the loosened flanges much more freely, now.

Quickly, he took hold of the pipe below the uncoupled union, and he pulled on it. The pipe rotated at the elbow at its bottom, and the two halves of the union separated completely.

After an initial spray that sent oil all over Narrow's hands, arms, chest, and legs, the oil poured out of the pipe in a straight stream.

He pressed his thumb over the hole to slow the flow, but the action momentarily created more spray, soaking him further. With the flow somewhat stemmed, he reached over with his other hand for the plugged union half. He needed to screw it in place against the ship's half of the union to act as a temporary cap to the escaping oil.

He quickly pulled his thumb away and thrust his union half into the stream of oil, up against the ship's half.

But the force of the oil stream was more than he expected—more than he had practiced with in the warehouse—and it drove the union from his slippery grip, sending it to the deck near his feet.

"Goddam*n!*" he muttered as he jammed his thumb back over the hole, receiving yet another shower of oil.

Unable to reach the union on the deck while still holding his thumb on the pipe, Narrow tried to pick up the fitting with his toes. Under ideal conditions he might have been able to wedge the fitting between his big toe and the next one, or even jam his little toe into the opening, but with the union and his foot both covered with oil he didn't have a chance, and it squirted out from under his foot, off the grating, and onto the steel decking, rolling completely out of sight.

"*God Damn!*" he repeated.

He contemplated letting go of the pipe, quickly bending down to pick up the fitting, and then getting back up to stop the oil. But without knowing exactly where the union was on the deck, he wasn't sure he could retrieve it in just a few seconds. Any longer and the pouring oil would overflow the drip can.

Muttering another oath, he resigned himself to reconnecting the pipe to stop the oil while he looked for the missing fitting.

A minute later, and with oil running down his chest and dripping from his elbows and every other body part, he had the pipe back together. By the time he did, the drip can was nearly full to the rim.

He unhooked the can, picked up the flashlight and walked, naked and dripping oil, forward toward the engine room. At each of the seven spring bearings along the way he poured some of the oil into the reservoir atop the bearing. Having recently been attended to by Billy, however, none of them could hold very much more, and Narrow found himself still with half a can of oil when he finished with the last bearing.

As much as he didn't want to, he had little choice but to distribute the remaining oil along the deck below each of the bearings as he walked aft. A little extra oil spread out along the length of the alley might go unnoticed, but he knew he was going to have at least another can to dispose of before he was done, and that concerned him. Excess oil on the deck would mean that something was leaking, and people would start poking around.

Back at the tail bearing, he hung up the can, and then crouched down with the flashlight to find the half of the union he had dropped. He ended up laying across the grating on his bare stomach before he could reach the wayward fitting tucked into an almost inaccessible corner. As he stood up he was thankful that he had not tried to retrieve it with the oil continuing to run.

Better prepared, Narrow got the pipe disconnected and the plugged union in place much easier—if no less messy—the second time.

With the pipe disconnected and the oil temporarily stopped, Narrow was able to proceed with the actual sabotage part of the plan.

He unscrewed the gate valve from the horizontal half of the oil line, and set it on the deck. That left the part of the pipe that passed through the aft bulkhead open and facing him ... and dribbling oil. He hung the drip can under it to try to reduce the already considerable mess.

He took the pipe he had used for a lever and unscrewed the plug from the coupling on one end. He threaded his pipe onto the end of the ship's oil pipe, and then he unscrewed the plug from the other end of his pipe.

Next, he took the wooden dowel and pushed it into his pipe. Not surprisingly, it went only about half way in and stopped. Narrow picked up the larger wrench and used it as a hammer to tap the dowel all the way in, which meant that its other end would be protruding out of his pipe and into the ship's oil line by about an inch.

What Narrow had just done was to push the contents of his pipe into a very critical oil line of the *Shea*. The contents was a special formulation of clay, fine aluminum-oxide grit, tiny metal shavings, silt, and some chemicals. Any one of those ingredients would be very bad inside of a bearing, but simple contamination was not the point of Narrow's sabotage.

The concoction had a more important property for this application. When mixed with oil, the powders would form a paste that would set to the consistency of cement within an hour.

The mixture would completely stop the flow of oil to the shaft's tail-bearing and in a short time, would stop the ship. But when the pipes were eventually taken apart in dry dock, assuming the ship survived being disabled at sea, it would look like the blockage had been caused by sloppy work practices when the ship was being built, because all of the contaminants Narrow had just injected into the line could be found in any shipyard in the country. The sabotage would look like an accident caused by the rush of war production. Genius!

Narrow unscrewed his pipe from the oil line, and reassembled the gate valve and the section of pipe that he had removed. He closed the valve, and then he was back to the messy part. He removed the fitting that was holding back the oil in the overhead tank, and then as quickly as he could, he rotated the pipe back into place, and reconnected the *Shea's* original union again ... all the while getting drenched with more oil.

Finally, he cracked open the gate valve to let the oil trickle into the dry powder inside the sabotaged oil line. If he had opened it all the way, the stream of oil might have washed the powder into the oil cavity of the bearing. It would do *some* damage there, but not nearly enough.

Now it was time to clean up. He took the rags and began wiping the oil from his body. Being work rags they were not exactly soft, and Narrow looked like he had a mild sunburn over his whole body before he was done.

He got dressed, and then took the already oily rags and wiped down the pipes, the bulkhead, the constantly rotating propeller shaft and flanges, and the deck as best he could. He wished that he had twice as many rags, but he made do with what he had.

The last thing he did was to hang the drip can under the gate valve rather than the petcock, and to crack open the petcock just a hair so that it let out a drop of oil every five seconds or so. This would help to explain to the next oiler why there was so much oil on the deck.

Finally, he rolled his sabotage kit into the oily rags and stuck them back inside his shirt and into his waistband. The oil would soak through his clothes, but that would be easily explained if it was noticed. There were plenty of places on the ship where one could lean against something and get a little oily.

He took a last look around with his weak flashlight, then turned it off, stuck it in his jacket pocket, and started up the ladder.

He was about half way up the escape trunk when he heard a faint noise from below and then saw the lights come on in the alley. He heard the noise again as the watertight door was closed, but the lights stayed on. Someone was inside the shaft alley.

Faintly at first, but then louder and louder, Narrow heard the sound of boots on the steel grating. He held himself perfectly still and opened his mouth wide to breathe as quietly as possible.

Looking down he saw a capped head appear and move around, apparently inspecting the area. Many of the officers wore the same style of cap, so he didn't know who it was.

As Narrow stood there, he felt one of the rolls of oily rags begin to creep downward from its place in his waistband. He pressed forward to pin it between his leg and the ladder, stopping its slide just as it slipped from the grip of his belt.

From below, Narrow heard, "Jesus H. Christ! These goddamned kids can't even turn off a goddamned spigot! Look at the oil on the goddamned deck!"

There was no mistaking the voice—or the cursing. It was the second assistant engineer. His name was Peter Moschella, but everyone called him Secondo because he was the Second Assistant Engineer and he was Italian.

Narrow didn't hear any reply to Secondo's ranting, so he guessed that he was probably alone and just cursing aloud to himself. He did that.

Finally, he moved out of view, heading back toward the engine room. He heard one more "Jesus H. Christ!" as his foot steps faded into the distance. After what seemed a very long time, he heard the hatch at the far end of the alley open, saw the lights go out, and heard the hatch close.

Once again in total darkness, Narrow reached down and took hold of the roll of rags through his pant leg. He knew it would be easier to work the roll out the bottom of his pants than to try to stuff it back up under his belt, although doing it while standing on a ladder in the dark was no easy feat.

As he pulled the rags out past his shoe, he felt the union squirm free from the bundle. He grabbed at it, fumbled it in his fingers, but then finally managed to trap it between his palm and the toe of his shoe.

With a sigh of relief, he put the union in his jacket pocket, tightened the roll a little, and stuffed it back inside his shirt and pants.

Two minutes later, he was standing inside the hatch at the top of the trunk. This was perhaps the most dangerous part of the plan.

When he had gone into the trunk he had been able to look around to make fairly sure that no one was watching. Now, however, anyone at all could be standing on the other side of the hatch and he would have no way of knowing until he opened it and stepped out.

He slowly turned the first three dogs, then he held his breath, turned the last one, and pushed open the hatch.

There was no one in sight. He released his breath as he stepped out onto the deck, and then he turned around to swing the hatch shut again. As it closed, a surprised Navy Armed Guard sailor came into view from behind it.

"Where the heck are you coming from?" the sailor asked. He seemed more bewildered than suspicious, however. With their quarters and all of their gun stations being topside, the Navy boys rarely went below decks, and would never have ventured into the shaft alley. He had likely never given much thought as to where the hatchway led, and may even have thought it was a storage locker of some kind.

"The shaft alley," Narrow said. "Way down below the waterline. That's the escape hatch in case it floods while you're down there." Playing on what he and Frank had been talking about, he went on, "I'm a little claustrophobic, so I wanted to see if I could climb all the way up in the dark without panicking."

"Looks like you made it," the sailor said as he walked over to the hatch. Narrow pulled it open so he could look down. With no lights on, it was a black bottomless pit.

"Shit!" the kid said. "Better you than me! I sure wouldn't want to be down there with a Kraut sub around firing torpedoes at us!"

"Yeah, thanks for reminding me of *that*!" Narrow said as he closed and dogged the hatch.

Narrow bade the sailor a good night, and then walked forward along the starboard side of the weather deck. When he reach the point where the bulldozer was lashed to the deck he squeezed between it and the rail. He looked fore and aft and saw no one. He pulled the two rolls of oily rags from inside his shirt, held them over the side, and let them fall together. The noise that they made hitting the water was easily absorbed by the noise of the ship churning through the cold Atlantic.

He looked at his watch. The hands showed 11:34, but aboard ship that meant 2334. He headed for the oilers' quarters where Billy would already be asleep. Narrow suddenly felt exhausted as the adrenaline rush of completing his mission began to wear off. He needed to get some shut-eye before relieving Frank at 0530. He was sound asleep minutes after he hit his bunk.

Secondo rapped on Rudy's office door, seeing the light on beneath it.

"Yeah, come in," Rudy answered from his desk.

"Hi Chief," Secondo began. "You said you wanted to hear about anything unusual, and I just came from the shaft alley. It's probably nothing, but there was quite a bit of oil on the deck, and I found the oil spigot dripping. It's probably a couple gallons, at most, so it's no big deal to the bearings, but somebody's either being careless or they thought they could drain the lube oil tank that way."

"Who's the oiler on watch?" Rudy asked.

"The new kid, Frank, right now, but he won't make his rounds in the alley until the end of his watch. The other new kid, Billy, was the last one in there."

"Where is he now?" Rudy asked.

"In his bunk, I guess," Secondo answered. "You want me to go get him?"

"Yes!" O'Hara's voice came from behind Secondo before Rudy could reply. "Better still, tell *me* where he is, and *I'll* go get him."

Rudy looked at Secondo, and said, "Yeah. Bring him up here, would you? Would you ask the captain to join us before you go down, too."

As Rudy's second assistant left, O'Hara stepped into the office and dropped down into a chair. "Told you so," he said. "You should have let me question him last night. I'd have had him telling the truth about everything all the way back to when he cheated on his math test in the sixth grade."

"I wondered how you kept in shape," Rudy said. "It's all that jumping to conclusions that you do, isn't it? And the leaps of faith you take in your own opinions. I always thought that the '*I*' in FBI stood for investigation, not inquisition."

"The kid made sure we were far enough from shore so we couldn't get help," O'Hara said, "and then he tried to drain your oil tank, which I assume would wreck bearings or something, right? So what more do you need? You want a signed confession? Would that do it for you? Well, give me five minutes with him, and you'll have your confession."

"I'll ask the questions," Captain Hill said from the doorway. As he stepped inside, he went on, "Until we establish—to *my* satisfaction—that he is your spy, the boy is a member of my crew and he'll be treated with respect."

"You can *start* the questioning, Captain," O'Hara said, but I'm not going to sit here quietly in the peanut gallery if you're not getting anywhere."

Just then, Secondo appeared in the doorway, and knocked on the open door. Billy stood behind him looking confused and a little scared.

"Come in," the captain said. As they stepped into the room, he went on, "Sorry to drag you out of your bunk right after you finished your watch, son, but there's some questions we need to ask you."

Billy had no idea what he might have done to warrant being called before the captain and the engineering officers, but the fact that one of the mess stewards was there really confused him. And he was not standing at attention, like *he* was in trouble; he was sitting down while the *captain* was standing.

"Did you check the spring bearings in the shaft alley at the end of your watch, tonight?" Captain Hill asked Billy.

"Yes, sir! Absolutely, sir!" Billy answered quickly. "The forward four were all fine, but I put a little oil in five and six. Seven was fine, and the last one took just a little more than the others. They were all running cool, though, sir."

"Did you use the tail bearing spigot to draw the oil for the other bearings?" Hill asked.

"Yes, sir," Billy answered a little confused. "That's what they taught us in Sheepshead Bay."

"Are you sure you turned the spigot all the way off when you were done?" Hill asked.

"Yes, sir!"

"You're absolutely sure it wasn't dripping when you left the alley?" the captain said.

Billy thought for a moment. "I ... I don't *think* it was dripping. I guess I really didn't check it, though. If it was I'm really sorry, sir. I'll be more careful from now on, sir."

"Why were you asking how far we were from land yesterday?" O'Hara suddenly demanded of Billy.

Hill rolled his eyes, but he let it go ... for now.

Billy was confused both by the question and the fact that a mess steward was asking it and in such an accusatory tone.

Billy hesitated but when the captain didn't intercede, he finally answered, "I don't know, I guess I was just curious."

"Curious, huh?" O'Hara said, straightening up in his chair. "You were curious about how far we were from shore, but not how deep the water might be. Or how cold it is, or how long 'til we make port. Why is our distance from shore the only thing that piques your curiosity about this whole voyage, huh?"

Billy hesitated again. To O'Hara that was a sure sign that he was trying to come up with some lie to cover his ass. To Hill, Billy just looked frightened and confused, which he saw as perfectly normal under the circumstances.

Billy finally turned to the captain, and as he tried to blink away the tears of fear that here welling in his eyes, he said, "I'm ... I'm scared, sir. I'm sorry, but I just am. I didn't think I would be ... I thought I'd be okay, but ..."

"What are you scared of," O'Hara asked. "Getting caught?"

Billy didn't understand what the steward meant, but he went on talking directly to the captain. "I'm scared of the U-boats, sir. They're like ... like cats in the water! And I *hate* cats. All sneaky and quiet and creepy." He glanced at the steward and then went on to the captain, "I heard that the U-boats don't attack when the ships are closer to shore anymore, because they're afraid of our airplanes. I was just hoping that we were close enough that the U-boats would stay away from us. I guess that's why I got out of the shaft alley without checking the spigot like I should have. I just really wanted to get back above the waterline. I'm really sorry, sir. It won't happen again, I swear to God."

"God?" O'Hara said, still unwilling to let go. "You people don't believe in God! You only believe in your precious *Fuehrer*."

"What?" Billy said as he wiped a tear from his cheek. "Fuehrer?"

"Nice act," O'Hara said as he pulled his wallet from his back pocket. Flipping it open to show his badge and ID, he said, "I'm with the FBI, and we know that you're part of a Nazi sabotage ring, so you can stop the lying and crying right now. It's all over."

"*What?!*" Billy blurted, his eyes wide with terror. He turned to the captain and said desperately, "I'm not a Nazi, sir, I swear to God! I signed up to *fight* the Nazis; I hate them! I swear to God, sir! You gotta believe me! *Please*?"

"I believe you, son," Hill said calmly. "Agent O'Hara was just testing you. That's his way." He gave O'Hara a look, and then went on. "But the fact is that we *may* have a Nazi saboteur on board, and now that you know about it, you're going to have to be sworn to absolute secrecy. We don't know who it is, yet—if there actually is one—so you can't tell anyone else on board about this, okay? Otherwise it might tip him off and he'd lay low and Agent O'Hara would miss his chance to arrest him. Can you keep it a secret? Do you swear?"

"Absolutely, sir!" Billy said, his eyes just as big, but now with excitement rather than fear. "What do you want me to do, sir?"

"Three things," Hill said as he put his hand on Billy's shoulder. "I want you to keep doing your job the best that you can as if this meeting never happened. I want you to keep all of this absolutely secret, especially that Mr. O'Hara—the mess steward—is really an FBI agent. And I want you to be extra vigilant. We believe that the saboteur is going to try to stop the ship by wrecking some part of it—not by blowing it up or something like that—so I need all the eyes I can get to be on the lookout for anything unusual. You think you can do all that?"

"Yes, sir! Absolutely, sir! You have my word!" he said as he held up his right hand.

"Thank you, Billy" Hill said shaking his hand. "Thanks for being honest with us. You can go back to your quarters now, and try to get some sleep. And don't worry about the U-boats. The Navy and the Air Corps have them more afraid of us now than we are of them."

That was an exaggeration, if not an outright lie, but Hill hoped it would allow the kid to relax enough that he could do his job the way he was trained.

When Billy was gone, O'Hara said, "That's it? He sheds a tear, says 'No, sir, I'm not a Nazi,' and you're just going to let him go back to destroying your ship?"

"He's not your spy," Hill said. "He's a scared kid, and why shouldn't he be? But if he was the saboteur, I've just completely defused him. He wouldn't try anything now, knowing that we're all watching him. He couldn't *hope* to get away with it."

"So, we're back to square one?" Secondo said.

"Not exactly," Rudy answered. "We know one more person that it's *not*." As Secondo turned to leave, Rudy added, "Just to be safe, let's have the oilers check the bearings every two hours, and let's have the officer of the watch take a walk down the alley a couple times while they're on duty. Make sure that gets passed on, will you, Pete?"

Back in the engine room once again, Secondo found Frank and told him, "The chief wants to start checking the spring bearings every two hours." He looked at his watch; it was quarter past midnight. "Why don't you go check them now, then at two, four, six, and then at the end of your watch."

Frank's heart sank. Obviously, he wasn't going to be able to get Narrow to come down and go into the alley for him every two hours.

"Did the chief say why?" Frank asked.

"He's the chief engineer," Secondo said. "He doesn't need to explain his orders to me any more than I need to explain mine to you."

"I didn't mean that, sir," Frank said. "I just meant is there anything special I should be watching out for? Is there anything wrong?"

"Just make sure the cups are topped off, that none of the bearings are running hot, and for God's sake when you draw oil from the tail bearing spigot, make sure it's turned all the way off."

"Okay, I'll be sure," Frank answered.

"You'd better," Secondo replied. "'Cause I'm gonna check, and if I find it dripping again, I'm gonna kick an oiler's ass the length of the alley and back again! Now, get going."

Frank opened the watertight hatch to the shaft alley, stepped inside and flipped the switch that turned on the row of overhead lights in their metal cages. He stood there for a moment staring down the narrow tunnel toward the far end, 130 feet away. He just stood there for several moments trying to get his breathing and his heart rate under control. He didn't understand how Narrow could actually *enjoy* being in a place like this. Being in one carved out of stone, hundreds of feet underground, without any lights, was *completely* beyond his comprehension.

Finally, he turned around and pulled the hatch closed, then spun the wheel to seal it. He would have felt a tiny bit better if he could have left it open, but regulations said it had to be secured at all times.

He began the walk aft, and put his hand on the first spring bearing. It was slightly warmer than the air temperature, but that was normal. Even with the film of oil between the steel shaft and the bronze bearing *some* friction would be generated. It was only when that friction became excessive that things started to go wrong.

He opened the cap on top of the bearing and looked at the oil level. It was right at the top, which is what he expected since Billy had checked it just two hours ago. As he waked aft, he checked each bearing, and found that only number five could hold any more oil at all, and that was very little. He considered leaving it until his next inspection, but the thought of Secondo's size-twelve against his butt motivated him to take care of it now.

He checked the rest of the bearings, topped off number five, and left the alley with great relief.

Two hours later he repeated the process—without needing to add any oil to any of the bearings—and then two hours after that he was back again.

This time, as he neared the aft end of the shaft alley, Frank began to notice a different smell. The whole cramped space always smelled of lubricating oil, but this smelled like *hot* lubricating oil. He put his hand on the last spring bearing, and even laid the back of his hand against the turning shaft. Neither one was particularly warm. He leaned over and smelled the bearing. The odor was not coming from there.

Being careful not to get caught by one of the bolts in the turning flange, Frank leaned over to lightly touch the short section of shaft between the flange and the aft bulkhead. Twisting at an awkward angle, though, he lost his balance and fell forward. Without really thinking, he tried to stop his fall by putting his hand on the rotating shaft. His hand no sooner made contact than it was flipped around and down, and Frank ended up in a small heap on the deck as if the propeller shaft had practiced a clever karate throw on him.

With his head against the bulkhead just a short distance from the shaft, he noticed that the hot oil smell was much stronger. And then he realized something else. The shaft had been hot when he touched it for the half second it took it to throw him to the deck. At least he thought it was. He reached up and lightly tapped the steel shaft with his fingertips to be sure.

"Damn!" he said out loud. It *was* hot! Far hotter that it ever *should* be!

As he scrambled to his feet, he tried to imagine what could be wrong. It was as if the tail bearing wasn't getting any oil. He reached up to make sure the gate valve in the oil line was all the way open. It was not, but that wasn't a major surprise. One of the old firemen at Sheepshead Bay had told him to never crank a valve all the way open, because it might get stuck. He advised opening it all the way and then closing it a quarter turn or so. So, as Frank turned the valve, he expected it to stop within a half turn at most. After a full turn, it kept opening, and Frank kept tuning. Two turns ... three turns ... almost four full turns before it stopped. The valve had been closed nearly all the way! But why?

Could Billy have closed it accidentally thinking he was shutting off the petcock? Could anyone make that mistake? Maybe Secondo had warned him about dripping oil, too, and it made him so nervous he screwed up.

Frank didn't really want to report his fellow oiler, and he *had* corrected the problem ... but he had no idea how much damage might have been done to the bearing in the six hours since Billy had been in the alley. He *had* to tell Secondo.

When he left the alley, Frank closed the hatch, but he didn't spin the wheel to seal it. He knew that Secondo would be heading back in there as soon as he told him about the hot shaft. He found Secondo in front of the boiler gauges at the other end of the engine room.

"Sir?" Frank said, getting his attention. "I think the tail shaft bearing is running kind of hot. I think maybe you should have a look at it."

"What do you mean you *think* it's running hot?" Secondo said as he started toward the shaft alley. "How hot?"

"Well, the aft end of the shaft was kind of hot, so I thought it must be the tail shaft bearing, you know?" Frank said following right behind Secondo.

"*How* hot?" Secondo repeated.

"I don't know in degrees," Frank said. "*Pretty* hot. I could keep my fingers on it for a little while, but just barely."

They reached the alley entrance, and Secondo pulled on the wheel to turn it, but the hatch swung open instead. "Did you close this hatch and not seal it?" he asked Frank. Without waiting for a reply, he went on, "If it ain't sealed it might as well be a goddamned screen door! Didn't they teach you anything?" As he stooped through the passage, he was muttering, "Goddamned kids ..."

Frank thought about explaining why he had left the hatch unsealed, but he knew Secondo wouldn't want to hear it. And he *had* been wrong even if he thought it was for a good reason. You *always* secured a watertight hatch after you passed through it. Period!

As Secondo made his way quickly aft he touched each spring bearing along the way, and mumbled rhetorically, "What the hell could be wrong back there, now?"

Not realizing that Secondo wasn't really looking for an answer, Frank said, "I think the lube oil got shut off accidentally. But I opened the valve before I went to get you."

"What valve? The gate valve in the oil line? It was *closed*? All the way?"

"Almost," Frank said. "I was just thinking that maybe Billy turned it the wrong way. Maybe he turned it with his left hand and got confused or something."

Out loud, but really talking to himself, Secondo muttered, "Goddamn! That little shit really *is* a sabot ..."

He caught himself before completing the word last word, but it was more than enough to allow Frank to fill in the blank. "*Billy is a saboteur?!*" he said to himself. "*It wasn't an accident?*"

"Goddamn!" Secondo repeated as he got near the end of the alley and could smell the hot oil. He reached in behind the flange and touched the rotating shaft.

"*Jesus H. Christ!*" he shouted, and then spun around, yelled, "Get out of the way kid!" and took off running up the alley, as well as someone his size *could* run in that tight of a space.

Frank was right behind him when he burst through the hatch into the engine room and shouted, "Telegraph the bridge we need to stop the engine!"

The fireman, Lonnie Hooker, grabbed the handle of the telegraph, swung it around to the center position, and then back to "All Stop." He didn't bother to ask why; it was obvious from Secondo's manner that something was very wrong.

By the time Lonnie had rung *all stop*, Secondo was at the voice tube to the bridge. "Engine room to bridge!" he shouted into the tube. "We have an emergency down here. The tail shaft bearing is overheated and in danger of seizing. Permission to stop the engine?"

Even though it was an emergency, Secondo couldn't just stop the engine without authorization from the bridge. For all he knew the PY escort could be right behind them, and stopping without any warning could cause a collision.

There was a few seconds of pause and then the bridge replied, "Permission granted, engine room. All stop." At the same instant, the needle on the telegraph swung around to match the engine room's.

Fortunately, Captain Hill had been on the bridge, and he was able to give permission to stop the ship immediately.

Secondo went quickly to the engine controls, spinning the throttle valve closed and opening the vents. The big engine kept right on turning, however, now being "back driven" by the propeller as the motion of the ship dragged it through the water.

Secondo engaged the reversing engine, cracked open the throttle, and gradually closed the vents. As he let the steam pressure build up in the cylinders, the engine began to slow down and then came to a stop, the force of the propeller being balanced with an exact amount of steam pressure.

But as the ship slowed, the force with which the propeller was back driving the engine decreased, and the engine began to turn backwards as the balance shifted. Secondo played a game with the throttle and vent valves, keeping the engine almost still until the ship came to a dead stop in the water.

"Throw in the jacking gear worm!" Secondo shouted, when he knew the propeller was no longer driving the engine. Lonnie and the other fireman jumped to it, and had the engine locked from turning in half a minute.

The effect of stopping the propeller while the ship was moving, of course, was like putting on the brakes, and every person on board knew that something must be wrong. It could be anything from a man overboard to a mechanical failure, but a loaded cargo ship that was part of a convoy didn't suddenly stop in mid-ocean without a very good reason.

While Secondo was twisting the valves of the engine back and forth, a shout came down the bridge voice tube. "Engine room. Report as soon as the engine is secure." It was the captain's voice.

At about the same time, Rudy's voice echoed from the voice tube connected to his state room, "What's going on down there? What's happened?"

With the firemen helping Secondo stop the engine, Frank was the only one left to answer the calls. Secondo shouted at him, "Tell the captain, *will do*, and tell the chief we got a problem with the shaft's tail-bearing, and he needs to come down here right away."

At the same time that Captain Hill gave the okay to stop the engine, he sent a seaman out onto the deck to send a silent message with the ship's signal light to the next ship ahead of them and to the PY behind them that they had a mechanical emergency and had to drop out of the convoy. The PY signaled back that she would circle in the area. The Liberty ship ahead of them signaled *good luck* as she pulled away from them.

Next, the captain contacted the Lieutenant in charge of the Navy Armed Guard and had him get all of his men to their battle stations. He then ordered all available seamen on deck to scan the waters for submarines.

As he stood on the bridge, Captain Hill swore to himself. Apparently, O'Hara's spy had succeeded despite their vigilance.

Less than a minute after the ship began slowing down, Rudy, Jones, and First were all in the engine room. They filed down the shaft alley to inspect the damage as well as that could be done with the ship sitting in the water.

Secondo carried a box-end wrench with him, and after everyone had touched the shaft and agreed that he had made the right call in stopping it from turning, he started to remove the bolts that held the cover in place over the access hole in the after peak tank. Leaving one loosened bolt in place at the bottom he rotated the cover out of the way. The hot oil smell, coupled with the smells left from the tank being periodically flooded by sea water were almost overwhelming once the tank was opened.

Being somewhat smaller than Rudy and Secondo, First volunteered to crawl into the tank with a flashlight to check out the cast iron tail bearing housing.

"She's hotter than the blazes of hell!" his voice echoed out of the steel cavern. "But I don't see anything wrong on the outside, and she's not leaking water."

While First was in the tank, Rudy took the drip can from the gate valve and held it under the petcock that was located below the shaft in the aft bulkhead. This spigot was connected by a pipe to the bottom of the tail bearing oil chamber, and was used to drain the oil from time to time to flush out any debris and to see if and how much seawater was leaking past the bearing.

Rudy turned the petcock and a geyser of steam blew out under pressure. He jumped back, having expected only a smooth stream of oil. The spigot gushed and sputtered for several seconds, and then settled into a steady full stream of water.

"Good God!" Rudy exclaimed. "There's no oil at all! It's just water. Where the hell did the oil go?"

Secondo answered, "Looks like Billy the Kid sabotaged the gate valve. The other oiler, Frankie, found it almost fully closed. It feels like it's open now, but maybe he did something inside it."

Rudy reached up and gave the valve a twist. "Sure feels open," he agreed. "But we can't trust it. We'll have to bypass the valve with a hose."

He looked down at the petcock, still pouring water and about to overflow the can.

"We've got a lot of water coming in past the bearing," he said, "Let's get a pump in the line here. We'll force oil into the chamber under pressure and drive the water out at the same time we're getting oil to the bearing." He thought for a moment, and said, "You know, it's a good thing we *are* getting so much water through the bearing; if it had gone dry it probably would have seized up and torn something all to hell."

Back in the engine room, Rudy telephoned up to the captain to report and explain the plan.

"You think we'll be able to restart the engine then?" Hill asked.

"A pretty good chance, sir, I should think," Rudy replied. "We may not be able to get full power out of her, but we should be able to make the nearest port under our own steam."

"Good," the captain said. "While you get your pump hooked up I'll have McCarthy fix our position and lay in a course for the nearest port with repair facilities. That could be Portland, Maine, but we might actually be just as close to Halifax, now."

By the time the engineers were making their way back up the alley, Narrow had made his way down to the engine room.

"Why'd we stop?" he asked Frank, knowing exactly why, but surprised that the bearing had seized up so quickly.

"The tail shaft bearing was overheating so we stopped the engine so they could inspect it," Frank answered. "All the engineering officers are in there now."

"*So, the bearing <u>hadn't</u> seized up,*" Narrow said to himself. It was a disappointment, but only a minor one. They had stopped because they knew the bearing was damaged and continuing on would only damage it more. And since there was no way to repair or replace the bearing while the ship was at sea, the end result was the same. The ship was dead in the water until a tug could be sent out for it.

While Narrow was smiling to himself, Frank looked around and then leaned in close to Narrow's ear. "Secondo thinks Billy's a saboteur!" he whispered. "He thinks he tried to wreck the bearing by shutting off the oil. But I discovered the tail shaft getting hot and I opened the valve back up. We'll probably get back underway again once the bearing and shaft cool down."

Narrow almost laughed out loud. He had forgotten to open the valve before he left the alley, but this was even better! Thinking they had fixed the problem by simply opening the valve, they would restart the engine, and in a couple of hours they would be stopping again with even more damage. And he didn't know why they suspected Billy—except for maybe the timing—but that was perfect, too. He began trying to think of some lies he could tell the officers that would cement their conviction that the chubby kid was a saboteur. He suddenly regretted dropping his tools over the side. If he still had them, he would plant them in Billy's gear.

Just then, the officers came out of the alley.

"Frank, Narrow! Come here!" Rudy called to the two boys. "Go with First to stores and help him bring back a pump and hose."

"What size hose?" Frank asked.

"First knows what we need; you just carry whatever he gives you."

"Get going," First said, "I'll be there in two shakes." As the boys headed for the ladder, First talked with Rudy and Secondo about the best way to splice the hose into the oil line.

At the top of the second ladder, Frank almost ran into O'Hara as he headed for the engine room.

"What's going on?" O'Hara asked as he brushed past them. "Why'd we stop? Where's the captain? Is he down here?" Without waiting for answers to any of his questions he headed down the lower ladder.

Frank thought it very odd that a messman would barge into the engine room looking for the captain just because the ship had stopped. He guessed that he was going to have a very short stay down there once Rudy saw him. A steward wasn't going to be anything but in the way in the engine room.

Ten minutes later Frank, Narrow, and First were back with the hose and a hand pump. As Narrow lowered the pump down the ladder to Frank on a short length of rope, Frank saw Secondo heading into the shaft alley with a tool pouch. Over by the boilers he saw the steward, O'Hara, talking with the First Officer, Jones. He couldn't hear what they were saying, but they appeared to be arguing. Frank thought it was very strange for a mess steward to be arguing with the second in command of the ship about *anything*, and even more so to be doing it during an emergency and in the engine room.

Narrow had no sooner made it down to the engine room deck when the captain appeared at the top of the ladder behind him. "Listen up!" he called out as he stepped down the ladder. "Our situation has just become more urgent." Everyone turned to listen.

He looked at Rudy, and said, "Do whatever you have to do to get us moving, Mr. Norcross. We just received a coded message from Halifax that one of their air patrols spotted a U-boat about thirty miles to our southeast."

"Is it headed our way?" Rudy asked.

"It seems to be," the captain answered, "so let's assume that it is, and not be here when it arrives."

"Aye, Captain!" Rudy said. He turned to Frank and Narrow, and said, "Get that stuff down to Secondo, and give him whatever help he needs."

The captain turned to Jones, and said, "Spread the word, Chief. And when you find that other oiler, bring him up to me. I'll be on the bridge."

Billy awoke from an odd dream about being chased by an ugly all-white cat that was wearing a rope collar with a swastika medal hanging from it.

Once he shook the sleep from his senses, he realized that the ship wasn't moving. The steady vibration of the propeller had been replaced by the eerie smoothness of the ship rolling gently in the sea instead of plowing ahead into the waves.

He hopped down from his upper bunk, but landed wrong and stumbled across the room, finally falling on Narrow's bunk. A sharp pain shot up his arm as his funny bone struck something very hard on the bed.

Muttering and rubbing his elbow, he looked to see what he had hit. After feeling around, he dug a pipe union from Narrow's jacket pocket. He thought that that was a peculiar thing to have in one's pocket, but when he noticed that both ends of the fitting had plugs screwed into them, it made even less sense.

Suddenly, the captain's words about a saboteur came back to him. He didn't know what a saboteur might use a plugged up pipe union for, but it was odd enough that he knew he should tell the captain and the chief. He stuffed the fitting in his pants pocket and headed up to the next deck to find the chief. His state room and office were empty, so he went up another deck to find the captain. He was not there either.

Then it occurred to him that the ship would only stop in mid-ocean if there was some kind of emergency, and if that was the case, the chief and probably the captain would likely be in the engine room. He was headed for the ladder when the next thought struck him. What if the emergency was caused by sabotage! He took off at a run.

As Billy went down the ladder on the starboard side of the ship, Captain Hill and Jones were coming up the port side, and they missed seeing Billy by seconds.

Billy reached the grating platform above the engine room, and descended the first ladder to the generator level. Below him, in the area between the boilers, he could see Rudy, the FBI agent, and First all gathered together, talking. He went down the second ladder and headed toward them.

O'Hara noticed him first, and with a grim glare headed toward him. "Come here you Nazi puke!" he said and grabbed him by the front of his shirt. "Your crybaby act might have fooled the captain, but I knew all along it was you. And now, you and I are going to find a quiet little room somewhere and you're going to tell me everything there is to know about the rest of your ring, or so help me, I'll tie a rope around your balls and I'll throw you over the side for shark bait."

"No! No! I'm not a Nazi! I swear to God!" Billy pleaded looking at Rudy, who, with the others had gathered around him and O'Hara. "I was just coming to tell you that I think *Narrow* is the saboteur." He dug in his pocket and pulled out the pipe union. He held it out to the chief, and said, "I found this in his jacket pocket!"

They all looked at it.

"A pipe union?" Rudy said. "What would he sabotage with that?"

"I ... I don't know," Billy stammered. "But look at the ends; they're both plugged. Why would somebody have that in their pocket?"

First took it from Billy and hefted it in his hand. "Nice weight; maybe he was going to make a monkey's fist out of it." he said.

"A what?" asked O'Hara.

"It's a kind of knot that wraps rope all around a small weight. It's usually used on the end of a heaving line. Some seamen make them just to practice knot tying, though."

Rudy took the fitting and looked at it closely. He then smelled it. "It's oily," he said.

"Meaning what?" O'Hara asked.

"I don't know," Rudy answered. "It just seems odd to carry an oily fitting around in your pocket or to plan on making a monkey fist out of one."

"See? I told you!" Billy said, looking around at the officers.

"How do we even know you got this from the other kid's jacket?" O'Hara said. "The last place *I* saw it was in *your* pocket."

"I swear to God!" Billy said. "I fell on his bunk and I hit my elbow on it. That's the God's honest truth!"

Rudy thought for a moment, and then said, "We'll sort all this out later when either Mr. Jones or the captain come back down here. For now, Billy, I'm confining you here to the engine room where we can keep an eye on you. Go sit down on the bench over there." He looked at O'Hara, and said, "You can stand guard, if you want, but if you touch the boy I'll throw *you* over the side for shark bait."

As Billy was falling onto Narrow's bunk, Secondo was pulling a pair of wrenches from his tool pouch inside the shaft alley. He also took out a marlinspike and handed it to Frank. The marlinspike was a long tapered spindle of wood that was used when splicing rope, but Secondo had a different use in mind for it, now.

Secondo put the wrenches on the union as Narrow had done earlier. As soon as he broke the nut loose the oil began to dribble. "Grab that can and hold it under here, kid," he told Narrow. "This is going to get messy." To Frank, he said, "I'm going to spin the nut off this union, and push the pipe out of the way. When I do, the oil's gonna pour out. As fast as you can, I want you to jam that marlinspike up the hole and stop the oil. Got it?"

Narrow wondered if that was going to work. It was a hell of a lot simpler than the half-union process he had gone through.

Secondo spun the nut and pushed the pipe away from the joint. As the oil gushed out all over his arms, he yelled, "Go kid!" to Frank.

With two hands, Frank jabbed the spike up into the end of the union, but the pouring oil threw off his aim, and the tip caught in the inner diameter of the union and didn't go up the pipe. With oil running down both of his arms he tried again ... and missed again.

"Jesus Christ! Does it need hair around it for you to hit the hole?" Secondo barked.

On the third attempt, the spike went up the pipe and stopped most of the flow.

Secondo took one of his wrenches and rapped upward on the bottom of the spike, wedging it solidly in the pipe and stopping the oil completely.

It worked, but Narrow still thought his method was better.

Secondo then took the smaller wrench and unscrewed the half of the union that was still attached to the pipe. Having a larger inside diameter, it came off and slid down to the fat end of the spike. He handed Frank the wrench, and then picked up the hose that was connected to the inlet of the pump. He held its open end next to the pipe.

"When I say go, you rap the side of the spike to loosen it, and then pull it out," he said to Frank. "Then I'll push the hose over the pipe."

"Okay, go!"

Frank lightly tapped the side of the spike with the wrench, and gave it a yank. It didn't budge.

"Jesus Christ!" Secondo bellowed. "Are you a little girl? Rap it like you mean it, not like you're afraid of it!"

Frank pulled the wrench back and took another swing.

"Not *too* hard!" Secondo shouted ... a second too late.

The wrench hit the spike and they heard a crack. The wooden shaft now sat a slight angle to the pipe.

"Oh, for God's sake!" Secondo growled. He took the wrench from Frank and threw it into the pouch. "Nice goddamned swing ya got there, slugger," he said. He handed him the hose and said, "Try not to break this, okay?"

Muttering and shaking his head, he took hold of the spike with both hands, and gently started to twist it. It broke off immediately, leaving a stump of wood up inside the pipe, sealing it off completely.

Narrow almost laughed out loud. Frank was doing almost as good of a job sabotaging the ship as he had done.

"Jesus H. Christ!" Secondo hollered. "Is everybody out to cripple this ship?" He grabbed the hose from Frank and handed it to Narrow. "Let's see if *you* can do something right," he said.

Secondo picked a hacksaw out of the tool pouch and set the blade against the side of the pipe a couple inches from the end.

"Couldn't we just drill out the end of the spike?" Frank asked. "It's just wood."

"We could if we had a drill in the pouch," Secondo answered without looking at him. "We don't, and I'm not waiting for one of you nincompoops to go find one." He pushed the saw forward and started the cut.

When the blade made its way through the first wall of the pipe oil started dribbling out and running along the saw. The deeper Secondo cut, the more oil ran out. As he was cutting through the final fraction of an inch of pipe, he said to Narrow, "Get in here close, and as soon as I finish the cut, you push the hose onto the pipe. Got it?"

"Ready," said Narrow as he moved in.

The end of the pipe fell off, taking the stub of the spike with it, and Narrow pushed the hose into the stream of oil and up against the pipe. But it didn't slide right over. It stuck against the sharp end leaving just a little crack for the oil to escape, and like holding a thumb over the end of a garden hose, it squirted the oil ... directly at Secondo's face.

He turned away, threw down the saw, and grabbed the hose away from Narrow. "*Jumped up Jesus H. Christ! The two of you are worthless!*" he bellowed as he twisted the hose onto the end of the pipe. He lifted his arm to wipe the oil off his face with his sleeve, but realized that his sleeve and everything else was already soaked. He grabbed Narrow, turned him around, and wiped his face on the back of his shirt.

Muttering, he picked up a wrench and put it onto the gate valve. In a few seconds, he had the valve and elbow section of pipe separated. He handed it to

Narrow, and said, "Don't lose this; when I'm done with this I want to see what he did to the valve."

Narrow was nervous as Secondo unscrewed the valve. He wasn't sure if his plugging concoction was going to be visible in the end of the pipe. When he removed the valve, a small amount of oil ran out, but Narrow couldn't see any of the compound. He breathed a silent sigh of relief.

The dribble of oil from the end of the pipe caught Secondo's attention. He had expected the pipe to be completely dry on the downstream side of the valve. "Let me see that," he said to Narrow, who was still holding the pipe and valve.

Secondo held one hand over the end of the valve and put his mouth to the end of the pipe with the union. He blew and immediately felt the air on his hand. "What the hell ...?" he mumbled. "This isn't plugged!" He turned back and looked at the pipe. After a moment's contemplation, he reached down and picked a long-blade screwdriver from the tool pouch. He slid the screwdriver into the pipe, and it stopped after just two or three inches. He pushed harder, but it didn't move. He picked up a hammer and rapped on the handle, driving the blade another inch or so, but no farther.

Narrow's heart began to beat faster and faster.

Secondo pulled out the screwdriver and wiped the tip off between his finger and thumb. He rolled the oily grit around between them.

"Son of a bitch!" he finally said. "*There's* our problem. The goddamned pipe is clogged up with shit that must have been in the tank since she was built. It's like goddamned cement."

Narrow's emotions were all over the map. He was disappointed that the plug had been discovered, of course, but impressed that it held so tightly. Good German chemistry! He was elated that Secondo was willing to blame the shipyard, and not suspect sabotage, but he was distraught that the crafty engineer would likely come up with some way of cleaning it out. And it crushed him to think that he was so close to succeeding in his mission for the Fatherland, and yet he was going to fail. The damage to the bearing had probably not been severe enough before the problem was discovered, and if they got the oil line reconnected—especially with the pump—the ship would be able to get underway and make it safely to the closest harbor.

"We're going to have to bypass all this and connect the hose as close to the bearing as we can," Secondo said. He looked at Frank, and told him, "You're the smallest of us, so you're going to have to crawl into the tank and cut the pipe in there."

Frank just stared at the small black hole in the bulkhead with his mouth open, unable to even reply.

Narrow saw Frank's reaction and an opportunity at the same time.

"Sir? Is it okay if I go into the tank, instead?" Narrow said. "Frank told me he's not real fond of small spaces, and I don't mind them at all."

Secondo looked at Frank. "Not fond of ... What goddamned next?" He turned to Narrow and said, "Fine. Get in there and I'll hand you the tools. Come on, let's go before that goddamned U-boat sneaks up on us."

"*The U-boat!*" Narrow said to himself. He had forgotten about that! If he could delay getting underway long enough for the sub to find them, he could still make his mission a success. Immediately, his mind started racing to figure out how to pull it off ... and still stay alive.

As he bent down to crawl into the access hole, Narrow secretly picked up the cut-off pipe with the piece of wooden marlinspike still jammed in it. He thought that if he could get the plug out, maybe he could wedge it into the pipe up close to the bearing, and still plug the line.

Once inside, Narrow called out, "Can you hand me the flashlight?"

Secondo passed the hacksaw in to him, and then crouched down at the opening. "I'll hold the light. You're going to need both hands on the saw."

He hadn't planned on being watched; that was going to make further sabotage much more difficult.

Standing on the slimy inclined surface inside the tank wasn't easy, but in an effort to buy additional time, Narrow made it appear to be more difficult than it really was.

After slipping and sliding a bit, Narrow turned his body to make it harder for Secondo to see, and put the blade of the saw against the oil line right next to the bearing housing.

He had completed two strokes before Secondo shifted his big frame well enough to see what he was doing.

"*No! No! Stop cutting!* You have to leave some pipe sticking up to connect the hose to! Jesus Christ!"

"Oh, yeah," Narrow said innocently. "How much do you think?"

"Two inches ought to be enough," Secondo said.

"How much is that?"

"Jesus Christ ..." Secondo muttered wearily. "Put three fingers up against the pipe." He watched Narrow do it. "Now, rest the blade against your top finger and start cutting right there."

Narrow began pushing the saw back and forth with one hand, leaving the fingers of his other hand against the pipe. At that rate, it would take him an hour to cut through the pipe, and he knew it. He didn't expect to get away with it for long, but every minute he could delay put the U-boat a little closer.

"Good loving Christ! Are you trying to give me an ulcer? Put both hands on the goddamned saw and cut like your life depends on it, because it damned well does!"

Narrow did as he was told, and as he cut he thought about the U-boat. With the *Shea* dead in the water, it would not have to get very close to make a good torpedo shot on the stationary target. It could possibly stand off far enough that the lookouts wouldn't see the periscope. If that was the case, the only warning he would get would be after somebody saw the bubble trail from the torpedo approaching and sounded the general-quarters alarm. He planned that as soon as he heard the klaxon start barking, he would dive out through the access hole—knocking Secondo on his ass if necessary—and launch himself up the escape trunk ahead of anyone else. It wasn't a *great* plan, and it depended on a lot of *ifs*, but even if it didn't work, and he died down here, he would go down as a hero to the Reich.

By now, the saw blade was two-thirds of the way through the pipe, and Narrow executed another delaying plan. He intentionally pushed the saw at an angle, binding the blade in the slot it had cut. The blade stopped, but he pushed hard enough on the saw to twist and break the thin steel blade. When the blade let go, Narrow's arm lurched forward, and the broken end sliced across his forearm. It wasn't a deep cut, and he had certainly not planned on it, but the blood added a nice touch of authenticity to the "accident."

"*Jesus-Joseph-and-Mary!*" Secondo hollered. "How the Christ did they ever let you out of Sheepshead Bay alive? Give me the goddamned saw!" He pulled the only spare blade from the tool pouch, strung it into the frame, and handed it back to Narrow. "You break *that* blade," he hollered, "and I'm gonna shove the sharp end up your skinny ass and pull it out your nose! Now be goddamned careful this time!"

Taking his time in the name of being careful, Narrow finally cut through the pipe.

"Now push the top piece out of the way," Secondo directed. "Just bend it."

Narrow was planning to struggle with the pipe, but it bent out of the way surprisingly easy.

Secondo passed the end of the hose in to Narrow, and handed him a screwdriver. "Twist the hose over the pipe and tighten the clamp real good. That side's going to be under pressure and I don't want any leaks."

With exaggerated difficulty, Narrow managed to get the hose over the pipe. Then, as he was tightening the clamp, he dropped the screwdriver. By the time Narrow had finally finished the job inside the peak tank, Secondo was so frustrated that he was about ready to beat his own head against the bulkhead.

Narrow began to crawl out through the access hole, but Secondo stopped him. "Stay in there in case there's any leaks," he said. He turned to Frank, and told him, "Start pumping."

Frank put his feet on the base of the pump, and started pulling the lever up and down. Secondo emptied the catch can that Rudy had used earlier, put it back under the drain spigot, and opened the valve. As it had before, water came running out.

"Put your back into it, kid," Secondo said to Frank. "We've got to pump *oil* into the bearing faster than the sea can push *water* in."

Frank began pumping harder, but he quickly realized that no one would be able to keep that up for very long. He wondered if the engineers had a plan to rig up a power operated pump or something.

Narrow watched the water flowing from the spigot and smiled inwardly. After all that, it wasn't working! He looked up, past Secondo, and watched Frank laboring on the pump. He almost laughed. How long did they think anyone could keep that up even if it had worked.

Suddenly, Narrow's attention was brought back to the spigot when Secondo shouted, "Yes! There's the oil! Good job, kid, you did it!" Narrow wasn't sure if he was talking to him or Frank, but it didn't matter; seeing the oil running from the spigot meant he had failed; the ship would soon be moving.

"Check around for leaks in there, kid," Secondo told Narrow as he handed him the flashlight.

"Looks good," he replied, though he was not at all happy that that was the case.

"Okay, come on out." As Narrow crawled out of the tank, Secondo said to him, "Run forward and find the chief. Tell him it's working and we're going to need the air pump, pronto."

As Frank had speculated—had hoped—the engineers knew that the hand pump would not work long-term. But the only compressed-air powered pump they had onboard would not fit through the hatch between the engine room and the shaft alley, so they would have to lower it down the escape trunk from above. In preparation, while Secondo and the oilers had been working on rerouting the oil line and testing the scheme, First had been on deck with other crewmen from the engineering department getting lines and pulleys run from a winch, under the gun tub, and over to the escape trunk hatch.

As Narrow approached Frank on the walkway, he turned back to Secondo and said, "Is it okay if Frank goes? He looks like he could use a break from this pump."

"I don't give a goddamn who goes, just somebody get your ass in gear!" he growled.

Narrow gave Frank a wink. "You've probably been in here long enough, huh? Go ahead; I'll take over the pump."

As Frank headed for the hatch, he thought about his claustrophobia. Oddly, he hadn't really been nervous at all the whole time they were in there. He wondered if that was because he wasn't alone, or if it was because he had been so completely occupied that he hadn't had a chance to think about the tight space.

Narrow began pumping at the same pace that Frank had, and Secondo said, "Slow down, kid. No sense busting your balls now that we know it works. Just keep a nice even pace and watch the spigot. Just keep a little oil dribbling out; just enough to keep the water at bay until we get the air pump down here."

As he pumped, Narrow began to think about how he could salvage his mission. Could he somehow sabotage the pump when it got down here? Perhaps he had acted too hastily in trading places with Frank. If he was up on deck, maybe he could have caused some "accident" that would drop the pump down the trunk, smashing it beyond repair. He heard the hatch open high above him, and heard metal clanking and indistinguishable voices echoing down the steel shaft. It was then that he knew that if he wanted to succeed for the Fatherland—for the *Fuehrer*, he had only one option left.

Secondo stood to one side of the escape trunk—lest some nincompoop topside drop a wrench or something—and shouted "encouragement."

"Get a move on up there! You think that goddamned U-bout is taking *his* time in getting here? Get that pump down here so we get our asses moving again!"

While Secondo's back was turned and his attention was up the trunk, Narrow unscrewed the handle from the pump—a steel bar about two feet long—and then walked up the alley, headed for the engine room hatch.

At the hatch, he made sure the wheel was spun all the way, forcing a tight seal, and then he slid the bar under the hub of the wheel, across one of the spokes, and beneath a steel lug that was welded to the bulkhead. He rotated the wheel in the direction to unseal the door, and the bar stopped it just as he planned.

But he wasn't sure if someone rocking the wheel back and forth might cause the bar to work its way out, so he slid his belt from his pants, and tied the bar in place. He rocked the wheel a couple of times, and nodded his satisfaction. He then turned around and walked back towards Secondo.

He was about half way back when Secondo noticed there was water—not oil—coming out of the spigot, again. He turned to find Narrow not at the pump. "What, you decided it's time to take a goddamned stroll? Get back on that pump before I boot your ass into next Sunday!"

As he approached Secondo, Narrow pulled down his fly. When he reached his hand into his pants, Secondo said, "What in God's good name are you doing? If you gotta take a leak, you ain't gonna do it here! This ain't no goddamned latrine!"

From a heavy cloth holster that was strapped to his inner thigh, Narrow pulled a small "skelatized" 25-caliber automatic pistol. Skelatizing removed the grips, the sights, and even the safety from a gun to make it as small and as easy to conceal as possible. It was a spy's weapon.

As Narrow pulled the slide back and chambered a round into the gun, Secondo said, "What the Christ are you doing with that? If the captain knew you had that peashooter he'd keelhaul your skinny ass! Give it to me, right now, and get back on that pump!"

Narrow aimed the gun at Secondo's chest, and said, "Tell everyone up there to get out of the trunk and seal the hatch."

Secondo just stared at him as if what he had said had been in some foreign language.

"Tell them now, or I'm going to shoot you!" Narrow demanded.

If they had been in a cartoon, a light bulb would have come on over Secondo's head at that moment. "*You're* the goddamned spy! I thought it was the baby faced kid, but it was you all along." Then something else clicked. "*That's* why you volunteered to go into the tank and why you were so goddamned useless in there; you didn't *want* to get the job finished. Christ almighty, I should have known nobody could be that stupid."

"Tell them!" Narrow repeated, shaking the gun at Secondo.

"What do you think's going to happen here?" Secondo challenged him. "The captain's not going to just sit around and let some snotty-nosed goddamned Nazi kid take over his ship. He'll break out the weapons and send the Navy boys in here after you. You gonna have a shootout between their rifles and your popgun there?"

"They won't try to come in here and get me as long as I have you as a hostage," Narrow answered.

"A *hostage*?" Secondo repeated with a laugh. "You really think the captain will put his ship and fifty or sixty men's lives in danger just to save *my* sorry ass?"

"He's American," Narrow said, "so yes. But even if he *does* decide to sacrifice you, and send in the Navy boys, it'll take him an hour to make up his mind. By that time the U-boat will have found us, and *it* will take care of making my mission a success."

Secondo just stared at him for a moment. "You're going to stand in here—thirty feet below the waterline—and wait for a torpedo to hit us? You're not just stupid, you're a complete goddamned lunatic!"

"No! Not a lunatic; a *hero* to the Fatherland!" Narrow said as he struck a pose with his head cocked and his chin jutting out.

Secondo jumped on the opportunity to lunge at him, but Narrow managed to step back and fire the pistol just before Secondo could get his hand on it. The bullet traveled inside Secondo's shirt sleeve, searing a line along left his arm, until it entered his shoulder where it splintered the bone and lodged in the tissue without exiting.

"*Suffering Christ!*" Secondo bellowed as he spun away in agony, gripping his shoulder with his other hand.

"Hey! What the hell's going on down there?" First shouted down from the top of the escape trunk.

"This skinny nimrod is the Nazi spy and he just shot me!" Secondo hollered back. "He wants to keep the ship adrift until the U-boat gets here. Send in the Navy boys and blast his ass straight to hell!"

There was a short silence—broken only by Secondo's groaning—while everyone contemplated what should happen next.

"Narrow?" First called down the trunk. "Is that you down there with Secondo?"

"It is," Narrow replied. "And everything he said is true. But I swear, if anyone tries to come down the escape trunk or sneak up on me from the engine room, I'm going to put a bullet in Secondo's head! Now, get out of the trunk and dog that hatch!"

"You can't get out of there, kid," First shouted down. "And you sure don't want to be down there if we take a torpedo. Let me come down and take care of Secondo, and we can talk about this."

"I said get out and close the hatch!" Narrow shouted. He reached his arm around and fired blindly up the trunk. The bullet ricocheted several times off the steel walls, but completely missed First.

First jumped back out of the trunk, and swung the hatch closed. "Dog 'er down!" he told two of the seamen standing there with him. "And make sure it stays sealed." He then took off to find the captain, muttering, "Lord love a duck!"

When Narrow took over at the pump, Frank left the alley, returning to the engine room. As he closed the hatch and dutifully spun the sealing wheel closed, he looked forward, past the engine—quiet and still. He saw Rudy standing next to the voice tubes, talking with the fireman Patterson. Farther to his right, he saw Billy sitting on the work bench, and he saw the mess steward, O'Hara leaning against a bulkhead not too far away.

As Frank made his way around the big thrust bearing at the aft end of the engine, he heard footsteps on the grating above him. He looked up to see the captain starting down the steps of the ladder. *Perfect!* he thought. *I can tell both of them at the same time that we got oil into the bearing.*

About half way down the ladder the captain stopped, and Frank turned to look up at him. He didn't look good. He looked like he might be dizzy. Suddenly, his eyes drooped closed and he fell forward.

Frank rushed to the foot of the ladder, yelling, "Captain! Look out!" He reached out his arms to catch the captain, and was knocked onto his back as the full weight of the falling man hit him.

Everyone in the engine room rushed over, and Rudy rolled the captain off of Frank. "Captain Hill! Captain Hill! Are you okay?" Rudy said as he knelt down and patted his cheeks.

No response.

He slapped a little harder, and repeated, "Captain Hill! Can you hear me?"

Nothing.

Rudy pulled open the captain's shirt and put his hand on his chest. Then he put his ear down to his mouth. Finally, he took hold of his wrist and felt for a pulse.

Rudy gently laid the captain's arm across his chest, and sat down on the deck. He looked up at the others, and said numbly, "He's dead. His heart must have gave out."

On his knees on the other side of the captain, Frank just stared down at him. He had never seen anyone die before, and had only ever seen one other dead person—his grandmother—who had also died from a heart attack.

Although Rudy had no medical training whatever, his diagnosis was a pretty good guess. Captain Jonas P. Hill died shortly after a massive arterial aneurism burst while he was coming down to the engine room after drinking a cup of coffee in the galley.

After several moments of shocked silence, Rudy said to Frank, "Go find Mr. Jones and tell him what happened. He's going to be in command, now." Rudy hung his head and shook it in sorrow and disbelief. "My God ..." he murmured. "What else is going to go wrong on this voyage?"

Frank got up, grabbed the railing, and was three steps up the ladder when he remembered.

"No, wait!" he said to Rudy. "Secondo sent me out here to tell you that we got oil pumped into the bearing and that he needed the air pump. And to get the engine ready to get underway, again."

"That's great, kid!" Rudy said. "Good job. First is up on deck rigging a line to lower the pump down the escape trunk, right now."

No sooner had he said that than First came running onto the upper grating above the engine room. "Is the captain down there?" he shouted.

He bounded down the first ladder and then saw the captain on the floor with everyone circled around him. "What the hell happened?" he said. "Is he alright?"

"The captain's dead," Rudy said, getting to his feet. "Heart attack, probably. He just keeled over."

First crossed himself in the traditional Catholic manner, and said, "God bless and keep you, Captain." Then he looked at the others, and said, "And God *help* the rest of us." Turning to O'Hara, he said, "The kid they call Narrow is your saboteur. He's got a gun and is holding Secondo hostage in the shaft alley. He shot him, and he took a shot at me, too. He's not going to let us near that tail shaft bearing; he wants us sitting here crippled until that U-boat finds us."

"I told you!" Billy said to O'Hara. O'Hara just ignored him.

Rudy looked at Frank, who was still standing on the ladder, and said, "Go find Mr. Jones. On the double."

Frank took two more steps up the ladder and looked up to see Jones coming down from the upper grating. It took about three minutes for Rudy, Frank, and First to explain the various situations to him.

Looking down at his captain, Jones took off his cap, and said, "I never wanted to get my first command this way." He looked at the others, and added, "And I certainly didn't think it would be a crippled ship with a Nazi spy on board and a U-boat sniffing us out."

He looked at Rudy, and said, "How long do you think we could run if we started up without getting oil to the bearing, Chief?"

"A couple hours, maybe," Rudy replied. "The sea water will probably keep the bearing from seizing up altogether, but the shaft will just keep wearing out the bronze until it's gone and the shaft is riding on the cast iron. By that time, though, the shaft and propeller will be so out of balance they'll be shaking us apart. We could even lose the propeller; it could break right off the shaft."

"Can't we just get the guns from the captain's safe and storm the alley?" Patterson asked.

"The kid said he'd kill Secondo if anyone came in through either hatch," Jones answered.

"I know it's a tough decision for you to have to make," O'Hara said, "putting your shipmate's life in jeopardy, but if we don't at least try to take the kid down, your whole crew is likely to die when that sub gets here. Maybe if we can distract him from above, somebody can open this door quietly, and I can get him with a rifle shot before he knows what's happening."

The officers all looked at one another. Finally, First spoke. "I probably know Secondo better that any of you, and I think he'd want us to take the chance for the sake of the ship."

"Alright," O'Hara said. "The captain said he had the trigger assemblies to the Navy boy's rifles locked up. That means they're probably Garands. Tell one of the sailors to bring one to the captain's office and we'll get it back in proper working order. Even standard issue, it will be a darned site more accurate than my pistol."

Jones didn't move. He turned from O'Hara to look at Rudy, and then First. "I don't know the combination to the safe," he said. "He never told me what it was. Did he ever tell either of you?"

"No," they both answered.

"You've got to be shitting me!" O'Hara said. "Well, if he didn't tell anyone, he must have at least written it down somewhere, wouldn't you think? Let's go search his office."

Rudy, First, Jones, and O'Hara combed every inch of the captain's office without finding anything that resembled a combination. They examined every piece of paper; looked on the bottoms and sides of the desk drawers; looked all over the safe itself; and even checked the backs of the framed photos that hung on the walls. Then they moved into the captain's state room.

They were performing an equally thorough search when Jones came across Hill's wallet in his night stand. He was reverently emptying the contents onto his bunk when he found a slip of paper with the number "10372248" hand printed on it.

"I think I might have something," he said to the others.

They went back into the office, and Jones spun the combination left-10, right-37, left-22, right-48 into the lock. He twisted the handle, but it didn't move.

"Maybe it starts to the right," First suggested, "not the left."

That didn't work either.

"Could the numbers be backwards?" Rudy said. "Start with 84."

The lock didn't budge.

For the next ten minutes they tried every arrangement of the numbers they could think of, but nothing worked.

"I give up. Maybe it's not the combination, at all," Jones finally said. He turned to Rudy, and said, "Can we get a cutting torch up here and just burn the hinges off the door?"

"Yeah!" Rudy answered. "We'll have to take the tanks off the cart, but we can get them in here."

"Don't bother," O'Hara said. "Cutting the hinges off won't get you anywhere. There are big steel bars inside the door that go out into the jamb. It'll take you hours—assuming you have enough gas—to cut deep enough to reach those bars. We might as well take the safe down below the waterline and let the first torpedo open it up for us."

"You have any better ideas?" Jones said.

"As a matter of fact, I do," he replied. He put his foot up on a chair, pulled up his pant leg, and unsnapped a snub-nosed .38 revolver from a leather ankle holster.

"I knew you gave in too easily to the captain," Jones said. "I told him you had another gun."

"And as it turns out, it's a damned good thing I do, isn't it?" O'Hara said. "Otherwise the only person on the ship who's armed would be that punk Nazi spy."

"So what do you plan to do?" Jones asked him. "I know enough about guns to know you can't make a sniper shot the length of the alley with that. That only happens in the movies."

"True," O'Hara said. "But I think we can still use distraction and the element of surprise to get him. Somebody needs to cause a commotion at the door to the shaft alley in the engine room while I slip into the escape shaft thing where you were going to lower the pump. Then I'll make my way down the ladder, quiet as a cat, and I'll drop out and shoot him before he knows what hit him."

"The *door* is called a hatch, and the escape *thing* is a trunk," Jones pointed out dryly.

"Tomato tomahto," O'Hara said. "Who gives a shit?"

"What kind of commotion?" Rudy asked, feeling the need to intervene between their clashing personalities.

"I don't care," O'Hara said. "Just keep him occupied for two minutes while I climb down the ladder. In fact, if you can get him talking or even hollering, that will be even better. That way I'll know where he is."

"But what if he hears you, or looks up the trunk?" First asked. "He said he'd kill Secondo if anyone tried to get in there. And you'd be a sitting duck, too."

"He won't kill his only hostage," O'Hara said flatly. "Your engineer's being alive is the only thing keeping the kid alive. As for me, I'll have to take that chance; that's my job. Since he kept it hidden from everyone, he can only have a small pistol down there. Probably no bigger than this one, and I'll bet it's smaller, yet. Spies like skinny little automatics that they can hide easily. They're not too accurate and not very deadly unless you're right up close to your victim."

Jones looked at his watch. "I don't have a better idea," he said, "and we better get doing *something*."

Before leaving the captain's office, they all coordinated their watches so they matched to the second. Then O'Hara and First went aft to the top of the escape trunk, and Rudy and Jones headed for the engine room.

As they passed the radio room Sparks called out, "Mr. Jones. When you see the captain, tell him that I picked up a weather broadcast that says there's a squall line headed toward us out of the southeast. From the location we got from Halifax on the U-boat, they could be right in it. It might slow them down, but it'll make him darned hard to see, too."

"Thanks, Sparks," Jones said. "So you know, the captain's dead. He had a heart attack down in the engine room just a little while ago."

"Oh my God!" Sparks said. "I didn't think he was that old."

"He wasn't," Jones said. "It was just his time, I guess. Keep listening and report any changes to me right away, okay?"

"Aye, Skipper," he replied.

Until Jones heard the words *Aye, Skipper* for the first time, the weight of the responsibility he suddenly shouldered hadn't really sunk in. In one brief instant he had become responsible for the ship, its cargo, and the lives of fifty-seven men. Fifty-eight, including O'Hara.

In the engine room, Jones explained the plan to the several members of the crew on watch. They were going to start a distraction at exactly five past the hour. But since O'Hara and First would not be able to hear it, they would wait precisely fifteen seconds after the appointed time, then quietly open the escape trunk hatch for O'Hara to get inside. The hope was that by that time Narrow would have been momentarily startled and disoriented, and then would focus on the noise from the engine room end of the alley. It was also hoped that the noise at the forward end would mask the noise at the aft end from the escape trunk hatch being opened.

Rudy turned to Frank, and said, "I want you to talk to Narrow. He might not be as suspicious of you as he would be of one of us."

"You want me to go back *in* there?" Frank said. "He might shoot me!"

"No. We'll crack the hatch an inch or two and you can shout to him through the opening," Rudy said. "Even if he shoots at you, the bullet won't get around the corner."

"What do I say to him?"

"What have you talked about before?" Rudy asked. "Baseball? Girls? Anything you can think of. You might want to stay away from world politics, though."

Jones interjected, "He knows we're onto him. Anything about baseball or dames is going to *make* him suspicious. But challenging him over his disloyalty to America might work. You don't have to be nice to him. If you get him angry it might distract him all the more." He looked at his watch. "We've got to get ready," he said.

The three of them made their way to the shaft alley hatch. Frank and Jones stood to one side while Rudy took hold of the wheel. Jones stared at his watch, and at exactly five after the hour, he said, "Now."

Inside the shaft alley, Secondo sat crosswise on the deck grating about ten feet forward of the escape trunk. His feet were underneath the unmoving propeller shaft, and his back was against the steel bulkhead. The coolness felt good. His shoulder ached continuously, but it was at least tolerable if he didn't move it. The wound continued to bleed, though, and he couldn't bear to put pressure against it to stop it.

Narrow was pacing up and down the alley, making sure that no one was attempting to interfere with his plan from either entry point.

A Kiss For Luck!

Rudy turned the hatch wheel, but it went no more than an inch and stopped hard. He tried again, pulling harder, but it stopped short, again.

"Shit! He's jammed the wheel with something! It won't open." Rudy said as he tried a third time.

"Rattle it back and forth!" Jones said, staring at the second hand of his watch as it passed the eight second mark. "Hurry! Make some noise!"

Narrow was about twenty feet from the engine room hatch when Rudy made the first attempt to open it. The sudden noise startled him, and he spun around and pointed his gun at the door. He almost pulled the trigger, but when he saw his belt-secured bar holding the wheel from turning he relaxed and even allowed himself a smile at his cleverness.

Rudy began twisting the wheel quickly back and forth. They could hear something clanging on the other side of the steel hatch, and knew it would be even louder inside the alley. And it suddenly occurred to Rudy that he might just shake loose whatever it was at the same time. He twisted, back and forth, all the harder ... but whatever was jamming the door, as noisy as it was, held fast.

Narrow jumped again when, Rudy began to rattle the bar stuck in the wheel. He crouched down and hid himself behind the middle spring bearing, pointing the gun at the hatch.

On the aft deck, below the gun platform, First and O'Hara stood with two seamen. Each seaman held one of the dogs to the hatch in each of his hands. First stared at his watch, and when the second hand hit fifteen, he said, "Go!"

The seamen rotated all four dogs as quickly and as quietly as they could, and First pulled open the hatch.

Secondo wanted to start hollering encouragement to his unseen shipmates and the Navy boys he assumed were coming to kill the little Nazi son-of-a-bitch, but something told him to stay quiet.

The sudden noise at the engine room hatch did exactly what is was supposed to do; it confused and disoriented Narrow ... but only for five or ten seconds. As soon as his brain snapped back into normal focus, it occurred to him that the crew and the Navy boys might try to get in through the engine room and the escape trunk at the same time.

Confident that his bar was going to hold the engine room wheel from turning, Narrow got up and ran aft. The bottom opening to the escape trunk would be easily defended, and although he only had five bullets left, *they* didn't know that. It would be pretty much suicidal for anyone to drop out of the escape trunk, not knowing where he might be, and they would hopefully stop before five of them died.

First barely had the hatch open when they heard running footsteps on the grating below echo up the trunk. Committed, O'Hara jumped onto the ladder, but was afraid that the distraction had not lasted long enough, and that the kid would appear below him before he even had a good grip on the rungs, much less had his gun out.

The only saving grace in the situation was that O'Hara knew that the kid's gun had to be a small "spy weapon"—maybe even a .22—and that at that range, even if he was hit, it was not likely to be fatal ... at least not right away.

Secondo sat perfectly still, his head against the bulkhead, his eyes closed. That, and the fact that he wasn't hollering oaths anymore, told Narrow that he must be unconscious ... or dead.

As Narrow leapt over Secondo's legs, the old faker threw up his good right arm and caught Narrow's ankle. He wasn't able to hold on, but it was enough to make Narrow stumble and fall on landing.

"You son-of-a-bitch!" Narrow barked as he got to his feet. He leveled the gun at Secondo's head, but the thought of being down to only four bullets and having no hostage stopped him from pulling the trigger. Instead, he swung his right foot and kicked Secondo in his wounded shoulder.

Secondo let out a long bellow, and toppled over sideways. The pain was so excruciating that it completely blocked the ability for his brain to form a blasphemous curse to hurl back at the little prick.

As the hatch closed behind him O'Hara heard what sounded like someone falling, followed by, "*You son-of-a-bitch!*" He correctly guessed that Secondo must have tripped Narrow somehow, and he whispered, "*Good work, you old Guinea!*" Two seconds later, he heard a grotesque scream of pain, and his blood ran cold.

Still at the top of the escape trunk, and hanging onto the vertical ladder in near total darkness with one hand, O'Hara used the few seconds of time that Secondo bought him to reach down to his ankle and unsnap his .38. His hand was around the grip when, between his legs, he saw Narrow's face appear at the bottom of the trunk. The kid's hand was next to his face, and although he couldn't see it, O'Hara assumed he was pointing his gun straight up at him. If he had had his gun out, he might have gotten a shot off, but he decided to just freeze, hoping Narrow couldn't see him in the dark. After a few seconds, Narrow disappeared from view.

With the kid no longer looking up at him, O'Hara slowly and quietly slid his gun from its holster. He wanted to pull the hammer back so that he could fire it more quickly, but he was afraid that even the small clicking sound it would make would be amplified down the hollow steel box he was in, and give him away.

He was about to take his first step down onto the next rung when Narrow appeared again down below. This time, however, instead of pointing a gun up at O'Hara, he was aiming a flashlight.

Fortunately for O'Hara, the batteries were getting very weak, and although he could see the light shining up, he was pretty sure that the beam was not powerful enough to light him up very well, if it reached him at all. He slowly moved his right arm to aim the pistol downward.

Apparently realizing that his flashlight was just about useless, Narrow began to back out of O'Hara's view, again.

Wishing to not miss another opportunity, O'Hara moved quickly, aimed and pulled the trigger.

The noise of even the small handgun inside the steel echo chamber was almost deafening, and it disoriented O'Hara for just long enough that he couldn't tell if he had hit Narrow with the round. There was no body lying below the trunk, but there was no return fire, either.

O'Hara stood on the ladder, motionless with the cocked .38 pointing downward. "Secondo!" he called out. "Can you hear me? Is the kid hit?"

His answer was Narrow's gun appearing around the corner, and firing two shots blindly up at him. Both missed, and O'Hara fired once to scare the kid back away from the opening. He then banged on the hatch, the signal to open it back up.

As the hatch swung open, Narrow appeared again, and this time, aided by the light from the open hatch silhouetting his target, he aimed and fired. The small but fast bullet hit O'Hara in the thigh, passing right through the flesh. He yelled, and fired blindly down the hole. He leapt for the opening and Narrow fired again.

It was a dumb-luck shot and it caught O'Hara in the right forearm, splintering one of the bones, and causing him to lose his grip on the gun and drop it. They heard it clang on the deck below as they slammed the hatch closed.

Jones, Rudy, First, and O'Hara met in the captain's office.

"So, now the Nazi has two guns and we have none," Jones said to O'Hara. "Great plan."

O'Hara, with his wounds bandaged and his arm in a sling, replied, "It was a lucky shot he couldn't make again in a thousand tries."

"I don't see how that makes any difference to the situation," Jones said. "He apparently only *needed* to do it once."

"Well, I'm not the one who took the combination to the guns to my grave!" O'Hara snapped, pointing at the safe. "At least I tried!" He held up his arm and said, "I put my life on the line for you and this ship!"

Jones closed his eyes and took a deep breath. "You're right, O'Hara. I'm sorry. You did the best you could. That was a pretty brave thing, actually. Thank you." He turned to Rudy and First, and said, "What do we do now?"

First said, "We could drop a couple of fire hoses into the escape trunk and flood the alley. He'd either drown or come floating up the trunk, right to us."

"That might kill Secondo, too," Jones said.

First looked down for a moment, and then met Jones' eyes. "I know."

Rudy said, "I don't think we have enough time to flood the whole alley and then pump it out again, and then get the oil pump set up before the storm and the U-boat get here."

"What about smoke?" O'Hara said. "Do you have a way to generate smoke? He'd either have to come out one of the hatches, or he'd suffocate down there. Clearing the smoke afterwards would be fast."

"There's still Secondo," Jones said.

Just then, Frank knocked on the open door. "Excuse me, Mr. ... um, *Captain* Jones."

"We're pretty busy, son," Jones said. "Can it wait?"

"Sorry, sir," Frank said, "but I overheard the chief saying down in the engine room that the only two ways into the shaft alley were through the engine room and the escape trunk. But I remembered a third. Through the aft peak tank. There's an access cover in the steering gear room, and the cover in the alley is already off."

Rudy, First, and Jones looked at each other. He was right! They had all forgotten that since that cover was almost never opened.

Frank went on, "I heard about the safe, but I heard that Mr. O'Hara had a pistol, so I'd like to volunteer to take it and go down through the tank and get Narrow. I'm a real good shot."

Jones replied, "Actually, the pistol is no longer an option, son. Unless you could carry a 20mm ack ack cannon down there with you, we have nothing to shoot him with. But I applaud your ingenious thinking and your willingness to volunteer. Maybe we can use the tank access in some other way."

"Um, sir," Frank continued. "I've sort of been looking at all the stuff we're carrying ... when I'm not on duty, of course! And well, there's a whole stack of rifles in hold number three. I don't know if they come with ammunition or not, but if they don't, we must be carrying that, too. Why would they ship guns without bullets?"

Rudy snapped his fingers. "You're right! I remember seeing that pallet swing past my porthole when I boarded!" To Jones, he said, "Look at the cargo manifest; see if it says what kind of rifles they are."

Jones pulled open a drawer in the captain's desk and was able to put his hands right on the manifest, having seen it while they were looking for the combination.

"Hold number three, port side, aft," Rudy told him.

He found the location on the manifest, and read, "Rifles; M1 Carbine."

"That's .30 caliber," Frank said.

"You've fired one before?" Rudy asked.

"I wish!" Frank said. "I've never even seen a real one, but I read all about it. Gas operated semi-automatic, fifteen shot clip, 850 rounds per minute, six pounds with ..."

"You *have* read about it," Rudy said, cutting of Frank's impromptu dissertation. To Jones, he said, "Any 30-cal ammo aboard, Skipper?"

Jones called Lieutenant Kendricks to the bridge and explained the plan. Since the Navy boys were assigned to protect the ship, Jones felt obligated to offer the "opportunity" to crawl down through the peak tank and try to get a shot at Narrow to the lieutenant. Kendricks pointed out that, to his knowledge, none of his men had any training for crawling around inside of Liberty ships, and that they were going to be much more valuable at their battle stations if the U-boat was sighted.

It took about fifteen minutes for two seamen to retrieve a crate of rifles from the top front corner of the pallet in hold number three, and for two others to get a drum of ammunition from number five. They met Rudy, First, O'Hara, and Frank on the aft deck.

One of the seamen pried open the crate, and folded back the heavy oiled paper that protected the contents. Rudy reached down to take out one of the rifles. He put his hand on one, and then something made him change, and he picked up the one next to it. That rifle carried the serial number 6,081,199, and a slip of paper with a kiss for luck on it, hidden inside. He handed it to Frank.

Frank removed the magazine, loaded fifteen rounds of ammo into it, and snapped it back into the rifle. He pulled back the bolt and released it, sliding a round into the chamber. He then rotated the safety to its on position.

"You sure you've never handled one of those before?" Rudy said.

"About every other kind of rifle and handgun," Frank said, "I've only dreamt about this one, though. I've dreamt about a Tommy gun, too."

"You want to fire it over the side just to make sure it's all working?" First said. "It's not like we're light on ammo."

Frank went to the rail, released the safety, and aimed at the crest of a wave. He squeezed the trigger, the gun went off, and then instantly snapped a new cartridge into the chamber. He then pulled the trigger three times as fast as he could, and watched the bullets zip into the water in a tight little circle. He reset the safety, and turned around with a wide grin.

"That's a nice rifle," he said. "I'd like to have this back home, come hunting season."

"Sorry," Rudy said, "No souvenirs. But if this works, I'll put you in for a commendation."

Rudy instructed one of the seamen to tie a couple of folds of rags around the steel butt plate and the muzzle of the rifle so that Frank could set it down without it clanging as he climbed through the steel bracing inside the peak tank.

Jones, Rudy, First, O'Hara, and Frank then went one deck down into the steering gear room. As the ship rolled in the sea, the rudder shifted back and forth slightly, but was kept in line by the massive semi-circular gear that connected it to the steering engine. It was this rocking and the rhythmic booming it created that they hoped would mask the noise of them opening the access hatch, and Frank's descent through the tank.

Rudy and First each held a large box-end wrench, and they fit them over two of the twenty hex-head nuts that were attached to a like number of studs welded to the deck, holding the access hatch in place. Timing their first pulls with the next boom of the rudder, they worked their way around the hatch until all of the nuts were broken loose.

Some of them were then able to be unscrewed by hand by the other men, but a few needed to be coaxed with the wrench the entire way. Finally, when all of the nuts were removed, Rudy told O'Hara to douse the light, so the bulbs in the steering gear room wouldn't light up the tank and possibly give away the surprise to Narrow. With only a red-lensed flashlight to cut the darkness, they pried the hatch loose from the gasket, and laid it carefully and quietly aside in time with the noise of the rudder.

Frank took the flashlight and looked down into the tank. He could just make out the first brace—a giant flat steel plate that spanned the tank from one side of the ship to the other, with myriad man-sized holes cut through it for lightening, and when it was used as a tank, to allow the water to fill all its levels.

Staring into the abyss, Frank's heart began to race, and he swallowed hard.

"You sure you can do this, kid?" Rudy asked him. "You sure you remember where all those plates are?"

Frank had told them that he had relentlessly studied the twenty-foot-long cutaway model of the Liberty ship that they used for teaching at Sheepshead Bay, and remembered vividly the arrangement of the bracing plates in the peak tank. It was not a complete lie, but it was certainly an exaggeration. He remembered looking at that section of the model, but since there was no machinery inside the tank, he paid it little attention. But he thought he remembered enough that he could carefully feel his way over, around, and through the bracing to get to the bottom ... to kill Narrow.

After he found out that Narrow was a Nazi spy, Frank realized that he had used his confession of claustrophobia to help sabotage the ship. By taking his own and Frank's watches in the alley, there would have been twice as much time for the bearing to be damaged before anyone discovered it. And on top of feeling personally betrayed, Narrow had shot Secondo, had probably contributed to the captain's heart attack, and had betrayed every member of the crew and the whole United States of America. As much as the dark closed area of the tank scared him, his hatred of the skinny little son-of-a-bitch down in the shaft alley more than overrode it.

"I can do it," Frank answered Rudy.

Before he dropped down into the opening, each of the men shook Frank's hand and wished him luck.

He lowered himself down through hole, and hung chest-deep on his arms. He timed his release, and let himself drop the rest of the way so that his shoes hit the steel plate at the same time that the rudder boomed. His feet slipped a bit on the slimy surface, but he caught himself. The first plate was only about five feet down, so he stood with his head sticking up through the hatch.

Rudy passed him the flashlight. "Use that sparingly," he whispered. "Good luck."

O'Hara handed him the padded rifle, and whispered, "Use *that* all you want! Good hunting!"

Frank ducked down with the light, and the men above him disappeared in the darkness.

In the dark musty gloom he took several deep breaths to try to get the panic that wanted to erupt in check. He then said a short silent prayer, asking for guidance.

He flicked on the red light for a few seconds to see where the holes in the deck were, and then moved carefully toward one of them. He laid the rifle down beside the hole, laid down on the slimy surface, and flashed the light down into the blackness below. This would not be a good hole to drop through; there was another hole directly below it.

Conserving his batteries, he crawled in the direction of the next hole, feeling for the drop-off with his hands. At the edge, a few seconds of red light showed him that this was a winner. The hole in the next plate below was offset to the port, and there was even a vertical brace to starboard with its own hole that he could use as a ladder.

He moved the rifle next to the opening, and he climbed down. Once on the next plate, he reached up and slid the rifle over the edge. He set it down, leaning it against the vertical brace he had been standing on, and moved carefully in the darkness to the next hole.

If his memory of the model served him correctly, there should be one more bracing deck plate, with the shaft's big tail-bearing assembly located just below that.

He peered over the edge of the next hole, but he didn't need to use the flashlight. Light spilled weakly into the tail bearing space through the open access hole into the shaft alley, and he could just see the last hole he would need to get through.

What he had forgotten from his "study" of the model was that as the tank went deeper, it naturally narrowed, following the curvature of the ship's underwater form at the stern. Therefore, the bracing plates naturally got smaller ... and the holes in them also got smaller.

He was pretty sure that he could fit through the hole in the next plate, but it would be a tight squeeze; he wouldn't be able to drop through it quickly, as he had through the others.

Being inside the dark closed area was bad enough; the thought of wedging himself in a tight opening inside that space was making him think about climbing back up, and giving the rifle to someone else.

Then he heard a low moan from below. It was followed by Narrow's voice.

"Jesus! Aren't you dead, yet? If I had more bullets, I'd put one in your head to put you out of your misery." Then he laughed, and added, "And mine!"

That was enough to steel Frank's nerves.

He crawled to the edge of the hole and swung his legs over. He reached out and picked up the rifle, resting it beside him on the plate. He slowly, silently, inched himself lower and lower, wiggling his toes like a bug's antennae to feel out the next plate. As well as being extra quiet, he had to be extra careful as well, because the next hole was directly below him, and he needed to straddle it to get a footing.

Finally, a toe tapped the edge of the hole and he was able to get his bearings. He silently planted his feet on either side of the opening, and then picked up the rifle.

He transferred the gun from his right hand to his left so he could lower it to the plate his feet were on. He gripped the rag-wrapped barrel and began to lower it when the rag started to slip. Suddenly, directly above the hole, the rifle began to slide from his grasp.

He squeezed his hand around the barrel with all of his might, but the rag on the oiled metal provided a very poor grip. As the rifle continued to slip, he was desperately trying to keep it from swinging, too, as the ship rocked. The butt was already in the hole, and it would have acted like a bell clapper if it started to bang against the plate.

The only thing keeping the rifle from falling onto the tail shaft bearing below was Frank's left index finger wrapped under the front sight ... but it was just enough. He slowly reached over with his other hand and took hold of the stock. He then squatted down, still straddling the hole, and gently laid the rifle on the plate.

As he crouched there, getting his breathing back under control after the adrenaline rush of almost dropping the rifle, he listened intently, hoping that Narrow would say something to Secondo, or make some noise so he would know where the traitor was.

If he was near the aft end of the shaft alley, and he heard the slightest noise, he might look in the access hole and see Frank's legs dangling down through the last hole. Nothing good could follow that.

He listened for a half a minute without hearing anything but the normal ship noises. He decided he couldn't wait any longer; he would just have to take the chance.

Holding himself up with his hands on the slippery plate, Frank lowered his legs through the hole. Just as his butt was squeezing into the opening, his feet touched the top of the tail bearing housing. Standing on the housing, he wiggled his hips, working his way down through the tight hole. Suddenly, his belt buckle scraped across the steel plate making a metallic grinding sound.

Trying so desperately to be silent, the small noise sounded to Frank like a coffin opening in a horror movie.

He couldn't know if Narrow heard the noise, but if he did, he might be coming right now to investigate. Frank decided that he had to move quickly.

With his chest and arms through the hole, Frank squatted down on top of the housing. He couldn't quite get his head below the plate, but that was okay. He reached up, and with a death-grip on the rifle, he turned it and worked it down through the opening without touching the sides of the hole.

He slipped the rags off the ends of the gun, wrapped his hand around the stock, and flicked off the safety. He put his finger across the trigger guard, and got ready to jump down off of the bearing.

He tried to get his breathing relaxed and even, but in the crouched position, it was difficult.

Just as he was about to jump, he heard a cough. It didn't sound close by—maybe half way up the alley—but was it Secondo or Narrow?

God, please let that be Narrow! he said silently, and he jumped off the bearing.

He held the rifle in his right hand, and steadied his landing by holding onto the bearing with his left. As soon as his feet hit the sloping and slippery bottom of the tank, he wrapped his finger around the trigger, and grabbed the front of the stock with his left hand. He let his downward motion bring him into a crouching firing position.

He was directly in front of the access hole and looking straight up the alley. Twenty feet away Secondo sat on the deck, not moving. Thirty feet beyond that, Narrow was turning to face him.

The sound of Frank's shoes hitting the tank alerted Narrow, and even before he finished turning around, he knew what was going on. The bastards had come down from above through the peak tank! He should have thought of that and closed the access cover. *Damn!*

He saw shadowed movement inside the tank, and he raised and fired the .38 that O'Hara had dropped.

Frank saw the flash of the gun that Narrow was pointing at him at the same instant that he pulled the trigger of the carbine. If he heard Narrow's gun go off, he couldn't tell because the sound was either mixed with or drowned out by the roar of his own rifle inside the confided space of the peak tank.

He pulled the trigger three more times as quickly as he could, and somewhere in the cacophony he heard Narrow's bullet clang against the steel bulkhead, The slug had struck right on the edge of the access hole and shattered.

With his ears ringing, and with his rifle trained on Narrow's chest, Frank watched him take three or four unstable steps back, and then fall over backwards onto the grating. He lay there without moving, but Frank knew from years of hunting animals that that didn't mean he was dead.

Lying on his back, Narrow provided a much smaller target, but Frank kept the carbine pointed at his crotch as he crawled out of the access hole. Once he could stand up, he pulled the rifle to his shoulder and took a more careful aim. Because he couldn't see Narrow's right hand, he didn't know if he was still holding the gun, so Frank watched him intently for the slightest move as he walked forward.

As he neared Secondo he could see in his peripheral vision that the gruff old engineer's left shirt sleeve, and the whole left side of his shirt was soaked with blood. Frank was pretty sure that he was dead, and it made him want to put another bullet into Narrow on general principle.

He walked slowly forward, now keeping the carbine aimed at Narrow's heart. At the tiniest movement, he was ready to put three more rounds into him.

As he drew nearer, he saw that Narrow's eyes were closed, and his mouth hung slightly open. He finally got close enough that he could see Narrow's right hand beside the grating and saw that the gun was still in it. His hand was open, his fingers simply cradling it, but Frank didn't trust him for a second.

Frank put the barrel of the rifle into Narrow's open mouth and pushed the sharp edges of the sight into his pallet. He didn't flinch. Still, Frank left the rifle there with his finger on the trigger as he bent down to pick up the handgun.

He put the .38 in his pocket, and stepped over Narrow's body, but he never stopped aiming the rifle at him. He walked backwards toward the engine room hatch so he would never have to take his eyes off him.

At the hatch he took a quick look to see what Narrow had done, and then, still facing Narrow, he slid the steel bar out of the wheel with one hand behind him. He banged on the hatch with the bar, two times, then paused and hit it again. It was the signal they had agreed upon that it was safe to open the hatch.

"I'm pretty sure Narrow's dead," Frank said to Rudy as he stepped through the hatch. "Secondo's back there." Sadly, he added, "He might be, too."

Rudy led two seamen down the alley. With his boot he rolled Narrow's body off the grating and under the propeller shaft. They found that Secondo was still alive, but just barely. They got him out of the alley and up to the medical cabin on the aft upper deck.

Twenty minutes later the crew had the air pump lowered into the shaft alley and forcing oil into the bearing. They brought the engine back on line, and everyone in the crew cheered as they felt their ship get underway, again.

They started slowly, and checked the bearing and tail shaft for any signs of excessive heat or vibration. When none was detected, they gradually increased RPM until they were eventually running at nearly top speed. A twenty-four hour watch was put on the bearing and shaft, and Rudy was amazed at how well the forced-oil scheme was working.

One of the Navy sailors was a medic, and he stopped the bleeding and prepared Secondo for a transfusion while Jones went through Secondo's records to find out his blood type. It was A-negative; a not very common type. Jones put out the word that they needed an A-negative volunteer, and at the same time, went through the rest of the crew's records.

Within minutes, six men showed up at Jones' door, with Billy at the front of the line. Four of the men were O-negative, so were universal donors, but Billy and Patterson, the fireman, were A-negative. Five minutes later, Billy was lying on a table next to Secondo.

They pulled Narrow's body from the alley, and brought it up on deck. O'Hara emptied his pockets, and performed a rough examination for his report. All of Frank's shots had hit him. Two went through his heart, one through his left lung, and the fourth hit him in the abdomen. O'Hara took several photographs of the body and then, with no way to preserve it, or reason to keep it, they heaved it over the side.

Over the new skipper's objections, O'Hara put his own pistol back in its holster ... just in case something else happened.

An hour after they got underway one of the forward lookouts reported a ship on the horizon, dead ahead. It was heading straight for them. As the distance between them closed, they could make out that it was a US Navy "tin can." Launched just two months earlier, she was a brand new destroyer named the USS Madden that was on shakedown and antisubmarine exercises.

Both ships slowed to pass, and as they drew near, the destroyer sent a message to the *Shea* with her signal light.

"Recd word of your breakdown. Came to lend assist and hunt sub sighted in area."

Jones had the *Shea* reply with her light, "Thank you! Back underway now but welcome assist re sub. Good hunting."

The Madden replied, "Our pleasure."

With the destroyer as well as the PY protecting her rear, the tension on the Liberty ship relaxed quite a bit. An hour after sunrise the following morning, the crew gathered for a memorial service for Captain Hill, after which, according to his wishes, his body—in dress uniform—was committed to the sea.

After those matters were attended to, and after his watch, Frank went to his cabin to clean the carbine he had used.

"Since I can't keep it," Frank had said to Rudy after the ship was underway again, "I sure want it to be in good shape for the next guy who has to use it."

Rudy had conferred with Captain Jones, and he agreed to let Frank hold onto the rifle until he had time to clean it, but he did take the ammunition back from him.

Although all Frank really needed to do to clean the carbine after firing only eight rounds was to push a cleaning rag through the barrel a few times and make sure everything was oiled, he couldn't pass up the opportunity to completely disassemble the rifle. He would probably never get another chance to touch all the parts of such a wonderful and ingenious weapon.

He had no owner's manual for the rifle, so he looked it over carefully before he started to take it apart. He had always been mechanically inclined, and the design of the weapon was pretty simple, so he was confident he could get it apart and back together without breaking anything, and without "extra parts" left over.

While examining it he noticed a small jagged hole between the two halves of the wooden stock. The edges of the hole were sharp and looked new, so he didn't think the rifle came from the factory that way.

With piqued curiosity, he used his pocket knife to loosened the bayonet clamp that also held the pieces of wood together. He depressed the retaining spring, and slid the clamp forward.

He lifted off the handguard, and looked at the grooves carved about equally deep in the top and bottom halves of the stock. In the bottom half, wedged tight against the steel barrel was a small chunk of metal. Frank used his knife to pry it out. He rolled it around in his fingers, recognizing it immediately as a bullet fragment.

In the adrenaline-powered excitement of the moment, he hadn't felt it, but he guessed that when the single shot that Narrow had fired hit the steel bulkhead, the bullet must have exploded and sent its pieces flying in all directions. The rifle just happened to catch this one.

Curious, Frank picked up the rifle and held it the way he remembered he had when firing at Narrow. The groove lined up on the right side of the stock with the palm of his hand on the left side. The gun had stopped the bullet fragment from penetrating his hand. If that had happened, he realized, he would never have been able to keep the rifle steady, and his shots might not have hit their target. Narrow might have gotten more shots off, and the outcome could have been completely different.

He stared at the grooves and the fragment for several moments, contemplating his good fortune. Finally, he set the fragment on his side table—a souvenir he would keep forever.

Looking at the wood, he decided that before he reassembled the gun, he would get some sandpaper and smooth the edges of the grooves to hide them as best he could.

He then went back to disassembling the rifle.

He looked closely to see if there were any other screws he needed to remove before he could take the barrel out of the stock. He saw none, so he gently lifted up on the barrel, and it, along with the receiver and trigger assembly, came out as a single unit.

He had to smile at how simple the inventors of this weapon had made such a complex little machine. Holding nearly all of the steel parts to the rifle in one hand, he moved to set the wooden stock on the bunk when he noticed a bright red pair of lips on a curled piece of paper in the barrel groove.

Frank had noticed the edges of the slip when he dug out the fragment, but he expected that it was some kind of inspection slip. Maybe even a little "Kilroy was here" cartoon.

He lifted the paper out and stared at the lip print with the words, "*A Kiss For Luck!*" written over it. The writing was smooth and flowing cursive, and Frank had to imagine it was written by the same girl who kissed the paper. In his mind he envisioned her looking like Bonnie Little, the auburn haired, freckle-faced, girl he had had a crush on since eighth grade.

He looked closely at the edge of the paper, and saw a small nick. He set the curled slip back into the stock, and easily got the nick to line up with the groove. The fragment had struck *directly* on the hidden talisman!

Frank didn't normally believe in rabbits' feet or anything like that, but this actually gave him a little chill.

As he took the carbine further apart, he kept looking down at the little slip. He wondered if all of the M1 Carbines they made had one. Probably not; that seemed a very un-military thing to do. Maybe just the carbines from that factory. Perhaps only the ones on "Bonnie's" assembly line.

The more he thought about it, the more special he believed the paper was. He eventually imagined Bonnie in a long line of pretty girls all assembling rifles, but she was the only one kissing and writing on pieces of paper to tuck under her barrels.

After he had taken the rifle completely apart, he used a cleaning kit he borrowed from one of the Navy boys to clean the bore of the barrel. He then wiped down the metal pieces and assemblies, oiled them, and put them back together. He set the trigger, receiver, barrel assembly into the stock, and placed the handguard on top of it. He was about to slide the bayonet band over the halves of the stock when he looked at the slip one more time.

A Kiss For Luck!

He had planned on putting the slip into his wallet and carrying it for the rest of the war as a good luck charm. It had certainly been that onboard the *Shea*. But what if the lucky charm wasn't meant just for him? What if Bonnie—or whatever the girl's name was—meant her kiss to bring good luck to whoever had the rifle? Would taking the slip from the gun break the spell of luck that went with it? Could it change the good luck to a curse for the person who took it?

He opened the stock back up, and picked up the slip. He touched his lips lightly to the kiss, and laid it back under the barrel where he had found it, even lining up the nick with the groove.

He also decided not to sand the grooves that the bullet fragments had made. Somehow it seemed fitting to him that the rifle should carry the scar as if it too would bring luck to the soldier who carried it into battle.

When he returned the rifle to Rudy, he didn't show him the hole that the bullet fragment had made, for fear that he would want him to repair it. He also didn't mention the lucky slip of paper. He didn't want the chief to think he was superstitious or something.

Thursday, May 18, 1944

The *Shea* steamed into Halifax only a half a day after the rest of her convoy arrived there. Her lubricating oil tank was nearly empty, but her stern bearing and propeller shaft had remained cool and smooth running the whole way. "Built hell for stout," Rudy observed.

After arriving, O'Hara left the ship to hand-deliver a detailed and highly classified report of what had transpired to his superiors in Washington, DC. Jones and Rudy talked with the commander who would be leading the convoy to England and discussed their options.

The ship could be unloaded in Halifax, but there was no dry dock open to make repairs. She would have to sail back to Portland for that. And there were no empty freighters in port, so most of her cargo would have to sit on the docks, maybe for weeks or more. That option would mean that the Nazi spy ring had succeeded. The material on the *Shea* would not make it to the troops in time to support the anticipated invasion of Europe .

The other option—favored by Rudy and the entire crew—was to fill the oil tank with heavy-weight oil, take on twenty or thirty extra barrels, and sail for England with the convoy. The convoy commander agreed, and local Canadian authorities at once turned to dealing with the many details required to close out the incident (which was kept secret for a decade afterwards). Two days later, the *SS Donald E. Shea* steamed out of Halifax harbor bound for Liverpool. She and her crew arrived without further incident seventeen days later. Frank always attributed that smooth passage to *A Kiss For Luck!*

End of Part II

A Kiss For Luck!

Part III:
Home by Christmas

Holabird Ordnance Depot
Baltimore, MD
Sunday, June 6, 1943
One year before D-Day

"How many times are you going to put in for a transfer, McCormick?" Major Lawes asked the sergeant standing in front of him.

"One more than the number of times you turn it down, sir," McCormick replied. "I believe this is number six."

"You know why I keep turning them down, don't you?"

"Because there's more paperwork involved in saying *yes* than in saying *no*?" McCormick answered, quickly adding, "Sir."

Lawes was pretty laid back for a man who was making the Army his career, and he laughed at the remark.

"That's why I have a secretary, Sergeant," he said. "No. The reason I've been reluctant to let you go is that you're the best damned mechanic and test driver that I've ever seen. You understand the machines the Army sends down here better than the folks who designed and built them. There's nothing that you can't break and then know how to fix.

"When the folks from Bantam brought that first Jeep down here in '40, you put it through its paces until it literally fell apart. But then you helped them figure out what they needed to do to make it right. Half the modifications that Willys and Ford are putting into all the Jeeps they're building are thanks to you. And you've done the same with trucks, trailers, and tanks.

"No, I've wanted you here because you make a big difference in what our boys will be using to fight Hitler when they invade Europe."

"Thank you, sir," McCormick said. "I hope what I've done here at Holabird will make a difference over there, but I really want to be more of a part of it. I'm as good with a rifle as I am with a wrench, sir."

"They can teach just about anyone to shoot a rifle," Lawes replied, "and those they can't, they can give a bazooka. What you have can't be taught; you have a natural gift."

"I take it then that you're denying my request, again, sir?"

"On the contrary," the major replied. "But I'm not about to let the Army, in its infinite wisdom, squander your talents by making you a foot soldier."

"Where would I be going, then, sir?" McCormick said with slightly mixed emotions. He was apparently getting his transfer, but going to another stateside assignment—like Aberdeen, the Army's other big proving grounds—wasn't what he had been hoping for.

"You're familiar with the 29th Infantry?"

"Yes, sir. The Blue and Grey," McCormick answered, referring to the nickname given the infantry division because when it was formed in 1917 it consisted of soldiers from states that fought on both the North and South sides in the Civil War. "But they're definitely a combat unit. Foot soldiers out the wazoo."

"That they are," Lawes replied. "But within the 29th is a unit called the 729th Ordnance Light Maintenance Company. That's where you're going."

"Can't say I've heard of them, sir."

"It's something new they've cooked up especially for *Herr Schicklgruber*. The Nazi army's *blitzkrieg* tactics mean the armies who have to fight them need to move quickly, too. That means supply lines become critical, so the Army has decided to make their repair facilities mobile, and keep them right up with the front lines. The idea is that if a truck or a Jeep or a tank breaks down, they fix it right there on the spot if they can, and it stays right in the action rather than being towed back to a depot somewhere."

"Good idea," McCormick said, wondering if it was actually someone in the Army who had come up with it.

"Same goes for radios, weapons, binoculars, rangefinders ... basically everything the Army needs to keep fighting. They're putting mobile workshops on the backs of deuce-and-halfs so everything you guys will need—including a place to work—will be right there."

"Thank you, sir," McCormick said. "That sounds like the perfect assignment for me. When do I ship out?"

Lawes stood up and handed the sergeant his new orders. "You need to be in New York on Friday. I'm giving you a five-day pass to get your affairs in order and to take a little R&R." He extended his hand, and said, "We're going to miss you around here, Kenny. Good luck."

McCormick shook his hand, and said, "Is it okay if I finish testing that Dodge deuce before I go? I think if we shorten a couple of the leaves in the front springs it's going to handle a whole lot better on the washboards."

The major smiled at McCormick's typical dedication. "Twenty-four hours, Sergeant" he said in a very official tone, "and then I want you off this base. Understood?"

Kenny snapped to attention, saluted, and said, "Yes, sir!"

Lawes returned the salute, and then in a more friendly tone he said, "I mean it. Take some time off to relax. You've earned it, and Lord knows you won't be getting any once you land in Europe."

Saturday, June 12, 1943

Six days later, Sgt. Kenny McCormick was sailing out of New York harbor inside the number three hold of the Liberty ship *SS Francis Grundstrom*.

The *Grundstrom*, like many Libertys, had been converted to a troop ship by adding fifty racks of four-high canvas bunks into four of the five holds. To the troops, the crude accommodations on a pitching and rolling freighter made boot camp seem like a resort vacation.

For the first four days the convoy was whipped by rain and wind, and nearly every one of the 800 troops—including Kenny—was seasick. When the weather finally broke on the fourth day, the captain encouraged all of his "guests" to spend as much time as they could on deck. With a flat sea, finally, he also had the crew use the deck cranes to lift the hatch covers from the holds to air out the stench of body odor and vomit.

In telling the story of the crossing, one of Kenny's shipmates would swear that he saw a seagull fly over one of the open holds and pass out from the smell, falling into the sea like a downed plane. In the hyperbolic *retelling*, it eventually became a whole flock of gulls.

Elated to be out of the bowels of the ship and in the fresh air and sunlight, 800 GIs crowded the weather deck sitting, standing, and lying down, wherever they could.

Leaning against the rail, watching the other ships in the convoy, a tall lanky fellow said to McCormick, "So, where ya from?"

The guy pronounced the word *where* as *way-ah*, and Kenny knew at once that the man was either from New Hampshire or Maine. His guess was Maine.

"Augusta," Kenny said. "You?"

"Kennebunkport," the guy said holding out his hand. "Jimmy McIntyre. Pleased to meet you. What outfit you joining?"

"Kenny McCormick," he replied shaking hands. "I'm joining up with the 29th Infantry."

"No kidding! Me, too!" Jimmy said. "What unit?"

"The 729th Ordnance Light Maintenance Company."

"Well ain't it a small gall-dang world! That's *my* unit!"

"So, you come out of Aberdeen?" McCormick asked. "I'm from Holabird."

"Nope. I was a cook at Camp Chaffee out in Arkansas," Jimmy said. "One day the CO was showing some VIPs around the base and he stopped at the mess hall. When it was time to leave, his car wouldn't start. I thought his driver—a corporal who just got his stripes—was going to pee his pants he was so worried about it.

"I happened to be outside taking a smoke break, and I walked over and told him to stop cranking the motor before he killed the battery. The CO asked if I knew anything about cars, and I told him I did; that it sounded like ignition to me. He asked if I could fix it, and I said probably; that I hadn't worked on a car yet that beat me.

"I opened the hood and pulled the coil wire and grounded it, and had the driver crank it over again. Sure enough, no spark. I pulled the coil from a Chevy delivery truck and jerry-rigged it into the CO's car. It fired up, and once it burned out all the extra gas the corporal had pumped into it, it ran like a top.

"Three days later I had orders to report to New York to join the 729th."

"I take it you were a mechanic before the Army made you a cook?" McCormick said.

"Yup. My Dad owns a service station in town. I been inside and under cars since before I could walk."

McCormick laughed. "Typical Army; they probably found a pastry chef to put in charge of the motor pool."

Tuesday, June 22, 1943

Ten days later—six of which included varying degrees of seasickness—McCormick, McIntyre, and the rest of the troops disembarked in Liverpool.

"If that's how we're getting back to the States when this is over," Kenny said as they walked down the gangway, "I think I'm going to become a Brit."

The two sergeants and all the other men from the ship were directed to rows of trucks—lorries, now that they were in England—that would either take them to the train station or motor on to the location of their assigned division.

Headed for southwestern England, the Devon-Cornwall peninsula, Kenny and Jimmy and a couple dozen others were deposited at the train station.

As they waited on the platform, two other sergeants wearing the blue and grey shoulder patch of the 29th Infantry walked by. They weren't carrying duffle bags, so they were obviously not new arrivals.

"Hey, buddy," Jimmy said to one of them, "I see you're with the 29th. Us, too."

The two men looked Kenny and Jimmy up and down.

"What company you with?" the tall one asked.

"729th," Kenny said. "Ordnance Light Maintenance Company."

The two strangers exchanged glances, and the short one said, "Great. More tens; just what the war needs." They both laughed, and walked off.

"Tens?" Jimmy said to Kenny. "What the hell's a ten?"

"Beats me," Kenny said, "but apparently they don't like them, and we're not the only ones."

A few minutes later a huge black steam locomotive belched and hissed into the station pulling a string of passenger coaches.

McCormick stood transfixed watching the wheels, levers, pistons, and cranks of the iron behemoth as it slowed to a stop in a billow of steam just beyond the platform. Kenny had always been fascinated by steam engines, and had even gotten a job in the engine house in Boston, working for the Boston & Maine Railroad. He was supposed to report for his first day of work on Monday, December 8th, the day after the attack on Pearl Harbor. Instead he enlisted in the Army.

When the train stopped it was already half full with other military personnel and civilians, so by the time McCormick and McIntyre filed on, they didn't even bother looking for a seat. Instead, they stood with their duffle bags on the rear platform of the last car.

As the cars began to move and pick up speed, a man in uniform came running out of the station. He wore lieutenant's bars on one side of his garrison cap, and a gold chaplain's cross on the other.

He ran toward the edge of the platform and the two sergeants, and Kenny leaned out from the step to grab the officer's hand. The lieutenant grabbed and leapt just as the platform disappeared from under him, but his shoe slid across the steel plate of the step on landing, and both Kenny and Jimmy grabbed him to keep him from falling back out onto the dirt.

Once he'd gained his footing and they all climbed back up onto the train's platform, both sergeants saluted, and McCormick said, "Welcome aboard, sir ... Father."

The officer returned the salute, and said, "Much obliged for the assist, gentlemen. Where you headed?"

"All we know is we're headed south to meet up with the 29th Infantry," McCormick answered.

"Ah! A few days at the beach, then," the lieutenant said.

"The beach?" Jimmy repeated.

"The 29th is training for amphibious landings down in Devon." The officer looked into the standing-room-only car, and added, "When some of these folks get off, you'll want to find yourself a seat if you can. It's a long ride."

Half a dozen men in uniform stood outdoors on the rear platform and watched the countryside rush past. Even though they could taste the soot being belched into the air by the locomotive 200 yards ahead, to McCormick and Jimmy it was like the air after a spring rain compared to the smell in the hold of the *Liberty* ship.

As the lieutenant lit his pipe, McCormick turned to him, and said, "Sir, do you happen to know what a ten is?"

"A ten? A ten of what?"

"Back at the station, a couple sergeants from the 29th referred to us as *more tens*. It didn't sound like a compliment."

"You with a fighting division or support?" the lieutenant asked.

"Support," McCormick said. "729th Ordnance Light Maintenance Company."

"Ah, yes," the officer said nodding his head. "Well, there's a saying among the fighting divisions over here that goes, *one shootin' and ten lootin'*. It means there are ten support troops for every one firing a rifle, and it's the ten who'll gather the spoils as the Army moves forward." He paused a moment, and added, "There's a variation that goes, *'one duckin' and ten ...* well, meeting the young ladies who've been liberated, if you get my meaning."

The two sergeants looked at each other.

"How far forward do they think they'll get without support, sir?" McCormick said.

"You don't have to defend yourself to me, Sergeant," the lieutenant said. "As a priest I'm one of the ten, myself."

"You can bet," Jimmy chimed in, "that the first time they're in a foxhole and their machine gun stops firing, they're gonna be looking around for us *and* for you!"

The lieutenant laughed. "True enough! They say there are no atheists in foxholes."

When the train reached Birmingham, a great exchange of passengers took place. The train pulled out of the station nearly as crowded as it had entered, but at least half of the men and women onboard were new to the train.

During the crisscross migration of passengers, McCormick, Jimmy, and the lieutenant made their way into the last car and found a seat. By the time the train had gone a couple of miles, however, the sergeants were already finding the air in the car stuffy and a little too heavy with combined cigar, cigarette, and pipe smoke. They decided to retreat to the rear platform, again, where they only had to breathe coal soot. The lieutenant, being one of the smokers, remained. Their seats were taken before they'd gone three steps.

To their surprise and delight, one of the fellow standees at the back of the train was a young woman.

Doffing his cap, McCormick said, "Evening, ma'am. Mind if we share the fresh air with you?"

Jimmy removed his cap, too, and said, "Ev'nin'."

She looked between the two men, and replied, "This is your idea of fresh air?"

"We've been stuck in the hold of a ship with 200 other men for fourteen days," McCormick replied, "so yes, this is pretty fresh."

She laughed. It was a high-pitched little twitter of a laugh, and although he would not have thought it possible, he swore there was an accent to it.

"On your way home from a hard day at the office?" McCormick asked.

"I'm a nurse, actually," she said.

He loved the way she said *ac-tually*! She said it like it was two words.

"Or I will be when I complete my training," she went on. "I'm on my way to Barnstaple to visit my Mum for the weekend. Then it's back to Queen Elizabeth for my final year."

"The Queen?" Jimmy repeated. "The for-real Queen?"

"Oh, no!" she said, laughing again. "Queen Elizabeth *Hospital*. It's where I'm taking my training. It's in Birmingham."

"So, is that where we just stopped? Birmingham?" McCormick asked. "I didn't see a sign, so I couldn't tell."

"Oh, yes, that's right," she said. "It's been that way for so long I'd forgotten the signs had been taken down."

"Why'd they take the signs down?" Jimmy asked.

"So Jerry can't find his way," she said.

"Jerry?" Jimmy said. "You mean the Germans?"

"Yes. Three or four years ago, when it looked like they were going to invade—especially right after Dunkirk—the government took down all the road signs and highway markers and signs for the train and bus depots. They figured if Jerry did land we might as well confuse him as much as we could. Of course with the way the government puts up their markers, some folks think leaving the signs up for Jerry would be *more* confusing." She twittered again at her little joke, and Kenny McCormick was head-over-heals in love!

He had heard that the women in England were cold fish, plain looking bordering on homely, had gaps in their teeth, and hated Yanks. Either this one was the exception that proved the rule, or all that was total malarkey! And Kenny didn't care which it was.

He stood transfixed as she answered Jimmy's questions about the signs. He absolutely adored her accent! That was another bit of hogwash, apparently; that you couldn't understand a thing they said. He understood every word and would have been content to sit and listen to the her read a service manual for a Ford tractor.

And her looks! My God, she was beautiful!

She wore a trim fitting suit of grey and brown tweed, with a smooth calf-length skirt and a blazer with four bone buttons down the front. Her white blouse, buttoned all the way to the top, had a crisp collar that fit close around her slender neck.

Perched on her head, cocked just slightly to her left, she wore a hat of deep grey fabric. The top was dome shaped, and fit close to her head, and it had a brim that went all the way around, sticking out slightly more in the front, and snapped down just a little. There was a short feather on the left side.

Her skin was fair and perfectly clear, her nose was small and straight, not pug, and certainly not the "typical" British hawk-beak that he'd heard about.

She had high cheekbones, but they weren't prominent, and they were accented subtly with a light touch of rouge. Kenny thought that she had either learned somewhere how to apply make-up to look natural, or she was running out because of war rationing, and didn't want to overuse it. Again, he didn't care which.

Her jaw was squarish and strong, but far short of being masculine. Her lips were full, colored bright red (apparently she was not running out of lipstick, thank God!), and were shaped in a gentle curve that made her look happy even when she wasn't smiling ... which was not often.

Her hair was brown, pulled back so her ears shown, but was long enough to cover the back of her neck in gentle curls.

And then there were her eyes. Kenny had never met anyone with true green eyes before. They made his heart somehow stop and race at the same time!

They were bright and sharp, and had a smile all by themselves, and when she laughed—that twitter—they twinkled so much it was almost as if they threw sparks.

Yup. Kenney McCormick was in love. But what the hell was he going to do about it on a train headed for war exercises?

Kenny, just 21 years old, was not a lady killer by any means. He had dated a couple of girls in high school and had almost lost his virginity in the back seat of his father's Studebaker, just before shipping off to boot camp. It was an experience that ended *prematurely*, so it really didn't even count as his first time. It would have been completely forgettable if it hadn't been so embarrassing.

He had met a few women during his time in Maryland. He had met them at various clubs while on leaves in Baltimore, but it was obvious that they were there for really just one reason ... the same reason as most of the men. He could easily have lost his virginity there, but the Army's VD films during boot camp made him overly cautious, and he limited his contact to dancing and kissing.

Standing next to Lily, Kenny remembered some advice his older sister had given him when he was nervously preparing for his first unchaperoned date in high school. "What do I talk about with her?" he'd asked his sister.

"Her," she replied. "Talk about school. Ask her what classes she likes the most, which teachers she likes. Ask her what she does after school; what she wants to do when she graduates. Ask her about her family. If she sees that you're interested in her, she'll be interested in you."

He decided that introducing himself was probably a good place to start ... right after getting rid of Jimmy.

Behind Lily's back Kenny made a hand gesture that told Jimmy to scram. He got the message, and said, "Hey, look! There's an empty seat in there. I think I'll go take the load off for a while. I'll catch you later, Kenny." To Lily, he tipped his hat, and said, "A pleasure, ma'am." And then he went inside the car.

"Right. Later, Jimmy," Kenny said. He turned to Lily, extended his hand, and said, "I'm Kenny McCormick, by the way. It's a pleasure to meet you."

The significance of his friend's hasty retreat was not lost on Lily, but she just smiled.

"Lily Thatcher," she replied, resting her hand in his. "Likewise, I'm sure."

He wasn't sure whether she expected him to kiss her hand or shake it. He closed his thumb lightly over her fingers, and shook it gently.

"Is Lily short for Lillian?" he asked without letting go of her hand. "I have an aunt named Lillian."

"Elizabeth, actually," she said.

That *ac-tually*, again!

"Just like the Queen," he said.

"In a round-about way," she replied. "I'm named for my grandmamma; *she* was named for the Queen, but the *first* Elizabeth."

"Interesting," he said, with a sudden and painful drought of adjectives. After an awkward gap, he asked, "So, how far is Barnstaple?" He was hoping it was a long way.

As she opened her mouth to answer, she was interrupted by a loud voice from the doorway of the car.

"Lily!" the man said, "How wonderful to see you! You look extraordinary!" He pronounced the last word, *ex-trod-in-ree*.

Facing Lily, with the platform railing to his right, Kenny turned to see a fellow exiting the car and stepping directly toward Lily. He wore a British Army uniform with sergeant's stripes on the sleeve. Kenny guessed he was a few years older than himself.

Lily seemed surprised by his approach and she pulled her hand from Kenny's and put it against the man's chest. It did nothing to slow his advance.

With her backside against the railing, she couldn't retreat, and he put his arms around her, taking her in a close hug. He tried to kiss her on the lips, but she turned her head and he kissed her cheek, instead.

Kenny was coiling up to hit this stranger for attacking his new friend, but the hug and the kiss, and the fact that she didn't scream kept him in check.

"Aren't you glad to see me?" the man said, still holding Lily. "No kiss for your old flame?"

Her hand still in between them, she managed to push him a few inches away from her body.

"I'm *surprised* to see you, Charles," she said, "And there'll be no more kisses from me; I told you that. You broke my heart."

"*Lily*," he said in a condescending tone, "I told you she meant nothing to me. She was the result of one too many bottles of wine and far too many miles away from you."

"Yes, you told me," she said, "and it means no more now than it did the first dozen times you said it. I've nothing else to say to you."

The man slowly dropped his hands to his sides stared at her for a long moment. At first Kenny felt a bit sorry for him, having been upbraided like that in front of strangers. But then he thought he could sense the man's anger rising, and once again, Kenny set himself to react if the guy made any aggression toward Lily.

If Kenny *had* seen anger in the man, it passed within seconds, and the guy broke into a smile. Kenny relaxed, but only a little.

"Well then, now that I've been properly set in my place," the man said, "why don't you introduce me to your friend, Lily?"

McCormick extended his hand. "Sergeant Kenny McCormick. US 29th Infantry. How do you do?"

"Sergeant Charles Haversham III," the man replied. "British 2nd Army, 3rd Infantry Division. I'm well, thank you ... all things considered." As he spoke he shook McCormick's hand with a grip that was far more forceful than necessary. Kenny had the impression that he was trying to intimidate him. After years of "knuckle-busting" work on cars, trucks, tractors, and everything else, however, Kenny's hand was more than up to the challenge.

Rather than escalating it into a grip-to-the-death struggle, Kenny simply matched the force of the grip—as if that's how everyone shook hands—and went on talking in a flat tone.

"So, are you headed for a few days at the beach, too?" Kenny asked.

"Right you are," Charles said, "I expect we'll be playing games down there, you and I. The question is will we be on the same side, what?" He relaxed his grip and let go of Kenny's hand, apparently through with *that* game.

"So, that's how they're training, huh?" McCormick said. "One army is the good guys and one is the bad guys?"

"Sometimes," Charles replied. "Other times it's everybody against mother nature as we storm a bloody great cliff or some such."

"Mind your language in public!" Lily scolded Charles.

Kenny had heard that the word "bloody" was a profanity in England, but he'd never heard why.

Charles laughed and looked at Kenny. "If you fancy this one," he said, cocking a thumb at Lily, "you'll have to mind your Ps and Qs, what? And in case you're wondering what to call that color in her eyes, old boy, that's jealousy-green."

He turned to Lily, and said, "Isn't that right, *my own Lili Marlene*?"

Lili Marlene was a popular song at the time—in both Germany and England—and spoke of the anguish of separation between a soldier being sent off to war and his girlfriend.

In a hearty baritone, Charles then sang a couple of the lines to the song:
"*Orders came for sailing somewhere over there;
All confined to barracks was more than I could bear ...*"

He then reached up quickly and took Lily's face between his hands and held her tight while he kissed her hard on the lips.

Her eyes went wide in surprise and then anger, and her hand came up to slap her assailant.

With his arms up high, it was easy for him to deflect her blow, and her fingers barely touched his cheek.

At the same time, Kenny cocked his right arm down and back and balled up his fist. He would rather have socked the Brit in the jaw or nose, but with Lily's face right against his, he would settle for the stomach.

Charles saw Kenny's motion out of the corner of his eye, and he let go of Lily's face and put his right hand out against Kenny's chest.

"No need for that, old boy," he said as he stepped back from Lily, and kept Kenny at an arm's length. "You can have her, and good luck to you on that count!"

He laughed, turned around, and walked back into the car.

"Are you okay," Kenny asked as he took both of her hands in his.

"Aside from being mortified, I'm just fine, " she said. "How rude!"

"If it's still the custom over here," Kenny said, "I'll be happy to go challenge him to a duel to defend your honor." He smiled at her, and added, "I may have to borrow a glove from someone, though."

She laughed—twittered. "That's very gallant of you, Sir Kenneth, but dueling *has* rather gone out of favor."

"Pity, he said. "Being a ten, I may not get to shoot anybody this whole war."

"A ten?" she asked.

He explained his job in the Army and how that made him a "ten."

She replied, "I think you should be a twenty or a thirty, or a one hundred. The fewer people there are shooting, the fewer boys are going to die or be wounded ... on *both* sides. When we do finally invade the continent, I've an idea that my fellow nurses and I are going to be kept busy day and night. I'm looking forward to finishing my training, and getting to work, but I'm not looking forward to that in the least."

"I'm sorry," Kenny said, "That was insensitive to say that I was disappointed that I wouldn't get to shoot anyone. You're right, of course. Shooting people is a very poor way to settle anything."

"More people at the tops of governments need to know that," she said.

"So, is the war what made you want to be a nurse?" he asked, steering the conversation back to her.

"I guess it was," she said. "I was 16 when war was declared, and we were all scared to death that Hitler was going to start bombing us at any time. ARP units sprang up all over, and I volunteered at the ambulance station that was set up in an old garage the next street over. I learned First Aid there."

"What's an ARP unit?" Kenny asked. "Ambulance rescue patrol?"

"Air raid precautions," she answered. "Our unit had two ambulances; some had only one, but nearer the big cities, units could have ten or more."

"Did you see a lot of action?"

"Far more than a young girl should," she replied, "It was a salutary experience, though, and it gave me a taste for medicine and for helping others. When I turned eighteen it was time for me to take up a job of national importance, so I applied for training as a nurse. I was so happy when I was accepted at Queen Elizabeth Hospital! It's part of the University of Birmingham's Medical School. It's rated as the most modern hospital in all of the UK!"

"Well, if I should get wounded," he said, "I'll insist on being taken there."

"Oh, you mustn't joke about such things," she said. "Don't go tempting the fates. They're not a lot to be trifled with. You'll want them well enough on your side when you make it to the continent."

"I'd say they're behind me, so far," he said. "They put the two of us on the same train, didn't they?"

Kenny found Lily very easy to talk to—not his strongest suit around pretty women—and even more pleasant to listen to.

After a few miles, he laid his duffle bag on its side and the two of them sat on it, their backs against the platform railing, as they continued talking.

When the conversation turned to her hobby of bird watching, she took a piece of paper from her purse, unfolded it, and showed it to him. In each of the four quadrants of the paper was a pencil-sketch of a different bird.

"You did these?" he asked. "They're amazing! I wish I could draw like that."

"And I wish I could fix a bicycle," she said with a laugh. "Seems everybody wishes for something other than what they have, don't they?"

"If you could have any wish," he asked her, "what would it be? Aside from being able to fix a bicycle."

"That Adolph Hitler and his gang of murderers had never been born," she answered.

"A worthy use of a wish," he said, "But let's take it as a given that we *all* wish for us to win the war—and do it very quickly. What else would you wish for just for you?"

She looked at him for a moment, and then with a grin, she said, "My wish is that I see you again, Sergeant McCormick. You're not at all like the other Americans I've met; all full of themselves, strutting in their uniforms like they're Clark Gable or some such.

"There's a saying about the Yanks, you know," she said looking around as if she was going to share a secret. She leaned close to his ear, and said, "That they're overpaid, oversexed, and over here."

She straightened up and giggled nervously as the color came up in her cheeks. She was not used to using such risqué language in public ... and with a near stranger on top of it!

He laughed, and said, "Well, I certainly can't deny that I'm over here, but I can guarantee that I'm not overpaid. And as for the last one ... well, it seems your friend Charles has me beat by a mile on that score."

She laughed. "He comes from a landed family, so he thinks that automatically makes him a gentleman. You're twice the gentleman Charles will ever be."

"I assume *landed family* means the aristocracy of some sort," Kenny said. "Is he wealthy?"

"His grandfather still owns acres and acres in the north and in Scotland, and his father runs a very successful paper mill. Charles, however, is just a beastly leech."

Kenny laughed. "Not to put too fine a point on it ..." he said.

"Enough about Charles. So, what is your one wish, Sergeant?" she asked.

"My wish is that *your* wish comes true," he said with a smile. "When I manage to get some leave—which won't be for a while—where could I look you up?"

"All of the nursing students live at the hospital," she said. "You'd have to call on me there."

"Can I write to you in the meantime?"

"I'd like that very much," she said. She took her bird drawing and wrote her address on the back in one corner. She carefully tore it off and handed it to him.

He read the address, and then turned the slip over. "What kind of bird is it?" he asked.

"It's supposed to be an American Goldfinch. That's the male; he has much brighter colors than the female," she said. "Hard to tell in black and white, though; I don't have any artist pencils. A nurse in training doesn't receive much salary, I'm afraid."

He put the slip in his wallet.

After another half hour of the calming rhythm of the train, Lily drifted off to sleep and her head lolled gently onto Kenny's shoulder. Kenny looked at his watch, It was nearing midnight, but he didn't feel the least bit tired himself.

An hour and a half later, the train began to slow as it approached the end of the line in Barnstaple. Kenny patted Lily's hand to wake her up, and she came around slowly.

When she saw that she was lying against Kenny, using his shoulder for a pillow, she sat bolt upright, and put her hand to her mouth in horror.

"Oh, dear me!" she said. "You must think me quite the tart to fall asleep all over you! I am dreadful sorry! Please forgive me!"

He laughed as he took her hand from her mouth and held it between his.

"Forgive you?" he said. "Hardly. I want to *thank* you! That may have been the most blissful hour and a half I've spent since I was about twelve years old and fell asleep in my grandma's hammock on a summer afternoon."

He helped her to her feet, and she straightened her clothes and adjusted her hat. He stood his duffle bag up, and they waited in silence for the train to come to a stop. They had been talking with the greatest comfort and ease for hours, and now, suddenly they felt awkward with each other.

And they each knew why.

He wanted so much to take her in his arms and kiss her lips before they parted! But what would she think of him? She was so much a lady that she had been horrified just to discover that her head had been on his shoulder while she was asleep.

She wanted so much for him to take her in his arms and kiss her lips before they parted! But she knew he was far too much of a gentleman for that. He hadn't even nudged her awake when she fell asleep on his shoulder for an hour and a half. Poor fellow, he must have lost all feeling in his arm!

She bit her lip and decided to take bold action! After all, he *was* going off to war!

He decided to take the gentlemanly approach, and ask if he could kiss her. Could she really refuse? After all, he *was* going off to war.

As he opened his mouth to speak, she leaned forward and placed her lips to his ... or rather *inside* of his.

They both pulled back, and looked at each other surprised and embarrassed by the awkwardness of the moment.

When he realized what she had been trying to do, he closed his lips and leaned forward to kiss her.

Realizing she had been far to forward, she began to apologize to him.

As she opened her mouth to speak, his lips went inside of hers.

Again, they pulled back.

"This shouldn't be this hard!" he said with a laugh. He took her face between his hands, and said, "Are you ready?"

With a big smile, she nodded her head, afraid to open her mouth again.

He leaned in and they pressed their closed lips together for a long moment.

They parted, and looked into each other's eyes. Suddenly, the silliness of the last thirty seconds vanished.

He wrapped his arms around her, cocked his head to the side, and found her mouth once again, this time soft and inviting.

She slid her arms around him, and welcomed the feel of his lips on hers.

They kissed passionately until the train lurched to its final stop, and they nearly toppled over.

Then, the most tender moment Kenny had ever had with a woman was shattered by the coarse, bellowing voice of a master sergeant on the station platform instructing the new arrivals to get their gear and get their butts into the waiting trucks.

Kenny kissed Lily one more time, and as he helped her down the steps, he said, "I'll write to you as soon as I can. Promise."

"Do be careful!" she said. "I'll look for your letter."

With that, a crush of civilians and soldiers exiting the train separated the two.

Wednesday June 23, 1943

Six o'clock roll call came very early the next morning. After breakfast in the mess tent with several hundred other soldiers, all of the new arrivals were sent to the quartermaster to draw their field equipment. McCormick and Jimmy and the rest of the men assigned to the 729th had turned in their standard-issue revolver side-arms before they left the States, and were now issued new Colt .45 automatics. And because they were technically in the infantry, they were also issued rifles.

Had they been combat troops they would have received the newer and more accurate semi-automatic M1 Garand. But being support personnel it was felt that they probably wouldn't be using their rifles much anyway, so they were issued the older bolt-action M1903 Springfield that originally saw action during the First World War.

Later in the day, McCormick and Jimmy were working in the armor staging area fitting Sherman tanks with huge rectangular snorkels that would allow the tanks to operate in water deep enough to wash over the top of the turret.

"This really works, huh?" McCormick asked the third member of their squad, Peter "Mack" McDonnely. Mack was also a sergeant, and was also from Maine, having been born and raised in Old Orchard Beach. The three Irishmen would eventually become known within the 729th as "The Micks from Maine."

"It looks like the biggest damn turtle you ever seen in your life crawling up onto the beach out of the water," he said with a laugh. "But if you want to see something *really* crazy, wait 'til you see a Donald Duck! It's a Sherman tank with two propellers on the back, sitting inside this *enormous* canvas bathtub. The damn thing actually floats! I've seen them tooling around out there a hundred yards off shore! Crazy!"

When they eventually broke for lunch and walked back to the mess tent, they happened to run into Lily's old friend from the train. He was walking towards them with two fellow British sergeants. They were all carrying trays of food.

McCormick nodded slightly, acknowledging him, and said simply, "Charles."

Charles stopped, turned, and said, "That's Sergeant Haversham, if you please. We're on a military installation now, not snogging in the moonlight on some forsaken train. Even you Yanks are expected to act like proper soldiers over here."

McCormick—and in fact, all three of the Micks—were "tech sergeants" or T/4's, so they were technically outranked by a "straight" sergeant—even from a different command. Most units treated the two grades as equals, but if push came to shove, Charles *was* his superior.

McCormick turned to look at Charles, but continued walking.

"My apologies, *Sergeant Haversham*," he said with another nod. He was *not* required to address him as sir. He then kept walking to the mess line with the other two Micks.

"You know him?" Mack asked.

"We met on the train, last night," he answered.

"What's *snogging*?" Jimmy said.

"It probably has something to do with talking to a girl," McCormick said. "And I'm sure it's derogatory. I met his old girlfriend on the train, too." Snogging was, in fact, British slang for what Americans referred to as making out.

"He seems like quite an ass," Mack said.

"I got that impression last night," McCormick agreed. "Now I'm sure of it."

Sunday, June 27, 1943

The following Sunday, the Micks attended Mass together, and then went back to work. There really wasn't much else to do, confined to base as they were, and there were plenty of tanks that still needed snorkels attached.

They were working on one of the Shermans when a Jeep roared into the compound, brushing so close to McCormick that he had to hug himself into the tank tread to keep from being hit.

The Jeep skidded to a stop with a cloud of dust, and Charles and one of his buddies climbed out laughing.

"Major Yardley sent us to get a wrecker," Charles said, addressing no one in particular. "A big one. Any of you Yanks know how to drive?"

"Good afternoon, Sergeant Haversham," McCormick said. "Nice of you to drop by. What is it the major needs a wrecker for?"

"I don't believe that's any of your concern, now is it?" Charles replied in his haughty accent. "You were given an order; follow it."

"Actually, Sergeant," McCormick said, "it sounds like you're the only one who's been given an order. So far, all *you've* done is to ask if any of us knows how to drive. The answer is yes."

As he stood there with his arms folded, just looking at the Brit, he saw the anger surface that he had first seen on the train. Again, Haversham seemed to have to force it under control.

"Just get your arse into the biggest bloody wrecker you have," Charles snarled, "and bloody follow me to the beach. *There's* your bloody order, Technical Sergeant!"

As the Micks climbed into the big Ward LaFrance M1A1 Heavy Wrecker, Charles took off, spinning the wheels of the Jeep and throwing gravel everywhere. Without the Jeep in four-wheel drive, it fishtailed in the dirt, and its rear quarter swung into the tank treads, bending the sheet metal of the Jeep and gouging its flat green paint. The tank, of course, was completely unfazed.

As Charles took off again, McCormick shifted the truck into gear, and they rolled out, following him ... and laughing hysterically.

Charles tore out of the compound as fast as he could, and McCormick guessed that he was going to try to drop them, and then somehow blame them for not keeping up. Kenny didn't care. He knew where the beach was and how to get there.

Earlier in the morning, Kenny had taken a Jeep he had finished working on for a test drive, and had followed the mostly-paved road that led from the encampment to Woolacombe beach where the landing exercises were taking place.

The road wound back and forth like a snake, skirting hills to stay as flat as possible for the four-legged draft animals that had been using the road for a century. As a result, it took three miles of driving to go between two points that were less than a mile apart as the crow flies. One also had to frequently share the road with herds of sheep, slowing travel even more.

Missing the kind of off-road driving that he had gotten so good at while serving at Holabird, Kenny had taken a "cross-country" return route with the 4x4 Jeep. He followed foot and animal paths over the hills, forded a couple of shallow streams, and with some strategic rock placement, he managed to crawl over a low but wide stone wall.

He was now going to take the same route—in the other direction—to beat Charles to the beach.

When Kenny turned off the road and into an open field, his two passengers thought he had lost his mind. They soon saw that the hills, streams and even the rock walls were no obstacles at all for the big 6x6 truck, and they began enjoying the crazy ride.

When they crested the last hill they were on a bluff twenty feet above the beach, and could see in the distance a Sherman tank—with its big snorkels—up to its turret in the sea. A dozen or so men stood around it and on it. They guessed that that was why the major sent for them.

Kenny put the truck in gear and began to drive forward.

Jimmy braced himself and shouted, "What the hell are you doing?!"

"I'm going down the hill," McCormick said wondering how that wasn't completely obvious.

"That's not a hill, it's a goddamned cliff!"

Kenny laughed. "Relax! It's 45-degrees, at most. This thing will go up and down bumps like this all day long."

Both Jimmy and Mack felt like they were going straight down, and they put their feet against the dashboard to brace themselves for when they crashed at the bottom.

With its transition in six-wheel-drive and low-gear, the truck crept slowly down the embankment, and then leveled out onto the beach, just as predicted.

Both passengers looked back to see what they had just driven down. Neither would have believed that a truck that big could come down such a steep slope without rolling over frontwards. Kenny laughed again at their expressions.

On the flat beach, McCormick shifted up through the gears and picked up speed quickly, heading toward the half-submerged tank.

Along their right, the embankment they had just come down ran the entire length of the beach. It was one of the features that made this stretch of shoreline valuable for landing practice.

In one area, the engineers had bulldozed a cut through the embankment that connected to the road on the other side. As McCormick passed the cut, Haversham's Jeep came roaring out through it, right at the truck.

Haversham had to brake and turn at the same time, and just missed slamming into the truck's huge rear tires. The Jeep spun around, and slid sideways until its tires dug into the packed sand of the beach, and the little vehicle went up on two wheels. It balanced there for a moment, deciding which way to go, and then finally dropped back down on its wheels.

Kenny watched the spinout in his mirror, and let out a sigh of relief when the Jeep settled down onto all four wheels. He really didn't want to have to repair a flipped Jeep.

As Charles swore at the truck, and cranked the Jeep's engine trying to get it restarted, Kenny pulled up in front of the tank. He looked down at a lieutenant, saluted, and said, "Afternoon, sir. Did someone call triple-A?"

"You think you can get that tank out of the mud before the tide puts it underwater?" he replied. "The major says he's going to take the cost of a new one out of our pay if we can't get it out."

Kenny laughed as he and the other two climbed down from the truck. "I hope you plan to be in the Army for life, then," he said. "I don't think these things come cheap."

They walked into the water and were surprised to find that the water that lapped at the bottom of the turret was only knee deep. Even the *tops* of the treads were under the sand!

"Wow!" McCormick said. "You really got this thing dug in! How the heck did you mire it like this?"

"Apparently, there was a big hole in the beach right where the tank drove off the landing craft, so it went pretty deep," the lieutenant said. "The driver panicked, thinking they were going underwater, and threw it in reverse to go back up onto the boat. But the treads wouldn't grab the ramp, and he dug himself deeper into the sand.

"Then some Brit sergeant on the beach thought he'd step in and help him," the lieutenant went on using quote-fingers on the word *help*. "He had him turning left and right; forward and back ... and every move he had him make buried the tank a little deeper. I swear the jamoke was doing it on purpose, just to see how stuck he could get the damned thing. He was laughing pretty good until he saw the major's Jeep coming up the beach."

"You happen to know who this Brit was?" McCormick asked, with a pretty good suspicion.

The lieutenant pointed down the beach, and said, "The same nimrod that almost ran into you with the major's Jeep. I don't know his name."

"It's Haversham," McCormick said. "Sergeant Charles Haversham III. You might want that for your report."

"I take it he's not a friend of yours?"

"Not exactly, sir," McCormick answered. "We've crossed paths a few times now; none of them what you'd call friendly. I don't want any trouble with him, though; it's kind of important that I get some leave before too long, and getting into a fight with a local won't help that."

"*Kind of important*," the lieutenant repeated with a smile. "Let me guess; you met a girl."

"Yes, sir. On the train coming down here. Turns out she's Haversham's ex-girlfriend."

"*Ah, oui!*" the lieutenant laughed. "*Cherchez la femme!*" (Look for the woman!)

"Yes, sir," McCormick said, "but *oh, la, la!*"

Eager to change the subject, Kenny said, "Looks like you tried pulling it out with another tank." He was looking up on the beach, past where the wrecker was parked, and saw the sand all churned up.

"Damn near got that one stuck, too," he replied. He nodded toward the wrecker, and said, "You really think you're going to pull it out with this?"

"Not a chance," McCormick answered. "But it just might give us enough leverage to get it to stop going deeper every time a tread spins."

He pointed to the embankment directly across the beach from the mired tank, and said, "Can you get two tanks up on that rise, sir? I think the ground is fairly solid up there, so they should be able to bite in pretty well. Have them line up one behind the other, directly in line with this one. Put the first one right on the top of the hill."

The lieutenant told one of his unit's sergeants to take his Jeep and drive farther up the beach to where assault exercises were still going on, and come back with a couple of tanks.

As that sergeant left, Sergeant Haversham pulled to a stop beside the wrecker. He leapt out and strode over to McCormick and the lieutenant.

He saluted, and said, "Lieutenant, I respectfully *insist* that you put this man on report for reckless driving, and willful damage to Army property. He nearly killed me and my passenger on the road out here when he ran into the side of the major's Jeep passing me on a turn. I would file a report myself, but he's not in *my* army." He looked McCormick up and down, and added with his British-accented arrogance, "*Thank-fully*."

McCormick smiled and turned to the lieutenant. "In case you haven't met, sir, this is Sergeant Charles Haversham III of the British 2nd Army, 3rd Infantry Division," he said. "He likes having his name repeated by others, by the way. Apparently he's a bit insecure about his rank, or something. And he is also full of what my granddad puts on his tomato plants to make them grow big and tall."

"Are you inferring that I'm *lying*, Sergeant?" Haversham said in his most thumped up indignant tone.

"No, that's what I was *implying*; I was hoping that the *lieutenant* would *infer* it."

Again, he saw the specter of anger dance in Haversham's eyes, and again he watched it recede without incident. He had a feeling that if they weren't always in a group when they met, the Brit wouldn't keep forcing the monster back in its box.

"I'll look into the matter, Sergeant Haversham," the lieutenant said. "But right now I'm more concerned with getting that tank out of the sand before the tide gets all the way in. If Sergeant McCormick gets it out, he will most certainly be in my report, and not for his driving skills."

McCormick said to Haversham, "Would you mind moving the major's Jeep before it sustains any more damage at your hands? You've parked right where I need to line the wrecker up."

Haversham and his fellow sergeant walked back to the Jeep, mumbling and chuckling. As Kenny climbed up into the cab of the truck, Haversham shouted to him.

"Are you a sporting man Sergeant McCormick?"

"What do you mean *sporting*?" he replied.

"Are you a gambler, old boy?"

"When the odds are even, I've been known to place the occasional wager," McCormick answered.

"Well, I'll wager you one pound—even odds—that you can't get that tank out of the sand with your truck," Haversham said.

McCormick looked over at the lieutenant. "You've been around here for a while, sir; what's that in real money"

"Around four dollars," he answered. "About what you make in a day."

To Haversham, he said, "Make it two pounds, and you're on. No sense betting if it's not fun to win and painful to lose."

The two Brits conferred quietly, then Haversham said, "The wager is that you can get the tank out of the sand before the tide is up using that truck, correct?"

"Couldn't have said it better, myself."

"Then you have yourself a bet, Sergeant." With that Haversham started the Jeep and moved it out of the way.

McCormick motioned Jimmy and Mack back into the cab, and asked the lieutenant to climb up onto the running board next to the open window. As he maneuvered the back of the truck into alignment in front of the tank, he explained what he was going to attempt to all three men. He'd never tried anything quite like it before, but given that there were no tank-wreckers in the area and that the tide was not going to slow down for them, he thought it was their best option.

Kenny left the truck idling—still on dry sand—and recruited some soldiers to help him with the wrecker's big steel tow cables. Jimmy and Mack climbed out and went to the rear of the wrecker. The lieutenant walked up the beach to direct the two tanks that were headed their way.

Jimmy and Mack got several of the soldiers who were standing around to help pull four lengths of "Marston Mat" from the bed of the truck. The ten-foot-long by fifteen-inch wide perforated steel plates had been developed for fast construction of temporary landing strips, but it was also useful for keeping heavy trucks from sinking into mud or soft sand.

Ten minutes later, McCormick had backed the wrecker onto the Marston Mats, right up against the nose of the half-submerged tank, and the cables and a couple of lengths of chain were attached to the tow rings on the front of the stuck tank. The rings were not only underwater, they were under the sand, as well, and took a while to excavate and hook up.

Finally, McCormick was ready to start orchestrating the operation. He had the crew in the stuck tank start its engine and wait for his signal.

He then directed the first tank on the hill to back up as slowly as it could. It had a cable attached to it that bobbed ten feet above the beach like a fat steel clothesline. The other end passed over the wrecker's cab and nested in the groove of the big pulley on the top of the wrecker's boom. From there it went straight down to where it was attached to the stuck tank's tow hooks. In theory, when the tank on the hill pulled the cable, it would be lifting the stuck tank straight up.

As the hill-top tank crept back, rather than the tank coming up, the wrecker was squashed down, compressing its massive steel springs until they were flat.

"It's not moving," the lieutenant said as he stood beside McCormick.

"I didn't expect it to, sir," he said, as he used hand signals to get the tank on the hill to keep creeping backwards. "I just want to put some upward tension on it for now."

When Kenny figured he had put as much stress into the wrecker's boom as it could stand, he had the tank on the hill hold its position. He then had the second hill-tank start crawling backwards. Its cable, which passed under the first tank, was attached to the frame of the wrecker at the front.

With the wrecker chained to the stuck tank at the rear, the wrecker didn't move very far as the hill-top tank pulled, and again Kenny directed the tank to pull until he thought they were nearing the limit of the cable and chains.

With the stuck tank being pulled upward and forward at the same time, Kenny then gave its crew the signal to try to drive slowly forward.

The engine roared and the water churned as the treads spun, but the tank didn't move. Kenny signaled the crew to stop.

"You have any other ideas, Sergeant?" the lieutenant asked McCormick.

"I'm not done beating this one, yet, sir," he said as he walked toward the still-mired tank.

He stood in the water and talked with the crew, then walked up the hill to confer with the other tanks crews.

As he walked down the hill, he announced to the troops who were standing around watching the show, "Everyone's going to want to get back about fifty yards. If one of these cables breaks it's going to snap around like the biggest bullwhip in the world, and it'll cut a man right in half."

As the two walked up the beach a safe distance, the lieutenant asked Kenny, "So, what's the plan, now?"

"Time for a Hail Mary," McCormick said.

"You mean a prayer?"

"That couldn't hurt," McCormick said, "but I was referring to the do-or-die football play."

He raised his arm, and saw an acknowledging hand signal from all three tank commanders.

"Here we go!" he said as he dropped his arm.

Immediately, all three commanders dropped into their tanks out of the way of a whipping cable.

A second later, the engines of all three tanks revved up.

The tanks on the hill inched backwards putting even more strain into the cables.

The truck scrunched even lower, and it let out loud mechanical groans.

The water at the sides of the stuck tank frothed as the treads spun at top speed.

And still the tank refused to budge.

Kenny began to raise his hand to stop the tanks before they crushed the wrecker or pulled it in half.

But then, he thought he saw the mired Sherman move.

He stared at it, not raising his arm any further, but not lowering it, either.

It *was* moving! *Everything* was moving!

The tanks on the hill were crawling backwards.

The wrecker was inching forward.

And the half-submerged tank was clawing its way up out of the water!

A cheer went up across the beach as the nose of the Sherman broke the surface.

Kenny raised his arm and spun it in a circle, meaning, *keep going, keep going!* and the four linked vehicles crept in unison, inch by inch, across the beach.

With the Sherman free of the suction of the sand and water, the driver had to back off on the throttle to keep from crawling up the back of the wrecker. It was at that point that Kenny put both arms over his head in an X, meaning *stop and hold*. He took off running, and waved Jimmy and Mack in, as well.

In two minutes they had the cables and chains disconnected, and Mack pulled the wrecker out of the way of the Sherman.

Again, the group cheered as the tank, under its own power, made it all the way out of the surf and onto dry sand.

As Jimmy and Mack, with the help of several soldiers, wound the cables back onto the winches, and put the Marston Mats back in the bed, the lieutenant extended his hand to McCormick.

"Thank you, Sergeant," he said. "You just saved a lot of asses from getting a serious chewing. No offense, but I wouldn't have bet a plug nickel that that was going to work, much less two day's pay."

"None taken, sir. Frankly, I wouldn't have either," McCormick said, "but I couldn't very well let a Brit intimidate the US Army."

At that moment they heard a Jeep start, and turned to see Haversham and his buddy driving away up the beach.

"Maybe he's going to *mail* me the two pounds," Kenny said with a laugh.

Monday, June 28, 1943

The next morning, Haversham and his two buddies approached the three Micks standing in the mess line.

"I've come to collect the two pounds you owe me," Charles said to Kenny.

"Small world," Kenny said. "I was hoping to run into you so I could say the very same thing to you."

"How do you reason that I owe you two pounds?" Haversham said. "It was those other two tanks that pulled the beast from the bloody sand, not your truck."

"They definitely helped," McCormick said, "but the bet was that I couldn't get the tank out *using* the truck. And I certainly used it ... I damn near killed it!"

"I meant using *only* the truck!" Haversham snapped in reply.

"Then you should have said that. Of course, I wouldn't have taken the bet in that case. That's just silly."

Kenny saw the embers of anger in Haversham's eyes, again, and had to decide whether to try to stoke them into a flame, or defuse the situation. He chose the latter ... mostly.

"Tell you what," Kenny said, "Because there was a misunderstanding—probably a language thing, old chap—you buy me a couple of packs of smokes—Camels—and we'll call it even." He extended his hand and added, "Sound good?"

"You can buy your own bloody fags!" Haversham snarled, and then stormed off.

Tuesday, June 29, 1943

Tuesday, the three Micks were again waiting in the mess line for breakfast when a British captain walked into the tent. A private noticed him, and called out, "At ease!"

Following protocol for a dining area, the talking in the tent stopped, but everyone remained seated and continued to eat. Those in line stood still, and waited for the captain to walk to the front of the line.

Instead, he said loudly, "As you were, gentlemen. Carry on." and fell into line behind the Micks.

"Good morning, sir," McCormick said. Then stepping aside, added, "Would you like to go ahead of us, sir?"

"I'm fine right here, son," Captain Noon replied. "If I wanted to be farther up in line I should have gotten here earlier, what?"

"If you say so, sir," Kenny replied.

As they moved along, the captain asked the sergeants where they were from, how long they'd been in England, what their hobbies were. In short, he was quite pleasant for a British officer.

While talking, Kenny glanced over the captain's shoulder and noticed Charles and his buddies standing at the far end of the tent. They weren't eating; they appeared to be just watching the line. Were they waiting for it to get short before coming over to eat? Did Charles have more antagonism in mind, but was put off by the captain's presence?

Kenny avoided looking right at them, but he kept them in view from the corner of his eye.

Finally, as they moved along the serving line, getting what the Army called breakfast slopped into their trays, Kenny noticed Charles pick up a full tray of food from a table, and start walking toward the line.

In his peripheral vision Kenny saw Charles passing by the line, a couple paces to his right. Relieved, he turned to watch the private serving oatmeal, and shifted his tray just in time to avoid it being dumped on top of his powdered eggs.

When he turned to go find a table, he ran smack into Charles.

It was obvious to Kenny that it was no accident. If they had been playing basketball, Charles would have just drawn a charging foul against Kenny.

The contact wasn't hard, and Kenny managed to keep his tray level, but Charles played his part brilliantly by throwing his tray up against his uniform and stumbling backwards, finally just standing there holding the tray in one hand hanging by his side, looking completely dumbfounded.

"Sorry, Sergeant," Kenny said, knowing he had been set up. "I didn't see you sneak up on me there."

"Sorry? Is that all you have to say you clumsy oaf?" Haversham blustered. "Who the devil's going to pay to have my uniform cleaned? Look at this mess!"

"Yeah, that is a shame," Kenny answered. "Tell you what; why don't you just take it out of the two pounds you owe me? How's that?"

Kenny wasn't sure where Charles wanted to take this. With the captain standing there, it seemed unlikely that he would knock the tray out of Kenny's hands and start a fight, but he readied himself for something like that.

Then it all came together.

"Here, here, now gentlemen," the captain said. "An unfortunate accident, but let's not have tempers flaring, shall we? You can both settle your differences in the ring Friday night. Seems it will do you both some good to let off a bit of steam."

"The ring, sir?" Kenny said.

"No one's told you, son?" the captain answered. "That's how we keep the peace around here. When two chaps have a row they put on the gloves and step into the ring on Friday night to settle it like gentlemen."

"I didn't know, sir," Kenny said. "That does sound quite civilized."

"Then you'll be there?" Charles said.

"You've gone to all this work to set it up Sergeant," Kenny said. "How could I refuse?"

"Good show," the captain said. "Friday night, then. Carry on." With that he slapped Charles on the shoulder, and walked off.

"You know, Sergeant," Kenny said to Haversham, "you didn't have to go to the bother of throwing food all over yourself to get me to spar a couple rounds with you. All you had to do was ask."

"Have you boxed before, Sergeant McCormick?" Charles asked.

"We had a similar set up when I was in boot camp. I was in the ring a couple of times."

"I can imagine," Charles sneered. "How was your record?"

"Draws. No knock-outs, if that's what you're worried about."

"Worried?" Charles chuckled. "I should think not."

"Good then," Kenny said and held out his right hand while holding his tray with the other. "Until Friday."

Charles shook Kenny's hand, and squeezed it again, as he had on the train. This time Kenny squeezed back, his grip more than a match for Haversham's.

"I don't know if you have it over here," Kenny said while maintaining his grip and watching Charles' eyes, "but there's a saying in the States that warns, to be careful what you wish for; you just might get it." With that he released Charles' hand and then slapped him on the shoulder as the captain had done. "Jolly good!" he said and turned to leave.

As he turned, Haversham's hand came up under Kenny's tray. But Kenny would have been surprised if he *hadn't* done something like that, and he easily rotated the tray out of the way.

"Careful there, old boy," Kenny said. "It'd be a shame if you ended up with *two* trays of food on your uniform."

"*Bloody tosser*," they heard Charles mumble as the Micks walked away.

"*Tosser*," Kenney repeated to his buddies. "I am going to *have* to find an English to American dictionary."

The rest of the week passed without any more emergencies or antagonism from Charles. Apparently, getting his captain to "suggest' that they settle their differences in the ring was all he had been looking for.

Friday, July 2, 1943

Friday at suppertime, McCormick stood in the doorway of the mess tent eating a cracker and watching a crew erect a very authentic boxing ring, complete with a canvas-covered floor that was raised four feet off the ground.

As the crew strung the ropes between the corner posts, Mack came up beside Kenny, and said, "You didn't eat very much tonight. You nervous?"

"No. I just don't want much in my stomach if I'm going to be taking punches there," he answered. With a nod toward the ring, he said, "The general sure is serious about fight-night. I heard he bought that ring with his own money. It sure is a damn sight fancier than the one we had in boot camp."

By seven o'clock a good size crowd was gathered around the ring. On one side, about twenty feet back, two flatbed trucks had been brought in, and a row of chairs was set up across each for senior officers. On the hood of one of the trucks was a blackboard that listed the ten fights scheduled for tonight. Haversham vs. McCormick was the last one. Kenny guessed that Charles had pulled some strings to make sure his bout was the main event.

Most of the fights were grudge matches between two soldiers who had some score to settle. Fortunately—for the combatants *and* the audience—the bouts were limited to three three-minute rounds. Those matches were strictly amateur-night brawls. Arms flailing, wild punches, a couple of bloody noses, and not a single knock-down. These were guys who were used to getting drunk and fighting in bar rooms. Wearing gloves, and with no furniture to bust up, they really had no idea what they were doing.

Two of the matches, however, were actually interesting to Kenny. The first was between two Americans, and the other between two Brits. There was no anger involved. These were just men who obviously enjoyed the sport of boxing. All four of the men were quite good in Kenny's opinion. Those matches generated a fair amount of betting, and Kenny guessed that they were probably in the ring every week.

Interestingly—and Kenny didn't think it was coincidence—the last bout of the evening, his, was the only one where a Brit was fighting a Yank.

When they climbed into the ring, Charles started dancing around and going through a shadowboxing show. His countrymen loved it. Kenny got the impression that he, too, was no stranger to this ring.

At one point he looked over to see Captain Noon, on one of the trucks, give Charles a thumbs-up.

Finally, the referee called Kenny and Charles to the center of the ring, and he explained the rules—for the tenth time. The two men bumped gloves and went to their corners.

Outside the ropes in Kenny's corner were Jimmy and Mack. Haversham's two buddies were outside his corner.

As he waited for the bell to ring, Kenny heard his name from ringside. He looked down to see the lieutenant from the beach.

"Show him what you've got, Sergeant!" he said. "We're all behind you! I've even got ten bucks on you. Don't let me down."

"I'll see what I can do, sir," Kenny said as the bell rang.

Charles danced out to the middle of the ring, and Kenny walked out ... and right into a right jab to the face. Fortunately, Kenny got his glove up quickly enough to fend off the blow, and he also managed to block the left cross that followed.

For the rest of the three minutes, it was pretty much the same thing. Charles danced and punched, and Kenny covered up and took the blows.

When the bell rang to end the round, Kenny walked back to his corner and sat down on the stool.

"Geeze! Are you okay, Kenny?" Jimmy asked. "You're taking quite a beating out there."

Kenny swished some water in his mouth, and spit it into a bucket, then said, "I've had worse."

"You ever consider throwing a punch yourself?" Mack asked him. "You do understand that you don't take turns every other round?"

"That's good to know," Kenny said as he stood up. "I'll keep that in mind."

Waiting for the bell, Kenny shook out his arms, and he happened to look down and see the lieutenant looking up at him with a questioning look.

"I'm okay," Kenny shouted to him over the noise of the crowd, "Don't worry about me."

"I'm not; I'm worried about my ten bucks!" he hollered back.

The second round went pretty much like the first, except that Kenny did throw half a dozen punches. Most had little effect, but one uppercut to the chin apparently caught Charles by surprise, and he actually had to take a few steps back away from Kenny. The Yanks in the crowd loved that.

He recovered quickly, and came at Kenny with that usually-suppressed fire in his eyes.

Kenny backpedaled staying just out of Charles' reach for several seconds, and then the bell rang.

Kenny relaxed, let his arms down, and turned toward his corner. That's when Charles let lose with a right hook aimed at Kenny's head.

Kenny caught the motion in the corner of his eye and managed to bend forward just in time to let the punch graze across the back of his head.

As the Yanks booed the late punch, Kenny shouted to the referee, "Can he do that?"

The ref wiggled his finger at Charles as he walked to his corner.

"Apparently, he can," Kenny said as he sat down.

"Okay," Mack said, "that was better, but you don't have ten rounds to pick up your speed little by little. You've got to give him everything you've got when you go back out there."

Then Kenny heard the lieutenant shout, "Now's the time for another Hail Mary, Sergeant!"

Jimmy leaned down close to Kenny's ear, and said privately, "I've been watching what you're doing out there; you're setting him up, aren't you?"

As Kenny stood up he looked at Jimmy and grinned.

Then the bell rang.

As Kenny expected, Charles came out of his corner burning mad and wanting to end the match with a quick knock-out.

While still charging at him, Charles threw a strong left jab at Kenny's face.

Kenny leaned to his right and down slightly, causing the punch to go beside his head and over his left shoulder. At the same time, he threw a left jab of his own, connecting solidly in Charles' stomach. Before Charles could bring his left glove back to protect his head, Kenny landed a hard right hook to the side of his head.

The combination was physically punishing to Charles, but more importantly, it surprised the shit out of him, and that was exactly what Kenny was going for.

The blow to his left caused Charles to take a step to his right. At the same time, he dropped his right arm and extended it to help catch his balance

With his right wide open, Kenny came around with a powerful left hook, twisting his whole upper body into the punch.

Charles staggered to his left and looked at Kenny as if he didn't know who he was; as if some other person—who knew how to box—had come out of his corner for the third round.

Still unable to believe what was happening, Charles charged Kenny and threw a left jab at his stomach. He followed it immediately with a right hook to Kenny's head.

Kenny rotated and leaned his upper body to his left. He took Charles' left in his side, and his right went over his shoulder.

Kenny responded with a right jab that slid under Charles' extended right arm and landed squarely on his jaw. He followed it with a left hook to the side of Charles' head, and completed the combination with a right uppercut that Charles managed to partially deflect as he brought his right arm back in to protect himself.

By this time, the crowd was going completely nuts. The Yanks were cheering, shouting, whistling, and the Brits were hollering instructions on how Charles should deal with the sudden change in the situation.

Kenny was sure that the suggestions, such as "*Don't let the blighter knock you about like that!*", "*Keep your bloody guard up!*", and "*Aim for his blooming chin!*" probably just made Charles more angry if he heard them at all.

Finally realizing that he was in an actual boxing match, Charles came at Kenny a little more cautiously the next time. He kept his arms in close to his body, and his gloves in front of his face as he watched Kenny's body movements very closely.

Kenny threw a couple of jabs that Charles easily absorbed with his gloves, and them Kenny saw Charles' right elbow come up.

After two rounds of fighting, Kenny knew that that was how Charles threw a right hook, and it had lots of follow through. Kenny knew that it was a flashy way to throw the punch—fun to watch—but it was far less effective than throwing the punch from the guarded position—arms close to the body—punching up and across, and then quickly pulling the arm back in for protection.

A Kiss For Luck!

The raising of the elbow did two things. It telegraphed the coming right hook to Kenny so he had plenty of time to prepare for it, and it left Charles' right rib cage wide open.

As the punch came across at the left side of Kenny's head, he easily ducked under it—another thing that would be difficult if the hook was thrown correctly. Starting from his bent and slightly rotated position, Kenny came up and across with a left hook that slammed into Charles' lower ribs—the ones most easily broken.

Charles took the blow better than Kenny expected, and Charles managed to come over the top of Kenny's right arm with his left. and connect pretty solidly with Kenny's head.

Kenny started stepping backwards, but Charles kept right after him, striking out at him with repeated right jabs that Kenny managed to block or deflect.

Finally, Kenny planted his feet and let Charles run into him. Charles' final jab passed over Kenny's left shoulder, and Kenny used the opening to bring his right fist up between their bodies in a powerful uppercut.

The blow snapped Charles' head back, stunning him enough that he dropped his left hand from in front of his face.

Kenny took the opening to plant a right, then a left, then another right jab to Charles' face.

Charles staggered backwards, but Kenny followed, hitting him with a right and then a left hook.

Finally, Kenny pulled his fists into a guarding position, and just looked at his opponent.

Charles stood on wobbly legs with blood running from his nose. He was barely able to lift his fists chest high. He seemed completely dazed.

The Yanks in the crowd were yelling, "*Finish him! Finish him!*" and the Brits were either booing or hollering for Charles to get his bloody fists up and *snap the sod out of it.*

Kenny knew he could knock him out with one good right hook, but he didn't. He stood there for another five seconds ignoring the crowd until the bell rang.

He then stepped up close to Charles, put his arms around him, and helped him back to his corner.

As he sat down heavily on the wooden stool, Kenny leaned down close to his ear, and over the noise of the crowd, said, "Let's call it a draw, okay?"

Saturday July 3, 1943

The next day, Kenny's entire body was sore. It had been a long time since his muscles had taken that kind of pounding.

He was under the hood of a Chrysler deuce-and-a-half truck pulling the cylinder head when he heard a Jeep enter the compound and stop. He looked up to see Charles walking toward him. He was alone, for once.

He walked up to the truck and looked into the engine compartment where tools and parts were scattered everywhere. "Giving her a tune-up?"

"A complete rebuild, actually," Kenny said. "Somebody drove it off the ramp of a landing craft when they were still in twenty feet of water. Went down like a rock. Hydrolocked the engine, probably bent a rod, and may have blown a hole through a piston."

"Ah, yes. I see," Charles said.

Kenny got the impression he didn't understand anything he had just said. And he seemed uncharacteristically uncomfortable.

"Are you okay, Sergeant Haversham?" Kenny asked, looking down at him from his perch on the fender of the truck.

Charles stared at the mechanical mish-mosh under the hood for a few seconds, then turned, and said, "I'd like to bury the hatchet, as you Yanks say." He held out his hand, and added, "And please call me Charles."

Kenny wiped his hand on his coveralls and shook Charles' hand. "My pleasure," he said. "I was afraid you were coming out here to ask for a rematch."

"Not a chance!" Charles laughed as he touched his tender nose. He thought for a moment, and then said, "You're a better man than I gave you credit for, Sergeant McCormick. Certainly a better boxer. You had me dead to rights in the ring last night, and you didn't press your advantage. Why is that?"

"The bell rang," Kenny said with a shrug.

"Bollocks!" Charles said. "You had plenty of time to set me on my arse." He thought for a second, and added, "And every reason to. I've been a wanker to you since the moment we met. I thought the match last night would be a doodle for me. I'd show you a thing or two in the first rounds, and then finish it quickly in the last. You turned the tables quite neatly. I *appreciate* that you didn't take the knock-out—my head hurts enough as it is—but I don't understand it. I didn't plan on letting *you* off so easily."

Kenny climbed down from the truck, and leaned against the fender.

"Cards on the table, there's three reasons I let the fight end the way it did last night," he said as he took a pack of Camels from his pocket. He shook one out and pulled it from the pack with his lips. He shook another out and offered it to Charles. Kenny lit both of them with his Zippo.

"Number one," Kenny began, "I didn't let *you* beat *me*, and that was my main goal when I climbed into the ring. Anything more than that would just be *piling-on*, as we say. Second, I figured that knocking you down in front of your home crowd would be rubbing salt in the wound and would be a little humiliating. I hoped that if I spared you that, you'd appreciate it enough to stay off my back for a while. I'm glad to see that I read you right about that."

"Quite magnanimous," Charles said as he blew out a lung full of smoke. "As I said, I do appreciate the gesture. What's the third reason?"

"The last person I knocked out boxing," Kenny said, "didn't wake up for three days. The doctors couldn't be sure if he ever would. That was my brother. It scared the living shit out of me. I swore I'd never get into the ring again, after that. But that changed in boot camp. They had the same kind of deal that you have here. If two guys have a beef, they settle it in the ring, and that's supposed to be the end of it. I didn't have much choice about getting into the ring unless I wanted to spend my whole time there cleaning latrines, but I did swear that I'd never knock anyone out again if I could help it."

"Did you fight with your brother a lot? Is that where you learned to box?" Charles asked.

"Actually, my Dad taught all three of us to box. He probably would have turned pro if he hadn't met my mother and started a family. But he never lost his love for it."

"He taught you well," Charles said. "Did he teach you the strategy of holding back until the end?"

"Not specifically," Kenny said, "but he did teach us that there's a lot more to boxing than hitting hard. He used to tell us to use our heads for something besides stopping punches."

"Good advise," Charles said as he crushed out his cigarette with his boot. "Well, I need to be getting back," he said. "But I'm glad we're all square." He extended his hand one more time.

"I am too," Kenny said as they shook. "I figure there're enough enemies on the other side of the Channel; I don't need any more on this side."

Half way back to the Jeep, Charles stopped and turned around.

"Do you intend to see Lily again, Sergeant McCormick?" he asked.

"Call me Kenny," he replied. "And yes, I do. As soon as I can get a few days of leave."

"Her favorite color is red, and her favorite flower is the gardenia," Charles said. "She likes crème-center chocolates, sweet wines, and Glen Miller." With a soft salute, he added, "Good luck, old boy," and headed for the Jeep.

It would be sixty days from his date of arrival before Kenny was eligible for leave, and during that time he wrote to Lily three or four times a week. The letters never mentioned the trouble he had had with Charles, or its eventual resolution.

When he was finally able to write that he was coming to Birmingham to see her on the following Saturday, he told her not to wait at the station for him, because he wasn't sure what train he'd be able to get on. He said he would pick her up at Queen Elizabeth Hospital as long as he got in at a decent hour.

Saturday, August 21, 1943

Saturday morning, wearing his dress uniform and carrying a cloth satchel with a change of clothes, Kenny skipped breakfast and hitched a ride into Barnstaple to catch the first train. While waiting, he bought a small loaf of bread from a vendor, and filled a flask that had once held whiskey, with black coffee. He would eat his breakfast on the train.

It was half past noon when Kenny got off the train at the Birmingham New Street Station. It was three and a half miles to the hospital from there, but he was well conditioned for the walk, and he wanted to do some shopping before he met Lily, anyway. He used the men's room to wash up and splash on some cologne, and then headed out onto Queen Street.

Kenny arrived at the lobby of the Nuffield House Nurses' Home at about quarter past two, and asked for Lily. While the girl used her telephone to "ring her up," Kenny looked at the photographs on the wall of Queen Elizabeth during the dedication ceremony just four years earlier.

When Lily came into the lobby a minute later, Kenny broke into a wide smile. Although he had thought about her every day, he suddenly realized that he hadn't remembered how beautiful she was.

She wore a simple one-piece dress that stopped about six inches below her knees. Although it was designed to meet the government's austerity regulations of "CC41"—the Civilian Clothing Act of 1941—it was well made and quite fashionable.

The dress narrowed at the waist and flowed over her figure like it had been made just for her. It was pale blue and had a wide black stripe, perhaps an inch and a half, that ran over the tops of the padded shoulders and down the outside of each arm. An identical stripe ran all the way down each side, from under the arms to the hem. A black fabric half-belt was tied in a bow at the front, and a narrow black placket with three buttons—all fastened—joined the black collar.

There was a small *faux pocket* cut into the fabric above the left breast and on the front of the dress at the right hip. The tops of the pockets were accented with a narrow black strip. To meet the fabric-saving austerity rules, there were no actual pockets below the slits.

On her feet she wore black leather sling-back pumps with two-inch heels, and over her left shoulder hung a fairly large, but thin, matching leather purse.

Her hair was rolled back above her forehead and on the sides, and lay lightly on the back of her neck, just reaching her collar.

"Wow!" he said as she walked toward him. "You look wonderful! Even better than I'd been imagining. I didn't know if you'd be wearing a nurse's uniform here at the hospital."

"Normally, yes, but never if we're going out," she said as she took his arm and he escorted her out through the door. "We're very strict about germ transfer here. We've a marvelous record when it comes to cross-infection in our wards. It's almost non-existent, actually!"

After savoring her *ac-tually*, he made a mental note about her apparent passion regarding infection and germs—or the lack thereof—in case their conversation stalled later on. He then fell back on another bit of his sister's advice; *you can never go wrong by complimenting a woman's hair or her clothes.*

"Well, I'm sure this is much prettier than any nurse's uniform, anyway," he said.

"It may be more the fashion," she said, "but our uniforms were designed by Norman Hartnell. Not every girl my age can say she wears a Norman Hartnell original every day!"

Kenny's blank expression told her that he had no idea who Norman Hartnell might be.

She laughed that little twitter, and said, "Mr. Hartnell is dressmaker to the *Queen*, as well as to half of London's society elite."

"Ah! Then you *are* a lucky girl," he said. "My attire was designed by Sears and Roebuck, I think. Clothiers to *everyone*!"

She laughed, but he wasn't sure she knew who or what Sears and Roebuck was. He thought maybe she was just being polite.

"I brought you something," he said to break the awkwardness of the moment.

He reached into his satchel and took out a box of chocolates.

"Oh! Why thank you," she said as she took it from him.

"They're all crème-centers," he said. "They were a bit hard to find, but not as hard as a gardenia corsage."

"That was sweet of you," she said with a smile. "Really. I appreciate it, but frankly, I'm glad you couldn't find any gardenias. I really don't care for them; there's a sad childhood memory attached to them." She looked at the box of chocolates, and said with a shrug, "And I'm afraid I'm allergic to chocolate."

"Son of a ..." Kenny laughed as the light came on. "Just out of curiosity, what's your favorite color?"

"Blue," she answered.

"And do you like sweet wines or dry wines?"

"I don't care for wine, at all, actually. It always seems to give me a headache. I much prefer a pint of ale."

"How about music?" Kenny asked. "Do you like Glen Miller, by any chance?"

"I didn't care much for American music, before," she said, "But it does rather grow on one."

Kenny laughed again. "Your friend Charles set me up," he said, "and I swallowed it hook, line, and sinker. I should have known better." He then told her the story of the encounters of their first week together, including the boxing match and his "bury the hatchet" visit the next day.

"That's terrible," she said. "I really must apologize for Charles' behavior. He really can be beastly." Kenny could tell she was amused, however.

"Go ahead and laugh," he said. "It's a funny story. He set me up with the chocolates and flowers just like I set him up in the ring. Turnabout's fair play."

She did chuckle, but then said, "I'm sorry. You were being very sweet ... or at least trying."

As they walked on, he took the chocolates back from her and returned them to his satchel. Then he took out another box wrapped in plain paper and tied with a string. It was seven or eight inches square, and less than an inch thick.

"I know I'm on solid ground with this one," Kenny said as he handed it to her. "Charles had nothing to do with it."

They were passing a small park at that point in their walk, and Lily decided to sit on one of the benches to open the package. She untied the string, turned the package over, and then carefully laid the paper open. She was looking at the bottom of a polished wooden box, but it had no markings on it so she still didn't know what she was holding.

She turned the box over, and saw the name "Faber-Castell" embossed in the lower right corner. She sucked in her breath in surprise.

She flipped the catch open and lifted the cover. Inside were twenty-four colored pencils. There was a charcoal black pencil at one end, and a white one at the other. In between were varying shades of violet, blue, green, yellow, orange, and red. Across the top was a pencil sharpener and an eraser.

Her mouth hung open as she stared at the gift and ran her fingers across the pencils as if she needed to be sure they were real.

"They're marvelous!" she finally said. "But ... but I can't accept them. I mustn't."

"What? What did I do now?" Kenny said. "You told me that you always wanted a set of artist pencils. Nobody I've ever heard of is allergic to pencils."

"I love them," she said, "but they're far too extravagant. We've only just met. What would people think if I accepted such gifts from you?"

"That you're a lucky girl?" he answered.

"That I'm a tart!" she replied.

"Okay, I think I can guess what a *tart* is—outside the context of a pastry—and I think you're wrong. It's a set of pencils; how could anyone read something *tarty* into that? If it were jewelry or nylon stockings then I could ..."

"You can get nylon stockings?" she cut him off.

He laughed. "No. They stopped making them in the States when we got into the war. All the nylon's going into parachutes now," he said. "The point is that this isn't a *romantic* gift, it's just a gift gift. Like a birthday present."

"But it's not my birthday," she said. "And there's plenty of biddies and old hags in the dormitory whose tongues would be wagging if I came back with something this fine."

"How about if we dump out the chocolates," he suggested, "and you hide the pencils in the box and smuggle them to your room that way?"

She laughed. "I don't think I could get away with it. I'm a terrible liar. My face would turn red and I'd give the whole game away the moment someone said, *'What a lovely box of chocolates. What kind are they?'*"

"Okay, if you're no Mata Hari and if the gift is too extravagant like it is," he offered, "how about if I just give you six pencils at a time? One of each color, each time I see you."

She looked at the pencils again, and ran her fingers over the whole set.

"I guess *that* would be all right," she said. "I mean it is just six pencils ..."

"Exactly!" he said. "Problem solved!"

"I'll carry them for now, though, if you don't mind," she said while closing the lid.

As she put the box into her purse, and then folded the paper to put in her purse, as well, he said, "So, is there any place nearby where we can get some lunch? I don't know about you, but I had a small breakfast a long time ago, and I'm starving."

"Do you fancy kidney pie?" she asked.

"I've never had it, but if you say it's good, I'll give it a try," he said. "I could sure go for a beer, too."

"Then I've just the place!" she said as she stood up.

As they walked, Lily explained some of the history of the old buildings they passed, and of Birmingham in general. Finally, they came to a dark old building with a thatched roof. Suspended above the door, hanging over the sidewalk, was a carved wooden sign featuring a standing bear wearing a bishop's miter on its head. Below the bear, the sign read, "Bishop and Bear Pub 1641."

As Kenny held the door open for her, he asked, "Is there a story behind the name of this place?"

"There's almost always a story behind the name of a pub," she said. "Some of them may actually be true, even," she added with a laugh.

There were a dozen or more people in the pub, mostly men, and mostly in the uniform of one army or another. Two Canadian's got up just as Kenny and Lily entered, so they took their places at a heavy wooden table near the window. Almost immediately the proprietor came toward them.

He was a big man; probably in his late forties or early fifties. He seemed to be quite fit, except for a pronounced limp, the product of an artificial left leg.

When he arrived at the table, Kenny realized the man was actually *huge*. He was tall and thick and wide, with every part of him well proportioned.

"Hello, Lily!" he said. "We haven't seen you 'round in a while. Who's your friend?"

"Tom Laughlin, this is Kenny McCormick," Lily said. "I'm showing him the finer sights of Birmingham."

"So you thought you'd show him the *Bishop* for contrast, what?" he kidded Lily as he extended his hand to Kenny. His deep voice went well below baritone and even bass, and into *basso profondo*.

"Pleased to meet you, Tom," Kenny said as they shook. Tom's hand enveloped his, and he knew he did not want to get into a squeezing contest with *this* man. "Are you the bear of *Bishop and Bear* fame?"

Tom laughed, and it sounded like something echoing from a deep well. "Long before my time," he said. "Lily'll tell you the story, won't ya lass? Now, what can I get for you two?"

"Two pints and two steak and kidney pies, please," Lily said.

"I'm afraid there's a lot more pie to that than steak and kidney, these days," Tom said. "What with all the rationing,"

"I'm sure Margaret is doing it up fine," Lily said. She then lowered her voice, and asked, "Do you have any pudding today, by chance?"

"Maggie made up a steamed chocolate pudding this morning; I believe there's a slice left."

"We'll take it!" Lily said to Tom. To Kenny, she said, "You'll love it!"

Kenny wondered what kind of pudding came by the *slice*, but he didn't say anything.

Tom came back shortly, and set the two glasses of ale on the table. "The pie'll be just a minute or two," he said and left.

Kenny raised his glass and waited for her to do the same.

"Here's to a short rest of the war, and a very long peace," he said.

She clicked her glass to his and said, "Cheers to that!"

He sipped the ale, and made a face.

"What's wrong?" Lily said.

"It's *warm*!"

She laughed, and said, "Oh, that's right. You drink your pints cold in the States, don't you?" She made a face of her own, and added, "Sounds dreadful."

"When in Rome ..." he said, and took a good swallow. "It does *taste* good," he admitted.

"So, tell me about the bishop and the bear," he said.

"Not far from here," she began, "in 1641, there was a bear-garden."

"Wait. A *bear* garden? Not a beer garden?"

"Beer gardens are in Germany," she said. "No, a *bear*-garden. It's where they used to have bear baiting contests. It was a horrible blood sport where they chained a poor bear to a post in the middle of a pit, and set dogs on it until they finally killed it."

"Didn't it fight back? I've seen a bear in the wild stand up to a whole pack of hunting dogs and live to tell his bear buddies about it."

"Oh, yes, he fought back. That was the *fun*," she said making quote fingers. "But if a dog was hurt badly or killed, they just sent in another dog. The bear never stood a chance." She shook her head and said, "Ghastly business!"

"I agree," he said. "Enter the Bishop?"

"Yes. As the story goes," she went on after a sip of ale, "a bishop made his way through the spectators one day, and climbed over the wall into the pit. He started shouting at the crowd how they were all sinners to be there laughing and cheering as they were.

"They began booing him and when no one left the arena, he began jabbing the dogs with his staff to keep them away from the bear. Apparently, he reasoned that if the dogs weren't attacking the bear there would be no amusement, and everyone would leave.

"Well, he wandered too close to the bear—who didn't recognize him as his benefactor—and the bear swiped his claws across the bishop's neck.

"A few men in the crowd—probably eager to make some points with God—dragged the bishop out of the pit and carried him to this pub—which had some other name at the time—and here he died."

"Bears one; bishops nothing," Kenny said. "At least he died for a noble cause."

"You might think that," she said, "but the reason he tried to stop the show that day wasn't to protect innocent animals from cruelty; it was because it was Sunday, and he thought it was a sin that they were there enjoying an afternoon of entertainment rather than being in church."

"So, was that the beginning of the end of bear baiting," Kenny said, "when people start dying, not just animals?"

"Hardly," she said. "Parliament didn't outlaw the sport until the 1830's sometime." She took another sip of her ale, and repeated, "Ghastly!"

Just then, Tom showed up with two pieces of steaming hot steak and kidney pie.

Even if Kenny had not been starving, it would have smelled wonderful. In the shallow bowl were pieces of onions and carrots swimming in a dark brown gravy. Also in the gravy were four small cubes of what Kenny assumed was the steak and the kidney. Perched on the edge of the bowl was a square of flaky, golden-brown pastry crust.

Tom leaned down and in what he probably considered a whisper, said, "Maggie pushed a couple extra cubes of meat into your slices, there. Enjoy yourselves!" He then walked away humming a tune that Kenny didn't recognize.

Lily picked up her fork, and said, "*Bon appétit!*"

"I hope it tastes as good as it smells," Kenny said, sticking his fork through an onion and into a carrot. He put it into his mouth, chewed a few times, and then looked at Lily with surprise.

"Is it okay?" she asked.

"That gravy is incredible!" he said around the chewed vegetables.

She laughed. "I hoped you'd like it," she said. "They make it with Guinness!"

"Well, that's too bad," he said after swallowing. "I was going to get the recipe to bring to the cooks back in camp. I don't think the brass would go for that, though."

By the time they had finished their pie, Kenny had also finished his ale. When Tom arrived with the pudding, he also brought another pint.

"That's pudding?" Kenny said, looking at what appeared to him to be a slice of a cake that had been baked in a round bowl rather than a square pan.

"A sweet pudding, yes," she said. "I think you call it dessert. We also have savory puddings, like Yorkshire, that are made with a meat stock."

He cut off a piece with his fork, and tasted it.

She watched his face closely.

He smiled, and said, "This is, without question, the best meal I've had in a year." He swallowed, and added, "And when I include the company, it may be my best meal *ever*."

She laughed, and turned just a little red.

"I'm enjoying myself very much, as well," she said as she took a bite of the pudding.

When Tom came to clear the empty plate, he set the bill on the table. "Unless you'd like another pint," he said.

"Not for me," Kenny said. "That was perfect. Would you like another?" he asked Lily, who still had an ounce or two in her glass.

"No, thank you. One is really my limit."

Kenny took out his wallet and drew out some bills. "Do you take American money?" he asked.

"I'll take just about anything but deutschmarks, lira, and yen," he said.

"I'm happy to go Dutch," Lily said. "Despite the crude saying, I don't believe you're overpaid."

"Not a chance," he said. "This is my treat. I may not be paid much, but I also don't have a lot to spend it on while I'm stuck on base." He handed Tom the money and he left.

Before putting his wallet away, Kenny said, "Would you take out your pencil set, please?"

As she took it from her purse, she said, "You're not going to take it back already, are you? You're not going to make me choose my six favorites."

"No," he said as he slipped something from his wallet. "I have a favor to ask." he handed her the piece of paper that she had written her address on; the corner of the page with a black and white sketch of a goldfinch. "Would you color it for me?"

Her smile positively beamed. "Oh, I should draw you a new one," she said. "Bigger and much better."

"No," he said. "Thank you, but this one is special to me."

"All right," she said happily, as she opened the case. She stared at the three shades of yellow for a moment, and then selected the darkest one.

She held the paper stretched between her finger and thumb, and began drawing dark lines on what to Kenny seemed to be random parts of the bird. After a while, she replaced the pencil and took out the next lighter shade. Again, she filled in pieces of the bird, here and there.

Finally, she switched to the lightest shade, and she began filling in the last of the white areas, but also going over the other shades so that they all blended together without being able to see where one shade ended and the next began.

He watched her face as she swished the pencil lightly over the paper. She was pure concentration; he doubted that she even remembered that he was there. This truly was her passion. He smiled as he saw the tip of her tongue peek out between her lips as she used shades of orange to finish the fine details of the beak and the feet.

Finally, she held the paper up to look at. She cocked her head one way and then the other, assessing it.

"I really wish you'd let me draw a new one for you," she said as she handed it to him.

"Wow!" he said. "It looks like something from a bird guide. You're amazing! I'd have just colored the whole thing with the same pencil. Yellow is yellow to me. This looks like it's ready to fly off the page."

"Thank you," she said, turning just a tiny bit red. "You're kind to say that, but I really can do better."

"Well, I'm happy to let you prove it, but even if you do, this little birdie is going to stay with me." He handed it back to her for a moment, and said, "Will you sign it for me? I'm sure it's going to be worth something someday."

She laughed. "Oh, I'm sure," she said as she wrote her name. "That and a rationing coupon will get you a pound of butter ... if you have a pound Sterling to go with it."

He put the drawing in his wallet, and she put the pencils in her purse. Having used them now, she knew that giving up all but six of them was going to be very difficult. He knew that, too, and he smiled inwardly.

As they got up from the table, she said, "I forgot to ask you; where will you stay the night, while you're up here on leave?"

"The train station, probably," he said. "I'm used to that kind of thing. They have plenty of benches and a good men's room where I can wash up."

"Are you being serious?" she said. "The *train station?*"

"I've slept in a lot worse places," he said. "At least it has a roof, and it's not made of green canvas."

"Wait here," she said, and left him by the door as she walked toward the back of the pub. She went around behind the bar and started to talk to Tom. He couldn't hear them over the noise of the patrons, but it was obvious they were talking about him. Tom looked over at him and nodded his head as Lily spoke. Then she pointed toward the ceiling, and he nodded again. At one point he could clearly read her lips saying, "*The train station, my God!*"

Finally, Tom raised his big right hand and waved him over.

"Yes, sir?" Kenny said as he leaned against the bar opposite Tom and Lily.

"Lily tells me you're planning to sleep in the train station. Is that right?"

"It seemed like an economical place to ..."

"Twaddle!" Tom cut him off. "You'll do no such thing. You've come to our little rock in the sea to help us defend her against that lunatic Hitler; the least I can do is give you a place to rest your bones." He pointed upwards, and said, "I've a room upstairs you can call your own tonight and whenever you're in Birmingham again."

"That's very kind of you," Kenny said. "What's your nightly rate?" he asked, reaching for his wallet. "I'm happy to pay in advance."

"I'll not take a blessed farthing from you," Tom said. "As long as you're here serving King and Country, you're a guest of Tom Laughlin." Then he added, "Of course, I can't feed you for free or keep you in ale; I do have to make a livelihood."

Kenny reached his hand across the bar, and said, "Thank you very much, Mr. Laughlin. I'm honored that you'd take me in."

"You're welcome, son. And it's Tom while you're under my roof," he said. "Lily'll show you the room and the loo. I have a hard time with those stairs, what with a tree-trunk for a leg and all."

Lily led Kenny through the kitchen and out the back door. To their right was a set of outdoor stairs that climbed the back wall of the old building.

She went up first, and Kenny was left to watch her bottom shift smoothly under the fabric of her dress as she climbed the stairs directly in front of him. He knew it was ungentlemanly to stare at her behind that way, but he rationalized that resisting the urge to reach out and *touch* it was somehow chivalrous.

At the top, Lily opened another door, and they stepped inside on the second floor of the building.

"Those *are* kind of narrow stair treads," Kenny said as he closed the door. "I can see why Tom would have trouble going up and down them with a wooden leg."

"Oh, he takes those just fine," Lily said. "It's the next set that gives him a pause."

She pointed to the end of the hall, and said, "The loo's down there on the right, by the way." She then opened a door that was both narrow and short, and stepped into what Kenny thought was a closet. She reached over to the wall and rotated a switch. It made a loud *clack!* and a single bare bulb came on way above them.

The stairs that the bulb illuminated could be more correctly described as a ladder with wide steps, than as a stairway. Kenny could see why Tom didn't want to scale these.

Holding onto the railing on either side of the steps, Lily started up. The stairs were steep enough that Kenny really had to wait for Lily to reach the top before he followed, but he realized that as she neared the top, he would have a pretty clear view up her dress.

He turned around, and said, "Let me know when you're at the top."

At first, she didn't understand, then she turned and looked down at him and saw him standing backwards. She flushed as it dawned on her how she was about to expose herself, and she was glad that he wasn't able to see that, either.

"Made it," she said as she stepped to the side and wait for him to make the climb.

They were standing in the middle of a room that resembled a large tent with plaster walls, and the middle was the only place where they *could* stand up straight.

The ends of the fifteen-foot long room were vertical, but shaped like triangles. The other two walls leaned inward, meeting a heavy wooden beam at the top that ran the length of the room. Two small dormer windows were set into one of the leaning walls, and let a surprising amount of light into the room.

Opposite the windows a wood-framed single bed was pushed against the wall. At the head of the bed was a small nightstand with a table lamp on it. Kenny pulled the chain, and the light came on.

"All the comforts of home," he said. "This is very nice. And a darned sight quieter than the train station, I might add. Thank you for arranging it."

"It didn't take much persuading," she said. "Tom was happy to help out."

"I get the impression you're more than just a customer to Tom," Kenny said. "Is he an uncle or something?"

"He might as well be," she said. "He and my father were in the Great War, and they met in hospital. Tom had lost his leg and Papa had lost an arm. They became close friends, so Tom's been around my whole life."

"Where's your dad, now?"

"He's with the Home Guard. We have a little cottage that's been in the family for generations, down on the Channel in Dover. They've set him up with a radio, and he watches the sky and the water for enemy planes and boats, and sends an alarm if he sees anything. He's very proud to be serving again."

"That's fantastic," Kenny said. "You must be proud of him, too."

"I am," she said. "I just hope he stays safe."

She was thoughtful for a moment, and then said, "You were quite the proper gentleman for averting your eyes when I went up the stairs just now. I'm embarrassed to say that I completely forgot myself." The color came up in her cheeks to be talking—however euphemistically—about exposing herself to him.

Being called a *proper gentleman*, he suddenly felt a bit embarrassed for having ogled her behind on the first set of stairs.

"I guessed you were probably unaware of ... well ... the *situation*," he said. With a little bow, he added, "I am happy to have protected thine honor, fair Lady."

She laughed, and replied, "The Lady doth believe that such gallantry should be rewarded. Wouldst thou be offended to receive a kiss from such a forgetful damsel?"

"On the contrary, my Lady," he said. "I wouldst be delighted to be thusly honored."

She took a step closer, and with her eyes open, she leaned in and placed her lips against his. The kiss quickly increased in intensity as their mouths moved against one another. She closed her eyes as their lips parted just a fraction of an inch, and she touched his lips with the tip of her tongue. Then she broke the kiss and looked into his eyes.

"The Lady doth admit," she said with a smile, "that she enjoys greatly rewarding her gallant knight thusly."

Suddenly, some impish inner voice inspired him to admit to his impure thoughts on the first stairs. There was no logical reason for telling her, but before that part of his brain could regain control, his mouth and lips were moving.

"Alas, Sir Kenneth has a confession that he must maketh," he replied with a hung head. "And his reward may be a slap to the face." He paused and added, "Which would be just and fitting."

She looked a little confused, but stayed in her whimsical character, and said, "Pray tell, Sir Kenneth, what is thy terrible transgression?"

"Sir Kenneth doth admit with—with appropriate shame—that, in a less-than-gallant moment of weakness, his eyes refused to be averted earlier, and they did taketh in the Lady's ... um, *backside* ... as she climbed the first stairs."

She blinked at him, but otherwise made no reaction.

Encouraged that he wasn't already feeling her hand on his cheek—and prodded on by that same impish voice—he leapt way out on the limb, and added, "In his defense—meager though it may be—he *did* respect the Lady's honor by withholding his *hand* from *its* temptation. The spirit was weak, but the flesh, at least, remained strong."

She looked at him for another very long moment as she replayed in her head the scene of them walking up the stairs. She could envision his eyes directly in line with her bottom. A smile crept across her lips.

Then, apparently the same imp that had fogged Kenny's logic decided to blur her sense of propriety, as well.

"One is left to wonder," she said looking into his eyes, "just *what* the Lady might have felt had Sir Kenneth not stayed his hand. A gentle caress of appreciation *could* be taken as a ... *compliment* ... is it not so?"

Immediately, she felt the color start to come up in her face. That may have been the most wanton thing she had ever said to a man; implying that she wanted him to touch her behind! And she didn't say it jokingly in the company of friends in the pub, but alone in the privacy of his bedroom!

Interestingly, she found that the ribald remark excited her as much as it embarrassed her. Perhaps more.

Somehow, the playful characters and speaking of oneself in the third person allowed the curtain of modesty that she always wore to part a little, and to let her deep, *forbidden*, feelings peek out.

The proper half of her mind quickly formulated the appropriate escape plan. Turn away from him, hope he doesn't see your embarrassment; head for the door; and get downstairs where the company of others will yank the curtain closed again.

The other half of her brain—the half that longed to take chances, but was kept bound and gagged by *propriety*—broke loose its chains and took command. It chose the *other* option.

She stepped forward until their bodies were touching, and then she wrapped her arms around him. She pressed her lips to his, and moved against them passionately. Her mouth opened a fraction, and she traced his lips with the tip of her tongue. Then his tongue appeared and the two danced and swirled between their undulating lips.

He wrapped his arms around her and ran his hands over her back while they kissed.

His hand felt the outline of the back of her bra, and his mind flashed back to that night in the backseat of his father's Studebaker. He remembered being surprised at how difficult the thing was to unfasten.

As they kissed and his hands roamed her back, he progressively made lower and lower circles with his right hand. He was pretty sure that she had invited him to touch her behind, but he wanted to give her the opportunity to correct him if he had misunderstood.

If anything, she kissed more passionately as his hand migrated lower.

Finally, he felt the outline of her underwear, and as if crossing the Rubicon, he continued on until his hand was lightly caressing the roundness of her buttocks.

She sucked in her breath, and bit down lightly on his tongue.

He let his fingers explore downward until he felt the curve where the bottom of her behind met her leg. He traced the line with a single finger, and then moved his hand back upwards making gentle circles, covering every inch of her left cheek.

As she exhaled, a small mew came with it, directly into his mouth.

With both hands, one on her back, and the other on her behind, he squeezed her close to him. He felt her bra-captured breasts press into his chest, and he was sure that she must be able to feel his hardness captured between them.

Suddenly, her body stiffened, and she bit down on his tongue until it was actually painful. Her breath came in short pants, and then she let out a little squeak. She froze like that for a few seconds, and then her body relaxed.

She broke their kiss, and dropped her forehead against his shoulder as she took several deep breaths.

Without a word, and without even looking at him, she pushed out of their embrace, turned, picked up her purse, and headed for the stairs. At the bottom of the stairs, he heard her footsteps fade down the hallway toward the loo.

Kenny was not very experienced when it came to women, but he was pretty sure what had just happened to Lily. He had read about these things in a men's magazine. Until now, he thought the stories were fiction.

He wasn't sure whether he should be proud that he had made Lily achieve an orgasm just by kissing and caressing her, or if he should be ashamed for having thrown her into what was obviously an embarrassing situation.

He took a few deep breaths to get *himself* under control, straightened his clothes, adjusted his tie in the mirror, picked up his satchel, and then went down the steps.

He waited for her in the hallway, and when she came out she walked toward him without making eye contact.

"Are you all right?" he asked her, opening his arms.

She skirted past him, said simply, "I'm fine," and went down the stairs and into the kitchen.

He let out a sigh and then he followed her down the stairs. At least he knew which way he should feel, now, he thought. Like a complete heel.

She was on the sidewalk before he caught up with her. She was walking at a quick and determined pace, heading in the direction of the hospital.

"Lily, I'm sorry," he said. "I didn't mean for that to happen. I lost control. I apologize."

"*You* lost control?" she snapped as she came to an abrupt halt. "You didn't have ..." She couldn't bring herself to finish the sentence.

She turned and began walking, again. "You must think I'm quite the trollop, now. Letting you ... *inviting* you to fondle my backside and then ..." again, she let the sentence drop.

"Assuming a trollop is like a tart," he said, trying to crack through the gravity of the situation just a bit, "and assuming that I understand what a tart is, I don't think that at all."

She stopped again and faced him. Tears were running down her cheeks this time.

She lowered her voice even though no one was anywhere near them, and snapped, "Do you know that I'm not even wearing *knickers* right now because of what happened back there? *That's* what trollop is! *That's* what a tart is!"

She began to turn away again, but he took her by the shoulders and stopped her.

"Elizabeth Thatcher!" he said in a serious tone, "I have two things to tell you. First of all, you are not a trollop, a tart, a tramp, or a floozy; what happened back there was entirely my fault, and I deserve to have my face slapped for it. I apologize, and I hope you'll forgive me.

"Secondly," he said, looking her in the eyes, "I love you! It breaks my heart to see you cry, and it scares me to death that if I let you get back to the hospital while you're still mad I might never see you again."

She sniffed and blinked away her tears.

Barely above a whisper, she said, "You love me?" No man had ever said those words to her before. It felt wonderful, but she was no silly school girl.

"How can you love me?" she asked. "This is only the second time we've ever seen each other."

"But we've been writing to each other for two months," he replied. "I've never felt this way about any woman before. Trust me; I know you're the only girl for me."

He took both of her hands between his, and he got down on one knee.

"Lily Thatcher, will you marry me?" he said looking up at her.

She stared at him with her mouth agape for a moment, and then said, "No!"

He blinked a couple of times, surprised at her definitive rejection.

"You can think it over, you know. I can wait. My train's not until tomorrow afternoon."

She giggled, feeling the tension of the past half hour finally leaving her body.

"I *can't* marry you," she said. "It's a rule of the nursing school. No one is permitted to marry during training."

"Then willst thou be my Lady in waiting," he said, "and wait to give thy fair hand to me upon graduation?"

She laughed her adorable twitter. "That's not what a lady-in-waiting is," she said. She pulled him up to his feet, and said, "But yes, I will wait for you, Sir Kenneth."

He pulled her close and kissed her. It was a warm and tender kiss, with just enough passion to stir the blood flow again in both of them. They each broke the kiss at the same time.

They looked at each other and laughed.

"I think we need to ration *those*," she said.

"Or at least learn how to adjust the throttle," he agreed.

He took her hand and they walked back to the hospital.

In the lobby, the woman behind the desk looked at Lily with surprise.

"I didn't expect you back so soon," she said. "I thought you had the whole day off."

"I do," Lily said. "I'm just back to pick up a sweater. I'm catching a little chill in the air." She glanced at Kenny as she said it, and her mouth curled into the tiniest of grins.

The woman looked at Lily curiously. She thought it was rather pleasant outside.

Kenny noticed the look, so he went over to her desk to try to distract her from thinking any more about it.

She was a plain looking woman, whose hairstyle—pulled back into a tight bun—and lack of make-up made her look even more plain. Kenny guessed he was several years older than Lily ... and quite possibly one of the tongue-waggers she had mentioned.

"You're not allergic to chocolate, by any chance, are you?" he said as he set his satchel on the corner of her desk.

When Lily came back into the lobby, Kenny was leaning against the edge of desk, laughing about something, and the woman was chewing her third crème centered chocolate.

"Looks like you made a friend," Lily said as they stepped outside.

"I figured that being on good terms with the sentry at the front gate can never be a bad thing," he said.

As they walked—hand in hand—Kenny noticed that Lily seemed to be holding her purse tighter to her side than she had before. It was as if she thought someone might try to steal her pencil set.

He smiled at how much she liked his gift. He didn't think there was any way that she was going to part with the set, now.

"Do you like the cinema?" she asked as they walked.

"Movies?" he said, "Sure. Is there a theater nearby?"

"A mile or so, if you don't mind the walk," she said.

"No problem. What's playing?"

"I'm not sure. I don't get to go very often. Are you willing to take the chance it's something you'll want to see?"

"I'll get to sit next to you, holding your hand in a darkened room for a couple of hours," he said. "It could be an Army training film, and I'd still enjoy myself."

She giggled. "Well, let's hope for something more entertaining."

As they walked, they talked about the kinds of movies they liked and their favorite actors.

She liked musicals, comedies, and romances, in that order.

He liked westerns, crime dramas, and then comedies.

She liked Fred Astaire, Leslie Howard, and Ingrid Bergman.

He liked Clark Gable, Rita Hayworth, and John Wayne.

When they turned the final corner, and they saw the marquee, he said, "You win. You get to see Ingrid Bergman."

The theater was playing *Casablanca*. The show started in twenty minutes.

"Are you sure you don't mind?" Lily said.

"Not at all. I like Bogey," he said. "I hear he plays a romantic leading man in this one. I'm going to have to see it to believe that, though."

Two hours later, they were back outside.

"I'm impressed," Kenny said. "Bogey played a better leading man that I thought he could have. *Here's looking at you, kid*," he said in a Bogart imitation.

Lily laughed. "And my gosh, Ingrid Bergman is so beautiful! *Play it Sam. Play 'As Time Goes By'.*"

"*Of all the gin joints in all the towns in all the world, she walks into mine.*" They both laughed.

"If I was Ilsa," Lily said, "would you have made me get on that plane? Would you have sent me away?"

"If you were Ilsa," he said, "you'd be married to Laszlo, so what choice would I have?"

"But Rick still loved her. That was as plain as day."

"That's why he made her do the right thing, and leave," Kenny said. "But if I were me and you were you, I'd *never* send you away. We'd travel all over France fighting the Nazis in every gin joint we could find."

"And we'd finally end up back in Paris, where it all began," she said laughing.

"I like the way you think. *Here's looking at you, kid,*" he repeated, Bogey-style.

As they talked and laughed, Kenny had no real sense of what direction they were headed, so he was surprised when he saw the *Bishop and Bear* sign up ahead.

Kenny looked at his watch. "Wow! It's almost seven o'clock," he said. "It's so bright out I had no idea."

"We're on British Double Summer Time," Lily said. "All the clocks are set two hours ahead."

"I know," he said. "It's just so strange to get used to.

"So, do you have a curfew or anything?" he asked her. "Do I have to get you back at a certain time? Or can we share a pint again?"

"I'm supposed to be back by dark," she said, "but that's almost ten o'clock this time of year. Besides, I think you greased the wheels pretty well with Anna. I don't think she'd turn me in if I was a little late."

"Great!" he said. "Plenty of time."

But as they approached the pub, Lily pulled him into the alley between it and the next building.

"Shortcut?" he said.

She stopped in the alley and he could tell that she was thinking about something. Finally, she looked at him, and said, "Did you ask me to marry you just to make me feel better?"

The question surprised him, but he replied, "No. I asked you to marry me to make you my wife. I wasn't joking, and I'm still not. I love you. I'll accept *later* as an answer, but I won't accept *no*. You're not going to get rid of me as easily as Rick got rid of Ilsa."

She replied by kissing him passionately.

"I have something I want to show you," she said when she broke the kiss. Then she led him by the hand into the backyard of the pub.

The pub had gotten quite busy, mostly with servicemen, and the noise spilled out through the open back door. Even so, Lily put her finger to her lips to indicate that they needed to be quiet.

Staying close to the building, and with Kenny right behind, she made her way to the foot of the stairs, making sure to stay out of sight of the doorway. She took off her shoes, and pointed at his, silently telling him to do the same thing. She then led the way upstairs.

Again, he was presented with the very agreeable sight of her behind, but he forced himself, instead, to look at her feet. But somehow, even watching her bare feet padding silently up the treads was arousing to him. He closed his eyes and shook his head to snap himself out of it.

At the top, she carefully opened the door, and they stepped inside. The noise from below easily filtered up through the old floor, and Kenny was pretty sure that he could have been in his combat boots and no one below would have been the wiser. But, following Lily's lead, he tiptoed down the hallway in his socks.

She opened the door that led up to his room, guided him inside, then stepped in and quietly pulled the door closed. The little landing was dark, but not black. The light from the windows in the room above spilled down to give them just enough light to see.

"We don't need the light," she said as she maneuvered around him and started up the steep stairs.

Again, he averted his eyes as she climbed, but in the dim light, he didn't think he could see anything embarrassing if he wanted to.

When he topped the stairs, he saw that she had set her purse on the bed and she was just standing in the middle of the peaked room, smiling at him. She seemed nervous for some reason.

She opened her arms inviting him into an embrace.

He wrapped his arms around her, and leaned down to kiss her. In her bare feet, she was two inches shorter than she was before. He liked that.

They kissed hungrily for a long while, holding each other tight and moving against one another in subtle but evocative ways. At no time, however, did his hands dip below the small of her back.

She finally broke the kiss and put a few inches of distance between their bodies. Their hands caressed each other's shoulders as they looked in one another's eyes. They each breathed deeply, trying to get their pulse rates back down to normal.

"A little of that goes a long ways," he said, letting out a sigh.

"Do you want me?" she asked him.

"Yes," he said. "Of course I do. I told you that I want you to marry ..."

"No," she interrupted him. "Do you want ... my body?"

Suddenly, there was no floor under Kenny's feet. He had no earthly idea what to say. He could recall nothing that his sister had ever told him that suggested how to answer a question like that.

In the time it took for him to blink twice he contemplated his choices.

If he said *yes*—which was the truth—would she think he was just another sex-hungry Yank, and leave?

If he said *no*, would she think he was lying, or would she be insulted that he didn't think she was attractive enough for him? Whether he answered *yes* or *no*, he saw himself ending up alone in the room.

Or ... was she actually asking him if he wanted to have sex with her?

He decided to play it safe.

"Sir Kenneth doth think that the Lady is *most* desirous," he said with a tiny bow. "But it would be less than gallant ..."

She laughed, and cut him off by putting her finger on his lips.

"When I was young," she began, "and I found out how babies were made, I swore that I would never have children if that was the only way to do it. How revolting!

"When I got a little older, and I understood my body a little better, I realized that the baby-making thing might not be all that disgusting after all. I left the possibility open, but I swore that I would only ever do such a thing with the person I married. And certainly *only* to have children."

Again, he had no idea what he should say, so he wisely kept quiet.

"Now that I'm in the medical field I understand that sex involves a lot more than intercourse for the sake of making babies. I think we demonstrated a little of that here this afternoon."

"I am sor ..." he began, but she pressed her finger harder against his lips to stop him.

"I'm *not* sorry," she said. "I was embarrassed at the time, because I certainly wasn't expecting that to happen, but ... well, truth be told, I enjoyed it. It felt marvelous!"

Once more, well chosen silence from him.

She moved her finger from his lips, and said, "Have you ever had an orgasm?"

A couple more blinks while his mind, once again, took off at full speed. Was she trying to get him to embarrass himself for some reason? On the other hand, s*he* had just admitted to *him* to having an orgasm, so he decided to be honest with her ... but to go for safety in numbers, just in case.

"I think every guy my age has," he said. "It's, you know, like part of growing up."

"Do you know that masturbating is actually healthy?" she said.

He just looked at her, unable to process any meaningful words. That was certainly contrary to everything his mother and the Army had told him. And no girl had *ever* used that word in conversation with him before.

"And did you know that women do it, too?" she added.

His mouth fell open.

She grinned and used her finger to push it closed.

"So, if it's healthy for each of us to do it by ourselves, how can it be bad if we were to do it together?"

His mouth moved to form words, but nothing came out.

She turned him and pushed back to the bed, and said, "Sit down. I want to show you something."

She sat next to him, picked up her purse, and took out a book and handed it to him.

It was titled *The Truth About Sex*, and was written by Doctors Marian and Walter Rogers.

"Are they doctors at your hospital?" Kenny asked as he opened the cover to look at the table of contents.

"No," she said with a little giggle. "I don't know where they're from, actually. Sweden, perhaps. I think they're a bit more ... *enlightened* there."

He scanned down the list of chapters on the first page of the index. They included subjects like *Why Kissing Feels so Good, Understanding Puberty, The Wonder of the Female Breast,* and *Exploring the Penis and Testacles.*

"Is this like a text book or something?" he asked. "Part of your training?"

She laughed. "Good heavens no!" she said. "If this were discovered in the house, someone would likely get expelled." She thought for a moment, then added, "But I guess maybe it is a kind of *unofficial* text book. It's been passed around among the girls to *round out* our education, you might say."

"Who's is it?" he asked, focusing on a chapter titled *Self Gratification; Masturbation demystified.*

"No one seems to know," she said. "Or at least no one will say. Each of us gets it for a couple of days to study a chapter or two—keeping it well hidden from the staff—and then we pass it on."

"So, there are no exams on these subjects or anything?" he said.

She giggled nervously, and turned red as she answered, "It's a self-graded course."

She took the book from him and flipped to a chapter with the heading, "*Enjoying The Wonder of Sex and Keeping Your Virginity.*"

"Read this," she said. "The first few pages, anyway."

As he read silently, she sat beside him, skimming over the words she had read several times over the past year.

He turned the page, and there was a black & white pencil sketch of a naked man and woman doing with their hands what had been described on the previous page. He swallowed hard and shifted nervously as his blood redistributed itself within his body.

As he continued reading, she stood up and walked to the end of the room. He breathed a little sigh of relief when she got up. He had been afraid to move the book from his lap for fear that she would see the effect her "text book" was having on him.

When he reached the break point at the end of the third page, he said, "That's ... very interesting. I can see how ..."

He stopped short when he looked up and saw that Lily had slipped out of her dress while he was reading, and was standing there in only her white bra and lace-trimmed "knickers."

She wore a nervous smile, and held her hands on the sides of her legs, against their natural inclination to rise up and cover her private parts.

"Do you think that's something you'd be interested in trying?" she asked, her voice barely above a whisper out of sheer terror. *My God, what if he says no?*

He didn't answer at all. He set down the book and walked toward her. He wrapped his arms around her and kissed her in a way that went far beyond mere passion. His hands roamed over the naked flesh of her back, and she ground her hips into him, feeling his unmistakable answer that he *did* want to try what he'd just read about.

Once again, he let his hand wander down until he was caressing her behind, this time with only a thin layer of cotton separating him from her skin.

She breathed deeply between kisses, and said on one of the breaths, "Put your hand inside."

He slid his hand up her back, and then down again, slipping his fingers beneath the waistband. He spread his fingers wide to hold as much of her soft flesh as he could. Then, he squeezed and pulled her tight against his body.

She let out a long moan as she tilted her head back and closed her eyes.

Suddenly, she pushed herself out of the embrace.

Startled, he was about to apologize again, but he stopped when she started tugging on his belt.

It was an Army-issued brass-buckle web belt, and she had no idea how to unfasten it. Her tugging only made it tighter.

Without exchanging words, he moved his hands inside hers, slid the bar back, and pulled the web from the buckle. He then unfastened the one button.

As he did that, she pulled his fly down.

They both finished at the same time, and his pants fell to the floor around his ankles.

She embraced him once again, pressing his thinly covered hardness between them. He slid his hand back inside of her panties and firmly massaged her behind.

She was panting and mewing as they ground together, and then she surprised him by pushing her hand between their bodies, and down into his shorts.

He rolled his head back and let out a long, "*Ohhh!*" as she wrapped her fingers around him.

He responded by pushing both of his hands into her panties and kneading her buttocks.

She withdrew her hand, and once more pushed away.

He sighed at the loss of her touch, but realized that it was probably just in time to prevent his ... *release*.

Panting, she reached her arms up behind her back, as she said, "Take your clothes off."

"What?" he said, not sure he'd heard her correctly over his own heavy breathing.

"Your clothes," she said, "take them off."

As she spoke she slid her bra down along her arms.

He stood there transfixed, looking at her naked breasts. The most perfect breasts that God had ever bestowed on any woman.

His open-mouth stare made her smile. She reached up to his necktie, and slid the knot down.

"You're way behind," she said.

As she undid the buttons of his shirt, he reached both hands behind his back to undo his cuff buttons. Putting his hands behind his back not only got them out of her way, but also kept them out of his view of her breasts.

She had just finished his third button down when he crossed his arms, took hold of his shirttails, and pulled his shirt and undershirt off over his head in one motion. He threw them inside-out into the corner, and stood there looking at her.

She slid her thumbs into the waistband of her panties, and said, "Together?"

"On three," he said as he positioned his thumbs in his shorts.

"One - two - three," she counted, and then pushed down.

Both of their underpants hit the floor at the same time.

They stood for a moment, looking at each other's nakedness. Simultaneously, they stepped forward and embraced once more. Their lips locked together, their flesh pressed against flesh, and their hands roamed, and caressed each other's backs.

Then, without speaking, they each reached down and began acting out the lesson from the book.

Two hours later, they lay together on the small bed. Lily's book lay closed on the floor after several other chapters had been studied, and exams taken. They were both still naked, completely exhausted ... and still virgins. And they were more in love than either of them ever thought possible.

Monday, August 22, 1943

Monday morning, Kenny and the other Micks were assembling Jeeps that had arrived from the US in crates. With the vehicle suspended in midair off the back of the wrecker, they bolted on the four wheels plus the spare.

On the ground, the steering column was rotated up to its driving position, and bolted to the dashboard, the hood and windshield were attached, and the driver's and passenger seats were bolted in place. Finally, the gas tank was filled with "petrol" and the completed "Truck, 1/4-ton, 4x4, Utility" was driven off to a staging area to join hundreds of others waiting for the D-Day invasion.

To get the engines to fire up without draining the batteries, it was common practice for one person to dribble a little gasoline into the carburetor while another cranked the engine. The engine would roar to life on the trickle of fuel, and with a steady hand, could be kept running long enough for the fuel pump to pull the gas from the tank and fill the carburetor, at which point the engine could be taken off of hand-fed life-support, and it would survive on its own.

As Kenny readied his tin can of gasoline over the carburetor of the next Jeep, Charles appeared at the fender on the opposite side of the engine compartment.

"So, Sergeant McCormick did you enjoy your weekend in Birmingham?" he asked.

Without acknowledging him, Kenny poured an extra helping of fuel into the engine, moved the can back out of the way, and held the throttle open with his hand.

"Hit it!" he called to Mack, who was sitting in the driver's seat, his view blocked by the open hood.

Mack flipped the ignition switch, and pushed his foot down on the starter button on the floor.

The engine cranked over, and then, just as Kenny knew it would, it backfired with a loud *Bang!* and blew a column of yellow flame three feet in the air.

Charles leapt back and cursed, "*Gore Blimey!*"

"Watch out for your eyebrows there, Sergeant," Kenny said calmly, "these things can backfire sometimes. I think it's the *petrol* we have to use over here; they're made to run on good old American *gasoline*."

"*Bloody twillip*," Charles mumbled. He stood three feet back from the Jeep as Kenny and Mack tried again—with success this time—to start the little four-cylinder engine. With the motor purring, Kenny closed the hood, and waved Mack off to the staging yard.

"So, what brings you out this way, Sergeant?" Kenny asked Charles as he walked over to the next Jeep in line. "Probably not for the fireworks, I'd guess."

"Just wondering if you enjoyed your weekend in Birmingham," he said, unsure if McCormick had heard him the first time.

Kenny had heard him; he just chose to ignore the question that was obviously meant to bait him. This time he answered.

"I enjoyed it very much—thanks for asking. Saw some interesting sights, met some nice people, and got to see that Bogart movie, *Casablanca*. Pretty good. You should take it in, if you can."

"Oh, really?" Charles said. "Did you see that with Lily?"

"Yes. She enjoyed it, too," Kenny answered. "She said to say *hi*, by the way. And to thank you for suggesting the chocolates."

"She ate the chocolates?" Charles said with obvious surprise.

"Oh, no. Funny thing; turns out she's allergic. Did you know that? But we did put them to good use, anyway."

Charles didn't quite know how to react to all that, so he mentally regrouped and fell back on the script he had been rehearsing in his head.

"One of my mates was in Birmingham, too. He tells me he saw you giving Lily quite a snogging in a back alley, Saturday night," he said. "But she rather likes that kind of thing, what? She always has been a bit of a slapper."

"*Snogging. Slapper.* You know, Chuck," Kenny said, "if you're going to insult Lily to try to make me angry so I'll agree to a rematch, you're going to have to use terms I'm familiar with; otherwise, it's kind of pointless, don't you think?"

"It means she's a tart, you bloody twillip!" Charles snapped.

"Ah! Now we're getting somewhere. *Tart* I know," Kenny said. "*Twillip* I'm not sure about, though."

"*It means you're a bloody fool!*" Charles shouted at him.

"Oh. Okay. Then for the record, I'm officially offended," Kenny said as he unscrewed the nut that held the breather tube onto the carburetor of the next Jeep. "But I'm still not going to fight you again. You have an unfair advantage. You know my strategy, and you know my weakness. It would hardly be a fair fight." He held his can of gas over the open carburetor, and said, "Watch your eyebrows!"

Charles jumped back a couple of steps as Kenny dribbled the gas.

"Hit it!" Kenny said to the corporal who had climbed into the driver's seat.

The engine started smoothly and Kenny kept it going by metering the fuel and twisting the throttle until he could tell that it was running on its own.

"Maybe the other one just didn't like you standing so close," Kenny said as he closed the hood. "I know you can have that effect on *people*."

"*Bloody bugger!*" Charles mumbled as he stomped off.

Wednesday, August 25, 1943

Wednesday afternoon, Kenny was testing the generator of a Sherman tank that kept letting the tank's main battery go dead, when he heard, "A-ten-hut!" called out from outside the open-sided work tent.

Kenny came to attention, and looked up to see the company's commander, Captain Davies, climbing out of his Jeep.

"As you were," the captain announced to the men, as he walked towards Kenny.

Kenny saluted, and said, "Afternoon, Captain. What can we do for you?"

"You can knock Sergeant Haversham's block off a week from this Friday night, Sergeant," the captain said as he returned the salute.

"Is that an order, sir?" Kenny asked.

"You know I can't order you to fight in the ring, McCormick," Davies said, "This is a *request*. But it's a request that originated with the major, who has been taking all sorts of flack from his British counterparts for not getting a rematch set up."

"Are you sure you want me to get in the ring with him, again, sir?" Kenny said. "That last match was pretty close. What if he knocks *my* block off?"

"It's a chance the major's willing to take," Davies said.

Kenny laughed. "That's very sporting of him."

"While I can't order you into the ring," Davies said, "the major *has* ordered me to do whatever it takes to get you to *volunteer* for a rematch."

"I see," Kenny said.

"How does seven days leave sound?" Davies said. "You'll probably need some R&R after the fight."

Kenny thought about it for a few seconds.

"Well, sir, it's like this," he replied. "I have this lady friend up in Birmingham who only gets one day off a week, so having seven days all at once won't do me much good, if you see my point. But if that leave were broken into, say, three three-day passes; now that might be more useful to me."

"Done," the captain replied. He thought a moment, and added, "If you win by a knock-out, I'll make it four."

"I'll see what I can do, sir," Kenny answered.

"Knock him out in the first round, and it'll be six."

"With one of them reserved for Christmas," Kenny countered. "Assuming we're still here then, of course."

"I can make that happen," Davies said. He extended his hand, and said, "Then we have an agreement?"

"And what happens if I lose?" Kenny asked as he shook.

"I'll give you three days to lick your wounds; that's it."

"Fair enough," Kenny said.

For the next eight days Kenny squeezed as much training in amongst his duties as he could. He had a feeling that Charles was going to be a lot better prepared for the rematch.

Friday, September 3, 1943

When Friday night rolled around, it seemed that the only men in the camp who were not massed around the ring were the unlucky few who were on sentry duty. More trucks had been brought in as viewing stands, and once again, "Haversham vs. McCormick" was the last match on the board.

The grudge matches were about the same as before, with one notable exception. A 150-pound big-mouth private from Mobile had challenged a small mountain of a corporal from Hoboken to a fight over some north versus south argument.

Apparently, the kid from Mobile was about the only person in the camp who thought the fight might turn out differently than it did. The kid was on the canvas, unconscious, after taking three well-landed punches to the head.

The other notable thing, in Kenny's opinion, was that the two regular American boxers were on the night's card, but the two Brits were not. He thought he knew why that might be, and his suspicion was confirmed when it was his turn to step into the ring.

While Jimmy and Mack were in his corner once again, Haversham's buddies had been replaced by the two British boxers.

When Kenny and Charles were called out to the center of the ring, Kenny said to Charles, "I see you're in better company, now."

Charles replied, "Now I'll show *you* some fireworks."

As he stood in the corner waiting for the bell to start the first round, Kenny turned and shouted in Mack's ear over the roar of the crowd.

"Watch the clock; when there's forty-five-seconds left in the round, shout out, *'You're hitting like a girl, McCormick,'* and shout it loud; I don't want to miss it. Forty-five seconds, got it?"

When the bell rang, Kenny came out prepared to do some real boxing. But even though he was expecting more from Charles this time, he was not expecting what he got.

Charles landed two fast left jabs, and then a textbook right hook that caught Kenny square in the side of the head.

Kenny saw a flash of white light as he stumbled to his right and felt his knee buckle. His vision came back just as he hit the canvas on his back.

He could see the referee swinging his arm and counting, but he couldn't hear him over the ringing in his left ear.

He rolled onto his side and managed to catch "*Three!*" with his right ear. On the canvas, he found himself almost face to face with one of the British boxers in Charles' corner.

"You boys taught him well!" Kenny shouted at him.

"You don't know the half of it, mate!" he shouted back. "Wait until the *second* round!"

Kenny was hearing "*Seven!*" as he pushed himself up to his feet.

For the next two minutes Kenny did a lot of covering up and backpedaling as Charles came at him relentlessly, and with well-executed punches. Although they were taking a toll, none of the punches had the same effect as that first set.

Finally, after what Kenny was sure had been ten minutes, he heard Mack scream at him, "*You're hitting him like a goddamned little girl, McCormick!*" Which, of course, wasn't true because Kenny wasn't hitting him at all.

The next punch that Charles threw was a left jab, and Kenny slipped to his left just enough to let it go over his shoulder. With Charles' left arm extended, Kenny came up with a right uppercut that caught Charles solidly under the chin.

Kenny had seen that Charles' favorite combination seemed to be *left jab, left jab, right hook*—the combination he had knocked him down with—so he had an idea of what was coming next, and the uppercut interrupted Charles' rhythm just enough for Kenny to step forward, and get inside of the hook.

Standing face to face with Charles, and with Charles' arm around the back of his neck, Kenny landed two hard, rapid punches to Charles' stomach.

Charles pushed away and drew his arms in low to protect his stomach, and Kenny used the opening to connect with a hard left hook to the head, followed by a right hook, followed by a left uppercut.

Charles staggered back from the quick barrage, and Kenny followed it up with the same thing in reverse order. Right hook, left hook, right uppercut.

Charles' staggering became more unsteady as Kenny kept battering him with the same combinations, and finally, Charles' knees both buckled at the same time, and he went over backwards onto the canvas.

It seemed to Kenny—and to every US GI there—that the ref took a long time to start his count. Kenny was afraid that Charles might be "saved by the bell." He didn't think he could take another round of that.

As the ref threw his arm down and shouted "*Ten!*" the bell rang.

The American's in the crowd went crazy, and they poured over the ropes to hoist Kenny onto their shoulders. Kenny looked over toward one of the reviewing trucks, and saw the major slapping Captain Davies on the back. He then turned to Kenny and gave him two thumbs-up.

Kenny never saw Charles again after that night. His company commander was so infuriated by Charles' first-round loss—and his own lost wager—that he had him transferred to a division on the Scottish coast.

McCormick used his passes to visit Lily once a month. With casualties continually coming in by ship from the campaigns in North Africa, Sicily, and now Italy, Lily wasn't always able to get time off, so Kenny volunteered his free time at the hospital when she was on duty.

Being completely untrained in anything but basic First Aid, Kenny was of no use in any medical capacity, but the staff quickly learned that he was able to fix just about anything mechanical. Several pieces of equipment that had broken down and had been collecting dust in a store room without any chance of being replaced, were suddenly back in service.

When there wasn't something to fix, Kenny spent many hours sitting with the wounded soldiers, many of whom were younger than himself.

When he had joined up, right after the attack on Pearl Harbor, Kenny was driven by patriotism and the notion that the war was almost a necessity to prove that good could triumph over evil. The killing, the wounding, the destruction were all pretty abstract while he was in the States. It wasn't until Lily had shown him some of the bombed out buildings in Birmingham that he began to get a sense of the reality of war and how it affected real people; people that Lily knew by name.

Now, sitting with young men who had missing arms or legs, who were permanently blinded, or who were burned beyond recognition by their own mothers, Kenny saw the true horror of the war, and it made him hate with an absolute passion, the Nazis and the Japanese, who had forced this atrocity onto the world.

Sometimes he would just sit and talk with the men; sometimes he would read to them; and sometimes he would write letters home as they dictated. That was the hardest.

One of the men—a boy, actually—or at least he had been when he *entered* the Army—asked Kenny to write to his mother and father back on the farm in Idaho.

> Dear Mom and Pop,
>
> The good news is that I'll be coming home pretty soon. The bad news is, it's because I was wounded.
>
> If you don't recognize my handwriting, it's because I can't use my hands right now. This letter is being written by a swell guy named Kenny McCormick. He's a sergeant who volunteers here at the hospital. (Hello, Mr. and Mrs.

Lenard. KM) I can't use my hands because they are both wrapped up after the surgery to take out all the shrapnel and stitch up the holes. The doctor said they should heal just fine, though.

He couldn't say the same thing about my legs, though, and they had to amputate them both, right above the knees. It sure makes me sad to think I'm never going to get to drive that old John Deere again. About the only thing I'll be good for in the fields now, is a scarecrow in the beans! I'll be too short for the corn! Hee Hee.
On the bright side, I <u>am</u> coming home. A lot of other fellows aren't so lucky.

I'll write again when I get the bandages off. I just wanted you to know that I'm alive and will be seeing all of you again, shortly.

Love to all of you! Give Cindy a kiss for me!

Your son, Henry

After Kenny read the letter back to Henry, he addressed the envelope and tucked the letter inside. He didn't seal it, however. Kenny took the letter with him when he left, promising to drop in the military post box downstairs.

That night, in his room above the pub, Kenny took the letter out of his pocket and wrote on the back of it.

Dear Mr. and Mrs. Lenard,

Your son is one of the bravest young men I have ever met! You should be very proud! The loss of his legs and his inability to go back to the life he left when he joined the Army would make many men angry and bitter, or simply make them give up. Although he doesn't know how yet, he told me that he is going to find a way to be useful on your farm. I have an idea about that, but first I wanted to share with you the circumstances that brought Henry here to Queen Elizabeth Hospital.

This story was told to me by Henry's platoon sergeant, who is also here at the hospital. I don't think Henry is ready to talk about it, yet. That happens, sometimes.

During the invasion of Sicily, Henry's 50-cal machine gun squad was defending one of the beachheads when they were attacked around midnight by Italian forces. A hand grenade was thrown into the nest, and actually bounced off of Henry's helmet. In the dark, no one knew where it landed, until Henry saw it, and jammed his helmet on top of it. When it went off, it ripped through the helmet, and caused the injuries to his hands that he described in his letter.

The sergeant said that if Henry had not shielded the rest of the men from the grenade, one or two might have been killed right away (including Henry), but the rest probably would have been injured enough that they would not have been able to fend off the attack, which they did. I will be very surprised if Henry doesn't get a Medal of Honor for his actions, to go along with his Purple Heart.

The next morning, he was being transported to a medical ship, when the landing craft that he and a dozen other casualties were in was hit by artillery fire. It was then that he received his leg injuries. He was one of only four survivors who were pulled from the water.

As Henry's medical ship passed through the Straights of Gibraltar, heading back here to England, it was attacked by a Nazi U-boat (even though it bore the red cross). It was damaged, but fortunately, not sunk. A US Navy destroyer chased and sank the U-boat.

Henry's ship made it the rest of the way under its own power, but very slowly. Sadly, many men died on board who might have lived if they had made it here sooner. As I said, your son is a remarkably brave man, and all things considered, a very lucky one, too!

Regarding my idea to help Henry on the farm, please take a look at the enclosed sketches. Since, as you know, most of the controls for your John Deere are hand operated, all that should be needed to allow Henry to operate the tractor is the addition of levers for the two brake pedals and the power lift pedal. I'm not sure of the model of your tractor (I'm most familiar with the Model-A), but if you have a clever mechanic or blacksmith

> around, I'm sure they can adapt the drawings I'm sending to most any model.
>
> I think it would be a swell surprise and a great welcome home if you could set up the tractor so he could drive it, before he gets back.
>
> Sincerely,
> Kenny McCormick
> Sergeant, US Army
> 29th Infantry

Kenny sealed the envelope and walked back to the hospital to put it in the post box so it would be picked up in the morning.

Friday, December 24, 1943

By some small miracle, Lily managed to be off duty on Christmas Day, 1943. On Friday, the 24th, Kenny met Lily's mother at the Barnstaple train depot, and they rode up to Birmingham together.

The two had first met a month earlier when Virginia came up to Birmingham to celebrate her daughter's birthday, and they had hit it off remarkably well. Unlike most of the American GIs she had met, Sergeant McCormick seemed to be an actual gentleman. Someone whom she could trust to visit her only daughter and not fear for her chastity.

Kenny had not met Lily's father, but by an extension of the same miracle, he was granted leave from his coast-watching duties, and he would be joining them in Birmingham. It would be the first Christmas the three had been together since war was declared in September of 1939.

"What's he like?" Kenny asked when they found out he would be able to come.

"He's a bit crusty, you might say," she answered.

"That doesn't tell me much," he said. "Steak and kidney pie is crusty, too. How's he going to feel about a Yank seeing his only daughter?"

"I suspect he'll see it a lot like Mum," she said. "It will all depend on the Yank. So be your most charming."

"Did your father ever meet Charles?" Kenny asked.

"Hated him," she replied. "Though him a boorish lout."

"Okay," Kenny said. "I have a pretty good idea how *not* to act, then."

"Be yourself," she said. "If you *act* this way *or* that, he'll know, and he won't trust you a bit."

On Christmas day, Tom closed the *Bishop and Bear*, and he and Maggie hosted the Thatcher family plus Kenny for Christmas dinner.

Kenny came down from his room early Christmas morning and helped Maggie in the kitchen. The food was different, and there was far less of it, but the controlled chaos of the kitchen reminded him of his childhood Christmases, and he felt as happy as he could possibly be, short of being home on that day.

When the Thatchers arrived at 11:00, Kenny gave Virginia a light hug and kissed both of her cheeks. He gave Lily's father, Mark, a firm handshake (fortunately, it was his left arm that was missing), and he gently shook Lily's hand and kissed both of her cheeks.

"Lily tells me your with the 29th Infantry, down in Devon," Mark said to Kenny as Tom handed the two men pints of ale.

"Yes, sir," Kenny said proudly. "The Blue and the Grey."

"Bunch of hooligans, as I hear it," Mark replied.

"That's mostly the Grey, sir," Kenny said. "I'm with the Blue."

Mark laughed. "Tom told me you was a quick one with the words."

"I try to keep up, sir."

Mark took a sip of his ale, then said, "Lily tells me you've met young Charlie Haversham; what do you think of him?"

"Oh, I don't think it matters too much what others think of Charles," Kenny said. "He thinks highly enough of himself that the rest of us don't need to be counted at all. But he insulted your daughter a while back, so I knocked him unconscious in the boxing ring."

Mark nearly spit his ale. "You're telling me porkies!" he said.

Kenny looked at Tom for a translation.

"He thinks you're pulling his leg."

"No, sir," Kenny said, holding up his right hand in an oath. "First round knock-out. It's how I arranged to get leave on Christmas day."

"Well, I'll be buggered!" Mark said with a laugh. He set down his glass, and slapped Kenny on the back. "Any man that gives a Haversham a bash and sets him on his arse, well, his blood's worth bottling, in my book!"

The main course for dinner was mock goose. Although Tom and Maggie owned a restaurant, and therefore had access to more food than individuals, they never hoarded it or took more for themselves than the rationing program allowed. The extra food was for paying customers, and even then, Maggie stretched it like she was a homemaker feeding her family.

Kenny would not have mistaken what they were eating for goose, but it wasn't bad tasting. It was made from potatoes, apples, cheese, flour, and vegetable stock, and was seasoned with salt, pepper, and sage. Maggie served it with carrots, parsley, and a fresh-baked loaf of bread. For dessert, Maggie made a steamed pudding, just like the one Kenny and Lily had eaten on their very first date in the pub.

After dinner and dessert, while the men sipped brandy and the women enjoyed sherry (one of the benefits of living in a pub), small Christmas gifts were exchanged.

Kenny gave Lily an artist's pad. He gave her mother an assortment of sewing needles in a leather pouch. He gave Tom a tin of Prince Albert's pipe tobacco, and Maggie got a small book of poems by Emily Dickenson.

Kenny had been around those four enough that he knew he was on solid ground with their gifts. But he had never met Lily's father before, and it had never occurred to him to ask what he might like for Christmas. He had, however, been paying attention when she told stories of her childhood, and how her family had celebrated Christmas, and how her father had adapted after losing his arm in the war.

He handed Mark his gift, and as he unrolled the plain paper, Kenny said, "The good Lord willing, all this will be over by next Christmas, and maybe you can use that to supply the family feast next year."

Mark held a stunning hand-carved duck call.

"Did you make this, son?" Mark asked.

"I wish I was that talented," Kenny said. "One of the guys in my outfit made it."

"It's beautiful," he said. "Thank you."

He put the call to his lips, but he hesitated without blowing. He lowered it, and said, "I'm going to blow this on the day the Germans surrender. Then I'm going to go shoot a duck, and we'll all celebrate."

"Here's to all of our boys being home by next Christmas!" Tom said raising his glass.

Everyone raised theirs, and agreed with a loud, "*Here here! Home by Christmas!*"

As winter gave way to the spring of 1944, Lily and Kenny were able to see less and less of each other. In her last year of training, Lily decided to specialize as a theater (operating room) nurse, so she was either in classes or on duty seven days of most weeks. And Kenny and his mates were up to their butts in alligators trying to get all the equipment that was pouring into the country ready for the invasion of Europe that everyone expected in early summer. They wrote letters almost every day, however.

Near the end of May, Kenny managed to finagle a two-day pass, and Lily talked her way into an entire afternoon and evening off.

They started toward the movie theater, but neither of them really wanted to see the show that was playing, a British-made mystery called *Candles at Nine*.

They walked hand in hand toward the pub, and went in the back way up to Kenny's room.

They laid down on his bed, fully clothed, except for their shoes, and held each other tightly. They kissed, but they weren't the hungry, desirous kisses like before. These were kisses of pure, deep love. They were tender, and filled more with longing than with lust.

Over the past year, Lily had seen thousands of wounded soldiers coming back from the front, and it scared her to death that sometime in the very near future Kenny could be one of them. But it terrified her even more that he could be killed in battle and she would never see him again at all.

Tears spilled from her eyes as she kissed his lips, and when he tasted the saltiness, he opened his eyes to look at her.

"Hey, what's wrong?" he asked quietly, knowing the answer full well because he had the very same fears. "Is my belt buckle sticking into you?" he joked.

She laughed and then sniffed, and gave him a playful swat on the arm.

"I *wish* that was all it was," she said. "I'd take your pants off and the problem would be solved."

"*More* of the world's problems should be solved that way," he said.

She smiled at his humor; she knew he was trying to kid her out of it. But it wouldn't go away that easily.

"I'm sacred, Kenny," she said, tucking herself into him tightly. "I'm scared for you. Maybe if I didn't see the results of this stupid war every single day of my life, I might be able to put it out of my mind, but I can't. It's all I can think about. I don't want anything to happen to you."

"You don't have to worry," he lied. "I'm one of the ten, remember? The Jerries aren't going to be shooting at me as long as the ones are up there on the front lines."

"Bombs don't know how to count," she said. "They don't care if you're a one or a five or a ten. I was here during the Birmingham Blitz; the bombs didn't care if you were young or old, if you were a mother or a child, if you were rich or poor. They killed and maimed and destroyed anyone and anything that was unlucky enough to be in their way."

"You told me you were in the street one night with your air raid unit when the bombs started falling," he said, "and a cluster of incendiary bombs went off in the sky above your head. You said you were too scared to even move, and the fuses hit the road all around you, but you weren't touched. Why do you think that is?"

"I'm a small target?" she said.

"No. It's because you're lucky," he replied. "And it's the same reason that I was on the back platform of that train on the one night in three months that you were able to travel to Barnstaple to see your mother. It's because *I'm* lucky, too. Do you have any idea what the odds must be against one certain girl from Birmingham, England meeting one certain boy from Augusta, Maine? And yet, here we are.

"I believe in luck," he went on, "and my theory is that when two lucky people get together, the good luck adds together, and they're both twice as lucky as either of them would be alone."

"Oh, I hope you're right," she said with a sniff.

He took her hand and moved it up to her face. He brushed a tear from her cheek with her finger. "Have you ever wished on a tear?" he asked her.

"I can't say I have," she said.

"It's something my grandmother taught us when we were kids," he told her. "She must have brought the tradition with her from the old country. Anyway, when we were all done crying from our skinned knee or bee sting, or whatever, she'd have us wipe the last tear from our cheek—and it had to be the *last* one or it wouldn't work. It's how she got us to stop crying. She'd tell us to make a wish, and then she'd kiss the tear from our finger.

"Care to give it a try?" he asked her, holding her finger.

"I wish for you to be home and in my arms by Christmas," she said. "And for all this deplorable nonsense to be over."

He moved her fingertip to his lips and gave it a tender kiss.

"Does it always work?" she asked him as he held her finger to his lips.

"Always," he said. "There was this one time I remember when I was in sixth grade," he went on. "I got hit in the eye with a snowball, and as if that weren't bad enough, it was a *girl* that threw it at me. My wish was that she would fall through the ice the next time she went skating on the pond. My Nana said that wasn't allowed, because wishing for something bad to happen to someone else is a sin."

"Even Hitler?" Lily said.

"The exception that proves the rule," he answered. "So anyway, I changed my wish. Instead of getting *rid* of Amy Kilroy—the biggest brat that Satan ever sent up to torture boys—I wished that there was a girl who was as good and pure as Amy was mean and evil to balance things out. It took me a few years to find her, but here you are."

She smiled at him, but something in *his* smile made her narrow her eyes, and ask, "Are you making that up?"

"You mean am I telling you porkies?" he said. "Maybe a little," he confessed as he kissed her. "My revised wish was actually that Amy would just move out of town, which she did in eighth grade. But see, it still came true. Just like yours will."

It was nearly 11:00 when he walked her home and he gave her a polite kiss goodnight in the lobby of the dormitory. He picked her up again in the morning, and she got enough time off to walk him to the train depot. Her supervisors knew pretty well that it was the last time she'd see him before he shipped out, and they were being unusually generous with all of the girls who were seeing off husbands, boyfriends, or brothers.

At the train station, among crowds of people—mostly men in uniform heading south—they held each other tightly, neither saying anything, but with a thousand thoughts pouring through their heads.

Finally, they both began to speak at exactly the same time.

They both laughed, and both said, "You go ahead."

They laughed again, and he said, "Lady's first. Please."

"I just wanted to tell you that I love you, Kenny McCormick," she said, feeling the tears welling in her eyes, but trying to fight them back. "I'll write to you every day that I can, and every night I'll pray that the Lord keeps you safe. And you don't have to worry that any other guy is going to catch my eye while you're gone. As far as I'm concerned, the only reason that I'm not Mrs. Kenny McCormick right now is because of that silly training rule."

He let out a little laugh as he used his thumbs to brush the tears—with which she had lost the battle—from her cheeks.

"See how meant for each other we are?" he said. "I was going to say almost the very same thing. And I promise to keep my eyes open and my head down over there. I'm going to do everything I can to beat the Germans as fast as we can, because the sooner they surrender, the sooner I can get back here and make you Mrs. Kenny McCormick. If liberating Europe isn't enough of a motivator, that sure is!"

Her tears flowed freely as they kissed a kiss that was going to have to last them for a very long time.

When they broke the kiss, he said, "Do you want to wish on another tear?"

"It won't do any good," she said with a chuckle. "I know me, and I'm pretty sure we haven't seen the last one."

He looked at his watch, and knew he was going to have to get on board in a couple of minutes.

As they walked toward the platform, she took a small envelope from her purse and slipped it into his jacket pocket.

"What's that?" he asked.

"A present," she said.

He started to reach into his pocket, but she stopped him.

"Please wait until you're on the train," she said.

His heart stopped completely.

"It's not a Dear John letter is it?" he asked.

"Don't be silly! I just told you I loved you and want to be your wife," she said. "Or did you think I was telling you porkies?"

He laughed. "I'm sorry. I guess I just keep expecting my run of good luck to run *out*."

"Don't even *think* that, much less say it!" she told him.

"So, why can't I see your gift now?" Then a thought struck him. "Is it a page out of that book?" he asked.

She blushed as she laughed. "*No!* I wouldn't send you into a country full of French women with something like that in your pocket ... not that they need any instruction *or* encouragement."

"Then why can't I see it?"

"I couldn't bear to see your face if you don't like it."

"Fat chance of that!" he said. "Now that I know it's not a Dear John letter, I can't imaging anything you could give me that I wouldn't love."

"Please?" she said.

From behind him a conductor hollered, "*All aboard!*"

"Okay," he said, and kissed her one last time. "As soon as I get to camp, I'll write to you and tell you how much I love it, whatever it is."

"No, I want the truth from you, even if you hate it. Promise?"

"Promise!" he agreed.

He started for the train, but she caught him by his lapels, and stopped him.

"One last kiss for luck," she said as she pressed her lips to his. Then she let him go, and he ran for the train.

She watched him through the car's windows as he walked forward and found a seat. All of the window seats were taken, so he had to sit on the aisle.

She waved to him, but then she froze as he took the envelope from his pocket.

She could see him mouth the words, "I'm on the train, now," with a big grin.

She scowled at him as he smiled at her and tore the top off the packet.

She put her hands up to her mouth nervously as he slipped the folded paperboard from the envelope. Folded in half, it was about as big as a wallet-sized photograph.

He opened it up and for a very long moment, just stared at it. She held her breath as she watched him.

Finally, he turned to face her, and as she swore she saw a tear roll down his cheek, he mouthed, "I love it! I love you!"

Fresh tears ran down her cheeks as she mouthed back, "I love you, too!"

Kenny nudged the soldier next to him and showed him his gift, then pointed to Lily.

The guy looked at the card, looked at Kenny, looked at Lily, and then looked back at the card. "Very nice!" he mouthed toward Lily, and gave her a thumbs up. She watched him give Kenny a slap on the back, and shake his hand.

Kenny and Lily waved until they could no longer see each other. Then Kenny sat back and looked at her gift once again.

"Your girl copy that from a photograph or something?" Kenny's companion asked him.

Inside the folded paperboard was a small full-color portrait of Kenny and Lily together. The detail in the eyes, mouths, and hair was astonishing to Kenny, especially considering how small the picture was. And the color was absolutely perfect, from the light tone of her skin to the red of her lipstick to the highlights in her hair.

"We never had any pictures taken, at all," Kenny replied. "And certainly none together like this. And I never posed for her, either. She must have done herself in a mirror, and me from memory."

"So, she's an artist?" the guy asked.

"She's a nurse," Kenny said, staring at the intricate detail in his face and uniform. "Drawing is just her hobby. But I think she might have missed her calling."

"Well, if she's half as good at nursing as she is at drawing," the guy said, "I think there's going to be a lot of guys in the next few months who're damn glad she chose the career she did. You can tell her to open a portrait studio *after* our business with Hitler is over, and we're all patched up, okay?"

"Home by Christmas?" Kenny said.

"From your lips to God's ear," the guy replied.

When Kenny returned to camp on June 1st, he found that all future leaves had been canceled. That meant that the invasion was probably very near. The mood in the camp was upbeat, if not exactly jubilant. Everyone was ready to get off the dime, but they also knew that the real thing was going to be a lot different than the war games they'd been playing for the past year. Each man knew that he might not make it back, and that if he did, he would certainly not get to see all the faces of the men with whom he'd trained so hard and so long.

Only ten days of each of the summer months would be at all practical for the invasion, with the two or three days surrounding the full moon being the best. The moon would give as much illumination as possible for the night operations such as paratrooper drops and glider landings, but it would also coincide with the lowest possible tide. This meant that although the beaches on which they were going to land would be much wider—by the length of two to four football fields—and would leave the first waves of troops exposed to enemy fire for a dangerously long time, it also meant that most of the anti-boat obstacles the Germans had planted on the beach would be exposed and able to be demolished or marked for subsequent landings as the tide rose.

The original date of the invasion, June 5th, had to be abandoned because of bad weather, even though thousands of men and tens of thousands of tons of materiel were already on landing ships bobbing in the English Channel. On June 6th, although the weather was only slightly better, the invasion was launched.

Very little information regarding its success or failure made it down through the ranks to the men waiting at the embarkation points, but the return of empty troop ships and the constant outflow of men gave a pretty strong indication that Operation Overlord was working.

Tuesday, June 6, 1944
D-Day

Before Kenny left camp on the afternoon of June 6th for his company's embarkation point in Plymouth, he was told to report to the quartermaster with his Springfield rifle.

"Gift from your Uncle Sam," the sergeant said to Kenny as he handed him a brand new M1 Carbine rifle. "These showed up this morning. Since the front-liners are already gone, the brass figured you boys in the rear might as well have them. Give me your Springfield, and sign here."

McCormick had just been issued United States Carbine, Caliber .30, M1; Serial number 6,152,649.

He looked the rifle over and he noticed a small splintered hole in the wood where the hand guard joined the stock.

"Hey, sarge," he said to the man who had just handed him the carbine. He pointed to the hole, and said, "This weapon is damaged. There's a hole in the stock that I don't think should be there."

The sergeant didn't bother to look at it. He just said, "It's brand new; right out of the crate, fella. If it's got a hole where a hole don't belong, it's a factory defect. Don't worry about it; I'm sure it shoots just fine."

"Yeah, but I don't want to get gigged for this when I turn out for inspection," McCormick said. "Write it down, will you? Weapon has defect on right forestock."

"Yeah, yeah, okay," the sergeant said, but didn't pick up a pencil.

"Hand me the form, and I'll write it down if you're too busy," McCormick said, "but I ain't leaving until one of us does it."

The sergeant looked up at McCormick, and then at the rifle he was holding out at him. He shook his head, and pulled the form Kenny had just signed from the stack of cubbies on his desk. He wrote something on it, but McCormick couldn't see what it was.

"What'd you write?" he asked.

Exasperated, he looked at Kenny and said, "That Sergeant K. McCormick is a pain in my ass!"

"Fair enough," McCormick said, "but can you add the part about the damaged forestock, too?"

The other sergeant finally laughed. He held up the sheet for Kenny to read. It said exactly what Kenny had asked him to write in the first place.

"Now get the hell out of here," the sergeant said, "before I do add the thing about the pain in my ass!"

Wednesday, June 7, 1944
D-Day+1

June 7th was a very long day for Kenny and his company. They had done all that they could to get the mechanized equipment ready for the invasion, and now that it was underway, there was nothing for them to do but sit and wait for their turn to go over.

With nothing else mechanical to work on while he waited, Kenny decided to take his new rifle apart. He was always curious about all things mechanical, but wondered especially about the hole in the stock.

Alone in the tent, he made sure there was not a round in the chamber, and then he used his pocket knife to unscrew the bayonet band. He pushed in the release lever, slid the band forward, and lifted off the wooden hand guard.

He looked closely at the two halves of the hole in the hand guard and the forestock. He had suspected that maybe a loose part—a firing pin or a screw—had gotten between the two parts during assembly, and the hole had been crushed into the wood. He could see now that that wasn't the case.

The grain of the wood was obviously pushed inward toward the barrel. Whatever made the hole had been driven in from the outside, between the two pieces of wood. He also noticed that the object had nicked a small tear in the inspection slip that was tucked under the barrel. That meant that the damage had happened *after* the gun passed final inspection.

He lifted the barrel and took out the paper, curious as to when it had left the factory.

To his surprise, the slip didn't contain a date and a rubber stamp, but was emblazoned with a pair of bright red lips, with the words "*A Kiss For Luck!*" written over them. He forgot about the hole and the rifle for the moment, and just stared at the slip.

Who had put it there, he wondered. That was the last thing Lily had said to him on the platform at the station! Could she have known about it? He quickly decided that that was impossible. It had to be just coincidence.

Kenny knew that virtually all assembly line work back in the States was being done by women and girls these days, and the lip print was definitely a female's. The writing probably was, too.

Could some accident have befallen the rifle, resulting in the hole, and its assembler wanted to make sure it didn't carry a curse, so she inserted the slip? No. The slip had a nick in it that meant it was already in the gun when the hole was made.

Maybe *all* of the rifles had this piece of paper, he thought. As un-Army-like as that seemed, Kenny put the slip in his shirt pocket, and left the rifle disassembled on his cot.

He went over to Mack's cot, took *his* new Carbine from underneath, and took it apart. No slip. He put it back together, and did the same to Jimmy's rifle. Again, no slip.

He went back to his own cot, sat down and thought about the mysterious piece of paper.

He finally decided that wherever it came from, whoever put it in there and for whatever reason, it was going to be a good luck charm for him. He would put it with Lily's miniature portrait in his wallet.

As he reassembled the rifle, something made him pause just as he set the hand guard in place. What if the little slip brought good luck to the *rifle*? Made it shoot straighter or miraculously made it jam-proof? It seemed to him that having a lucky rifle heading into war might be a lot better than a lucky slip of paper in your wallet. Either way, he would have it with him.

He opened the rifle up and put the slip back where he had found it.

When he had it back together and stowed under his cot, he took out some paper and a pencil, and wrote Lily a letter to tell her about the slip. He decided not to tell anyone else.

Thursday, June 8, 1944
D-Day+2

On the morning of June 8th, the second day after the invasion began, Kenny and the men of the 729th boarded troop-transport landing-crafts and headed for Normandy. It would be afternoon before they set foot on the European continent.

A Kiss For Luck!

Thursday, June 22, 1944
D-Day+16

Two weeks later, as US troops pushed toward Cherbourg, Major Lindel, the CO of the 729th, stood in the radio truck and listened to the almost constant *thud!*, *thud!, thud!* of the shelling that was an impossible-to-ignore reminder that there was a war on ... and that it was very close by.

He read over the radioman's shoulder as the corporal transcribed the message he was hearing in his headset.

When he stopped writing, Lindel said, "Reply this: *'Roger, wilco. Will send a wrecker immediately. 729th over and out.'*"

The corporal repeated the major's words into his mike, then switched the mike off. "Maybe you'd better send a medic too, sir," he suggested. "From the hollering in the background, I think the colonel's going to shoot his driver!"

Lindel slapped the corporal on the shoulder acknowledging his joke, then he stepped down from the truck, and looked about for the 6x6 wrecker. He didn't see it in camp, and it was hard to miss. He saw McCormick leaning into the engine compartment of a Jeep, and called to him.

"McCormick, where's the wrecker?"

"Captain Shelby sent it out to pick up that deuce with the broken axle, sir. Should be back in a half hour or so," McCormick replied.

As he spoke, he plugged the coil lead back into the distributor, then swung into the driver's seat. He flipped the ignition switch, and pressed the starter button with the toe of his boot. The engine cranked, and he pumped the gas peddle once with his heal. The 4-cylinder "Go-Devil" engine came to life. He listened to it for about thirty seconds, was satisfied with its sound, and shut it off. By that time, Major Lindel was at the side of the Jeep.

"Colonel Grier's on his way down to see how we're *getting on*." the Major began, mocking the Colonel's use of the British vernacular. "Only his car seems to have gone off the road about ten miles east of here ... stuck in the mud. We need to go rescue him."

"Shouldn't need the wrecker to pull a staff car out of the mud," Kenny replied. Patting the steering wheel of the Jeep, he said, "Eugene here should be able to get him out okay."

"You think so?" the Major asked, having very little experience with Jeeps aside from their use as "little trucks."

"Sure of it, sir" Kenny answered without a doubt in his mind.

"Okay. Take two men, and go get him out." He pulled out a strip-map and showed McCormick where the Colonel was.

Kenny grabbed his Carbine from the tool truck, and set it into the scabbard on the inside of the Jeep's windshield. He fired up the Jeep, and then pulled along side a deuce that was getting its fuel tank repaired.

"Hey, Mack," he called out. "Scare up a length of tow chain, will you? We need to go rescue a colonel. I'll find Jimmy and be right back."

A minute later, Kenny was head east at top speed, following the major's map. About two miles out, however, he missed an unmarked fork, and ended up heading more south than east—right toward the slow-moving front line.

After traveling for about fifteen minutes, Mack recognized a landmark on the map and realized they were way off course.

Kenny stopped the Jeep, looked at the map, concurred with Mack's assessment, and prepared to turn around.

The dirt road was narrow where they stopped, with a deep ditch on one side and an eight-foot tall 45-degree banking on the other. To get a better view of their surroundings, Kenny pulled the lever that engaged the Jeep's front axle, and they crawled up the embankment in four-wheel drive. At the top of the burm, he turned the Jeep back in the direction they had come.

The three men looked back across the long ribbon of dirt road they had been traveling, paralleled almost out of sight by the irrigation ditch on its left side. What caught their attention, however, was the setting sun.

The sun had just dropped below the thick cloud-cover, and peeking out from the clear band between heaven and earth, it created the most spectacular illumination of the underside of the clouds. For that brief moment, it was hard for them to remember that a war was being fought less than a mile away—probably *much* less, with their recent wrong turn!

Their reverie of the idyllic moment was broken when Jimmy, in the back seat, yelled, "*Holy crap!*"

The two others spun around to see what had spooked Jimmy.

They were staring down on a Nazi Panzer tank at the bottom of the other side of the embankment.

It was back to them, and about twenty yards behind them. Its motor was off, and the tank commander stood chest-high in the open turret, facing away from them and unfolding a map, apparently as lost as the Micks were.

He had surfaced at the same time the Jeep stopped on the top of the hill, so he hadn't heard them. He *did* manage to hear Jimmy's startled yell however.

He turned around, looked at the Americans for a few startled seconds, and then dropped down quickly into his steel rabbit hole, swinging the hatch closed as he went down.

In that same few seconds, Jimmy had drawn his .45-automatic, and squeezed off three quick rounds. He was pretty sure the last of his bullets hit the guy.

Almost instantly, the Panzer's huge V-12 engine roared to life and the turret started to swing around bringing the cannon in their direction.

Mack and Jimmy started yelling, "*Go, Go, Go!!*"

Kenny hesitated just a moment before pulling the shift into first, and turning the steering wheel hard to the left to start back down the side of the embankment. But instead of going down the hill, he held the wheel until the Jeep had turned completely around and went over the top of the hill heading down the side where the tank was.

Almost in unison, Jimmy and Mack yelled, "*What the hell are you doing?!*"

170

Kenny shifted through second and into third, floored the gas pedal, and the little Jeep flew down the slope. He downshifted, braked, and turned hard when they got to the bottom, and then drove straight at the hundred-thousand-pound beast, up-shifting once more, and picking up speed.

Even more emphatically, his passengers screamed, "*WHAT THE HELL ARE YOU DOING?!*"

"Boxer's trick!" he yelled over the roar of the little four-banger engine. "Get in close and it takes the power out of their punch!"

Kenny drove the Jeep right up to tail end of the Panzer, and skidded to a stop with the hood nearly touching the inch-and-a-half thick armor plating under the tank's "duck-tail". The barrel of the 75mm cannon hung out over the top of the Jeep, directly above Jimmy's head.

Over the rumble of the big V-12, McCormick yelled, "She can't fire on us if we're in a clinch with her! We wouldn't have gotten a quarter mile down that road if we'd run!"

McCormick wasn't suicidal. He had played "Jeep tag" with some of the tank drivers back at Holabird, so he knew a lot about the weaknesses of tanks in general, and he knew a little about the Panzer, specifically, through reports he'd read on ones that had been captured.

Eyes wide in disbelief, Mack hollered back, "Well, she's gonna squash us like a bug if we sit *here*!"

In his down-Maine accent McCormick replied, "We'll see about that! She may be bigger, but we're a darn-site quicker than she is, and she has an Achilles' Heel. Jimmy, take that chain and throw it over the cannon!"

"*Do what?*" he bellowed.

"Throw the chain over the barrel," he repeated. "And hurry! Mack, grab the ends and jump out. Hook them onto our tow hitch. Make it snappy, before that Kraut figures out what we're doing! But hang on tight—if she starts to move I'm gonna take off fast!"

They quickly did as they were told, fueled by the gallon or so of adrenaline pumping through their veins. As soon as Mack had the chain hooked to the Jeep, he hollered, "Done!" and leapt back in.

While they were setting the chain, McCormick shifted the Jeep's transfer case into low range, so he would have plenty of power. With Mack onboard, he backed away from the tank a couple of feet, and then shifted into first, turned the wheel left, and floored the gas pedal.

The chain went taut as the tank's enormous turret tried to stop the Jeep from going anywhere. But Kenny knew that this was the behemoth's weakness.

Back at Holabird, Kenny had seen two Sherman tanks pass close to one another when one of them had the turret turned so its cannon was hanging out sideways. The barrel hit the passing tank, and acting like a long lever, drove the turret backwards. The force being backfed into the turret motor blew apart its gears, leaving only the very slow hand wheel to turn the five ton turret. Kenny was betting their lives that the Panzer had the same weak link.

The bewildered tank commander, looking through the tank's narrow periscopes, could not see what the *verrueckt Amerikaner* (crazy Americans) were up to, but because they were too close to fire at, he ordered the tank into reverse—toward the Jeep—to try to crush them.

The tank's sudden movement actually worked in Kenny's favor, putting even more strain on the chain and into the Panzer's turret.

Just when Kenny thought the tank was going to start dragging the Jeep backwards, the eight and a half ton turret broke free and swung lazily around to the side of the tank.

"Unhook the chain, *quick!*" Kenny hollered just as the tank came to a shuddering stop.

Kenny shifted back into high range as Mack reached over the back of the Jeep, and unhitched the chain, leaving it dangling from the cannon.

With the tank's two front-mounted machine guns facing away from the hill, and its unpowered cannon pointing sideways, Kenny knew it was their only chance to make a run for it.

He spun the Jeep around, and headed up the hill at full throttle.

Jimmy and Mack watched as the turret slowly turned in their direction, powered only by a tiny hand wheel.

"Hurry up! Hurry up!" Mack shouted to Kenny.

To speed up the aiming, the tank commander told the driver to move forward and turn the tank at the same time that the gunner was spinning the hand wheel as fast as he could.

As the cannon came around farther and farther, Jimmy and Mack watched it start to elevate.

"We got about three seconds!" Mack shouted.

Kenny knew that the cannon would be coming around to bare on them from the right, so he veered the direction of the Jeep left to make the gun have to follow them farther around.

All of a sudden, Mack and Jimmy saw the turret stop turning and the barrel stop elevating ... but it wasn't lined up on them.

Jimmy let out a roar of laughter when he saw that the tank had driven over the chain they left dangling from the cannon, stopping the turret dead. His levity lasted only a couple seconds, until the fifty-ton beast snapped the chain like kite string.

The tank made one more sideways lurch, and just as the Jeep crested the hill, the cannon roared.

The Jeep's speed caused it to go airborne over the top of a hill and the three men had to hold on tight to keep from flying up and out.

Just as the Jeep's wheels touched the hill on the far side, the tank shell exploded into the other side, probably two feet from the top. The Jeep was showered by flying dirt and rocks, and the windshield shattered. It was the first time the Micks were happy to be wearing their steel helmets.

Bouncing down the embankment, one of the shift levers on the Jeep's transfer case popped out of gear, leaving the engine disconnected from the wheels. At the bottom, Kenny downshifted and gunned the engine, but they didn't go anywhere.

As he scrambled to figure out what was wrong, and then to get the lever back in gear, they felt as much as they heard the approach of the tank as it thundered up the other side of the embankment.

Just as Kenny got the gears engaged the steel behemoth appeared above them. It paused on its vantage point to see which direction the Jeep had gone, not knowing, or able to see, that it was directly below them.

McCormick saw that the tank had come up backwards, cannon first. A lucky break for him and the other Micks. Had it come over frontwards, with its machine guns staring at them, Kenny could probably not have dodged the bullets very long. But facing only its human-powered cannon, he felt he could outrun and outmaneuver the beast. He gunned the Jeep and took off down the dirt road at full speed.

Perched at the narrow top of the embankment, the tank couldn't maneuver well, so as soon as the commander saw the running Jeep, he rumbled down the hill to take his next shot from level ground.

With a mile-long tree-topped embankment on one side, and a deep ditch on the other, McCormick had little choice but to stay on the road. He swerved from one side to the other in an erratic patter to make it harder for the tank to line up on them, but he knew that even a near-miss could kill all three of them. He wondered what their chances would be as smaller targets on foot and split up.

The tank came down the hill fast, and as it skidded around on the road to line up on the Jeep, its left tread ended up right at the edge of the ditch on the far side of the road.

The commander decided to use the whole tank to aim the cannon rather than the pathetic hand crank, so he called out steering orders to the driver as he adjusted the cannon's elevation. The tank inched forward, maneuvering "... left, left, left ... back right ... GOOD! Hold there!"

Suddenly, the embankment of the ditch yielded to the 50 tons of steel creeping along its edge.

Just as the commander yelled "Fire!" he felt the tank begin to tip slowly to the left. His shot went to the right of the Jeep, and over the top of the embankment, blowing apart a tree. The recoil from the cannon helped the tank to settle deeper into the ditch.

Jimmy and Mack watched mesmerized as the big Panzer tilted over into the ditch, then struggled to get free. Its right tread was off the ground, and its left could not dig into the soft mud of the ditch ... it was a condition known as *high-centering*, and it could be fatal to a tank.

Mack yelled at McCormick, explaining what had just happened, and he stopped the Jeep and turned to see the great monster throwing mud and water first frontward, then backwards ... to no avail.

The thrashings served only to dig the ditch deeper, and cause the tank to lean farther. As it jostled to get free, the weight of the cannon caused the unpowered turret to swing around, until the muzzle plowed into the ground. The gunner tried to crank it back up, but the tiny hand wheel was no match for the cannon's weight.

McCormick spun the Jeep around, and sped back toward the tank. Once again, that nagging question popped up. *"What the hell are you doing?!"*

McCormick hollered back, "We're gonna capture us a Nazi tank! Get out your weapons!"

He stopped the Jeep next to the underside of the tank and the two men jumped out. Kenny grabbed his carbine from the windshield scabbard, and followed. They leapt across the ditch, and made their way cautiously around the entrapped beast.

They spread out and kept their weapons raised. If the hatch opened, they were ready to start firing. But it didn't open.

Kenny soon found himself standing next to the mired steel giant, with Mack several yards to his left, and Jimmy to his right, in covering positions.

He pulled his Army-issued German/French/English dictionary from his jacket, and laboriously called out to the tank, "*Übergeben Sie oder wir werden Sie in Brand gesetzt!*" (Surrender or we will set you on fire!)

Fire was a tank crew's worst nightmare, and McCormick knew it from his days at Holabird. He waited for half a minute—which seemed an eternity—then repeated his demand as loudly as he could. A moment later the hatch opened slowly, and a hand with a white rag appeared.

The commander was the first to appear. As he climbed out through the hatch, they could see his left arm was soaked with blood.

"I *knew* I hit him!" Jimmy boasted.

As the wounded man made his way over the top of the sloping turret, his foot slipped, and without the use of his left arm he had a hard time stopping himself. Instinctively, McCormick reached out and grabbed the man's boot, pushing it toward a hand-hold.

"*Vielen Dank!*" (Many thanks!) the officer said.

As the commander readied himself to jump to the ground, the next crewmember appeared in the hatch.

The commander jumped, but stumbled when he landed, and once again, McCormick reached out to help him. Holding the carbine by the forestock in his left hand, he grabbed the man's right shoulder, and kept him from face-planting in the dirt.

At that moment, McCormick heard Mack shout, "*He's got a gun!*"

Assuming he was talking about the commander, Kenny pushed the man down as he took a step back, and swung the rifle up to get his right hand on it and his finger on the trigger.

Suddenly, pistol fire erupted. Jimmy, Mack, and the man in the tank were all firing at once.

Holding the rifle waist high, McCormick swung around and fired three quick shots up at the tank without the luxury of aiming.

The man in the tank fired at McCormick at the same time he was squeezing off the first round.

McCormick's first shot hit the man in the left lung, but the recoil of the carbine and McCormick's poor firing stance allowed the barrel of the gun to jump up, and the second and third shots sailed over the man's right shoulder.

The enemy's shot, although hurriedly aimed, was deadly accurate. It traveled a straight path toward McCormick's heart.

And had it not been for the carbine leaping up as it recoiled, it would surely have killed him.

The German's bullet grazed the top of the M1's bayonet band, deflected a fraction of a millimeter, struck the front of the wooden hand guard, and deflected just enough more to send the slug tearing into McCormick's left shoulder rather than his chest.

Kenny stumbled backwards, managing to stay on his feet, but saw the commander getting to his feet and lunging in his direction.

Holding the carbine with only his right hand, Kenny pulled the butt plate into his hip, and managed to get the barrel up and level as he took a step backwards.

He pulled the trigger twice, and then spun to the side as the commander fell toward him and sprawled lifelessly into the dirt.

At the same time, Jimmy and Mack had each put another bullet into the man in the hatch of the tank.

McCormick fell to his knees, trying hard not to pass out from the un-Godly pain in his shoulder.

"Jesus, Kenny! Are you okay?" Mack yelled when he finally took his eyes off the tank to look at McCormick.

"I think I'll live," he groaned.

"Hey, how did you say '*set their asses on fire*,' Kenny?" Jimmy asked, still pointing his pistol toward the hatch.

"*Sie in Brand gesetzt*," Kenny said.

"*Sie in fucking Brand gesetzt!*" Jimmy shouted. "*Schnell!*"

Slowly, a pair of gloved hands extended up through the hatch behind the dead man hanging half out of the opening.

Mack pantomimed pushing the dead soldier out of the way, and man did so. He then climbed out, and stood facing the tank with his hands on top of his head. His two other crewmembers did the same.

As Jimmy stood guard with both his and Mack's .45's, Mack took out the First Aid kit and field-dressed Kenny's wound as he sat on the ground. He cut open his shirt, and found that there was no exit wound.

"I don't wonder it hurts so much," Mack said as he sprinkled sulfanilamide on the wound to prevent infection. "The bullet's still in there."

He placed a gauze pad against the bleeding hole, and while Kenny held it, Mack wrapped a cloth bandage around his arm and shoulder to keep it in place.

While Mack and Jimmy herded the three Germans into the back of the Jeep, Kenny got on the walkie-talkie and called into camp to report what had happened. He used the code letters, numbers, and words on the strip map to explain where they were, without letting any eavesdropping Germans know at the same time. Then they pulled out.

With the windshield down, Mack drove, Kenny sat in the passenger seat cradling his arm and groaning with every bump, and Jimmy sat backwards atop the dashboard, pistols drawn, guarding their prisoners crammed into the back seat.

After Kenny's call, another vehicle was dispatched to rescue the Colonel, and within ten minutes they passed a truckload of GI's being sent out to guard their prize until a tank-wrecker could be brought up to extricate it.

And what a prize it turned out to be! It was one of several dozen *Panzer Nachtjäger* that had been tearing up the Allied troops in the dead of the night.

The *Nachtjäger* (night fighter) was a Panzer tank equipped with a powerful infra-red search-light, and an infra-red night-scope atop its turret. The light from the search light was invisible to the naked eye, but lit up the night like green-tinted daylight when viewed through the scope.

With one of these scopes, the Americans would now be able to see the Night Fighters as soon as they turned on their IR search lights. It would be like the Germans were driving at them with their high-beams on!

When the Jeep pulled into camp it was immediately surrounded by cheering GI's hailing the "Micks from Maine" as giant-killers and heroes. The trio also got the new nickname, "The Maine-iacs!"

Kenny was lying on the Major Lindel's cot in his tent while they waited for the ambulance that would bring him back to the beach and an evacuation ship. As they waited, the major and Captain Shelby quizzed him, and marveled at his crazy David and Goliath stunt.

"You know, son," the major said to Kenny, "when they dig that bullet out of your arm make sure they keep it and give it to you. That's a million-dollar piece of lead you've got there."

He was referring, of course, to Kenny having a "million-dollar wound." An injury bad enough to send you home, but not bad enough to kill you.

"I don't know, sir," he replied. "I spent the last three and a half years waiting to get here and do my bit, now I'm shipping out when we're just getting started."

"Be careful what you wish for, son," the major said. "Besides, once you lay your butt in a bed with a real mattress and clean sheets, and you get those pretty nurses around you every day, I think you'll manage to forget all about us over here."

"The nurse thing *had* crossed my mind, sir," Kenny said. "Do you know if I get to choose what hospital I go to?"

Just then there was a rap on the wooden frame of the tent door.

"Come," the major said.

An officer walked in, saluted, and introduced himself as Captain Peter Scotts.

As Kenny began to get off the cot to come to attention, the major said, "As you were, McCormick."

"McCormick?" Scotts said. "The third of the trio who just captured that tank? I've just been enjoying your compatriot's story in the mess tent. Damned gutsy maneuver." He laughed. "A Jeep and a Panzer toe to toe, and the Jeep won! Imagine that. Well, congratulations. When the war's over, we'll have to see if we can get some medals for the three of you."

"When the war's over?" Lindel repeated. "I was going to push that paperwork through this week."

"Sorry, Major," Scotts said. "We're going to need to keep this a secret as long as we can. If the Jerries know that we can see them in the dark, now, they may send the whole *Nachtjäger* group somewhere else. And then, of course, we'll want to send the scope stateside and copy it. Better if they don't know that, too."

"Aren't they going to figure it out when one of their tanks goes missing?" the major asked.

"Missing and in-enemy-hands are two different things," Scotts replied. "They've got their tanks going every which way, right now. We don't think they have a very organized plan, and if they do, nobody's following it. It's probably why that tank was out there all by itself."

Major Lindel looked at the captain curiously. "What outfit did you say you were with?" he asked.

"I didn't. But I'm with the OSS," he replied. "The tank is most interesting, of course, but I actually popped in to beg a favor." [The OSS, Office of Strategic Services, was the WWII equivalent to the CIA.]

"Is it okay if the sergeant hears it?" Lindel asked.

"Oh, no problem at all," Scotts said. "That we're supplying the French Resistance with arms is certainly no secret."

"Then what can we do for you?" Lindel asked as he motioned the captain toward a chair.

"We had a bit of bad luck last night," he began. "We had an air-drop scheduled for one of the marquis south of St. Lo. They're out there trying to blow up bridges and cut telephone lines, and just make it as hard as they can for Jerry to get reinforcements north.

"Anyway, the plane that was to make the drop developed engine troubles over the Channel, and had to ditch. We rescued the pilots, but we lost all the guns, ammo, explosives, and the radio we were delivering.

"So, I'm on a mission to beg, borrow, or steal anything I can get my hands on that will make Jerry's life a little less pleasant, and get it to *la Résistance* tonight."

"Sounds like you should be talking to the quartermaster," Lindel said. "They're in charge of all the supplies."

"Yes," Scotts replied, "and a small mountain of paperwork, as well. If I *can* get what I need from them, it will take days. I have hours. So what I'm doing is officially unofficial."

"What do you have in mind?" the major asked.

"Well, I understand that one of the things the 729th does is to process weapons that come back from the front with a wounded or a deceased soldier. You clean it, repair it, if necessary, and then send it on to the quartermaster for reassignment.

"Now, I've also heard that transportation of these recycled weapons to the rear is not always Johnny-on-the-spot, owing to all the vehicles you have being used to move the Army forward.

"So, in the spirit of inter-unit cooperation, I'm offering my time and the use of my personal Jeep to help you boys out and get these weapons out of your way."

The major laughed. "I had heard that OSS stood for Obsessed with Sneaky Shit, now I know it's true. But if you want to sign for the weapons, nobody here is going to check with the boys at quartermaster to see if they showed up."

"A pleasure doing business with you, Major!" Scotts said as he stood up and extended his hand. And the men and women of *La Résistance* thank you, too."

As the captain turned to leave, Kenny said, "Excuse me, sir. I'd like to make a donation, if it's okay with the major."

With his good arm, he slid his carbine out from under the cot. "I'd like you to take this, if you would, sir. It just saved my life, and I have a feeling it has some pretty special qualities that the resistance can use."

"Thank you, son," the captain said as he took the rifle. He looked it over, and he noticed the gouge in the metal bayonet band and the splintered end of the wooden hand guard. He also noticed the hole in the side of the stock.

"A little the worse for wear," the captain said. He turned to Captain Shelby, and said, "Can we get this cleaned up while I load the other weapons?"

"NO!" Kenny snapped, then quickly added, "... Sir."

They all looked at him.

"Like I said, sir, there's something special about that rifle," Kenny said, "and I think it needs to go back into battle just the way it is, scars and all. It shoots just fine, I guarantee that."

"If your CO has no objection," Scotts said, "I certainly don't. And I'm sure our French freedom fighters won't mind."

"The last thing I'm going to object to is less work for my men," Lindel said. "If McCormick says the rifle's fit for duty, then it's all yours."

"Thank you, again, gentlemen," Scotts said. "All of you."

With the carbine in hand, he headed for the door, but then stopped, again. He turned back to face Kenny.

"When I walked up to the door a little while ago," he said, "did I overhear you asking if you could request a certain hospital when you get back to England?"

"Yes, sir," he said. "I have a lady friend who's a nurse at Queen Elizabeth in Birmingham. I thought it might be nice to see her again."

The three officers laughed at his understatement.

"... nice to see her, again, huh?" Lindel repeated. "I should think so!"

"*Cherchez la femme!*" Captain Scotts said with a chuckle. "Raise your right hand," he said to Kenny.

He did as he was told, but his confusion was obvious. Neither Lindel or Shelby knew what was going on, either.

"Say, *I swear*," Scotts said.

"Swear what, sir?"

"I can't tell you; it's a secret. Just say it."

"I swear," Kenny said obediently.

"Good. You're now a temporary member of the OSS." He turned to Lindel, and said, "If I could borrow your desk for a minute, and a sheet of paper, I think we can get Sergeant McCormick his wish."

They all watched as he wrote a short letter, and then signed it with a flourish.

He handed it to the major, and asked, "What do you think?"

Lindel read the letter out loud.

> To whom it may concern:
>
> Please be advised that the bearer of this letter, Sergeant Kenneth McCormick, is on a special assignment for the Office of Strategic Services (OSS), and must be directed to Queen Elizabeth Hospital in Birmingham as quickly as possible, and with as little notice as possible.
>
> To understand the importance of this assignment, you should realize that the wound in the sergeant's left shoulder, while very genuine, was intentionally received as part of his cover. DO NOTHING THAT WILL JEOPARDIZE THAT COVER OR HIS MISSION!
>
> Daniel M. Scotts, Captain, US Army, OSS

The major laughed. "It's just outrageous enough to work."

"Of course it will work," Scotts said. "It's one less decision those poor souls sorting the wounded will have to make, and what difference is it to them, anyway? It's not like I'm trying to sneak the sergeant into Buckingham Palace."

"Did you write you own notes when you played hooky from school?" Shelby asked.

"I got so I could write my mother's name better than she could," he answered with a laugh.

Eight hours later, McCormick was aboard a troop transport with hundreds of other wounded soldiers heading across the Channel, back to England.

While the pain in his shoulder was excruciating he refused to let the medics give him any morphine for fear that he would be asleep when he needed to present his letter to someone, and he would end up in the wrong hospital.

He showed the letter to half a dozen different people, none of whom questioned it at all. When he was finally on the train heading for Birmingham, he recognized the countryside, and only then did he let a corpsman give him a shot.

Friday, June 23, 1944
D-Day+18

Kenny woke up in a bed in a stark white room with at least two dozen beds in it.

The first thing he noticed was that he was wearing a hospital johnny. His uniform was neatly folded and at the foot of his bed.

The second thing was that his shoulder had a fresh bandage on it, and his arm was strapped to his body. He didn't know if it had been operated on or not, but it sure still hurt.

The third thing he noticed was that he had to pee!

He managed to get the attention of an older nurse, and when she came over, he said as he swung his legs out of the bed, "Ma'am, I hate to be crude, but I have really got to use the loo! Can you point me in the right direction, please?"

"It's nearer than you think," she said as she reached under the bed and slid out a bedpan. "Here you go, soldier. We can't have you boys wandering all over the place. Getting you back into your beds would be like trying to herd cats."

He wasn't happy about the bedpan, but he knew if he argued the point for more than thirty seconds, he might not make it to the latrine, anyway. He wrapped the sheet around himself, and as he maneuvered onto the pan, he asked the retreating nurse, "Do you happen to know Lily Thatcher, by any chance?"

"Never heard of her," she said without looking back.

Kenny's heart skipped a beat.

"This is Queen Elizabeth Hospital in Birmingham, isn't it?" he called out to her.

She either didn't hear him, or chose to ignore him, and walked away.

After he finished draining his bladder—and worrying that he would overflow the bedpan—he slid the pan back under the bed and got up to find out where he was.

Four beds down, he found a man propped on one elbow, reading a paperback.

"Hey, Buddy," Kenny said, "Do you know what hospital this is?"

He looked up at Kenny, looked around the room for a moment, and then said, "I can't say that I do. I don't think anybody's ever told me."

He moved on to another bed where two men were playing cards, one of them with his head bandaged and only one eye showing.

"You guys know where we are?"

"You're in a hospital in England, fella," the man with one eye said. "No need to worry."

"I'm not worried," Kenny said. "I just want to know *which* hospital."

"What's it bloody matter," the other guy said with a British accent, "as long as it's in bloomin' England!"

Kenny turned to find someone else to ask, but he stopped cold when he saw another nurse coming toward him.

It was Lily.

They walked toward each other, smiling ear to ear, and trying desperately not to run.

They each wanted to throw their arms around the other, and share a long passionate kiss to celebrate their reunion. But they didn't. Not in such a public place, and not while she was on duty.

They shook hands, and Kenny kissed her cheek.

"God, it's good to see you!" he said.

"Mind your language," she said, touching her finger to his lips. "This isn't a battle field, you know. It's wonderful to see you, too, I only wish it didn't have to be here. How does your shoulder feel?" she asked looking at the dressing.

"It still hurts a lot. Do you know if they've taken the bullet out, yet?"

"We haven't," she said. "Your wound isn't life threatening, so you're scheduled for later on tonight or in the morning."

"Are you going to be there when they operate?" he asked.

"I'm on duty in theater tonight," she said, 'but I won't be if they put it off until the morning."

"Well, can you make sure they keep the bullet when they dig it out?" he asked. "I'd like it as a souvenir."

"A lucky charm?" she said. "That's pretty standard, actually. Everyone wants a keepsake of their million-dollar wound."

"You remember me telling you about that *Kiss for Luck!* piece of paper I found in my rifle just before I went over?" he asked her.

"Of course," she said. "I thought it was a wonderful omen. Apparently, it wasn't lucky enough, though."

"It was luckier than you can imagine," he said. "That rifle probably saved my life."

He then told her the story of the tank encounter, and how the German's pistol shot was deflected by the rifle into his shoulder when it was probably heading for his heart.

"Oh, my gosh!" she said. "I had no idea! What a *marvelous* bit of luck! What a marvelous gun! Will they let you keep it, now that it's ruined? Or at least the lucky slip of paper?"

"The rifle wasn't ruined at all ... part of its luck, I think. It has a couple of scars, but it's still quite fit for service. So I donated it—lucky slip and all—to a captain who was gathering weapons to send to the French resistance fighters. I figure they can use all the luck they can get if we're going to get this thing finished by Christmas."

Unfortunately, the war in Europe would drag on for almost another year, during which time Lily would be kept dreadfully busy ministering to thousands of wounded soldiers.

Kenny never regained full motion of his left shoulder, and was therefore never redeployed to Europe. He was transferred to the Quartermaster Corps, and remained stationed in England for the duration of the war.

On May 8th, V-E Day, Kenny and Lily were married in a small church in Dover, a few miles from Lily's family cottage. Discharged from the service, Kenny made good on his vow not to take a Liberty ship back home, and opened a bicycle shop in Hockley, just north of Birmingham. A few years later, he moved it to Birmingham, within cycling distance from their home.

Lily remained a nurse until the couple had a daughter, three years later. When Margaret entered school, Lily opened a small portrait studio in the parlor of their home to bring in a little extra income.

End of Part III

A Kiss For Luck!

Part IV:
La Résistance

Agen, Vichy France
Thursday, May 6, 1943
One year and one month before D-Day

The bell above the front door jingled, and with a Pavlovian grasp of the obvious, Marie Renaud called out, "*Client!*" (Customer!) in her native French.

"I know, Mama," her daughter Joyce said with a chuckle. "I have ears, too." She turned and looked through the round window in the door that separated the kitchen from the shop-half of the bakery.

The young German *Oberfähnrich* (senior ensign) was looking directly at her. He smiled, and she smiled back. Before pushing open the door she reached up, and below his view through the window, she unbuttoned another button on her blouse and tugged it open a shade more.

"Franz!" she said brightly as she swung the door open. "You look so dashing today. The cap is so much more stylish than your helmet." She spoke in intentionally muddled German hoping to impress him with her attempt to learn his language. In fact, she spoke fluent German already. It was just part of the act she put on to show how much she cared for him.

He smiled dopily at her for a moment, taking in her beauty ... and her cleavage.

He touched his garrison cap, adjusting it unnecessarily, and said in French that was worse than her German, "Thank you. But I think it is silly looking. Now that I have graduated from officer's school I will be getting my lieutenant's uniform and cap, soon. You will think me very handsome then, no?"

"I think you are very handsome, now," she said. "But yes, an officer's uniform will fit you well. I'm sure you will make a fine officer."

Their flirtatious chitchat continued for several minutes, until another customer, a stoop-shouldered old woman, came in.

Joyce wrapped a croissant in paper and held it out to Franz. He took a 100-reichsmark note from his pocket and handed it to her. "I believe that is correct," he said as he clasped her hand and the croissant between his two hands. He leaned in quickly and kissed her on the cheek. "*Auf wiedersehen*," he said as he slipped the roll from her fingers and turned toward the door.

Joyce looked at the crisp bill in her hand. 100 reichsmarks was twenty times what any other German soldier would pay for a croissant. But the German currency that had been forced upon France since the occupation was inflated twenty times over the franc, so it really worked out just about right.

As the door closed behind Franz, Joyce turned to the old woman, and with a smile said in French, "What can I get for ..."

Her question was cut short by a slap across the face.

"*Putain*!" (Whore!) the woman snapped. "You should be ashamed! You're *mother* should be ashamed! You carry on with a Nazi pig! I will buy *nothing* from your whorehouse bakery!" She spit on the floor, then turned, flung open the door, and repeated "Whore!" as she stormed out.

Joyce stood there with her hand on her cheek watching the woman leave. It hadn't been a hard slap—it had been more humiliating than painful, and she knew that that was the old woman's intent. Joyce couldn't blame her for her reaction, but she couldn't very well explain that she was wrong, either.

She rebuttoned her blouse, got a rag from behind the counter, and wiped the old lady's spit from the floor. She then went back into the kitchen to help her mother. She showed her the bill that Franz had given her.

Her mother laughed. "Herr Franz is smitten with you. You play your part well. But it is easy when you have such breasts, no? I remember when young men looked at *my* breasts."

"Is that how you lured Papa?"

"*Oui*. And my derrière," she said slapping her rump, which had grown generous with time. She laughed again, and said, "Men are so stupid when sex is involved."

Joyce chuckled. "It is a good thing, no?"

"Have you made love with your young soldier?" her mother asked.

"No," Joyce answered, not the least bit shocked by her mother's personal question. "I let *him* make love to *me*, but the feeling is far from mutual. That old lady was right; he is just one more Nazi pig." She chuckled again. "He is so funny. When we lie together naked, he tells me of his dream to be a great general one day, like his hero, Rommel. Like that is the kind of pillow talk a girl wants to hear. But it is so easy to pretend I'm interested and get him to tell me all sorts of things about the army. If he did not talk so freely in bed, I would not let him even look at my breasts, much less touch them."

"Well, just be careful, my love. If he suspects your pillow talk is making its way to the Allies even your perky breasts will not save you."

"I know, Mama. But I cannot just sit on my hands and let Hitler and Mussolini divide up our country. I know it's not much, and the Allies probably already know all that I can offer, but at least I feel I am doing something in the name of France. The *real* France; not that groveling Petain's puppet show."

"I know, my dear," her mother said, turning to give her a hug. Tears spilled from her eyes as she kissed her daughter's cheek. "God bless you, my love. And God keep you safe."

Two days later, shortly after Franz had come in to buy his daily croissant and get his morning fix of cleavage, a young man in a Basque beret entered the store and hurried through the swinging door into the kitchen. Joyce stood at the sink drying her hands. She had been washing the mixer when she heard the shop door's bell ring.

"Pierre!" she said, surprised to see him in the store at all, much less rushing into the kitchen. She looked around him through the still swinging door to see if anyone else was in the store. "Is something wrong?"

"Where are your mother and father?" he asked hurriedly.

"Upstairs. What is it? What's wrong?"

"Get them! You must leave. Now. All of you."

"Why? What's happened?" Joyce asked as she tossed the towel into the sink and headed for the stairs with Pierre right behind.

Pierre was a fellow member of the rural resistance group. To keep each other safe, the members of their group rarely had any public contact, so for him to come to the shop like this meant that there was serious trouble.

"The Milice (the Nazi-controlled French militia), have gotten on another round-up kick," Pierre said as they mounted the steps two at a time. "Jacque has seen the list of names they've given the police; your mother's name is on it."

"Oh, God!" was all Joyce could say as she made the top landing and rushed down the hall.

Joyce's father was pedigree French as far back as anyone cared to look, but her mother was Jewish. The family had fled Paris and headed south when her father first heard that the German's had invaded France through Belgium, completely avoiding the "impregnable" Maginot Line. If France's military leaders were stupid enough to think that a single line of concrete bunkers—no matter how large their guns—would keep the Nazis out indefinitely, then he had no faith whatsoever that they could keep the Germans from marching to Paris almost at will.

The family had been very careful not to let anyone in their new city of Agen know that Mama was Jewish, but there was always a trail, and always people who were willing to barter such information to the Nazi's for money, to save their own necks, or out of pure spite.

"Mama! Papa! We have to go!" Joyce shouted as she ran down the hall. "The Milice are coming!"

Marie and Vincent needed no further inducement. Virtually every Jew in France lived in fear of that sentence. They each grabbed a jacket, and Vincent pulled a leather travel case from the top shelf of the bedroom closet. It had been packed months ago, against just such an emergency. It contained the necessities for hasty travel, including warm clothes, soap, a razor, and all of the cash—francs and reichsmarks—that Vincent had been able to hoard after paying the bills.

Also in the case were forged travel papers and passports for Marie and Vincent; a contribution made by Joyce through her resistance connections.

Mama, Papa, Joyce, and Pierre hurried down the stairs and turned to head out through the back door into the alley. As they opened the door they heard the tinkle of the bell above the shop's front door.

"Go!" Pierre said. "I'll see to whoever it is. And lock the door behind you."

Joyce walked down the alley ahead of her parents, checking to see if the police had stationed anyone to prevent just such and escape attempt. They had apparently not.

Joyce didn't consider the local police very bright; they were just thugs and stooges, taking orders. Most were unable to think on their own, and the rest were unwilling to.

She quickly led her parents down alleys and streets they had never even seen before, and into the outskirts of the city.

From the kitchen, Pierre peered out into the shop through the crack at the edge of the swinging door. Two local policemen were standing there, looking at the few pastries in the glass case. He pulled off his beret and stuffed it into his pocket, and quickly tied an apron around his waist. He picked up a loaf of bread and pushed the door open.

"*Bonjour*!" Pierre said brightly, extending the loaf to the taller man. "Here is the bread you requested, fresh from the oven." He added with a wink, "Compliments of the proprietors, of course." He was acting in as flamboyant and effeminate a manner as he could.

Confused, the two men looked at the bread and then at Pierre. "We are not here to pick up bread," the tall one said, although he didn't hand the loaf back, either. "Where are the owners? Vincent and Marie Renaud."

"Ah!" Pierre said, throwing up his hands. "You *just* missed them. They have taken a basket over to the widow Lafourche over on Rue Clair Matin. The poor woman lost her husband in the Great War, and now her son, up in Sarrebourg. Do you know her? Always so strong and straight! But I don't know if she will be able to withstand this blow. Her daughter, Eva—the little tart—has run off ..."

"We are not here to listen to your gossip," the shorter man snapped. "When will they be back?"

"Oh," Pierre mused for a moment, "an hour I should think. It is a fair walk over to her house, you know, and Vincent has that knee that acts up when the weather gets like this. They will probably want to visit, of course. Mrs. Lafourche is quite lonely, I'm sure. Perhaps if you ..."

"Never mind!" the tall one said. "We'll be back." They turned and left ... taking the bread with them.

Pierre took off the apron, put his beret back on, and rummaged in the kitchen until he found a cloth sack. He put several loaves of bread and all of the croissants he could find into the sack and left through the front door. He headed down the street in the opposite direction from the police. He would meet Joyce and her parents at the safe house tonight, and they and the others in the group would plan the Renaud's escape to Spain while they enjoyed the bread and a bottle or two of wine.

Two weeks later, Joyce kissed her mother and father good-bye and left them in the hands of a resistance band that specialized in smuggling downed Allied airmen across the Spanish/French border. It would be almost two and a half years before she would see them again.

When France fell to the Nazi's in 1940 the resistance movement sprang up almost immediately. But the movement lacked nearly any kind of organization, and was primarily a propagandist faction, rather than a fighting force. Small bands of French patriots published leaflets and underground newspapers to expose the traitorous acts being carried out by the Vichy government that had handed over the whole of northern France to the Germans ... and who, they felt, received substantial personal rewards for doing so.

Little by little, and with the aid and encouragement of the Allies, *La Résistance* became militaristic. Those groups became known as *maquis*. Literally translated as "thicket" the word more generally referred to "the bush" where the bands hid out and launched their harassing raids against the occupying Nazi's and the capitulating French secret police, the *Milice*.

Rather than risk returning to Agen, and ready to take a more active roll in fighting the Germans, Joyce headed north toward the border between the Nazi-controlled *Zone occupée* (occupied zone) and what was laughably called *Zone libre* (free zone).

Like a fish swimming upstream, Joyce followed what was known as the Pat O'Leary Route northward. The route, which typically flowed southward from Paris to Marseilles, Barcelona, or Perpignan on the Mediterranean Sea, was one of several established "underground railroads" by which the resistance groups escorted and handed off Allied airmen who had been shot down on bombing raids. Like her parents, they would be smuggled across the border into neutral Spain. Eventually, the flyers would make their way back to England, and many would end up back in the skies over France.

Monday, June 7, 1943

Just south of the line of demarcation between the free and occupied zones, was the town of Issoudun. South of that was the village of Saint-Août, where Joyce met up with a maqui that was planning to sabotage a German supply train in two night's time.

The group's founder and leader was Julien Arsenault. Two or three years older than Joyce, he was a tall, broad, and implausibly handsome man whose egotistical image of himself went even beyond the already extraordinary reality. He was immediately attracted to Joyce, but almost entirely because of her looks rather than her patriotic spirit.

Joyce took a very quick dislike to Julien, and only stayed with the maqui because it offered her her first chance to actively fight the Nazi's.

Performing her keenly honed part as the *enjeneau*, Joyce played Julien as skillfully as he thought he was playing her.

In the evening of the first day that she met up with the maqui, the group sat around a heavy wooden table in a small farmhouse, eating bread and drinking wine.

"How do we know you're not a spy," Julien asked Joyce, "sent here to betray us to the Milice or the SS?"

"I thought my letter of introduction from Pierre Sousa took care of that," she answered, pretty sure that he was just trying to put her on the spot and show the others how in-charge he was.

"Such a letter could easily be stolen or even forged," he said. "Tell me, how many German's have you killed? I have sent at least seventy-five to their graves."

"Wow!" she said, feigning astonishment at his feat. She was sure that it was an exaggeration, or perhaps a tally for the entire maqui for which he felt he deserved all of the credit.

"In such company," she went on, "I'm almost ashamed to say that I haven't killed any. Not yet, anyway. That's why I came north; it's why I want to be part of your group ... if you'll have me. I'm tired of just preaching and handing out fliers about defying the Germans. I want to help destroy them."

"Are you any good with a rifle?" Julien asked.

"I'm pretty good with a shotgun," she said. "Before the war I used to go hunting with my Papa."

Julien laughed. "This war isn't some leisurely duck hunt, chéri," he said. "Unless you're standing close enough to almost poke your Nazi target with the barrel, your pellets will hardly get through all of his clothes. All you'll do with a shotgun is piss him off. And this prey shoots back if you don't kill it."

"Then you must teach me to shoot a rifle. I'll never be as good as you, of course," she said, stroking his ego, "but even if I am only a little bit as good it can make a difference, no?"

He looked her in the eyes for several seconds, and she held his stare. She could almost see the wheels spinning in his head, trying to formulate the advantage he could take in the situation.

"I'll teach you what I can in two days," he finally said. "You can prove your loyalty to France then by shooting Germans when we stop the train. Assuming you can be taught to shoot straight in that time, of course."

"I have faith that you can teach me," she said with a seductive smile. She was picturing in her mind the image he was probably thinking about of his arms wrapped pleasantly around her showing her how to hold a rifle.

"I'm not sure that my faith in you is as strong," he replied.

She looked at him quizzically.

"You know where we eat and sleep and you know our plans for the train," he said. "What if you *are* a spy? At the first opportunity you could run and tell the authorities and we would all be shot before we ever heard the train whistle blow."

"Show me a German, and I'll shoot him tonight," she said.

"That would draw attention we don't want," he replied. "I have a better idea. Until we take the train two nights from now, you'll stay right by my side. We'll see how good of a pupil you are and I can keep an eye on you at the same time."

"What better company could I ask for?" she said, turning to look at the other men at the table. "I'm accustomed to sleeping on the floor, so I won't even take anyone's bed."

"You'll sleep in *my* bed," Julien said.

"Oh, I couldn't ask you to give up ..." she began.

"With me," he continued, cutting her off. "Sneaking off while we're all asleep would be especially easy."

She almost laughed. She didn't believe that he really distrusted her that much—not with the letter she had; he was just using it as a way to get her into bed! She had no interest in having sex with him, although she imagined it might be quite pleasant ... and it had been a long time. But after Franz, she had developed a very strong aversion to having sex with men she didn't like. For once, however, her biological calendar was working in her favor. She had started her period a few days earlier.

"You needn't worry about me sneaking off," she said. "I'll prove my loyalty at the train, you'll see." She then added with a coy smile, "And in the meantime, I won't have to worry about being cold, no?"

Julien's bedroom was at the back of the farmhouse. It was the only room with just one bed in it. All of the other men slept three to a room. Joyce wondered if that was because, as the leader, he felt he was entitled to that privilege, or because he "entertained" women there often. She noticed that his bed was the only one large enough for two people to fit on—although just barely.

Joyce had a single change of clothes and a heavy wool sweater in her backpack. Certainly nothing that would pass for pajamas.

If she had her own bed, she would probably have slept in only her underpants just for a chance to be out of her clothes for a while. Being in the same bed with Julien, she didn't think that was a good idea. He certainly didn't need any more encouragement. She decided to sleep in her underwear and her shirt.

She sat down on the bed, and took off her boots and her socks. She then stood, and pushed off her pants.

She turned to find Julien completely naked and pulling back the blanket on the bed. He climbed in, and without covering up, he laid there waiting for her.

To her dismay—but not her surprise—he was even better looking without clothes on. He was lean, muscled, and well proportioned—in all aspects. He had an attractive amount of hair on his chest, and a dark, tangled island of it father down.

She turned her back on him and bit her lip as she sat down next to him, and began to swing her legs onto the bed.

"That's how you're going to sleep?" he said. "Half dressed? That won't be very comfortable. What's the matter; don't you trust me?"

"I don't trust *me*," she lied. "I don't want to start something I can't finish."

He looked at her curiously.

"It's my time of the month," she said with a shrug. Then she added, "But all should be well by the time we take the train. It will give us something to celebrate, and a great way to do it, no?"

A look of disappointment came into his eyes that almost made her laugh.

"Well, surely you will be more comfortable without your shirt," he said. "And still able to control yourself, I expect."

"I'm sure you're right on the first count," she said. "And I can only *hope* you're right on the second."

"Don't worry," he said in such a dejected tone that she nearly laughed again. For such a fine example of a man, he was such a little boy.

She tossed her shirt on the chair with her pants and lay back down in her light cotton bra. Her breasts were not small, but they were not heavy and pendulous like her mother's, either—at least not yet. She was proud of her breasts, and she wore a bra—something her mother never did—to try to keep them appealing for as long as possible.

She pulled the blanket up over her chest and rolled onto her side, facing away from him.

"Good night, Julien," she said. "Thank you for letting me share your bed."

"You're welcome," he said as he lay there on his back. His tone nearly made her laugh again.

An hour later, she was awakened when he rolled onto his side, facing the same direction that she was. His naked body spooned against hers, and she found the warmth welcome.

He let out a single gurgling snore and shifted his body slightly. His right arm ended up draped over her, with his open hand resting on her left breast. She had to wonder if he was really still asleep, but his breathing made it seem that way.

She began to relax and drift off again under the warmth of his unconscious embrace. But then he began making little moaning sounds.

She rolled her eyes, knowing she would not be able to go back to sleep with him moaning in her ear, and she contemplated nudging him with her elbow. Then, she suddenly realized that she could feel his manhood stiffening against her buttocks!

She had to smile, wondering what kind of dream he was having. Such a little boy!

Then she wondered if he was dreaming about her. She rather hoped so. It would be more than a little deflating to have him lying there with his hand on her breast and his erection pressed against her behind while he dreamt about some other woman!

After a few minutes of being physically entangled in what she imagined was his erotic dream, his whole body suddenly jolted, and it startled her. She knew that falling feeling that snaps you awake suddenly, and she had to wonder how that played into his dream.

He didn't appear to come fully awake, but groaned, swallowed hard a couple of times, and rolled over onto his other side.

She missed the warmth of his body almost immediately, although not the intimacy of the contact. She was tempted to roll over herself and cuddle into his back, but even the thought of the warmth didn't override her desire to not encourage him if he should wake to find her snuggled against him. She settled for lying with her back against his, and pulling the blanket up under her chin.

Tuesday, June 8, 1943

She was awake and dressed and sitting in his chair when the rooster in the yard proclaimed the beginning of a new day.
　　She watched Julien stir, open his eyes, and apparently get his bearings. Then he looked over at her.
　　"Good morning," she said. "Did you sleep well?"
　　"I did," he answered, tossing back the blanket to reveal a full erection. "But sleeping next to you, see how I have awakened?"
　　Joyce knew that it was not uncommon for men to wake up with an erection. Erroneous though her conclusion was, she felt it was amusing that they were apparently always dreaming about sex.
　　"I'm flattered," she lied.
　　He got out of bed and crossed over to her, making no attempt to cover himself.
　　She smiled, but not because she was pleased at his display or even impressed by it, but because he reminded her of a peacock, flaunting his plumage to impress his hoped-for mate.
　　"It is obvious," Julien said, "that he thinks you are a very beautiful woman, no?"
　　She reached out and cradled his erection in her hand, and leaned over and kissed the top of it. "Patience, my friend," she said to it, "the time for celebration is near."
　　She then stood up and put her arms around his naked body, trapping his erection between them, and kissed him on the lips.
　　She lingered there only for a moment, and then said, "I should let you get dressed," and then turned for the bedroom door.
　　As she closed the door behind her she smiled to herself wondering if he was going to realize that he had just shared a kiss with his own penis.

Breakfast consisted of fried eggs, fresh from the chickens that roamed the yard, freshly baked bread, and ersatz coffee. The eggs were wonderful—she had not had an egg in months. There was nothing she could do about the substitute coffee, but she felt she needed to teach whichever one of the men had baked the bread how it should actually be done.
　　The cook turned out to be a sweet and easy-going young man named Luc. He was perhaps a year younger than Joyce, and was not the least bit offended by her suggestion that his bread could be better.

"If I had known I was going to become a baker one day," he said, "I would have watched my mother more closely, and maybe asked some questions. I have only my memory of her tossing things together in the kitchen to guide me."

With Julien standing at the door waiting for her, she said to Luc, "When I come back, I'll show you some of the secrets my mother shared with me. She is a fantastic baker!"

As they left the farmhouse, Julien handed Joyce a pistol in a leather holster.

"Put that on your belt," he told her. "I'll teach you to shoot that first. We have many more bullets for it than for the rifle."

As they walked and she strung the holster onto her belt, she said, "Giving me my own gun, I guess you've decided that you can trust me, no?"

"No," he said. "It's not loaded."

When she had rebuckled her belt, he handed her the rifle he was carrying. She slung it over her shoulder, and then he handed her the cloth satchel of ammunition, as well.

"Anything else I can carry for you?" she asked as she lifted the strap over her head and across her chest and back.

"Each of us carries his own weight in my maqui," he said. "If I let you join us, you may as well get used to it now."

They hiked two kilometers (a mile) or so, ending up in a shallow valley with a stream at the bottom, and an untended orchard of fruit trees along one bank.

Julien was nearly a head taller than Joyce, with legs proportioned to match, and she found herself almost having to trot at times to keep up with him. She wondered if he was doing it intentionally to test her endurance. Or maybe just to make sure that she knew that she wasn't his equal.

In the shade of the trees, he had her set the rifle and satchel down. She wanted to sit and rest for a while, but he didn't suggest it, and she'd be damned if she'd ask.

"Have you ever fired a pistol, before?" he asked as he reached into the satchel for a handful of ammunition.

"No," she said as she took the gun out of the holster.

He shook his head wearily as he spread the bullets out on top of the bag. "This may be a very long day," he said, exaggerating his burden.

"I'm sure I hate to be so much trouble to you," she said, laying it just as thick, "but it is for the good of France, no? I promise to try my best."

"I suppose that's all I can ask," he said as he took her right hand, in which she held the gun.

It was a French made *Modèle* 1935A semi-automatic, which bore a close resemblance to the Colt Model 1911 automatic that the US Army carried. One big difference between the two weapons was that the bullet for her gun was about 2/3 the size of the .45 caliber bullet fired from the Colt. On one hand, it meant that her gun had much less stopping power, but on the other, it meant that it had less recoil and would be easier for her to handle.

It also happened to be the only extra weapon of any sort that the maqui had, and at the farmhouse they had nearly a thousand rounds of ammunition that fit none of their other guns.

He held the pistol and her hand so that the left side of the gun was facing up. He curled her thumb across the grip and positioned it over a small button behind the trigger.

"Push that button, and pull the clip from the grip," he said. "I'll show you how to load it."

She held the empty clip in one hand and the pistol in the other. "Put the gun back in the holster," he said. "You'll need two hands for this."

He pointed to the cartridges he had spread out on the satchel, and asked her, "Which ones do you think fit your pistol?"

She may not have known a lot about guns, but it was obvious that the fat casing that tapered down to a small bullet would not fit in the clip she held. She reached down and scooped up half a dozen of the .30 caliber pistol cartridges.

"Sometimes the larger size has trouble fitting in, no?" she said making an obvious *double entendre*.

"The larger size always fits where nature intends for it to fit," he said. "In *this* case smaller is better, however."

He wrapped his hand around hers so that the clip was pointing upward. He showed her how to slide one of the cartridges onto the spring-loaded platform, back end first.

"Now you try it," he said.

Her first attempt didn't go well. Using her bullet, she had to push the first one down against the spring at the same time that she pushed it back under the top lip of the clip. But the back edge of her cartridge kept catching on the first one where the casing met the bullet. Twice her cartridge went over the top of the clip, and the third time it slipped from her fingers and fell to the ground.

Julien groaned. "Here, let me show you how it's done," he said.

"No. I see what I was doing wrong," she said as she manipulated another cartridge from the handful she held up to her fingertips.

This time, she didn't try to push the bullet straight back against the first one, but rather she started at an angle and then rolled her bullet parallel as it went past the sharp edge. It worked perfectly. She loaded the next four the same way. She picked up three more rounds, and by the time she had loaded the eighth cartridge she was doing it in less than a second.

"You learn fast when you set your mind to it," he said, unwilling—or unable—to give her unqualified credit for doing something well. She wondered if that was a trait reserved for women, or if his standards were such that only *he* could ever attain them.

"Okay, now push the clip into the grip until you hear it click," he told her.

When she had done it, he reached over and rotated the safety, which was located above the hammer, upward to its safe position. "We don't need any accidents," he said.

"Now, take hold of the slide with your other hand," he said, "right on those ridges there. Now pull the slide back, and let it go."

She pulled it about half way back and it slipped from her fingers. It was harder to pull than she had expected.

"No!" he said rolling his eyes. "You have to pull it back *all* the way before you let it go!"

"I didn't let it go; it slipped. And you didn't tell me how far!"

"Until it won't go any farther!"

"And how far might *that* be?"

"About forty millimeters!"

"Thank you!"

She gripped the slide again, as tightly as she could, and yanked it back. This time she felt it stop against something hard and she let it go. The slide snapped forward and pushed a cartridge from the top of the clip into the firing chamber. It also left the hammer back in its cocked position.

"Good," he said. "You're listening to me. Now, aim it that way, and get ready to fire it."

"What should I aim at?"

"It doesn't matter; you won't hit it," he said. "I just want you to see what it feels like when the gun goes off."

When firing her father's shotgun, she would pull the butt against her shoulder, and with her finger on the trigger, her right arm would be bent at about a 90-degree angle. She decided to do the same thing with the pistol.

Holding the gun with both hands around the grip, she bent both arms and positioned it about twenty centimeters (eight inches) in front of her face. She looked across the sights at a tree ten meters away, and before Julien could say anything, she pulled the trigger.

Clack!

The hammer snapped forward, but the gun didn't go off.

"It didn't work," she said.

"Good!" he replied. "You'd have hurt yourself. It didn't fire because the safety is on ... thankfully."

"What do you mean I'd have hurt myself?"

"You're holding the gun way too close to your face. And with the way you're holding your arms, if it went off it might have kicked back and hit you right in the nose."

He moved behind her and put his arms around hers, cradling her hands between his.

Here comes the groping, she said to herself.

To her surprise, he did nothing the least bit sexual.

"Straighten your right arm all the way out," he said, stretching the gun out in front of her. "Lock your elbow. Just like that. Now turn your body about half way, like this." He held the gun, and pushed on her left shoulder until her body was at about a 45-degree angle to her arm. "Good. Now wrap your left hand around the bottom three fingers of your right. Your left arm will stay a little bit bent."

When he had her posed correctly, he released her and stood back to look at her. "Does that feel comfortable?" he asked. "Natural?"

"I guess so," she said. "The sights are a long ways away."

"They still work the same. Just line up the back one with the front one with the target."

"Should I close my left eye?" she asked.

"I leave both eyes open," he said, "but many close one eye. You'll have to try it both ways and see which way is better for you."

"Can I shoot now?" she asked.

"You have to cock the hammer, again," he said, "and release the safety."

She reached up with her right thumb and pulled the hammer back. But she couldn't stretch her thumb high enough to reach the safety without releasing her grip on the gun.

He watched her struggle for a moment, and then said, "Keep your grip on the gun with your right hand at all times. Use your left hand for the safety. It is a terrible idea putting it on top like that. I think it was designed by a Belgian ... one with fat hands."

With the hammer cocked and the safety off, she once again lined up on the tree. She squeezed the trigger as her father had taught her to do with the shotgun.

Blam!

The pistol had far less kick than the shotgun, but held at arm's length rather than against the shoulder it jumped more than she expected.

He saw the surprise in her face, and said, "That's why I wanted you to fire it without trying to hit anything. A pistol takes a little getting used to."

With the gun still in front of her, she began to turn toward him, saying, "It jumped more than I ..."

"Whoa! Whoa!" he said reaching out to stop her turn. "Be careful! That's ready to fire, again! Every time it goes off it loads a new bullet and cocks the hammer. That's why they call it an automatic."

"Sorry," she said, turning back toward the tree. "I was just going to say that it jumped more than I expected. Was I holding it wrong?"

"No," he said. "The problem is that you're about half as big as you need to be to hold the gun steady. I don't think there's anything you can do to keep it from jumping. You'll have to practice getting it back on your target as quickly as possible after each shot. Try it again."

She raised the gun and looked along its sights with both eyes open. Then she lowered it again, and stared at the tree.

"I hit it!" she said. "Look! I hit the tree with my very first shot!"

He looked over her shoulder, and saw the hole in the middle of the small trunk.

"Beginner's luck," he teased her.

"Natural skill," she countered.

"Brought out by a good teacher."

"Who has a talented pupil," she concluded.

They both laughed.

"Perhaps we make a good pair," she said. She immediately regretted saying that, fearing he would take it as romantic encouragement.

If he did, he didn't say or do anything to acknowledge it.

Instead, he said, "The test, chéri, will be to see if you can hit it twice, no?"

She got in her stance one more time, sighted on the tree, and squeezed the trigger.

This time the jumping of the gun didn't surprise her and she did as he suggested, bringing it back on target as quickly as she could.

Then she lowered the gun to see if she had hit the tree again.

About twenty-five millimeters (one inch) from the first hole was a second one.

"I did it! Look at that!"

He looked, and said, "Chéri, I *am* impressed. I have never shown anyone how to shoot a pistol who has done that. I think the Germans have much to fear from you."

She noted that he said *I have never shown anyone how to shoot a pistol ...* rather than *taught* anyone. Was he really giving her credit for the accomplishment?

"Thank you," she said. "I hope you're right. But I think the sights need adjustment ... if that's possible. I was aiming at that knot well above the bullet holes, both times."

"You missed because the bullet starts to drop as soon as it leaves the gun," he explained. "The farther away the target is, the more it will drop. The sights are not adjustable; you have to compensate by aiming above where you want to hit."

"How do I know how much?"

"Experience," he said. "See how far below the knot your holes are? Aim that far *above* the knot this time."

She got into her stance, and aimed at her bullet holes. Then she raised the gun up until she was sighted on the knot, and then raised it the same amount again and squeezed the trigger.

When she looked, she saw a hole at the top edge of the knot.

Even before she could point out her accomplishment to Julien, he said from behind her, "My God! Are you this good at everything you do?"

Last night she would have been sure that there was a sexual innuendo in that question. This morning, his male ego didn't seem quite so all-consuming. She decided to give him the benefit of the doubt that perhaps not every thought he had—awake or asleep—was about sex.

"I haven't tried that many things," she said humbly, "but I've been told I'm a fast learner."

"To say the least!" he said. "Try that next tree farther out. Aim at the scar where the branch has broken off."

It was an oval-shaped scar about eight or ten centimeters (three or four inches) long. She lined up on her target, and then moved the gun up a little, and then a tiny bit more for the added distance. Where she was aiming was odd, because the gun was pointing at nothing—into the air between two branches that formed a Y.

She squeezed the trigger, the gun jumped, and she quickly brought the sights back to the scar. Then she lowered the gun and stared at the tree for a bullet hole.

"There goes my record," she said sadly. "I missed."

"No you didn't," he said from behind her.

She turned and saw him looking through a pair of binoculars.

"You hit right at the bottom of the scar; right on the edge," he said.

"Really? Let me see?" she said reaching out for the binoculars with her left hand.

"Put the gun away, first," he said. "Set the safety, aim at the ground, and pull the trigger."

She did as he instructed, and the hammer clacked forward without firing the gun.

"Now, put it in you're holster."

She did, and he handed her the glasses.

She looked, and said, "Wow! Look at that!"

"You are remarkable, chéri," he said, shaking his head. "You're the most natural shooter I've ever seen."

"Thank you," she said. "It *seems* natural to me; like I've done it in a previous life or something. Can I practice with the pistol some more before we try the rifle?"

"Let's save the rifle for tomorrow," he said. "I'm curious to see what else you can do with the pistol."

For the next three hours they went through almost a hundred rounds of ammunition, practicing everything from standing, sitting, and prone shooting positions, to quick-draw shooting without aiming. She was at least good at everything he had her try, and she was down right amazing at some of them.

Finally, Joyce rooted around the inside of the satchel but could only come up with six more bullets.

"I guess we're just about done with the pistol," she said as she slid the cartridges into the clip without even looking.

Julien looked at his watch. It was almost noon.

"Just as well," he said. "There are some men I must meet this afternoon. Besides, I'm getting hungry, aren't you?"

"I hadn't really noticed," she said. "But now that you mention it."

"I want you to try one last thing before we go," he said as he stooped to pick up a large stick, about the size of his forearm.

"You said that you used to be pretty good with a shotgun," he said. "What did you hunt? Duck? Pheasant? Quail?"

"Duck," she said. "Before Papa moved us to Agen, there was a small pond ..."

"Do you think you can hit *this* duck if I throw it in the air?" he asked her, showing her the stick.

She laughed. "I doubt it!" she said. "One bullet is a lot smaller than a whole pattern of shot. Why? Are there a lot of flying Germans I'm going to have to worry about?"

"Maybe not flying," he said, "But plenty of them will be running when they see how you shoot at them."

He walked about six meters (six yards) to her left and stopped. "This will be like the shotgun," he said. "Don't use the sights; just follow the log with the barrel. But don't shoot this time, okay? Just try to stay on the *duck* to get a feel for how you have to move the gun."

He lobbed the log across in front of her, about four meters off the ground.

She followed it and pulled the trigger as it reached the top of its arch. With the safety on, the gun only clacked.

"Do you think you'd have hit it?" he asked.

She walked over to where it had landed, and said with a laugh, "I think your pet duck is safe, and that we'll be having vegetable stew for supper."

She threw the stick back to him and returned to her spot.

"Ready?" he said. "Safety off?"

"Safety's off," she replied. "I'm as ready as I'll ever be, I guess."

He lobbed the stick; she followed it and pulled the trigger.

Both of them watched a spray of wood chips erupt from the back end of the stick.

"Oh my God!" she shouted as she jumped in the air. "I hit it! Did you see that? I hit it!"

"Unbelievable," he said, shaking his head. He walked over and picked up the stick. "I don't think you killed it, but my poor friend no longer has any tail feathers."

She flicked the safety on, shoved the gun in the holster, and ran to him.

"I am so excited!" she said as she threw her arms around him and gave him a kiss. "Thank you so much for teaching me to shoot! I can't wait to meet a German!"

He looked down at her smiling face, and licked his lips. "You taste much better without the essence of penis."

Her mouth hung open for a second and she felt the color come up in her cheeks.

"I ... um ... I'm sorry about that. I was ..."

"No," he said as he put a finger on her lips. "I deserved it. I was being an ass. *I* apologize to *you*. My big male ego sometimes gets ahead of my better judgment. I'm sorry."

She smiled, stretched up, and gave him another kiss, much longer and much harder than the first one.

As they walked back toward the farmhouse, he said, "You know, I was tying my boots before I realized what you'd done to me this morning. At first I was angry, but then I laughed out loud. That was damned clever of you. No woman has ever put me in my place quite like that before."

"My mother used to tell me I was too clever for my own good sometimes," she said. "I'm glad you saw the humor in it."

"Yes, well just the same, we won't share the joke with the others, okay? Our secret."

"Don't worry," she said. "I'm part of *La Résistance*; I know how to keep a secret."

At the farmhouse, the whole group ate a small lunch of cheese, bread, fruit, and wine. The bread was left over from breakfast, and had certainly not gotten better with age.

As Julien prepared to leave with most of the men, Joyce asked if she could go along, as well.

"I'm afraid not, chéri," he said. "You should stay here, with Luc. Some of the men we are meeting would be suspicious of *any* newcomer." Then he added, "And the others would be so distracted by your beauty that we would not get any business done." He gave her a wink, and headed out the door.

She smiled as she watched him leave. It was a corny line, but she was sure he meant it as a compliment. At least he was trying to be charming, even if he had a long way to go. She decided it might be fun to be his guide on the journey.

"Care to let me in on the secret?" Luc said from behind her, snapping her out of her thoughts.

"Secret?" she said turning around. "What kind of secret?" Did he know something had happened in Julien's bedroom this morning? She was quite sure Julien wouldn't have told him.

"Your mother's secret for making bread," he said.

"Oh, yes! Of course, of course," she said, relieved. "Show me what you have for ingredients and we'll see what we can do."

For the next half hour she watched and corrected as Luc made enough dough for two loaves of bread. He had expected Joyce to actually do the baking, or, at very least, to help, but she taught him the way that her mother had taught her; by doing.

When he was done mixing the dough, he set a wide metal baking sheet on the table, and tossed some flour on it.

As he reached for the ball of dough, Joyce said, "Wait, what are you doing?"

"I'm going to bake it," he said, obviously surprised at the question. "Why? Do we need to add something else?"

"Gas bubbles," she said, knowing before she had even tasted his bread last night that not letting it rise was one of its problems.

"Gas bubbles?" he said.

"You haven't given the yeast a chance to work, yet," she said. "It reacts with the sugar and flour and makes all the little bubbles that make the bread fluffy."

"Okay," he said stepping back from the table. "How long do we have to wait?"

"Oh, an hour," she said, "Maybe a little more."

"An *hour*?" he laughed. "They rarely give me that much time to cook a whole meal. You haven't heard these men grumbling about how hungry they are, have you?"

"This will be better," she said, "trust me. They'll be happy to wait."

She took a large crockery bowl down from a shelf, wiped it out with a towel, and set it on the table. As she wet the towel and wrung it out, she had him place the dough in the bowl. Then she placed the towel over it.

"Set the bowl on the box behind the stove there," she told him.

"Are we hiding it?" he asked. "There are better places."

"The heat from the stove will make it rise faster," she said. "It also keeps it out of the drafty air."

She had him add a couple of small logs into the belly of the stove to get the temperature up, and then she noticed a pair of cast iron Dutch ovens in the corner, stacked one atop the other.

"Do you ever use those?" she asked walking toward them.

"Sometimes when a chicken has outlived its usefulness," he said, "we'll have a big stew."

"Well, they're also great for baking bread," she said. She carried one, and had him pick up the other. They placed them both on top of the stove to warm up.

"Show me around your farm," she said to him as she walked toward the back door. "Watching bread rise isn't very interesting."

They walked down the three stone steps into the back yard. Even before the war, this was no commercial farm, Joyce could see that. It looked to her like its couple of acres had probably been supporting whatever families had lived here for the past hundred years.

"There's really not much to show you," he said. "You can see pretty much all of it from right here."

A dozen or so hens wandered in their seemingly aimless chicken way around the yard, as a lone cow munched hay from a manger in front of a small stone barn.

The stubble in one of the fields told her that the winter wheat had recently been harvested, which explained the abundance of flour in the kitchen. Another field was covered in the early green of spring-planted vegetables.

To one side of the farmhouse was a circular stone well with a peaked roof above it. She could see where a crank once mounted to raise and lower a bucket, but the well was now covered over with boards, and had the modern convenience of a hand pump.

To the other side of the house stood a small and very old orchard of what Joyce assumed were different fruit trees. But they could also have been olives, for all she knew.

She sat down on the stone step, and said to Luc, "It seems odd, but I feel so ... comfortable here. I grew up on the fringes of Paris—a real city girl—and since I was so high, I knew all the best places to *buy* fruits and vegetables, but never really knew anything about growing them. I used to wonder what it would be like to live on a farm, but this is the first time I've actually set foot on one. I love it! It's so ... idyllic. Like something out of a story book."

He laughed. "That's because there's not much work to be done at the moment. It'll wear you out during planting and harvest."

"I suppose," she said, thoughtfully. "But it seems like it would be invigorating, too. Spending your days outdoors, in the warm sun, growing your own food, depending on no one, least of all the idiots in government."

"And standing in the cold rain," he said, "and the blistering heat. And watching a million grasshoppers descend like a black cloud and eat every living thing you spent the whole year growing."

She laughed. "That sounds like experience talking. How long has the maqui called this their home?"

"About a year," he said. "But it's been *my* home for almost thirty. I was born here; in Julien's bedroom. The farm was my parents', and before them, my grandparents lived here."

"You have more experience than I thought," she said. "Where are your parents now? I helped mine escape to Spain."

"They passed away just before the invasion. I'm glad they didn't have to see what France has come to."

"I'm sorry to hear that," she said. "Do you have any other family?"

"Just my brother, Julien," he answered.

"Julien is your *brother*?" she blurted. That would never have occurred to her. Apparently, each of them got all of his traits from a different parent. Where Julien was tall, muscular, and unfairly good looking, Luc was average in all of those areas. Julien was loud, outgoing, brash, and full of self-confidence, and Luc was reserved to the point of almost being timid.

Luc chuckled. "That's the reaction most people have ... especially the women."

"I'm sorry," she said. "I didn't mean to ..."

"Don't worry about it," he stopped her, smiling. "After almost thirty years, I'm used to it. Julien has always cast a pretty long shadow."

Luc might have *said* that he was okay living in his brother's shadow, but Joyce wasn't convinced. His tone and even his face belied his words. The smile on his lips wasn't one of amusement, but more like one of tolerated acceptance, and there was certainly no smile in his eyes. She tried to imagine how it would be to live in the shadow of someone like Julien. If Luc's input within the maqui was any indication, it was like being almost invisible.

But there was something she liked very much about Luc. Maybe it was the fact that he *was* so opposite his big brother.

"I don't have any sisters or brothers, myself," she said to him, "but if I did have a brother, I'd want him to be more like you than Julien."

"Thanks," he said with a genuine grin. "I think you'd make a nice sister."

She made a mock pouty face. "Not a girlfriend?" she asked.

"You could only be my *sister* by birth," he said. "You would my *girlfriend* by choice. And with Julien around, I know how the choice would go."

She looked into his eyes and saw at least sadness, and probably bitterness. He quickly turned away from her.

"I think Julien's shadow is colder and darker than you'd like to let on," she said. She took his hand, and went on, "Talk to me. Just between the two of us. Brother to sister."

After a long silent pause, he let out a sad sounding sigh, then glanced at her for a moment, and turned back to stare out into the distance.

"Sometimes I think I truly hate him," he said without looking at her, almost as if talking to himself. "I hate how he treats other people ... good people." He looked at her again, and added, "Like you."

"Me?" she said. "I think he's treated me okay. He came on a little strong last night, perhaps, but when he was teaching me to shoot this morning, he was a perfect gentleman. He has a long way to go to be as sweet as *you*," she added with a smile and a pat on his knee, "but maybe he just needs the right guide, no?"

Staring back out at the fields, Luc asked. "Did he apologize to you this morning?"

"For what?" she said, once again wondering if he knew what had gone on in Julien's bedroom.

"It doesn't matter," Luc said. "That's his *system*. He taught it to me, but I can't do it."

"What do you mean *system*?" Joyce asked.

"His first approach with women is to come on strong, just like you said. Some women seem to like that. He calls it the caveman approach.

But if he finds that they don't react well to that, he will do some rude thing, and then later apologize for it. He says that no woman alive can resist a sincere sounding apology. If he doesn't bed them shortly after that, then he assumes they belong in a convent and he moves on to greener pastures."

He turned to see her staring at him with her mouth open.

"He did, didn't he?" he said. "I'm sorry, Joyce. I shouldn't have stuck my nose ..."

But she got up and walked away from the farmhouse, toward the fields.

He sat and watched her walk away.

She stopped at the edge of the wheat field, and stood there staring into the distance with her arms folded across her chest.

He pushed himself up, and walked out to stand beside her. Neither of them said anything for a long time. They just stared out at the hills of France, not really seeing anything, just lost in thought.

"Please don't be mad at me," Luc said finally. "I like you; I didn't want to see him use you like all the others."

Still looking out at the hills, Joyce said, "I'm not mad at you. I'm not even mad at Julien." She turned toward him, and went on, "I'm mad at *me*. He did exactly what you just told me, and he had me completely fooled. I'm a grown woman who wants to go out and kill Germans for God's sake; I shouldn't be able to be taken in like a bubble-headed schoolgirl."

"I'm sorry," he said. "I didn't say it to make you feel bad." He grinned, and added, "I'm just trying to look out for my sister."

She smiled at him, leaned over, and kissed his cheek. "Thank you. I'm glad that you told me," she said. "I would have been a lot madder at myself if I'd found out about his *system* in a few day's time."

"What will you do?" he asked. "Please don't tell him that you figured out his system; he'll know that I told you."

"Don't worry," she said. "I'm well versed in keeping secrets."

"Will you leave us, now? Leave the maqui?"

"*Hell* no!" she said definitively. "Your brother still owes me a shooting lesson. And just *maybe*, I'll be able to teach *him* something, too. Besides, if I left now, everyone would believe I *was* a spy, and they'd track me down."

"I'd tell them the truth before I let *that* happen," he pledged.

"Well, I'm staying at least until we derail that train and I shoot my first German," she said. "But thank you for the offer. You're the sweetest brother I've ever had."

She leaned over, and kissed his cheek again.

He surprised her by turning, putting his arms around her, and pulling her close. He then found her lips with his own.

Surprised by his advance, she didn't respond in kind right away, and his kiss was awkward against her unmoving lips.

He began to pull away. "I sorr ...

But she put both of her hands on the back of his head, and pulled him back, stopping his apology with her lips. This time when their mouths met they were each ready for it, and there was no awkwardness at all.

As timid as he seemed to be, Joyce was surprised at how good of a kisser he was. It had been a very long time since Joyce had been with a man that she enjoyed kissing, and without any conscious thought of doing it, she found herself weaving her fingers into his hair, and moving her body sensuously against his as their lips and tongues flowed through the choreography of their visceral dance.

After some period of time that neither of them could have guessed, he broke their kiss and put a few inches of distance between them. He did not let go of her completely, however.

Holding her by her sides, he smiled at her, and said, "That's probably not how a brother and sister should act, is it?"

"It's okay," she said with a provocative smile, "I'm adopted." Then she leaned in and gave him another quick kiss. "But I do think it's better if the other's don't see us doing that."

"I'm sorry," he said, looking down at the ground. "It won't happen again, I promise."

"The hell it *won't*!" she said. "I haven't been kissed like that since I left Paris! I just don't think we should be seen doing it. Not just yet, anyway."

He smiled at her, and they kissed again, quickly and without embracing.

Turning back toward the orchard beside the farmhouse, she said, "Come. Tell me about your fruit trees before we have to go back inside and bake bread. Did you climb in them when you were little?"

When Julien and the others returned from their meeting in town, they brought back a fat sausage that they all enjoyed with the fresh baked bread and some wine from the cellar below the kitchen.

Everyone made comments about how good the bread was, and one of the men said, "I nominate Joyce to be our official cook from now on!"

The others all shouted their agreement.

"Don't look at me!" she said. "Luc did all the baking. All I did was to suggest he use those cast-iron pot things with the covers to cook the bread in. And that's only because I used to see my mother do it that way."

After the meal, Julien led Joyce out through the kitchen and the backdoor, and into the moonlit yard.

The yard was more beautiful at night than it had been in the daylight, and Joyce wanted to sit on the stone step and just take it in.

But Julien didn't want to sit. He took her hand and guided her into the shadows of the orchard.

They stopped next to a gnarled fig tree, and Julien said to her, "Do you know what I think?"

"What is that?" she said with a smile, expecting some sort of come on.

"I think you're lying," he said.

"Lying?" she said with a start. "About what?"

"Making the bread," he said. "Luc has been cooking for us for nearly a year, and the first time you set foot in the kitchen he suddenly discovers the secret to edible bread is putting it in a pot? Perhaps you are as good in the kitchen as you are with a pistol, no?"

"I swear on my mother's head that I never touched a grain of flour or put my hands on that bread in any way until I ate it at the table with you," she said.

He looked down at her, and even in the darkness she could tell that he still didn't believe her. But then he laughed, and said, "Well, you know what else? I really don't care. As long as he keeps making bread like that he can have a *fairy Godmother* in the kitchen with him."

He took her in his arms, bent down, and kissed her lips.

She had enjoyed his embrace and his kiss this morning in that other orchard, but now she had to turn on the actress in her to respond the way he expected her to.

As she kissed him—not the least bit caught up in the throes of passion—she found herself detached and analyzing his kiss. She decided that he was pressing into her lips too hard; his mouth gyrated in almost a chewing fashion; and he seemed to like to bite her tongue. His technique was aggressive and taking, where Luc's was passionate and inviting.

She wondered if their lovemaking would have the same differences. She suspected it would, and while she welcomed the thought of *researching the subject* with Luc, she hoped that she could find a way to *avoid* any benchmark research with his brother.

After a thankfully short while, one of the other men, Yvon, came to the backdoor and shouted for Julien.

"Over here!" he called out as they walked from the deep shadows.

Yvon made no apologies for interrupting, and Joyce got the impression that it was probably not uncommon for them to find Julien out there, *entertaining guests*.

"Ramon is here," Yvon said. Glancing at Joyce, he added, "About the you know what."

Julien left her without a word, and went back into the house, followed by Yvon.

Alone, Joyce then did what she wanted to do in the first place. She turned and sat down on the stone step, and looked out at the billion stars in the sky.

As Julien and Yvon went inside, Luc came out and joined her.

As he sat down, Joyce pointed into the sky, and shouted, "Look! Look!"

He looked up to see the last second of a shooting star.

"Did you make a wish?" he asked her.

"The same one I've been making for years," she said. "That all this would be over, and we could all go back to our real lives."

"Amen!" he said.

They sat in silence for a while, each feeling content to just be next to the other, somehow sharing their thoughts without actually saying anything.

"Hard to believe that the same God who created all that," Joyce said without taking her eyes from the sky, "would allow something as stupid and awful as war, isn't it?"

"It tests one's faith, that's for sure," Luc said. He turned to her, and went on, "And then he sends someone like you into my life, and all my doubt vanishes."

She smiled at him. "And yet, He has me sleeping in Julien's bed," she chuckled. "He *does* work in mysterious ways."

A half hour later, Julien appeared in the doorway, and looked down at Joyce and Luc as they sat on the step, talking.

"Is your fairy Godmother telling you how to make a soufflé, now?" Julien said with a laugh.

"What?" Luc said as he and Joyce got up. "Fairy Godmother?"

"He's joking," Joyce said. "He somehow believes that I made the bread. I told him that I never set a finger on it."

"God's truth," Luc said. "The lazy thing stood around and watched me the whole time."

"We'll see," Julien said, obviously unconvinced. "While chéri is with me learning to shoot the rifle tomorrow, you can bake the bread all by yourself. That should tell us, no?"

Julien reached out his hand to Joyce. "Come. It's time for bed."

As she took Julien's hand and walked up the steps, she said, "Goodnight, Luc. Sleep well," and followed it with a wink.

"I'll have to be *careful*," Julien said with an amused tone of sarcasm. "It seems you may be taking a liking to Luc."

"Luc is sweet," Joyce said as Julien closed the bedroom door.

"Luc is like a schoolboy," Julien replied making no effort to hide his contempt. "He couldn't kill a German if his own life depended on it. He has a hard time killing the chickens when the time comes. Some cook, no?"

Joyce wanted to defend Luc, but she decided to hold her tongue. She was too new to the group to get into family politics. Especially when Julien didn't seem to want her to know that they *were* family, for some reason.

In the bedroom Joyce undressed down to her underwear again, and Julien once more stripped naked. She turned to find him standing there with a full erection ... again.

Does he ever think of anything else? she asked herself.

"He would like so much more," Julien said in a sad, resigned tone, gesturing toward his penis, "but he will settle for a goodnight kiss like the one you gave him this morning."

She was glad—and just a little surprised—that he wasn't asking her for more than a simple kiss. The way she had felt about him when they were walking home from shooting, she was sure she would have obliged. Now, even a *kiss* on his manhood was distasteful to her ... on more than one level.

But she figured that if the gesture would appease him for another night, she could do it and pretend to like it. She had pretended to like far worse.

She leaned down, and he cradled his penis in his hand, offering it to her as if to worship.

"It is only a couple more nights, my pet," she said to it sweetly. "And then we will both have our reward for our patience."

As she pursed her lips and drew near to the smooth skin, he surprised her by putting his hand on the back of her head and forcing the head of his erection to her mouth.

She closed her lips tightly, and turned her head away. She pulled out of his grip and stood up, fighting the urge to punch him.

He groaned. "*Please!*" he said, almost begging. "You are driving me *insane*! Don't tell me a woman as beautiful as you has never pleasured a man that way before."

"I want you, too, dear Julien," she lied in her best imploring tone. "But I don't want to just *service* you. I want to make love *with* you. I want to feel you deep inside me where a woman needs a man. Please. It's only a couple more days, and then I will give myself to you until the rooster tells us to stop."

He clasped his hands on top of his head and let out a low growl. He turned away from her and looked up at the ceiling.

She watched him closely. He was angry, and she didn't want him angry. She needed him to teach her to use the rifle, and to bring her on the train attack.

She moved up behind him, snuggled her body against his nakedness, and put her arms around him.

"I know you're trying to be patient," she whispered into his ear, "and I promise it will be worth it."

He just grunted.

"I hate to see you so *tense*," she cooed. "It must be terribly uncomfortable to try to sleep that way." She lowered her hand, and took hold of him gently.

"Maybe I can help you to relax," she said as she started moving her hand slowly back and forth.

In an amusingly short time, he was done, and they were both crawling under the covers. He was asleep in less than a minute, and Joyce snuggled herself against his warmth. She drifted off contentedly, and enjoyed an uninterrupted night's sleep, waking only when the rooster called the sun into the sky.

While Julien continued to sleep, she poured some water from the ceramic pitcher on the wash stand into the shallow basin. She then stripped naked, and washed herself with the small cloth that hung on the table.

The water was cold but invigorating, and it felt wonderful to be clean again after nearly a week of traveling. She dressed in her only other set of underwear—which she had washed yesterday while the bread baked—and was pulling on her pants when Julien stirred.

He tossed back the covers, and she was surprised to see that he was not erect, for once.

Standing there in her bra, she soaked the washcloth in the basin and wrung it out as he stood up from the bed. "Come here," she said. "We didn't get a chance to clean you up very well last night."

She squatted down as he walked to her, and she noticed that he was starting to grow. When she wrapped the cold washcloth around his penis, he sucked in his breath and went immediately limp. She had to fight to keep from laughing.

After toweling his penis dry, she cradled it in the towel, and gave it a quick kiss. Making a show of wiping her lips, she stood up and kissed him on the mouth. "Very soon," she whispered to him.

She pulled on her shirt, and as she turned for the door, she said, "You'd better hurry before all of Luc's bread is gone, no?"

Wednesday, June 9, 1943

After breakfast Julien left through the kitchen, and returned a short while later with the rifle, the pistol she had used the day before, and the cloth satchel of ammunition. She wondered where they kept the weapons. In the barn, perhaps? It might be difficult to explain seven men living together on this small farm if the Milice were to catch wind of it. With a cache of weapons and ammunition, it would be obvious that they were a resistance maqui, and they would be arrested and turned over to the SS immediately.

The morning was brisk, and the fast paced walk to the orchard felt good.

As they walked, Julien said, "I want to apologize for last night. It seems I am always forcing myself on you. You are a very desirable woman, chéri, and parts of me seem quite unable to control themselves."

"Don't apologize, Julien. I understand," she said, with far deeper meaning than he could know. "The truth is, I'm actually quite flattered by the attention your *parts* show me," she lied.

At the orchard, Julien took a piece of cloth from the satchel and unfolded it. It was about a meter square, and had a crude outline of a man's head and torso painted on it. In the middle of the face area was a toothbrush mustache.

A piece of heavy twine was tied to each of the top corners. He tied the ends to a couple of tree branches and let the cloth hang down. Not far behind the tree stood the one remaining wood wall of what had once been a small storehouse.

"Do you think you can hit *Adolph*, here?" he asked.

"It will certainly be my pleasure to try!" she said.

"Let's see if you are as dangerous with a rifle as you are with the pistol," he said as they started walking away from the target.

He had her carry the big rifle and the satchel of ammunition, again. "I'll show you how to load the magazine while you walk," he said to her. "Later we'll see if you can do it while you're running."

The rifle Joyce was carrying was a *Lebel Modele 1886/M93*. It had been designed in 1886 and was the first rifle in the world to use smokeless powder, which had been invented two years earlier.

Joyce's rifle had the manufacturing date of 1887 stamped into the barrel; it was 56 years old, but it was a remarkably robust and accurate weapon in the right hands. It had seen action in many battles during the Great War, including the Battle of Verdun, and although no records of such things were kept, bullets fired from the rifle that Joyce was carrying had killed more than fifty Germans during that "war to end all wars."

The Lebel weighed more than nine pounds and was four-feet-four-inches long—2/3 of that being barrel—so it could be awkward for a lot of men. But Joyce's father had taught her the trick of nesting the butt of their shotgun into her left armpit, and supporting the rest of the gun with her crooked left arm while she reloaded it with her right hand.

Of course reloading the Lebel was a lot different than sliding two shells into two wide open holes in the end of the shotgun barrels.

As they walked, Julien had her rotate the bolt up and pull it back, opening the receiver. Then she scooped three or four of the big rifle cartridges from the satchel, and pushed them, one at a time, down into the gun and into a tube located directly below and parallel to the barrel. That tube—the magazine—held eight cartridges.

"Now, put one more round down in the elevator there," he told her. The elevator was the mechanism that lifted cartridges from the magazine up to the barrel. When she'd done that, he said, "Now put the last one into the firing chamber, and close the bolt. You now have ten shots before you need to reload. But be very careful, chéri, it's ready to fire, and there is no safety on that gun."

"Is it broken?" she asked.

"It was designed without one," he replied. "They expected the soldiers to carry it into battle without a bullet in the chamber."

That didn't seem like a very good idea to her, but she wasn't a gunsmith, so maybe there was a reason.

When she was done loading, she looked back to see how far they had walked. Adolph was getting smaller, but she felt that she could probably hit him with even the pistol from here.

"Where are we going?" she asked.

Julien pointed ahead, and said, "That stone wall. It will be about a hundred meters (100 yards)."

If she hit the target with her pistol at *that* distance, she knew there would be as much luck involved as skill.

"How far will this rifle shoot?" she asked. "The bullets aren't much bigger than the pistol's, but the cartridge is huge."

"I'm told more than four kilometers (two and a half miles)," he said.

"My God!" she said. "How could you ever hit anything at that distance?"

"You can't," he said. "I think that was probably a test to see how far it would make a bullet fly. A waste of ammunition, really. Once you get used to the sights, though, it can be quite accurate out to four or five hundred meters. I've hit a German at nearly a thousand meters with that gun."

Once at the wall, he had her lay the satchel on top of it, and sit behind it. She laid the rifle across the satchel to cradle its weight, and he showed her how to set the rear sight for one hundred meters. Having a short shoulder-stock, the rifle fit her surprisingly well, and she felt very comfortable with it.

While he watched Adolph through his binoculars, Julien had her squeeze off her first round.

Considering the rifle cartridge was enormous compared to the pistol round, she was surprised at how little the rifle kicked. That, of course, was because the rifle was nearly six times heavier than the pistol.

"That hit a little high and a little to the left," Julien said, having seen the spray of splinters as the bullet struck the wall behind the target.

She actuated the bolt and got another round into the chamber. She made the slight sighting corrections, and squeezed the trigger.

"Well, he won't be doing that stupid Nazi salute anymore," Julien said. "You hit him in the right shoulder."

She reloaded, corrected again, and squeezed the trigger.

"*Magnifique*, chéri!" Julien shouted. "Right in the middle of the chest! *Magnifique!*"

For the next four hours they practiced at greater and greater distances, and in all different shooting positions. She found that she got her best accuracy while lying prone on the ground with the rifle resting on the satchel, but it was just a little slower to work the bolt that way. And it was a lot slower to reload the magazine.

Her worst marks came when she was standing and holding the rifle unsupported. It was simply too long and too heavy for her arms. Her accuracy improved somewhat when Julien had her put her left hand against a tree trunk, and rest the rifle on her arm. But working the bolt one-handed was impossible for her, and letting go of the tree to use her other hand, and them setting up again made it a very slow way to shoot.

"We should be heading back," Julien said finally. "It is a long walk to catch the train tonight, and we should all rest." He looked at her with a slightly raised eyebrow, and added, "And I am anxious to see if Luc's fairy Godmother showed up again to help him make bread."

"You don't seem to like Luc very much," she said. She decided not to ask why, but to just leave it as a statement. She was curious to see if Julien would tell her that they were brothers.

"Oh, Luc is alright in his place, I guess," Julien said. "Someone needs to tend the farm while the rest of us are off fighting the Germans."

"He doesn't go on raids with you?" she asked. "He told me that you taught him to shoot, too. He said he's pretty good with a rifle."

"And if we were fighting an army of cloth targets, he could win medals," Julien said. "But Luc is a coward."

"A coward? What happened to make you say that?"

As they walked away from the orchard, Julien explained.

"We had gone out one night to cut telephone lines, and we surprised a German patrol. There were three of them, so we outnumbered them two to one. We jumped them before they could use their weapons, and we killed two of them with just our knives.

"The third one ran away, and I shouted to Luc to shoot him. He pulled his pistol and aimed, but he didn't fire. I kept shouting, 'Shoot him! Shoot, damn it!' but he just stood there pointing the gun. By the time I realized Luc wasn't going to shoot him, I had to use the rifle—that one—to kill him. It made much more noise than was safe, so we had to abandon our sabotage and just make for home.

"Luc claimed he couldn't get a good bead on him because he was running and it was dark. But I managed to hit him in the same light."

"Maybe he couldn't shoot him in the back," Joyce offered.

"A Nazi's back is a better target that his front," Julien scoffed. "He carries less crap there that could deflect the bullet."

"Will Luc be going on the raid tonight?" Joyce asked.

"Yes. There is much that we need to carry, and it's a long way," Julien answered. "And if he fails to pull the trigger when he's told to again, I might shoot him myself."

"Will you shoot me if I fail to kill a real German?" she asked.

He laughed. "The only reason that you would fail to kill the first German who crosses your sights would be if you were a Nazi or Milice spy," he said. "In which case, yes, I would shoot you."

They walked a while more, and then Joyce stopped and looked back at where they had been shooting. She could still see the wooden wall in front of which Adolph had hung, and guessed that it was at least one and a half kilometers (1500 yards) away.

"Do you think the Lebel could hit the wall from here?" she asked.

He took out his binoculars, and looked off at the wall. "I know the *rifle* is capable," he said. "The question is whether or not the *shooter* is capable."

"Do you think you can make the shot?" she asked.

"Yes," he said without hesitation. "But I'd rather see you do it. Put a round in the chamber, and lie down."

She found a grassy spot, laid the satchel down for support, and got down on the ground with the rifle.

"How far away do you guess the wall is?" he asked.

"Fifteen-hundred meters, maybe?"

"Give or take a hundred," he agreed.

She flipped up the rear sight and slid the cross bar up until it was on the 1500 line. She pulled the stock to her shoulder, and with both eyes open, she lined up the sights.

"What are you aiming at?" Julien asked as he looked out through the binoculars.

"The *wall*," she said.

"Which part?"

"The *middle*," she said thinking that would be completely obvious.

"There aren't many Germans who are the size of a wall," he said. "... with the exception of Herr Goering, of course. But you aren't likely to get a shot at *him*. Why don't you aim for that whitewashed board toward the top?"

"You have binoculars," she said, "I can just barely *see* that."

"And you know what I see through the glasses?" he said. "I see the face of the Milice officer who put your mother's name on his list to be rounded up and sent to the work camps in Germany. Oh, and look ... I can see him laughing."

"It's beginning to seem clearer to me," she said with a little chuckle.

She relaxed as much as she could, she got her breathing nice and steady, and she focused every bit of concentration that she had across the two sights and that laughing whitewashed board.

She slowly squeezed the trigger.

She squinted her eyes, but there was no chance that she could see a bullet hole at that distance.

Julien took his eyes from the binoculars and looked down at her. "Remind me never to make you mad, chéri," he said. "Even from a great distance."

"Did I hit it?" she said. "The board, not just the wall?"

He handed her the binoculars as she stood up. "Not only should the blimp Goering be afraid of you," he said, "but skinny little Herr Goebbels, as well."

Back at the farmhouse, they found two perfect loaves of bread on the table for lunch. In the kitchen, another two cooled while two more baked in the Dutch ovens.

"We'll take those with us tonight," Luc said pointing to the cooling loaves, "and we'll have two more for when we get back," he added pointing to the stove.

Also on the stove was a simmering pot of soup. "I used the rest of the sausage and some vegetables to make a soup for supper," Luc said. "It's going to be a long walk tonight."

Standing in the kitchen with Luc and Julien, Joyce made a showing of looking under the table, then on the far side of the stove, in the cupboard, and even behind the door.

"What are you looking for?" Julien finally asked.

"Luc's fairy Godmother," she said with a grin. "But he appears to be all alone here, as far as I can see."

After lunch, the men checked their weapons, and the supplies they would be bringing with them. Joyce disassembled her rifle and her pistol, and cleaned them both thoroughly. She loaded the Lebel with nine rounds, leaving the chamber empty, and loaded both of the clips for the pistol.

Most of the men were able to nap for part of the afternoon, but Joyce was far too excited to sleep. She slipped quietly outside, and found Luc in the yard pushing hay into the cow's manger.

"You can't sleep, either?" she said to him.

"The chores still need to be done," he said. "The cow and the chickens can't feed themselves while we're gone."

"Can I do anything to help?" she asked.

"You could fill the water trough, if you don't mind. There is a bucket inside the barn next to the door."

"Are you nervous about the raid?" she asked him as she retrieved the bucket, and he dug a scoop of chicken feed from a wooden box.

"I haven't been on a raid in a long time," he said. "I don't want to let the others down."

"I know what you mean," she said. She was sure that he was referring to not shooting the soldier in the back, but she decided not to let on that Julien had told her the story. She was becoming a master at keeping secrets.

"I've *never* been on a raid," she went on, "so you can imagine how nervous *I* am."

"I heard Julien telling Carlos that you're almost as good a shot as he his," Luc said. "I'm sure you'll do fine."

"Targets and tree branches don't shoot back," she said.

"And they don't run away from you into the darkness," Luc replied. "The last time I went with the group we had gone to cut telephone lines, and we surprised a Nazi patrol. Carlos and Craig killed two of them with their knives, but the third one got away.

"I shot at him three times with my pistol, but I couldn't hit him. I finally had to yell for Julien to use his rifle to try. The guy must have thought he had run a safe distance, because he stopped to look back, and it was just long enough for Julien to hit him. With all the noise from the shooting, we had to abandon the sabotage and return home."

"It sounds like it was an impossible shot," Joyce said. "It doesn't seem to me that you let anyone down."

She wondered which of the brothers was fabricating details about what really happened that night. She wanted to believe that Luc's version was the truth, but if it wasn't, she could see why he would fictionalize some of the fine points. She wondered if she could get one of the other men to tell her the story to break the tie.

Standing near the door, she looked around the inside of the barn, and said, "Is this where you hide the weapons in case the Milice come snooping around?"

"The hen house," he said. "Come. I'll show you in case you ever need to get to them."

On the far end of the barn was a small wooden lean-to structure. They ducked under the low roof, and stepped inside. All of the hens were outside, pecking at the grain that Luc had just scattered.

"Under the nesting?" she said, looking at the row of hay nests that lay on a low wood platform against the wall of the barn.

"See for yourself," he said.

She lifted a nest, and found only a solid wood plank.

"Is it a false bottom?" she said.

"No. A false roof," he said, knocking on the boards above their heads. "Come outside and I'll show you."

They walked around and stood next to the low edge of the sloping roof. It was a simple board-and-batten style where narrow strips were nailed on top of the wider boards where they joined to cover the openings. It wasn't waterproof, but it minimized the dripping inside. It was fine for animals.

Luc took hold of the low edge, and lifted up on it. The whole roof hinged up like the lid of a big trunk. Luc picked up a short stick from inside, and held it straight up and down, then let the roof rest on it.

Inside there was a space about 100 millimeters (4 inches) deep. Aside from a large piece of cowhide with the hair still on it, the space was empty because all of the group's weapons were in the farmhouse at the moment.

"This kind of roof isn't exactly rainproof, so we cover the weapons with the cowhide," Luc told her.

"This is brilliant!" Joyce said. "Who would ever think to look for a false *roof*?"

"The best place to hide something is in a place that nobody would ever guess *is* a place," Luc said.

"Did you make this?" she asked. That seemed a good bet from the pride he was taking in showing it to her.

He answered with a smiling nod. "I built it when the others were away for a couple of days one time. When they came back I put all the weapons in here—we used to keep them under the hay in the barn—and then I asked them to try to find them. Nobody could, so I knew it was a safe place."

"Very clever," Joyce said, guessing that Luc probably had a number of talents that lay hidden because of the long shadow his big brother cast.

Around nine o'clock the group left the farmhouse on their 15 kilometer (9 mile) hike to the rail line.

It was a cloudless night with a three-quarter moon, so there was enough light to follow the narrow paths and game trails that would keep them off of the roads. The seven men and one woman spread out and walked in single file. Carlos led the group, and Julien brought up the rear, with Joyce in front of him, and Luc in front of her.

There was no talking at all, except when they would huddle up once in a while to make sure they were going the right way. Even then, the talking was in very hushed tones.

Joyce was wearing brown slacks and a tan cotton shirt that was a lighter color than she would have liked while trying to be stealthy at night, so over it she wore a dark blue denim jacket. To keep her shoulder-length hair out of her way, she tucked it up under a brown worker's cap. From a distance she could easily be mistaken for a man.

Over one shoulder she carried the Lebel rifle, and over the other the satchel of ammunition. On her hip she wore her pistol, and on her back was a rucksack with the loaves of bread and a large wedge of cheese. She felt a little like a pack mule, but all of the men carried their own weapons and assorted tools and rucksacks of supplies, as well. She also felt quite proud to be part of this patriotic little group and on the way to derail a Nazi train.

Thursday, June 10, 1943

It was nearly two o'clock in the morning before they came out of the tree line at the top of the last hill and could look out on the section of rail they were going to sabotage. It was 150 meters away across a downward sloping open field, and on the far side, 20 meters beyond the rails, was another line of trees.

"You and Luc will stay here as lookouts," Julien said to Joyce. "One of you watch east and the other west. If you see any patrols coming along the tracks, shoot at them to draw their attention away from the rest of us. Kill as many as you can," he said, looking at Luc, "but it will be our warning signal. Fire on them for about thirty seconds, and then run like hell, and let them see where you've run.

"Go down the trail we just came up, and take cover at the fork. If they follow you into the woods, you should be able to pick them off. If they don't go into the woods, we'll take them from behind."

From behind the dry-stone wall that ran along the top of the hill, Joyce and Luc watched the six others spread out and make their way across the field.

While watching to the east, Joyce occasionally glanced down at the men who were now working along the rails. She couldn't make out what they were doing at that distance and in the low light, but at least she knew where the train would be derailed. She would have a perfect view.

All the while watching for any sign of a patrol, Joyce walked back and forth along both sides of a short stretch of the wall adjacent to where the train would be stopped. She stole ten or fifteen second glances at the wall every minute or so, and eventually found what she was looking for.

She knelt down on the back side of the wall, and while still watching the tracks over the top, she wiggled a couple of small stones that were at ground level out from among their larger brothers. She climbed over the wall, and did the same thing at the front.

She took a long look at the east end of the tracks, and then quickly laid down on the ground on the far side of the wall. She stuck her rifle through the hole she had just made among the stones at ground level, and found that she could shift back and forth and cover several hundred meters of track.

Luc—who had been wondering what the heck she was doing—looked down at her, and said in a whisper, "Brilliant! Like an arrow-slit in a castle wall!"

"Exactly," she said. "You should find a place to make one. I'll keep watch while you look."

An hour later, Julien and Carlos, and two of the others returned to the hill top.

"Where are Paul and Craig?" Joyce asked Julien.

"In the woods on the other side," he said. "They need to be nearby when the train stops."

"Why?" she asked.

He looked at her for a long moment, and decided not to explain, but simply said, "You'll see."

While two at a time took turns as lookouts, the others rested as well as they could behind the wall. When Julien nudged her some time later, Joyce awoke with a start, surprised that she had actually fallen asleep.

"No rooster out here," Julien said, "but the sun manages to make it into the sky even without him. We all need to be awake and alert now that the night no longer hides us."

Joyce opened her rucksack and broke one of the loaves of Luc's bread into large chunks. She gave some to each man, and let them take a bite of the cheese, as well. Each had his own canteen of water to wash it down with. She wondered if Paul and Craig had anything to eat in their hiding spots on the other side of the tracks.

It was nearly an hour before Luc said to everyone, "Quiet! Listen! I think I hear the engine."

They all strained, and one by one, they began to hear it also.

Julien looked at his watch.

"She's a half hour late," he said.

Everyone peeked their head up over the wall to look for the train, but because of the bend in the tracks, all they could see was its smoke above the trees.

Then Joyce, looking through Julien's binoculars, said, "What the heck is that?"

Just coming out of the trees, well ahead of the engine, was a tiny handcar being pumped along by two German soldiers. On the front edge of the car stood two more soldiers, staring intently at the track ahead of them.

216

"That's why she's going so slow," Julien said when he looked through the binoculars. "They're inspecting the tracks closely as they go."

"Won't they see that you've sabotaged the rails?" Joyce asked.

"I hope so," he said.

"What?" she replied.

"During the first months of the occupation," he explained, "before we had many weapons, we would descend like locusts on an unguarded stretch of track, remove scores of spikes in a row from one or both rails, and throw them into a river or even bury them.

"At first we were rewarded with many derailments, but the Nazis quickly learned to guard the rails more closely, and to inspect them more frequently. The train crews would even carry their own supply of spikes to replace the stolen ones. We have not used this type of sabotage in half a year or more.

"That's why I hope they find that we've stolen their spikes," he concluded. "Otherwise all we would have to show for our efforts is a derailed engine. Not much of a prize."

"I don't understand," she said.

He handed the binoculars back to her, and said, "You will. Watch."

As the chugging engine came into view from the trees, one of the inspectors on the hand car suddenly shouted, "*Stoppen Sie den Zug! Die Schienennägel fehlen!*" (Stop the train! The rail spikes are missing!)

One of the pumpers on the little car pulled on the brake lever, and the other shouted and waved at the locomotive.

The slow-moving steam engine screeched, hissed, and groaned as the engineer vented the steam to the drive wheels and threw on its brakes. The dozen cars behind it clunked together in a domino effect, each bumping into the one in front of it as its own brakes tried to stop its forward momentum.

The hand car made its way slowly to the edge of the last rail that still had all of its spikes, and the four soldiers jumped off to walk the tracks and see how many spikes were missing.

Behind them, even though the train had been moving slowly, it still took a long while for its hundreds of tons of mass to slow down.

When the train reached walking speed, the big doors on the box car right behind the coal tender slid open, and a swarm of twenty or thirty soldiers, rifles and machine guns in hand, piled out of both sides of it.

"François told me they were moving something important!" Julien said in a low but excited voice. "Look at the guard they've put on the train!"

As the train continued to creep along, slowing all the while, Julien looked back along its length.

"Look at the three flatcars covered by tarpaulins," he said. "Those are artillery pieces! I can tell by the shape!"

He swung back to look at the engine. It was still moving forward, but just barely.

"Come on," Julien encouraged the engineer in a whisper, "just a little farther. Go ahead you lazy Kraut-lover, get up close to the handcar so your friends don't have to walk so far."

But the engine and the train ground to a standstill and a cloud of steam erupted from the drive cylinders indicating the finality of the stop. The engine was still fifty meters from the handcar.

"Dirty bugger!" Julien growled under his breath.

Then they watched as a Nazi lieutenant trotted up next to the cab and shouted something up to the engineer.

The engineer just threw up his hands in a very typical French "*c'est la vie*" gesture.

The lieutenant shouted again, this time pointing forward in a demanding manner.

The engineer said something, but did nothing to make the train move, which was apparently what the German wanted.

The lieutenant pulled his pistol and aimed up at the engineer. This time they could hear him shout, "*Déplacez le train maintenant, cochon français!* (Move the train now, you French pig!)"

Shaking his head wearily, and giving the officer a dismissive wave, the engineer nonetheless reached for the throttle. He left the cylinder vents open, and when he pulled the throttle open, huge jets of steam blasted out both sides of the engine.

The lieutenant jumped and yelled something at the engineer.

Even from their distant vantage point, they could see the engineer laughing as he closed off the vents and the big drive wheels slowly started to turn.

The train crept forward. Ten meters. Twenty meters. Then the engineer opened the vents again, and let the train coast another ten meters before he began to apply the brakes.

Suddenly, the ground beneath the engine exploded with a thunderous *Boom!*

Joyce jumped at the sight and sound of the explosion, and at first she thought something had happened to the engine. When she heard Julien shout, "Yes! Perfect!" she understood why he had wanted the engineer to pull farther forward.

The explosives that Julien and the others had planted blew the rails out from under the engine, but the blast also punched a hole up through the engine between the boiler and the smoke box. Weakened by the TNT explosion, the boiler tubes split under the 250 pounds of pressure inside them, and let loose a tremendous steam explosion that blew burning coal embers twenty meters in all directions. Within seconds, smoke, steam, and fire enveloped the entire engine.

Also within seconds, the air was filled with shouts in German as the soldiers fanned out to guard the now disabled train and its cargo.

"Time to go?" Joyce asked Julien.

"No," he said. "We need to cover François' group while they attack. *Stopping* the train is only half the job."

No sooner had he spoken then Joyce heard gunfire erupt from the woods far to her left at the back end of the train.

A number of German soldiers fell, but the rest threw themselves down and began firing blindly into the woods.

Then Joyce heard the deep *Whump!* of a mortar, and the whistling of the round as it sped through the air. She wasn't sure which side had fired it until she saw the explosion at the back end of the middle flatcar.

The German's firing intensified, but was answered a few seconds later by another mortar round. This one hit squarely on the covered artillery piece on the same flatcar.

The German lieutenant ran towards his men shouting orders, and a dozen of them got up and charged the woods, firing their weapons as they ran.

Every one of them was cut down before they got half way to the tree line.

"How many men does François have?" Joyce asked in amazement. "It seems like a small army!"

"He is well connected with the British OSS," he replied. "He has more than fifty men, all well trained, and well armed."

The German officer yelled more orders, and the men lying in the grass continued firing into the woods. At the same time, the tarp over the last flatcar was thrown back, and revealed two four-barreled anti-aircraft cannons.

"*Merde!* (Shit!)" Julien said. "Those things will cut the trees down like a sickle through grass!"

They were *2cm Flakvierling 38* cannons that fired 20mm (3/4-inch) rounds at more than 800 per minute. At that range, François' men wouldn't stand a chance against one of them, much less two.

Even before the tarps were all the way back, the gun crews were swarming over the two cannons. With practiced precision, a soldier swung up into the seat of each of the guns, and began spinning the hand-wheels to swing the gun's barrels around toward the trees and down to ground level. Another two men stood on each side of both guns, ready to swap out the 20-round magazines as the cannons chewed through the ammunition.

Julien laid his rifle across the top of the wall and got down behind it.

"I'll take the man shooting the far cannon," he said. "Chéri, you take the man on the near one. Luc, watch closely and if either of us misses, take a second shot. The rest of you shoot at anyone standing on the flatcar and keep firing. Set your sights for 200 meters."

Julien was certainly a good teacher, and he appeared to be a good leader, Joyce thought. Too bad he was such a barbarian when it came to women.

"Ready?" Julien asked.

Five voices replied, "Ready!"

The *Flakvierlings* were built with armor plating across their fronts, so the group had to wait until the guns rotated far enough toward the woods for the operators to come into their sights from the side.

"Fire!" Julien called out finally, and five rifles went off almost simultaneously, followed a couple of seconds later by the sixth.

A moment later, four of the men on the flatcar were dead or dying, and another was badly wounded. Only Carlos' shot missed, but he made up for it with hits on his next two shots.

Joyce's shot hit the gun operator under his left arm while it was raised cranking the cannon around. The bullet ripped through both of his lungs and his heart, and he fell over sideways, dead before he was on the deck of the car.

Julien's shot struck the other operator a little low, shattering his hip. The wound was not fatal, but it caused him to roll off the seat in crippling pain.

Seeing both of the shooters fall, Luc took aim on the middle of the back of one of the loaders, and pulled the trigger. The man fell forward, and then sideways off the car and onto the ground.

They all reloaded and fired at least two more times before the surprised Nazi lieutenant directed rifle and machine gun fire up at the hill, and they had to take cover behind the wall.

While Joyce and her group were pinned down, two more of the gun crew soldiers jumped into the seats of the cannons. As the far gun continued its swing towards the woods, the lieutenant directed the other one to aim up at the hilltop.

As bullets ricocheted off the stones and zipped over their heads, Joyce yelled to Luc, "The arrow slits!"

They both dove to the ground and pushed their rifles through the holes they had made.

"*Merde!*" Joyce exclaimed when she saw the near cannon aiming toward them. "Everyone get down!" she shouted. Then to Luc she said, "You take the far one!"

Just as Luc fired, the new man on the far gun moved, and his bullet missed. He quickly reloaded and fired, just as the man pushed the firing pedal. The cannon roared, sending half a dozen rounds into the woods, and then the man fell off the seat, hit by Luc's second shot.

With the gun's armor facing them, Joyce aimed at the wire aiming reticule of the first cannon, located between the barrels, but the operator's face was not behind it. He was wisely keeping his head down.

All of a sudden, the barrels erupted with jets of fire as the shooter fired his first rounds.

She heard the rounds whistle overhead, and she kept her aim on the reticule, expecting the man to pop up and take another aim.

But she saw the gun lower slightly without the shooter making an appearance. Apparently, a spotter that she didn't have time to search out was telling him that he was too high.

With no operator to shoot at, Joyce decided to try an impossible shot. She aimed at the bore of one of the cannon barrels, and pulled the trigger.

Apparently, the shot *was* impossible. She saw her round hit the armor just low and to the left.

Before she could make another try, the cannon started firing again. Fortunately, the inexperienced shooter had overcorrected, and the rounds exploded into the hillside below the wall.

As she aimed at the cannon barrel again, the gun moved up slightly. She didn't think he was going to miss this time.

She pulled the trigger, and a ball of flame engulfed the *Flakvierling*. It rocked forward, slid off the flatcar, and crashed onto the ground.

Her mouth hung open for a second, until she realized that her bullet hadn't done that, but that the gun had been hit by a mortar round from François' group.

Luc's shot had killed the operator on the other cannon, and none of the other soldiers were foolhardy enough to jump up and take his place.

Joyce quickly searched out the soldiers firing rifles and machine guns at them, and returned their fire until she was out of bullets.

As their bullets continued to ping off the rocks and zip overhead, Joyce shoved ten rounds of ammunition into the rifle, and then stuck it back out through the hole.

She got four shots off at the men laying in the grass when another mortar round hit in the middle of them, and silenced half their guns. Moments later, a second round hit ten meters away from the first.

The German lieutenant was screaming orders, but there were few men left to carry them out. The gunfire into the woods and up at the wall was reduced to almost nothing.

The return fire from the woods increased, and the other men in Joyce's group went back to shooting over the top of the wall, as well.

Suddenly, machine gun fire opened up from Joyce's right.

The two rail inspectors, having survived the explosion of the engine, had circled around and had crawled up along the wall from the east while the fighting went on to the west.

While one of the two sprayed bursts of bullets to keep everyone down, the other jumped up on top of the wall and let loose a volley of shots at the enemy hiding behind it.

Joyce *felt* as much as she *heard* a bullet thud into the dirt below her leg, missing her by only a centimeter.

Yvon was hit in the neck, and rolled over, falling into a sitting position against the wall. He died almost instantly.

Julien took a bullet in the chest as he was spinning around to get a shot off at the attacker. His rifle round blew the man's shoulder apart, and he dropped his machine gun and fell off the wall.

Instantly, the other soldier popped up and began firing, but he quickly ran out of ammunition.

As he rushed to change clips, Luc rolled away from his rifle, which was still sticking through the wall, and drew his pistol.

Just as the German raised his machine gun again, Luc fired. One ... two ... three ... four times. The soldier's uniform had a tight grouping of holes in the chest as he dropped to his knees and fell over on his face.

As Luc looked down at the man he had just killed, the other one rolled over and reached for his machine gun with his left hand. Luc fired two rounds into his back.

Joyce no longer had any doubt which version of the runaway-soldier story was true. She just wondered why Julien had lied about it. Perhaps just to discredit Luc in her eyes?

In all the excitement, no one had noticed that the shooting from down below, and from the woods had completely stopped.

They all looked over the wall, and saw that the Nazi lieutenant had done something that would have earned him a bullet in the head by *Der Fuehrer*. He had surrendered.

In the sudden quiet, Joyce could hear shouts in German coming from the woods, telling the remaining soldiers to turn and walk back to the train with their hands up.

Leaning heavily on the wall, Julien said, "Keep your guns on them in case it's a trick."

Joyce looked up at him, from her arrow slit and noticed that his hand was red with blood.

"Julien! You're hit!" she exclaimed jumping up. "Where?"

"In the chest," he said looking down at his blood-soaked shirt. "But I am happy—and a bit surprised—to say I am not dead."

Carlos looked at his back, and said, "My God! The bullet went right through you!"

They all craned to look.

Then Joyce noticed Yvon sitting against the wall, staring down at the ground, but not moving.

"Yvon!" she cried as she rushed to him, noticing the blood on his neck.

It didn't take a doctor to realize that he was dead, and she lightly kissed his forehead, and closed his eyes. "Good bye, my friend," she said quietly. "God be with you."

"We'll care for Yvon later," Julien said. "Everyone, back to your rifles. I don't trust them as far as I can spit."

He reached down and slid Joyce's rifle from the hole between the rocks. "Once again, you show how clever you can be, chéri," he said. He groaned loudly from the pain in his chest as he stood up. He handed her the gun, and said, "But I think you can shoot over the top of the wall safely, now. Keep an eye on the other cannon in case some Nazi hero decides to sneak into its seat and win himself the Iron Cross."

As she looked back down at the train, Joyce saw that a dozen or more of François's men had come out of the woods with their guns ready to fire, and were moving towards the Germans in a wide line. A second, smaller group went among the dead and wounded and collected weapons.

The Germans were herded toward the box car they had come out of, and after being frisked for weapons, they were told to climb back in. The door was closed and locked from the outside, and a single guard was posted on either side of the car.

As François's men then opened the other box cars in the train, and climbed in to examine the contents, Joyce asked Julien, "What the heck do you do with prisoners?"

"I don't know," he said. "I've never seen a German surrender before."

A short while later, Paul and Craig had rejoined the group carrying their dynamite detonation box and what they could salvage of their wire.

As they watched boxes being unloaded from the train, they saw a lone man separate himself from the group and start to walk up the hill toward them.

"Is that François?" Joyce asked Julien.

"François de Gaulle," he answered. "He claims to be a cousin of the general, Charles de Gaulle, but I have my doubts. His ego is big enough, but not his nose."

Joyce chuckled, and watched the man approach. He moved up the hill with the confident stride of a young man, but his full head of pure white hair, and his white Van Dyke style mustache and goatee made him look much older. As he neared, she could see that his face was marked with the lines of age, but only to a point where it gave him character. She guessed that he was probably in his sixties, and she considered him rather handsome ... for an old man.

"François!" "Julien!" the two men greeted each other.

François climbed nimbly over the wall and opened his arms to embrace his brother-in-arms, but when he saw the blood on his chest, he stopped.

"Julien! You're wounded! Are you alright?" he asked.

"Apparently, I am," he said. "The bullet seems to have gone clear through me without hitting anything of importance." He looked down at Yvon, and added, "Not all of us were so lucky."

"I'm sorry," François said. "I lost three good men, as well, with another three wounded. But if it had not been for you up here, those anti-aircraft cannons would have cut us to bits. My sources told me nothing about *those* being on the train."

"You can thank Joyce here for keeping them inactive," Julien said.

"Ah!" François exclaimed. "You are Mademoiselle Renaud! Julien has told me of your shooting prowess! I thought he was bragging, but now I believe!"

He embraced her, and kissed her on both cheeks.

"Thank you!" he said. "You saved many lives this morning!"

"But not alone," she replied. "Luc and Julien, and all of us helped to keep the cannons quiet. And if it hadn't been for your mortar, you would be up here looking at corpses."

"*Oui.* We are all in this thing together. Thank *all* of you," he said nodding his head solemnly. "*Vive la France! Vive la Résistance!*" he added, raising his fist in the air.

"*Vive la France! Vive la Résistance!*" they all repeated.

Looking down at the men unloading the box cars, Joyce thought about the locked one.

"What will you do with the prisoners?" she asked François. "You're not going to set the car on fire, are you?" As much as she hated the Nazi's, that kind of death for *anyone* caused her to shudder.

He looked at her in surprise, then he laughed. "No, child," he said. "Such barbarism is a *German* invention. I intend to do nothing with them. Literally. After we leave, someone will come along before too long and let them out. I can only hope it is one of the young lieutenant's superiors. When they discover he surrendered his supply train to *La Résistance*, they will pack him off to the Russian front ... if he is lucky!"

"What have you found in the other cars?" Luc asked.

"Rations, mostly," he said. "Now that the German's have eaten all the food in France, they have to resort to bringing in their own canned *dachschwein* from home."

"Roof pig?" Joyce translated François' German phrase. Back in Agen, Fritz had told her about *dachschwein*. It was rumored to be a sausage made from cats that were raised on rooftops for food. She doubted that the story was true, but living on a diet with almost no meat of any kind, she wondered if it could really be all that bad anyway.

"Is there enough that we might take some back with us?" Joyce asked.

"Of course! Of course!" François said. "Take all you can carry. The booty here is as much yours as it is ours." Then he asked her, "*Sprechen Sie Deutsch?* Or do you just know their delicacies?"

"*Ich weiß, ein wenig Deutsch.* (I know a little German.)," she replied modestly. "But I have heard rumors about their roof pig."

"I thought you were told there would be weapons on board," Julien said. He closed his eyes and grimaced against the increasing pain in his chest.

"Yes. We had hoped for rifles, machine guns, and grenades, but all we found are shells for the artillery pieces. Not much use to us on foot. We will have to settle for what we have taken from the soldiers."

Suddenly, a thought struck him. He removed the Zeiss binoculars that hung from a leather strap around his neck, and held them out to Joyce.

"A token of my esteem," he said. "And a remembrance of your first battle. If I had my tools and my loupe, I would engrave the date for you."

"Thank you," she said. "I'm honored. Are you a jeweler, then?"

"I was," he said, "and I hope to be again one day."

Shouts from below called him away, but before he left, he hugged and kissed all of them. "*Vive la Résistance!*" he said again, and headed down the hill.

After Julien's group had collected as many cans and boxes of German rations as they could carry, they returned to the top of the hill to bury Yvon. They chose a spot in the woods that Luc paced off from a small rock outcropping.

"After the war," he said, "I will come back and put a marker here."

"A nice sentiment," Carlos said. "I only hope there are enough markers to go around when all this is over."

Twenty minutes into their long trek back to the farmhouse, the group heard a series of explosions behind them. Joyce looked at Julien questioningly.

"François is blowing up the cannons. If we can't use them, he doesn't want the Germans to have them either." Again he grimaced from the pain, and he had to lean against a tree for a minute to regain his strength.

"Perhaps there is more damage inside your chest than you know," Joyce said. "Is there a doctor you can trust in the village?"

"Let's just get back so I can lay in my own bed," he said. "I don't need a doctor. I'll be fine in a day or two, trust me."

In fact, the 9mm bullet that had gone through Julien *had* done remarkably little damage. It had gone between his ribs—front and back, had passed to the right of his trachea and spine, and had narrowly missed his heart ... almost. A tiny nick in Julien's aorta left him bleeding internally, slowly filling his plural cavity with blood.

The walk back was long and slow, with Julien needing to take many rest breaks. Although his entrance and exit wounds were not bleeding badly, he seemed to get a little weaker and a little slower with each kilometer. At one point Luc suggested they build a litter out of some tree branches and their coats so they could carry him, but he staunchly refused.

It was nearing seven o'clock in the evening when they reached the farmhouse; almost twelve hours from the time they left the train.

Joyce and Luc took Julien into his bedroom, stripped him of his bloody clothes, and cleaned and dressed his wounds. They laid him in his bed, and he was asleep—or unconscious—within seconds.

While they took care of Julien, Paul gathered the weapons and ammunition, and hid them in the hen house. He then left for the village to get the doctor.

Carlos slid the kitchen table back and opened the trapdoor that led to the farmhouse's root cellar—which also served as their wine cellar. With Carlos in the kitchen, Craig on the ladder, and Henri down below, the men hid away all of the rations they had brought back. With such an attack on the train—even so far away—they knew the Milice, and probably the SS, would be scouring the countryside tomorrow for those responsible. Having cans and boxes of food in the kitchen cupboards with *Heeresgut* (Army Property) stenciled on the side would be hard to explain.

As Carlos handed Craig the last can, a banging came on the front door. It was not a pleasant company-call knock; it was unfriendly and demanding.

"Get down!" Carlos quietly told the other men. They ducked into the cellar, and Carlos closed the trapdoor and silently set the table back on top of it. The banging came again, followed by, "Open up!"

Joyce and Luc heard the banging, as well, of course, and as she closed the bedroom door—all but a tiny crack—she quietly asked Luc, "This could be trouble. Is your pistol loaded?"

"A full clip," he answered, taking it out, cocking the hammer, and releasing the safety.

She peered out through the crack as Carlos went to the door, and she drew her pistol, as well.

Carlos went into a befuddled-old-man act, and opened the door.

Outside stood a man in a Milice uniform, complete with beret and the twisted-ribbon "gamma" insignia. Behind him stood two German soldiers, each carrying a machine gun.

Carlos looked at the men with a bright smile, and said, "*Bonsoir, messieurs! Bonsoir! Comment allez-vous ce soir?* (Good evening, gentlemen! Good evening! How are you tonight?)"

"Not well! The partisans have blown up a supply train!" the man said as he stepped through the doorway, pushing Carlos aside. "Who are you? Where is Julien Arsenault?"

Joyce moved away from the crack at the door, and whispered directly into Luc's ear. "There are three of them—two with machine guns. I don't know where Craig and the others are, but I think we can do this alone. We'll shoot the two with guns, first. You take the one on the right, I'll take the left. Then we'll both take care of the other one. Be careful; he's right next to Carlos."

She went back to the door, ready to fling it open and start shooting, but when she looked only the unarmed man was visible, and he had moved so he was partially blocked by Carlos.

She strained her ears, and she thought she heard footsteps to the left of the door. But were both of the other men there, or only one?

She waved her hand at Luc, silently telling him that they weren't going to go. She then handed him her pistol and quickly began to take off her shirt.

"My name is Carlos Santiago," Carlos replied proudly to the man's question, not slipping from his befuddled character. "Julien is my nephew ... on his mother's side ... she was my sister, you see. Did you know her? She lived in this very house for many years. Margarite was her name, God rest her soul. Did you say that you knew her?"

"I don't give a damn about your sister!" the man snarled. "Where is Julien?" He pointed toward the kitchen and the one other bedroom, and the two soldiers went to check them out.

Luc looked at Joyce undressing with a furrowed *what-the-hell-are-you-doing* look.

As she hurriedly pushed off her slacks and underpants, she leaned to his ear, and said, "I need to see where they are. I'm hoping they won't start shooting at a naked prostitute when I step out into the room." She added as she unhooked her bra, "Drop your pants and stand behind me. Keep your gun ready but hidden."

She disheveled her hair, took her gun back from Luc, and reached for the doorknob.

"Are you a friend of Julien's" Carlos asked the man innocently.

"Where is he, you old fool!?" the man demanded.

"I'm afraid Julien is ill, *mon ami*," Carlos told the man. "He will not be able to come out and visit this evening. A warm bed is the best thing for typhoid, no?"

"In there?" the man said, as he pointed to the bedroom door.

Just as the soldier reached for the knob, Joyce pulled the door open, and stood in the doorway, stark naked and breathing heavily.

As if steadying herself from overexertion, she had her right hand against the wall just inside the door frame. In that hand she held her gun out of sight. Her other hand was on her hip.

The man and the soldier—as well as Carlos—looked at her in dumbfounded surprise.

"What the hell are you doing *now*, you horny old man?" Joyce said to him in an angry voice. "You didn't tell me you were inviting *others*!"

Hearing a woman's voice, the second soldier stepped from the kitchen, and stared at her with his mouth open.

"You will each have to pay the same amount," she said to them collectively. "I have to earn a living, you know."

The man with Carlos looked past Joyce, and saw Luc with his pants down.

"Is your brother in there with you?" he demanded. He turned to Carlos, and snapped, "Typhoid, huh?"

He started to move toward the door, and Joyce pulled the gun from the wall, turned, and shot the soldier to her left. She spun back and before the other man could get his mouth closed, much less get his gun raised, she shot him in the chest, as well.

She had hoped that she had gotten far enough out of the way for Luc to shoot the other man, but she didn't hear his gun go off.

When she turned toward the man, she saw why. He had acted with surprising speed, and had pulled Carlos in front of him as a shield. He pulled a small caliber pistol from his pocket, and held it at Carlos' back.

With his gun leveled at the man—and Carlos—Luc stepped out of his pants and walked forward.

Naked, Joyce held her gun aimed at the man, as well, although he presented way too small of a target, hiding behind Carlos.

"Put your guns down or I'll shoot him through the spine!" the man demanded.

"Go ahead," Luc said. "Only shoot him in the head, please. Uncle Carlos is an old man who has lost his mind anyway."

Clearly, Luc's reply took the man aback, and it gave Joyce just enough of a chance to step to the side where a bit more of the man's head became visible, and she pulled her trigger.

The bullet missed Carlos' ear by a couple of millimeters, and entered the man's right eye. His scream turned to a gurgle as he fell, but he made no more noise after he hit the floor.

"Did he leave any men outside?" Joyce asked Carlos as she went to the front door.

Again, she hid her pistol beside the door frame, and pulled open the door, completely naked. She had intended to shout, "Help me! Help me!" if anyone had been out there and had heard the shots. But the yard was empty, except for the old Citroen that the soldiers and the man had driven up in.

"Apparently, they came alone," she said as she stepped back inside and closed the door, "but they came in a car; that's how they got here so fast."

When she checked the yard, Luc had stood behind her, ready to join in if there had been any shooting, and Carlos had rushed to the kitchen to let the other men out of the cellar.

Joyce, completely naked, and Luc, with his pants off, stood in the main room of the house as the two men who had only heard the shooting stared at them, bewildered.

"It's how babies are made," Joyce said to them, "and how Milice pigs are killed." As she headed for the bedroom to get dressed, she added, "Carlos will explain."

"Help me get these swine outside, and their blood cleaned up," Carlos said to the men, "and I'll tell you the story of *Crazy Uncle Carlos and the Naked Prostitute Assassin.*"

In the bedroom, Luc checked on Julien as Joyce got dressed.

"He's still breathing," he said, "I hope Paul gets here quickly with the doctor."

Luc had told her that he sometimes hated his older brother, but she knew that was born of rivalry and resentment. She could hear in Luc's voice that the love that connected them by blood was still there, though. She was happy for that.

While Luc pulled on his pants, she asked him, "Do you know the dead Milice officer? He seemed to know you and Julien."

"Maurice Savreux," he said. "He was a barber in the village when the Germans invaded. To curry favor he offered his ears to the SS. For some reason, men seem to talk freely about their political views when having their hair clipped, and he passed along what he heard.

"When a dozen men were rounded up and sent off to work camps, his secret was out, and the SS had to protect him. So they made him a captain in the Milice. You'll be a hero in the village for having shot him."

"And at the same time, I'll have a price on my head," she said.

"We all will," Luc replied. "Maurice wasn't bright enough to have figured out that Julien and I might have been involved in the sabotage this morning. Somebody sent him out here, and when he doesn't return, someone much smarter is likely to pay us a visit."

"Is there a place we can go?" she asked.

"We could join François," Luc suggested. "He apparently knows how to keep even a large band of men out of sight."

"Do you know where to find him?" she asked.

"No. But, Carlos might," he answered. "He was with François for a few months before he joined us. But I know he's not nearby; getting to him might be hard. There will be roadblocks, so it will be traveling through the woods, again. I don't think Julien will be strong enough for that for weeks."

"Then perhaps we should drive," Joyce said. "Maurice was kind enough to leave us his car, no?"

"And do we shoot our way through the roadblocks?" he said skeptically.

"I hope it doesn't come to that," she said. "I'd rather lie our way through. I think Carlos is pretty close in size to Maurice, and he seems to be quite a good actor. I think he should dress in Maurice's clothes, and drive us through as his prisoners. Do any of the others speak German? One of them could dress in one of the soldier's uniforms, and pretend to be guarding us. That way they would have a machine gun ready in case something goes wrong."

Luc thought about the plan for a moment, and then said, "I think Julien was wrong when he said you were clever. You're downright devious."

"I'll take that as a compliment," she said with a smile.

"*Und ich spreche Deutsch.* (And I speak German.), he added. "My Mémé and Pépé were from Austria."

"Perfect!" she said. "Now, let's go tell the others. But we'll have to say that it's your idea, okay? They may not be ready to take such a suggestion from a new recruit ... and a woman."

In the back yard, they stripped the clothes off of Maurice and one of the soldiers. One of them had fallen forward when Joyce shot him, so the front of his jacket was soaked with blood, making it pretty useless to them. The other, however, had fallen backwards, so from the front, the only outward indication that he'd been shot was a small bullet hole.

Having been shot in the face, Maurice had only a few splatters of blood on his dark-colored jacket and beret, which virtually disappeared after Joyce cleaned them with cold water.

By the time they had stripped the bodies, Paul and the doctor appeared in the back yard. Seeing the car out front, they had made a wide circle around the orchard to come in from the back. Paul was ready to get his gun from the henhouse and rescue his comrades, but that was obviously unnecessary.

While the doctor went inside with Joyce and Luc, the men carted the bodies out into the woods, quickly dug shallow graves, and covered them with brush and leaves.

In the bedroom, the doctor examined Julien while Joyce and Luc looked on. At one point, Luc helped to roll his brother onto his side so the doctor could examine his back, and Joyce noticed that Julien's body seemed completely limp as he was moved. He also looked extremely pale.

Finally, the doctor pulled the blanket back up under Julien's chin, and motioned for all of them to go out into the main room.

All of the men were gathered there, and they sat or stood in silence, waiting for the doctor to speak.

He shook his head sadly, and said, "I don't think Julien will last the night. I believe the bullet must have struck a blood vessel inside his chest—perhaps a small one, or just a small cut—but he has been bleeding internally for hours now. It's a testament to his strength that he has made it this long."

"We're the same blood type," Luc said, pulling up his sleeve. "You could give him a transfusion from me."

"It wouldn't help," the doctor said. "At least not for very long. He needs surgery to stop the internal bleeding, and that type of operation requires a hospital. I doubt that he would survive the trip to Le Claire, and if he did, his wound would be reported to the Milice and the SS, so if he did survive, he would probably wish that he hadn't."

Putting his hands on Luc's shoulders, the doctor said, "I'm sorry, Luc. I've known you and Julien all your lives; this is almost as hard for me to tell you as it is for you to hear. But you will always know that your brother died for a great cause; he is a hero to the real France; the France that will one day rise again because of men like him." He looked around the room, and added, "Because of men—and women—like all of you. *Vive la France! Vive la Résistance!*"

"*Vive la France! Vive la Résistance!*" they all repeated.

"I can't just leave him here to die all alone," Luc said. "The rest of you go on; I'll catch up."

"You don't know where we're going," Joyce said. "How will you find us?"

"You need to go, Luc," the doctor said. "There's not a thing you can do, and it won't be safe for you here. I'll stay with Julien. I won't leave him alone."

"It won't be safe for you either," Joyce said.

"I'll be fine," he said. "If they show up while I'm here, I'll say you kidnapped me and forced me to help your friend. I'll say that I could have saved him, but only pretended to help, and let him die. I'll tell them that you are coming back in a day's time to get him. That will keep them here waiting for you, rather than chasing you, no?"

Joyce gave him a hug and kissed both his cheeks. "I wish you could come with us," she said. "I like the way you think."

"I'm afraid I'm too old to run through the woods killing Germans," he said. "So I'll just stay here and give them as much grief as I can, in my own way."

Ten minutes later, they had all said their good-byes to Julien and the doctor, and they got ready to leave.

Maurice's uniform fit Carlos like it was tailored for him, but the soldier's uniform was a little baggy on Luc. They reasoned that with him sitting in the car the poor fit wouldn't be easy to see, however, so they went ahead with the plan.

They got all of their weapons from the henhouse, and loaded them into the trunk. Inside the trunk they found several short lengths of rope, and black cloth hoods. They correctly guessed that Maurice would have used them to tie up and blind his prisoners while he transported them.

With the car packed, they all climbed in. Carlos and Luc took the front seat, while their "prisoners," Craig, Paul, and Henri, sat in back. The prisoners each had a pistol and a black hood. If they came to a roadblock, they would pull on the hoods and hide their guns behind their backs, as if they were tied up.

With the car's spare tire mounted on the outside of the lid, there was a reasonable amount of room inside the trunk for Joyce. Although not to be confused with comfortable, Joyce was able to make something of a nest for herself using Carlos' and Luc's regular clothes as well as the men's jackets and a couple of blankets from the house.

The only part that she truly dreaded was when the doctor closed the lid and rotated the two handles locking her inside.

They had discussed leaving the lid unlocked, but the rotated handles would be obvious if they were stopped, and a curious guard might wonder why the trunk was left unlatched. Another problem was that if the car should hit a bump, the lid could fly open by itself, exposing Joyce, if not throwing her out altogether. Joyce was not happy to hear the latches click, locking her inside, but she knew it was the best decision.

Settled into her nest, and with her pistol in her hand, Joyce heard the motor start, and then the car began to move. She wondered if she would ever see the little farm again. She hoped so.

Although she couldn't stretch out, Joyce found that the ride in the trunk of the old Citroen was not nearly as bad as she had anticipated. In fact, she was surprised to realize that she had been sleeping when she was awakened by the car coming to a stop.

She silently let the safety off of her pistol, and strained to listen to what was going on up front. With the car's motor still running, it was difficult to hear, but they appeared to be at a roadblock.

She heard someone speaking in German, whom she suspected was the guard. Then she heard Luc translate into French, after which Carlos answered in French, and Luc translated that back into German. Joyce shook her head. It was just like the Germans to man a roadblock in the middle of France with soldiers who spoke no French.

The ruse worked, however, and in a couple of minutes they were on their way, again.

A short while later, she felt the car slow again, and then the ride got very rough. Something was wrong!

As the car bounced on for a minute or two, she felt around, and found one of the black hoods, and rolled it up. She put it across her mouth, bit into it, and tied it behind her head, making a gag.

Suddenly, the car stopped, and the engine was shut off. Joyce's heart was pounding as she heard the doors open, but didn't hear anyone speaking. She put her hands behind her as if she was tied up, but she kept a tight grip on her gun.

She heard the handles rotate, and then the trunk lid was slowly pulled open.

She looked up to see Carlos and Luc looking in at her.

Carlos laughed when he saw her trussed up like another prisoner. "You're a quick thinker, aren't you, Jo? I wasn't so sure about a woman joining us, but Julien was right about you; you're a definite asset to the maqui *and* to the resistance. I'm glad you're on *our* side!"

"Why did we stop," she asked, pulling the gag from her mouth.

"We thought you could probably use a break," Luc said. "We've still got a long ways to go."

"It is getting a little stuffy," she said as she crawled out into a dense stand of woods. "Thanks for remembering me back here."

After stretching for a while, they all had a few bites of bread, relieved themselves, and got back into the car.

To make sure that Joyce wasn't suffocating in the trunk, they made a couple more brief stops as they drove westward, but they encountered no more roadblocks.

After driving for nearly three more hours, Carlos announced that they were nearly out of petrol. Rather than let it stall on the road, they decided to drive the car a short distance into the woods again, and hide it with brush.

As Carlos and Luc changed back into their civilian clothes, Carlos explained that there was a small town up ahead, about two hour's walk. It was where he had first met François, so he hoped to be able to make contact, again.

"We should take the rifles and ammunition," he said, "but we'll hide them before we enter the town. It's been months since I've been here. It could be crawling with Milice by now. We'll just have to play it by ear."

When they had walked close enough that they could make out the steeple of the church in the town, they left the dirt road and walked a hundred meters or so into the woods.

"We'll stay here until daybreak," Carlos said. "There will be few people awake at this hour, and those that are may not welcome strangers sneaking into their town, no?"

In the last thirty-six hours, none of the group had gotten anything more than a nap, so they were all exhausted.

"The rest of you sleep, if you can," Joyce said to them as they entered a circle of trees where the ground was thick with pine needles. "I had a little nap in the car; I'll stand watch."

She got no arguments. Only Paul remained standing, saying, "I dozed off in the car, as well; I'll keep you company."

Joyce stood at one side of the circle, and Paul at the other. As quietly as they could, they kept moving, knowing that if they sat down, or even leaned against a tree, they too would be as fast asleep as their comrades.

Although she could see little of it through the trees, the sky was just beginning to lighten in the east when Joyce thought she heard something in the direction of the road.

She picked up a pine cone and tossed it at Paul to get his attention. In the dim light, she pantomimed listening in the direction of the road.

A moment later, he nodded that he heard something, too.

She motioned for him to get down and stay there, and she drew her pistol and crept away from the group, moving swiftly and quietly from tree to tree.

When she was about twenty meters from the group, she saw a figure moving between the trees in the near darkness. As he passed behind the next tree, she ran to the next one in front of her, getting a few meters closer to the figure.

Then, from the other side of the group, she heard, "None of you move! And don't touch your guns; we have you surrounded!"

There was murmuring and rustling of leaves, and she could faintly make out eight or ten figures standing around the clearing. She could also see the figure she had been stalking, walking toward the group.

She moved two more trees closer, and waited to see what was going to happen.

"Where is the other one?" the man that she was stalking asked. "There were six of you."

"I'm behind you with a gun pointed at your back," Joyce said ninety-percent hidden by a fat pine tree.

The man laughed as he turned around with his hands up. "Mademoiselle Renaud, I presume," he said. "François told me to watch out for *you*." He turned back to the group, and said, "We've come to pick you up. It is better for strangers not to wander through the village unescorted." He found Luc, and said, "I'm sorry to hear about your brother. He was a good man; a true patriot."

"How did you know that he's hurt?" Luc replied.

The man paused a moment, and then said, "I'm sorry, my friend. I thought you already knew. Julien passed away a few hours ago."

"How do you know that?" Luc asked.

"Doctor Poullard called François to tell him you were coming," the man explained. "He said you were dressed as the Milice and a Nazi soldier. He didn't want there to be any accidents when we ran across one another."

"François has a *telephone*?" Joyce said. "Out here?"

"No," the man laughed. "But there are a few in town, and François will always get the message in short order."

"Will you take us to him?" Carlos asked.

"That's why we are here," the man said. "I am Pierre, by the way." He doffed his hat and made a slight bow. "At your service."

As the combined group walked toward the road, Pierre said, "We found your car, by the way. We'll go back for it with extra petrol. It could come in handy. The uniforms, too."

Friday, June 11, 1943

The sun was well above the horizon when, an hour later, the group walked down the gravel driveway of a large farm. Joyce looked at the farmhouse in awe.

In contrast to Luc and Julien's stone-walled, thatched-roof little cottage, the building was enormous. It was two-story with an obvious attic, was wood framed and covered in whitewashed shingles, had a slate roof, and had to have at least ten rooms inside. It made perfect sense for housing a group the size of François', she thought.

But they walked past the farmhouse, and toward one of the two big wooden barns. Perhaps François wasn't ready to receive them, yet, she thought.

Pierre knocked—in what Joyce assumed was a code—on the small mandoor next to the big sliding one. She heard it being unbolted, and when it swung open, she was surprised to see twenty or thirty men milling about. She was also surprised to be hit with the rich smell of good cooking.

"Ah! Just in time for breakfast!" François called out from Joyce's left.

He walked straight to Luc and opened his arms to him. They embraced, and François kissed him on both cheeks. "I am so sorry for your loss, Luc," he said. "Julien was a good friend, a credit to the resistance, and a credit to the name of Arsenault. God bless and keep him."

"Thank you," Luc said. "And thank you for taking us in."

"It is my pleasure as much as my duty," he said.

François turned to Carlos, embraced him, and said, "It's good to have you back, my friend!" He faced Joyce, opened his arms, and said between kisses on her cheeks, "Welcome to our humble abode."

"Thank you," she said, "but why aren't you staying in the farmhouse instead of the barn?"

"Because that is where the family who owns the farm lives," he said. "We are merely temporary guests. We're not like the Germans; we don't take what isn't ours just because we can."

"I'm sorry. I didn't mean to imply that ..."

"No offense taken," he said holding up his hand to stop her apology. "Come. Sit and have breakfast with us, and tell us how you escaped from Monsieur Savreux's clutches, and ended up with his uniform."

As a cook slid a nearly perfect over-easy egg onto her pie-tin plate, she said, "You should really have Carlos give the account. I'm not much of a story teller, especially when the story's about me."

A second cook ladled some stew onto her plate, and she quickly tilted it to keep the juice from overrunning her eggs. She hated it when different foods touched.

Carlos' retelling of what was a tense and literally life-and-death situation had the whole group roaring with laughter as he mocked Maurice's pumped up self-importance, reenacted his old-fool's act, and then struck a pose and strutted about shaking his butt, playing the naked prostitute shooting Germans.

Joyce's face was red as all the men looked at her, but she couldn't help but laugh at the story, too.

When Carlos was done, everyone stood, turned to Joyce, and clapped. François had her stand up on the table and take a bow.

One of the men called out, "Show us your prostitute disguise!"

The rest of the men whistled, and roared their approval.

She laughed. "I don't think so," she said, stepping down. "Most of the men who saw the last show are dead. I'd hate to repeat *that* kind of performance."

When they sat back down, Joyce asked François how he happened to know Doctor Poullard.

"From the last war," he said. "He treated me after my unit was gassed by the Germans. More than half of them died before making it to the hospital. I'm the only one still alive today.

"I saw the Doctor most every day, for months. We became close friends, and he later attended my wedding, and delivered both of my sons. They are out on guard duty at the moment. I'll introduce you when they return." He wiggled his eyebrows, and added, "They are both single."

Joyce was certainly no stranger to men being interested in her, and she had long ago figured out how to use that to her advantage. But in this time and place she was not interested in playing the games of pursuit.

"If they are like their father," Joyce said, "I'm sure they are most eligible. I, however, am not."

"Luc?" he said.

She nodded her head.

"Hmm. I would have thought that you were more Julien's type," he observed.

"I think *all* women were Julien's type," she said with a smile. "But Luc is *my* type."

François laughed. "A woman who thinks for herself!" he said. "Bravo!"

"*Jeanne d'Arc* (Joan of Ark)," she said, raising an imaginary sword.

"I assume then," he said, "that you are not a believer in Monsieur Petain's edict of *femme au foyer* (women at home)?"

She laughed. "I'm not a believer of *anything* that man says," she replied. "Least of all that."

"Are you familiar with the lineage of your family name, Renaud?" he asked her.

Her father had told her the story, but François seemed to be enjoying talking to her, and it was the first time that she had felt so relaxed in a long time. So, she said no.

"The name comes from medieval literature," he began. "The hero's name was Renaud de Montauban. He and his three brothers fled from the court of Charlemagne after Renaud accidentally killed the king's nephew in a brawl. Charlemagne eventually gave pardon to the brothers on the condition that they enter the Holy Crusades, which they did, and which they survived.

"So, you see, you come from a long and proud history of fighters," he concluded. "*La Résistance*, was your destiny!"

They chatted for a little while longer, then Joyce said, "Please don't think me rude, François, but I am quite exhausted, and you have made me feel so comfortable here, that I'm sure I'm going to fall asleep any minute. Is there a corner where I can throw down some hay and take a short nap?"

"Of course! Of course!" he said. "Where are my manners? With all of your adventures, I should have known that you've had no time to sleep since before the train."

He stood up, and led her to the other end of the barn. Along the way, she found Luc, and looped her arm through his to get him to follow.

"Come and sleep with me," she said quietly into his ear.

"An irresistible invitation," he replied in a whisper, "and I know I'll regret saying this, but I hope you're talking about actually sleeping. I'm ready to fall asleep standing up."

"So am I," she said. "But we need to share a bed because I told François that we were lovers, to keep his eligible sons at bay—and probably a third of the other men here, as well. I hope you don't mind."

"Mind which?" he asked with a smile. "Being used to protect you from unwanted advances or sharing a bed with you?"

"I hope that neither one is *too* painful for you to put up with," she said with playful sarcasm.

He let out a theatrical sigh, and said, "For the good of the cause, I'll pretend that I'm not deeply offended. *Vive la France!*"

She chuckled, and said, "I'll try to make it up to you ... but only for the good of France, you understand."

François directed them to a ladder in the far corner of the barn. They climbed up to find a large loft with a pile of loose hay at one end. They each grabbed a big armload, and threw it down near the wall, making a double-size bed out of it.

They could still hear the men down below, but neither expected to have any trouble falling asleep. Fully clothed, they laid down on their straw mattresses. As Luc fluffed up a little pile behind his head to act as a pillow, Joyce leaned over him, and kissed his lips.

It was not a kiss of burning desire, but neither was it a simple good-night kiss. He put his arms around her, and responded in kind.

After several long seconds, she broke the kiss, and said, hardly above a whisper, "I'm glad I'm with you ... no pretending."

"I'm glad, too," he replied. "And it has nothing to do with the good of France."

She cuddled next to him, with her head on his shoulder, and both of them were asleep in less than a minute.

Wednesday, August 18, 1943

Over the next two months, Luc and Joyce slept together nearly every night, but they never became intimate. Not that both of them weren't interested, but sharing quarters with so many men, there was simply never enough privacy for that.

Although most of the men respected that Luc and Joyce were together, there were a few that continued to make passes at her. It became tiring saying no to them all the time, but Joyce knew that those were the type of men that would be trying to bed her even if she had been wearing a wedding ring and had been there with two or three children.

Far more frustrating than the unwanted advances, however, was the lack of respect shown her by François, which naturally set the tone for all of the others.

After it was discovered that her family had owned a bakery, she spent a good part of most days cooking for the group. Not that she minded pitching in with the others who helped to cook for the men, but *they* rotated in and out of the duty, where it seemed to have become permanent for her.

The few times that she did go on raids with the men, it was because François had a need for her prowess with the Lebel as a sniper.

She was rarely able to sit in on any of the maqui's planning sessions, and when she did, it was made clear that she was there to listen and take instruction, not to speak. Her thoughts, observations, and opinions were plainly unwanted.

But it was political ideology that became the last straw. Eventually, it became apparent to Joyce, Luc, and the others, that François was one of the many resistance leaders who, because of their communist leanings, did not want to restore a democratic government to France after Germany had been forced out. They wanted a new French revolution and a socialist government.

Some serious arguments on the subject ensued, and it was mutually agreed that Joyce, Luc, Carlos, Craig and Paul should part company with François' group. Henri, who had been a communist even before meeting Julien, chose to stay with François.

La Maqui de Julien, so named in honor of their fallen founder, moved north, into the occupied zone. Life there would be much more dangerous, but their harassment of the Germans would be more keenly felt there, and would be much more supportive of the Allies' eventual invasion of the continent.

By April of 1944, the maqui had gained three more men, Jon, Peter, and Richard, bringing the total to eight. Despite being such a small group, however, they were remarkably effective in their sabotage of train tracks, telephone and telegraph lines, and even roadways. And perhaps *because* of their size, the group was able to evade capture by the Germans by living in small very temporary encampments in the woods, rather than seeking refuge in a village where anyone could be a Nazi collaborator.

That danger was made evident by the fact that the SS and the Gestapo knew the names of the original five maqui members, and had put a price on the head of the group's *flintenweib*, Joyce Renaud, as being a *scharfschütze* (sniper).

The term *flintenweib* literally meant "shotgun woman," but was used to denote a woman who was good with any gun, and although it seriously decreased her odds of surviving the war, Joyce was actually proud of the title, and of the reward.

While British agent Nancy Wake was the Gestapo's most wanted female of the war—with a five-million-franc price on her head—compared to Joyce's meager reward of ten-thousand—Joyce was one of only a handful of females who were such thorns in the side of the Germans that they were offering a no-questions-asked reward for their capture. It was an exclusive if very dangerous club that Joyce was honored to be part of.

South of Saint-Lô, France
June 23, 1944
D-Day+17

It had been two and a half weeks since the Allies had successfully landed on the continent, and Joyce and the seven men who constituted *La Maqui de Julien* continued to focus all of their energies on hindering German reinforcements from getting to the battlefront quickly enough to make a difference.

And, of course, the Allies wanted to assist them and all of the other resistance groups in any way they could. To that end, word had been spread by OSS operatives to three local maquis that there would be an airdrop of supplies on the night of June 23rd.

The operation did not go well, however.

The three groups—a total of about 35 freedom fighters—hid in the tree lines surrounding the designated field. Thankfully, the rain had stopped, but it had apparently delayed the take-off of the plane. They had been told to be ready for the drop at around midnight, but it was nearly 2:30 before they heard the sound of the low-flying aircraft.

They had expected a single or twin engine plane, but what appeared out of the darkness over the treetops was a huge four-engine Lancaster bomber.

The bomb bay doors were open when the plane came into sight, and it flew so low that when the four barrels of supplies were released, their parachutes could not fully open before they hit the ground. All four of them burst open, spreading their contents over 100 meters of open field.

As the bomber banked off to be swallowed by the darkness once again, the maquisards swarmed onto the wet field and began collecting whatever was not smashed beyond repair. Two radios and two sets of rangefinder binoculars were a particularly sad loss.

Two recent additions to one of the other maquis had been trained in England and parachuted into France to use the radios and binoculars to direct precision bombing and artillery strikes from observation points behind the enemy lines.

As the men and women scavenged all they could carry, another sound suddenly came from the end of the field.

Alerted by the impossible-to-miss roar of four Rolls-Royce Merlin engines not 30 meters off the ground, a German motorized patrol burst into the open area, washing the scattering freedom fighters with headlights and spotlights, and spraying machine gun fire at them.

Some were able get to the trees and fire back, giving a little cover to the rest, but many were caught in the middle of the field.

When the Germans opened fire, Joyce dove into the grass, dropping a canister of .30 caliber ammunition, and a carton about the size of a shoe box, of unknown contents.

She landed on something long and hard, and it took her about two seconds to realize it was a rifle. Lying flat, she pulled it from the grass and dirt and was surprised to see how small it was compared to the Lebel that was leaning against a tree at the edge of the field.

She had never even heard of, much less held an American M1 Carbine.

At first, when she didn't feel a traditional bolt lever sticking out the side of it, she thought the little rifle had been broken in its hard landing. But in the flash of a spotlight she saw the detail of the streamlined bolt, and realized that the rifle must be semi-automatic like her pistol. What a brilliant idea!

There was a magazine hanging out the bottom of the gun, and when she pulled the bolt back she was just able to make out a bullet being slid into the firing chamber. The magazine was loaded! At least the OSS had gotten *that* right.

On her belly, she shouldered the rifle and aimed at one of the bouncing spotlights that was fortunately not aimed directly at her at the moment. She squeezed the trigger. Nothing happened. It took her a second to find the safety in the dark, and to flip it off.

Again, she lined up on the light and squeezed the trigger. *Pop!* A miss. Now knowing how comfortable the gun was to fire, she aimed again, and pulled the trigger three times in quick succession like she would her pistol. *Pop! Pop! Pop!*

The light went out, and Joyce was totally in love with a little rifle bearing the serial number 6,152,649. She gave it a light kiss on top of the dirty wooden hand guard, and then lined the sights up on the soldier behind the truck-mounted machine gun.

Before she made it all the way off the field on her belly—pushing the mystery box and the canister of ammunition that she didn't even know fit her new best friend—she had emptied the fifteen round magazine and killed or wounded at least six Germans. Sadly, an equal number of *maquisard* were killed or captured.

The whole of *La Maqui de Julien* made it out intact, but with far fewer supplies than they had hoped for. When they got far enough away from the drop zone to feel safe, they stopped to examine what they were all carrying.

Along with Joyce's carbine and ammunition were a satchel of hand grenades, four pistols with no bullets other than what were in the clips, half a dozen containers of assorted rifle ammunition that fit none of their guns, and a crank-type explosives detonator with no explosives.

When Joyce looked at the olive-drab pasteboard box she had rescued, she noticed that there was a pattern of holes cut in one end of it. She cut the string that held the box closed, and opened the top. The inside was completely filled with a white cloth that looked like a towel. She folded open the towel to find something made of paper, more or less tube shaped, and nestled cozily within the cloth.

She put her hand around the paper to lift it from the towel, but she let it go and jumped back when the package moved in her fingers. Then the package cooed.

"Oh my God!" she said. "It's a pigeon! And it's alive!"

She carefully lifted it out, and unwrapped it.

Richard laughed, "Is that supposed to be dinner?"

She saw that it was wearing a message capsule on its leg, and said, "It's a homing pigeon."

"They must have suspected they were going to smash the radio," Carlos commented sarcastically.

"What kind of message are we supposed to send them?" Joyce wondered aloud.

"How about, '*Try again, and fly higher next time, Anglo-idiots.*'," Carlos suggested.

His comment got a laugh, but it didn't really answer the question.

"Maybe it was meant for somebody else," Jon offered. "Aren't you supposed to have a code book to send messages like that?"

"Well, we can't very well go running around the countryside asking if anyone's missing a homing pigeon," Joyce said. "We could send them a message that they messed up the drop, but I think we should hang onto her for a while in case something more interesting comes up."

"How do you know it's a *her*?" Craig asked.

"Did you see how calm she was when I opened the paper?" Joyce said. "If it was a boy, he would have shot out of that tight little space like a hunting falcon, and gone and found a cat to kill. Trust me, it's a girl. And her name is Bridgette."

"Is her name on the capsule?" Jon asked.

"I actually just made it up," she said as she removed the towel and set the bird back in the box. "She reminds me of a customer we had back in Paris. Big puffed up breasts and a long pointy nose."

Saturday, June 24, 1944

Later that morning, when the sun came up, Joyce could see how dirty her new rifle was. When the group took a break from the trek back to their hideout, she decided to clean it up.

She wiped it off with the towel from Bridgett's box, and that's when she noticed that the front end of the wooden cover that went over the barrel was splintered. She guessed that it had probably happened when it hit the ground from the airplane. *Idiots*, she thought. *It's lucky the gun works at all.*

After wiping it down, she could see that there was still dirt between the top cover with the splinters and the bottom part of the stock, so she decided to take it apart.

She loosened the screw on the bayonet band with her knife, slid it forward, and lifted off the hand guard. She wiped off the guard, and set it in the grass beside her.

As she went to wipe the bottom half of the stock, she noticed the edges of what looked like a piece of paper sticking up a couple of millimeters on each side of the barrel.

Curious, she carefully lifted the barrel up, not knowing if there might be another screw or clip holding it in place. She was surprised and happy with how easily the barrel and the whole trigger assembly lifted out.

She found herself looking at a slip of paper with a bright red pair of lips curled into the barrel groove.

Jon, who was fascinated by the obviously state-of-the-art little rifle, sat next to Joyce watching her take it apart.

"What does it say" he asked when he saw the slip with what appeared to be English writing on it.

Joyce, who had grown up in cosmopolitan Paris, spoke and read a little English, and the four words on the slip happened to be in her vocabulary.

"*Un baiser pour la chance!*" she told him.

"Do all English rifles come with such a note?" he asked.

"I don't know," she said as she lifted it from the stock.

Jon called Luc and Carlos over. "Look what is inside the new English rifle," he said. "Do you think that's their new secret weapon?" he asked with a laugh.

"If it is, it works," Luc said. "We all made it from the field in one piece, thanks at least in part to that gun."

Carlos looked at the markings on the top of the barrel, and said, "This is an American gun, not English." He took the slip from Joyce and looked at it closely.

"Wait a minute! I *recognize* these lips," he said. He closed his eyes and smiled, as if recalling a pleasant memory. "Her name was Roseanne. We met in Madrid in the spring of '36. Ah, what a time we had!" Then his face turned sullen, and he went on, "And then the civil war came. I could not bear the thought of her in danger, so I sent her back to America. I have not heard from her since ... until now."

Joyce reached out and took the slip back from him. "You are so full of shit!" she said with a laugh.

He made a hurt face, and said, "Don't rob an old man of his happy memories." Then, with a smile, he added, "Especially the ones I make up. Those, most times, are the *best* ones!"

Joyce looked at the slip closely. "If they put these in all of the guns—probably thousands of them—wouldn't they *print* them? This was obviously written by hand. And the kiss looks real, too."

"Well, if that's the case ..." Luc said, reaching out for the slip.

Joyce handed it to him, and he went on, "I think Roseanne meant it for all of us." He touched the slip to each of his cheeks, and then handed it to Jon, who did the same thing. When Carlos took it, he put it under his nose, and inhaled deeply. "Ah, my sweet Rosie," he said, and then touched his lips lightly to the slip.

Joyce chuckled as she took the slip back. She looked at it for a moment, and then kissed it, herself.

"Ooo!" Carlos said, "I didn't know that my Rosie was that kind of girl! ... nor you, for that matter, Jo!"

"Don't get too excited, old man!" Joyce said with a laugh. "I'd kiss a toad if I thought it would bring us good luck."

As she cleaned the parts of the gun she noticed a small gouge in the two halves of the wood, as if something—a fragment of hand grenade shrapnel, maybe—had hit the side of the gun and was stopped by the barrel. She wondered if she had knocked the piece loose when she took out the barrel. She looked in her lap, and on the ground where she sat, but quickly realized that finding it would be hopeless. Besides, she had to get the gun back together so they could start moving, again.

She set the slip back in its place in the stock, put the barrel assembly on top of it, and closed it up with the hand guard.

When she slid the bayonet band back over the hand guard and stock, she saw the gouge in the top of the metal bracket. It lined up perfectly with splintered damage. *That* looked like it could have been caused by a bullet.

With the rifle back together, she stood up and the group moved out.

As they walked, she wondered about the gun's history. At first she had assumed that it was a new weapon, procured—however they did that—by the OSS specifically to supply the resistance. Now, seeing that the rifle was obviously used, she had to wonder about its previous owner—or owners. In order for one's gun to be given to someone else, she imagined, the first person probably had to be dead. That didn't seem very lucky.

Then, another more positive option occurred to her. What if the rifle had stopped the shrapnel and deflected the bullet, and had saved the shooter's life? That would certainly be lucky.

Immediately, a new thought challenged that solution. Why would the soldier have given up his lucky weapon if it had just saved his life?

Perhaps the answer was somewhere between the two, she thought optimistically. Perhaps he was only wounded, and was sent to a hospital!

She decided that she was going to believe in her last explanation. As unlikely as the scenario was, she *did* sense an aura of good luck about the gun.

Tuesday, June 27, 1944

Two nights later, Joyce and three of the others formed a wide circle of night-time sentry positions around a small bombed-out barn where the rest of the group slept in the cellar.

They were all tired after a night of successfully sabotaging telegraph lines, but the German patrols made it far too dangerous for all of them to sleep at the same time.

Joyce didn't mind sentry duty; the quiet gave her time to think of new ways to antagonize the Germans.

Because they had no explosives—aside from hand grenades, which made poor demolition devices—Joyce was thinking of a variation on the missing-rail-spike theme that the Germans would not have encountered before.

A Kiss For Luck!

The resistance groups knew that the Allies were heading south toward the city of Saint-Lô, and would need to take it in order to break out of the coastal region and push into the heart of France. And they knew that the Nazis would be sending troops and armament to the city to prevent that break out. Slowing that reinforcement for as long as possible was paramount.

Joyce assumed that the Germans would still be using the hand-car advanced-guard in front of the trains, so her strategy had to outsmart that defense.

Wednesday, June 28, 1944

"What if we could take the screws from the rails," Joyce offered the next morning when they were all together for a short while, "cut off the screw part, and put the heads back where they belong? I don't think the handcars weigh enough to push the rails aside, so the soldiers riding them would think all was well. But when the engine came along, it *would* push the rails apart, and the train would be derailed."

"The vibration from the approaching train will cause the heads to bounce around like children's tops," Carlos said dismissively. "It would fool no one. A waste of time."

Carlos was in one of his grumpy moods, brought on by a recurring stomach aliment.

"Maybe if we didn't cut the heads all the way off," Jon, who happened to be the youngster of the group, suggested. "If we cut them *almost* all the way through, they would stay together, but be too weak to hold the rail with an engine going over it."

"When you screw the spike back into the hole you will twist the head off," Carlos said, wondering why they continued to discuss a plan he had obviously rejected as impractical. "Either that or you will not have cut deep enough to make the spike sufficiently weak."

"What if we don't cut off the full length of the spike?" Luc said. "We would leave just enough to bite into the first few millimeters of wood. It would hold the spike from bouncing out, but not be strong enough to hold the rail under the weight of the engine."

Several heads nodded.

"And how do you plan on cutting all these spikes?" Carlos asked. "You'll need dozens for just one length of rail. If we *had* a hack saw that would take days." Carlos was as fond of exaggeration when he was being negative as he was when telling a humorous tale.

Joyce smiled to herself. Carlos was obviously not yet willing to agree that it was a good idea, but he had changed his objections from "it won't work" to "how are you going to do it?" She knew he would be on board before they were done, and probably even taking credit for some part of the plan. She didn't care who got the credit, as long as the plan took its toll on the Germans.

"How long is a length of rail?" Joyce asked Peter, who had worked for the railroad before the war.

"Six meters," he replied. "They put their sleepers every half meter, and use two spikes on each sleeper for each rail. So, that's twelve sleepers, times two spikes, so, twenty-four spikes you'll need to cut for each length of rail."

"I think we should do it on the Laroche trestle, southwest of Saint Lô," Joyce said. "If we can get the engine to drop even two or three meters—especially upside down—it will take them a lot longer to get it back on the track. But I think they use more spikes on trestles and bridges, don't they?"

"Two on the outside, and one on the inside," Peter replied. "So you're up to thirty-six per rail."

"I should think that one rail would be enough, wouldn't you Carlos?" she asked, allowing him to get behind the plan without having to admit that his initial objection might have been wrong, which would never *ever* happen.

"But it's still going to take you some time to cut them ... *if* we had a saw ... and *if* we had the spikes."

"The spikes are easy," Joyce said. "That whole spur on the east side of the Toulom River is never guarded since we blew up the bridge. But where can we get a hacksaw and maybe some extra blades?"

"There is a blacksmith I know of outside of Saint Gilles," Richard said. "About four kilometers (two miles) west from here. He has a power saw run by his water wheel. Or at least he used to."

"Will he let us use it?" Joyce asked.

"I think he will," Richard replied, "as long as his wife doesn't know. He is a loyal Frenchman, but she is scared to death of any trouble with the Nazis."

Joyce thought about that for a moment. "Not that I blame her for her caution, but maybe we can use her paranoia to our advantage," she finally said.

Friday, June 30, 1944

Two nights later, with the quarter moon heading quickly for the western horizon, Joyce, Luc, and three of the others set out to harvest screw-in rail-spikes from the Toulom River spur while the others reconnoitered the Laroche trestle to see if it was being closely guarded.

With the moon setting a half hour after midnight, they didn't have a long time to work before darkness made their tasks nearly impossible. And using flashlights would be suicidal.

After the six kilometer walk, she and her four compatriots stood at the edge of the narrow line of trees a hundred meters from the spur, and watched two German guards walk along the length of track they had come to pillage.

"Why are they guarding the track on this side of the bridge?" Jon asked quietly. "It's completely cut off from the main line by the bridge we blew up months ago. What use can it be?"

Looking through binoculars, Luc said, "It appears that they are trying to fix the bridge. I think I can make out rails, tools, and timber on the flatcar on the other side."

When the group talked about having "blown up the bridge" they were technically correct because they had used the last of their dynamite to do it, but the result was far less spectacular than the phrase made it sound. On the far side—where the flatcar was—the bridge had been knocked off its pilings, dropping its edge about a meter below the grade of the track. The rails had been ripped free and were bent beyond any hope of straightening, but on the whole, the damage was very repairable with the right equipment and enough manpower.

"Why do you think they want to fix it now?" Joyce wondered. "They looted every storehouse in the village by truck after we wrecked the bridge."

"Maybe they had hidden something in the village that they now need to move before the Allies get here," Luc suggested. "We'll have to go and see later on."

"Art treasure?" Jon suggested.

"I was thinking arms and ammunition," Luc said, "but you could be right. I would put nothing past them."

"What do we do about the guards?" Peter asked. "Just shoot them?"

"No," Joyce answered. "I have a plan for their uniforms, but they can't be bullet-riddled and bloody. Let's take them by hand."

"*La prostituée?*" (The prostitute), Luc offered. They had successfully used the diversion several times since Joyce had invented it back in the farmhouse.

"They're privates, so they're probably young enough for it to work," Joyce agreed. "We'll use the switchman's shack. Jon, you stay here with the rifles and tools until we're done. Use my rifle and keep it trained on them in case anything goes wrong."

"Should I shoot for the head to save the uniforms?" he asked.

"Not in this light," Joyce said. "If you have to shoot them, just hit them in the biggest spot you can see. Even if you just wound them we can probably take it from there. But hold your fire until you hear one of us call out to you."

Joyce, Luc, Peter, and Craig set out from the tree line while Jon spread out on the ground in a prone position to cover them with the carbine.

The quartet hunkered down and ran low while keeping their eyes on the guards, ready to throw themselves onto the ground if they started to turn around.

The guards continued to walk away from them along the track, about a hundred meters or so beyond the switchman's shack. The bridge lay another seventy-five meters in the other direction.

They guessed that the two would turn around and begin their march back when they reached the siding where an elevated platform had been built many years ago to unload rail cars. The platform was now dilapidated and useless, and needed no guarding, but it would be a convenient landmark—the bridge being the other—to march between. The Germans did that kind of thing.

On the other hand, for all they knew, the two soldiers could keep right on marching back into the village, this foray to the bridge being a once-a-night patrol.

The group made it to the little building with no sign that the guards knew that anything was amiss behind them.

The shack, about four meters (12 feet) square, with windows on all four sides, had been built about the same time as the platform, but with much more care. As a result, although it had not been used since before the war, it was still in good shape, with—surprisingly—all of its windowpanes intact, if dirty.

The dirty windows were an advantage to the troupe, as they could peer through the little building and see, in the dim light, the shapes of the guards coming toward them, now that they had turned around at the platform. Because of the distance, the dirt, the darkness, and the fact that they weren't actually expecting anyone to be there, there was little chance that the guards would see them.

On the side of the shack facing the bridge—the side away from the guards—the building's door was set into a shallow alcove, perhaps 1/3 of a meter deep. It was there that Joyce and Luc would set *la prostituée* trap.

While the others kept an eye on the approaching guards, Joyce took off her beret, released her hair from its ponytail bun, and shook it out. She then stripped out of all of her clothes, except for her shoes, and set them in a neat pile.

"*Oh là là!*" Peter whispered, shaking his hand as if he had touched something hot. "I have always liked *la prostituée*!"

Joyce playfully cupped her naked breasts and jiggled them. "You wouldn't if you were on the other end of it," she whispered in reply.

Luc backed into the alcove of the doorway, and unfastened and dropped his pants and shorts. He stepped out of one leg, but left the trousers gathered around the other. It was part of the look they wanted to create.

Joyce then got into the alcove with Luc and leaned her naked body against him. His back was to the door, and she could see over his shoulder. Through the dirty windows she watched the two German's coming closer.

Crouching, Peter and Craig hid behind the small building, moving around it as the guards approached to keep the shack between them.

At the tree line, Jon kept the rifle aimed at the soldiers, but he couldn't help stealing glances at Joyce. God, she was a beautiful woman! One half of him wished that he had a telescopic sight, but the other half knew it was a good thing he didn't. If he had one he would probably not be able to keep it trained on the guards.

It was only the fact that the stakes in the game they were playing were literally life and death that kept Luc from becoming aroused at the intimate contact he was having with such an attractive, naked, woman. It certainly didn't mean that it meant nothing to him, however.

"One day," he whispered in her ear as she looked past him, "we will have to do this for real."

"You want me to become a prostitute?" she teased into his ear.

"I want to make love to you again," he said, giving her a slight swat on her naked behind in mock punishment for being fresh. "It seems like forever."

"On the day that the Germans surrender," she whispered in his ear quite seriously, "we will make love until the sun rises and sets on the *next* day."

"From what I hear about the Americans," he replied, "such motivation would have the war over in a week."

"They will have to find their own motivation," she said. She pulled herself close against him, and whispered, "Enough now. Here they are."

She began gyrating her pelvis against him, and he began rocking his hips while he grabbed her naked buttocks and pulled her tight. They kissed passionately and moaned loudly.

As the two young Germans passed the shack, their attention was drawn by the noise, and then riveted by the sight of a shapely French whore plying her trade in the doorway of an abandoned railroad shanty.

One of them just stood with his eyes wide and his mouth open, but the other said in stern German, "Hey! What do you think you are doing? You can't do this here!"

So surprising was the sight, that neither of them bothered to raise the rifles they carried, nor did it immediately occur to them that there was no logical reason that a prostitute should be working way out here. Such was the power of sex over young men's minds.

Joyce turned at the waist so that her pelvis remained against Luc, but so that the two guards could see her bare breasts. She glared at them as if she had no idea what the one had said, and replied in French, "*Allez-vous les petits garçons! Je suis occupé!* (Go away little boys! I am busy!)"

Luc scowled at the two as he continued to rock his hips and hold onto Joyce's rear end.

"I am almost done here, you stupid fools!" he said in German through gritted teeth. "Leave us alone and you can have her when I am done." He grunted and pulled her hard against him.

The silent one continued to just stare at Joyce's naked bottom, held tight by Luc's hands. The other one began to raise his rifle and said, "You must leave now! *Schnell!* You cannot be ..."

His sentence was cut short when Peter leapt from the side of the shack and drove an ice pick into the base of his skull from behind. He rocked it back and forth quickly, completely severing the German's brain stem, and the lifeless body crumbled to the ground.

Craig's attack on the silent one didn't go as well. He was slightly farther away from his victim when he leapt from hiding, and it gave the German just enough time to turn away so Craig's ice pick pierced the skin of the soldier's neck, but did no mortal damage.

The youngster screamed in pain and panic, and tried to raise his rifle.

Luc spun Joyce to the side, took one step forward—his pants dragging from his ankle—and punched the kid in the face with a powerful right fist.

The young German staggered backwards, moaning. Craig spun him around while he was off balance and pushed him, face first, into the ground. He jabbed the ice pick into his neck and rocked it as Peter had done, and the soldier stopped moving.

"Try to keep the blood off the uniforms," Joyce said as she waved for Jon to join them and bring the tools.

"At least they died seeing something enjoyable," Luc said as he pulled up his pants.

As Joyce got dressed, she pointed to the talkative one, and said, "I was beginning to wonder if maybe he liked boys, instead. I've never had a man get so angry seeing me naked." As she fastened her bra, she added, "Or am I getting too fat for *la prostituée*?"

The three men laughed. "Trust us," Peter said. "The fault was with him, not you. *Oh là là!*" he said, and shook his hand again.

Twenty minutes later, using three wrenches, they had collected forty screw-spikes in three heavy canvas sacks. They removed them in scattered spots on both rails from 100 meters of track in the hope that it would not be terribly obvious that they were missing.

Carrying the two dead guards, they headed back to the tree line. Before the night was out, they would strip them, and bury the bodies. They would be missed, of course, but without the bodies, their superiors would not be sure that they hadn't deserted in the face of the coming Allied advance. They would be neither the first nor the last.

Saturday, July 1, 1944

Just after dark on the following night, the entire group headed for Saint Gilles. They stayed in the woods and followed paths and small back roads until they got within sight of the blacksmith's home and separate barn.

"The waterwheel is not turning," Carlos observed. "We've come all this way for nothing."

"Look at the stream," Peter said. "It's almost dry. Rommel must have it dammed up and flooded another field for one of his great defense strategies."

"What do we do now?" Jon asked.

"Even without the waterwheel for power," Joyce said, "he must be able to cut steel, somehow. There's smoke coming from the chimney, so he's still working."

They continued on until they were at the tree line next to the property.

Luc removed the tunic he was wearing, took a cap from the leather satchel he carried, and placed it on his head to complete his transformation into a lieutenant in the Nazi army. The uniform he wore was a greatly valued possession of the maqui, obtained more than six months earlier, during another performance of *la prostituée*.

Next to him stood Jon and Craig, wearing the rail guards' uniforms, complete with helmets and rifles slung over their shoulders.

Just as the imposters were about to leave the cover of the trees, the door to the barn opened. An old man came out and headed toward the house. He was a big man, but he walked with a heavy limp on his left side. It was probably why he wasn't in a slave labor camp somewhere in Germany.

"Must be suppertime," Joyce whispered.

"Good luck for us that they have anything to eat," Luc said, "Having them together to start will make this easier."

Leaving Peter and Carlos in the woods as sentries, the imposters made their way down the short drive and stood at the front door to the house. Joyce and Richard, carrying the spikes, went to the barn, and slipped in through the door.

"Lieutenant Luc" stood at the front door, with the two soldiers side by side behind him. He knocked loudly, assuming that the kitchen would be in the back of the house, and that that was where the couple would be. They heard footsteps approaching across a wooden floor. The pace of the steps was even, so it must be the wife, Luc thought. Good.

The door opened slightly, and a slice of female face appeared behind the crack. The one visible eye went wide in surprise that bordered on panic.

"*Guten Abend, Frau Bouvier*," Luc said in German as he removed his cap and bowed slightly.

The wife's one eye just stared at him.

"*Pardon*," he said, switching to well acted German-accented broken French, "You perhaps do not speak German. My French is only fair, so please forgive me if I struggle. *Bonsoir Madame Bouvier*," he said with another bow. "Please excuse the interruption, but may I come in to ask a personal favor?"

"*Qui est-ce*? (Who is it?)," her husband called from the kitchen.

She opened the door slowly, and with her eyes still on Luc, she turned her head slightly to answer her husband. "It is a German officer, here to ask a favor."

"What? A favor? What favor?" the old man said as he pushed himself away from the table and clumped across the floor to join his wife in the front room.

By the time he was at her side, the three "Nazis" were inside, and Jon had closed the door.

The wife's look of panic softened somewhat with her husband at her side, but Luc could tell she was still very afraid. The husband's look was a cross between suspicion and anger. Luc saw no fear there at all. He wondered if the old man's leg had been injured in the Great War. Between that war and this one, it would give him ample reason to loath and distrust the Germans.

With his cap under his arm, Luc bowed again, and said in French, "Good evening Mr. Bouvier. My name is Hans Schubert. I apologize if I am interrupting your dinner, but I have a personal favor I would like to ask."

"What do you mean a *personal* favor?" the old man asked.

"I mean that it has nothing to do with the army or the war, and that I am willing to pay for your services," Luc said.

"What do you want then?" the wife asked.

"I would like your husband to repair a part for my car."

"He is not a mechanic. He is only a blacksmith," she replied.

"I know. I *have* a mechanic." Luc said with a gesture indicating Jon. "What I need is someone who can mend a broken part. I believe your husband has the skill and the facilities required."

"I make horseshoes and nails," the old man said, minimizing his true skills to the German. "I know nothing about automobiles."

"Nor do you need to," Luc said. "Perhaps if you would accompany Joseph to the barn, he can show you exactly what we need." With a wave toward the door, he added, "*S'il vous plaît?*"

Luc was ninety-nine percent sure that the old man would go along with his "request." Even though he had explained that it was personal, it was still coming from a Nazi officer with two armed soldiers behind him. Once he was outside, away from the wife, Jon would explain who they really were and what was really going on.

The tactic of separating loved ones to ensure the cooperation of both of them was typical Nazi policy, and Luc noted the look of nervousness returning to Mrs. Bouvier as her husband left with Jon, and Craig stayed inside by the door. Luc had no interest or need to terrorize the woman now that her husband was with the others, so he softened his approach even more to try to allow her to relax.

"Perhaps a cup of tea while we wait for them," he suggested in his make-believe broken French.

That did nothing to abate her fear. "I ... I'm sorry, Herr Lieutenant," she said, wringing her hands, "we have had no tea since the ..." She stopped herself short of saying *the occupation*, which would imply that it was the Germans' fault that they had no tea—which, of course, it was. Instead, she finished with, "... for some years, now."

"Yes," he replied, nodding sadly, "the war has produced many hardships." He reached into his satchel and took out a small metal tin. It had a swastika on the side and the word "*Schnitttabaks*." He handed the tin to the woman.

"Do you read German, by any chance?" he asked her.

She shook her head.

"It says *cut tobacco*," he told her. "But really it contains English tea. I would probably be in more trouble for having that, if my superiors knew, than for being here asking your husband a favor," he said with a chuckle. With a charming smile, he added, "I have been saving it for some time, now, waiting for a suitable occasion to enjoy it."

That part was not a lie. The tin had been in the satchel when they acquired the uniform. It had been almost full then. They had celebrated a few times with it, but then decided to save the rest in case some extraordinary situation should come along.

She opened the tin and looked inside. She took a deep sniff. Her eyes closed and her face relaxed as if her nose had transported her to some long-ago, far-away place of peace and tranquility.

She returned momentarily, however, opened her eyes, and said, "I will make you a cup, Herr Lieutenant. Please, come into the kitchen." As she led the way, she added, "I'm afraid we have no milk or lemons, if that is how you take it."

He followed, and said, "Please call me Hans. And I insist that you make a cup for each of us. Tea must be shared to be truly enjoyed, no?"

She looked at him curiously with a hint of cautious suspicion on the side. The words *gracious* and *Nazi* were never used in the same sentence.

Luc almost laughed at her puzzled expression. "And please set some aside for your husband," he said. "After all, he is the one doing all the hard work."

Still a bit dubious, but with really no other choice, she indicated a chair at the table, and said, "Please have a seat, Herr Hans."

She turned and slid a small cast iron pot to a position at the back of the stove, and set a well-worn kettle on the vacated spot. She then opened a door on the front of the stove, and using a small stick, she poked at the embers below the kettle. She tossed the stick on the coals, and closed the door.

Luc guessed that the pot she moved was the couple's dinner. Probably soup or stew of some kind. He doubted that it contained any meat.

From a cupboard shelf that was covered by a lacy curtain, the woman took down a china tea pot. She set it on the table, and returned to get two matching cups. The set was delicate, pretty, and in perfect condition. It had probably not been used in years—certainly not to make tea—but it was as spotless as the day it came from the store—very likely in Paris. This was a prized possession, and he hoped he could use that fact to get her to relax.

He picked up one of the cups and examined it. Looking at the mark on the bottom, he saw that it had been made in London. "This is a magnificent set, Mrs. Bouvier," he said. "Let me guess; a wedding present?"

She looked at him again, perhaps even more curious, but just a shade less skeptical.

"Why yes, it is," she said. "From my mother ... God rest her soul," she added, crossing herself.

"I am honored," he said with a slight bow of his head.

She opened the tin and sprinkled a few leaves into the pot.

He looked into the pot and then up at her. "Are you making tea for the sparrows?" he asked her with a mock scowl. "Put enough in there that the steam doesn't blow it away and we are left to drink nothing but hot water."

She tapped a few more flakes in, and he inspected the pot again. He looked at her and gave a theatrical shake of his head to indicate his disappointment. Without a word, he held out his hand, and she passed him the tin.

He shook a liberal helping into the pot, and then set the tin on the table and snapped the lid closed, indicating the finality of his actions.

She looked at the pile of leaves covering the bottom of the pot. It was more than she would use for three pots of tea in the *good* times!

"You are too generous, Herr Lieutenant," she said.

"*Nein*," he replied. "It is you who are being generous. You have loaned me your husband, you have invited me to sit at your table, and you are allowing me to drink from a tea set that is obviously quite special to you."

He sat back in his chair, and folded his hands on the table. "Looking at me in my Nazi uniform, I can understand and appreciate that you dislike and distrust me," he said. "But wearing these insignia does not mean that I believe in what they stand for. There are very few of us in Europe today who are not trapped in a place or a situation where we would rather not be. You have a lovely country here, but I would like to be back in my own Germany just as much as you would like to see me there."

She said nothing, but he knew she was dying to agree.

"The English and the Americans have finally landed, and they will not easily be pushed back into the sea. The war will soon be over. A few weeks, a few months, who knows. Perhaps then, all of our lives will begin to get back to normal."

She made no reply, but she was obviously thinking about his remarks. She heard the water boiling, and turned to get the kettle. She filled the tea pot with bubbling water, set the lid in place, and put the kettle back on the stove, off to one side. She then sat down opposite Luc.

For a minute, she stared at the steam rising out of the pot. She leaned forward, closed her eyes, and inhaled deeply. It had been a long time since that aroma had filled her kitchen.

Finally, without opening her eyes, she said, "What will you do when you get back to Germany?"

It was the first thing she had said to him that could be regarded as conversation. He smiled to himself. Even as a Nazi he could be charming, he thought.

"I was a printer before the war," he said, not lying. "Text books mostly. With what some of my less-enlightened countrymen have done, I believe there will be a big demand for book printing when civilization returns to Europe."

For the next twenty minutes they talked and sipped their tea. At one point Luc even managed to make her laugh by saying, "You know, you can always tell a true Aryan because he is as blond as Hitler, as fit as Göring, and as tall as Goebbels." It was an old joke, and she had probably heard it before. But she had certainly never heard it coming from a Nazi officer.

Forty minutes after they had arrived, a knock came at the front door. Two knocks, then one, then two more. It was the all-safe signal.

Craig opened the door and let Jon and the old man back in.

"Were you able to repair my part?" Luc asked, getting up from the table.

"As good as new," the blacksmith replied. "Repaired by a Frenchman, perhaps it is *better* than new."

Luc laughed. "As long as it will get my car headed south, once again."

He picked up the tin of tea and put it in his satchel. "If any maquisard should pay you a visit, we wouldn't want them thinking you were collaborating, would we?"

He considered leaving her more tea, but he knew that they would use the tea in the pot over and over until every molecule of flavor had been boiled from every leaf.

Luc clicked his heels, bowed to his hostess, and said, "*Auf wiedersehen.* That means '*until we meet again*,' Mrs. Bouvier. And I hope that we shall one day, when this uniform has been long burned."

He turned to her husband and extended his hand. "*Merci beaucoup*," he said. He took a folded stack of bills from his jacket pocket—a prize also found in the uniform—and pulled out ten one-hundred reichsmark notes.

He handed the bills to the blacksmith, and said, "I wish I could pay you in francs, but ..." he shrugged, and said, "*C'est la guerre* (It is the war). If I were you—and I could find something to buy—I would spend those as quickly as possible. They may not be worth anything in a week or two."

The three German imposters walked down the drive and then cut into the woods to join the rest of the group.

"How did it go in the house?" Joyce asked. "Did you make any friends?"

"Unfortunately, it was Hans the Nazi who made the friend," Luc said as he took off his officer's cap and returned it to the satchel. "But at least she wasn't afraid that her husband was being tortured the whole time." As he swung the tunic over his shoulders, he asked, "How did it go in the barn?"

"Without the waterwheel," Joyce replied, "his saw is now *human*-powered. He has rigged up a big handle on one of the machinery pulleys, and we all had to take turns cranking it around to get the saw to move. Then we had to slow down on the last ten spikes, because we broke the blade, and he only had one extra." She pointed to the sacks that three of the other men were carrying, and said, "We got it done, though. Tomorrow we'll install them, and see if we can topple a train."

Sunday, July 2, 1944

Early the next morning, everyone in the group, except Peter, headed for the train tracks and the Laroche trestle. Peter set out for a hilltop a couple of kilometers away, where he could see another couple kilometers south along the tracks. Because the emergency supply trains were not running on any kind of schedule, Peter would use a signal mirror to warn the others if a train was approaching.

As they had been the night before, Luc was dressed as Lieutenant Schubert, and Jon and Craig wore the soldiers' uniforms.

While the others took up hidden sentry positions in the brush on the hill, Luc, Jon, and Craig walked out onto the trestle. As "Lieutenant Schubert" stood supervising, privates Jon and Craig began unscrewing rail spikes, and replacing them with their cut-off substitutes.

The plan was as dangerous as it was bold. The idea, of course, was that the three of them, working in broad daylight, should look like they belonged there and were doing some repair work if a German patrol should happen by. If that happened, and Luc was not able to talk his way out of a challenge, the rest of the maqui would come to their rescue by opening fire on the patrol. Depending on the outcome of that eventuality, they would then have to decide whether or not to abandon the rail sabotage.

It took about half an hour for the two men to swap all thirty-six spikes, but when they were done, the rail showed no signs that it had ever been tampered with.

As they walked from the trestle back towards the dirt road that paralleled that part of the tracks, a boxy little open-topped *kübelwagen* (bucket car) came flying around a corner, trailing a plume of thick dust. Luc and the others forced themselves not to break stride as it approached, and they breathed a sigh of relief when it sailed past, perhaps not even noticing them.

But ten meters beyond them, its brakes suddenly came on and it skidded to a stop, becoming engulfed by its own dust cloud. It then backed up until it was abreast of the three imposters.

"*Wer sind Sie? Was machst du denn da?* (Who are you? What are you doing there?)" the SS captain in the passenger seat demanded.

"*Heil Hitler!*" the three maqui men said, raising their arms in salute. The captain raised his hand to about shoulder height, and repeated, "*Heil Hitler*," but seemingly with more irritation than enthusiasm.

As the officer opened his door and began to step out of the car, Luc said, "My name is Lieutenant Hans Schubert, Captain. I got word last night that this section of track had been damaged by the partisans. And it's a good thing I came out to inspect it." He turned to Jon, and while gesturing toward the bag and then the captain, said, "Show the captain one of the sabotaged spikes." Luc knew that Jon didn't speak German, but the pantomime was enough to get the point across.

As Jon dug one of their extra cut-spikes out of his sack, the captain looked around, and then asked, "Where is your vehicle? How did you get here?" He was clearly suspicious.

"My car is about two kilometers that way," Luc said, pointing in the direction that the captain had been traveling. "We walked here along the tracks, of course. Perhaps the captain would be good enough to give us a ride back, now that we are done here."

"Let me see your identity papers, all of you," the captain demanded. The soldier who was driving the car just watched what was going on, but the one in the back raised his machine gun over the side of the car and aimed it in the direction of the group.

"Of course, Captain," Luc said as he removed his cap with his left hand, and wiped his brow with his sleeve. "I understand your suspicion. The partisans are a devious lot." He switched the cap to his right hand and placed it back on his head. He then reached into his jacket pocket for the dead lieutenant's papers.

Removing his cap with his left hand and replacing it with the right was a signal to the others hiding in the bushes on the far side of the road to get ready to start shooting. But where Luc and the others stood put them directly in the line of that fire.

Luc turned to Jon and Craig. While they didn't know enough German to know what was being said, they understood the hat signal, and Luc said in French, "*Maintenant!* (Now!)"

The three men dropped to the ground, and four rifles fired simultaneously from the top of the hill.

The captain's eyes went wide and his mouth opened silently as a bullet struck him in the middle of the back. And then he fell over nearly on top of Luc.

The driver slumped over sideways, but was apparently only wounded, because Peter could see him struggling to get to his pistol. He shot him again, and he stopped moving.

Both Joyce and Paul had taken aim at the soldier in the backseat, because he was the only one holding a weapon. Both of their bullets hit him in the back, but he still had enough time or reflex to squeeze the trigger. Fortunately, he didn't have enough time to take aim, and his ten-round burst went well above the men lying on the ground.

From behind the car, Luc waved his cap to make sure they didn't fire anymore, and then the three men got up.

With pistols drawn, they examined the three Germans to make sure they were all dead. The SS captain was still breathing, so Luc fired another shot into the back of his head.

He gave a thumbs-up sign to the group up on the hillside, and then, after stripping them of their weapons, he, Jon, and Craig loaded the bodies into the back of the car. The uniforms were of no use with bullet holes and blood.

"What do we do with the car?" Jon asked Luc. "If we leave it here it might tip off the train crew that something is wrong, and they'd inspect things more closely."

"I know," Luc said. "It's a little big to hide in the bushes, and I hate to give up such a prize, anyway. But if we drive it down the road we could run into another patrol."

"Do you think we could drive it along the footpath?" Craig suggested. "Aren't these things supposed to be made for driving where there is no road?"

"I guess we'll find out," Luc said as he slid behind the wheel.

To avoid leaving tire tracks too close to the sabotaged trestle, they drove up the road a short way before turning off and into the brush. The others, including Peter, met up with them, and a kilometer or so into the woods, they stopped and buried the dead Germans.

As much as they would have liked to watch the result of their sabotage—if it worked at all—they were far too small of a group to resist an attack like the one the Germans mounted when they blew up the train with François, so they knew they needed to be kilometers away when the next train came by.

While they were stopped, however, they heard the chugging of a locomotive in the distance. They all climbed into the car, and started off again, but as soon as they started, Jon jumped back out.

"All of you go on," he told them. "We have to know if the cut spikes worked so we can use it again, no? I think I can see the trestle from up in this pine. As soon as the train either derails or passes by, I'll catch up to you."

Luc tossed him the binoculars. "Be careful! And make sure you're not being followed before you head back to the barn." With that, he pushed the stick into first, and started off again.

The little two-wheel-drive *kübelwagen* did a remarkably good job of carrying the group cross-country. Twice they had to pile out so that it could make it up a steep hill, and once they had to virtually lift it out of a ditch, but all in all, it was a darned sight better than walking.

They parked it beside their shell of a barn, and covered it with fallen timbers, boards, and hay. They didn't have any plans for it, yet, but with half a tank of petrol in it, they were sure they'd think of something.

It was nearing sunset when Jon finally made it back to the barn. Richard, Paul, and Peter were on sentry duty, but the rest of the group was huddled in the cellar, and eager to hear his story.

"*Mon oui!* I wish you could have seen it!" he began after taking a long sip of wine. "As we thought, the little handcar was way out ahead of the train, but it stopped just as it reached the ravine! All four soldiers got off and two began to walk across the trestle, while the other two climbed down the little cliff to walk down below and look up. I'm sure they were looking for explosives.

"At one point, one of them up above stopped right in the middle of the rail we sabotaged, and he kicked one of the spikes. I have no idea why he did it, but I thought my heart would stop, and I'd fall out of the tree. But the spike held! Then, of course, I worried that the whole idea wouldn't work; that the spikes were still too strong.

"Finally, they all made it to the other side, and as they ran back to their little car, they waved the engineer the all clear sign. They jumped on their car and pumped like hell with the engine not five meters behind them, and not slowing down a bit. Of course, it wasn't going very fast to begin with, but if it hit them it would have pushed them right off the tracks and into the ravine.

"The handcar made it all the way across, and again, I worried that the whole scheme was not going to work.

"Then the engine started across, and it was right on top of our rail, and nothing was happening. My heart sank. Then, all of a sudden, *ping, ping, ping,* the spikes began to sail out of the rails! Just like a zipper! One after the other they went flying!

"Then the rail flew off the side of the trestle, and the engine's wheels started smashing up the trestle. But the train stayed upright!

"I could hear the brakes screeching, but the engine kept going and splintering the sleepers. It finally came to a stop out in the middle of the ravine, leaning to the side, but apparently not enough to tip over.

"I swore and began to climb down to get the hell out of there, when I heard a loud *crack!* I looked up to see the engine moving in slow motion, tipping out over the edge of the trestle." As he spoke, he leaned to one side demonstrating the slow list.

"Finally, it rolled right off, and pulled the coal tender with it. It crashed upside down, the boiler blew to pieces, and the burning coal in the fire box flew everywhere! I'm sure it caught the trestle on fire, but I didn't stick around to find out.

"When the brakes came on, soldiers started leaping out of the cars, so as soon as I saw the train crash, I flew out of the tree, and took off. I went way out around the lake to make sure I didn't lead anyone back here."

The SS investigation into the cut-spike sabotage included anyone in a wide area with the ability to saw steel. It eventually led them to the blacksmith shop of Mr. and Mrs. Bouvier.

The old man held to the story that he had welded and machined a car part for a Nazi lieutenant—whose name he did not know. But when his petrified wife confessed to having tea with the officer, told them that his name was Hans Schubert, and that he said he was driving south, the SS officer all but forgot about the spikes. They had been looking for Lt. Schubert for months, and had *suspected* that he had deserted.

Tuesday, July 4, 1944

Two nights later, the group resolved that they needed to find out why the Germans were repairing the bridge on the Toulom River, where they had stolen the spikes.

Knowing that the SS stick was still in the hornet's nest over the train sabotage, they decided that only Joyce and Luc should risk going into the town to investigate. There was a dusk 'til dawn curfew, but they figured they could use *La prostituée* to explain why they were out after dark if anyone stopped them. It was another reason that only the two of them should go.

They made their way cross-country through the woods, and when they reached the edge of the town, they hid their pistols and their rifles in a culvert under the road. It was a huge risk going into town unarmed, but if they were stopped *with* weapons there would be no chance at all of talking their way out of a firing squad ... naked or otherwise.

At the far edge of the town, away from the railroad tracks, the curfew was obviously not strictly enforced. While the streets were not crowded, and those who were about didn't stop to chit chat, there were enough others around that Joyce and Luc felt comfortable being there.

Within five or six blocks of the tracks, they noticed that there were less than half as many civilians, all of them hurrying wherever they were going, and staying in the shadows as they did. While continuing to act as casual as possible, they stayed out of sight as best they could, going from one darkened doorway to the next, ready at any time to go into the prostitute routine. To be ready to launch the act quickly, Joyce had even removed all of her underwear before leaving the barn.

Two blocks from the tracks, they saw the first of the two-man patrols. They dared not go any closer, but from the end of a dark alley, they could see all the way down a street to a big warehouse two blocks away. Although there was a complete blackout—enforced much more severely than the curfew—there was a nearly full moon. And although it was only a couple hours from setting, it still gave more than enough light to see that there was a great deal of military activity around the warehouse.

"What do you think is in there?" Luc whispered to Joyce.

"I don't know, but the Nazi's obviously think it's pretty important," she answered, "which means the Allies need to bomb it to hell. I think this is the message that Bridgette has been waiting to carry back to England."

It was a little before 1:00 a.m. when Joyce and Luc made it to the outskirts of the town, half a kilometer (1/4 mile) from where they had hidden their weapons.

As they passed the alley between the last two buildings on the last street, the headlights on an automobile hidden in the alley snapped on. The sudden glare startled them almost as much as it blinded them.

"Stop where you are! Put your hands in the air!" a voice called out in German-accented French from behind the lights.

Joyce and Luc recovered from the shock quickly, but instead of raising their hands, they started shouting at each other.

"You see!" Joyce yelled at Luc. "I told you we should stay in my room! Now see the trouble you've caused!"

"Oh, like I could get it up with your sister and her kid in the next room!" he shouted back. "Obviously, I want my money back!"

"Bullshit!" she spat. "I've spent the last hour entertaining you. Nobody is guaranteed a climax if he can't get his own dick to stand up!"

"You filthy whore!" he shouted at her, and raised his hand to slap her.

"You will stop your acting now!" the voice behind the headlights shouted. "We have your weapons from the culvert. We know your are partisans!"

"Weapons?" Luc said, shielding his eyes and trying to see past the lights. "What the hell are you talking about? We have no weapons."

"An American carbine, a Belgian sniper rifle, and two French pistols," the voice replied. "You were seen putting them there an hour ago, and you were discreetly followed through the town."

"You're mistaken," Luc said. "There has been some mix up. I am Gene LeBeau, I live right here at 45 Rue de Lyon. This is Maria ... something. I don't even *know* her last name. She is a common whore. I can show you my papers," he said, reaching into his back pocket.

"Halt!" the voice shouted. "Put you hands up where we can see them!"

Luc complied, saying, "*Pardon!* I just wanted to show you my papers."

"Forgeries, no doubt," the voice said. "You are the Sniper of Sebastian. I believe that your rifle proves it."

"Me? A sniper?" Luc laughed. "I've never fired a rifle in my life. I am a printer of books."

"A book printer, eh?" the voice mocked. "Then you will know all about poetic justice, no?" The voice turned hard, and went on, "Like the justice in being executed with your own rifle."

"He's telling the truth," Joyce said. "I pretended to be a whore so I could make my way through the town and see who I should kill next. He is just a poor French slob with a fat wife. I am the Sniper of Sebastian."

The voice laughed.

"Seven dead," Joyce said, recounting the attack the group had made on the crossroad village of Sebastian. "A captain, a lieutenant, a sergeant, and four soldiers ... two of them SS. One shot each." The tally was actually the total from three different rifles, but she was gambling that they wouldn't know that.

There was silence from behind the headlights.

Out of the corner of his mouth, Luc whispered to Joyce, "What the hell are you doing?"

"If you don't believe me," Joyce said to the lights, "give me a target and a singe bullet."

"You admit then that you are a partisan?" the voice said. "Why?"

"This so-called Frenchman is innocent," Joyce answered. "As much as his groveling weakness makes me want to puke, I can't stand by and let him be shot just because he has a wandering penis and chose the wrong whore to satisfy it. That's the difference between us and you; we only kill the enemy, not innocent bystanders ..." she looked at Luc and added, "... no matter how worthless they might be."

"Bra-vo!" a second voice from behind the headlights said with an accompanying clap. "A first rate performance! Your acting has only gotten better, Mademoiselle Renaud."

Joyce's blood ran cold. She recognized the voice instantly. It was her "boyfriend" Franz from Agen.

"If you know my name," she said, not letting on that she knew who was speaking, "then you know I'm telling the truth. Let this worm go, and take me to the SS to collect your reward."

"There is a reward for you?" Franz said, "I did not know you were so famous. But alas, the reward would only be for civilians. As soldiers and officers, it is our *duty* to find and dispose of *freedom fighters*, as you call yourselves."

He walked out in front of the headlights, and off to one side where the lights lit him up for her to see.

"Franz!" she said in perfectly acted surprise. "My God, I never expected to see you again! And look at you! A captain! I'm impressed. I knew you would go far!"

"I almost didn't recognize you," he said. "Your hair is so much longer. And you are much thinner than I remember."

"Meals are not as regular as they were in the old days in Agen, no?" she said. "You are looking well, though. I was right about how handsome you'd be in an officer's cap."

To the other German, Franz said, "Turn off the lights before we attract a bomber."

Shining a small flashlight on the two of them, he said to Joyce, "So, *you* are the Sniper of Sebastian, huh?"

She shrugged, and said, " *C'est la guerre*. We each do what we feel we must."

"Only, I don't believe you," Franz said. "I think you are lying to protect your friend here. Your latest lover, I presume?" He looked at Luc, and went on, "Did she tell you that she used to sleep with me? The enemy. I will admit that she was good in bed ... but I'm sure that came from lots of practice, no?"

"You hurt me, Franz," Joyce said with a pout. "I liked you. I was sorry that I had to leave without saying good-bye."

He laughed. "I believe that as much as I believe that you went from being a baker of pastries to a *tireur d'élite* (sharpshooter)."

"I told you, I'll prove it," she said. "Point out a target, and give me one bullet. If I hit it, you'll know, and you can let Monsieur LeBeau go back to his fat wife."

Franz laughed, again. "You are much too eager for me to let your friend go," he said. "But I am a betting man, and I will make you a wager. If you can hit a target of my choosing, I will let your friend go, and I will turn *you* over to the SS—a win that you will surely regret.

"If you miss, we'll know that you are lying, and that *he* is the Sniper of Sebastian. Of course, in that case, he will have to be executed, no?"

"I accept," she said, not really having a choice anyway.

"There is one more stipulation, however," Franz said. "If you miss the target, you will be given one more bullet, and you will be your lover's executioner."

"Once again, Monsieur LeBeau is not my lover," Joyce replied. "Although he thought he was going to be."

"And once again, I don't believe you," Franz said.

Franz waved, and the other man stepped forward from the car. He was a sergeant; probably Franz' driver.

As Franz took his pistol from its holster, he told the sergeant, "Search *Monsieur LeBeau*—or whatever his name is—to make sure he has no more weapons. I'll cover you." To Joyce, he said, "Step to the side. I will search *you* myself."

When the sergeant was done, he stepped back and drew his side arm to guard the two prisoners.

"Put your hands on top of your head," Franz told Joyce as he put his gun away. He moved behind her, and ran his hands over every part of her body in a very ungentlemanly search. When he put his hands on her breasts, naked under her shirt, he said, "You've given up wearing a bra, I see." He fondled them a little, and added, "I've missed these. Most French women are endowed either like boys, or cows."

"I've missed your expert touch," she lied.

He laughed, and said, "I'm sure you have."

He drew his pistol again, and gave her a small push toward the car, a Renault *décapotable* (convertible) perhaps ten or twelve years old.

"You will ride in the front with my driver. I will ride in back with your friend, with my pistol in his ribs. We will need to get away from the town a little ways so your shots don't excite the guards at the warehouse unnecessarily."

"What's in the warehouse that's so important?" Joyce asked as she walked.

"The truth is," Franz said, "I don't know myself. I expect it is one of the Fuehrer's *waffes merveilleux* (wonder weapons), hidden there some time ago ahead of the Allies' inevitable invasion."

They drove about four or five kilometers out of town, and pulled off the road into an open field. Franz had his driver stop, and Franz and Joyce got out. He went to the car's trunk, and took out Joyce's carbine.

"The other one is the sniper rifle," Joyce informed him.

"Be thankful I'm not making you take the shot with one of your pistols," he answered.

To his driver, he said, "Take him to the trees at the other end of the field, and tie his hands behind a stout one." He reached into a wicker basket in the trunk, and took out an apple. "Place this on his head," he added.

"You're daft!" Joyce said. "That's seventy-five meters! I won't even be able to *see* the apple in this moonlight!"

Franz thought for a moment, and then said, "Perhaps you're right." To his driver, he said, "Leave the car ten meters or so away from him with the headlights shining on him. Then come back here."

As the sergeant drove off across the field, Franz had Joyce stand a few meters away, and he unloaded her carbine, ejecting the cartridges into the grass. He picked up the bullets, and put them in his jacket pocket.

He handed her the rifle, and said, "You'll use a standing position."

She glared at him. "You're making the shot impossible for *anyone*."

"The prize is your friend's life," he said. "You didn't expect I would make it easy, did you?"

They watched in silence as the driver tied up Luc, set the target on his head, and moved the car around to light it up.

When he got back to them, Franz told him, "Stand behind her, cock your pistol, and point it at the back of her head. If she turns away from the tree, pull the trigger."

Franz handed her a single bullet, and said, "*Bonne chance*." He then stepped back to watch her.

Joyce lightly kissed the top of the hand guard, and whispered, "You heard him, Rosie; bring me good luck."

She set the L-shaped flip-site to its short position. By experimenting, she knew that this setting was apparently meant to be accurate at about 150 meters. That was twice the distance she was shooting, so it meant that the bullet would hit well high of whatever she aimed at. But there was no shorter adjustment, so she was going to have to aim low—at Luc's nose—to hit the apple on his head.

She pulled back the bolt, pushed the bullet into the firing chamber, and let the bolt go. As she made sure the safety was off, she wondered if she could duck and spin fast enough to shoot the sergeant before he got his shot off. Probably not. But even if she did, Franz had the rest of her bullets, and his own pistol.

She wrapped her left arm tightly through the rifle's web sling as Julien had taught her long ago, and pulled the steel butt plate into her shoulder. She relaxed as much as she could, taking slow, deep breaths with her mouth wide open.

She looked through the tiny hole in the rear site, and lined up the flat-topped front site on Luc's nose.

She began to put finger pressure on the trigger, but then stopped. She raised the rifle to site directly on the apple, and squeezed the trigger.

Bark exploded from the tree 10 centimeters (4 inches) above the apple.

Joyce slowly lowered the rifle, and looked at the ground in defeat.

Franz let out a little chuckle. "The Sniper of Sebastian, huh?" he said. "Frankly, I'm impressed that you hit the tree." To his driver, he said, "Take the rifle. We'll walk closer for her executioner's shot. We wouldn't want her to have to shoot him twice."

In the corner of her downcast eye, she could see the sergeant put his pistol in its holster, and at the same time saw Franz stepping closer.

With both hands still holding the rifle, she swung its butt plate back and upward as hard as she could, and caught the sergeant under the chin.

Blood splattered, his jawbone splintered, and his teeth cracked apart like ice cubes. He fell over backwards, unconscious before he hit the ground.

Joyce spun and lunged at Franz, driving the barrel of the gun towards his throat as if it was a bayonet.

But his left hand had already been on his pistol as he approached her, so as she attacked the sergeant, he had just enough time to get it out and flip the safety off before the rifle barrel was thrust at him.

He pitched back to avoid the barrel and he pulled the trigger at the same time.

His pistol went off and the barrel of the carbine carved a slice of skin out of his chin.

His bullet hit the right side of rifle's stock at a shallow angle, just behind where Joyce was holding it. It burrowed itself into the wood and was stopped from entering Joyce's stomach by the steel butt plate.

Franz screamed in pain as he stumbled backwards and brought his right hand up to his bleeding chin. With his left hand he fired two more times, but both shots went wide.

The momentum of Joyce's jab with the rifle had brought it up across her chest, almost vertical, and she now brought it back down, smashing the butt plate into Franz' gun hand. The impact fractured the bones in his thumb, and caused him to drop the gun with another yelp of pain.

She rotated the gun again, bringing the barrel over her own left shoulder, and drove the butt at him as he tried to back away from her.

The steel plate hit him in the throat, and crushed his windpipe. Clutching his throat with his blood-covered hand, he fell over backwards, choking and sputtering.

Joyce exhaled deeply, and then calmly reach down and picked up Franz' pistol.

He looked up at her with wide eyes, as she shot him in the forehead. She then walked over and did the same to the unconscious sergeant.

She fished her bullets from Franz' pocket, and as she ran across the field to Luc, she reloaded the carbine's clip.

As she untied him, Luc said, "You didn't actually try, did you? I think you could have made that shot."

"I think I would have," she said. "But why take the chance. There was no way that he was going to let you go even if I did."

Freed, he took her in his arms, and kissed her hard. He then gave her a hard swat on the ass.

"Ouch! What the hell was that for?" she said, rubbing her butt. "I just saved your life!"

"And don't you ever do it again by trying to sacrifice your own!" he said pointing a scolding finger at her. "We're in this together!" Then he kissed her again.

They climbed into the still-running car, and Luc drove back to where the bodies were lying.

As they bumped across the field, Luc asked Joyce, "Do you know how to drive?"

"In Paris we didn't need a car," she answered, "and in Agen, we couldn't afford one, so I never learned."

"Then I guess I have to be demoted to sergeant," he said. "It would be a scandal for a captain to be seen driving a sergeant around."

"We're taking the car?" she said.

"I thought we should drive back to the river and see if there is a place where we can sink it," Luc said. "The longer it takes them to find the bodies, the better."

They stripped the two Germans, and put their uniforms on over their own clothes. There was blood on both of them, but if they did run into someone, they hoped it wouldn't be easily noticed in the dark.

After taking out their weapons and the food basket, they folded the bodies into the trunk.

Franz' officer's cap was too big for "Captain Joyce," but by piling her hair up on top of her head she managed to keep it from falling over her ears as she rode in the back seat. "Sergeant Luc," behind the wheel, had no such trouble with the soldier's helmet.

Driving in blackout mode in the waning moonlight, Luc was less than 50 meters from the oncoming car before he even saw it. The other car was a newer Mercedes that neither slowed nor moved from the center of the road to pass.

Luc braked and drove onto the shoulder to avoid a collision, but he still saluted the passing car, guessing that only a high-ranking officer would have such a car in France ... and a driver with no manners.

As it passed with its windows rolled down, Luc caught a glimpse of two generals in the back seat. He wondered if they had just come from inspecting the mysterious warehouse.

As soon as Luc spotted the other car, he had shouted a warning to Joyce, and she pulled her cap down low and put her chin on her chest, pretending to be asleep, so her feminine face wouldn't be easily seen. It was probably unnecessary; the generals paid no more attention to them than their driver did.

Three or four kilometers later, Luc turned off onto a rutted road just before the main road crossed over the river by means of an old wooden bridge.

A short distance downstream, the road ran close along the steep riverbank, three or four meters above the water. Luc stopped, and they both took off their bloody uniforms, throwing them into the trunk with their rightful owners.

Luc released the parking brake, and they both pushed the car over the edge. It rolled down the embankment, picking up speed quickly, and burst into the water with a huge splash. It rolled out into the river until it was two or three meters from shore, and then stopped. The backs of its seats, its hood, and the windshield were all still above the water.

"That's not what I had in mind," Luc said as they stared down at the car. "I've seen good sized boats on this river; I thought it was a lot deeper."

"Maybe it is farther out," Joyce offered. "Should we go down and push it? Sitting there, it will be easier to see than if we left it in the woods."

He started looking in the darkness for some good footing to get down the banking.

"Wait! Look!" Joyce said.

He turned to see the car moving slowly sideways as the water pushed against it. Then gradually it tipped to the side and then rolled over, completely out of sight under the water.

"There must be a hell of a hole right there!" Luc said. "I'll bet the catfish love to hang out there."

"Or they did until we dropped a car on them," Joyce said.

Wednesday, July 5, 1944

It was well after sunrise when Luc and Joyce made it back to the barn. Luc immediately went to their hay-mattress bed and fell asleep.

As tired as she was, Joyce got out a pencil and the slip of paper that had been in Bridgett's capsule. The paper was about the size of a dollar bill, and in her smallest printing—stopping to sharpen the pencil several times—she wrote a detailed message about the warehouse in the town, its high level of army activity, and its direct connection to the railway spur. On the flip side, she drew a map of the town, with an arrow indicating north, and another pointing to the warehouse.

She folded and rolled the message, slipped it into the Bridgette's capsule, and took her outside. She kissed the top of her head, whispered, "*Bonne chance!*" and gently tossed her up into the air.

"Well, that was silly," Carlos said, standing in the broken doorway of the barn.

"What do you mean?" Joyce said. "You don't think I should have sent the message?"

"The message is fine," he said. "But you wished her *bonne chance*. She's an English pigeon, Jo; what makes you think she speaks French?"

Joyce laughed. "I'm sure she got the message from my kiss for luck on her head," she said. "And speaking of kisses for luck," she went on, "Wait until I tell

A Kiss For Luck!

you about the luck your sweet Rosie delivered to me with the rifle ... after I wake up."

Major John Waverly walked into his boss' office at SOE (Special Operations Executive) headquarters on Baker Street in London carrying a small piece of paper.

"Good news, sir. Looks like we might have stumbled upon that Jerry railway gun that we lost track of back in March," he said as he handed his boss the slip. "This arrived an hour ago over at the Bletchley loft. It was on one of the birds we dropped to the resistance a week ago Friday."

"Are we sure it's real?" the colonel asked after reading it and looking at the map.

"No reason not to think so," Waverly answered. "We haven't received any phonies in a long while, and when we used to get them they were usually bogus tallies of troop strengths or locations of non-existent Panzer divisions. This one wants us to bomb a specific warehouse that happens to be connected to a rail line."

"Do we know this Joyce Renaud who signed it?" the colonel asked. "Is she one of ours?"

"We know *of* her, sir, but she's not ours, per se," the major replied. "She runs with a small group called *La Maqui de Julien*. The Gestapo has a price on her head. She's supposed to be quite good with a rifle from what we hear."

"How good is the map?" the colonel asked.

"Quite good, actually, for it's size. We should see if we can recruit her for the cartography branch," he added with a chuckle. "We checked it against an aerial photo from a year ago, and it's all quite precise. The tracks even run right into the building she points to, just like it shows."

"Good show," the colonel said, handing back the message. "I'll give bomber command a call and see if they can spare a dive bomber or two. Head over there so they can see the map."

Early that afternoon, July 5th, three American A-36 Apache dive-bombers took off from an RAF base in the south of England. Under each wing of each aircraft was a 500 pound bomb.

The flight of precision bombers flew over the Channel and over the fighting south of Normandy with a squadron of B-17 bombers. After the bombers had dropped their cargo, and turned for home, the Apaches kept flying south over and beyond the city of Saint-Lô.

"Target in sight at one-o'clock. Range two miles," the flight leader, Commander Jim Lucy, said over his radio.

"Roger," came back two replies. "Visual on target."

Although the raid on this particular target was supposed to be a surprise to the Germans, with so many Allied aircraft in the air over northern France, radio silence was really not necessary. In fact, it would have been more of an alert to the Nazis if radio communications suddenly did go silent.

A mile later, the leader radioed, "Beginning dive."

He reached down and pulled a lever to arm the two bombs under his wings, and keeping his eyes fixed on the roof of the big building ten-thousand feet below, he banked his plane to the right rolling over until he was flying upside-down. He directed the aircraft into a wide arc that would bring him into a nearly vertical decent over the top of the warehouse. The other two aircraft followed, separated by a hundred yards.

As he began to pick up speed in his dive, Lucy opened his dive brakes to keep his speed to about 300 miles an hour. His eyes flicked back and forth from the target directly below, to his airspeed and altimeter instruments.

He could see three antiaircraft guns firing up at him, but they didn't worry him too much. He knew that they were designed to hit planes flying past them, not directly at them. And their flak shells were set to go off at a specific altitude, which was decreasing by almost 600 feet every second. The head-on profile of his plane also presented a fairly small target, so if he *was* hit he knew it would be through dumb-ass bad luck.

At twelve-hundred feet, he pulled the lever releasing both of his bombs, and spoke into his oxygen-mask microphone, "Bombs away!"

He then "horsed back" on the control stick—a pilot term for pulling with all your might—to pull the plane out of its dive. The pull-out drove his body into the seat with almost five times the force of gravity, causing the blood to drain from his head. His vision rapidly went grey and then he went completely blind.

The condition didn't worry him, though, because he knew it would only last until the plane leveled out—two or three seconds—and his heart was once again able to overcome the G-forces and pump blood back up to his head.

The other two planes followed in identical fashion, and then all three headed for the coastline to the west at 350 miles an hour.

Photo analysts would later examine the combat film taken by the third bomber, and determine that the outline of a railway gun could be seen among the smoke and ruins of the warehouse just before the second plane's bombs hit.

When Joyce and Luc woke up later in the afternoon of the 5th, they told the others who were not on sentry duty about their narrow escape from Franz. When she showed them her rifle, and the damage it sustained saving her life, they were in complete awe.

"That little kiss inside certainly does carry luck!" Richard said.

"I knew there was something very special about my Rosie," Carlos said. "And all this time I thought it was just her *pechos grandes* (big breasts)!" he added with a laugh while pretending to cup them with both of his hands.

Luc looked closely at the damage to the rifle. The carbine was unique in the way that its web sling was attached, and it looked like it played a part in stopping the bullet.

The sling, used for carrying the rifle over the shoulder, actually passed *through* the stock near the butt plate, being held from pulling back out by a hollow steel cylinder that nested into a groove in the wood.

The cylinder, with a screw-on cap and steel dipping needle, was filled with oil and was used for field maintenance of the weapon. It proved much more important for Joyce.

Entering at an angle, the bullet dug a groove into the wood just ahead of the canister, right at the top edge of the webbing. Exiting the wood, it shredded the webbing, went straight through the steel cylinder and its steel pin, and then burrowed a hole through the last inch of wood, to be stopped by the stamped-metal butt plate.

Had the webbing and the cylinder not been there to absorb some of the bullet's energy, it would have had just enough additional force to have broken through the thin metal of the butt plate, and to have entered Joyce's stomach.

Looking at the bulge in the butt plate, Luc said, "The bullet's probably still in there. You should take it out and keep it for a good luck charm."

Using her knife, she unscrewed the single screw that held the butt plate to the stock, and pried it off. Bulging out of the wood was the squashed nose of a 7.65mm bullet.

She wiggled it out with her fingernails, and looked at it closely. As many bullets as she had handled and fired, this was the first one she ever held *after* it had *been* fired ... and at *her*, at that!

As the others passed the bullet around, marveling at her good luck, she screwed the butt plate back onto the rifle.

"I wish we had a drill," Joyce said when got the slug back. "I'd like to string it onto my necklace to keep my cross company."

"I would be afraid that a hole would let out the good luck," Luc said only half joking. "I have a better idea." He reached out his hand, and asked, "May I have it for an hour or so? I promise I won't lose it or let its luck escape."

In the afternoon sunlight, Joyce sat beside the barn, cleaning the oil from the ruptured canister off of her rifle. High overhead, she heard the drone of airplane engines. She looked up and searched the sky, and finally found three small shapes traveling in a southerly direction. She hoped they were headed for the warehouse; it was in that general direction.

Knowing they couldn't see her even if they were looking for her, she waved and called out, "*Bonne chance!*"

Half an hour later, Luc came around the corner of the barn with the rest of the group behind him.

"Did you see the planes?" Joyce said excitedly as she stood up. "They should have dropped their bombs, by now. I wish we were close enough to hear the explosions."

"I heard them, but I was inside," Luc said. "How many were there?"

"Three," she said. "They looked small; dive bombers, I think. I wished them good luck."

"Speaking of good luck," he said, "I have your lucky bullet, and I also have a question to ask." He set the bullet in her hand, and she beamed as she stared at it.

Working alone, and using a length of bailing wire he found in the barn, a board with a nail through it, and a pair of pliers that they had found in the tool kit in the *kübelwagen*, Luc had fashioned a tiny wire cage around the bullet, with a loop at the top for Joyce's necklace.

"It's wonderful!" she said, holding it in her fingers and turning it all around. "I love it!"

She reached up, unclasped her gold necklace, and threaded the charm onto the chain. She put it back around her neck, and pressed her hand over the caged bullet, holding it close.

"Thank you!" she said with wet eyes. "It's perfect!"

"There is one more thing," he said. He took her left hand in his, and he got down onto one knee. He opened his right hand and produced a small dull-silver-colored ring.

Using the same bailing wire, he had curled a circle three times around, and then polished the ends of the wire smooth.

Holding the ring in front of her left ring-finger, he said, "Joyce Renaud, will you marry me?"

Completely surprised, she was momentarily speechless. Then her eyes overflowed as she broke into a wide smile, and managed to reply, "Yes, Luc Arsenault, I most certainly will!"

The rest of the group clapped, and Carlos asked, "When is the joyous occasion? I need time to prepare a speech and have my suit pressed."

Luc slipped the ring onto her finger, and answered, "On the day that Germany surrenders. That way we will never forget our anniversary." With a grin at Joyce, he added, "We already know what we're going to do on our honeymoon."

He took her in his arms, and they kissed passionately as the others clapped and cheered.

The city of Saint-Lô had not had an easy history. Born as a fortified settlement of the Gaul's in the 500's, it received support from Charlemagne in the 800's in the form of a defensive wall, but was nevertheless sacked by the Vikings in 890.

After rebuilding, the city enjoyed several centuries of growth and prosperity, until the 1300's when, during the 100-years-war, it was sacked and claimed by England. Shortly thereafter, in 1347, it was struck by the plague.

In 1378 it was again under French rule, but in 1418 it was back in English hands, and stayed that way for 31 years.

During the Wars of Religion, from the mid to late 1500's, the city went violently back and forth between the French Catholics and the Huguenot Protestants.

After the Edict of Nantes in 1598, Saint-Lô once again settled into a long period of relatively peaceful growth.

On June 17, 1940 it was occupied by the German army. On July 7, 1944, two days after Joyce and Luc's engagement, the Allied armies began an attack on Saint-Lô to displace the Germans so that the Allies could break out of the confinement of the Normandy area.

The Battle of Saint-Lô lasted fifteen days, during which time ninety-five percent of the city was destroyed by artillery and aerial bombardment from both sides.

When the victorious Allies finally marched through the ruined city, one American GI was quoted as saying, "We sure liberated the hell out of this place!"

Although the Allies would probably have prevailed in the Battle of Saint-Lô without the help of resistance groups like Joyce's, there is no question that the campaign would have been longer and more costly, both in materiel and in lives.

From D-Day, June 6, 1944, to V-E Day, May 8, 1945, the war in Europe would last for 335 more days.

As the status of France changed from "occupied" to "liberated," the majority of the resistance groups joined an umbrella organization created in exile by General de Gaulle, called the *Forces Françaises de l'Intérieur* (French Forces of the Interior or FFI), and *La Maqui de Julien* was no exception.

While Joyce and Luc and the others were more than happy to hinder the Germans on the larger and more organized scale that the FFI provided, they strongly disliked the politics of the larger group.

Through the landings at Provence, on August 15, 1944, the Free French Army was back in France, and after October of that year, when most of France had been liberated, a program was begun to merge the FFI resistance units with the regular army.

The members of the former *Maqui de Julien* flatly refused. Considering that the little group was a bunch of rebels, they were remarkably democratic, and although they were one hundred percent loyal to France, none of them had the temperament to survive the rules and regulations of formal military life. Another reason was that women were not allowed into the French Army at that time, and if they could not all go together, they would not go at all.

Within months of the August 1944 recognition of de Gaulle's *Gouvernement Provisoire de la République Française* (Provisional Government of the French Republic) by all of the Allied governments, relative normalcy slowly returned in the areas where there was no active fighting. Unless, of course, you had been a Nazi collaborationist, in which case there was a good chance that you would be executed-without-trial by a vengeful citizenry.

By Christmas of 1944—by which time everyone had hoped that the war would be over—the group had returned to Luc's family farm. It had been ransacked—probably by the Milice—and showed the signs of more than a year and a half of abandonment, but was mostly the way they had left it, if terribly overgrown.

They hid their transportation, the little *kübelwagen*, in the barn, and cleaned and oiled their rifles, and then hid them in the henhouse roof. They kept their pistols as protection against desperate collaborationist or marauding loyalist mobs. Neither of which—thankfully—ever materialized.

During the winter and spring of 1945, the group slowly broke up and each went his separate way, with the exception of Carlos, who stayed on to work the farm with Joyce and Luc. As agreed, however, when the former members of *La Maqui de Julien* heard the news that Germany had surrendered, they all hurriedly returned to the farm.

Tuesday, May 8, 1945

On May 8, 1945, V-E Day, Joyce and Luc were married in the small church in the village. In attendance, along with the maqui members and many of the villagers who had known Luc since childhood, was Dr. Poullard.

Nine months and three days after the wedding—in the same bedroom where Luc had been born—and delivered by the same doctor—a son was born to the couple. They named him Julien Vincent, after Luc's brother and Joyce's father.

Before Julien's first birthday, "Grampa Carlos" had traveled to Spain and returned with Joyce's parents. They opened a bakery in the village, and lived in the four-room flat located above.

Joyce's carbine hangs on the wall in the farmhouse, and is regularly used by the family to hunt game for food. The *Kiss For Luck!* slip is still inside the gun.

End of Part IV

A Kiss For Luck!

Ken Blaisdell

Part V:
The Homecoming

Chicago, Illinois
Tuesday, May 4, 1954

Damn! May 4th already, I said to myself as I drew an X through May 3rd. Not that I have anything against May 4th specifically, or that I mind May in general, you understand. In fact living in Chicago May is usually pretty welcome, weather-wise. It's just that June is right behind it, and I don't have a story, yet. Worse, I don't have an *idea* for a story, yet.

    I looked at the painting of the pin-up girl on the calendar. She was trying—with just the appropriate lack of success—to hold her skirt down against a gust of wind. For no logical reason, she made me think of all the girls in the streets the day the 2nd French Armored Division marched into Paris after liberating the city from the Germans.

    I was a war correspondent then, and stories were easy to come by. You had to pick *which* extraordinary thing-of-the-day you were going to write about, and discard the dozen others. Living with the front-line troops was hell, but the writing came easy.

    When I made it back to the States after the war, I had a few pretty good offers to choose from, and I picked the Chicago Sun. The Tribune had made me a better financial offer, but I didn't like their right-wing politics. Three years later, in '48, the Sun merged with the Times, and I got an editor that I couldn't stand. By that time I was pretty tired of assignment writing anyway, and was longing for the old days of picking my own stories, so I quit and went freelance.

    The first couple years were damned good. Enough editors remembered my name that I had no trouble selling almost anything I wrote.

    But things are different now. The decision to buy a piece is usually made by some committee, so I have to pitch my ideas a lot harder just to get a maybe. Then, half the time the editors—yes, that's plural—want so many rewrites that I end up working for fifty-cents an hour.

    The telephone rang, snapping me out of my trip down memory lane.

    "Rich Lawson," I answered.

    "Richard Charles!" came the voice from the other end. It was Dave Cartwright. We'd known each other for twenty-odd years, and he always called me by my first and middle names. I don't even remember how it got started, anymore.

    "How's that tenth-anniversary of the liberation of Paris piece coming?" Dave asked. "You got a first draft for us to look at?"

    "Not exactly," I said.

    "So, that's a no?"

"Well, I did have something, but ..."

"But what?" he interrupted. "Did the dog eat your homework?"

"I don't have a dog," I told him. "*I* ate it."

"Things getting that tight, huh?"

"I didn't like it," I said seriously. "It was just a rehash of what everybody—including me—wrote ten years ago. The celebrating in the streets, the German sniper fire, General de Gaulle's march down the Champs Elysees, the 28th Infantry marching down the same street, the pretty girls kissing every guy in sight, blah, blah, blah. I even threw in Ernie Pyle's comment that anybody who didn't sleep with a woman that night was an exhibitionist. It just read like a ten-year-old newspaper."

"Well, what else do you have in mind?" Dave asked me. "I'm holding two and a half pages in the August edition for you, and I'm going to need time to dredge up photos to go along with whatever it is you write. The galleys need to put together and approved before July 4th if we're going to make it."

"I know," I said. "And I appreciate that. I really do. But I want this to be good, not just filler, you know?"

"I do too, Rich," he said. "But there's two other guys here—well, one of them's a woman, but there's two other editors who'd like to take those pages. I'm going to need to show the old man something pretty quick, or we're going to be SOL."

"I hear you. I've got a couple of ideas I'm trying to flesh out," I lied, "and then I'll send you an outline, okay?"

"Next week?" he said. It was really more of a statement than a question.

"Next week," I repeated. It was really more of a desperate hope than a promise.

After I hung up, I sat down and stared at my typewriter for a while, waiting for something to start flowing. The Remington wasn't being the least bit helpful.

I got up, pulled on my coat, grabbed my hat, walked past the elevator, and took the stairs the three flights down to the street. I turned west and headed for Banyan's. If I has Hemingway, there would probably be a glass of scotch in my near future, but seeing as it was only ten in the morning—and my only similarity to Hemingway was that we were both once war correspondents—I was looking forward to a cup of Maxwell House.

I passed Mike Delaney's news stand on the way, and a tabloid-size newspaper in his foreign language section caught my eye. The headline, in French, read, "*Dixième Anniversaire!* (Tenth Anniversary!)" the sub-head read, "*Parisiens Se Préparer Pour La Fête!* (Parisians Get Ready For Celebration!)." Below that were some of the iconic photos of the occupation and the liberation. A grown man crying, Hitler and his entourage walking in front of the Eifel Tower, Charles de Gaulle, looking a foot taller than everyone around him, strutting in his uniform, and a French girl kissing a GI.

I bought a copy of the paper and headed for Banyan's. Maybe the spark I was looking for was waiting inside.

Cliff McCoy, the proprietor, waved at me as I entered, and pulled my cup from its spot under the bar. He filled a cup for himself, as well, and came over to join me in the window booth. He didn't usually get much business before 11:00 or so, and at the moment I was the only other person in the place.

"You speak French?" Cliff asked me, looking at the paper upside-down. "I *assume* that's French."

"It is, and I do," I answered, translating the headline for him. "I took French in high school, and when I got to France during the war I was surprised at how much of it had apparently gotten lodged in parts of my brain that I wasn't using for processing whatever I could about the opposite sex. By the time I left, I could speak pretty fluently—if not exactly like a native—and I could read and write the language almost as well as English. Mrs. Kelley would have been proud."

"So, you read French newspapers just to keep your hand in?" Cliff asked.

"I haven't read one since I've been back in the States ... almost ten years," I told him. "But this almost jumped off Mike's rack as I walked by. I'm trying—desperately—to find a hook for a story I need to write for the tenth anniversary of the liberation of Paris. I'm hoping there was something in here calling my name."

Cliff's wife, Claudette, called to him from the kitchen.

"Duty calls," he said sliding out of the booth. "Talk to you later. Good luck."

"Thanks. I have a feeling I'm going to need it," I said.

The paper—a weekly—seemed to offer mostly gossip-type stories about French celebrities and politicians. There was an editorial—and I use that term loosely—about the recently elected president, René Coty, which used more space discussing his clothing and his eating habits than talking about his politics.

There was a half-page ad that was promoting the appearance of Marlene Dietrich at the *Café De Paris* on the 21st. I remember hearing her recording of *Lili Marlene* countless times over there, and I had even walked in front of the *De Paris*. If I didn't have more pressing business, I could sit here and get all nostalgic.

On the last page before the personals, the winners of an essay contest were printed. In the run-up to the anniversary celebrations in August, the paper was sponsoring a weekly prize—actually, first, second, and third prizes—to school kids who submitted stories about what their folks did during the war.

After reading them, I had the distinct impression that the first and second-place stories had probably been written—or at least dictated—by the parents themselves. But the grammar and the style of the third-place finisher was unpolished enough that you could believe a kid wrote it. And the story was actually more intriguing. Even its title, *Un Baiser Pour La Chance!* (A Kiss For Luck!), grabbed my attention.

It was written by an eight-year-old kid named Julien Arsenault, and briefly told the story of his mother in the French Resistance. The story was unique from the other two, because it didn't tell of all of her daring and patriotic exploits fighting the Nazis, but rather it talked about the rifle she used during the last year of the war.

According to Julien's story, she ended up with an American rifle after an Allied supply drop, and later discovered a slip of paper inside it with a woman's lip print and the words, "*A Kiss For Luck!*" written across it. Later on, when she was captured by the Nazi's, she managed to escape—along with Julien's future father—aided by the good luck that came with the gun.

Empty of bullets, she used the rifle to coldcock her two captors, but not before one of them fired a pistol at her. The rifle intercepted the bullet, lodging in the butt of the gun, undoubtedly saving both his mother's and his father's lives.

Later, Julien's father dug the slug out of the rifle, and made a good-luck charm out of it that his mother wears every day.

Here was the hook I'd been searching for, serendipitously dropped into my lap by a morning stroll past Mike's news stand! And obviously, there had to be a lot more to the story than the hundred and fifty words I sat there rereading. The kid mentioned railroad and communication sabotage, that his folks were part of a larger *maqui*, and even a carrier pigeon named Bridgette. If his mom and dad weren't *in* Paris when it was liberated, they surely contributed to the fact that it *was* liberated.

I flipped the paper over to the front page and looked at the masthead for the publisher's information. There was a Paris address and a phone number. I looked at my watch and did some mental math and calculated that it would be a little after three in the afternoon in Paris. There would probably be someone there on the news desk to answer a phone call, but I wondered if the folks who handled kids' essay contests would still be there.

In a much better mood than when I came in, I left a generous quarter on the table for my ten-cent cup of coffee, took the paper, and headed back to my apartment.

With my yellow legal pad on the kitchen table in front of me, and a cup full of sharpened number-twos to one side, I dialed the operator and asked for international long-distance. It took almost a full minute for the call to get connected. Severely testing my rusty conversational French, I finally got put through to the circulation department, which—logically, when I thought about it—sponsored contests and promotional gimmicks for the paper. The woman who answered sounded young and pretty—whatever pretty sounds like.

"Hi, my name is Rich Lawson, I'm calling from the United States," I began in French. "May I ask who I'm speaking with?"

"My name is Charlene," she answered, "How may I help you?"

"I would like to get in touch with the young man, Julien Arsenault, who won the third-place prize in your recent essay contest," I told her. "Actually, I want to get in touch with his mother," I corrected myself.

"May I ask the reason?"

"Of course," I said. "I'm a writer in Chicago, and I'd like to do an interview of Julien's mother for a local magazine. Naturally," I added, "I would mention that the story originated with your paper."

"Hold on a moment, Mr. Lawson, and I'll see what we have."

I heard the phone clunk onto the table, and faintly, over four-thousand miles of wire, I could hear what I assumed were file drawers being opened and closed.

After half a minute at long-distance rates—during which time I was doodling dollar signs on my pad—Charlene came back on.

"I have a box number at the village post office, but no phone number," she said. "There are a lot of farms down in that area and few farmers have much need for a telephone. But there is a note here that says a message may be passed on to Mrs. Arsenault through a bakery in the village. Would you like that number?"

"Yes, please," I answered, wondering what the connection to the bakery might be.

I wrote the number down as she dictated it, then I asked, "Do you happen to know what the mother's name is? Julien only calls her Mamma in the essay."

"I have Joyce Renaud-Arsenault listed as his mother here," she told me.

"Thanks, Charlene, you've been a great help! You have a nice night," I said and then hung up, stopping the flow of dollar signs.

But I started it again, almost immediately, as I dialed the operator back, and gave her the bakery's number. The woman who answered sounded older ... nothing registered on how pretty she might be.

In French, I introduced myself, and said, "I'm trying to get in touch with Joyce Renaud-Arsenault. I was told that she could be reached through this number."

"Thursday," the woman said.

"Pardon?" I replied.

"Thursday," the woman repeated. "Joyce comes in to help on Thursday. You call back then."

"I see. Well, is there any way ..." I stopped talking when I realized I was talking to a dial tone. She had hung up.

I decided not to call back right then, but I didn't want to wait five days until Thursday, either. Maybe if I called in the morning, I'd get someone more cooperative.

I opened the paper, and as I read the essay again, I started jotting down questions on my pad that I wanted to ask Joyce when I finally connected with her.

Each question I came up with seemed to spawn two or three follow ups, the answer to each of which could potentially lead to another and another. It didn't take me long to realize that I was going to need to have Julien's mother on the phone for quite a while to get a decent story put together.

Beyond thinking about the long-distance phone call cost on my end, it was obvious that if she was on the phone with me for hours, she wouldn't be getting much "helping" done around the bakery. I had a mental image of the woman I'd talked to taking the phone from Joyce and hanging it up mid-question.

I thought for a while, and then pulled the Yellow Pages out of a cabinet drawer.

I made a couple of calls, and when I was done I sat there staring at the numbers I'd written on my pad. I decided to call Dave.

"Your ears must have been burning, buddy," he said after hellos. "I just came out of the old man's office, and he said if he doesn't have something in his hands Friday, Stewart and Happy-Bottom are going to get to fight over the space."

"Happy-Bottom?" I asked.

"Yeah, That's the other editor," Dave said with a chuckle. "Her name is Gladys, but she made the mistake of telling us that kids in school used to call her Glad-Ass when she was little. So now I call her Happy-Bottom. Pisses her off, no end."

"Cute," I said with a laugh. "You never finished that copy of *How to Win Friends and Influence People* I sent you, did you?"

He laughed. "Charm is for the babes in the *Miss America Pageant*," he told me. "Like Truman said, if you can't stand the heat, get out of the kitchen."

"I'm going to stretch your reference to charm," I said, "into a segue for my story idea. It's about a *lucky* charm."

"Hit me," he replied. "I'm on the edge of my seat."

I told him about the French newspaper, the kid's essay, the *Kiss For Luck!* slip of paper, and the Mom's lucky slug.

"What do you think?" I asked. "I'm sure I can pull a connection to Paris out of it."

"I like it," he answered. "It's a different angle; I think it could be interesting. So, are you going to interview the old lady over the phone, or what?"

I told him about my phone calls to the newspaper and the bakery.

"If she doesn't have a phone," he said, "and you can't talk to her at the bakery for more than ten minutes every Thursday, I'm seeing the deadline as a little hard to hit."

"That's where you come in, old buddy," I told him. "I want to fly to France to meet with her. I've wanted to go back since the war, anyway, only the advance you gave me won't cover the ticket, and I'm still waiting for the checks for the pieces I did for *The Saturday Evening Post* and *Colliers*. Can you spot me a couple hundred until I get back?"

"*A couple hundred?*" he repeated like I'd asked him to donate a kidney. "That's like two weeks' pay. You don't expect me to eat while you're writing this story? It's the artist who's supposed to starve, not his editor."

"Oh, come on," I pressed. "You've probably got that in your wallet, right now. Shoot, if I had your money, I'd burn mine because it was just in the way."

"Who the hell have *you* been talking to, my ex-wife?"

"Seriously, Dave. This is a dynamite story, I can feel it. It's just a loan, not a gift. I'll give you whatever you want as collateral, but I really need to do this story. Please?"

There was a long pause and then a heavy sigh from the other end of the phone.

"The things I do for my friends," he moaned finally. "Come over to the office and I'll write you a check. And I'll take the key to your apartment as collateral, because if Gail finds out I'm handing out hundred dollar bills, she'll throw me the hell out."

"You're exaggerating," I said. "Gail likes me."

"Yes, but she likes that portrait of Franklin more," he replied.

"Okay. Our secret. Thanks, Dave. I really appreciate this," I said, heaving my own sigh of relief. "You won't regret it, I promise."

"Yeah, that's what my girlfriend told me when she talked me into taking her to Miami," he said. "Only when my first wife found out, I *did* regret it ... and still do every time I write her that alimony check."

Thursday, May 6, 1954

Two days later I was at Midway Airport, bright and early, walking up the steps into a PanAm StratoClipper. When I left France after the war ended, I flew in a twin engine C-47 Army cargo plane. We hopped from France to England, England to Greenland, Greenland to Nova Scotia, and finally Nova Scotia to New York. I was so sick of airplanes at that point, I took the train back to Chicago.

Comparing the two, the plane I was stepping into now made that C-47 look like a Model-T next to a Lincoln. It was a close civilian cousin to Boeing's big B-29, like the ones that dropped the A-bombs on Japan to end the war. Only this baby could carry 114 passengers ... in comfort, had a full kitchen, had sleeper births like on a train—not that I could afford one of those—and even had a lounge downstairs in its belly. It had about every luxury you could think of, and it took you where you were going at more than three hundred miles an hour. And I've read where Boeing's next trick is a plane like this with four *jet* engines. What a time to be alive!

Friday, May 7, 1954

I landed at Orly Airport, a little south of Paris, about five the next morning. I hopped a taxi to the train station, and fours hours later I was in the city of Issoudun. My final destination—or at least where the bakery was—was forty-five minutes farther south; the town of Saint-Août. From what I'd been able to find in my travel guide, the whole place had a population of about 1,100, so I wasn't surprised that the train didn't go there.

Rather than jump right in another taxi, I decided to find a cup of coffee, first. It was a little after 9:00 a.m. local time, but my body apparently didn't know I was in France, so it thought it was three in the morning. I'd fallen asleep on the train, and if it wasn't for an attentive conductor, I'd be half way to Châteauroux right now.

I found a café with sidewalk tables, ordered black coffee and a croissant, and then lit up a Winston. While I ate and drank, a delivery truck pulled up in front of me, blocking what had been a rather pleasant view. After carting some boxes inside, the driver came out with the proprietor, and I overheard him say that he had a delivery to make down in Saint-Août.

Five minutes later I was sitting in the passenger seat of the old Citroen van, heading south.

The guy was pleasant enough to talk with and he gave me a chance to brush up on my French as I explained that I was in France researching a story for an American magazine. But when I fell asleep again, ten minutes into the trip, he just let me sleep. Bless his soul.

When I opened my eyes we were stopped and I was alone. It took me a moment to remember why I was sitting in an old truck in an alley, but when it clicked, I climbed out and looked for the driver. He was in the back, pushing some boxes to the edge of the van.

"Let me give you a hand," I said as I hefted one of the boxes. "So, is this Saint-Août?"

"*Oui*. If you don't mind carrying that inside, it would be a big help," he said as he jumped down and grabbed a box himself.

We were parked behind a clothing store, and when we finished the delivery, I asked if he was familiar with the little town.

"I come here three or four times a month," he told me.

"Well, I'm looking for a bakery, but I don't know its name," I explained. "But I figure a town this size can't have *too* many."

"Only one that I know of," he said. "Walk to the end of this alley, look to your left across the street, and you'll be looking at *Le Parisien*. I can personally recommend the *profiterole*. It is the best between here and Paris ... and I've tried them all."

"Thanks for the recommendation," I said. "I'll give it a try." I knew from my short stint in Paris during the war that a *profiterole* was what we called a crème puff back in the States, and it was one of my favorite pastries.

"Can I give you something for gas?" I asked as I reached for my wallet.

"Certainly not. I was coming here anyway, and I enjoyed the company," he said. "Well, for ten minutes, anyway," he added with a laugh.

"Sorry about that," I said. "My eyes still think they're in Chicago, and think they should be shut right now."

I grabbed my suitcase from the van, and headed up the alley.

Le Parisien occupied a slender, three story, building, wedged tightly between two fatter ones. The lace curtains in the upstairs windows made it look like it might have been one of those places that had an apartment above it. You couldn't get a much shorter commute to work than that.

The bell above the door jingled as I stepped inside, and the woman behind the glass display case looked over, smiled, and said in French, "*Bonjour!* I'll be with you in just a minute. Please look around." She then went back to waiting on the elderly man who, based on the conversation I picked up, was a regular.

The shop was long and narrow, with a display case on both sides of a three-foot wide center aisle. I set my suitcase down at the end of the case on the right, and then looked over the pastry inside. I had to be careful not to drool on the glass, and it wasn't easy. Fresh French pastry in a bakery called *Le Parisien*, smack in the heart of France. Even the *smell* was heavenly. To a dessert junkie like me, they could have charged admission for the aroma alone.

The old man finally left with a loaf of bread that I could have *eaten* in half the time it took him to buy it. But then I reminded myself that life was lived at a different pace here than in America.

As the old man opened the door, the woman happened to notice my suitcase. I saw her eyes narrow either in curiosity or in suspicion.

She turned to me, smiled again, and said, "*Bonjour*. Welcome to *Le Parisien*. This is your first time visiting us, no?"

She was a pretty woman. She had dirty-blonde hair cut short, and her skin was smooth, but well tanned, like she spent a good deal of time outdoors. I took her to be in her mid-thirties.

I was about to introduce myself when I noticed the piece of jewelry she wore around her neck. It was a small wire cage with a deformed bullet inside it.

"Madame Arsenault?" I said. "What a pleasant surprise! You are just the person I've come to see."

"Do we know each other?" she replied. I picked up on the same reaction in her voice that I saw in her eyes when she noticed my suitcase. But I still couldn't tell if it was curiosity or suspicion.

"Pardon my manners," I said as I took off my hat, the glass case still separating us. "My name is Rich Lawson. I'm a writer for a magazine in America. I read about you in your son's essay."

"My son's ess ..." and then it clicked for her. "Oh, yes. The newspaper contest." And then something else clicked. "Did you call here looking for me earlier this week?"

"I did," I said. "Your son did a great job of whetting my appetite with his story. I'd like to write a feature article about you and the rifle he wrote about, if you have the time to talk with me."

"I don't usually have much time for conversation when Papa's off delivering and it's only me and Mamma here," she said.

As if on queue, the bell over the door jingled announcing another customer, a woman who appeared to be about the same age as Julien's mother.

"I understand completely," I replied as I stepped back to let her wait on the customer. As she put half a dozen éclairs into a box, the two women chatted about the new teacher the town had just hired. I got the impression they were glad to see the old teacher leave. I was happy to find that I could follow the conversation; my French was coming back nicely.

When the customer left, she came around the case and extended her hand.

"Please call me Joyce," she said.

"Rich," I replied, shaking her hand. She had a strong grip.

"So, what fascinated you so much about my son's little story that you would travel half way across the world to talk about it?" she asked me.

"Everything from its title, *A Kiss For Luck!*, down to that bauble you have around your neck. I was a war correspondent over here from D-Day to V-E Day, and I know that the real story of the war isn't in battle plans, troop movements, and body counts; it's in the kind of personal details that your son wrote about ... and that you obviously lived."

She didn't reply right away. There were a lot of soldiers and others who had lived through the war who, even ten years later, couldn't talk about it. It was that traumatizing for them. I hoped she wasn't one of them.

Finally, she said, "Where are you staying while you're here?"

"Actually, I haven't figured that out, yet," I told her. "Maybe you could recommend a hotel or a boarding house for me."

"You'll stay with us at the farm," she said. Her tone didn't imply that it was a suggestion, but that it was a simple fact. "You'll want to talk to my husband, Luc, and to Carlos, as well. We were all in the thing together."

"Thank you! I'm honored!" I said genuinely surprised by the offer. "You're sure your husband won't mind? There's enough room?"

"Luc will put you to work if you're not careful," she answered. "And you can sleep in Julien's bed. He'll sleep in the barn."

"The *barn*? That hardly seems fair," I said. "I don't want to displace the boy to the barn when he's the reason I'm here in the first place."

"You'll be doing him a favor," Joyce said with a chuckle. "He has a whole fort built out there in the loft. Sleeping there is a treat for him."

"And Carlos? Who is that?"

"Carlos Santiago. He was a member of our maqui. He stayed with us to help on the farm after the war ended, and he's adopted Julien as his grandson. He will *love* your company and your fresh ears. Every man, woman, and child in town has heard all of his stories at least five times." She gave a theatrical head shake, and added, "Some of us many many more."

The door opened again, and a young couple came in, followed half a minute later by an elderly lady. I stood out of the way, leaning against the wall while she waited on everyone.

I don't even remember closing them, but when I *opened* my eyes Joyce was standing in front of me, smiling. She was gently shaking my shoulder. I had fallen asleep standing up!

"You're exhausted," she said with a chuckle. "Come. I'll take you upstairs where you can lay down until it's time to go."

"No, no. That's not necessary," I protested against my own better judgment. "I'll be fine."

"And when you fall over sound asleep, some customer will think you were poisoned by bad filling, and they will run screaming from the shop," she said. "I insist."

I'm sure she was exaggerating about the screaming thing, but it *would* be embarrassing to fall over in the middle of the shop.

"Well, I guess if you *insist*," I gave in easily, "it would be just rude of me to refuse, wouldn't it?"

She laughed, and led me through the kitchen where I was introduced to her mother—whom I had met on the phone—and then up a flight of narrow stairs. A few minutes later, I had my jacket and shoes off, and I was lying on a couch. About thirty seconds after that I was dead to the world.

When I woke up, I looked at my watch—which was still on Chicago time—and added six hours to its 9:00 a.m. I splashed some water on my face in the bathroom, put on my shoes and jacket, and headed back down to the bakery.

An old man was just coming in the front door as I entered the shop from the kitchen, and he gave me a surprised look.

"Who are you?" he asked in a less than friendly tone.

Joyce intervened, and said, "Papa, this is Mr. Lawson, from America. He's come all the way here to write a story about Julien's essay from the newspaper."

His appearance, brightened immediately.

"Julien?" He said looking at me with a sudden smile. "You're gong to write a story about my Julien?"

I stole a quick glance at Joyce, and she gave me a wink. If I was reading all the signs right, Julien was the key to Papa's heart, and Joyce was dangling it in front of me.

"Well," I said, "the story isn't so much *about* Julien as it was *inspired* by him. I read his essay in the newspaper, and I couldn't believe an eight-year-old had written it. He has a natural talent, alright."

"He does! He does!" his grandpa quickly agreed. "He gets it from me, I think. I used to write his Mémé poetry when we were young." Then he paused a moment, and a slight frown replaced the smile. "If your story is not about Julien, then who?"

"Julien's mother," I said, deciding not to say *Joyce* or even *your daughter*. "Your grandson seems very proud of his Mamma. I think he will be thrilled to see her story in an American magazine, no?"

"Oh, he will! He will!" he agreed. He looked up at the cuckoo clock on the wall, turned to Joyce, and said, "You should go and take our friend to meet Julien. He will be home from school soon, no?"

"He will, Papa," she said. "Are you sure you and Mamma won't need me?"

"We'll be fine," he said with a wave of his hand. "You should take the car; it's out front. My deliveries are all done."

"Are you sure Papa?" Joyce said while at the same time taking off her apron.

"Go!" Joyce's mother said from the kitchen door. "Before he wants to go with you and leave me here alone."

Before I could turn to pick up my hat and suitcase, Joyce's father grabbed me and did the French two-cheek kiss thing. Then her mother followed suit. I've never had a problem with kissing women, but when it comes to men I'm very much a handshake kind of guy. But what are you going to do? When in Rome …

Joyce and I stepped out the front door and I found myself looking at a boxy, bright yellow convertible with a huge French flag painted on the door. I recognized the shape, but had certainly never seen one in that color. Officially, the vehicle was called a Type-82. It had once been a German Army field car, better known to both the Germans and the Allies as a *kübelwagen*, which translates to "bucket car." It had been the Nazi counterpart to the American Jeep.

I set my suitcase in the back, and climbed into the passenger seat. As Joyce pulled smoothly away from the curb, and made a u-turn, I said, "I'm sure there's a story behind this thing."

As we drove, she told me a story about derailing a steam locomotive off of a wood trestle that burned in half as a result. The *kübelwagen* was a prize taken when they killed a trio of SS soldiers who stumbled upon the saboteurs—who included Julien's father—shortly before the train arrived.

"Is that the train sabotage that Julien gives about one sentence to in his essay?" I asked.

"I'm not sure," she said, downshifting to make it up a long hill. "There were a number of train attacks, and he's heard all the stories from his Grampa Carlos." She listed the geographic location of half a dozen attacks, but I didn't recall any of the places.

"What can you tell me about Bridgette the pigeon," I asked her as we accelerated down the other side of the hill and I held onto my hat.

"A hero with feathers," she said. "I found her tucked into a box the same night I found the rifle that Julien wrote about. It's a miracle she survived the landing. The plane dropped the supplies so low the parachutes didn't open. Later on, I sent her back with directions to a warehouse the Nazis were very interested in, and the next day the Allies sent dive bombers to blow it up."

"What was in it?" I asked.

"At the time, we didn't know," she said. "After the fighting moved on, we went and looked, and there was one of Hitler's railway guns inside, bent and twisted and burned from the bombs."

"Is it still there?" I asked, knowing that the vestiges of the war still lingered all over Europe.

"It was cut up for scrap iron years ago," she answered.

"I can see that you still have the bullet Julien talks about in the essay, but do you still have the rifle?" I asked. Out of sight, I had my fingers crossed that she did.

She looked at me like I had asked if she knew where babies came from.

"Of course," she said. "Why wouldn't I?"

I shrugged, and said, "Some people want to forget the war. They don't want things around to remind them."

"Then they're fools," she said. "If you forget the last war then you might as well be making plans for the next one."

"I agree," I said. "That's pretty much what the philosopher George Santayana said. *Those who cannot remember the past are condemned to repeat it.*"

"See?" she replied. "That's just what I mean. I'm not crazy."

"Someone thinks you're crazy because you want to keep the rifle?"

"Papa. He thinks that every sign that the Germans ever set foot in France should be erased without a trace."

"Yet he uses one of their field cars to make deliveries."

"If he could afford another car—a French car—he would push this one in the river. He wouldn't get near it until Luc and Carlos and I painted it yellow and put the flags on it."

"But he seems proud of the essay Julien wrote about the war."

"That's because it's about pushing the German's out. Besides, I think you noticed that he's automatically proud of *anything* Julien does."

"I got that, yeah," I said. "And you use it masterfully."

"It's a gift," she said with a smile. "No offense, but men are pretty easily manipulated by the women in their lives."

"None taken. I've been a victim of that fact since about eighth grade. I just didn't recognize it until twenty-five years later."

We pulled along side of an old stone farmhouse, and came to a stop in front of a small barn. The location of Julien's fort, I assumed.

Before we were out of the car, a boy about four feet tall bounded out of the back door of the house.

"*Pépé!*" he shouted as he leapt off the step. He hit the ground and came to a comically sudden stop when he realized I wasn't his grandfather.

"Julien, this is Mr. Lawson from America," Joyce said as she came around the car. "Mr. Lawson, my son Julien."

The boy's eyebrows went up, as he said, "From America?" He stepped forward, extended his hand, and said in struggling English, "It's a pleasure to meet you, sir."

"The pleasure is mine," I said shaking his hand. His eight-year-old grip was nearly the equal of his mother's. Back to French, I said, "I read the essay you wrote about your mother, and I decided I had to meet the two of you."

His eyebrows went up even farther. "Did you read it in *America*?"

"Chicago, Illinois," I answered. "I guess that makes you internationally published, huh? I didn't make that milestone until I was thirty-something."

"You are a famous writer?" he asked me.

I chuckled. "I guess if you have to ask that question, the answer is probably no," I answered humbly. Out of the mouths of babes ...

I saw Joyce grimace a little at her son's innocent *faux pas*. "Where is your father?" she asked Julien. I think she asked as much to change the subject as to find out where her husband was.

"He and Grampa Carlos went to the pond to check the traps," he answered.

"Is dinner cooking?" she asked.

"Yes. It should be ready in about an hour, I think," he answered. "The bread is all done."

She looked at me, and asked, "Do you like rabbit stew?"

"I can't say that I've ever had it," I answered. "But if that's what I'm smelling, I look forward to trying it." Actually, I was so hungry that if she said it was old-sock stew, I think I'd have eaten it ... as long as it had some vegetables.

She looked at Julien, and said, "Why don't you run down to the pond and tell Papa and Grampa we have company for dinner?"

"Maybe I should drive the car!" he offered. "Grampa Carlos will probably be tired you know."

With a grin, she said, "Yes, I suppose he will be. That's *very* thoughtful of you."

"And they'll have animals to carry if the traps caught anything," he added to his reasoning. Apparently, the manipulation gene didn't skip a generation in the Renaud-Arsenault family.

"Yes, that would be quite a burden, wouldn't it?" she agreed with a smile.

She looked at the car and then back at him, giving a show of mentally debating her answer. I think she had made up her mind; she was just giving him a hard time.

"*Please?*" he said. "I'll be careful."

"Okay," she gave in with theatrical reluctance. Then she smiled and gave him a hug. "But no faster that second gear, understand?"

"Okay!" he said, and shot around to the driver's side.

I reached into the back and picked up my suitcase. The vision of assorted dead animals lying across it flashed through my mind, and it wasn't pleasant.

With a driver's seat designed for the average German soldier, Julien had to sit forward to reach the pedals, but he quickly had the car started and in gear. It just began rolling forward when he stopped, pulled it back into neutral, and turned to look at his mother.

"Can Mr. Lawson come with me?" he asked.

Joyce and I looked at each other. I shrugged, and said, "He can't drive any worse than the cabbies in Chicago. I've survived *that* for years."

She looked at Julien, and with a stern look and serious tone that mothers the world over can conjure up, she said, "You be extra careful, young man. Mr. Lawson is a guest. And you're to go straight to the pond and back. None of your side trips, do you understand?"

"Yes, Ma'am," he said. Then he looked up at me, and said, "Hop in, Mr. Lawson! Wait until you see my raft!"

"A raft?" I said to him as I slid into the passenger seat. "Is it big enough for two?" Not that I had any intention of getting on it; I can't swim. I just wanted to show interest in something he was obviously excited about. Unlike my buddy Dave, I *had* read the book, *How to Win Friends and Influence People*.

"You better not set one foot on that raft! *Either* of you!" his mother interjected. "You pick up Papa and Grampa, and you come right back. If I see wet feet when you get back you won't drive the car for a month, young man, and *you* won't hear any more stories, Mr. Lawson."

Julien and I looked at each other. I made a worried face, and said, "You know her better, but I don't think she's kidding."

"She's not!" he assured me.

We pulled out, and despite not being able to sit back in the seat, Julien maneuvered the pedals so smoothly that the shifting felt almost like a hydromatic.

We drove along the edge of one of the farm fields, and then turned onto a twisting dirt road that cut into the woods and weaved through the trees. The kid's driving skills were impressive. Comparing him to a Chicago cabbie was an insult to *him*.

"Did you really come all the way here from America just to talk to me about my essay?" he asked as he negotiated an S turn between two substantial trees.

"You and your mother, yes," I answered. "The title you chose, *A Kiss For Luck!*, caught my attention, right away. And you did a great job of setting the hook in just a hundred and fifty words."

"What do mean, *setting the hook*?" he asked as he downshifted into first to climb a short, steep hill.

"Making me want to read more about the subject," I answered. "Or in this case, making me want to *write* more about it."

"Is my Mom going to be famous?"

"I don't know," I said. "The magazine I'm writing for has millions of people who read it every month, so I guess you could call that famous."

We crested the hill, and I saw the pond down below. At the southern end, I could see the low manmade dam that created it. Tied to a tree on the near bank I saw Julien's raft. I laughed to myself thinking that Joyce certainly didn't need to make any threats to keep me off *that* thing!

As we descended the hill, I saw two men walking toward us, one behind the other. Between them, over one shoulder, they carried a stout tree branch, from which hung a dead animal. It appeared to be a wild bore. Over the other shoulder of the first man—whom I assumed to be Julien's father, Luc—was slung a short rifle.

As we approached, the two men stopped, and—quite understandably—stared at me curiously.

Julien pulled to a smooth stop beside them, and I lifted my hat, and said in French, "*Bonjour!* My name is ..."

But my self-introduction was cut off by Julien.

"Papa! This is Mr. Lawson from America! He's going to make Mamma famous!"

That did little to dispel their curious stares. In fact, I think it ratcheted them up to *wary*.

I opened the door, and stepped out of the car. I doffed my hat once again, and started over.

"*Bonjour!* My name is Rich Lawson. I read your son's essay about his mother in the newspaper, and my magazine sent me over here to see if you would all agree to do a more in-depth article on your exploits during the war."

"Why?" Luc asked. He had the same combination of curiosity and caution that Joyce had exhibited. The reaction was certainly understandable. Living in an occupied country for years would take a long time to get out of anyone's system.

"The tenth anniversary of the liberation of Paris is coming up," I explained, "and my magazine wants to do a special tribute to the men and women who contributed to that."

"None of us was in Paris," Luc said.

"All the same ..." I began, but was cut off by Grampa Carlos.

"Can we talk about this in the car?" he said. "This pig is getting heavier and heavier the longer it hangs from my old shoulder."

They hefted the animal up onto the hood of the car, into the indentation where a spare tire should have been. They tied it down with some cord from under the seat, and tossed the pole into the woods.

Luc and I climbed into the back seat, and Grampa Carlos took the front. Julien pulled out, and had to drive a little farther down the road before it became wide enough to turn around.

"Where is your mother?" Luc asked Julien as he drove.

"Home," he said. "She sent me to pick up you and Grampa Carlos."

Luc turned to me, and said, "Then you've met my wife?"

"At the bakery, in town," I said. "You're a lucky man; she's a delightful woman."

I was still getting the feeling of distrust from him. I wasn't sure what to do next. Then Grampa Carlos helped me out.

"Now, what were you saying about writing an article about all of us and making us rich and famous?" he asked as he twisted in the front seat to look at me, equally twisting Julien's words.

"No guarantees on wealth or fame, " I replied with a laugh. "The idea behind the article is to spotlight some of the unsung heroes who made the liberation—not just of Paris, but of all of France and Europe—possible. Julien's essay about his mother's lucky rifle struck an immediate chord with me. I think it's just the kind of unique story that readers want to see."

"You're right! You're right!" Grampa Carlos agreed with me. "They're tired of the old stories of de Gaulle, and Montgomery, and Eisenhower. It's time they heard that they were not the only ones in the fight to free France."

"Exactly!" I said. I turned to Luc, and said, "In a hundred and fifty words, your son did a remarkable job of whetting my appetite—and that of my editor—regarding the extraordinary part that you, your wife, Carlos, and your whole group played in defeating the Germans. I think that by now everyone knows that the Allied victory would have been longer in coming, and cost many more lives without *la Résistance*, but I don't think they know enough of the personal stories; the dangers that you and your grouped faced without the support of a big army behind you.

"You read Julien's essay in America?" Luc asked me. I got the impression that his scale was starting to tip slightly in the *curious* direction, and away from the suspicious.

"Do you believe in fate?" I asked him. "That some things are somehow meant to happen?"

"I guess," he said. He held the rifle that had been over his shoulder between his legs, now. I recognized it as an American M1 Carbine. Julien's essay only mentioned that his mother's "lucky" rifle was American and small. I guessed that it was probably a carbine.

As I talked about fate, Luc moved his hands over the gun in what looked like reverence. The group could certainly have come up with more than one carbine during the war, and I couldn't see the butt end of the stock on this one, but I'd have been willing to bet my airplane ticket back to the States that he was holding the rifle that Julien wrote about. They were still using it to hunt!

"The newspaper happened to be on a news stand in Chicago, Illinois as I walked past on my way to get a cup of coffee," I went on. "I've walked past that stand a hundred times, and I never even noticed that it had a section with foreign newspapers in it. But that day, not even a week ago, that paper all but jumped off the rack and into my hands.

"Sipping my cup of coffee, I'd read through all of the articles and even a lot of the ads, and figured that I'd just wasted my dime. Then I turned the page and found the essay contest, and it was like Julien's words were the only ones on the page. His title, *A Kiss For Luck!*, leapt right out and grabbed hold of me. I read his essay, and I knew I had to write this story. *Your* story."

"This is the rifle, you know," Luc said, picking the gun up into his lap. "It still has the slip of paper inside it."

"May I?" I asked holding my hands out.

He checked that the safety was on, and handed it to me. "Careful. It's loaded," he said.

I turned it so I could see the right side of the stock.

There was a groove dug into the wood, and beyond the slot where the sling came through the stock, the groove turned into a hole. In my mind's eye, I had seen these features all jagged and splintered. The reality was that they had been sanded smooth. Which made perfect sense if you were going to continue to use the gun for its intended purpose.

I picked it up so I could see the end of the metal butt plate. I could see where a bulge had been hammered more or less flat again.

"When we get back to the house," I asked Luc, "will you open it up so I can see the slip?"

"It will give us something to do after dinner," Grampa Carlos answered, "while I tell you the history of *La Maqui de Julien*."

I looked quizzically at Julien and then at Luc.

"He's named after his uncle—my older brother—who died in the war."

I nodded solemnly. "I'm sorry to hear that," I said. "Will I hear that story?"

"You most certainly will!" Grampa Carlos assured me.

His grin made the phrase *Be careful what you wish for* leap to mind.

Dinner was excellent! I'll admit that I had my reservations about wild rabbit, but it was delicious. It cut with a fork, and had a slightly sweet, mildly gamey taste that reminded me—at the risk of being cliché—of chicken, only stronger. The stew was rounded out with carrots, onions, celery, and mushrooms. The bread was wonderful, and there was a red wine from the cellar beneath the kitchen. Five stars, all the way!

After Julien and Joyce had cleared away the dishes, Grampa Carlos began telling me his stories. Just from his theatrical style, I got the impression that he was embellishing somewhat, and every once in a while, Joyce would call out from the kitchen, "Now tell him how that *really* happened, Grampa," to keep him on track.

I was scribbling highlights on my note pad as fast as I could, and hoped that the notes would jog my memory for the details, later on. It had been a long time since I'd felt an article almost write itself like this one was doing.

When Joyce and Julien came back to the table, she stopped on the way and took the carbine down off of its hooks on the wall above the potbelly stove. Julien had cleaned and oiled the rifle as, I assume, part of his normal chores, so the magazine lay on the shelf above the stove. She nonetheless pulled back the bolt to make sure there was not a round in the firing chamber. She then laid the gun on the table in front of me.

"Would you like to see the slip of paper that Julien wrote about?" she asked me.

"I've spent my next paycheck and traveled halfway around the world to do *just* that!" I replied.

With an old, wooden-handled screwdriver, she loosened the bayonet band, pressed the release spring, and slid the band forward. She lifted the top half of the stock away, and then, holding the rifle so I could see, she lifted the barrel assembly.

There, cradled by the curve of the stock, nestled a piece of paper about an inch wide by about two inches long.

"Can I take it out?" I asked.

"Sure," Joyce said. "It's been out many times ... but it always goes back in. I couldn't imagine shooting the rifle without it anymore than without its sights or its trigger."

The way it fit, I half expected it to be stuck to the curve of the wood, but the slip lifted out easily. I suspected that the paper had started out perfectly white, but it was now a slight tan color, a little dirty, and slightly edge-worn. Age alone would probably have discolored it, but I guessed that sitting right against the hot barrel as the gun was being fired accelerated the process.

The lip print, too, was darker than I imagined it was when it was fresh. My mental image had been one of the bright red lipstick style of the '40's. The cursive words, *A Kiss For Luck!*, were still perfectly visible.

"Do you know if they put a slip like that into all of those guns?" Joyce asked me.

"I seriously doubt it," I said. "This would be completely out of military character, based on my experience with the Army."

"Would a soldier have done it?" she asked.

"Maybe one with very pretty lips?" Grampa Carlos suggested with a chuckle.

Joyce gave him a look, and said, "Very funny." She looked at me, and said, "You know what I mean."

"I guess that's possible," I said. "Maybe he clipped it off the bottom of a sweetheart's letter, and stuck it in there." I thought about that for a few moments, and said, "It seems unlikely, though. If I were going to keep something like that as a talisman, I'd put the slip in my wallet, not my gun. I'm thinking this might have been put in right on the assembly line."

I looked at the stamping on the barrel assembly, right behind the rear sight. Above the serial number the word "ROCK-OLA" was imprinted.

I chuckled, and said, "Well, that's a small world for you. This gun was made right in Chicago, not ten miles from where I live, and I had to travel over half the globe to see it."

I wrote the serial number on my pad.

As I sat looking at the disassembled rifle, imagining its parts going down an assembly line of young women—with pretty lips—a new thought began to take shape regarding the story I wanted to write. What if the slip *had* been put in back in Chicago? Could I trace its route through the war all the way from the Windy City to an old farmhouse in the middle of France? Now *that* would be a story!

I set the slip back into the stock, and started to reassemble the gun.

"Do you remember the date that they dropped the gun to you?" I asked Joyce.

"They darned near dropped it *on* her!" Grampa Carlos said.

"June of '44," she said. "It was a couple weeks after the Allies landed."

"June 23rd," Luc said. "I remember because that's my mother's birthday."

"God rest her soul," Grampa Carlos said, "I wonder if she had a hand in guiding the rifle to Joyce's hands."

After setting the barrel into the stock, I saw a small gouge in the top edge of the wood. And then I noticed that if I slid the slip down just a bit, the gouge lined up with a small tear in its corner.

I picked up the top of the stock, and saw a matching groove there. I looked closely at the barrel and saw a tiny dimple in the metal right next to the gouge and in the middle of the tear in the slip.

"Do you know how this happened?" I asked Joyce.

"No. It was there the first time I took the gun apart to clean the mud from it. The same time I found the note."

"There was no piece of shrapnel or anything inside?" I asked.

"I don't think so. I didn't find anything," she replied. "And look at this," she said. She set the top of the stock on top of the barrel and slid the bayonet band into place. "Doesn't it look like it's been hit by something here, too? More shrapnel, or even a bullet?"

There was a shallow indentation in the metal band that lined up with a groove of missing wood on the front of the barrel cover. The edges of the groove had been sanded smooth, but it sure did look like the two features could have been caused by a bullet passing through.

"I always wondered how the gun made it from the American Army to me," Joyce said. "It was obviously not new. Did somebody have to die for it to be sent off to us?"

"Unfortunately," I said, "that's how a lot of weapons changed hands. But there's something peculiar about this.

"When I was a correspondent near Normandy, not too long after D-Day," I explained, "I spent some time with an ordnance group that traveled just a little behind the front-line troops, and repaired anything that got broken. I sat and watched a dozen men one day, fixing rifles. They had a stack of about a hundred and fifty.

"How they did it was to take every gun apart, and throw all of the same kinds of pieces into separate steel pans. After they got all the guns apart, they cleaned everything in gasoline, and then they started putting them all back together, like an assembly line. All the pieces are interchangeable, so no gun ever went back together exactly the way it came in. Parts that were bent or broken they sent to one of their shops to be fixed, or they threw away. But by the end of the day they had a hundred or more good rifles put back together, ready to start shooting again."

"Do you think one of them might have put the slip in there?" Julien asked.

"Not a chance," I answered with a laugh. "They were far too busy to even think of something like that, and if they had, the slip would have greasy fingerprints rather than pretty lips."

"And that's the peculiar part," I went on. "As far as I know, a gun *always* went through small-arms repair before it was reissued. If a soldier was killed or even wounded, he couldn't tell anyone whether his gun might have jammed or misfired or something. And if it went through repair, there is no chance that that slip could have stayed inside the gun. That tells me that this rifle has an even more unique history than we think."

Saturday, May 8, 1954

The next morning the Arsenault household was awake with the sun. I looked at my watch and tried to remember the last time I'd gotten up before six in the morning. When I factored in the time-zone changes, it was quarter to twelve midnight; just about bedtime back home.

Being a city boy, I wasn't too much help with the daily chores, so I pitched in where I could, but mostly just stayed out of everyone's way.

After chores, breakfast consisted of coarsely-ground oatmeal, a fat sausage link—stuffed mostly with boar meat—and fried eggs that could only have been fresher if the hen had laid them directly into the pan.

A little later—still before I would normally be awake—I rode into town with Joyce. She was going to help out in the bakery, and I had a phone call to make.

As it was still not even two in the morning in Chicago, I had some time to kill before I could make my call if I expected Hank to answer without a string of expletives. So, once again, I figured I would help out where I could.

While I could say that I was more at home in a bakery than on a farm, that would only be true from an eating standpoint. So, I offered my services to Joyce's father, helping him load up the *kübelwagen* and make deliveries.

We made deliveries to a café and a small restaurant in Saint-Août, then drove north to Ambrault where we delivered a cake for a wedding reception. We then headed west to Sassierges-Saint-Germain, where *Le Parisien* came to the rescue of a hotel whose brick oven had collapsed, by dropping off a dozen loaves of bread. The final destination was the city of Ardentes, where we supplied three cafés with pastries.

The entire circuit was probably less than twenty miles, and during the drives between towns I tried to engage Vincent in conversation about Joyce as a young girl. I could have extracted his eye teeth more easily. I switched to his supposedly favorite subject, and was surprised at how difficult it was to get anything more than a yes or no answer from him even about Julien.

I finally realized that he wasn't being stoic, but that he was concentrating so hard on his driving that he almost couldn't answer. And even at that level of concentration, his skills were pretty marginal. It was obvious that his mother, and not his Pépé, had taught Julien to drive.

When we got back to the bakery, I still had at least four, and probably five hours to kill before I could expect a civilized answer from Chicago. I asked Joyce's mother if I could use her parlor, again, to sit and start putting my thoughts for the story on paper.

I had packed a new yellow legal pad so I'd be able to take notes when I got here, but I was now kicking myself for not having brought along my typewriter. It wasn't that I'd forgotten it; I had only envisioned doing research and interviews while I was here, not any actual writing. But the story was so alive in my head, right now, that it was almost bubbling out of my ears.

Four hours later, Joyce came upstairs with a plate of sandwiches, a cup of tea, and a pastry of some sort, covered in powdered sugar.

"I thought you might be hungry," she said as she set the plate down. "You've been busy, I see."

Almost half of the pages in the pad were flipped over, filled with my scrawling cursive and scratch-outs.

"Thank you! I hadn't really noticed," I said, putting the pad down, "but now that you mention it, I'm starving."

I reached for a sandwich and noticed her craning her neck to see what was written on the pad. I picked it up, flipped the pages back on top, and handed it to her.

"It's not polished, yet," I said. "I'll probably rewrite it twice before my editor gets *his* hands on it, and then make more changes after that."

As I chewed, I watched her face for a reaction. She worked her way down the first page—the grabber—and then with a disappointed look, handed the pad back to me.

I swallowed, and said with more than a little surprise, "You don't like it?"

"I don't know," she said. "I can't read it."

"Oh," I said with a relieved chuckle. "You don't read English." I had been speaking French since I landed—and it was getting better all the time—but I was writing in my native tongue.

"I read English," she said. "I can't read your writing."

I laughed. "And that's exactly why typewriters were invented," I said. "Maybe I'll read it to you after dinner, tonight."

She went back down to the bakery, and I finished two sandwiches while reading over what I had written, so far. I finished the pastry, and then looked at my watch. It would be half past seven in the morning in Chicago.

I got up, stretched my legs a bit, and then put on my jacket. I put a couple of pencils in my pocket, picked up my pad and hat, and headed downstairs.

Joyce directed me toward the post office, *La Poste*, where there would be a public telephone. Her mother offered to let me use theirs, but I didn't know how long I might be on the line, and I didn't want to tie up the bakery's only phone.

I waited until two o'clock—eight a.m. back home—before I dialed the operator. I had Hank's number in my address book, so that saved a little time by not having to go through directory assistance, but it was still a long process before I heard his voice on the other end of the line.

Sitting somewhere in between us, I could hear the long-distance operator in the US ask Hank, "Will you accept a collect call from one Rich Lawson in Saint-Août, France?"

"*France!?*" I heard him say.

"Just accept it, Hank," I said around the operator. "I'll pay you back."

"You'd better!" he told me. Then, with a distinct lack of enthusiasm, he said to the operator, "Yes, ma'am. I'll accept the charges."

"You may go ahead," she said to me, and then clicked off.

"Hi, Hank. Thanks for taking the call," I said. "I didn't wake you up, did I?"

"No. Half a dozen fire trucks going past did that about an hour ago," he said. "Why are you in France?"

Because I could almost hear the long-distance charge meter ticking with every word, I gave him a very brief version of my discovery of Julien's *A Kiss For Luck!* essay, meeting his mother, and seeing the actual rifle.

"So, what I need from you," I said spreading an absolutely true compliment on top of my request, "is your incomparable, never-failed-me-yet research talents."

"Flattery will get you everywhere," he said. "That and my usual fee."

"I wouldn't have it any other way," I said. In fact, there were researchers I'd used who charged half what Hank did per hour, but I'd found out—painfully—that you get what you pay for. They always took longer, and were never as accurate.

"What do you need?" he asked.

"I'd like to find out how this rifle—I have the serial number—got from the Rock-Ola plant in Chicago to a field in northern France. If you can dig it out, I'd like to know exactly when it was built, and the name of the soldier it was issued to. Then I need to know what happened to him. It's a good bet he was in the D-Day invasion, or arrived shortly after. I suspect he was killed or wounded. If you can follow the gun after that, it would be great, but I have a feeling the trail will go cold then." I then read the serial number to him, and had him repeat it back.

The thought of him wasting his time—and my money—chasing the wrong rifle was not the least bit amusing.

"Okay," he said. "You remember that this is Saturday, right? I won't be able to get into the military records I need until Monday."

"Damn!" I said. "I did forget that."

"So, will you be back by then?" he asked. "You want to come by and see what I have Monday night?"

"My ticket back is for tomorrow," I said, "but I think I'm going to change it. My gut tells me there's still more story over here. I'll give you a call Monday night, okay?"

"Okay," he said. "It's your dime."

"It's a whole boatload of dimes," I said, "but I really think this story is going to be worth it."

I walked back to the bakery, and asked Joyce if I could stay another day or two with her.

"Absolutely!" she said. "We've all enjoyed your company. And Julien mentioned this morning that you hadn't gotten the chance to cruise the pond on his raft."

I laughed. "Well, I hate to disappoint him," I said, "but I can't swim, so I don't see that happening. I'll try to make it up to him some other way."

"I think I know just the thing," she said, and shared her thought with me.

"That I can do," I agreed.

"I'll get Sylvia, a young girl in town here, to help out in the bakery tomorrow," Joyce said, "and we'll drive up north, and I'll show you some of the places where the stories you're writing about actually took place. Would that be helpful, do you think?"

"That would be fantastic!" I said. "Thank you!"

I used the phone in the bakery to call PanAm at Orly Airport, and cancel my reservation for tomorrow. The girl told me that the next open seat they had back to Chicago was next Thursday, the 10th, but that if I wanted to leave earlier, I should call to see if there were any cancellations—like mine—in the meantime.

I went back upstairs, and got back into my writing.

About 4:30 Joyce came up to get me, and we drove back to the farm.

We pulled into the yard and Joyce didn't even have the engine turned off before Grampa Carlos came up to her door carrying two five-gallon US-Army Jerry cans.

"I have to drive into town to get some kerosene for the stove," he said. "the tank sprung a leak last night, and we have only about a gallon left. Luc is fixing the hole."

"Where is Julien?" Joyce asked as they swapped places.

"He went down to check the traps," Grampa Carlos said. "I think the boar we shot yesterday had been scaring off all the rabbits. Maybe the traps will have better luck now."

Joyce went inside, and I went around the side of the house to see if I could help Luc. Not that I'm very mechanically inclined, mind you, but if he needed some gum chewed to stick in the hole, I figured I could be of assistance.

The kerosene tank was an old 55-gallon drum that was still mostly olive drab from it's time in the Army. It lay on its side on top of a pair of X's made out of wood. Luc was on his knees, working on the bottom near one end of the tank.

In his hand he held a stick that, judging by the knife lying on the ground and the shavings all around it, he had just sharpened to a point. He was twisting and pushing the stick up into the bottom of the tank. I noticed the stubs of two similar looking sticks on the top of the tank.

Noticing me standing there, he said, "Damn water gets into the barrel, and sits there on the bottom until it rusts right through." He pointed to the sticks on top, and said, "We turned the barrel over not a year ago. I thought we'd get a lot more time out of it."

"Hmm," I said, having absolutely nothing that I could contribute. I didn't actually have any gum, and doubted it would stand up to kerosene, anyway.

Just then, Joyce came around the corner.

"You need any help, Luc?" she asked.

"No. I'm about done. We need to find a new tank, though. This one's going to look like a porcupine before too long."

"We knew it was coming," she said. "We can't complain about getting eight or nine years out of a free barrel."

"Unfortunately, new one's aren't free," he said, getting up.

"Well, while you wash up," she said, "Mr. Lawson and I will walk down and see if Julien needs any help with the traps."

When we walked back around the corner of the house, she picked the carbine up from where she had leaned it against the back steps, and handed it to me.

"If you're going to be writing about it," she said, "I thought you might want to shoot it."

"Hell yes!" I said. "Thank you!" I caressed the gun, and felt probably the same way that Julien felt the first time they let him drive the car.

I slung the rifle over my shoulder, and we set off.

We followed the road that Julien had driven only about twenty yards, and then veered off onto a footpath. A short way in she stopped, and pointed to an area to our left.

"Its all grown over, now," she said, "but there are two SS soldiers and a Milice traitor buried right there."

She then proceeded to tell me a story that they intentionally withheld while Julien was with us last night. I knew that the French were a lot more liberated about all things sexual, but I understood why she might not want her eight-year-old son to hear the story of *La prostituée*, just yet.

Walking behind her in single file along a narrow part of the path, I was lost in thought about how to phrase the story she had just told me to get it past the magazine's censors. When we crested a small rise, she stopped so suddenly, I almost walked into her.

"*Ce vieux bâtard fou!* (That crazy old bastard!)" she whispered with an emphasis that went way beyond the volume of her words. "Give me the gun," she said quietly.

The expletive coming from her stunned me. I had never even heard her say *damn*. I slipped the rifle from my shoulder, and I looked over hers.

Down below, at the edge of the dirt road stood an old man. He was holding a shotgun ... which was pointed at Julien, who sat on a large rock with his back to us.

As Joyce took the magazine from her pocket, and snapped it quietly into the rifle, I asked into her ear, "Who the hell is that?"

She pulled the bolt back, and eased it forward, loading and cocking the gun almost silently.

"Gérard Cousteau," she answered me quietly through curling lips that added weight to the obvious hate in her voice. As she took hold of a small tree, and rested the rifle across her forearm, she went on, "He owns the farm next to ours, and is always accusing us of poaching his game."

"Keep your sights on him, but don't shoot," I whispered into her ear. "His gun could go off when you shoot him. I have an idea."

With that, I left her, and made my way, as noiselessly as I could, through the thirty feet or so of woods to the dirt road.

I began walking down the middle of the road, and whistling *The Happy Wanderer*, loud and clear ... and mostly in tune.

Apparently, the old guy was hard of hearing, because I was within about twenty yards of him before he heard me. He was yelling something at Julien—who still faced away from me—but over my own whistling I couldn't make it out, and I didn't want to *stop* whistling, because I wanted to give the old codger plenty of warning I was coming. Surprising an angry old man with a shotgun was not part of my plan.

Finally, he looked up and saw me. He swung the shotgun up at me, and demanded, "Who the hell are you?"

I held up my hands to show that I wasn't armed, and I have to admit that having a shotgun pointed at me by a lunatic didn't make me feel very comfortable—but at least it wasn't in Julien's face anymore.

Recalling Joyce's story about how they came into possession of the *kübelwagen*, I imagined that all I had to do was drop to the ground, and the old man would be dead. But I thought this could be resolved in a better way.

At the sound of my voice, Julien spun around. "Mr. Lawson! What are *you* doing here?"

There were tears streaming down his face, and I seriously contemplated dropping to the ground.

But I stuck with my original plan.

"I've come to collect you," I said in a stern voice. To the old man, I said, "What's the little son-of-bitch been doing now? Poaching, again?"

"Exactly!" the man bellowed. "And this time his mother and father are going to pay me for my rabbits or they'll not get their son back, by God!" As he spoke, the gun lowered a little, and I felt better having him thinking I was on his side.

"You know who his mother is, don't you?" I asked.

"Of course. Joyce Arsenault," he answered.

"Joyce *Renaud*-Arsenault," I corrected him. "The Nazis called her the Sniper of Sebastian. She's a crack shot with a rifle ... and she's up on the hill right now, aiming right at your chest."

His eyes went wide, and he spun his head to look up into the woods. Joyce wasn't trying to hide in the least, and he found her right away.

I reached out and took the shotgun away from him. Julien jumped up and ran to my side.

In less than a minute, Joyce had joined the little group.

She jabbed the barrel of the carbine into the old man's chest, and snarled, "If you *ever* threaten my son again, no one in this world will stop me from filling your worthless body full of holes! Do you understand me?"

Not as full of fear as I might have expected—certainly not as much as I would have been facing an enraged Joyce Renaud—he replied, "The boy stole from me! He's poached my rabbits, *again*! I am within my rights to protect my property!"

"All of his traps are on *our* farm!" Joyce shouted back. "How do you think that's poaching?"

As she spoke, I slowly reached over and guided the barrel of the carbine away from the old man's chest, lest there be an accident.

"The rabbits' warren is on *my* farm! They are *my* rabbits!" he yelled back.

"You old fool!" she shouted as I gently removed the gun from her hands. "They're *wild* rabbits! They multiply and they find new homes! How do you know where *any* of them live? And where they run is up to the rabbits. They don't see any property lines. You don't own them any more than we own the ducks who land on our pond and that you shoot when they fly over your fields!"

Somehow, that simple logic had eluded him until just then, but it was obvious from his softening expression that the argument made sense.

Then, in one of those gestures that gives you faith in the younger generation, Julien said, "I caught four, Mr. Cousteau. You can have two, if you need them."

He looked down at the boy, and just stared at him for several seconds. Finally, he reached out and tousled his hair, and said, "Thank you, son. But you went to the work of catching them; you should keep them."

He looked up at Joyce, and said sadly, "I'm sorry, Mrs. Arsenault. I suppose you're right. The game is wild, and there is plenty for everyone, now. Sometimes I find myself remembering the occupation days."

I handed him back his shotgun, but kept the carbine in my hands. I like to have faith in humankind, but I wasn't dumb enough to think that one sunshine moment like that was going to melt the ice from a seventy-year-old curmudgeon. But I also didn't think that *he* was dumb enough to shoot at three people who were armed with a semi-automatic rifle, when he had only a single-shot breach-loading 20 gauge shotgun.

As we walked away from each other, Joyce hugged Julien to her side, and said to me, "Thank you, Mr. Lawson. I was quite ready to kill him, you know."

"I got that," I said. "But as much as I enjoy your company, staying around for who-knows-how-long to testify at a French murder trial would probably have made me miss my deadline."

As we walked, Joyce said to Julien, "Let's not tell your Papa and your Grampa about all that, okay? They might worry about you going down to the pond alone."

She gave me a wink that I took to mean that that wasn't the real reason. At least not all of it. My guess was that if Luc and Grampa Carlos knew that old man Cousteau had threatened Julien with a shotgun, there would be *four* bodies buried in the woods.

As we came out of the woods near the house, Luc was walking toward us.

"I was getting worried," he said. "I thought somebody might have fallen off the raft."

"No," Julien said. "We ran into Mr. Cousteau."

I don't know about Joyce, but *my* heart stopped.

"We caught four rabbit's," Julien went on, "so I said he could have two, if he wanted. He said he didn't."

Luc looked at Joyce. She just shrugged.

"Interesting old guy," I said.

Luc looked at Julien, and said, "That was very nice of you, son. Very nice."

He looked at me, and said, "Gérard is not always the most pleasant of neighbors."

"Really?" I said. "Hmm."

After dinner, Joyce announced that everyone was going to pile into the car in the morning, and drive north so they could show me some of their battlefields.

"Aw!" Julien complained. "I wanted to take Mr. Lawson on my raft tomorrow."

"I have to be honest with you, Julien," I said as I helped him clear away the dishes, "I'm afraid of water. I can't swim."

"Really? But you're a grown up."

"In most regards, I usually am," I said, "But I just never learned to swim when I was a kid."

"I could teach you!" he offered.

"Thanks anyway, but I think I'm getting to be too old of a dog to learn that new trick," I told him. "But something I'm not afraid of is heights. I'd really like to spend the night in your fort in the loft, if you think there's enough room."

"*Really?* The whole night?"

"Yeah, why not? There aren't too many haylofts in Chicago anymore since Mrs. O'Leary's cow burnt the city down."

"A cow burnt down your city?" he said.

"I'll tell you about it, tonight," I said. "Let's get the dishes done."

A Kiss For Luck!

Later on, approaching nine o'clock, while Julien and his mother were rearranging the bedding in the fort, Luc pulled me aside out in the back yard.

"What went on down at the pond today?" he asked me.

"Pretty much what Julien said," I replied.

He just looked at me waiting for more.

"Look, Joyce didn't want you to get angry, or worried, okay? When we got there, Julien and Mr. Cousteau where having a ... *disagreement*. But Julien didn't run away from him or anything. He held his ground. You'd have been proud of him, I think."

"A disagreement? Did the old man threaten him?" he asked.

"Not that I heard," I answered honestly. "When Joyce and I got there she got into a debate with him about who owns the rabbits and the ducks, and eventually they agreed that they're fair game. Your wife can be quite persuasive, you know. That's when Julien offered him the rabbits, just like he said. He turned them down, and that was about the end of it."

He looked at me without saying anything for a long few seconds.

Finally, he said, "The old man's crazy, you know. I don't trust him."

Then, from the barn Julien's voice called, "Mr. Lawson! It's all ready!"

"Coming!" I answered. To Luc, I said, "Wish me luck," and then headed toward the barn.

While I climbed the vertical ladder to the loft, Julien held a flashlight above me, shining down on the rungs ... and into my eyes. Very helpful.

I crawled through a small door, and was then able to stand up, more or less straight, inside the fort. A hurricane lantern hung from a nail in a rafter, and threw off a surprising amount of light.

Julien gave his mother a hug and a kiss, and she started for the ladder. I peeked out to make sure Luc wasn't down there, and then quickly recounted my conversation with him to both of them. In case he felt the need to continue asking questions, I wanted us all on the same page.

Not that I had any reason for wanting to deceive Luc, I just had a strong interest in preserving the family peace. My mother ran interference on my dad more than once, and I'm probably able to sit for long periods today because of it. God bless her!

As Joyce descended the ladder, she stopped with her head at door height.

Looking up at Julien, she said, "Don't leave the flashlight on for a long time. You'll wear out the batteries, and you're not getting any more." She looked at me, and said, "No smoking in here."

I clicked my heels, and snapped a salute as I said, "*Oui! Mon Capitaine!*" I nudged Julien, and he snapped a salute, too.

She laughed. "Try to get some sleep; it'll be an early morning," she said as she climbed down out of sight.

Julien closed the little door, and I looked around *Fort Julien*. The corner of the loft had been walled off using old doors and planks nailed into place, and there was one window with four small panes of glass that allowed for observation of an enemy approaching from below. At the moment, it had a burlap curtain drawn over it. At the back wall, where the roof pitched down to about four feet, was a small table. Next to it was a three legged stool, and a wooden crate. The banquet hall, I presumed.

"This is quite a place you've got here. Did you build it yourself?"

"I thought it up," he said with obvious pride. "But Grampa Carlos helped me with the doors and the big stuff,"

I stuck my hand through a two-inch space between two of the doors, and asked, "Why the gap?"

"It's an arrow slit!" he said. "That was my Mom's idea. Cool, huh?"

"Ah, yes. I see that, now. Very clever. Shoot at your attacker without exposing yourself."

I walked over and sat down on the crate. I stretched my legs out and leaned back against the wall. "So, where did all the doors and the window come from?" I asked him.

"There's an old house, way past the pond, that got hit by a bomb during the war," he explained. "Nobody lives there."

He sat down on the stool, and said, "Tell me about how the cow burnt down your city."

About an hour later we were both storied-out, and decided to hit the hay ... literally. Two beds had been fashioned from armloads of hay with a couple of blankets spread over it.

Julien crawled between his blankets, I turned out the lantern, and he turned on the flashlight while I tucked myself in.

The hay mattress was surprisingly comfortable, and it brought me back to one of the more comfortable places I ever slept during the war. Most nights it had been under a pup tent, stretched over a fox hole, with nothing but a thin bedroll separating me from the often-wet ground. We correspondents lived just like the front-line troops we were covering. Thinking back on that experience, this was downright palatial.

Julien was asleep in about two minutes, but my mind was churning with thoughts about the story.

If I was going to put in all of the vignettes of Joyce's wartime experiences—which I wanted to do—the article was going to get too long, pretty quickly. And if Hank was able to come through for me with more background on the rifle, there might be—would *hopefully* be—even more stories to tell. I wondered if Dave could arrange a serialized story in the magazine, over two or three months.

As I laid there with my hands behind my head, staring up into the darkness, the thought of turning the article into a book began to form.

I've always wanted to write an actual book, and even started a few times. The first one—before the war, when I wasn't even living there—was going to be a history of Chicago. Which is how I come to know so much about Mrs. O'Leary's cow, I guess. The war pulled me away from that, and I was never able to get into it again after I got back. Somehow the fascination with the city waned when I was actually living there.

After the war, I started a book about my time as a correspondent, but quickly realized that it was going to look like a me-too copy of Ernie Pyle's books, and I lost interest.

The third was a hard-boiled detective novel titled *Dead Letter Delivery*, a la Mickey Spillane and Dashiell Hammett. I was happy with how my characters were developing in that one, but the plot never really gelled for me. I realized that fiction was just not my forte.

The more I thought about it, the more I liked the idea of *this* book, however. Of course, it all hinged on what Hank would be able to pull together for me. I had faith in *him*, but it was whether anything that he came up with would be as remotely interesting as Joyce's story that would make the difference.

Sunday, May 9, 1954

We headed north, early in the morning. I sat in the back seat of the *kübelwagen* with Joyce and Julien, and was surprised at how comfortable it was ... at least compared to my memories of riding in the back of a Jeep with two soldiers.

The first stop was the site of Joyce's first-ever military action as a freedom fighter.

Luc parked the car near the railroad tracks, and we walked up the hillside to a stone wall. I had already heard the story, but seeing where it all happened made it come alive.

I brought my Leica 35mm camera along, and I took a number of pictures. I wanted to take a lot more, but I had only brought three rolls of Kodachrome with me, so I had to be careful.

Julien had to pull away some weeds to uncover them, but he found the "arrow slits" in the wall that his mother and father had made, and pointed them out to me. He then proceeded to lie on his belly and aim along the stick that had become his imaginary rifle.

I looked at the front of the wall, and could clearly see the marks where bullets had struck almost eleven years ago.

We walked a short distance into the woods behind the wall, and came to a clearing that seemed out of place among the growth of brush, vines, saplings, and weeds.

As I watched, the four of them began to "police the area." They yanked saplings out of the ground, pulled weeds, and dragged vines that couldn't be broken off back into the undergrowth. On their knees, Joyce and Julien cleared away the grass and leaves from a spot near the center of the clearing to reveal two stone markers set flush into the ground.

I stepped forward, and read the carved lettering on them. The one on the left read, "*Yvon Lamont; Died June 10, 1943.*" The other read "*Julien Arsenault; Died June 11, 1943.*" They both had the same inscription under the dates. "*A True Patriot Who Gave His All to His Beloved France.*"

I had no idea what to say. I just stood there staring at the markers.

Finally, Joyce stood up, and said, "Yvon died here during the attack on the train. Julien was wounded at almost the same time as Yvon, but he died the next day. We know he'd have wanted to be buried up here, so after the war we moved his body and set these stones. We come up every month or two to keep the woods at bay."

"Do you mind if I take a picture?" I asked.

"No, of course not," she said. "I'm sure they would be honored if they were mentioned in your article."

"Oh, they will be, " I said as I set the aperture for the shade of the woods.

With the grounds-keeping done, the four of them formed a circle around the stones, and joined hands. They bowed their heads, but then Julien looked up, and said to his mother, "Can Mr. Lawson be in the circle?"

She looked at me, and asked, "Would you like to?"

"It would be my privilege," I said as I stepped forward. I took Joyce and Julien's hands, and we bowed our heads.

"Heavenly Father," Grampa Carlos began, "Hear our prayer that no more like Yvon and Julien need perish to bring about your promise of peace on earth. Please guide us and all of those in the seats of power to find peaceful means to settle our differences, to forgive transgressions, and to live in harmony on earth until it is our time to be at Your side in Heaven. We ask these things in the name of the Father, of the Son, and of the Holy Ghost. Amen."

"Amen," we all repeated. I didn't look closely at the others, but I had tears in *my* eyes.

On our way back down the hill, I asked Joyce quietly, "Did you tell him about Julien's *differences* with Mr. Cousteau?"

"No, of course not," she answered.

"Spooky," I said.

The next leg of the journey took almost seven hours. Although I thought the *kübelwagen* was reasonably comfortable when we started out, it lost it's charm before we made it to Tours, two hours farther away.

We drove through Tours, Le Mans, and Caen, needing only one fuel stop, but numerous stretching breaks.

It was close to five o'clock in the evening when we reached the area south of Saint-Lô where they had toppled the train off the trestle and acquired the *kübelwagen* .

None of the former *Maqui de Julien* had been back since that day, and young Julien had never seen it at all.

The wood trestle had been replaced by a steel span over the ravine, and there were now two sets of tracks, so that trains could travel north and south at the same time.

To satisfy my own curiosity, we drove north into the city of Saint-Lô. I was surprised at how much it had been rebuilt. When I walked through the city almost ten years ago, it was a complete ruin. I don't believe there was a single building that was not hopelessly damaged. I had heard that they—whoever *they* are—had talked about leaving it in ruins as a war memorial. I'm glad they decided against it.

We had dinner in Saint-Lô, and then headed south. We drove through Sebastian, and Joyce pointed out the rooftop from which the "Sniper of Sebastian"—all three of them—fired. Farther south and east we followed an overgrown road to the barn they used as a hideout. It had completely collapsed into the stone basement.

Our last stop was the town where Joyce and Luc had been captured by Franz on the night that the rifle saved her life. The ruins of the bombed-out warehouse were completely gone, replaced by a block of apartments.

We drove out of town on the road that Joyce and Luc had taken that night, and with a little difficulty found the field where Franz found out he was screwing with the wrong woman. It was now mostly filled in with small trees and brush.

It was almost three in the morning before we made it back to the farm, with all of us—except Julien—taking turns driving. And that wasn't because Julien didn't *ask* every time we stopped to switch drivers.

Monday, May 10 1954

Life on a farm, even a small one, has little respect for what time you went to bed. The rooster began crowing before 6:30, and everyone groaned their way out of bed to start the day.

It was going to be a long day for me. In order to let Hank have enough time to work his magic after the records archives opened, I would have to wait until about ten at night—four p.m. his time—to call him. Of course, at ten p.m. *La Poste* would be closed, so Joyce's mother graciously agreed to let me use the bakery's phone.

I pitched in where I could around the farm, but to say that I was being very helpful was generous, indeed. Probably my greatest contribution was pulling vegetables straight out of the garden, and cutting them up to go with the wild-boar roast that Luc was cooking for dinner.

Aside from that, I spent most of the day working on my long-hand draft of the story. About mid-day, I took a break to bring the carbine outside, disassemble it, and take half a roll of photos of it in the sunlight.

I also took a nap up in Julien's fort.

After dinner—during which I concluded that wild rabbit tastes better than wild boar—I decided to walk the mile and a half into town, if for no other reason than to burn some time.

I got to the bakery about 9:30, and of course it was closed. I found the key under the flowerpot, and let myself in. When the connection finally made it through to Hank, he accepted the charges, right away, and I asked, "Any luck?"

"This may be the easiest assignment you've ever given me," he said. "God bless the Army's obsessive record keeping."

"Seriously? That's fantastic! What have you got," I said, with my pencil poised above my pad.

"United States Carbine, Caliber .30, M1, serial number 6,152,649," he began. "It was assembled at the Rock-Ola Music Company in Chicago, Illinois, on May 9th, 1944, on the swing shift. It shipped to Boston, Mass. the following day on the New York Central rail system, and left Boston Harbor aboard the Liberty ship *Donald E. Shea* on May 16th.

"The *Shea* apparently had some mechanical difficulties at sea, because she fell out of the convoy, and arrived in Halifax a day late. She left Halifax with the convoy on the 21st, and arrived in Liverpool on June 5th—one day before D-Day.

"On June 6th your rifle was issued to one McCormick, Kenneth William, a sergeant with the 729th Ordnance Light Maintenance Company of the 29th Infantry. The form he signed has the note, 'Weapon has defect on right forestock.' written on it in pencil. It doesn't say what kind of defect."

"It's a little hole," I said, "between the two halves of the wooden stock. I'm surprised anyone even noticed it, much less bothered to write it down. But it's good information; it means it happened before the rifle ever saw combat."

"And that's where the trail ends, I'm afraid," Hank said. "From there the rifle is listed as lost."

"Well, it's been found," I said. "Did you happen to find out anything about McCormick? Was he killed or wounded, or MIA?"

"Wounded on June 22nd," Hank said. "Evacuated to Queen Elizabeth Hospital in Birmingham, England. He recovered, but was listed as unfit for combat duty, and reassigned to the Quartermaster Corps. He served the rest of the war in England, and was discharged on October 11th, 1945."

"Do you know where he is now?" I asked. I'm sure the anticipation in my voice made it through, even across four thousand miles of telephone cable.

"When the Army was done with him," he answered, "they stopped keeping records on him."

"Damn," I said. "Well, can you see what you can dig up in some other way?" I asked, mentally watching another day drag by.

"Somehow, old buddy," he said, "I just knew you'd want to know that. He lives at 717 King's Lane, Birmingham, England. He has a wife and a daughter."

"That is *fantastic*, Hank!" I said. "You are the best!"

"A fact that will be reflected in my bill," he said. He wasn't joking, but at the moment, I didn't care.

"Did you happen to stumble upon his phone number?" I asked.

"I don't *stumble* upon anything," he said with overacted indignance. "I plan, I research, I find."

"Sorry. I stand corrected," I said, humbly. "You should translate that into Latin and put it on your letterhead. So, did you happen to ascertain Mr. McCormick's telephone number during your explorations?"

"I like the letterhead idea," he said with a laugh. "And yes, I did ... of course. That's what I do." He read it off to me, and I wrote it down.

"Thanks, Hank. I really appreciate this," I told him. "I don't know how you do it, and I'm not going to ask."

"Just as well," he said. "I wouldn't tell you. Once you know how the trick is done, it isn't magic anymore, and you'd no longer see me as the God I am."

I laughed. "Well, I promise to genuflect the next time I see you," I said. "In the meantime, don't close out the bill. Can you see if you can find out what happened to that Liberty ship. It's a long shot, but somewhere between the Rock-Ola plant and when McCormick got the rifle something put a hole in the stock."

"Factory defect?" he offered.

"Possible, I guess," I said. "Do you think you can excavate the name of anyone at Rock-Ola who might know if that kind of thing could happen, and if it would pass inspection if it did?"

"I'll see what I can do," he said. "At least that's in my own time zone."

"I'll give you a call about the same time, tomorrow, okay?"

"Talk to you then. Happy writing!"

I hung up, and looked at my watch. Although Birmingham would be in *my* current time zone, it was quarter to ten at night. As much as I wanted to talk to Sergeant McCormick, getting him out of bed to do it probably wouldn't be very ingratiating.

I turned off the light, and headed for the front door. Through the window I saw Joyce sitting there in the *kübelwagen*. I closed the door, locked it, and put the key back where I'd found it.

"This is a pleasant surprise," I said as I climbed into the car. "Nothing's wrong, I hope."

"There's no moon tonight," she said, pulling from the curb and making U-turn. "I didn't want you getting lost."

"Thanks. I hoped to avoid that, too. I didn't think to bring a flashlight."

"So, how did your call go?" she asked.

"Great! I think I found out who had the rifle before you got it. And he's still alive *and* he's in England."

"Fantastic! Did you call him?"

"Tomorrow. I don't want to drag him out of bed if he's sleeping. But I'm just going to introduce myself, I think. I want to actually meet him before I talk about the rifle with him."

"Why?" she asked.

"A few reasons, really," I said. "First, it's likely to be a long conversation, and it is still long-distance even if it's not to America. Second, I want to see his reaction when I tell him what the rifle's been through since he had it. But the third reason is probably the biggest.

"There's no doubt in my mind," I told her, "that your part of the story is going to be far better—more alive—for my having been here and meeting you and your family and experiencing the places where the rifle has been. I can only hope that meeting McCormick, face to face, adds that kind of spark to his piece of the story, as well."

"Well, it's been a pleasure having you here, Mr. Lawson," she said. "Julien is so excited that his essay is going to make his mother famous."

"His lips to God's ear," I said. "His mother deserves it. You're a remarkable woman, Joyce Renaud-Arsenault. Luc is a very lucky man. I like to think that if I'd met you while I was over here then, I'd have had the good sense to try to marry you, too."

"I'm flattered, but unless you had been prepared to live in France, I'd have said no. I didn't risk my life to leave."

"Understandable," I said. "And I couldn't wait to get back to the States ... no offense to France. So, was it love at first sight with you and Luc? You certainly seem well suited."

"I think Luc might have been interested in me when I joined the maqui, but in all honesty I hardly noticed him, at first. His big brother, Julien, was a commanding presence in the group, and he made it pretty obvious that *he* had his sights set on me."

"Was the feeling mutual?"

"There were a few fleeting moments," she laughed. "God rest his soul, Julien was the most overbearing womanizer I think I've ever met. But I pretended to be interested in him so I could cut my teeth killing Nazis with his maqui."

She then told me about having to share a bed with him, and what that was like, but later tricking him into sharing a kiss with his own incorrigible manhood. I laughed out loud at the image she painted.

"You must have really wanted to kill Nazis," I said, "to have put up with that."

"Don't get me wrong," she said. "Julien was a true patriot, a great leader, and even a great teacher—I'd never even held a rifle before I met him. He just had a weakness for women that caused his groin to do all of his thinking whenever one was around."

I laughed again. "I've known a few men like that," I said. "In English, we call them *sex-oholics*. I don't know if you have a direct translation, but it's someone who gets just as stupid about sex as an alcoholic gets about booze. All control, all logic goes right out the window."

"That's a good description," she said as we descended the hill toward the farmhouse.

"Should I put that story in the article," I asked her, "or do you want to keep it private? I understand it's kind of personal."

She thought about it for a few moments, and then looked at me, and said, "I guess if I really wanted to keep it a secret any longer, I wouldn't have told a globe-trotting author, would I? I'll leave it up to you if you want to include it."

"What do you mean *keep it a secret any longer*?" I asked as we pulled to a stop by the barn. "You mean from young Julien, right?" I had an idea that was not what she meant.

"Luc and Carlos have never heard that story, either," she said.

"And you're leaving it up to *me* to decide whether or not they should hear it? Thanks a lot!"

She laughed. "Sometimes knowing the truth is a burden, no?"

Tuesday, May 11, 1954

If all went well, I would soon be on my way to England. I packed and said good-bye to everyone, complete with the two-cheek kissing thing. Julien hugged me so tight, he actually made me cry, the little bugger.

He wanted to skip school to ride with his mother and me up to Issoudun where I would catch the train north, but she nixed that. Apparently he had a history test that morning, and she didn't want him to have to repeat the exam any more than repeating history.

Joyce drove me into town, and stayed to help at the bakery while I headed for one of the phone booths at *La Poste* with a pocket full of change.

The connection to Birmingham went through far faster than my calls to the States, and I soon heard the other phone ringing.

"4467," I heard when the phone was picked up. I had completely forgotten that folks in England answered the phone with the last four digits of their number, and it threw me for a second. And until I heard the British accent, I had been ready to introduce myself in French.

"Good morning," I said in English for the first time in days. "My name is Rich Lawson. I'm trying to reach Kenneth McCormick. Is he in by chance?"

"May I ask what it's concerning?" she asked with an almost musical lilt. I always loved a proper British accent ... especially from women.

"Yes, of course. I'm a writer with an American magazine, and I'm researching an article on GIs who stayed in England after the war," I fibbed.

"*Life Magazine*?" she asked.

"Not the one you're thinking of, I'm sure," I said. "It's a monthly called *Global Life*."

"I see," she said. "Well, he'll be at the shop, at this hour. You can ring him up there, if you like, but I dare say he won't have much time to talk with you. He's been without a helper for a fortnight now, and he's dreadfully busy."

"I understand," I said. "I'll be very brief, I assure you. Do you happen to have that number?"

She told it to me, and I wrote it down.

The phone at the shop was answered on the third ring.

"Hello. Birmingham Bicycle. Kenny speaking. What can I do for you?"

"Good morning, Mr. McCormick," I said. "My name is Rich Lawson. I'm a writer for an American magazine, and I'm researching an article on GIs who stayed in England after the war. I wonder if you'd be interested in talking with me."

"Are you the Rich Lawson who was a correspondent in Europe during the war?" he asked.

"I am," I said, surprised at his question. "I'm flattered that you remember my name."

"I was with the 729th Ordnance Company," he said. "You spent some time with my outfit. I was back in England with my arm in a sling by then, but I remember reading your dispatch about us in *Stars and Stripes*."

"My God! You're right! I knew the 729th sounded familiar!" I said. "What a small world! I was just talking about your outfit the other day. I was telling some folks how you repaired and reissued rifles."

"I was with the motor pool," he said. "but that was my company, alright. So, what is it you want to talk about?"

Half an hour later I was standing next to the *kübelwagen* at the train depot in Issoudun. I hugged Joyce, and kissed both of her cheeks.

"It is a pleasure and an honor to have met you, Joyce Renaud-Arsenault," I said. "I truly hope that we'll see each other, again. I will definitely keep in touch as my article takes shape."

"Thank you," she said. "From all of us, but especially Julien. I'm sure he could never have imagined this when he was writing that essay for the newspaper."

"Don't be *too* sure," I said with a chuckle. "He showed me a pretty limitless imagination when I spent the night in his fort with him. I think he's going to go places. You're a lucky mom, and he's a lucky son."

She leaned in and surprised me with a light kiss on the lips. "That's a kiss for luck," she said.

I smiled kind of dopily, and my eyes welled up.

She smiled, a little damp-eyed herself, and pointed to the train. "Go," she said, "you have an article to write."

As I took my seat by the window, I watched her weave the bright yellow car through the traffic, and head for home.

It was 3:00 in the afternoon when I reached Calais on the French side of the English Channel. I made my way to the ferry terminal, and then found a public phone so I could check in with Hank.

"I talked with an Army inspector who worked in a Garand factory," he told me, "and he said he couldn't speak for all of his counterparts, but he personally would not have passed a rifle with the kind of defect that you told me about. Something like that, the guy said, even though only cosmetic, would have been relatively easy to repair with wood filler, so *he* would have made sure it was done.

"Which makes the next piece of the puzzle all the more intriguing," Hank went on. "It seems that just before the Liberty ship *Shea* left Boston Harbor, an FBI agent boarded, and rode with her to Halifax, where he got off and returned to New York. I poked around a little, and that was very uncommon, apparently. Agents *boarded* ships all the time, but they never *sailed* with them."

"No record of *why* he sailed with them, huh?" I asked.

"I'm sure there is," Hank said, "I just haven't found it, yet. The FBI is even more obsessive about recordkeeping than the Army, they're just a lot more tight-fisted."

I thanked him, told him where I was and where I was heading, and said that I'd check in with him tomorrow, if I could.

It was almost 4:30 when I got off the ferry in Dover on the English side of the Channel, and another four hour train ride finally brought me to Birmingham New Street Station.

I found a pay phone and called the McCormick residence. Kenny suggested a place to meet, and I hailed a taxi that dropped me in front of a pub called the *Bishop and Bear*.

I was met at the door by a huge man who could have inspired the bear half of the pub's name. He led me to an empty booth in the back corner.

"Lily and Kenny will be along directly," he said in an accent so thick it was a wonder he didn't have to chew the words to get them out. "They told me to make you feel at home. So, what'll it be, mate?"

"A pint of your darkest ale," I said. "Thanks."

Five minutes later, a couple walked in who appeared to be the right age. They had a little girl with them who looked to be six or seven. She held her mother's hand, and was carrying a cloth doll under the other arm. Cute kid.

They walked straight to my table, and the man stuck out his hand. "Kenny McCormick," he said. "This is my wife Lily, and our daughter Margaret."

"Rich Lawson," I replied standing up. "It's a pleasure to meet all of you," I said as I shook hands down the line. I was surprised to find that I actually missed the cheek-kissing thing. "Thank you for meeting with me."

The *bear*—whose name I learned was Tom Laughlin—returned and took our order of kidney pie, all around.

"I used to have the kidney pie when I was in London in '44," I said. "As I recall, there was a lot more pie than kidney, back then."

"Oh, it's *wonderful*, now!" Lily said. "You shant be disappointed, I promise!"

Not wanting to admit that I had lured them there under the false pretence of an article I wasn't really writing, as we drank our pints, and Margaret her ginger ale, I asked Kenny about his decision to stay on in England when the war ended. He told me about his year-long courtship with Lily, and his rivalry for her affections with a Britt named Haversham, whom he eventually knocked out in a boxing match in their Army camp.

"Tell him the bit about your rifle," Lily said to him.

"Yes, the rifle," Kenny said as the kidney pies showed up. "That's another reason why I'm here. And not just here in *England*, but here at *all*. I was issued an M1 Carbine on D-Day, and it saved my life when a couple guys from my company and I chased down a Panzer tank in a Jeep."

"In a Jeep?" I repeated. "That seems rather risky. You must have done some fancy shooting to have pulled that off with a carbine."

"I did kill the commander of the tank with the it," he said, "but what saved my life was that the rifle deflected a bullet that was heading for my chest, off into my shoulder. When I was evacuated back here, I even ended up in the same hospital where Lily was a nurse."

"You *ended up*," Lily scoffed. "You made well and sure you'd *end up* at Queen Elizabeth," she said with a delightful chuckle. "Tell him that part of your story now."

"Well, when I was waiting in the CO's tent for an ambulance to bring me back to the beachhead," Kenny began, "This OSS captain comes in looking for any weapons he can scavenge to parachute to the French Resistance. I still had the carbine with me, so, with my CO's permission, I donated it to the cause, since it was only going to get reassigned anyway.

"In conversation I happened to mention that I had a sweetheart working at Queen Elizabeth Hospital, so in return for my rifle, he wrote me a letter that said I was a part of some secret OSS operation, and had to be delivered to that hospital, and none other."

"And that worked, huh?" I said with a chuckle.

"The rest is history," he said with a slight nod toward Margaret.

"Do you know what happened to the rifle after that?" I asked.

"No idea," he told me. "I've often wondered, though."

"Tell him what you found inside it," Lily said to him.

"Well, I was just killing time in the staging area down south on D-Day, waiting to be called up to board one of the ships. So, just out of curiosity, I decided to take my new rifle apart, just to see what made it tick, you know? Mechanical things fascinate me. Well, you know what I found inside it, tucked underneath the barrel?"

"A slip of paper with '*A Kiss For Luck!*' written over a pair of lips?" I answered.

Kenny and Lily both stared at me with their mouths open. I love surprises!

"How did you ..." Kenny began to ask, but then it clicked, and he said, "You found it! You found my rifle!"

I nodded with a big smile. "It ended up in the hands of a remarkable young woman—a freedom fighter named Joyce Renaud—that I have just spent the past few days visiting. It saved her life, too."

"*She still has it?*" he asked excitedly.

"She does," I answered. "Her family still uses it to hunt game for the dinner table, *and* it still has the slip inside it. I've held it in my hand."

"You're joking!" Lily said. "After all these years?"

"It's a little dark from age, but she says it's as much a part of the rifle as the trigger or the sights."

"My God," Kenny said thoughtfully as he leaned back in the booth. "It really did carry good luck with it."

"It sure seems that way," I said.

"You know," Lily said, leaning forward almost conspiratorially, "It seems to me that a story about this *kiss for luck* rifle might be more interesting to your readers than talking about Yankee expatriates."

"I think you may be onto something there, Mrs. McCormick," I said. "It has certainly piqued *my* interest."

I turned back to Kenny, and said, "When you found the slip, why didn't you take it out and keep it? Put it in your wallet, or something?"

"I thought about it," he said. "But then the same thought struck me that occurred to Miss Renaud; the slip is part of the rifle. If the slip brings good luck, it's a package deal."

"When you had the rifle apart," I asked, "did you notice a gouge in the wood of the stock between the upper and lower halves?"

"Yes! Yes, I did! Do you know what caused it?"

"I was hoping *you* could tell *me*," I said. "I guessed—correctly, apparently—that the gouge in the bayonet band and the top of the stock were caused by a bullet, but the groove between the halves of the stock seems too small for that."

"And where would it have happened?" he said. "The sergeant that issued me the rifle said it was fresh off the ship, right out of the crate."

I looked at Lily, and said, "An element of mystery is added to our story."

She chuckled, and said, "I love it!"

We enjoyed a slice of pudding for dessert (yes, a *slice* of pudding), and another pint as Kenny and Lily filled in details about their year before D-Day. I wasn't sure how much of it I might use in my final story, but it was obvious they were enjoying reminiscing.

While Kenny reenacted the Jeep-versus-tank episode with a pack of cigarettes for the tank, the top off the salt shaker for the turret, a toothpick for the cannon, and a box of matches, for the Jeep, Margaret stretched out in the booth, and using her mother's pocketbook as a pillow, went to sleep with her doll hugged under her arms. I suspect she had heard the story many times before, but I could only imagine how enthralled Julien would be with it, if *he* were here.

Finally, Lily announced that they needed to be going home. Tomorrow was a work and school day. And she had an early appointment for a portrait sitting.

"Do you have a place to stay for the night?" Kenny asked me.

"The whole trip over here from Saint-Août happened rather fast," I said. "I didn't have a chance to call ahead for reservations. Can you recommend something?"

He and Lily looked at each other and smiled.

"I believe we can," Lily said as she waved to get Tom's attention.

"There's a small room upstairs that Tom rents out," Kenny said. "It's where I stayed the first time I came up to visit Lily."

"Perfect!" I said. "Maybe it will give me inspiration for the story."

"I certainly hope not!" Lily giggled quietly to Kenny. The lighting was dim, but I thought I saw the color come up in her cheeks. If my story was going to be a work of adult fiction, I thought to myself, I could probably come up with a whole chapter based on that giggle alone.

Wednesday, May 12, 1954

The next morning, after breakfast downstairs in the pub, I sat at the booth in the front window, and wrote in my pad until it was full. Tom gave me directions to a store where I could probably get another pad, and also pointed out that Kenny's bicycle shop was not far beyond it.

It was about three miles to the shop, and I could have taken a taxi, but I did some of my best thinking when I walked, and I had plenty of time to kill before I could call Hank, again.

The store Tom sent me to had exactly what I wanted, and I bought two pads, just in case, and a better pencil sharpener than the one I'd brought with me. They also had a nice little Underwood typewriter in a handy carrying case. I was very tempted to buy it, imagining myself typing away on the long flight back to Chicago. But then I thought about how the clicking and clacking would probably annoy the heck out of whoever was sitting next to me, and decided against it. Besides, what would I do with two typewriters when I got home?

As I left the store, I noticed a big display of art supplies. Oil paints, brushes, colored pencils, that sort of thing. I wondered if this was where Kenny had bought the set of pencils that he told me about giving Lily on their first date.

Kenny's bike shop wasn't hard to find. It had a three-foot tall model of an old fashioned "penny farthing" bicycle—the kind with a huge front wheel and a tiny rear one—hanging out over the sidewalk.

I looked around as Kenny waited on a couple of customers, and put the chain back on the sprockets for a little girl.

"Nice place you've got here," I said when he was free. "You seem to keep pretty busy."

"*Too* busy with my helper gone," he said. "You know anything about fixing bicycles, by any chance?"

I laughed. "I can ride one," I said, "and that's about the extent of it."

"Pity," he said. "I have a pair of coveralls that would fit you just dandy."

"What happened to your helper," I asked. "He quit?"

"Broke his fool leg in a bicycle race. I'll be lucky to see him back in a month," he said. The front door opened, and a man dragged in a bike with a badly bent rear wheel. "The tenth anniversary of D-Day is coming up," Kenny said as he went to assist the man. "I have a lot of bikes I can rent to the tourists, but I'm going to need help keeping up."

"Well, I'll get out of your way," I said, "But if I meet any mechanically inclined people on the way back to the pub, I'll send them your way."

As it turned out, I did. About halfway back, a girl—perhaps 17 or 18—zipped past me on one of those bicycles with all the gears on the back wheel for shifting speeds. The bike wasn't a racer—at least not anymore—because it had a wire-frame basket mounted on each side of the rear wheel, and a whicker one on the handlebars. There were small packages and envelopes in the baskets. I got the impression that she either was, or worked for, a delivery service.

A little way up the street I watched her slow down and come to a stop at the curb. I expected her to carry something into the nearby building, but instead, she got off and crouched down by the rear wheel.

As I got closer, I could see her fiddling with the gizmo that moves the chain back and forth over the gears. Apparently satisfied with whatever she was doing, she strung the chain back over the sprockets, stood up, and pulled a rag from her pants pocket.

"You look like you've done that before," I said as I came abreast of her.

"I've a frayed derailleur cable that keeps stretching," she said as she wiped her hands. "One of these times I'm not going to be able to adjust it any further."

"You should buy a new one," I said, giving Kenny a plug. "There's a bicycle shop about a mile back that way."

"I know," she said. "I pass it every day. The problem is being able to afford it. I'm lucky to have enough for my share of the rent every week." She swung her leg up over her trusty steed, and said, "And talking isn't getting deliveries made. Been nice chatting with you, though."

"He's hiring, you know," I said just as she was about to shove off.

She checked her launch, and said, "Who's hiring?"

"The guy who runs the bike shop," I said. "You look like you know something about bicycles; you should drop in and talk with him."

She looked up the road—although the shop was out of sight—and then at her baskets full of packages. "I will!" she said to me. "Thanks! Who can I say sent me around?"

"Rich Lawson," I said.

She extended her hand, and as I shook it, she said, "Darcy Haversham. Pleased to make your acquaintance."

"My pleasure," I said after a split-second of shocked pause that I don't think she noticed. I had to resist the urge—which wasn't easy—to ask if she had an uncle or a brother or something who fancied himself a boxer during the war. "Good luck!" I called after her, as she pushed off into the road. She gave me a wave in reply.

It is truly a small world! I chuckled to myself as I walked on.

When I got back to the *Bishop and Bear*, I ordered a ham sandwich and a cup of coffee for lunch, and took it upstairs to my room. The pub was beginning to see its lunch crowd wander in, and I didn't want to take up a table while I sat and wrote. Besides, it was beginning to get a little noisy.

In the quiet of my little attic retreat, I filled up a few more pages while I ate, and then stretched out on the small bed to relax and think about how I would arrange all of these vignettes into a book if I decided to go that way. I think I was asleep in about a minute and a half.

I looked at my watch when I woke up. It was three o'clock. I didn't realize I was that tired. I decided to blame it on farm living and having a rooster for an alarm clock.

I took a short walk to get the blood pumping again, and then went back to writing up in my room.

About four-thirty, Tom's wife shouted up the stairwell to tell me that Lily was on the phone for me.

She invited me to dinner at their house at 6:00, and gave me directions.

I took a bath in the washroom a floor below. The tub was bigger than the one in Joyce's farmhouse, but I really missed the pounding spray of the shower in my apartment. I shaved, ran some Brylcreem through my hair, made myself otherwise presentable, and then went downstairs to mingle in the pub.

About quarter past five, I decided to give Hank a call. It would only be eleven-fifteen, his time, but maybe he had had a lucky morning searching for details about that Liberty ship.

The pub had a phone booth in the back that shut out most of the noise.

"You're going to *love* this!" Hank said after the call was connected. "I managed to actually talk with the FBI agent who was onboard the *Shea* when she sailed out of Boston Harbor."

"You're kidding me! How did you find him so fast?"

"Sometimes it's knowing where to look, and other times, it's knowing who to ask," he said.

"What's his name?" I asked, pencil poised.

"I can't tell you that."

"What?"

"He would only talk to me if I guaranteed that his name would never show up in connection with anything he told me."

"I know how to protect sources," I said, "I won't print it if he doesn't want me to."

"I know you won't," Hank said, "because I'm not going to give it to you, old buddy. Look, this guy could be a really good source for me in the future—he kind of likes to talk. On top of that, crossing an FBI agent, in general, is not a good idea, if you know what I mean. So, do you want to hear what I have from an anonymous source, or should I flush it?"

"Take your fingers off the lever and back away from the toilet," I said. "I'll take it."

"Well, it seems there was an unidentified Nazi saboteur aboard the *Shea* when she sailed, and my guy was sent onboard—by Hoover himself—to infiltrate the crew and figure out who it was.

"He figured it out, but when he did, the guy took a hostage and barricaded himself inside the long compartment where the propeller shaft goes. He called it the shaft alley. The spy managed to stop the ship dead in the water, and the word was that a U-boat was in the area.

"My guy had a shootout with the Nazi, but he ended up the loser when he took a bullet through the wrist closing a watertight door to protect the rest of the crew.

"Finally, he recruited the smallest guy in the crew to crawl down through this bulkhead labyrinth thing with a rifle he had them borrow from the hold of the ship. The guy killed the Kraut by emptying a whole magazine into him."

"*And it's the same gun?*" I asked, nearly shouting I was so excited.

"I don't actually know that," Hank said. "My guy didn't think to write down the serial number. But he did say that he was sure it was an M1 carbine. He doesn't know what happened to it when everything was over."

I just sat there in the booth, completely deflated. So close!

"But cheer up," Hank said. "All is not lost just because my guy didn't write down the serial number. Remember who you hired for this job. I have someone digging for the *Shea's* crew manifest even as we speak. My guy remembers the kid's first name being Frank, so that should narrow it down when I get the list."

"He didn't even write down the kid's last name?" I said, not hiding my displeasure very well. "I thought FBI agents were supposed to be all meticulous and everything."

"It's in his report," Hank said, "he just doesn't remember it from ten years ago. And the file is still classified, so he couldn't very well go and pull it out to refresh his memory. Don't worry; I'll figure out who Frank is."

"Sorry," I said. "I didn't mean to question your sleuthing abilities. This is actually really good information. I appreciate it."

"Don't worry about it," he said. "Give me a few more hours—oh, let's say four o'clock, my time. Can you call me back, then? I think I should have the names off manifest by then."

"I'm off to dinner at the McCormick's," I told him, "I can't imagine it running later than that—that's ten o'clock over here. And I'm finally staying in a place that has a phone."

I thanked him again, and hung up.

I sat there for a minute and tried to imagine how the hole I had seen in the side of the gun—which I had convinced myself was made by shrapnel—could have gotten there aboard a ship that wasn't bombed or torpedoed.

A knock on the phone booth door snapped me back to the then and there, and I forced the question out of my mind, and put my faith in Hank.

On my way to the McCormick's I had the taxi stop so I could pick up a couple of bottles of wine—a red and a white—and a box of chocolates; can't-miss gestures when invited for dinner, according to Emily Post. Except, of course, when you don't know that your hostess is allergic to chocolate and wine gives her a headache.

Kenny and Lily were gracious in accepting my gifts, but they had to laugh. "You needn't fret over it," Lily told me. "You couldn't have known. And goodness knows Margaret will enjoy the chocolates, and Kenny the wine."

Kenny then told me the story of how his rival had set him up for failure more than ten years ago by telling him that wine and chocolates were Lily's favorite things.

As Kenny opened the white, he said to Lily, "I had someone pop into the shop this afternoon asking about a helper's position."

I had planned on asking him about that.

"That's wonderful," Lily said as she sliced a loaf of bread. "And you hadn't even taken out an advertisement. Does he seem right?"

"It was actually a young woman," he said, "but she seems to know her way all around a bicycle. Her name is Darcy Haversham."

"Oh my," Lily said as she stopped slicing and turned to look at Kenny. "Do you suppose Charles would have sent her 'round?"

Kenny looked at me.

"Actually, I did," I said with a kind of stupid smile.

"Good heavens, why?" Lily asked.

I told them the story of seeing her fix her bike on the sidewalk after leaving Kenny's shop. "It seemed like one of those out-of-the-blue serendipitous moments," I said, "so I suggested she drop by. I didn't even know her name until she was pedaling off."

Kenny chuckled. "What a crazy coincidence," he said. He turned to Lily, and went on, "She told me she's a distant cousin to Charles. She's only met him at a family wedding and a funeral. Says she doesn't care much for him, but that it's okay because he cares enough for himself to make up for it several times over."

Lily laughed. "Well then, you should hire her straight away if she has the talents you need," she said. "Goodness knows she's a good judge of character. She should get on fine with your customers."

Before we sat down to dinner, Kenny took his watch out of his pocket and handed it to me. It was a fairly ordinary watch on a short leather fob. But on the other end of the fob hung a deformed bullet.

"I meant to show that to you last night. It's the slug they dug out of my shoulder," he said. "My million-dollar wound. It's a 7.65mm, fired from a Mauser pistol."

"An interesting good luck charm," I said, and I told them about Joyce's.

"Every time I look at my watch," he said with a nod toward Lily and Margaret, "it reminds me how lucky I *am*."

While we ate, I noticed a frame, about a foot square, on the dining room wall, with what I thought were two wallet-sized photographs matted in the middle of it. Later on, I looked closer, and saw that they were both pencil sketches. The top one was a goldfinch, and the other was a very small portrait of Kenny and Lily.

Kenny saw me studying them, and he said, "Lily did those. The goldfinch even before we met, and she gave me the portrait when I left her to go join the troops for the invasion." He then proceeded to tell me their stories.

Dinner was a pork shoulder with cabbage. I had recognized the smell as soon as I walked into the house, and it sent me back in time and space all the way to my grandmother's kitchen for Sunday dinner. And the taste was exactly the way I remembered. What a marvelous evening!

I walked back to the pub to kill time, and to think. It was a quarter to ten when I got there. I went upstairs to get my pad and some pencils, and head back down to the telephone. It was occupied, so I ordered a pint while I waited.

"When did you say you were leaving for home?" Hank asked me after the normal pleasantries.

"I didn't," I said, "but I think I'm pretty well done over here. Why?"

"That kiss for luck thing must be rubbing off on you," he said. "Do you know what date the *Shea* sailed out of Boston with your gun onboard?"

"If you told me, it's in my notes, but don't make me look."

"Well, I did. It was May 16th, 1944. Do you know what this coming Sunday is?"

I did some quick counting, and answered, "The 16th."

"Ten years to the day that she sailed with your rifle, and was almost sunk by a saboteur. The crew is having a reunion in Boston this weekend. You think you can make it?"

"If I have to swim!" I said. "That's fantastic! Do you know if Frank whatever-his-name-is is going to be there?"

"I talked with a guy named Rudy Norcross, who was the Chief Engineer on the *Shea*, and he told me that as of a month ago, Frank—his last name is Hendricks, by the way—was going to be there. They were in port on different ships in New Orleans, and Frank told him he was going to arrange his next few trips to make sure he was there."

"Did you tell him about me, and what I'm doing? I wouldn't want to just show up and crash their party."

"I did, and he said you'd be welcome. These guys love telling their war stories, apparently. They're meeting at the Lenox Hotel in Boston."

"Fantastic!" I repeated. "You were the best before, now you're even better!"

"And closer to home," he said, "I also have the name and phone number of the girl who was the assembly-line lead on the shift when your gun was put together. Her married name is Maggie Olson, but she was Maggie Kelly at that time." He gave me her phone number—a South Bend exchange, but at least she was in the Chicago time zone. I was getting pretty tired of traveling.

After I hung up from Hank, I dialed the operator, and had her connect me to the PanAm office at Heathrow. There was no answer. At a little after ten at night it was a long shot.

The next morning, I got my return-flight ticket changed, packed, and headed for the train station. I stopped at Kenny's bike shop on the way, because I wanted to take a picture of his "million dollar" watch fob. While I was there, Darcy gave me a kiss on the cheek for giving her the tip about the job.

The train ride to Heathrow took two hours, and I had to wait around another three before the airplane started to board. The flight to Boston took almost twelve hours, but I got a fair amount of writing, and a lot of sleeping done while in the air.

Friday, May 14, 1954

Because of the time-shift thing, it was eight o'clock Friday night when I landed at Logan Airport in Boston.

"Lenox Hotel?" I said to the cabbie leaning against his yellow car in front of the terminal.

"Sure thing," he said as he opened the back door for me. I climbed in with my suitcase, and he ran around to slide in behind the wheel.

"So, what're you in town for?" he asked as he dropped the flag.

"A ten-year reunion," I answered, opening up a brand new pack of Winstons. I lit up and cracked my window to let the smoke out.

"School reunion?" he asked, "or something to do with the war?"

"War," I told him. "A Liberty ship named the *Donald E. Shea* sailed out of Boston Harbor ten years ago Sunday. The crew's in town this weekend to reminisce and catch up."

"Hey, thanks for your service, pal," he said, "I had a brother that sailed on Liberties and Victories; I know you merchant marines didn't get nearly the credit you deserved for sailing those floating targets, and dodging torpedoes."

"I'll be sure to pass that on to the crew," I said, "but I'm a writer here to interview some of them."

"*Life Magazine*?" he asked.

"A book, if everything keeps going as well as it has been," I told him.

Ten minutes later—which included an unnerving trip through the Sumner Tunnel under Boston Harbor—I was walking across the lobby of the Lenox toward the registration desk.

"Hi, I need a single room for tonight and tomorrow night," I told the clerk, a very efficient looking gentleman with a pencil mustache. Then I added, "I'm here for the *Donald E. Shea* reunion." Can't hurt to mention that, I figured; sometimes groups get a discount. I didn't.

I put my stuff in my room, and went down to the dining room. As I passed the registration desk, a big guy was checking in, and I overheard him say the name Donald E. Shea. Since Liberty ships were almost always named after people who had died—usually at sea—I figured it was a good bet that he wasn't introducing himself.

I waited until he was done, and as he turned around, I said, "You're here for the *Shea* reunion?"

He looked me up and down, and then said, "You Lawson? The writer guy?"

"Then you must be Mr. Norcross," I said as I extended my hand. "Pleased to meet you. Thanks for letting me crash your party."

"Rudy," he said shaking my hand. "You may be sorry before you're done; these guys'll talk your ear off then pick it up and keep talkin' into it."

I laughed, and said, "Well, just call me Vincent Van Gogh then, as long as I get the scoop on your trip ten tears ago."

He laughed and slapped me on the arm. "Hank said you were a likeable guy," he told me. Then he leaned in, lowered his voice a little, and said, "He also said you'd buy me dinner."

"Well, I'd hate to make Hank out to be a liar ... on either count," I chuckled. "You want to put your stuff in your room, and meet me in the dining room?"

Ten minutes later we were at a corner table, and a shapely young waitress came over to take our drink order. When she leaned over to set the little napkins on the table, I swear you could see between her breasts all the way to her belly button. We ordered two beers, and then watched her behind wiggle its way back to the bar.

"It's rude to stare like that, you know," I told Rudy.

"If we weren't lookin', she wouldn't be doin' her job," he said. "She didn't paint that skirt over her butt tonight to be comfortable. You know where the word *tips* comes from, don't you? It's a contraction of *tits* and *hips*."

I laughed, and said, "Somebody told me it stood for To Insure Prompt Service."

"Not in any waterfront bar I've ever been in," he said. "And I've been in a few."

He held up his left hand, and said, "You see those two missing fingers?"

"Not really," I said, "they're missing. I do see the other ones, though."

"Hank told me you wrote for a magazine, wise guy," Rudy said, "not the funny papers. So, you know how I lost 'em? I was in Baltimore, and I got in a bar room fight over a babe that would make tootsie here look like Olive Oyl. A guy smashed a bottle on the edge of a table, and I put my hand up to keep him from slitting my throat."

Suddenly, Rudy's story was interrupted by a deep voice from behind us. "A busted beer bottle brawl over a babe in a bar in Baltimore?" the man said. "Try saying *that* three times fast."

We both turned to see a tall thin man walking up to the table.

"God save us!" the man said. "Another how-I-lost-my-fingers story."

"Howard! You skinny old son of a dog!" Rudy said as he stood up. They wrapped their arms around each other, and slapped each others backs ... there was no cheek kissing.

I stood up, and Rudy said, "Rick Lawson, this is Howard Walsh. One of the least capable first assistants I ever had the misfortune to sail with."

"And Rudy taught me every single thing I know," Howard said. We shook hands, and he said, "Pleased to meet you Rick. Were you one of the Navy boys onboard? Can't say I recognize you."

"It's Rich," I said. "And no, I wasn't on the *Shea*. I'm a writer ..."

"He's finally going to tell the world about how we almost got sunk by a Nazi spy," Rudy told him. Then he turned to me, and said, "You think they'll make it into a movie? I want William Powell to play me."

"*William Powell*?" Howard said. "William Powell doesn't look anything like you."

"I know," Rudy laughed, "that's why I want him!"

"Well, then I'll get Jimmy Stewart for me," Howard said.

The waitress returned with our beers, and broke up the Hollywood fantasy.

"Who's your friend?" Howard asked Rudy while staring at the waitress.

"Name's Holly," she said with a big smile—equal, I'm sure, to the size of the tip she was hoping for. "What can I get you from the bar?"

"Beer," answered Rudy as he dragged out a chair for Howard. "Then wait about five minutes, and bring another round. I'll tell you when to stop."

I sipped my beer and listened to the two sailors catching up. In the last eight years—since the last time they'd seen each other—Howard had apparently gotten his Chief's rating, and the two of them threw names of ships and captains back and forth like namedropping at a Park Avenue cocktail party.

Just before Holly came back with the second round of beers, a different waitress—a little older, and a lot more modest—came over to take our dinner order.

By the time the meal came, I had to ask my dinner companions, "So, did you guys actually sail on the *Shea*? I think I've heard the name of about every ship in the merchant fleet—at least on the Atlantic side—*but* the *Shea*."

"What do you want to know?" Rudy asked as he sliced into his prime rib.

"Tell me about your saboteur," I said breaking my cod apart with my fork.

When Rudy had told me that *they'll talk your ear off* he wasn't kidding. But he should have said *we'll* talk your ear off, because he certainly had no problem eating and talking at the same time.

The story they told me was the unabridged—read as *long-winded*—version of the synopsis that Hank had passed on to me from his FBI guy. The general outline was the same, but I had the feeling I was getting more accurate detail from the two sailors, especially when it came to the FBI agent's part in the drama.

To clarify a point, but also to do a little fishing, I asked, "So, the FBI agent ... what was his name again?"

"O'Hara," Howard said.

"Yeah. Craig O'Hara," Rudy confirmed.

"That's right!" I agreed with a snap of my fingers. "O'Hara." I had to smile to myself for getting the name without Hank's help. Not that I would use it without permission, but it felt good having it in my pocket.

I went on with my question, "So, O'Hara lost the only gun that the crew had to the Nazi saboteur—this kid they called Narrow—down in the shaft alley. Is that right?"

"You got it!" Howard said as he wiped the spaghetti sauce off of his plate with a slice of bread.

"To be fair," Rudy said, "He dropped it when he got shot in the arm trying to ambush the kid, but the result was that the kid had two guns and a hostage, and we had a U-boat coming up our butt."

"Whose idea was it to use one of the rifles from the cargo hold?" I asked, suspicious that it might not have been O'Hara's.

"That whole thing was Hendricks' idea," Rudy said. "He remembered seeing the rifle crates in the hold, and volunteered to climb down through the peak tank. I think he was extra pissed off, because the Nazi kid had used him to get more time down in the shaft alley to do his dirty-work."

"So, what do you know about the rifle that Hendricks used?" I asked, finally getting to the million-dollar question.

"Standard issue M1 carbine, as far as I know," Rudy said as he finished his salad. "Not much else *to* know."

"Did it go back in the hold when everything was over?" I asked.

"Yeah. Hendricks cleaned it, oiled it up, and we put it back like nothing ever happened," Rudy said. "O'Hara said the whole sabotage thing had to be kept top secret."

"Are you aware of there being anything *unusual* about the gun?"

"Like what?" Rudy asked as another round of beers appeared.

"Something tucked inside it?" I said. "A slip of paper?"

"Not to my knowledge," Rudy said. "I never saw the gun while Hendricks was cleaning it, and I can't speak for him, but if he found anything inside the gun, he didn't tell *me* about it."

That was *not* the answer I was hoping for.

"How about some damage to the front part of the stock?" I tried. He wouldn't have needed to see the gun taken apart to have seen that. "A small hole on the right side, just between the upper and lower halves of wood?"

He thought for a few seconds with his beer glass to his lips, but not drinking.

"Nope," he said, finally, then pulled a swallow of beer. "I don't remember any hole in the gun. As far as I know, it went back into the crate exactly the way it came out."

My heart sank. If I'd been in a cartoon, there would have been a drawing of a book with wings on it, over my head and flying away.

"You look disappointed that the gun didn't have a hole in it," Howard said.

I never did have a poker-face.

"Just 'cause Rudy here says he don't remember a hole," Howard went on, "don't mean it didn't have one. He don't even remember where he lost his fingers!" he laughed loudly, and followed it by draining his glass.

Rudy backhanded him across the arm. To me, he said, "I will say that I didn't *inspect* it before we put it back. The only one who'll know for sure, will be Hendricks, probably."

"He is coming, isn't he?" I asked, trying to lift my hopes back up.

"He said he was a month ago," Rudy told me. "But that old rust-bucket he was going out on when I saw him in New Orleans could'a broke down or even sunk between there and Brazil."

I'm sure my mouth hung open at that prospect, and both Rudy and Howard burst out laughing.

"Don't worry," Rudy said. "Ships these days don't keep radio silence like we had to on the *Shea*. If anything had happened, he'd be able to let us know. And his ship is no rusting tub, either. It's only about three years old. Twin steam turbines."

When we finished eating and talking, it was about eleven at night. By then, after a week overseas, I was adjusted to European time, so it felt like four in the afternoon to me. They went up to their rooms, and I picked up the checks.

I charged it all to my room after adding tips to both the dinner and the bar tabs. I left a little extra for Holly. She was a pleasant, professional, and efficient waitress ... not to mention very easy on the eyes. My generous tip was just one more example of us men being easily manipulated by women. I wouldn't have it any other way.

Saturday, May 15, 1954

The maid knocking on the door to come in and clean at 10:30 woke me up the next morning. I washed up, shaved, and went down to the dining room.

I was in that grey area where I could order either breakfast or lunch. I got two eggs, over easy, and an English muffin. The eggs were okay, but *nothing* like what I had been eating on Joyce's farm. The English muffin—which, interestingly, isn't even call a muffin in England, but a crumpet—was a little overdone. A little extra butter and some strawberry preserves made up for it, though.

When I was done, I went to the registration desk to see if Hendricks had checked in last night or this morning. His reservation was still open. Don't panic, I told myself. There's still 24 hours.

I found a quiet corner in the lobby—where I could see the front desk—and sat down with my pad to sort through the notes I had jotted down before going to bed last night ... actually this morning.

The details Rudy and Howard gave me about the sailing of the *Shea* were great, but the one connection I really needed—that the *Kiss for Luck!* gun was used to kill the saboteur—was missing.

From Hank's research, I could be reasonably sure that the gun had traveled from Boston to Liverpool on the *Shea*, and I could probably make the story work with that alone, but the real grabber to the book I had in mind was an uninterrupted chain of lucky events spanning the whole life of the gun.

And of course, I could always lie and *say* it was the same gun, and who—with the possible exception of Hendricks—could say otherwise? But I wouldn't do that. Non-fiction should never have the qualifier "mostly" attached to it.

As I flipped my pages of notes, the name Maggie Kelly-Olson caught my eye. Hank told me that she was the lead on the assembly line when the gun was put together. I wondered what she might know about the slip being put inside. Was it something they put into all of the guns they built? Or was it an Irish Sweepstakes one-of a-kind thing that they did for just one lucky GI?

I found another chair next to a lobby phone, and asked the hotel operator to put through a call to Indiana, and charge it to my room account.

When she put me through, a man answered the phone. "Hello, is this Mr. Olson?" I asked.

"Yes. Who is this?"

"Hi, my name is Rich Lawson," I said. "I'm a writer, and I'm doing a story on ..."

"Are you the war correspondent?" he asked.

"It seems like a lifetime ago," I answered, "but yes, I was. Did we meet once?"

"No," he said. "I was stationed stateside. But I used to read your stuff all the time. You and Ernie Pyle."

"Ernie was a hell of a guy," I said. "We shared a tent in France more than once. It's a shame he didn't make it to see the end."

"Yeah," he said. "So unfair. So, what can I do for you?"

"I'm doing a story about M1 carbines that were made in the Rock-Ola plant, and ..."

"You're the second guy that's called about that in just a couple days," he said.

"That would have been Hank Logan," I said. "He was doing some background research for me."

"Yeah, that was his name," he said, "So, what can I tell you?"

"I'd actually like to talk to your wife, formerly Maggie *Kelly*, if I could," I said. "I understand she was a lead on one of the assembly lines at Rock-Ola."

"She was. It's where we met," he told me. "I'm afraid she not in, right now. She's visiting her sister over in Gary."

"You worked at Rock-Ola, too, huh? What'd you do there?"

"I was a final inspector with the Quartermaster Corps.," he said.

Final inspector? My heart skipped a beat. I had to wonder why Hank didn't tell me that. Had I really uncovered something he'd missed? There would be some ribbing about *that*!

"Let me ask you," I said, "as a final inspector, you'd know all the parts that went into one of those guns, wouldn't you?"

"Absolutely," he said.

"Was there ever anything *extra* put into any of those guns, by any chance?" I asked.

There was a long pause, and then he answered, "Extra? Like what?"

"Like a slip of paper with a note on it?"

Another long pause.

"You found one of them, huh?" he said.

I didn't know what emotion I should attach to *that*. On the one hand, he apparently knew something about the slip, but on the other hand he said *them*, rather than *it*.

"So, how many were there?" I asked, not really wanting to know.

"I have no direct knowledge of any slips aside from the one that I found and removed during a random lot inspection," he answered.

I was intrigued by his *official-ese* phrasing. "And would you have any *indirect* knowledge of such slips?" I asked.

"My career is still with the Army, Mr. Lawson," he said, "so no; none that I would care to comment on."

"I see," I said, understanding that nothing ever happened too early in one's military career that its later discovery couldn't screw up the next promotion.

"But I *can* put you in touch with someone who *would* have knowledge of multiple slips ... if they did, indeed, exist," he said. "Her name is Betty Driscoll. She was Betty Hancock, at the time. We've stayed friendly with her and Josh over the years." Then he gave me her phone number in Chicago.

It looked like I had pulled off yet another coup over Hank!

I charged another call to my room, and had the operator dial Betty's number. No answer after fifteen rings. I was disappointed, but not despondent. I'd try again later.

I went back to organizing my notes, but then changed my mind. I put my pad back in my room, got a map from the concierge, and headed out to walk the *Freedom Trail*.

By the time I was done exploring the USS *Constitution*—Old Ironsides—I decided I'd walked enough, and took a taxi the three miles back to the hotel.

I asked at the desk about Hendricks, but he still wasn't there. Then from my room, I tried Betty's number, again, but still got no answer. On the off chance I wrote it down wrong, I had the operator check the number for me. Naturally, the phone wouldn't be listed in Betty's name, and I had to wrack my brain to remember what Olson had said her husband's name was, since I didn't think to write it down. Then it came to me; Josh!

I had the number right, and while I had her on the line, I asked the operator to try to connect me. Still nothing.

The rest of the afternoon included a sandwich from room service, organizing my notes about the *Shea* into an outline for that part of the story, and a nap.

Before I went down to dinner, I tried Betty, again. Nothing. At the desk, I asked about Hendricks, again. Nothing.

That I couldn't reach Betty didn't worry me at all. She was probably just away for the day, and she lived in my home town. But the thought of Hendricks as a no-show was beginning to concern me. If I missed him this weekend, tracking him down and arranging another meeting could be difficult. His job took him, literally, all over the world.

In the dining room. I looked for Rudy and Howard, but they weren't there. I suspected that more of their shipmates may have shown up during the day, and they were out hitting some of their old haunts. It was a pretty safe bet that they wouldn't normally stay in a place like the Lenox while they were in port.

I got a table for two for one, and settled in on the side where I could watch the rest of the room, and look out into the lobby. I didn't know what Hendricks looked like, but I was going to react to just about any male who looked the right age.

Holly came over, and said with a big smile, "Good evening, Mr. Lawson. I'm glad you decided to join us again. What can I get you from the bar?"

"I'm thinking of the T-bone, tonight," I said. "What's your house merlot?"

"It's a 1953 Awful," she said in a low voice. "The cab is good, but I think the shiraz is the best red we have."

"Thanks for the warning," I said with a laugh. "The shiraz it is."

While she was gone, the other waitress came and took my dinner order. When Holly brought the wine back, she hovered around the table, needlessly adjusting the centerpiece, folding the napkin and straightening the silverware for a nonexistent dinner partner. I got the impression she wanted to say something to me, but was stuck in one of those circles of inner debate.

She finally said, "I'll check back to see how you're doing in a little while," and walked off.

Two-thirds of the way through my steak, she apparently noticed that my glass of wine was nearly empty, and brought over a full one. "On the house," she said with her usual smile. Again, she lingered, and again, she left without saying anything.

After dessert of crème brulee and a cup of coffee, I signed both of the checks—with Holly's insider tip about the wine reflected in *her* tip—and headed for the front desk to check on Hendricks, again.

As I left the dining room, Holly came out behind me. "Mr. Lawson, could I talk to you for a minute?"

"Sure," I said, never one to turn down a conversation with a pretty woman. "What can I do for you?"

"Well, I wanted ... I just ..."

It was strange to see her tongue-tied after the way she had chatted so easily with the three of us last night, and with me just a little while earlier.

"I wanted to thank you for the tip last night," she finally managed. "And tonight, too. That was very generous of you."

I wasn't sure why *that* was so hard to say, but I replied, "You're very welcome, but you deserved it. You're a great waitress. You should give lessons."

"I'm even better at other things," she said.

I didn't know what that was supposed to mean, at first, but after a moment, the pieces finally clicked into place for me. The extra glass of wine; her special attentiveness tonight while I was alone; pulling me aside outside of the dining room; her nervousness. She was *propositioning* me!

"I see," I said. "Well, thank you anyways, Holly. I do find you quite attractive, but I have some notes I need to work on tonight, and then I'm going to turn in early. I think I walked over half of Boston today."

She looked at me curiously for a few seconds, and then *her* light bulb went on. Her eyes went wide and she said, "Oh! No, Mr. Lawson! *That's* not what I meant! Oh, no! No! That came out *all* wrong, didn't it?" she hid her face in her hands, and mumbled through them, "I am *so* embarrassed!"

"I guess I should be embarrassed, too, then," I said. "And I apologize. I apparently misunderstood *something*. What *did* you mean? What *other things* are you better at?"

"Secretarial things," she answered. "You know, typing, shorthand, editing, those kinds of things."

"Oh, I see," I said with a tone that indicated, *I have no idea why you're telling me this*.

"Well, I know you're a writer," she said, "and I saw you in the lobby with a legal pad and pencil, and I thought maybe you could use somebody to type up your notes and help you keep things organized."

"Waitressing isn't keeping the bills paid?" I asked.

"It's okay," she said, "but I have a degree from Smith that's collecting dust while I wait tables."

"Really?" I said. "In what?"

"Education, actually," she said. "But I found out I really don't like teaching, so I became a secretary."

"So, this is part time?" I said, nodding toward the bar.

"No. I got fired, and I'm doing this while I'm looking. I have to pay the rent, you know."

"Fired?" I said.

"Oh, not because of my work," she said quickly. "My boss's wife made him fire me because she didn't think he could be trusted around me."

"And could he?"

"Hell no! I never encouraged him, and I certainly never gave in to him, but he was always trying to put the make on me. I was actually a little relieved when he fired me. Although he has called me a couple of times, *since* he let me go ... the jerk."

"I see," I said, as my eyes flicked for just a second to her low-cut blouse. She noticed, and brought her hand up to cover her chest.

"This is *not* what I wore to the office, I assure you," she said. "This is ... well, it's ..."

"What's expected of a barmaid by businessmen with company expense accounts, and other lecherous old men," I finished for her. "I understand. And I apologize for judging you the way I did ... and for acting like one of those lechers. Please forgive me."

"No harm done," she said. "I guess I can't blame you. Everybody judges books by their covers." She smiled, and then said, "Which brings me back to my original question; do you need any help with *your* book? My spelling is excellent, I take shorthand, I taught English grammar, and I can type 130 words a minute."

"Wow! I'm lucky to hit 50 with the wind at my back," I said. "But as much as I might *need* help, I'm not in a position to hire any, right now."

"Well, let me show you what I can do, okay? Then if you change your mind, you'll know who to call."

"I don't have a typewriter handy," I said.

"I do. Let me take some of your notes home," she offered, "I'll type them up and make them shine like gold, and bring them back first thing in the morning."

I looked at her a little bit puzzled by her persistence. "I really don't need a tryout," I said. "I'll take your word for it. Besides, if and when I do find myself in a position to hire some help, I'll be back in Chicago."

"That's okay," she said. "I don't have family or anything tying me to Boston. I've always wanted to see Chicago."

"Why is working for *me* so important to you? There must be a thousand secretary jobs you could get in a city like Boston."

She stared at me for a moment with a pretty dejected look. Suddenly, I felt sorry for having called her out so bluntly. She started to turn away, but then stopped and turned back to face me.

"Two reasons," she said, "since you asked. The first is that I overheard some of what you were telling your sailor friends about the book you're working on with the lucky rifle. My father was in the Army in Africa, so it intrigued me. The second is, Mr. Lawson, that I like you. And it's not because you tip well. I don't spend my nights picking up big-spender customers; I'd get fired if I did, *and* I wouldn't be able to look at myself in the mirror. But I'm an excellent judge of character, and you seem like a guy that I'd like to get to know better."

Now it was my turn to just stare. Finally, I managed, "I'm flattered, Holly. On both counts. But you realize that I'm old enough to be your father, don't you?"

"How old do you think I *am*?" she challenged me.

I laughed. "Sure, and when I get done offending you with that one, I'll guess your weight and then your dress size."

"I'm thirty-three," she said. "How old are you?"

"I'll be fifty this year."

"Okay, you're just *barely* old enough be my father," she said. "You'd have to have gotten very romantic in the backseat of your old man's Buick back in high school."

I laughed. "I never got lucky enough in high school to get that unlucky," I said. "And I'd have put you at about twenty-five, by the way. But I'm still not going to guess your weight."

"Good," she said with a chuckle. "And I'm not going to tell you, either. And thank you; I try to take care of myself."

We looked at each other with the awkwardness of two teenagers at the spring dance. The moment was mercifully broken when a man called out from the bar, "Hey, Holly! You working tonight, or what?"

"Duty calls," she said. "I'll talk to you later, okay? When are you leaving?"

"Probably Monday," I told her. "I'll make sure I see you before I go."

She went back into the bar, and I stood there for a little while, digesting all of what had just happened. I looked in, and saw her leaning over a table, smiling at two men in business suits. One of them was obviously looking right down her blouse. I actually felt a twinge of jealousy.

As if she could feel me watching, she turned, looked at me, and gave me a wink. Then she went back to taking their order.

Refocusing, I went to the front desk, and found out that Hendricks had still not checked in.

The reunion party didn't start until 1:00 the next afternoon, Sunday, but it seemed to me that Hendricks was cutting it awfully close. Too close for *my* comfort.

From my room, I tried Betty's number again, and finally got an answer. It was her husband, Josh.

I introduced myself, and briefly explained that I was doing a story on Rock-Ola rifles. He said that he had just gotten back from putting Betty and their two kids on a train for Buffalo to visit her aunt. She would be back Tuesday morning.

That was probably just as well, I figured. I really wanted to talk to her in person, anyway. I get so much more from a face-to-face interview. And at least I knew she was alive and well. More than I could say about Hendricks.

I decided not to ask him if he knew anything about the *Kiss For Luck!* slip. I'm not entirely sure why. I think I just wanted to hear about it first-hand from his wife.

Sunday, May 16, 1954

I met a couple more of the *Shea's* crew at breakfast the next morning, including an Italian guy named Peter Moschella, who was the Second Assistant Engineer on the trip. Back then, apparently everyone called him *Secondo*. He was now a First Assistant Engineer, and they called him *Primo*.

After breakfast—at which point Hendricks had still not checked in—the desk clerk made a deal with me to keep me out of his hair every time a male guest walked in. I would sit quietly in the lobby, and he would give a signal if Hendricks showed up. I worked on my notes when not anxiously studying each new patron.

I went upstairs about noon to clean up and dress for the reunion party without having received any signal from the clerk.

I was impressed by the room that the hotel had set up for the group. Apparently, a number of the crew had sent photos and other memorabilia ahead, and a very efficient event coordinator, named Judy, had set them out on display. Also, posted on a couple of easels, were letters sent by several crew members who were not able to make it. I scrutinized the names for Hendricks', but it wasn't there. I took that to mean that he hadn't changed his mind about coming.

Of the forty crew and the seventeen Navy Armed Guard who had sailed out of Boston Harbor on the *Shea* ten years earlier, thirty-eight of them made it back.

Most of the missing simply couldn't arrange or perhaps couldn't afford to get to Boston, but a few, apparently, had since passed away.

At a little after 1:00 the *Shea's* former captain, Adam Jones, stood up and clinked his glass for silence. He gave a short speech welcoming everyone back, and thanking them for contributing to the reunion fund. He then gave the floor to Roberto Delano, who had been the *Shea's* chief steward, and who was now an ordained minister.

Reverend Delano said a prayer for all of the crewmates who had passed, with a special one for Captain Hill, who had been the ship's original captain, and who had died of a heart attack during the sabotage incident. He then gave a blessing for the food that was about to be served, and the wait staff began carrying plates in from the kitchen.

There was a five piece band that included a female singer, a drummer, a guitarist, a pianist, and a guy who could apparently play any instrument that had ever been bent out of a piece of brass. While lunch was being eaten, they played soft background music, mostly from the forties, and they were quite good.

The room had been arranged so there was a dance floor in front of the band, but with only five or six wives in the group, it seemed to me its use was going to be quite limited.

As the dessert dishes were cleared away, the band started playing Glen Miller's *In The Mood*, and the crew with partners took to the floor.

I was tapping my foot to the beat, and watching one couple who could have entered a dance contest. After a while, I turned to look at the door—hoping to see Hendricks—and what I saw was a dozen women walking into the room. It looked like they ranged from their late teens to their forties, but they were all good looking women.

As I watched, they filtered throughout the room, locked their sights onto a man, took him by the hand and led him to the dance floor.

I waved Judy over and asked her what was going on.

"They're taxi dancers ... at least that's what we used to call them in the thirties," she said. "Girls who like to dance and can use a few extra dollars."

"Is the hotel paying them?" I asked.

"No. The band," she told me. "They play these kind of things all the time, and they know there's often not a lot of women in the group. They pay the girls so there's somebody dancing to their music. It's all part of the package."

The song ended, and the band started into *Pennsylvania-Six-Five-Thousand*, and a thirty-ish girl walked over, took my hand, and tugged me toward the floor. I protested that I couldn't dance and that I was just an observer, but she completely ignored me.

On the floor, she showed me a few steps, and actually got me feeling quite comfortable, but I was glad that *Fred and Ginger* had decided to sit this one out.

As I gave her a spin, I looked around the room, and I noticed a knot of men all standing around the captain's table. They all seemed to be talking to a man that I hadn't seen before. He was tall and lanky and wearing a dress-blue uniform. It had to be Hendricks!

I wanted to run from the dance floor and go make sure it was really him, but two things stopped me. One, he was obviously enjoying the company of his old shipmates and didn't need some stranger trying to horn in. And two, I was really enjoying dancing with Lori!

The song ended, and the band went right into the nice slow *Begin the Beguine*. I asked Lori to teach me that one, but she told me that they were only allowed to dance one song in a row with each guy. She assured me that she'd find me later on.

I sat down and looked over at the captain's table. They had pulled in another chair for Hendricks—at least who I *hoped* was Hendricks—and they were all laughing and swapping stories.

I couldn't hear what they were saying, but it didn't matter. I could see that they were enjoying the same kind of camaraderie that I'd experienced among the soldiers on the front lines during the war. It was such a contrast to the petty office politics that I ended up having to endure working at the papers.

I saw no need to intrude, now that Hendricks was in my view, but if he tried to leave I was going to tackle him before he made it to the door.

I danced with a couple of the other girls, and then finally got my slow-dance with Lori. As we glided across the floor—okay, *she* glided, I stomped—to *Moonlight Serenade*, she asked me why I was *observing* a sailors' reunion.

"I'm a writer," I said, "I'm working on a story about something that happened on this ship ten years ago, during the war."

On a first name basis up until then, she looked at me, and said, "You're not Rich *Lawson*, are you? The war correspondent?"

"Guilty as charged," I said as I stepped on her toe. To my credit, it was a *light* step. I was getting better.

"Well, it's an honor to meet you!" she said. "We used to read your dispatches all the time while my Dad and my brother were over there. It really helped for us to know what they were going through. The bad parts, and the good."

"I'm glad I could help," I said. "It was quite an experience. I hope nobody else ever gets the opportunity to do it."

The song was nearing its end, and I said to her, "How'd you like to take on a secret mission to help me out?"

"Anything!" she said.

I explained what I wanted, and as the band went into *Cab Driver*, I went back to my table, and Lori flitted among her fellow dancers, whispering in their ears.

I watched as she and six of her friends descended on the captain's table like a small swarm of locusts, and a few seconds later had stripped it clean of every man there ... except Hendricks.

He sat there watching his buddies being led away, looking a bit confused. He looked around, and he saw me watching him. He pointed his thumb at his retreating friends, and raised his eyebrows in a silent question.

I just nodded.

He broke into a wide grin, and waved me over.

He stood up as I neared the table, and as we shook hands, he said, "Frank Hendricks. Pleased to meet you. Rudy said you've been waiting since Friday night to talk to me. I was going to come over in a little while, but Shanghai-ing half the crew to get me alone was clever."

"Rich Lawson," I said. "The pleasure is mine." I looked at the dance floor, and said, "It doesn't look like they're minding too much. But I won't keep you from them. I know you've got ten years of catching up to do with a lot of them. I just wanted to introduce myself, and see if maybe you'd have some time tomorrow to talk with me."

"I've got a one o'clock train back to New York tomorrow," he said, "but I can eat breakfast and talk at the same time. It's a trick Rudy taught me a long time ago. How's seven o'clock in the dining room sound?"

"I'll be there," I said. I shook his hand, again, and said, "Enjoy yourself, and I'll see you in the morning."

Before I left, I wrangled one more dance with Lori. As the singer performed a wonderful rendition of *The Very Thought of You*, I thanked her for *forcing* me to dance, and for conspiring with me to abduct the captain and his crew.

I went into the bar, and looked for Holly, but she wasn't there. I finally asked the bartender.

"Sunday's her night off," he said as he poured a draft beer along the side of the glass, ending up with the perfect head. "She's on for lunch tomorrow, though. Should be here around ten-thirty or eleven."

Monday, May 17, 1954

Pad in hand, and pencils in pocket, I was in the dining room at quarter to seven the next morning. Frank showed up on the dot of seven.

The waitress filled our coffee cups and took our order, and as he stirred sugar into his black coffee, Frank asked, "So, what can I tell you that you haven't already heard from the rest of the crew three times?"

"I think I have a pretty good picture, *in general*, of what went on during that trip with the saboteur, but you're the only one who can tell me *specifically* how the whole thing ended that day down in the shaft alley. Primo told me about the sabotage to the oil line, and about getting shot, and even how the kid shot up the escape tube and hit the FBI agent. But he was pretty out of it by the time you crawled down through the empty water tank with the rifle."

Frank went through that hour or so in minute detail for me. As I scribbled my notes, I got the impression that he hadn't replayed that specific time period in his life—in that detail—for a very long time, if ever. Staring out into the dining room as he spoke, I was sure he was mentally seeing the insides of the *Shea*, rather than tables and chairs and coffee cups.

Afraid of getting an answer I didn't want to hear, I finally asked him about the gun.

"Rudy told me that you cleaned the rifle before it was put back in the crate," I said. "Is that right?"

"Yup," he said and took a swallow of coffee.

"Did you just clean the bore, or did you take it all apart?"

He paused for a moment while looking at me. I don't think he was trying to recall the answer; I got the impression he was trying to decide *whether* to answer.

He finally said, "I took it apart. Mechanical things always fascinated me."

"Did you happen to find anything unusual inside it?" I asked with my heart in my throat.

Another pause while my heart refused to beat at all, regardless of its location.

"You mean the slip of paper with the lip print on it?" he asked finally.

I let out my breath and my heart restarted. "Exactly!" I said. "And please tell me that it had *A Kiss For Luck!* written on it."

"How did you know? I never told anyone about that slip."

"I've been following a rifle with a slip like that half way around the world," I told him.

"So it's *not* the only one," he said. "I always wondered how many there might be."

"There's more than one," I told him, "but I don't actually know how many. Not yet, anyway."

He nodded thoughtfully, as if knowing that his rifle wasn't unique sapped its specialness.

Little did he know.

"So, when you had it apart, did you happen to see any damage to the gun?" I asked just barely containing my excitement. "To the stock where the top and bottom halves meet, specifically? Right about where you'd hold it with your left hand?"

He looked at me for a long moment, and then slipped the ring off of his right hand, and passed it to me.

"See the stone?" he said. "That's a bullet fragment that hit the rifle—right between the halves of the stock—just as I was aiming my first shot. If the stock and the barrel hadn't stopped that fragment from going through my hand, I probably would have dropped the gun, and that Nazi kid's second bullet probably would have killed me. None of us would be here this weekend if it wasn't for that gun being in exactly the right place at exactly the right time."

"That's happened more than once," I said.

"So, I figured that slug was my lucky charm," he went on, "and I dug it out and kept it. A few years later, I had it cast into a piece of Lucite, and set into that ring."

"You didn't think to keep the slip?"

"Oh, I thought about it," he said, "But somehow I figured it belonged with the rifle. I'm sure it sounds crazy, but I imagined the slip making the rifle lucky for whoever was using it. And I knew the D-Day invasion was going to happen pretty soon, and whoever had the rifle on *that* day was going to need all the luck he could get."

"It's not as crazy as you think," I said, and proceeded to give him a synopsis of the stories I'd spent the past week and a half chasing down.

"Well, I'll be damned," he said when I got to the present. "And you know where the rifle is now?"

"Hanging on a wall in a farmhouse in the middle of France," I said.

"Wow! It really did carry luck with it. I'm glad I *didn't* put that slip in my wallet."

"And hopefully," I said, "it's got one more piece of luck in it for me, and this book I'm putting together will be a best seller. Your piece of the gun's story ties it all up. Now, I just need to talk with the girl who's responsible for putting the slip in there in the first place, and find out why she did it."

"And you're sure this is the same rifle?" he asked. "You said there was more than one with a slip in it."

"The damage from your bullet fragment clinches it for me," I said. "The only better proof I could want is if you had written down the serial number."

"Look inside the ring," he said.

"You're kidding!" I said as I twisted the ring around.

There, engraved neatly into the gold was the number 6,152,649.

"Why?" I said.

"I have no idea," he said. "Or I didn't until just now. I wrote it down before I gave the rifle back to Rudy, and kept the little piece of paper in the cloth pouch with the bullet. When I had it set into the ring, something told me to keep the number together with the slug. *This* turn of events certainly never entered my mind."

"This is amazing! You couldn't make something like this up," I said. "You mind if I take a few pictures of this before you leave? My camera's in my room, and I have a close-up lens that I bought with it, and never had a use for until this week. Another one of those impulse things that had no rhyme or reason until now."

After breakfast, I spent some time in my room, neatening up my freshly scribbled notes. Then, after the maid knocked on the door, I finished packing, and went downstairs and checked out.

It was quarter past ten when I went into the bar, and looked around for Holly. She wasn't there, so I climbed up on a stool, and ordered a Coke to wait.

I was lost in thought about Hendricks' part of the story when a familiar voice came from behind me.

"Hey, sailor. Come here often?"

I turned around on the stool, and made a show of looking Holly up and down appreciatively. "If the likes of you will be servin' up the grog," I said, almost pirate-like, "you can bet your bilge-water I'll be coming back."

The guy a couple stools down gave us a funny look, and Holly and I both laughed.

"I have to head out pretty quick," I said. "I just wanted to stop in to say good-bye."

"I'm glad you did," she said, putting something in the breast pocket of my jacket. "That's my phone number. I hope it's just *so long*, and not good-bye. Don't forget my offer."

"I won't," I said as I stood up. She surprised me by giving me a hug, which I returned, and then surprised me again, by giving me a quick kiss on the lips.

I wasn't the only one surprised. I caught another funny look from the guy on the stool, and a scowl from the bartender—who I guessed was Holly's boss.

"Holly's my niece," I said to them. To Holly, I said, "You remember to call your Aunt Polly, now. She's lonely there on the farm, with me gone all the time."

"I will, Uncle Rich," she said with a smile that was just one tick removed from a laugh.

I met Hendricks in the lobby and we shared the fifteen minute cab ride to South Station.

He boarded a train for New York, and I bought a ticket for Chicago, aboard *The New England States*. Between the money I'd spent in France and England, and the checks I'd written for the hotel bill and the coach seat on the train, I knew my checking account was going need emergency resuscitation when I got back. I sure hoped the checks from *The Saturday Evening Post* and *Colliers* were going to be in my mail. I hated to start borrowing from my savings account; that always seems to be a one-way affair. But I felt strongly enough now that if I had to live under a bridge with just my typewriter, I was going forward with this book ... and I finally *was* calling it a book.

Tuesday, May 18, 1954

It was Tuesday afternoon when the train pulled into LaSalle Street Station. I was stiff, and not too well rested after having tried, with little success, to sleep in my coach seat. The good news was that the 24-hour ride—without the pesky distraction of sleep—had given me plenty of time to work on the book.

On the ride back to my apartment block on the trolley coach, just about all I could think about was flopping down in my own dear, sweet bed. The one thing that was going to postpone that glorious reunion was a call to Betty.

Sitting at my table, I dialed her number—the first number I'd called in two weeks without the help of an operator—and it was picked up after the second ring.

"Hello," a pleasant sounding woman said. Then, before I could reply, she said, away from the phone but not out of ear-shot, "I've got it, Josh! Randy, put that down!" Then back to me, she said, "Sorry."

"No problem. Is this Betty Driscoll?"

"Yes, it is. Is there something I can help you with?"

"Hi, Mrs. Driscoll. My name is Rich Lawson. I'm a writer ..."

"Oh, yes. Josh said that you called. Something about the rifles we made at Rock-Ola during the war."

"Yes. I was wondering if I might be able to arrange some time with you to talk about your time on the assembly line there. Perhaps I could ..."

"Would you like to come to the house for dinner tomorrow night? It's just spaghetti and meatballs; nothing fancy."

"Um, ah, sure," I answered, caught completely flat footed by her invitation. "Can I bring a dessert?"

"That sounds wonderful," she said. "Six o'clock?"

"Perfect," I said. "Just give me directions, and I'll be there."

"We're about four and a half miles from the Rock-Ola plant," she said, and gave me directions.

Wednesday, May 19, 1954

Wednesday morning I had to pry myself out of my bed, but I knew I had work to do. I rewound the film that was still in my camera, and took it, along with the two other rolls I'd exposed, and headed across town to the photo lab. I paid the extra money for three-hour processing, and then went home to organize an outline for my book.

Around noon, I picked up the photos, and headed uptown to see Dave at the magazine.

"I thought you'd gone AWOL on me!" he said when he got back from lunch and found me waiting in his outer office, showing his secretary, Ellen, my photos. "Where the hell have you been? Is that my article?" he asked when he saw the manila envelope in my hand.

"France, England, and Boston." I answered, "and no, it's not."

"Then you should be sitting behind a typewriter," he said, "not standing around showing your vacation snapshots to my secretary." Looking at her, he added, "Who has other things to do."

As I scooped up the photos, she said to me, "I *love* it! Good luck!"

In his office, Dave dropped down in his chair, and said, "I'm not going to be able to keep Happy Bottom's hands off those pages without something to show the old man, Rich. What the hell have you been doing for two weeks?"

"Let her have them," I said. "I've got something much better."

I then pitched my book idea to him, running down the outline, and showing him the photos. "The only part I have left," I told him, "is how and why the slip got into the gun in the first place, and I'm having dinner with the woman who can tell me that, tonight."

"I like it," he said, "but we put out a monthly magazine, remember; we're not a book publisher."

"I know," I said, "but you have connections. I've heard you talk about people you know at HarperCollins and Simon & Schuster. Just get me in to see someone, and I know I can sell this."

"And what do I get out of it?" he said.

"My undying gratitude, and top billing in the acknowledgements," I answered.

"I already own your gratitude," he reminded me. "You promised me that for the pages you just told me to give away. And it's hard to buy cigars with acknowledgements. Thirty-percent," he said. "Of the gross, not the net."

"You're saying you'll be my agent?" I asked.

"I think I can get some people to look at a draft of this when you've got it done," he said.

"Isn't the standard fee for a literary agent fifteen-percent?" I asked. "Thirty seems a little steep. How about twenty because of our deep abiding friendship?"

He looked at the pictures spread out on his desk, and made some little humming noises. Finally, he said, "Okay, twenty-percent. But I want a draft of your first two chapters and a polished outline on my desk in one week."

"Done!" I said as I reached out to shake his hand.

As I gathered up the photos, I said, "Now, about my advance ..."

There was a lot of whining, a little cussing, and several comparisons of me to his ex, current, and future wives, but I left the office with a check.

I gave Ellen a thumbs-up as I walked past her, and she blew me a kiss. "Use that on your cover," she said.

I took a taxi to Betty's, arriving with a Devil's-food cake, a bunch of flowers, and a bottle of Chianti.

Standing on the front porch, I twisted the old crank-style bell in the middle of the door, and heard a male voice call out, "I got it!" from inside.

Josh invited me in, and introduced himself, then led me into the kitchen. Betty was stirring a big pot of spaghetti sauce, and it smelled wonderful. It triggered another trip back in time, to my *other* grandmother's.

She wiped her hands on her apron, and then shook mine. Her hand was small, but the grip was strong. I got the impression that this was a woman who was not afraid of physical work.

"Welcome to our humble home, Mr. Lawson," she said. "I almost feel like I should say, welcome *back*. My Dad used to sit out there in the living room and read your dispatches during the war, and then your columns in the *Sun*. He never could understand why they let you go when they merged with the *Times*."

"I left in search of greener pastures," I said.

"And did you find them?" she asked me while stirring the sauce. Before I could answer, she turned to Josh, and said, "Will you set the plates on the table, please, honey? Let's use the dining room, okay?" At a little higher volume, she called out to her unseen kids, "Randy! Jessica! Help your father set the table. Hup to!"

She turned back to me, apparently wondering why I hadn't answered her question. This woman was obviously used to getting a lot of things done at the same time! I envisioned her pulling rifle parts from different boxes, and almost throwing guns together one after the other.

"Sometimes the pastures were very lush," I said, stepping back as she carried a pot of boiling water to the sink to drain the spaghetti, "and other times it was like foraging in the dust bowl. But I think I've found myself a patch of clover, finally."

"A story about Rock-Ola rifles?" she said as the steam billowed up from the sink. "No offense, but it sounds a little boring."

"None taken," I said. "But I imagine you feel that way, at least partly, because you put thousands of them together. I'd probably feel the same way, but I think I have an angle you might find interesting. I'll tell you about it after dinner. I'm starving, and that smells delicious."

"It will take an awful lot to make me interested in rifles," she said, sliding the spaghetti from the colander into a bowl. "If every one of them suddenly disappeared from the face of the earth, it would make it just that much harder to start the next war. Oh, would you mind slicing the bread over there? The cutting board's under here, and the knife is in that drawer."

Josh poured the wine—with a shot-glass full for each of the kids—and then we all joined hands, and Randy said grace.

Betty's sauce and meatballs were fantastic! I would never say it out loud, and I'd deny, under oath, even thinking it, but hers was actually better than my grandmother's.

As I cleaned the sauce from my plate with a piece of bread, I asked Josh, "So, did you work at Rock-Ola, too?"

"No," he said. "I was on the other end of the rifle. I was in Italy with the Fifth Army."

"That must have been rough," I said. "I was in northern France, but I know the Fifth took a lot of casualties getting Italy back from the Germans."

"It was. But I think the worst part was missing food like this," he said giving Betty a wink. "You'd think you could get a good meatball in Italy, wouldn't you? Well, not during the war, I can tell you that."

I helped clear away the dishes, and was given the honor of cutting the cake. The kids were given the unusual treat of being able to eat their dessert in front of the TV, and as Betty poured coffee, she said, "So, what can I tell you about assembling carbine rifles that could possibly be of interest to your readers?"

I slid an envelope out of my inside jacket pocket, and took the top photo off the stack.

"Do you recognize that?" I asked, handing her the picture.

Her mouth hung open as she stared at a close-up of the *Kiss for Luck!* slip curled in the stock of Joyce's rifle.

"Oh my Gosh! I had forgotten all about this!" She looked at me, and said, "Wherever did you find it?"

"In a farmhouse in France," I told her. "So, you *do* recognize it?"

"Yes!" she said. She looked at it closely, and then said with a laugh, "Those are *my* lips! It's one of mine!" She passed the photo to Josh, and said, "Remember I told you about doing that?"

"Well, I'll be darned," he said. "It does look just like one of your letters."

"Letters?" I asked.

"That's how the whole thing got started," Betty said as I showed her a couple more shots of the slip taken out of the gun. "I used to sign my letters to Josh and my brother that way; with a bright red kiss, and *A Kiss For Luck!* written over it." Then she told me the story of her brother's infantry company, and their miraculous escape from harm after kissing her lucky lips. "So, I talked the girls on the line into making these slips and putting them inside our rifles."

"How many did you make?" I asked.

"One of the Army's inspectors found out, and made us stop after one shift," she said. "Oh, but we put a few in the night before that, too. So, probably around 450, give or take."

"How many other girls made these slips," I asked.

"There were five of us all together," she told me.

"And you're sure those are your lips?" I asked.

"Absolutely." She held one of the pictures for me to see, and said, "See that little line in the lipstick? I had a split lip that week."

"And that's definitely her hand writing," Josh added.

Betty sat smiling at the photo, no doubt recalling the *fond* memories of those days of rationing, and worry, and round-the-clock work.

"Do you have the rifle, now?" she asked.

"It's still hanging on the farmhouse wall in France," I said.

"When did you find it? And how?"

"I first found out about it just a couple of weeks ago, right here in Chicago. But let me tell you what happened to it after it left your assembly line, before I tell you that part."

I took the stack of photos—which were arranged in careful order—from the envelope, and asked Josh to come around and sit next to Betty.

I told them the story of the *SS Donald E. Shea*, and showed them photos of Frank's ring, and the fragment damage to the rifle.

Then I went into Kenny McCormick's story, and showed them his watch-fob slug, and the damage to the front of the rifle. I also showed them a picture I'd taken of the family, pointing out that their daughter, too, was six years old.

Finally, I gave them a brief accounting of Joyce's story, and showed them the photos of her lucky necklace, and the hole in the butt of the rifle. The last picture was one of Julien, whom, I told them, was about the same age as Randy.

"There are a number of people, spread across the world," I said finally, "who firmly believe that that slip of paper with your lips on it saved their lives. And that if it hadn't been for your lucky charm, those two adorable kids wouldn't be here today."

Betty had tears running down her cheeks. "It's unbelievable," she said. "Wonderfully, crazy, unbelievable! I would never in a million years have imagined anything like this!"

She got up from her chair and came over to me, and opened her arms. I stood up, and she embraced me hard. "Thank you so much for bringing all this here and sharing it with us," she said. "I take back what I said in the kitchen. I don't think this is the *least* bit boring!"

As we sat back down, Randy came into the dining room, apparently unglued from the TV by an uninteresting commercial. He looked at one of the pictures of the rifle, and said, "Hey, cool!" He looked at me, and asked, "Is this yours?"

"It belongs to a woman in France, now," I said, "but before you were born, your mom put that rifle together for soldiers like your dad."

"Really?" he said looking at his mother.

She nodded with a smile.

"Cool!" Then he turned to his father, and said, "Can *we* get one?"

"No. Those are just for soldiers," he told him.

Randy looked at the photo for a moment, and then replied, "But he said a *woman* has this one."

"Sometimes women can be soldiers, too," Betty said.

"Really?" Randy said as if she had just told him that dogs are really cats sometimes.

"I'll tell you about it tomorrow," she said pulling him into an embrace. "Why don't you go get your sister, and go up and get yourselves ready for bed?"

"Aw!" he said. "But I'm not tired!"

"You can stay up a little longer," she said, "but get ready, now. Hup to!"

As he left under over-acted duress, I said to Betty, "If it's okay, I'd like to get a picture of you and the family before they go to bed. I've got to take my documentation full circle."

Over a couple more cups of coffee and the rest of the cake, I told her about Julien's essay in the French newspaper that started the whole adventure, and she went into more detail about her days at Rock-Ola, including a great anecdote about getting rid of a lecherous supervisor by giving him credit for something he had no hand in, and watching him get promoted right out of the plant.

Wednesday, May 26, 1954

The next week flew by for me. I spent so much time in front of my typewriter that I often forgot to eat. Which was really okay, after the way I'd been stuffing myself for the *previous* two weeks.
    When I finally had my work in presentable shape, I called Dave at his office.
    "Richard Charles!" he answered, true to form. "I hope you're calling to tell me you've finished your opus."
    "Hardly," I said. "But I have the first of the five parts done—at least in draft—and outlines for the other four. I want to bring them by for you to read, and I also want to run the pitch by you that I want to use when you get me in to see a publisher."
    "Since this doesn't have anything to do with the magazine, anymore," he said, "why don't you come by our apartment for dinner tonight? I told Gail about your book, and she's dying to hear more. And that's a good sign; she's not usually interested in anything but romance novels."
    "What time, and can I bring anything?" I asked.
    "Cocktails at seven," he said. "And we're ordering in Chinese, so whatever wine goes with that."

Gail let me in with a smile, a hug, and a kiss on the cheek. I knew Dave was exaggerating about that $200 loan. Either that, or he really didn't tell her.
    "Dave's in the living room," she said as she took my hat, overcoat, and the bottle of Riesling. "Is that your book?" she asked looking at the fat envelope I'd set on the side table.
    "Part of it," I said. "It's a long way from the *whole* book."
    "Do you mind if I read it while you and Dave have a drink? From what he told me about it, I just can't wait. I never thought I'd want to read a book about a *rifle*."
    "Sure," I said. "There's a stack of pictures in there, too. They're numbered and it tells on the back which part of the story they go with, and what or who they are."
    She led me into the living room, where I could already hear Dave talking. I was a little surprised to see Ellen, his secretary from the magazine, sitting there sipping on a martini. And I guess it showed.

"Hi Rich," she said, getting up to give me a hug. "I hope you don't mind me being here, too. Dave said you were coming over tonight to unveil your book, and I blackmailed him into inviting me along."

"The more the merrier," I said, accepting a gin and tonic from Dave. "I need all the constructive criticism I can get." I took a sip, and asked, "What'd you blackmail him with, just out of curiosity?"

"I told him if he didn't let me come, I'd tell Gail we were having an affair."

From behind me Gail laughed. "With that old fart?" she said. "Good luck!" She held up the envelope, and said to Ellen, "Come on; let's go in the kitchen and read Rich's opus."

Dave motioned me toward the sofa, and he dropped down in his leatherette easy-chair.

"So, how long do you think it will take for you to finish the thing," he asked as he took a cigarette out of the silver holder on the coffee table. He slid it over to me, and I took one as well.

"At the rate I was working this week," I said, "maybe a couple months if I decide not to eat and bathe regularly."

I took my Zippo from my jacket pocket, and lit his cigarette. He took a long drag of *throat comforting pleasure*—at least that's what the Kool ads called it—and blew it out through his nostrils. "That doesn't leave much time," he said.

"Until what?" I asked, lighting my own cigarette, and snapping the lighter closed.

"Publication. This has to be on the shelves before May of next year. This will tie in perfectly with the tenth anniversary of V-E Day."

"Of course!" I said. "I hadn't even thought about that. That *is* perfect." Then I said, "But that's *plenty* of time."

"If it were a magazine article, it might be," he said. "But by comparison, book publishing speeds along like a glacier. It usually takes a year, and sometimes two for one of the big-six publishers to put a book in the stores after they buy the rights."

He then proceeded to explain the arduous tasks involved in book publishing to me.

"And it has to be finished with enough time left over for the marketing and publicity before it actually goes on sale," he concluded. "This horse will have to be on a damned fast track to get to the finish line on time."

Just then, Gail and Ellen came back from the kitchen.

"I love it!" Ellen said. "Why are you sitting here instead of writing the next part about the ship and the Nazi spy?"

"You're sounding more like your boss all the time," I said. "Just don't start *looking* like him, please."

"Is all of this true?" Gail asked.

"As far as I know," I said. "Most of it's been corroborated through direct evidence or multiple sources, and I haven't found any reason to doubt what any of the players have told me."

"You know who'd love this?" she said to Dave. "Marion Jameson. This is exactly her style."

"By God! You're right!" Dave said, getting up. "I hadn't even thought about her. And *she's* right here in town!"

"Who is she with?" I asked, grinding out my cigarette and standing up to join the others.

"Harper & Faust," Dave said.

I'd heard of them, but didn't really know much beyond their name and that they had a address over on Lake Shore Drive, overlooking Lake Michigan.

"You think they could whip the horse faster than one of the big boys?" I asked.

"Don't the smaller jockeys usually win the race?" he answered. "Speed and agility are what we need, here."

"Are they big enough to do it up right?" I asked him. "I don't want this to look like some dime-store novel."

"They may not be one of the big-six, but I think they're in the top twenty," he told me. "And they do everything *from* dime-store novels to text books to big novels. They published that one by Steve McGuire that just came out ... what's the name of it?"

"*The Prince's Lady*," Gail said. "How they get away with printing some of those love scenes, I will *never* know."

"Just be thankful they do!" Ellen said, and both women giggled.

"I'll call Marion, first thing in the morning," Dave said.

"You know her very well?" I asked hopefully.

"She was Dave's first boss out of college," Gail said. "He started as a copyeditor, and left as an assistant manager, five years later, when *she* got promoted."

"I hope you didn't burn the bridge when you left," I told him. "I've seen how tactful you can be."

"Nah," he said with a wave, "We still exchange Christmas and birthday cards. She's the one who actually pointed me towards magazines. She knew that the guy who replaced her was a complete butt hole, and I wouldn't be able to work for him very long without punching him."

"I've been *there*," I said.

The doorbell rang, and Gail and Ellen went to get the food, while Dave set out plates on the kitchen table, and I opened the wine.

Thursday, May 27, 1954

Dave and I were at Harper & Faust the next morning at 11:30 for a 12:00 appointment. I'm not sure where Dave borrowed the charm to do it, but Marion had agreed to eat lunch in so that she could squeeze us into her overbooked schedule.

"Now, I need to warn you," Dave said as we rode up in the elevator to the sixth floor, "Marion can be a little ... shall we say ... abrupt. Don't take it personally. And don't tuck your tail between you legs, either. Wishy-washy people—but especially men—light her fuse like a blowtorch."

We waited in her outer office until exactly noon, when her secretary led us inside.

"Well, you certainly appear to be eating well, David," she said as she came from around her massive mahogany desk. "The magazine business must be good."

"I can't complain," he said with a laugh as he patting his stomach. It *had* grown somewhat in the years that I'd known him.

They hugged, and he said, "When I left Harper & Faust your office was on the third floor, and didn't have a window. This is spectacular! Look at that view! How many more floors can you still go up?"

"Until Mr. Harper retires, and Tom Young moves into the penthouse, none," she said, "But when that happens, there will four of us trying to get our nameplates on Tom's old door."

"Well, I'm sure having the cover of another bestseller hanging on your wall will certainly help your chances, won't it?" Dave said.

"Not as much as the sound of a flushing toilet full of money will hurt them," she answered.

She turned to me, extended her hand, and said, "Marion Jameson. Pleased to meet you."

"Rich Lawson," I replied returning the very businesslike handshake. "Pleased to meet you, as well. Dave told me that you and he ..."

"You have twenty-five minutes left, Mr. Lawson," she said as she turned and went back behind her desk. "I suggest you not waste it with small talk. Please, show me what you have."

She sat down, and sprinkled some dressing on the salad that had appeared on her desk while we were looking out her window.

I was glad that Dave had warned me that she could be *abrupt*, otherwise I could have mistaken her behavior as something like *rudeness*.

From the portfolio case I had carried in with me, I took out a two-foot square poster, on which I had mounted a dozen of my photos this morning. I stood it on her desk, and motioned for Dave to come over and hold it up.

"These are photographs of the actual rifle that I talk about in the book," I told her, "and the people whose lives it affected."

I took the manuscript of the first part from the case, and I held it out to her. "This is part one of the book," I said. "It tells the story of when the rifle was first assembled—right here in Chicago, by the way—and the origin of the title, *A Kiss For Luck!*"

She looked at it but she didn't take it from me. "That's all you have?" she said, as she speared a tomato slice with her fork. "And how many parts *will* there be?"

"Five," I said, as I set the manuscript on her desk, and took the outline from the folder.

I offered the outline to her, and to my surprise, she took it. Then she doubled-down on the surprise by saying, "Read me part one, please."

"Excuse me?" I said.

"Part one of your story, Mr. Lawson," she said, looking at me over the top of her reading glasses. "Please read it to me."

This was going *nothing* like the way I had rehearsed my big pitch!

"I'm really not much of speaker," I began to protest.

"I'm not asking you to run for office," she said while looking at the outline. "Nor to try out for Hamlet. But I assume that you are able to read—aloud—the words that you've written."

I gave Dave a quick glance, and he just shrugged.

I picked up the manuscript, and I began reading.

"A kiss for luck, by Rich Lawson. Part one. 'For those of you who never saw an assembly line of women putting weapons together during the war, it was a wondrous thing to behold. This story begins with just such an assembly line in Chicago, Illinois, but it is really about one special M1 Carbine rifle that was made on that line in May of 1944.'"

As I got going, I found myself getting more and more comfortable with the reading, and even began to put inflection into it. I decided not to try doing different voices for the different people I quoted, however; I do know my limits.

About halfway through, I got the impression that Marion wasn't even listening to me. She was flipping back and forth through the pages of the outline, and studying the poster of photos.

Suddenly, she interrupted me in mid sentence. "Wait a minute. Who are you referring to there?" she asked. "Is that Maggie, or Betty?"

"That's Betty," I answered.

"Confusing," she said. "Too many *shes*. That needs to be tightened up."

"I'll make a note," I said as I dog-eared the corner of the page.

"Please go on," she said, now looking directly at me.

I began again, but I quickly found that I'd felt more comfortable when she seemed to be ignoring me.

It took almost twenty minutes for me to finish, and when I did, she made a showing of looking at the clock on her wall.

"Well, what do you think, Marion?" Dave asked her. "Isn't this perfect for the V-E Day anniversary next year?"

She didn't reply. She flipped through the pages of my outline one more time, and looked over the photos. Finally, she reached over and pressed a button on the intercom on her desk.

"Yes, Miss Jameson?" her secretary answered.

"I'm done with lunch, Crystal. Would come take this away, please?"

I don't know whether I was more disappointed that she wasn't interested, or angry at her callousness for the past half hour. I thought seriously about telling her what I thought of her lack of professionalism, but I checked myself. She *was* an old friend of Dave's, after all, and I didn't want to queer that for him ... though I couldn't guess how having her as a friend would do him any good.

Then, she continued to her secretary, "And find Charlie Michael for me. Tell him I need him in here, right away."

Who was Charlie Michael, I wondered. The bouncer?

She let go of the button, and let out a long sigh as she slowly shook her head. She then looked up at me, and said, "You are going to have to work balls to the wall, Mr. Lawson, if we're going to make V-E Day next year."

"Then you're going to do it?" Dave said, sounding every bit as surprised as I was.

"With the proviso that Mr. Lawson makes the deadlines that we put in front of him," she answered.

"Oh, no problem with *that*!" Dave said. "He's almost given up eating, and he can type in his sleep. And since he won't be going out, he won't even need to waste time bathing."

She smiled at Dave's eagerness to make a commitment on my behalf, but then turned to me and asked, "What do *you* think?"

"As long as the deadlines are humanly possible," I said. "It's not like I have a social life or anything."

"Good!" she said. "Charlie Michael, whom you'll meet in a minute, will be the project manager. If anyone can put a team together that can get this done, it's Charlie.

As if she'd been listening to hear his name mentioned, Crystal buzzed, and announced that Charlie was there.

"Send him in, please," Marion said.

"Charlie," she said as we shook hands, "this is Rich Lawson. Mr. Lawson, Charlie."

"Are you the war correspondent Rich Lawson?" he asked.

"That's me," I said. "Did you read my dispatches from the front?"

"Actually, you *wrote* about me," he said. "Well, my company, anyway. You spent a couple of nights in our gun pit with us—a 90mm—three or four weeks after D-Day."

"I remember *that*," I said. "Firing up into the blackness at planes we couldn't even see. I'm sorry to say I don't recall your face, though."

"It was dark," he said. "And it's a pretty forgettable face, anyway."

"Well, now that you two have concluded your reunion," Marion said, "perhaps we can get to the matter at hand."

She explained to Charlie what the concept for the book was, that I had a draft of part-one of five and an outline for the other four, and that she wanted to have books on the shelves by June 1st of the following year, and advanced copies for a marketing launch by April 2nd.

"I don't have to explain the challenges to you," she said to Charlie, "but you might want to explain them to Mr. Lawson. This goes to the top of your list, so pick the best people for your team. Give me the list tomorrow morning, and I'll get them reassigned."

She stood up, handed me my poster of photos, and extended her hand. "It was nice meeting you, Mr. Lawson," she said. "I'll see you at the launch in April."

"Thank you," I replied. "You won't regret your faith in me, or in the story. I think that ..."

She cut me off, addressing Dave, "I'll have the contract messengered over to you this afternoon. Standard terms and rates for a first-time author. I need it signed and back here by end of day, tomorrow."

Dave and Marion said their good-byes, and as we walked through her outer office, I heard Marion's voice over the intercom. "Crystal, would you come in here with your pad, please. Leave the door open in case Mr. Anderson shows up early."

Dave left to get back to the magazine, and Charlie and I went downstairs to his office. On the way, he had Photostat copies made of all of my pages.

In his office, he looked over what I had, calculated backwards from the April 2nd launch date, and asked, "Do you have an assistant?"

"You think I'll need one?" I asked.

"Once stuff starts going back and forth and back and forth between you and our editor, there's no way you'll keep your sanity if you're making corrections and revisions to one part of this while you're trying to write the next part. And then when our design team, the copyeditor, the printer, and marketing get involved, you'll really lose your mind." He held up the manuscript, and added, "And no offense, but you really need someone who can proofread."

"None taken," I said. "I've always paid more attention to the words in a sentence than the letters in a word. That's probably the one thing I agreed with the *Trib* about. Their campaign to modify spelling; changing words like *although* to a-l-t-h-o, and *height* to h-i-t-e like they sound."

"Sadly," he said, "for you, anyway, it hasn't caught on. So keep your dictionary handy. If—or rather *when*—you decide to put on an assistant, I can give you a few names."

"I think I know someone," I said.

He picked up his phone and dialed a three-digit number. "Hi Norma," he said. "Can you come in here, please? I'd like you to meet a new author I need you to work with." He listened to the reply, then said, "Yup. Another priority shift from the sixth floor."

A minute later, she stepped into the office. "Norma, this is Rich Lawson. Rich, Norma," he introduced, and we shook hands. "Norma will be your editor." To her, he said, "Rich is writing a book that needs to launch on April 2nd of next year."

"Is this your first book?" she asked me.

"First *book*, yes," I said, 'but I *am* a professional writer. Newspapers and magazines. I was a front-line correspondent during the war."

"That's good, but not great," she said. "Books are different; they're not just really long articles. How much of it is done?" she asked.

Charlie held the manuscript out to her. "That's the first of five parts," he said. "Beyond that, it's outline. I have copies here."

She flipped through several pages of the manuscript, then looked up at me, and said, "Do you have an assistant?"

"Not yet," I said with a little laugh.

"Good," she said. "Because if you did you'd have to fire her."

She turned to Charlie, and said, "Start now?"

"That's the word from upstairs," he said.

To me, she said, "Make sure that Lucy, out there, has your address. When I get done marking this up, I'll have it sent over by messenger. Use a messenger to send everything back to me, too. If we use the mail, this won't get done until *Christmas* of next year."

On the bus ride home, I thought about Holly—and not for the first time since I'd been back. I hoped she was serious about seeing Chicago, because I sure wanted to see her, again. I was still unsure what she saw in me, but it seemed to be genuine—not just the big-spender thing, because, boy would *that* be a disappointment. On the slip with her phone number that she had given me in Boston, she had also written her work schedule, so I'd know when I could catch her at home. I would give her a call about 10:30 tonight.

Once at home, I began work on part two of the story, which I titled, *The Crossing*.

I had set my alarm for 10:30 in case I fell asleep in front of my typewriter, but I had no problem staying awake. The words were flowing pretty well, and if not for the alarm, I probably wouldn't have remembered the call until midnight.

I have to admit to some trepidation as I dialed Holly's number. What if she'd found a real secretarial job in the week and a half since I'd left? What if she'd come to her senses about dating a father figure? What if she'd been lying the whole time in the hope of bigger tips?

The phone had rung six times, and the image of her out dancing with some guy her own age was becoming more and more defined in my brain. So fixated had I become on why Holly wasn't home, that when the phone *was* answered, it actually startled me.

"Hello! I'm here!" she answered, followed by heavy breathing.

"Hi. This is Rich. Are you okay?"

"A bit winded," she said. "I was on the landing below with an armload of groceries when I heard the phone. I ran up the stairs, and then couldn't get my key in the lock. I don't know why, but I had a feeling it was you."

Hearing her voice actually gave me a little tingle. Which was going to make me feel like even more of a doofus if any of my fears came to pass.

"I'm glad you made it," I said. "I was about to give up."

"Well, I'm glad you didn't," she said. "What's going on?"

"I just called to tell you that I have a publisher," I said. "The book's going to come out next April, just in time for the tenth anniversary of V-E Day. Pretty good, huh?"

"That's great!" she said. "I'm so happy for you!"

I was really hoping that she would ask me if I still needed her help, so that I wouldn't feel so stupid if I asked, and she had changed her mind. No luck. So, I just jumped in with both feet.

"So, are you still interested in coming out here and giving me a hand?" I asked.

"Absolutely!" she answered. "I was afraid to ask if that's why you were calling, in case you found somebody closer to home."

"I didn't even look," I said. "Who could I possibly trust to do a better job than my own niece? So, when can you be out here?"

"How's Saturday night?"

"*This* Saturday?" I said. "As in the day after tomorrow?"

"Sure," she said. "I'll pack my car in the morning, and I should be in Buffalo by nightfall. That's about 450 miles. Chicago's about 530 miles beyond that, so if I get an early start, I should be *there* by nightfall on Saturday."

"You've given this some thought, haven't you?"

She laughed. "A little," she said. "Fantasizing might be a better word for it. I can't wait to see you again, see a new city, and use my office skills, again."

"What about your current job?" I asked. "You don't strike me as the type to just walk out and leave them shorthanded."

"Covered," she said. "I have a friend named Lori who's subbed for me a few times. She's been dying to get in full time. I'll call her and Dwayne in the morning, and set everything up. The hotel won't even miss me."

"Is your friend Lori a sometimes taxi-dancer, by any chance?" I asked.

"Yeah. How'd you ... ? Oh, that's right! She worked the reunion at the hotel when you were here."

I laughed. "I can see how the two of you could be friends. She's a good sport."

We chatted for a while longer, I gave her directions to my apartment once she made it to Chicago, and then we said good night.

Working off of the adrenaline of knowing that Holly was coming, I put in about another hour ... and then I crashed.

Friday May 28, 1954

About nine the next morning, a messenger rang from downstairs, and I went down to sign for a package with my manuscript in it. I took it out on my way up in the elevator.

I had never seen so much blue pencil in my life! And there were editing symbols in there that I didn't even recognize. I literally had to dig out a reference book to see what it was she wanted me to do to my baby.

At first, I was really ticked off. Norma was obviously miffed at her bosses for overworking her, and she was taking it out on me.

The typos and the spelling errors were one thing—and admittedly, there were plenty of those—but her wonton blue-pencil slaughter of nearly every sentence I had typed was simply an abuse of power.

Since there was little room left on my manuscript to write anything else, I took out a pad, and began to write my rebuttals to her editorial directives.

I was rolling along pretty well, making pithy—bordering on snide—comments as to why what I had written in the first place was better than what she wanted me to change it to, when on the sixth page, she rewrote all but about eight words of an entire paragraph, and then drew an arrow in the margin, indicating *more on other side*.

I flipped the page, wondering what more she could possibly do to one paragraph.

She had written a note in regular black pencil.

> "Rich: I like the concept of your book-in-multiple-parts, and I <u>love</u> the "Kiss for Luck" thing. But what I've read, so far, focuses too much on the rifle. That would be great in a magazine article - even necessary for brevity, but it just won't work for a whole book. Your book has to be about <u>people</u>. The people whose lives were affected and changed by the rifle. We might sell the <u>rifle</u> book to a lot of soldiers, but we'll sell the <u>people</u> book to soldiers, <u>and</u> to women. And trust me, there's a lot more of us than there are of them. Norma."

I thought about that for a while, and then went back to the beginning and looked at the changes she was suggesting. They made much more sense in that light. There were still a few I didn't agree with, but on the whole, she was right; I had to change my focus. Damn! That meant virtually starting over! Where the hell was Holly?

With a less adversarial attitude, I read all of Norma's mark-ups through the whole manuscript. Beyond the changes to focus, she also picked out every single typo, spelling error, missing punctuation mark, and split infinitive. She didn't miss a thing. She could probably spot fly poop in pepper at thirty yards.

With my work cut out for me, I set the pages of Part-Two aside, rolled a new sheet of paper into the typewriter, and began anew on Part-One.

About 7:30 Holly called to say that she had reached Buffalo. We had an enjoyable ten minute conversation, and then I got back to work. I couldn't wait for her to be here ... on *many* levels!

Saturday, May 29, 1954

After a long Friday night, by noon on Saturday, I had a new draft of Part-One, which I was now calling *The Assembly Line*. I called the messenger service to come pick it up. Norma had been pretty explicit that when I had something done I had to send it to her right away, night or day, weekend or not.

I headed back upstairs with the intent of recrafting my outline with the new focus, but when I walked into my apartment, it struck me that it was a complete disaster. An image of Saint-Lô after its liberation flashed through my mind.

I'm not normally a slob, but I'm not exactly a spit and polish kind of guy, either. I don't get a lot of company dropping by, so if there are more dishes in the sink than in the cupboard, the bed's not made, and there's a blob of toothpaste in the sink, who's to know but me, right?

But these past couple of weeks since I've been back, I've really neglected the place. I certainly didn't want Holly thinking this was how I *always* lived.

While I was washing the dishes, it suddenly occurred to me that Holly wouldn't have any place to stay when she got here. Even staying the night here with me—with me on the couch, of course—would be pretty scandalous if any of the neighbors saw her come in and not leave.

If something like that were to get back to Marion, who knows what could happen. Bigger careers than mine have been ruined by that kind of thing. Most people aren't as prudish nowadays as they were in the '40's, but Marion didn't come across as the liberal type.

After I put the last plate away, I went to the phone book, and looked up the number for the Bastion Hotel. I'd never had occasion to go inside, but it was located on the next block, and although it wasn't top of the line, like the Ritz or something, it appeared to be nice enough. And it would be a lot more *affordable* than the Ritz.

I called, and reserved a room with an attached bath for three nights. Hopefully, by Tuesday, we would be able to find Holly a nice studio apartment, nearby.

As I headed for the bathroom to give it a long overdue scrubbing, I looked at the kitchen table. It was strewn with half-typed pages, crumbled sheets of paper, my yellow note pads, a dictionary, a thesaurus, pencils both sharp and dull. Like a nagging boss, it reminded me how much work I had to do, and that I had no time for distractions like cleaning an apartment.

Which led me to consider *why* I was cleaning the apartment. If I didn't have time for the distraction of *cleaning* for Holly, how was I going to manage the distraction of Holly herself?

I suddenly found myself contemplating what I had gotten myself into. I was forced to admit that even if Holly was as good of a typist and proofreader as she claimed, at least half of the reason that I had asked her—a woman I had known for a total of about three hours—to quit her job and drive a thousand miles to come and work for me was that I wanted to date her. When the hell was I going to have time for that?

And she had said that she wanted to date me too, so asking her to forget all that and just sit and type probably wouldn't make for a very warm relationship.

What the hell had I been thinking? Okay, when I recall the skirt and blouse she was wearing the night I met her in the bar, I *know* what I was thinking ... and that was the problem.

Sure I needed help with the book, but there were plenty of local women whose cleavage I had not ogled who could fill that bill. Charlie had even offered to recommend some.

I looked at the phone, and I knew I could call the hotel and cancel the reservation I just made, but without a Dick Tracy 2-way Wrist-Radio, there was no way I could reach Holly on the road, and tell her that she should turn around and pretend she never met me ... which would certainly have been easier as a disembodied radio voice than face to face.

Resigned to the fact that there was nothing I could do to change the situation for now, I headed for the bathroom with my can of *Bon Ami*.

An hour and a half later, I had the place in pretty nice shape, and was back at the table—which was arranged like an actual desk—working on my rewrite of Part-Two with the new people-focus.

At five o'clock, as I continued working, I began expecting Holly at any minute. By six o'clock I was wondering if maybe she had broken down or something. Then there was also the scenario where *she* came to *her* senses, and she was headed back to Boston.

About six-thirty the intercom buzzed from the lobby. My heart move up about six inches, right into my throat. I wanted it to be her, and I didn't want it to be her, and I couldn't decide which one I wanted more.

I went over and pressed the *talk* button. "Lawson," I said generically into the box on the wall. There *was* the possibility that it was the messenger service bringing me something from Norma.

"Hi! It's Holly. I finally made it!" came the reply.

"Hey! I was getting worried. Welcome to Chicago!" I said, "I'll be right down."

As I got into the elevator, Mrs. Giondelli came out of her door. "Hold that, Mr. Lawson!" she instructed me, and then struggled her two-wheeled shopping basket out through her self-closing apartment door. Mrs. G. was a round little woman in her seventies, who stood about four-foot-five, and who was one of the building's busier bodies.

"Good evening, Mrs. Giondelli," I said as the doors slid shut. "Off to do some shopping, I see."

"I have to get my roast for Sunday dinner," she said. "Mr. Koepenick gives a discount after six o'clock, you know." She looked up at me, and observed, "No hat?"

"Oh, I'm not going out. I'm just meeting someone in the lobby," I said. Then, picturing Holly giving me a big hug and a kiss—and the reaction that would get from Mrs. G.—I quickly added, "My niece, from Boston."

When we came around the corner from the elevator, Holly was looking at the prints of 1900 Chicago on the lobby wall. "Holly! How's my favorite niece?" I said with a quick wink. "This is Mrs. Giondelli. She's one of my neighbors upstairs."

"Hi, Uncle Rich," she said without missing a beat. "I'm fine." She turned to Mrs. G., smiled, and said, "Please to meet you, Mrs. Giondelli. How are you?"

"Fine," she said flatly, then added, "You need to comb your hair, young lady." Then she trundled on out of the lobby.

As the door closed, we both laughed. "Don't listen to her. You look great!" I told her.

"Liar," she said. "I've been stuck in a car for the past twelve hours; I must look like something the cat *wouldn't* drag in. And walking up the street from where I had to park, I found out why they call this the windy city."

"Okay," I said, "How about, it's great to see you?"

"You, too, " she said with that big smile. We each opened our arms to hug, which, in my mind's eye, was a tight embrace and included a kiss on the lips. Reality—as is so often the case—fell short.

The hug was one of those leaning-forward contact-at-the-shoulders things, and the kiss was on the cheek. And even that was just a cheek to cheek touch with the kiss sound actually out in midair.

I didn't know what to think. I had expected her to be a lot happier to see me after driving a thousand miles across six states to do it. Then it occurred to me—in a clutching at straws kind of way—that maybe she was just worn out from the long trip.

"You must be tired from that drive," I said. "Come on upstairs and relax. Have you eaten dinner, yet?"

"I haven't," she said. Then in a lowered voice, she added, "But what I really need is a powder room."

Ah! That explained it! Who can be romantic when they have to pee?

In the apartment, I pointed her toward the shiny-clean bathroom, and asked if she wanted anything to drink.

"I have Coke, ginger ale, some red wine, a couple cans of beer, instant coffee, or tea," I told her.

"Tea would be nice, thank you," she said just before the door closed.

When she came out, the water was just boiling. I told her to make herself comfortable on the sofa.

"That was quite a drive in two days," I said as I poured the water into two China cups that I probably hadn't used in three or four years. "I took the trip on the train, and *that* was no picnic."

"I'm just glad the old Plymouth didn't leave me stranded out there on the road somewhere," she said.

I put the tea, a cup of milk, and my sugar bowl on a tray that I don't think I had *ever* used, and brought it into the living room. I set the tray on the coffee table, and I sat in the chair opposite her. She had worked some magic on her hair in the powder room. She looked wonderful, and I just had to smile.

She poured a dribble of milk into her tea, and as she sprinkled in a little sugar, she said in a pretty flat tone, "We need to talk about something, Rich."

Now, I don't have a *lot* of experience with women, but that vague semblance of a hug and kiss downstairs, and the fact that she wasn't looking at me as she spoke just now, gave me a pretty good idea of what that *something* was. She was calling it off before it ever got started. I was about to get a verbal "Dear John" letter.

My smile evaporated and I felt like I'd been punched in the stomach. Which, I realized, was pretty contradictory considering that only a few hours ago I wanted to call her and tell her to turn around.

As she gently swished her spoon back and forth, she said, "I'm not sure that my being here is a good idea."

"Oh, *that*," I said, brightening. "You had me worried for a moment, there. But don't worry about *impropriety*. I took the liberty of getting you a room at a hotel a block over. Just for a few days, until we can find you a place of your own."

"Actually, I did, too," she said. "The Bastion. But that's not what I'm talking about. I mean Chicago.

"This book can be a big opportunity for you," she said, "and you told me how critical it is that it gets done on time. You don't need me here distracting you with a budding romance."

"Distracting me?" I said as if the exact same words hadn't been front-and-center in my brain just a little while ago. "No! I'm *glad* you're here," I countered, leading with my male ego, and leaving my logic kicked into the corner and gasping for breath. "I sure can't do this without help."

"And I'm sure that with a single call to your publisher, you'd have a whole list of girls who could help you."

I just looked at her for several long seconds. "I see," I said finally, as I set my cup on the table. Even if had *wanted* to take a sip, I'm not sure I could have kept it down. I forced a little chuckle, and said, "I think you're the first woman who's ever thrown me over *before* I went on a date with her."

"*Throw you over?*" she repeated. "I'm not trying to throw you over! It's crazy considering that I've talked with you in person and on the phone for a total of what? An hour? But I really like you. I'd *like* to date you and get to know you better, but I don't think that's a good idea for *you*, right now. I'll drive back to Boston, we'll keep in touch, and when you get out from under all this, we can give it another try."

Again, I just looked at her. Finally, I stood up, walked around the table, and held out my hands to her. "Would you stand up, please?" I said calmly.

With a questioning look, she took my hands, and I helped her to her feet.

"About five or six hours ago," I said to her, "I told *myself* exactly what you just said to me about the distractions of a relationship."

"Then you know I'm right," she said. It wasn't a triumphant statement. It had more resignation in it than pride.

"Yes, you are. About everything but leaving Chicago," I said. "If I have to flatten all four tires on every Plymouth on the block to do it, I'm not letting you drive away."

She narrowed her eyes, and said, "We both agree that me being here will be a distraction to you, but you won't let me leave?"

"I've never met anyone—man *or* woman—who seems to think as much like me as you do. You even booked a room for yourself at the same hotel where *I* booked a room for you. I think we were meant for each other, Holly.

"Before I started researching this rifle story, I didn't believe too much in luck or in fate. But learning about that slip of paper tucked into that carbine, and all the people that it affected, changed my mind. I'm even beginning to think that that *Kiss For Luck!* slip played some mysterious part in making sure that you and I were both in the dining room at the Lenox two weeks ago."

"You may be right about that," she said. "I wasn't supposed to be working that Friday night. But Gwen came down with a sudden case of laryngitis, and they called me in."

"See? There you have it; fate! You *have* to stay. Otherwise the whole *Kiss For Luck!* mystique goes right out the window."

"Along with your ability to finish the book in time."

"No. I think the slip also brought us together for its own *selfish* reason; to *get* its book written," I said.

With a raised eyebrow, she said, "You really think the slip is *conniving*? Not just lucky?"

I laughed. "Not really. But see? I couldn't even get *that* past you we think so much alike. Look, we're both rationally thinking adults, not a couple of hot-blooded teen-agers, right? If we were working together for a publisher in some office somewhere we could do it and get our work done, couldn't we?"

"So, no romance until the book is published?" she said.

"How about, no head-over-heals can't-think-of-anything-else infatuation until the *editing* is done?" I countered. "Let's not get all crazy about this."

She laughed, and said, "I think I could handle that." She stepped forward and put her arms around me. "You think we should seal our pact with a kiss?"

"Two minds with a single thought," I replied.

If that kiss had been an actual signature, it would have been John Hancock on *The Declaration of Independence*. Wow!

I took her over to Banyan's to get some dinner. It wasn't fancy, of course, but it would be quick, and she said she wanted to get checked into her room and get some sleep. It also seemed apropos, because it was where I read the French newspaper that got the whole thing started.

As we ate, I told her the whole story of the rifle, and our quick dinner lasted for more than an hour.

We walked back to her car, which was parked about half way between my place and the hotel, so we didn't see any reason to move it. As I hefted her two suitcases from the passenger seat, I asked, "How did you happen to pick the Bastion out of all the hotels in Chicago?"

"The Boston Public Library is about a block from the Lenox," she said, carrying her make-up case, "so I went over and got a street map of Chicago and a *Yellow Pages*, and found the closest hotel to your address."

"Clever," I said, "But disappointing. I was hoping I could pin the coincidence on the lucky slip, again."

Sunday, May 30, 1954

The next morning, Holly was in my lobby at six o'clock. I buzzed her in, and waited in my doorway for her to come up.

I almost laughed when I saw her, but she looked wonderful! She wore a light jacket over a simple blue dress with a pleated skirt that ended six inches or so below her knees. It tapered in at the waste behind a narrow black belt, and she had a string of pearls around her neck, just visible with the one button that she had left undone. Her hair was pulled back into a bun, with not a strand out of place, and she wore a curved little hat on top of her head. If C.B. DeMille had been casting for a prim and proper secretary for one of his movies, Holly would have gotten the part.

"Good morning, Miss Dillon," I said in my best professional tone. "You're looking well, today."

"Thank you, Mr. Lawson," she said, with equal propriety. "You look very smart in your suit, as well. I like that tie."

"Thank you," I said, holding the door for her. "Welcome to your first day at Lawson and Associates."

I had carried her typewriter from her car last night, and if weight was any indication, it was at least twice as good as the one I used. It was also electric. I'd have been jealous if my typing skills wouldn't have made it a complete waste on me.

I had set her up at the kitchen table, and moved my stuff to a card table I opened in the living room.

"So, what is my first assignment?" she asked.

I picked up a small stack of papers, and handed them to her. "This is my outline for the third part of the book. As you can see, I've made quite a few revisions to it. Would you mind typing it up so that I can send it over to Norma? And would you make a carbon, please, so we can have a copy here?"

"And what's the name of your book, again?" she asked.

"*A Kiss For Luck!*" I said, surprised that she had forgotten.

"Oh, yes, I remember now," she said as she put her arms around me and gave me a big kiss.

I was in no special hurry to end the kiss, but when we did, I shook my finger at her, and said, "We have rules at Lawson and Associates, Miss Dillon. There will be no more of that in this office ... until noon when we break for lunch."

We both laughed, and then I helped her off with her jacket, took mine off, and we got to work.

As I sat down in the living room and continued my pecking away on Part-Two, her machine came to life out in the kitchen. I couldn't believe how fast she was going, so I leaned over to where I could see her. She sat there, her back perfectly straight, her eyes never leaving my scribbles while her fingers flew across the keys. It suddenly occurred to me that I wasn't going to be able to keep her busy very long.

By lunchtime, she had finished with my outline, and had started typing up the handwritten notes from my legal pads, then filing them according to which part of the book they belonged to. I'd never had a writing assignment so organized in my life!

We went out and had sandwiches at the deli around the corner, and when we got back, a kid on a bicycle was just pulling up with a package from Norma.

I slid out my second attempt at Part-One on the way up in the elevator, and was surprised to find almost as much blue pencil as the first time. I thought I had done a *much* better job with the rewrite.

We sat down in the living room, and as I finished reading Norma's notes on a page, I would hand it to Holly. About half way through, she said, "Wow! She is good! She doesn't miss *anything*, does she?"

"And I only sent this to her last night about an hour before you got here. Apparently, she doesn't sleep, either."

"So, do you want me to type it up with her edits, or do you want to make some changes, first?" Holly asked.

"What do *you* think of the changes she's asking for?" I asked. "You can see what I wrote, and what she's suggesting. Which do you think is better?"

She looked at the page in her hand, and it was obvious she was thinking. But I had the idea that she was thinking less about her actual answer than how to phrase it so she wouldn't offend me.

"Well, let me put it this way," she finally said. "If I was reading this in *Life Magazine*, what you wrote would be great. But if I was curled up in front of the fire with a cup of tea, and reading this in a book, I'd want the extra detail and the dialogue that Norma's asking you for. Does that make sense?"

"It does," I admitted "... damn it! I'm beginning to see why book publishing takes so long. Oh, well. The third time's the charm, right?"

"Do you want to dictate while I take it down in shorthand?" she asked.

"I've never been too good at dictating," I said. "Even letters. I really have to write it out to get my thoughts across well."

"Nonsense!" she said. "Just tell me the story like you did at Banyan's last night. Don't worry about form or punctuation, or any of that; that's what I'm here for."

She went to the kitchen, and came back with her pad, the folders of my notes, and half a dozen pencils. She handed me the notes for Part-One, and said, "To jog your memory." She then sat down, stuck five of the pencils into her hair bun, and said, "Ready when you are, Mr. Lawson."

The process did not start out too auspiciously. I kept trying to craft my sentences as if I were committing them to paper, and she kept telling me to relax and just tell the story. It took us forever just to get a few paragraphs done. When I asked her to read it back to me for about the sixth time, she tore the sheet off her pad, and pulled all of the pencils out of her hair.

I watched completely perplexed as she unpinned the bun and shook out her hair, and then unfastened three more buttons on her blouse. She then leaned forward, looked me in the eyes, and said in a seductive tone, "Hey sailor. What's a girl have to do to hear about your *rifle*?"

I burst out laughing, and it was just the ice breaker that we needed.

In my best Bogie impression, I said, "Give me a kiss, sweetheart, and I'll tell you everything I know."

She leaned across the table, and gave me a kiss—and a view—that would make the Pope question his vows, and then she sat back down.

"There's one of those waiting at the end of each episode," she said in a pretty good Ilsa imitation. "Ready when you are, Rick."

It went *much* faster after that. Once in a while, I would slip into my descriptive mode, and she would stop me, and simply say, "He said - she said," to remind me to include dialogue.

About three hours later, she was at her typewriter.

While she was typing, I was making notes to my notes for Part-Two. Adding dialogue to the story on the Liberty ship was a little more difficult than when a handful of girls were interacting. A lot of the action in *The Crossing*, took place when people—all men—were alone.

About two hours after she began, Holly called out from the kitchen, "Done!" and she had the double-spaced first draft neatly stacked on the table.

I looked at my watch. It was after 6:30. "Let's let the ink dry while we get something to eat," I suggested. "Then you can go home and get some sleep while I read it through, and see if I want to make any changes."

"You will," she said as she got up, fixed her hat onto her head, rebuttoned her blouse, and slipped on her jacket. "I'll show you where when we get back."

We had a light dinner at Banyan's—which quickly became "our place"—and when we returned, we sat side by side on the sofa, and read through the draft. She pointed out the places where she thought it could be better, including excising some stuff altogether, we agreed on the revisions, and she went back to typing.

It was almost ten by the time she finished retyping and we had read through it a final time. I called the messenger service, and seven minutes later, we heard the buzzer.

On the too-short ride down in the elevator, we shared a goodnight kiss for as long as we could, and after I handed the manuscript to the kid, I walked Holly down the block to the hotel. In front of the lobby elevator, I gave her a final goodnight kiss on the cheek. That's what uncles do.

Monday, May 31, 1954

Apparently, Norma had other authors to terrorize, or was sick, or something, because the entire day went by without a return package from the messenger service.

Assuming we were on the right track, Holly and I went to work on the new version of Part-Two, using the same story-telling-and-stenography process, including—at my insistence—the four unfastened blouse buttons. You don't mess with a successful formula.

By early afternoon we had a draft knocked out that Holly and I could review together as we had for Part-One. We left it sitting on the table, and celebrated by going out to do some sightseeing.

It was after dark before we got back, and we had had such a wonderful time just being together that neither one of us really felt like getting back into the editing.

I put on some Sinatra 45's, opened my bottle of wine, and we just relaxed on the sofa, telling each other stories about growing up. Her in a little town north of Boston, named Rowley, and me in an equally small town southwest of Muncie, Indiana, named Middletown.

Our series of goodnight kisses started on the sofa, had a second application at my door, continued in the elevator, and ended, finally, with an uncle-kiss in the hotel lobby.

Tuesday, June 1, 1954

Around ten o'clock Monday morning, Holly and I had finished reviewing and re-editing the draft of Part-Two, and had it in an envelope waiting for Norma's return of Part-One.

It was quarter to twelve before the messenger arrived, and I had him wait while I looked over Norma's mark-ups. If it was another bloodbath of blue pencil, I wasn't going to send him off with Part-Two.

With Holly looking over my shoulder, I slid the manuscript from the envelope. Across the top, in red ink, was written, "*Magnifique!*"

I suddenly remembered how I felt when I had gotten a gold star on my summer vacation report in fifth grade. I quickly flipped through the pages, and while I don't recall seeing any pages with *no* markings, they were far fewer and much farther between.

"Yes!" I said. "We did it!"

Holly hugged me from behind and gave me a kiss on the cheek as I handed the kid his return envelope, and a bigger than usual tip.

We went upstairs, and read through Norma's edits, and it was funny to see Holly getting a little miffed at some of the corrections to her punctuation.

"What the heck has this woman got against semi-colons?" she asked. "Almost every one that I put in, she wants taken out."

I had noticed that when Norma was editing my own drafts, but with the wholesale changes she wanted me to make to actual content, I didn't worry at all about a few periods perched atop commas.

"I don't know," I said. "Some childhood trauma? Maybe a truck with a semi-colon in the middle of the name on the door ran over her bike when she was a little girl."

Holly pulled out my *Manual of Style*, and became less and less miffed as she checked the usage of each semi-colon, and saw that Norma was right ... in *most* cases.

"This one is right!" she would say when she found one that she could successfully challenge. "I am *not* changing that into two sentences!" I found it amusing.

For my part, I was okay with most of Norma's changes, and Holly got to work on what we hoped was finally the final draft of Part-One.

From there on, with our formula well established, we became a regular writing machine.

That night, Dave and Gail invited us over for cocktails, and it came up that Holly was still staying at the hotel, and that we needed to get her an apartment.

"I think Ellen is looking for someone to split expenses with," Gail said. "The girl who was sharing her apartment got married a couple of weeks ago." She got up, went to the phone, and called Ellen. When she came back, she motioned for all of us to get up, and said, "Come on. We're all going over to Ellen's so she and Holly can meet." To Holly, she said, "You'll love Ellen. And I think you'll like her place. It's not walking distance to Rich's, like the hotel, but it's a quick bus ride."

Friday, August 20, 1954

By the middle of August, Holly and I had gone through all of the rounds of editing with Norma on all five parts of the book, and were scratching around for something to keep Holly busy.

This time, Norma came through for us. Impressed by the quality of my drafts after Holly joined the team, and the speed with which we turned them around, she recommended her services to another of the authors she was working with.

It got kind of lonely, not having her in the apartment all day, every day, but it made the evenings and weekends more special.

The book writing process was not done, of course. Every time a new department at Harper & Faust got involved in the project, they wanted changes. Fortunately, Holly was so fast and well organized with her other clients, that she could juggle her time so that she would work her magic for me as a top priority.

Wednesday, January 5, 1955

Less than a week after the new year started, I got called into a meeting at Harper & Faust, and was pleasantly surprised to see Holly there, as well.

We sat next to each other at a big conference table with eight other men and women. On the table were half a dozen copies of an oversized, soft-bound book. Printed on the cover, in block letters was "A Kiss For Luck" Under that was printed, "ARC only." Below that was, "Harper & Faust," and finally, in the smallest line of text, was my name.

Holly slid one over and opened it up. I could see from her expression that she was not impressed. The words were grouped together in the middle of the page with wide margins all around.

Charlie, who was sitting across from us and must have been watching her face, said, "That's a galley proof, Holly. It's for a final round of editing before we set the type for printing. Since it's all single-spaced now, the margins are wide so there's room for notes."

"Oh. That makes sense," she said. "What about the cover? I hope that's temporary, too. What's *ARC only?*"

"We'll get to the cover in a little while," he said. "ARC means advanced reading copy."

He then got up and said to everyone, "Alright, let's get started. We have our galley proofs, and ARCs so it's time to start driving in the brass tacks.

"Each department has a copy or two, Rich has one—has everyone met the author, by the way? This is Rich Lawson."

I nodded, and said, "Hi," and got a chorus of "Hi, Rich" in return.

"The ARCs will go out tomorrow to some reviewers and magazines, including *Look*, *Life*, and *Saturday Evening Post*. Marketing's also making a hard push at *Good Housekeeping* and *Ladies' Home Journal* because the story has so many women involved. If we can get any or all of *them* hooked, the advertising folks will be able to take a couple of weekends off."

There was a round of chuckles, and then Charlie said, "Keith, tell us about your marketing plan."

Keith Little, a trim middle-aged man with thick, wavy, salt-and-pepper hair stood up and began, "Well, like Charlie said, we're going to try to get interest percolating about this special *Kiss For Luck* carbine right away, but the real publicity spike will come when we do the book launch on April 2nd."

He looked at me, and went on, obviously excited, "The grabber is going to be a first-time meeting of all the folks you wrote about in the book, *with* the rifle, *right here* in the Rock-Ola factory! Is that killer, or what? You think they'd all be willing to do that?"

"That *is* quite an idea," I said. "They might be *willing*," I went on, "but none of them is wealthy. I don't know that Kenny in England, or Joyce in France *could* get here."

"Oh, H&F will pick up all the bills!" he said with a wave. "That's what marketing budgets are for."

Someone else quipped, "I thought they were for trips to Miami in February."

Everyone laughed, including Keith, and he said, "Well, not *this* February, apparently. Not with *this* deadline."

Again, at me, he said, "So, can you contact all of them and see if they can make it? We'd want them here the last week in March, probably. We'll put them up downtown, take them to a show, wine 'em and dine 'em, the whole nine yards."

"What about husbands, wives, and kids of the main players?" I asked.

"Hell yes!" he said. "The *extended* connection will make it all the better!"

Keith went on for a while, talking more to his H&F counterparts than to me, about the nuts and bolts of the marketing campaign.

When he finally sat down, Charlie said, "Jimmy, what's the design look like?"

Jimmy turned to the woman next to him—who I guessed was his assistant—and said, "Let's show them what we have, Mona."

Mona got up and walked to a row of three easels that were standing at the end of the room. She was a tall brunette, perhaps in her mid-thirties, who could have been a model for those pin-up babes they painted on the noses of bombers during the war.

The easels all held a two-foot-wide by three foot tall poster of the company's H&F logo. She stood beside the first one and said, "We have three different contenders for the cover art. We're going to do some testing with a number of readers, both men and women, and see which one turns out to be the favorite. It's a new technique called a focus group."

Someone joked, "Yeah, and then Old Man Harper will tell you which one *he* likes, and that'll be that."

Everyone laughed, and then Jimmy said, "Well, we're going to *try* to be scientific about it, at least. Go ahead, Mona."

She slid the H&F poster off the first easel to reveal a giant blow-up of the book's cover. It was a black & white photo of Allied troops in action, probably taken on D-Day. Over the top of the picture, in large black font, were the words A Kiss For Luck!, one word under the other. Below that, in much smaller text, was my name.

"This is a scene from Omaha Beach on D-Day," Mona said, confirming my guess. "We chose this background because it represents the reason that the girls were assembling rifles in the first place."

There were comments around the table, and everyone generally agreed that they liked it.

Mona moved to the second easel, and revealed a completely different cover

In the background was one of the inspirational posters from the war. It featured a full color painting of a young woman with her hair in a red bandana, and holding a wrench in one hand while she looked up at a black & white image of a soldier going into battle. On top of the poster was a picture of the center section of a carbine rifle, and lying atop the rifle was the *Kiss For Luck!* slip. In the bottom left corner was my name.

"We went with this background," Mona explained, "because of the obvious connection with the girls who made the rifle, but we also feel it will target the female audience better than the battle shot."

Again, there was some discussion, with about a 50-50 split on which background was better.

The last cover she unveiled was a complete departure from the others. It was a black & white drawing of the rifle—apparently copied from one of my photos—with a full color drawing of the slip, with its bright red lips, lying next to the it. The title was arranged in a straight line, and my name was bigger on this cover than on either of the others.

Once more, the pros and cons were discussed. Finally, Mona looked at me, and said, "You're the author, Mr. Lawson; what do you think?"

"Well," I said, "I'm a less-is-more kind of guy, so I'd have to pick number three. I like the simplicity, and I think the basic white background makes the lips really stand out."

"Doesn't hurt that your name's the biggest on that one, either," somebody joked, and everyone laughed.

"Well, it probably won't matter anyway," Charlie said, "because, like Mona said, they're going to do their testing, and then Mr. Harper will decide."

Charlie turned to his right, and said, "William, I think you had something?"

The man was probably the oldest at the table, had a bald pate, neatly trimmed white hair, wore a blue stripped bow tie, and rimless spectacles.

"Yes," he said. "Thank you Charles." Then he looked at me, and said, "William Addison, Mr. Lawson; H&F's legal department."

That fit perfectly with his looks. "Pleased to meet you," I said.

"Likewise. Now, what you've written is a work of non-fiction, and you've used the names of a number of real people, most or all of whom, I gather, are still alive."

"That's right," I said.

"And I assume that everything you've written about them is true and can be substantiated."

"To the best of my knowledge," I said.

"Well, just to be on the safe side, we're going to ask you to provide us with a list of names and addresses so that we may send them each a copy of the galley proof—which will need to be returned, of course—along with a release form. We'll provide standard cover letters explaining that when they sign the form it will give H&F permission to use their names within the context of this publication. In the case of minors, the parent's signature will suffice. It will probably be a good idea if you write a short letter of your own, basically introducing H&F to them."

A man on my side of the table asked, "Does *every* person in the book need to get a copy? We don't have an unlimited supply."

"Not if they're just mentioned in passing or in some benign manner that could not be seen as libelous in any way."

The meeting went on for about another hour, with the people around the table using book publishing and marketing jargon that, as a newspaper and magazine man, went mostly over my head.

Holly left with me, and we settled down on my sofa to read through the galley proof.

Considering that we had gone over every word in that book at least half a dozen times, it was amazing how many things I wanted to change. Not because they were wrong, but because I felt I could make them just a tiny bit better. Holly kept me in check, and pointed out that no artist is ever finished with his creation, he simply stops working on it.

Shortly after midnight I woke up with my open mouth feeling like the Nebraska dust bowl. Sometime after ten—the last time I remember looking at the clock on top of the TV—we had apparently both fallen asleep reading.

I nudged Holly, and twenty minutes later we were in a taxi, riding back to her apartment. She objected to my going with her, but there was no way I was going to let her travel across town alone, at that hour.

We kissed goodnight at her door, and she crept inside so as not to wake Ellen.

On the ride back, I thought about the big book launch that Keith had planned, and a thought about how to make it even better occurred to me. I took the note pad from my jacket pocket, and wrote down my idea, afraid of losing it to a good night's sleep. While I was writing, a second idea for the launch party popped into my head. I didn't bother writing that one down; I was pretty sure I wouldn't forget it.

Thursday, January 6, 1955

I set my alarm for six so that it would be noon in France when I called the bakery. Expecting that I would have to arrange a time for a callback, I was surprised when Joyce answered the phone.

"*Bonjour! Le Parisien,*" she said. I had forgotten I was going to be speaking French.

"*Bonjour, Joyce. C'est Rich Lawson. Comment êtes-vous?*"

"Rich! What a surprise! I'm wonderful. How are you?"

"Very well, thanks. And how is everyone else? Luc, Grampa Carlos, Julien? Your mother and father?"

"Everyone is doing just fine. Julien is doing so well in his math classes that I think he's going to become an engineer one day."

"Recalling his fort in the barn," I said, "I'd think maybe an architect."

"I like that, too," she said.

"Well, I'm calling because I have a favor to ask ... and a surprise for you," I began. "A publisher, here in Chicago is going to publish my book about your rifle, and ..."

"Really? That's *wonderful*! I'm so happy for you! Julien will be thrilled to hear that! Congratulations!"

"Thank you," I said, "But there's more. The book is going to be released on April 2nd, and before that, my publisher needs to have a form signed that you and the others agree that it's okay to use your real names in the book."

"Of course it is," she said. "Why wouldn't it be?"

"Well, this is all a request from their legal department, just to keep the i's dotted and the t's crossed. You should be getting an advanced copy of the book by mail, very shortly. I remember you saying that you read English, so if you could go through it and make sure that your part of it is all correct, that will make the lawyers over here very happy."

"Julien's English is better than mine, I think," she said. "I probably won't be able to get the book out of his hands. Thank you! That's a *wonderful* surprise!"

"Actually," I said, "that's not the surprise. My publisher is going to throw a big party on the day of the book launch, and they want all of the people in the story to be there. They want to fly you over, put you up in a hotel and pay for everything, and then fly you home when it's all over. That means Luc and Julien and Grampa Carlos, too."

Silence. For a moment I thought we'd lost the connection.

"Are you serious?" she finally said. "*All* of us?"

"They told me to invite the whole family," I said, "so I guess that means your mother and father, too."

"I can't believe it!" she said. "How wonderful! Oh, Julien will be so excited!" Then she said, "Oh, but Mamma and Papa won't come, I'm afraid. When they made it back to France after the war, they vowed they would never leave again."

"I can understand that," I said. "But it will be great to see you and everyone else again. They want you to come over the last week of March so you'll be adjusted to Chicago time before the party on the second of April. Do you think you can arrange to be away then? That's about six or seven weeks from now."

"Oh, my goodness, *yes*! One way or another, we'll *be* there!"

"That's great!" I said. "And in the meantime, do you think Luc or Grampa Carlos could build a box for the rifle, and ship it over to me? They want to put it up on display during the party. There will be all sorts of magazines and newspapers there, and they'll want pictures of it."

"Why don't we just bring it with us?" she said. "When you take it all apart, it's small enough to fit in a suitcase."

"I thought of that, too," I said, "But the publicity department wants to take some pictures of it ... better ones than what I took. They might use a picture of it on the cover.

"Apparently, there's a company over there near Orly Airport that will put your package on an airplane for you, and fly it to wherever it needs to go. Much faster than putting it on a ship. My publisher will be mailing you the customs paperwork and a check to pay for the whole thing. And speaking of customs, is that enough time for all of you to get passports?"

"We'll certainly find out!" she said.

After Joyce and I said our good-byes, I called Kenny at his home number in Birmingham. I wasn't surprised that Lily answered, since I figured Kenny would be at work in the bike shop.

I explained the situation to her as I had to Joyce, and she was equally thrilled.

"How splendid! Kenny's helper has returned, and the Haversham girl is getting on fabulously. I'm sure Kenny will be able to steal away for a week!"

With my time-lag calls out of the way, I went back to bed for a little while.

Holly showed up a little after eight, and we went back to reviewing the galley proof.

We broke for lunch at Banyan's, and when we got back I found the number of the Merchant Seaman's Union in the phone book, and gave them a call. Of all of the people we wanted to bring to Chicago for the reunion, I was sure that Frank Hendricks was going to be the trickiest.

I got passed from the operator to one gentleman who couldn't help me, then back through the operator to a pleasant woman named Agnes.

"Well, son," she said, "I can't say that I've ever tried getting a message to someone when I didn't even know what ship they were on or what port they sailed from, but if you're not in too big of a hurry, I'll certainly give it my darnedest. Your Chief Hendricks didn't sign on here in Chicago, so I'll have to make some telephone calls to other union halls. Why don't you give me your number, and I'll call you if I find him."

"That would be fantastic!" I said. "Thank you so much. But, you know, while you're calling, perhaps you could ask about a few others at the same time." I then gave her the names of some of the other crewmembers I'd met including Rudy, Jones, and "Primo."

Lastly, I called Betty.

"Hello," she answered, then through a covered mouthpiece, I heard, "Jessica! If you're sick enough to stay home from school, you need to be in bed! Hup to!"

"Hi, Betty. This is Rich Lawson. How are you?"

"Oh, hi! I'm doing great. How are you? How's the book coming along?"

"That's actually why I'm calling," I said. "It's ready to be released in April."

"Fantastic! I can't wait to read it!"

"And you won't have to wait even that long," I said. "I have an advanced copy that I'd like to drop by." I then explained about the release form.

"And I also want to invite you and your family to the book launch party," I told her, and explained all of that. Then I asked, "Do you still keep in touch with any of the other girls you worked with on the line back then? I know about Maggie, but how about the others?"

"Oh, sure," she said. "We always swap birthday and Christmas cards, and usually see each other around the holidays."

"That's great!" I said. "Well, would you mind passing the invitation to the launch party on to them, as well?"

"Oh, they'll be tickled! When I told them I'd met you and that you found one of our rifles, they couldn't believe it. They'll be so excited!"

My final call before getting back to reviewing was to Keith at Harper & Faust. I explained the idea that I had jotted down last night—actually early this morning—and he loved it. "Leave it to me!" he said. "This'll really ice the cake!"

About two o'clock, Agnes called from the union hall. "You must be a very lucky person, Mr. Lawson," she said. "I found your Chief Hendricks on only my fifth call!"

"That's great!" I said. "I do have a lucky charm that seems to be working for me."

"He sailed out of New York the day after Christmas, heading for Columbia," she went on. "He's on a ship named the *Augustus D'Elia*. The folks at the union hall can't get a message to him, but they gave me the number for the shipping company. If you call them, they'll be able to pass it on."

She gave me the number, and I thanked her profusely.

"I'm still looking for those other names," she said. "This detective work is kind of fun!"

I called the shipping company, and although it wasn't as easy as Agnes made it sound, I did finally find someone who could get my message radioed to the ship. To keep it simple, I only asked that Frank call me as soon as he was near a telephone.

Holly and I finished our review of the galley proof in another day, and got it back to Charlie. He told us that we were the first to finish, so as a reward, I took Holly out to dinner in lieu of sticking a gold star on her forehead.

On Saturday night, I got a call from Frank. He had just gotten off his ship in Cartagena. I told him about the reunion, and he promised to arrange his schedule to be there. Over the course of the next week, Agnes tracked down all of the others I had asked about, and a week after that, I had received replies from all of them. Unfortunately, none of them were going to be able to make it.

The first week in February, small notices began appearing in newspapers all over the country, with the bold headline, "*Did you get A Kiss For Luck! during the war?*" The notice then went on to solicit responses from any GI who had come across one of the 450 or so slips. That was the bright idea that had come to me that night riding back from dropping Holly off at home. As the weeks went on, the notices got larger, and even appeared in several national magazines.

I was at Harper & Faust one day in early March, to sign yet another piece of paper, and I happened to run into Keith in the lobby.

"I've seen the *Kiss For Luck* inquiries in the paper," I said. "How is that working? Have you gotten many responses?"

"Yeah, some," he said, "I don't know how many, though. And frankly, it doesn't matter. What's more important than finding any of those GIs, Rich, is the curiosity that the notices are generating. We put one in a paper in East Podunk, Anywhere, and the next day there's a story editor calling to find out what it's all about. And readers are calling and writing, too. We give them a little teaser, and then tell them they can read the whole story when the book hits the shelves, April 2nd. We couldn't get this much buzz if we bought full *advertising* pages for the book. Fantastic idea, Rich! I wish I could claim it as my own."

A few days later, I heard that Keith's idea to hold the book launch in the Rock-Ola factory fell apart. With the company in stiff competition for jukebox sales with the industry leader, Seeburg, as well as Wurlitzer, the factory floors bore no resemblance at all to the assembly lines during war. With the nostalgic point completely dulled, it was decided to hold the gala in one of the Drake Hotel's lavish ballrooms. Not coincidentally, the Drake was where H&F was putting up all of the reunion guests for the launch party. I'm sure they arranged a discount.

Tuesday, March 22, 1955

I was still in my pajamas when I got a call from Holly. "I have to go home," she said.

Assuming she was at work at H&F, I asked, "Are you sick? You want me to come get you?"

"No, I'm fine," she said. "I mean home to Massachusetts. I got a call last night that my grandmother passed away. The funeral is this Saturday."

"Oh, Holly. I'm so sorry. Do you want me to go with you?"

"Thank you," she said, "but you need to stay here. I should be back in plenty of time for the launch—it's not for a week after the funeral—but I'm sure Keith will have plenty of things for you to be doing between now and then."

"Well, I will take you to the station," I said. Then I added, "You're *not* driving again, are you?"

"Oh, no!" she laughed. "Once was *more* than enough for that. Thanks. I'm on the 8:15 tomorrow morning."

The following Monday, the 28th, just as Holly had predicted, I got called into H&F because they needed my signature, again. Only this time it wasn't on a piece of paper; it was inside a couple hundred copies of the book! Keith wanted to hand them out at the launch party, and send them to buyers and reviewers all over the country.

It was exciting to finally hold a finished ready-for-sale copy of my book in my hands. Whoever made the final decision on the cover had chosen the one with the WOW poster in the background. I had to admit that it probably was a better choice than the one I would have picked.

I felt pretty proud to be signing my books ... for the first thirty or forty. Then it got to be a lot like work.

At least I had help, though, so it went quicker than if I'd been there alone. One young guy took the books out of the boxes and put them on the table, then a young lady flipped each one open to the right page, and slid it in front of me. I signed, and slid it to the side, where another girl scooped it up, and put it back into another box. I got a little feeling of what it must have been like for Betty and her friends on the Rock-Ola assembly line.

"So, have any of you read this?" I asked as we all went through our mechanical motions.

"I wish I had the time to read a tenth of the books that we put out," the restacking girl said.

The opener said, "I sat down with a page proof one day, and read the first part where they put the gun together. I really liked it. I'm going to buy a copy."

"They don't give you free copies for working here?" I asked as I signed.

All three of them laughed. The guy said, "Old man Harper didn't build this place with his penthouse office overlooking the lake by being generous to his employees. Most people think that H&F stands for Harper & Faust, but it really means Harder & Faster." Again, they all laughed.

"Well, I only live on the third floor with a view of the street," I told them, "but I'll make sure each of you gets a signed copy from the promo stack they told me I'll get."

The Tuesday night before the party, Kenny, Lily, and Margaret landed at Midway Airport. Keith arranged for the hotel's Cadillac limousine to go out and pick them up, and asked me to ride out to greet them.

The plane was about an hour late in landing, and the three of them looked pretty bedraggled as they stood in the customs line. Margaret looked like she was going to fall asleep standing beside her mother, with her doll hanging limp on the floor.

Bob, the chauffeur, and I took their suitcases as soon as they made it through, and Kenny scooped up his little girl, and she fell asleep with her head on his shoulder before we reached the car parked at the curb. I certainly couldn't blame her; if she'd been home in Birmingham, it would be after two in the morning.

They got checked in, and I told Kenny to call me when they got up, and I'd show them some of the sights of the city. Kenny had never been to Chicago, and Lily and Margaret had never even been out of England.

The phone woke me up about six the next morning. I answered it expecting it to be Kenny. It would feel like *noon* to them.

"Hi, Rich, this is Joyce. Did I wake you up?"

"Hi, Joyce. Don't worry about it; I had to get up to answer the phone, anyway," I said rubbing my eyes. "Have you landed already?"

"No. We haven't left, yet," she said. "I don't know if we're going to be able to."

That woke me up.

"What's happened? Is everyone alright?"

"They took Papa to the hospital last night," she said, and I could hear the fear in her voice. "We think he had a heart attack."

"Oh, Joyce! I'm so sorry. Look, don't even think about the trip; your place is there with your father. I'll keep him in my prayers, and please call me with any news, okay?"

"I will," she said. "Thanks for understanding. I know this book launch is important to you, and I hate to let you down."

"Don't be silly," I said. "Your father's *much* more important. Go and be with him. Say hi to everyone else for me, too. You're all in my prayers."

"I will. Thanks again, Rich. I'll call you if there's any change. Bye, now."

I set the phone down, and just stood there for a while. I wondered if Keith had a contingency plan for something like this.

Realizing that there was no going back to sleep after a call like that, I got naked, and climbed into the shower.

While I was shaving, the phone rang. It took several rings before I could wipe off and get to it.

"Hey, Rich. I didn't wake you up, did I," Keith asked. "I hope not, 'cause you're due over here in half an hour."

"I am?" I said. "I'm supposed to be taking the McCormick's sightseeing today."

"No," he said. "You're supposed to be here for the magazine and newspaper interviews. Don't you remember I told you about that?"

"Vaguely," I said after a short pause. In all honesty, I had gotten very used to Holly keeping track of my appointments for me. She is *so* organized! "What about the McCormicks?" I asked.

"They're fine. I sent an actual tour guide over to take them around the city."

"Good. That's good," I said, stalling with the hope that our conversation about the interviews would suddenly reappear. Finally, I gave up and said, "So, tell me about the interview thing, again."

"Just get your butt over here, and I'll explain it all then."

In Keith's office, twenty minutes later, he offered me a cigarette, and then said, "We've got interviews set up for you every half hour. Each one should last about twenty minutes, give or take. These'll be entertainment reporters, not newshounds, so you don't have to watch every little word. I know you used to report for the *Sun* and the *Times*, yourself, but this isn't like what you did. Don't try to outthink these folks; they just want some happy fluff to fill a column or two."

"Fair enough," I said. "I think I can do that. You said an interview every half hour? Why not put them all together in one room? I know you have the space."

"Again, this isn't like your press conference days," he said. "Each of these folks wants to feel like they're getting an exclusive scoop on you ... even though they know darned well they're not. It's how the entertainment side of the reporting game is played. They'll ask you a lot of the same questions—that you'll get tired of answering—but each one will be able to write their piece from an actual one-on-one perspective. Again, it's all part of the game."

"How many are there?" I asked.

"I cut it off at an even dozen, today." he said. "Eight of them are out of town papers or magazines, so those'll be on the phone."

"Six hours of talking about myself? I don't think I'm that interesting."

"It'll amount to about a half hour's worth of talking about yourself," he chuckled. "Repeated over and over."

"Are you going to set up interviews for the others? Betty and Kenny and Joyce ... Oh shoot! I forgot to tell you that. Joyce called me this morning, and said her dad is in the hospital with a heart attack. They're probably not going to make it."

"Damn!" he said. "I knew things were going too well. There's always *something* that comes flying out of left field." He looked at me, and said, "You're going to have to do her part."

"What do you mean, *her part*?"

"In answer to the question you were asking," he said, "no, the others won't go through this same interview ordeal. We're trying to keep the reporters away from them until the launch party, to build the suspense.

"At the party, I'll introduce each person from the book, and when I'm done, I'll let each of them take questions from the group. Since you know more about her than anyone else, you'll have to stand in for Joyce."

That wasn't the kind of contingency plan I was hoping for, and I think he saw that in my face.

"Don't worry; you'll be fine. It's not like we're going to put you in a dress and wig, and try to fool someone. And we certainly can't postpone at this late date."

The intercom on his desk buzzed, and his secretary said, "Mr. Little, Miss Grange from *The Boston Globe* is holding."

"Thanks, Marcia," he said. "Wait thirty seconds, and put her through." To me he said, "I'll sit in on your first one, but I'm sure you'll be fine. Pick up the extension over there, when I answer. Any last questions?"

"Can't think of any," I said moving to the chair at the small round table. "It's going to feel funny on the other side of the questioning, though."

The phone rang, and he answered, "Hi Abby! How are things in Bean Town?"

"Hi Keith," she answered. "Not too bad. March is going out like a lamb, just the way I like it."

"About the same, here," he said. "It's supposed to hit 60 today, so we can't complain.

"Abby, I have Rich Lawson on the extension. Rich, this is Abby Grange with *The Boston Globe*. Go ahead, Abby."

"Hello, Mr. Lawson," she said. "It's a pleasure to get to talk with you. I used to read your dispatches from the front lines. If this book is anything like those, I can't wait to read it."

"Thank you," I said. "I actually traveled back to some of those places I saw in France and England researching it. I got to stand on a lot of the spots where pieces of the story took place, so I've tried to convey that same sense of being-there."

I looked over at Keith, and he gave me a big smile and a thumbs up.

The rest of the day went pretty much like that, except that Keith left me in a vacant office to fend for myself after Abby's call. By the time I was heading home, I never wanted to use the word *I* again.

About six o'clock, I made myself a sandwich. Knowing that Holly's train would be arriving in the next hour or so, I didn't want to go out and chance missing her call from the station. I had just taken my first bite when the phone rang.

"Hi, Sweetheart. How are you?" Holly said when I answered.

"Hi! Wow! You're in early," I said. "They must have laid some downhill tracks between Buffalo and here. I'm glad, though; I've really missed you."

"I've missed you, too," she said, "but it looks like I might miss the launch party, on top of that."

My heart fell into my stomach.

"Oh, no. What happened? Are you alright?"

"I'm fine," she said. "My *grandfather's* crazy, but *I'm* okay. I called a few times during the day to let you know what's going on, but I guess you were out with the McCormicks, huh?"

"Actually, I was at H&F doing interviews all day," I told her. "I'm so tired of talking about *me* that I couldn't wait to hear about *you*. Now I'm not so sure. So, what's up?"

"Right after the funeral my grandfather started saying that he didn't want to live anymore; that without Marsha his life was over. We tried to tell him that that was a natural feeling, and that we all loved him, and wanted him around for a long time. By Sunday afternoon, he was so depressed we were afraid he might try to hurt himself. So, several of us have been taking turns staying with him."

"Holly, I'm so sorry. That must be awful to see him that way," I said. "But take as long as you need. We'll all miss you at the launch—especially me—but family comes first." Then I told her about the call I'd gotten from Joyce.

After we said our good-byes, I stuck the sandwich in the refrigerator, and put on my coat and hat. I'd have dinner at Banyan's ... in a glass with two olives.

Thursday, March 31, 1955

Thursday, Keith had more phone interviews set up for me, and one face to face. They ran the full spectrum from a call with an editor at the venerable *Ladies' Home Journal*, to sharing a cigarette and talking with a book reviewer for a relatively new men's magazine being published here in Chicago, called *Playboy*.

That evening, as I took yesterday's sandwich out of the refrigerator, the phone rang. I actually dreaded answering it, wondering what else was going to go wrong.

It was Joyce.

"*Bonjour, comment est votre père?* (Hello, how is your father?)" I asked as my stomach lost all interest in the sandwich, fearing the worst.

"He's fine, actually," she said. "It was apparently something he ate. He gave us quite a scare."

"Indeed," I said.

Finally, a tiny ray of sunshine.

"On top of that good news, it means that we can come, after all!" she told me. "We have reservation on the plane leaving at eight o'clock tomorrow night."

"That's wonderful!" I said, as the ray of light spread out into a full beam. "What time do you land?"

I heard a crinkling of paper as she apparently looked at her ticket. "Arrive Midway, 3:45 p.m. Saturday, April 2nd," she read.

I whistled, and said, "That doesn't leave much time. The party starts at five. By the time you get through customs and out to the hotel, you'll barely have time to change your clothes."

"Is it far from the airport to the hotel?" she asked.

"About half an hour," I said. "I'll talk to my publisher, and they'll make sure there's a car and driver waiting for you."

"I'm so excited, Rich," she said. "This is all so difficult to even believe. And Julien will burst if *he* gets any more excited."

"I can't wait to see all of you," I said. "I hope you have a great flight."

I sat down, and finally ate my sandwich, washing it down with a can of Pabst Blue Ribbon.

Friday, April 1, 1955

Friday morning I got another unsolicited 6:00 a.m. wake-up call. I knew it wasn't an April Fools prank, because nobody *I* knew would get up that early just to pull a joke on someone.

It was Holly.

"Sorry to wake you, sweetheart," she said "but I wanted to catch you before Keith dragged you off somewhere."

"That's okay. I'd much rather hear your voice than his." With that old familiar anxiety knot forming, I asked, "Is your grandfather okay?"

"He still needs watching," she said, "but his sister—my Aunt Janis—is going to take him back out to the Cape with her. We all think getting him out of the old house will help him to start moving on."

"That's great," I said, seeing the clouds finally parting and the sun pouring down. "So, are you on your way back?"

"Later this morning," she said. "I leave Boston at 10:25, and get into Chicago tomorrow at about 5:30 at night. I'll hop in a taxi, and be there as quick as I can."

"I'll make sure there's a car waiting there for you," I said, figuring the hotel limo could drop Joyce and her entourage off, and get to the train station in plenty of time. "I can't wait to see you, honey! This wasn't going to be half as much fun without you."

True to Holly's prediction, Keith called me at a little after eight.

"Hi, Rich," he said. "I need you over here at 9:00 to talk with Mary about the itinerary for your book-signing tour after the launch. You can you make it, right?"

"Sure," I said. "And while I've got you, I got a call from Joyce last night, and they're going to make it after all. They're scheduled to land at Midway at 3:45 Saturday afternoon. Can you have the hotel car waiting for them?"

"That's great!" he said. "Sure. No problem."

"And Holly called, and *she's* going to make it, too," I went on. "So can you make sure the car is at LaSalle St. Station at 5:30 tomorrow night?"

"Done and done!" he said. "See you at 9:00."

Saturday, April 2, 1955
The Launch Party

As requested, I was at the hotel ballroom at four o'clock. Keith and half a dozen of his team were there making last-minute adjustments to what looked to me to be perfectly fine arrangements.

Along both opposite walls of the room stood a number of easels, each holding a poster-size blow-up of a photo with some relevance to the book. There was a photograph of the Rock-Ola plant, and a poster showing a helmeted GI holding a black & white photo of his girlfriend with her hair up in a bandana, as he announced, "*My girl's a WOW.*"

I was surprised to see a photo of the Liberty ship *Donald E. Shea*, at sea, since this photo had not been at the *Shea's* reunion. Then I looked closely, and I could see that someone had retouched the photo and added the *Shea* name over whatever the real name of the ship was. There was a photo of the engine room, and a shot of the long dark shaft alley, and I would have been very surprised if they were of the actual *Shea*, either. But since all Liberties were virtually identical, who would know?

On the other wall was an aerial photo of the bombing destruction in Birmingham, a shot of the *Bishop and Bear* sign—that was my photo, one of the D-Day landings showing a pair of snorkel-equipped Sherman tanks, and another retouched photo that put a Jeep next to a Panzer tank.

Next to that was a picture of the ruins of Saint-Lô, followed by a locomotive on its side billowing smoke and steam. I seriously doubted that it was one that Joyce and her group had destroyed, but like the Liberty ship, one looked pretty much like the next. The next poster had a picture of a messenger pigeon, and an A-36 dive-bomber, both in level flight. The final one was of Joyce's farmhouse—again, my photo.

At the front of the room was an elevated stage. In the middle was a podium with the H&F logo on the front of it. To each side of the podium was a circular red curtain, about four feet in diameter, and suspended from where it touched the stage to about six feet high.

I climbed up onto the stage to take a peek.

I pushed through the overlap in the back, and inside the left curtain was a polished wooden pedestal about four feet high, with two clear Lucite rods sticking up out of it another foot. On top of those rods, almost as if suspended in mid-air, the rifle was perched. It was quite an effect. *I* had seen the gun before, and it almost took *my* breath away.

I went and looked inside the other curtain, and saw a giant-size blow-up of the book's cover. I had to admit that I liked looking at it. You could certainly see my name on *this* one.

I looked at my watch, and wondered if Joyce and the family had made it to the hotel, yet. I had also not heard anything from Frank since I talked to him a week ago when he confirmed that he would be here.

I headed to the front desk to find out, and passed Keith heading back into the ballroom.

"I'm going to see if Frank and Joyce have checked in, yet," I told him.

"Don't bother. He has, she hasn't," he said. "I just talked with the manager, and his driver called in to say that Joyce's flight is late, *and* that they're sending it to land at another airport, for some reason."

"Where?" I asked as the clouds rolled back in over my sunny day.

"Whoever the driver was talking to didn't seem to know," Keith said. "The manager has somebody calling the airline to see what he can find out. He's going to pull out all the stops to get them here, if it's at all possible." He put his hand on my shoulder, and added, "Let's hope for the best, Rich, but be ready to come on stage and talk in her absence."

"What about Holly?" I asked. "Is there still going to be a car at LaSalle Street for her?"

"All set," he said. "It won't be a limo, but it is a Caddy."

"I don't care if it's a Studebaker," I said, "as long as it runs long enough to get her here."

About quarter to five, soft music started playing. I looked around, and saw that the main curtain on the stage had parted just enough to reveal a tuxedoed string quartet. By five o'clock, there were probably a hundred or more people in the ballroom, and I had to wonder what a book launch party for a Hemmingway novel must look like.

At about quarter past five—allowing time for the fashionably-late to arrive—Keith took the stage, and the quartet faded to silence. With that, most of the guests moved to the round tables that were arranged throughout the room, but a handful—mostly photographers—remained standing along the walls.

Keith took the microphone from its holder on the podium, and walked out to the edge of the stage.

"Ladies and gentlemen, thank you so much for coming out tonight to help us launch Rich Lawson's first book, *A Kiss For Luck!*"

There was a round of applause, and Keith took that time to point at and wave to a number of the guests that he apparently knew personally.

"In October of 1941," Keith began when the applause died down, "less than two months before the Japanese bombed Pearl Harbor, the US Army approved the design of what, in official military jargon, was called the *United States Carbine, Caliber .30, M1*. It quickly became known simply as the M1 Carbine.

"During the war, 6,221,220 M1 Carbines were produced, with almost a quarter-million, being turned out by our own Rock-Ola Manufacturing Corporation." He stretched his hand out toward the audience, and said, "David Rockola, would you stand up, please?"

He stood, and everyone turned to look at him.

"On behalf of a grateful nation," Keith said, "and people the world over who can celebrate their freedom, today, *thank you!*"

The audience applauded enthusiastically, then Keith bowed slightly toward Mr. Rockola, who nodded and said thank you, several times, before sitting down.

Then Keith went back to his speech. "Of the 228,500 M1's made by Rock-Ola, 487 of them left the factory with a little *unofficial-something* inside. Something that David probably never even knew about.

"On the night of May 9th, 1944, one of the girls on the assembly-line swing-shift had the bright idea to add a lucky charm to each of the rifles they built."

From behind the short curtain above Keith's head, an eight-foot long copy of Betty's slip slowly lowered into view.

The audience burst into applause, and Keith stood to the side, looking up at the giant lips.

After a little while, he began, again, "All of the girls on the line used their precious war-rationed lipstick to kiss a slip of paper, and then write over their lip print, *A Kiss For Luck!* as a little reminder of what those soldiers overseas were fighting for ... and what was waiting for them when the got home!"

The audience laughed.

"Ladies and gentlemen," Keith said, pointing to the sign, "I'd like to introduce you to the owner of those lips, the inventor of this wonderful good luck charm, Miss Betty Hancock!"

Betty walked out onto the stage with a huge smile as the audience got to its feet, applauding.

Keith shook her hand as if he'd never met her before, and then after what he apparently deemed the proper amount of clapping, he motioned the audience to sit back down so he could continue.

"Unfortunately for our GIs," he went on, holding Betty's hand, "that unofficial-something was strictly against Army regulations, so only a little more that a single shift's worth of those special carbines ever made it out the door."

There were low murmurs, and groans, and even a boo for Army regulations, which drew a round of laughs.

"Well, about a year ago," Keith went on, "war correspondent and former reporter for the *Chicago Sun* and *The Times*, Rich Lawson, was looking for a story to write for the tenth anniversary of the liberation of Paris. By pure chance—or perhaps guided by some *lucky charm*—he happened upon an obscure French newspaper that featured the eight-year-old winner of an essay contest. That unlikely literary find led Mr. Lawson to the discovery of one of these special carbines in a small farmhouse in the middle of France.

"That rifle carried the serial number 6,152,649 ... and it is right here!"

With that, the curtain around the rifle went up and the audience applauded, again.

While they clapped, he said into the microphone, "Rich. Come on up here."

He had told me that he wasn't going to bring me up until the end, but it was obvious that he knew how to work a room, so I didn't question his change in plans.

I went through a side door, and emerged on stage. I shook his hand, and I gave Betty a hug.

"Ladies and gentlemen, the author, Rich Lawson!"

More applause. It made me feel a little self-conscious, but at the same time, it was very heady stuff!

"Why don't you do the honors, Rich?" he said. "Go on over there, and push the curtain up."

We hadn't rehearsed this, so as I took hold of the curtain, I hoped the stagehand with the rope could see me from wherever he was.

I tugged upward, and at the same time that the curtain magically rose to reveal the giant cover of my book, the quartet struck up the chorus of *Luck be a Lady*, from *Guys and Dolls*.

"Ladies and gentlemen," Keith said, "I give you ... *A Kiss For Luck!*" and he blew them a kiss.

As the audience clapped, he motioned me over, and I went and stood beside him and Betty.

Using whatever applause timer he had in his head, Keith settled the audience down, and then went on.

"While I can't possibly do justice to the story that Rich has spent the last year meticulously researching and putting together as he traveled half way around the world, I would like to introduce to you the main character in each of the parts of the book. I'm also going to be introducing them to one another," he said. "You see, none of them have ever met Betty *or* each other before right now.

"Part-One of Rich's book chronicles the efforts and the lives of Betty and her fellow WOWs during the spring of 1944. In Part-Two, the rifle—*this* rifle" he added pointing, "is loaded onto a Liberty ship for delivery to England to help support the fast-approaching D-Day Invasion. Unfortunately, also aboard that ship is a Nazi saboteur bent on *stopping* that delivery.

"Now, I'm not going to ruin any surprises in the story that Rich has put together by telling you how they figure out who the saboteur is or how they stop him, but I am going to introduce you to the man—a young farm boy on his first trip to sea, at the time—who used this very rifle to save his ship, its vital cargo, and the lives of every one of the crew.

"Ladies and gentlemen, Mr. Frank Hendricks!"

The audience applauded as Frank, dressed in his dark-blue chief's uniform, strode onto the stage. He shook Keith's hand, and then mine, and then opened his arms as he stepped over to Betty. He took her in an embrace and was saying something into her ear that even I couldn't hear over the doubled volume of the clapping. When they separated, I could see that both of them had tears running down their cheeks. My eyes were none too dry, either.

While the audience applauded, I stole a glance at my watch, and then looked out at the ballroom door. I desperately wished that Holly could be here to see this. I also wanted Joyce to show up. Her introduction wasn't far away. Not that I had any problem at all being her stand-in, but this would be her big moment; she should hear—*feel*—the applause that she so deserved.

Keith quieted the audience, and then went on. "In Part-Three of the story, after the rifle made it to England, it was issued to a young sergeant who was serving with the 29th Infantry in a unit called the 729th Ordnance Light Maintenance Company. Basically, he and his company were there to fix anything that the Army broke—and they were kept plenty busy!

"About two weeks after D-Day, a little south of Normandy, this young mechanic from Maine and two of his buddies engaged in a fight-to-the-death with a Panzer tank. It is the first and only time in the chronicles of the war that a Jeep tangled with a Nazi tank and the tank lost. That young sergeant had this rifle in his hands that day, and it saved his life when one of the surrendering tank crew drew a pistol and shot at him.

"Ladies and gentlemen, Mr. Kenny McCormick!"

Kenny walked out to the audience's clapping, shook all of our hands, and gave Betty another emotional embrace. More tears all around.

I looked over at the vacant ballroom door, wishing I could ask Keith to call for an intermission.

"With the approval of his commanding officer," Keith went on, "Kenny donated our rifle to the OSS for an airdrop behind enemy lines to supply the freedom fighters in the French Resistance.

"It ended up in the hands of a young lady whose patriotism and devotion to her native France could probably fill a book all by itself. She became a superb marksman, an inventor of new ways to sabotage Nazi trains, a pigeon handler, and an intelligence gatherer for Britain's Special Operations Executive.

"During one of her spying missions, she and a compatriot—her future husband—were captured by a Nazi officer, and she managed to effect their escape with the help of our lucky rifle, here. Which, at the time, didn't even have any *bullets* in it! At least not until her captor fired his pistol at her, and it stopped *that* bullet from killing her.

"Now, unfortunately, due to difficulties with overseas transportation, our hero of the French Resistance isn't able to be with us at the moment ..."

The audience let out a disappointed, "Oh," almost in unison.

I looked over at the door, one last time, and there stood Holly and Joyce, side by side! Joyce's family stood right behind her.

"She made it, Keith!" I shouted, pointing at the door. "She's here!"

Everyone looked toward the door, and then started clapping.

"Well, you certainly know how to make an entrance," Keith said with a laugh. "Your timing is perfect! Maybe our rifle is still exerting its lucky force! Come on up here."

Not knowing where the backstage door was, she walked to the front of the stage, and Frank and I each took one of her hands, and hopped her up with us as the audience continued applauding.

Over the clapping, Keith almost shouted into the microphone, "Ladies and gentlemen, Miss Joyce Renaud!"

I took her across the stage introducing her to the other men, and finally to Betty. They stood for a moment, smiling at each other, and then they embraced and kissed each other's cheeks like long-separated sisters.

The audience was on its feet clapping and cheering, and if there was a dry eye in that room, that person needed to see an eye doctor or a psychiatrist.

After a good deal of clapping with Betty, Frank, Kenny, and Joyce lined up across the stage, holding hands, Keith quieted the audience, and said, "Now, when I introduced Betty and Joyce, I used the maiden names by which everyone knew them when their stories took place. The former Betty Hancock is now Betty Driscoll, and Miss Joyce Renaud has become Joyce Renaud-Arsenault.

"Frank and Kenny have also married, and collectively, the group has five children between them ... three of whom would not be here today without the intervention of this lucky rifle into the life of one of their parents.

"Ladies and gentlemen, please welcome to the stage the husbands, wives, and children of our heroes!"

A Kiss For Luck!

From behind the curtain at both sides of the stage, all of the family members came forward. The only two that I had never met were Frank's wife and the eighteen-month-old son that she carried.

After an appropriate length of applause, Keith continued.

"Almost as much a part of her family as her husband and kids, and certainly no less a part of our story, are Betty's coworkers back at Rock-Ola. Ladies and gentlemen, please welcome Maggie Kelly, Sally Higgins, Lucy Katz, and Lydia Howe!"

In the original plan, Keith had told me that after introducing the Rock-Ola girls he would ask me to say a few words. After the applause for the girls quieted, he broke from the script again.

"A while ago," he began, "I told you that 487 of Rock-Ola's rifles contained a slip of paper emblazoned by the lips of one of these lovely ladies. Well, over the course of the past two and a half months, Harper & Faust has searched far and wide to see how many of those slips, besides this one, could be accounted for.

"We received calls and letters from more than 250 GIs who remembered seeing one of those slips, and responses from 48 who still actually *had* the slip they found in their rifle.

"Ladies and gentlemen, please welcome some of the luckiest GIs to ever don a uniform!"

The curtains parted the rest of the way, and as the quartet played *As the Caissons Go Rolling Along*, 44 men came onto the stage from the wings. Most wore their old uniforms, but those who had expanded beyond that limit in the past ten years wore suits decorated with their company insignias, ribbons, and medals. They all wore an Army garrison cap, and they held their individual *A Kiss For Luck!* slips in front of them, displayed in identical 8 x 10 matted frames, obviously provided by Keith and company. The condition of the slips ranged from almost like new to barely recognizable multiple-pieces.

Another standing ovation, and tears that completely exhausted the room's supply of tissues.

After each of the men had given Betty and the other girls a hug, it was finally my turn. And that was something about which I had very mixed emotions. I felt humbled by the company I was with up on that stage, and felt that anything I could say might almost be distracting. There was, however, one important thing that I did want to say.

"Ladies and gentlemen," Keith said, "I give you the man whose eye for a story, whose diligent research, whose tireless traveling, and whose unsurpassed skills as a writer have brought all of these people together for the very first time ... the author of *A Kiss For Luck!*, Mr. Rich Lawson!"

I stood there for what seemed a very long time as both the audience, and the people on the stage applauded me. What a thrilling moment!

Finally, Keith quieted the room, and he handed me the microphone.

"Thank you for being here, today," I began, "thank you for your interest in my book—*our* book," I corrected myself, with a wave to everyone on stage, "and thank you for your show of support to all of these brave and dedicated men and women.

"When Keith was introducing the families of Betty, and Frank, and Kenny, and Joyce a little while ago, he failed to mention an interesting coincidence among their marriages. He failed to mention it, because I never told him about it. And it's not in the book, because I only discovered it, myself, a couple of weeks ago.

"It turns out that every one of their anniversaries is on May 8th—V-E Day. Only Kenny and Joyce were each married on the actual day in 1945, but Betty and Frank both chose that day, as well. Betty in 1946, after Josh got home from overseas, and Frank, three years ago. It's interesting to think that the rifle—and Betty's lucky slip—that play such an important roll in allowing them all to *see* V-E Day, could have had some influence in their decisions. At any rate, happy anniversary, in advance, to all of you."

The audience applauded, and then I went on.

"With regard to the book, I have a bit of a confession to make," I began. I pointed to the giant cover, and said. "I can't take credit for this. If this were a work of fiction, I could say, 'I created this. This is a product of my imagination, and this belongs to me.' But this story belongs to the men and women you're looking at up on stage, here. They were generous and open enough to share with me the intimacies of their lives ten years ago, so that I could share them with you. I am just the messenger, here; *they* are the story."

With his master's sense of timing, Keith started a round of applause.

"But there are a lot stories out there that never get told," I went on, "and this could have been one of them if not for someone willing to take a chance on an old war correspondent who'd never written a book in his life. That person is Harper & Faust's Marion Jameson. Marion, would you stand up, please?"

She did, and I said, "On behalf of all of us up here, thank you for giving me, and their story a chance."

When the applause settled, I went on, "I'd also like to thank the creative and skilled folks at Harper & Faust who took the stories that I collected, and turned them into a polished book. I think they deserve a huge round of applause, and I *know* they have my undying admiration and gratitude."

The audience responded enthusiastically to my request.

"But even before Harper & Faust could work *their* magic," I went on, "all of my scribbled notes had to be put onto paper and made readable. And if that had been left up to me, we'd all be lucky to be in this room a year from now.

"A year *ago*, while I was in Boston researching the story, a young woman happened to overhear me talking about the rifle with some of Frank Hendricks' shipmates, and she offered her first-rate secretarial skills if I needed them. And boy, did I!"

I looked out, and found Holly standing next to the door. Guessing what was coming, she was criss-crossing her hands in front of her, and shaking her head, no.

Like I could be that easily dissuaded.

"Holly, would you come up here, please?" I waved, and added, "Come on, if not for you, this would still be a stack of yellow legal pads!"

The audience clapped, and as she made her way to the stage, I said, "Ladies and gentlemen, the person without whom—literally—this book would not be here today, Miss Holly Dillon!"

I took her hand, and as the audience applauded, she said into my ear, "I'll get you for this."

I whispered back, "You ain't seen nothing, yet."

When it quieted down, I went on, to the audience, "With regard to the creation of this book, I honestly don't know what I would have done over the past year without Holly's tireless effort, her excellent office and proofreading skills, her organization, and her unflagging support.

"And with regard to my life in general," I went on, "I can't imagine what I would do without her from here on."

Still holding her hand, I bent down onto one knee in front of her, looked up, and said into the microphone, "Holly Dillon, will you marry me?"

Her free hand went up to her mouth, which hung open in surprise.

After a few seconds of gasps and murmurings, the room went quiet, waiting for her reply.

Tears filled her eyes, and as she nodded, she squeaked, "Yes!"

As they say on the radio, *the crowd went wild*!"

I stood up, we wrapped our arms around each other, and kissed as the quartet played *Here Comes The Bride*. I then took a ring out of my pocket, slipped it on her finger, and kissed her again.

When it settled down a little, I turned to the audience, and asked into the microphone, "Would anyone care to guess what day the wedding will be?"

Almost as one, they shouted, "*May 8th!*" and another round of cheers went up.

I gave a thumbs up, and kissed Holly, once more.

The End

Epilogue:

A Kiss For Luck!: Rich Lawson's first book made it to the number two spot on the *New York Times* non-fiction best seller list, but was ironically kept out of the top spot by Norman Vincent Peale's, *The Power Of Positive Thinking*. In France, it made it to number one, where it stayed for eight weeks. The French movie rights were purchased by a small studio that wants to film *La Résistance* with Simone Signoret staring as Joyce. The US movie rights are still available.

Betty Hancock (Driscoll): Betty remained in her childhood house in Chicago raising her children and being the woman behind her successful man. She would often meet up with Rich when he was doing a local signing, and kiss the page of the book with bright red lipstick before Rich signed it. It is estimated that about 150 such copies exist, and are highly prized by collectors.

Frank Hendricks and Kenny McCormick: After meeting at the launch party, Frank and Kenny struck up a close friendship. A year later, when Frank's second child, a daughter, was born, he decided to abandon the sea, so that he could be a more active part in his children's lives. Playing on his fascination with, and aptitude for, all things mechanical, he and Kenny formed a partnership to manufacture racing bicycles, designed by Darcy Haversham. The Birmingham factory has produced a number of bikes for the *Tour de France*. Each year, prior to the race, the Hendricks and the McCormicks get together with the Renaud-Arsenaults.

Joyce Renaud-Arsenault: After the book was translated into French, Joyce became something of a celebrity, and was recruited by the French Olympic Committee to coach the women's shooting team. With typical French pride, and certainly with PR in mind, the Renault company replaced her battered German *kübelwagen* with a brand new Dauphine sedan. She continued to live on the farm, and eventually sent Julien to university where he became an aeronautical engineer. He was the youngest member of the team that designed the supersonic transport, *Concorde*.

Holly Dillon and Rich Lawson: Holly and Rich were married on May 8th, 1955, in a small private ceremony in between publicity engagements. The couple do not have children, and travel extensively. With Holly's vigorous encouragement—referred to by Rich as *encoura-nagging*—he is writing his first novel. Set in World War II England, it is a story about a female pigeon handler and her run-in with a Nazi spy.

United States Carbine, Caliber .30, M1, serial number 6,152,649: After traveling with Rich on his signing tour, the rifle was returned to Joyce, in France, as agreed. Years later, a fan of the book, contacted her and offered to buy it for $2,000 (Half the price of a new car at the time!) and a replacement rifle of her choice. She accepted with the stipulation that the *Kiss For Luck!* slip stay with the gun. The rifle is now in a private collection in Arizona, owned by Erik Knudson.

Major Technical and Historical References:

1. *American Rifleman Magazine*; April 2008; "Making A Different Kind Of Music; The Rock-Ola M1 Carbine." By Bruce N. Canfield.
2. War Department, Ordnance Office: *Ordnance Field Service Technical Bulletin Number 23-7-1; Carbine, Cal. .30, M1.* March 17, 1942.
3. *The Liberty Ships of World War II*, by Bill Lee.
4. *Acta Non Verba* by Bill Lee
5. *This is Sheepshead Bay*, by John L. Beebe.
6. *Troopships of World War II: Liberty Ships*, at www.skylighter.org.
7. *Navy Manuals And Documents Online* at Historic Naval Ships Association (www.hnsa.org). *Engineering Branch Training; Liberty Ships.*
8. *Arnold Hague Convoy Database* at www.convoyweb.org.uk.
9. *WWII: We Crossed The Atlantic In A Rolling Freighter*, by Tom Dillon
10. *29th Division Living History Group* at 29thdivision.com.
11. *The (Very) Best of British: Slang* by Mike Etherington.
12. *British Anti-Invasion Preparations Of The Second World War* at www.wikipedia.org.
13. *The Battlefields That Nearly Were. Defended England 1940* by William Foot.
14. *US Troops In Amphibious Training At Crow Point In Devon, England, during World War II* at www.criticalpast.com.
15. *Recollections Of A Nurse During WW2* by Mary Goodhand at www.bbc.co.uk.
16. *Christmas Under Fire* by Mike Brown at www.bbc.co.uk.
17. *French Resistance* at www.wikipedia.org.
18. *Map of Major Escape Routes Through France* at www.wwii-netherlands-escape-lines.com.
19. *FUBAR: Soldier Slang of World War II* by Gordon L. Rottman.
20. *Ernie's War: The Best of Ernie Pyle's World War II Dispatches* by David Nichols.

Acknowledgements:

I would like to express my gratitude to all of the people who inspired and supported me during the writing of this novel. A few, whose contributions were singularly important, are mentioned here.

Erik Knudson: Erik is my good friend and next door neighbor, and he is the owner of the real M1 Carbine rifle that inspired this fictional story. One summer evening, while he was cleaning the weapon after a day at the shooting range, I happened to drop by. While I was admiring the vintage WWII rifle, with its years of scratches, digs, and wear, he commented, "Wouldn't it be interesting if she could talk, and tell us all of her stories?" I thought about that for a few moments, and replied, "You know, I think I can make that happen." I then spent the next two years researching and writing this novel.

Bill Lee: Bill is a retired shipbuilder turned writer, who is an authority on almost anything that floats. He was part of the engineering and test team that developed the nuclear power system for the Navy's NIMITZ-class aircraft carriers. During my research on *Part II: The Crossing*, I read an article titled *The Liberty Ships of World War II* written by Bill. I contacted him to ask some specific questions, and he took the time to answer them in great detail. We have been communicating ever since. Bill has become one of my invaluable proofreaders, finding not only spelling errors and typos, but challenging me always to prove my accuracy with regard to historical details.

Philip O'Mara, Rich Hill, and the entire crew of the *SS Jeremiah O'Brien*: Birthed at Pier 45, Fisherman's Wharf in San Francisco, the *O'Brien* is a National Liberty Ship Memorial, and one of only two surviving Liberty ships in the world, of the 2,710 that were built. During my research I made the pilgrimage to San Francisco, and with an introduction from the shipkeeper, Philip O'Mara, I received a personal guided tour from one of the ship's volunteer crewmembers, Rich Hill. Rich had served on Libertys during the war, and was part of the all volunteer crew that sailed the *O'Brien*, under her own steam, from San Francisco Bay to the beaches of Normandy, France for the 50th Anniversary of the D-Day invasion in 1994. Rich showed me through the entire ship, answered my myriad questions, and allowed me access to specific areas that are featured in the story, all in the name of accuracy. During lunch with the crew, I explained my writing project and asked how *they* would sabotage the ship. While they had never considered that before, it sparked some interesting debate among the men whose job it is to keep the ship *going*.

Joyce Stevenson: I would like to thank Joyce, another good friend and neighbor, for inspiring some of the qualities and talents for the character Joyce Renaud in *Part IV*, and also for the editor, Norma, in *Part V*. She knows what qualities and talents I'm talking about.